BROAD ARROW
JACK.

BROAD ARROW JACK.

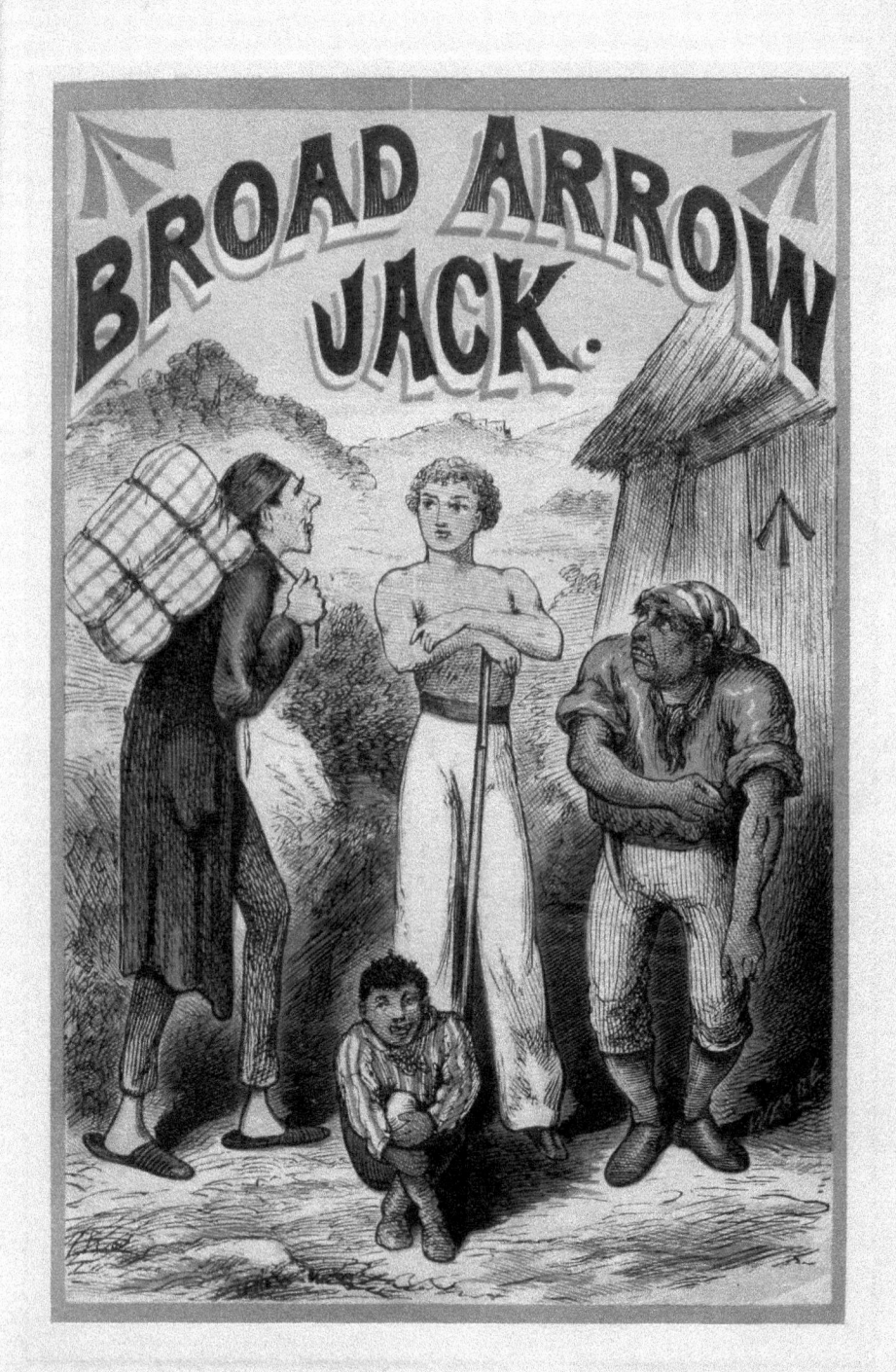

ONE PENNY WEEKLY.

24 PAGES OF SENSATIONAL ROMANCE.

WITH

MAGNIFICENT PICTURE PRESENTED GRATIS.

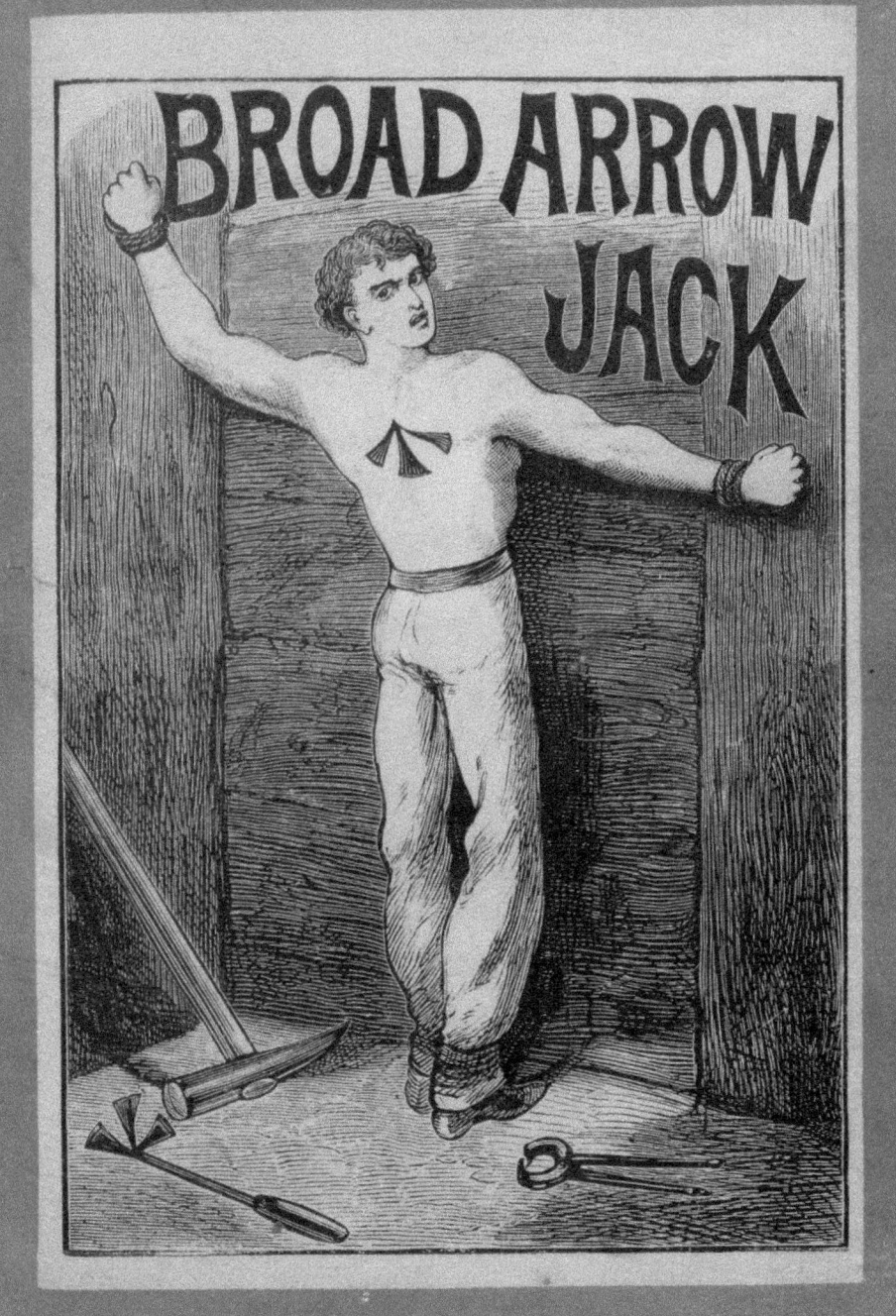

BROAD ARROW JACK

LONDON: CHARLES FOX, 4, SHOE LANE, FLEET STREET, E.C.

Sold by all News agents.

"Stand back!" cried Broad-Arrow Jack.

BROAD-ARROW JACK.

BY THE AUTHOR OF
HANDSOME HARRY and CHEERFUL CHING-CHING.

"THERE, YOU ACCURSED BRITISHER!" YELLED THE OGRE—"YOU ARE BRANDED, AND I NOW RE-CHRISTEN YOU 'BROAD ARROW JACK.'"

No. 1

BROAD ARROW JACK.

CHAPTER I.
A FATHER AND TWO SONS.

"SHE has struck! Heaven help us!"

A hundred voices spoke as one; but the sound was lost in the storm. The sky was black as the grave, and the sea roared in the darkness unseen, save where the lightning flashed. Two hundred souls, gathered aft of the emigrant ship Esmeralda, clung to each other in despair. All order was lost—passengers and crew were hopelessly mingled together in that terrible hour.

The captain was a brave man, but he could do nothing. When first the storm broke out he had ordered the passengers to be battened down below, but ere his orders could be obeyed some mad reckless men—quick to see danger, and quicker still in sacrificing the good of others to their own advantage—refused to go below. Hot and angry words ensued. The captain drew a revolver from his pocket, and threatened to shoot them one by one if they did not obey; other weapons were produced, and a struggle which stretched two men stark and stiff upon the deck took place.

The noise of the quarrel alarmed the rest, and a rumour ran round the ship like wildfire to the effect that the ship was sinking, and that the captain and crew were bent upon cooping up the passengers, and making good their own escape by means of the boats.

When once a crowd of people get hold of an insane idea, all reason and argument is in vain. The captain implored, threatened, and urged them, for their own sakes, to leave the deck; but, with a few exceptions, they refused. Among the coolest and most reasonable were a father and two sons.

"We can go below," said the father, "and die, if it must come to that. To remain here is to work the sure ruin of all. Come, my sons, let us go."

"No," hurriedly whispered the captain; "remain here. I may want you."

Once more he made an appeal to the terrified crowd; but half his words were lost in the roar of the elements, and the rest fell on unheeding ears. Huddled together like frightened sheep, they cowered on the deck.

It was not quite dark when the storm came upon them with the suddenness and power of a white squall, and the spectacle the poor creatures presented was very pitiful. The captain—a strong man, and a stern one—clasped his hands, and turned away to hide his tears.

Men, women, and children mingled together—mothers holding their little ones to their breasts, and wives clinging to their husbands; children shrieking and crying, clutching their parents with their little hands as if they saw grim death at hand; lone men who had left a friendless land behind them, and were going to see if warmer hearts could be found in other lands, knelt with clasped hands, striving to breathe a prayer they had not thought of for years; young girls sent out by friends to better themselves in the prosperous country across the sea lay stretched out upon the deck, weeping and moaning; and in the midst stood one man, like a rock, with a fixed face and thoughts far, far away. He had left wife and children behind, and was going out to make a home for them in a land wide enough for all. "I will send for you in a year," he said at parting, and in less than a month his lifeless body was being carried to and fro by the many currents of the sea.

A sad scene!—and who can wonder that the captain turned sick at heart? He knew that all the energies of himself and his crew were needed to save the ship from the power of the storm—the most furious and terrible he had ever known.

Great gusts of wind, that came now from one point of the compass, now from another, split the sails into ribbons, and bent the masts like whipstalks; mighty waves, tearing along like mad beasts, rushed at the Esmeralda, striking her with a force that threatened to tear every plank to matchwood, and rolling over the deck, carrying away each time some living creature to a watery grave. They must have cried out as they went; but the storm drowned the puny mortal voices even in the strength which despair can give.

The captain took the wheel, and hurriedly signalled to the father and two sons previously alluded to, to stand by and keep a clear space for him to work in. There was need of the precaution, for some people seemed to think that the captain had in himself power to save, and came creeping up, begging mercy of *him*—and many, while they breathed the futile and blasphemous prayer, were carried away by the sweeping waves, and hurried into eternity.

"God have mercy on us all!" was the father's prayer as they were carried off, and a big sigh heaved his mighty chest. He was a tall powerful man—almost a giant, being quite six feet six, and broad and muscular. His face was of the Saxon type—blue eyes, fair hair, and well shaped nose—slightly aquiline—with the calm expression which true bravery alone can give. Only when others suffered did his looks change. When the waters beat upon him, and threatened to bear him away as they had done others, there was no ruffle to be seen. The man was like a pillar, firmly fixed, and by means of sheer strength held his ground. He stood with his right foot well advanced, and body slightly bent in the direction where the danger lay, his arms linked in those of his sons.

There was a strange contrast between these two boys. The elder of the two was not more than fourteen, but he was already taller than the general run of men. He had his father's features and bearing—the same indifference to his own fate, and sympathy for the misfortunes of others.

The second lad was about ten years old, and, save in the Saxon cast of his countenance, bore no resemblance to his father or his brother. He was barely the average height of boys of his years, and looked less than he was, owing to his delicate—almost sickly—looks and spare form. His brother was a young oak; he was but a tender flower.

But a deep love lay between these two, and their eyes were seldom removed from each other until the darkness came; and then each passed a hand in front of his father, and held together with a grip that only death itself could have broken.

What a night, and what a world of misery on board that good ship! She fought against the waves—rode over them when she could—broke through them when they came too suddenly upon her; she creaked, and groaned, and gave forth deep sobs, as if she knew how much depended on her gaining the victory over storm and tempest.

But it was not to be. An hour after the deep darkness fell she suddenly pulled up with a crash, and heeled over upon her side. Then the great cry went up—"She has struck! Heaven help us!"

Many who shrieked out the words never spoke again. The breakers, angry at their useless beating upon the rocks, dashed up with devilish joy, and wrapped the mass of agonised humanity in their cold embrace.

Some were stunned, and spared the last struggle; others fought out a brief desperate battle for dear life, and lost; a few clung to spars, hencoops, life-belts, and such things as they had been able to secure; but the mighty breakers, flushed with victory, laughed at their efforts, and beat out the spark which makes up living beings—the spark which hides so well from the anatomist's seeking, and defies man to tell from whence it comes, and whither it goes.

Of all living creatures on board the Esmeralda that night only three were saved. The rest went down—some to find a last couch upon the sands under the sea, others to be carried to the shore, tossed up, and left to bleach in the sun, but nearly all, on sea and land, to become the food of those creatures whose office it is to consume the cast-off habit of the departed soul.

All dead save three!

A father and two sons, clinging to each other, with the youngest in the middle, and the father and eldest son holding on to a spar, and swimming vigorously with their feet. A flash of lightning revealed the direction of the shore—white as a land of snow with breakers—giving but little chance of being saved, but it was their only chance, and they made towards it.

"Be strong and brave, Cecil," cried the elder boy in the ear of the younger.

The delicate lad gave him a slight pressure of the hand he grasped in reply. He had indomitable courage in his frail form, even as the other had in his stronger one.

The father never spoke, but kept his eyes fixed ahead, so as to be ready to take advantage of every flash of lurid light. Again and again it came, but revealed nothing better than hill-tops of foam, and great hills beyond.

"There is no hope," he thought; but he held on his way. It mattered little to him whether he lived or died unless his brave boys were spared. On them were centred all his hopes—he had no other tie in the wide world.

More than one line of breakers became visible in the short intervals of light as the struggling trio neared the shore. The first line was soon reached, and they found themselves in a whirlpool of foam. A terrible blow upon the knee told the father that he had struck upon a rock. The agony was great, but he held to the spar and to the hand of his sickly son.

On—on through the waters, growing each moment more turbid and terrible. Now on the summit of a great roller—now in the midst of a great plain of bubbling water—on towards the shore, where the sea was strongest, and the danger greatest.

"No hope!" thought the father again, and the forked lightning danced about the sky.

But he held on with his powerful arm, and his strong brave son never relaxed his hold upon the piece of timber which stood between them and death; and the delicate boy, confident in their strength, rode calmly between them, with his tiny hands clasped by their strong brown palms.

It was perfectly marvellous how they held together. Strength alone could not have done it. It was pluck—sheer pluck and determination—that won the day. Beaten and buffeted about, choking with salt water, cast up on the rocks, dragged down to be cast up again, tossed and turned about—bruised, and bleeding—they were never sundered, and at last the furious sea, angry at its own impotence to disunite the brave three, cast them up on the shore and left them there.

There they lay for half an hour or more, unable to speak, and scarcely believing that they had reached the land, but still hand in hand, as they had been through all. The storm had spent its fury; the lightning flashes came fewer and farther between; the thunder rolled in the distance; the clouds broke, and sped away; the stars shone out, and naught was left to tell the story of the great commotion, and what it had done, but the still heavily-rolling sea, the many fragments of the wreck floating about and lying on the shore, and three worn-out castaways stretched out in the helplessness of utter exhaustion.

CHAPTER II.
A KNAVE AND FOOL.

"DON'T be hard on me, Mr. Jaundice. I can't help it—indeed I can't! It's all nerves—I'm nothing else—indeed it is! I never could abide a thunderstorm. As soon as it comes on my limbs get as loose as one o' them ere figgers as we used to work with a string in our hearly days."

The speaker—a short stout man about forty years of age, with a flabby face, wherein were a pair of colourless shifty eyes, a pug nose, and a mouth wide enough for a man ten times his size—turned an appealing look towards the man he addressed, licking his dry lips, and quivering with the remnants of a great bodily fear, or, in other words, a terrible funk.

There were but two together, sitting under the shelter of a rock where they had taken refuge from a storm—the storm of the previous night, which, after venting its fury upon the sea, had turned its attention to the land, and rained great torrents, torn down trees, and covered the level lands with great sheets of water.

"You are the most confoundedly cowardly beggar that ever lived," was the reply.

He was a man of much better mould—good figure, handsome face, slight sinewy limbs, and a general look of good blood and breeding about him, but over all the shadow which a vicious life casts, and that marred all. The first speaker was not a very agreeable-looking object, but he was not one whit more repulsive than the other. Mr. Jaundice was the sort of man one would not care to meet with in a lone place on a dark night, and was certainly not likely to address a stranger without laying himself open to a suspicion that he was up to some game or other not usually played by honest men.

The pair were dressed in rough velveteen suits, and slouch hats, such as settlers wear. Close behind them two rifles were tucked away to keep them from the wet, and in a belt round the waist of Jaundice were a brace of pistols.

"This is a precious place to have passed the night in," continued Jaundice, with a savage frown. "If you had moved those legs of yours we could have got to the village before the storm came on. I had a good mind, Wobbles, to leave you behind."

"If you had," replied Wobbles, turning pale at the very thought, "I should now have been a cold corpse lying on the sandy plain for the crows to peck at."

"As good a thing as could happen to you," said Jaundice; "for what good are you? I often wonder I had anything to do with you."

"It's wery kind o' you, Mr. Jaundice," replied Wobbles, "and I shall never forget the honour as you showed me in old England, when you helped me to get through the little money my mother left, and showed me how to make real golden suv'rins out of brass door-knobs."

"Hush, you fool!" cried the other. "Do you want *that* to be known?"

"There isn't anybody anigh us," replied Wobbles.

"How do you know?" asked Jaundice. "The very air will sometimes betray us. Besides, if you don't want your head knocked off, you will let the past rest."

"So I would, if it would only let *me* alone," replied Wobbles; "but it won't, and when I thinks of that three hundred pounds which my mother raked and scraped up for me in twenty years, and the six silver teaspoons, silver teapot, and warious other articles, which all went in a month, my wery heart do bleed—indeed it do!"

"You shouldn't have backed the wrong horses, then."

"Which the tips come from you, and I puts the money on with a friend o' yourn," said Wobbles, softly.

"What did you say?"

"Nothing," said Wobbles, hastily. "I was only taking in a hextra breath of this fresh morning hair."

"Air, you beggar—not hair."

"Not being hedicated," said Wobbles, "little herrors might be overlooked."

"Come," said Jaundice, rising, "there is the sun, and I think we may be moving. You won't be blessed by the Ogre for keeping me away, as I was to have given him his revenge last night."

"That Ogre," said Wobbles, as he stretched his podgy legs, "is a most dreadful party. I never looks at him without a curdling all over me, and a general feeling about the legs as if the calves had gone round on their own axis."

"You are all calves—and calf," said Jaundice. "A curse upon this weather! I am stiff as an iron bar. If we hasten we shall be back in an hour."

He stepped lightly over a narrow brook close to the rock, where the water ran rapidly, and strode on. Wobbles regarded the brook attentively for a moment, and then retreated a few steps, to make a running jump of it.

It could have been done easily enough; but that dreadful limpness to which he alluded so pathetically came over him as he took his spring. and into the water he went, with his chin and shoulders on the bank opposite.

"Murder!" he gasped. "Help! Save a drowning sinner!"

"What now?" cried Jaundice, turning back. "What! not able to get over that! Come out, you lubberly son of a cook."

He seized Wobbles by the collar, and jerked him out upon his back, then strode on, leaving the other to follow at his leisure.

Wobbles shook himself, and trotted after him, uttering short gasps expressive of discomfort. Their way was rough—over a broken plain, with rocks and bushes scattered about, and here and there a rising hill. Far away in the horizon was a line of blue misty clouds; but these were mountains, a good two days' journey away.

An hour passed without the pair exchanging a word. Jaundice led, and Wobbles followed—Jaundice with his head bent down, brooding like a man who had a very big skeleton in his cupboard at home.

An exclamation from Wobbles woke him from his day-dream, and, looking up, he beheld his follower in a fixed attitude, staring away to the left, and, following his gaze, saw three figures crossing an open part of the plain.

Seemingly there were two men and a boy—the boy riding on the back of the man who was taller than the other. They were approaching the path taken by Jaundice and Wobbles in an angular direction.

"What now?" cried Jaundice. "Who is here?"

"Some dark and desperate villains, I'll bet," gasped Wobbles. "Shall I fire off my gun, to let them know that I am not to be trifled with?"

"Yes, if you want me to blow off your head, to let you know *I* am not to be trifled with," replied Jaundice. "These are strangers—one is a sailor, by his dress—and I dare say that they have something about them worth having."

"Don't!" cried Wobbles, sinking suddenly on his knees—"don't, for goodness sake! I can't stand it—I can't abear it!"

"What's the matter with you, ass?" said Jaundice.

"I've seen too much of it!" gasped Wobbles, "and too many of 'em. They haunt me—I see 'em in the night, with their throats cut; and when the wind blows I seem to hear moaning, as that poor fellow did who——"

"Silence!" cried Jaundice, striking him with his open hand. "What next will you blare about? Confound you, do you think I'm going to murder these men?"

"I hope not," said Wobbles, as he got up. "It's too dreadful—indeed it is—it's hawfull!"

"I am only going to see if they are worth anything," returned Jaundice; "and, if they've got any pluck, I'll take them to the village, and play a game of euchre—that's all."

"I hope it will be all," said Wobbles, with a wild eye. "But if they win——"

Jaundice suddenly cocked his gun, and Wobbles collapsed. But, if he said nothing, he evidently thought a great deal, for, if ever a heartfelt fear was written on the face of man, it was upon his.

"You keep up with me, and say nothing until I speak to you," said Jaundice; "and rub your face to put a little colour into it, you lily-livered hound."

"It's all very well to be brave when you ain't haunted," murmured Wobbles; "but, if you got the curdles I do in the night, you'd sing another song."

"Do you think that I am free?" asked Jaundice, bitterly. "Do you imagine I have no grim shadows by my side?"

"If you have," said Wobbles, "you seems to like 'em."

"I am a man, and defy them," replied Jaundice.

"He's a livin' wonder," soliloquised Wobbles, as they moved on—"hard as a stone, tough as leather, and remorseless as the tropical halligator. If I could only get away from him, I'd go to some place as he don't know of, and try to get a respectable living. But where is that place? I don't know—he'd find me out if I was to dive into the bowels of the hearth. It's no use—I'm with him until somebody knocks him on the head; and Lord end a henergetic man to do it as soon as possible!"

The three strangers by this time were aware of the approach of Jaundice and Wobbles, and stopped to let them come up. As he drew near, Jaundice saw that what he took for the second man was only a boy—hatless, but otherwise dressed in sailor's garb.

"By Jove!" he exclaimed, "that's a fine young fellow; and the other is a strong one. What cheer, my fine friend? Whither going?"

"Can you direct me to a town?" asked the man addressed.

"I can direct you," replied Jaundice, smiling, "but I am afraid you would never get there. The nearest town is three hundred miles away."

"Then we are lost!"

"Not so. We have a small settlement here—of jolly good fellows."

"Oh, lor'!" gasped Wobbles.

"Will you be quiet?" hissed Jaundice. "We have a small settlement close by, and shall be very glad to give you such shelter as we can."

"Thank you very much!"

"Your name, stranger?"

"Ashleigh; and these are my two sons—Jack

and Cecil. We were wrecked on the coast last night, and, finding nothing but barren rocks there, came inland in search of friends and shelter."

"You shall have both," said Jaundice, with assumed heartiness, which jarred on the listener's nerves, in spite of his desire to accept the offer graciously. "My friend Wobbles here knows the place."

"I do to my sor——" began Wobbles; but a look checked him, and he hastened to say, "and a jolly good sort you'll find 'em—so free and heasy, and haffable."

"Can I help you to carry that lad?" said Jaundice. "You seem to be rather lame."

"I was shaken a good deal last night," was the reply. "No, thank you. Jack will take his turn now."

Cecil, who had received the offer of Jaundice with anything but pleasure, was relieved when his brother took him on his back, and strode on ahead with a wide firm stride.

"Son of yours?" said Jaundice.

"Yes," replied Ashleigh.

"Fine lad!"

"Yes, and as good and brave a one as ever lived."

"No doubt," returned Jaundice; "he looks like it. You come from the old country?"

"You mean England?"

"Yes."

"I do. We were going to Australia, and got wrecked on this coast."

"Ah! just so. You might have been wrecked on a worse."

"I don't think so," muttered Wobbles from the rear.

"Were you speaking?" asked Jaundice, with great suavity, and a glittering eye, full of venom.

"It's a kind o' cough as hacts spontaneous," replied Wobbles.

"I'll give you some physic for it when we get home," said Jaundice.

The knees of Wobbles met, and his eyes turned up towards the clouds. Only by a strong effort—a tremendous one for him—did he succeed in stifling a groan.

"How is it that you have settled so far from here?" asked Ashleigh.

"It is on the road to the newly-discovered diamond-fields," replied Jaundice. "Some of the returning miners find our village convenient to stop at."

"Conwenient or ill-conwenient, they stops—for ever," muttered Wobbles.

Jaundice took a pistol from his belt, put it behind his back, and presented it at Wobbles, who looked straight down the muzzle, with every hair on his head stiff as a wire broom.

"A more lovely willago," he said, "can't be—good beds, good hair, and lots of agreeable company. Oh! it's a lovely place for invalids like the little chap ahead."

"My Cecil," said Ashleigh, "is not strong, and the heavy work of last night has proved too much for him—he is almost helpless."

"But he bears it well," said Jaundice. "How many beside you three escaped?"

"None. Nearly four hundred souls perished."

"Awful!" said Jaundice, trying to look sympathetic, and failing most dismally. "Oh! what a sad thing! The shore must be strewn with them."

"Alas! it is—with the old and young—men, women, and children."

"And their property?"

"The shore was covered with wreckage, but I saw no signs of anything that would be of service to us."

"No, I suppose not. You came here in a straight line?"

"In a straight line."

Jack turned round at this point, and suggested a few minutes' rest—more on account of his father than himself. The party sat upon the ground, Jaundice by the side of Jack.

"You've got some muscle, youngster," he said, feeling his arm.

"I suppose so," replied Jack, with a smile. "They used to tell me so at school."

"I don't think I ever saw a boy of your make before. What's your age?"

"Fourteen."

Jaundice whistled, and Wobbles opened his mouth about five inches.

"I gave you sixteen, at the least," said the former. "May I feel your arm again?"

"As you please."

"The biceps of a giant!" muttered Jaundice—"bigger than they look. What will you be when you have reached manhood?"

"A man, I hope," replied Jack, quietly.

"He will be a whopper!" said Wobbles.

"I hope we shall be friends, youngster," said Jaundice, after a pause.

"Much better for you if you are," put in Wobbles—"that is, I meant to say, better for all parties; for there's nothing like being friends. It saves a world of trouble, and a heap of gory—noses."

He was going to finish with something else, but a glance at Jaundice showed that it wouldn't do. Cecil—who was lying down, with his head upon his brother's knee—looked from Wobbles to Jaundice with a keenness often found in the young who are delicate.

"I don't like you two," he said, suddenly.

Jaundice was too wary to ask why; but that blundering ass, Wobbles, put the question.

"Why not, my little chap?" he asked.

"Because one is a knave, and the other a fool," replied Cecil.

The candour of childhood could not be resented by men, and the pair referred to were obliged to swallow it as best they could. Jaundice affected to laugh, but Wobbles ventured on a little mild expostulation.

"Come," he said, "that's not perlite. When I was your age, if I had said such a thing before my sainted mother—which she left me three hundred pounds, three spoons, a teapot, and sundry harticles; and in less than a month the b'iling lot was gone, as Mr. Jaundice knows, for it was him as ——"

"Shut up, will you?" growled Jaundice. "That blessed teapot was only Britannia metal."

"But we made shillings of it," said Wobbles; "and I passed 'em off one by ——"

"Shall we be moving on?" said Jaundice, hastily. "Nothing jars on me so much as the babbling of a fool."

"I am ready," said Jack, as he hoisted his brother on his back.

His father got up slowly and painfully, and on his forehead there were small drops, which came of intense agony, silently borne.

"He's got his machinery put out somewhere," thought Jaundice, regarding him. "All the better. It will save us a world of trouble. I wonder whether he has any ready about him?" and he walked on meditating.

CHAPTER III.

THE VILLAGE.

"THERE'S the village," said Jaundice, pausing on the summit of a rising piece of ground, and pointing into a valley below, where about a dozen huts could be seen.

It was a pretty spot, with grass, and flowers, and beautiful trees, and a small stream winding about like a broad band of silver—an oasis in the rugged and almost sterile plain.

"That's our place," continued the speaker, "where a few good fellows dwell like brothers, living in peace and harmony. You might almost call it the abode of innocence."

Wobbles groaned.

"What's the matter with you?" demanded Jaundice, with an angry frown.

"It's that cough as comes in sudden spasms," replied Wobbles. "I can't help it."

"There is nobody moving about at present," said Jaundice, turning from him. "Up late last night, perhaps, playing a friendly game of cards—for love mostly, I should say. But come down and rest in my little crib. It is that but nearest to us."

None of the residences seemed to be more than hovels, but on a nearer approach they improved in appearance. The structures were rude, but comfort had not been forgotten. The residence of Jaundice had, to all appearance, about half a dozen rooms, and there were two good glazed windows on the side in view.

Jaundice went forward and knocked at the door. A woman with the remnants of great beauty still upon her opened it quickly, and stood in the opening, with arms folded across her breast. She was clad in the short silk dress and long mantilla of a Spanish lady, and the masses of rich black hair, drawn smoothly back, shone like ebony in the morning light.

"So you've come back," she said. "Where have you been all night?"

"That fool detained me," Jaundice replied, pointing to Wobbles. "He had one of his nervous fits, and would have died if I had left him."

"It is false!" she cried, passionately. "Where have you been?"

"If you won't believe me," said Jaundice, indifferently, "ask Wobbles."

"Come here," said the woman, beckoning to the most unwilling Wobbles. "You, at least, cannot lie with your face. Has he spoken the truth?"

"Hevery word is hauthentic," replied Wobbles, fervently.

"Speak plainly. Is it the truth?"

"It is, Mrs. Jaundice."

"You may go."

"Now that you are satisfied, Maggie," said Jaundice, "let me introduce you to some new friends, who are in need of shelter."

She had not noticed them before, but she saw them now, and, by her face, was favourably impressed, but she did not ask them to come in.

"Cannot they get food and shelter elsewhere?" she asked.

"Maggie—Maggie, I have asked them in," urged Jaundice.

"As you have asked others," she said, and his face darkened: "but let them come in. Ah! what is this?—a sick child! Give him to me. I want something to care for. I live in a wilderness of wasted love."

"Don't say that, Maggie," said Jaundice, in a wheedling tone.

"Give the boy to me," said Maggie, "I can carry him. I am strong. Ah," she added, looking at Jack, "you are very handsome; you have a noble face."

"Who ought to be jealous now?" asked Jaundice, laughing.

She paid no heed to him, did not hear him perhaps, but, taking Cecil in her arms, carried him in; the rest followed, and the visitors were astonished to find the place well-furnished with modern things. There was even a carpet on the floor.

"My humble home in the woods," said Jaundice, lightly; "you are welcome."

"How got you these things so far from a town?" asked Jack's father.

"Friends brought them for us on their way to the diggings," replied Jaundice, and Wobbles gave vent to another groan.

"Go and see if the others are up," said Jaundice to him, "and bid them come to breakfast."

Wobbles seemed glad to get away, for he skedaddled with much precipitation, and Jaundice asked Maggie what there was for breakfast.

"Bread, coffee, and cold meat," she said.

"Will you spread it in the arbour?" he asked.

"You must spread it for yourselves," she replied. "I have work here. This child is very ill."

"Come with me then," said Jaundice, "and let her look to the boy."

"Yes, go," said Cecil, answering a look his father gave him. "This lady has a kind heart."

"My heart," she replied, "has been ashes these many years. The fires of sorrow and suffering have destroyed it."

"Oh, no," said Cecil, throwing his arms around her neck, "it is not all gone yet."

"Now she is happy," said Jaundice. "Give her a child to spoon over, and she is content."

"The child, at least, will not deceive," she replied—"nor slight—nor beat—nor curse—nor wring her heart with coldness and falsity—but take your friends away. This child wants food and rest."

Behind the house there was an arbour formed by the entwining of branches of half a dozen willow trees, with a beautiful creeping passion flower running over all. Inside was a long table, and seats for about a dozen people.

"This is our reception-room," said the host, "for the house is small at the best. Here we give our little dinner parties, and get the advantage of the fine air. You see we command a view of a pretty piece of the river and those far-off mountains. It is really very pleasant to sit here and smoke a cigarette when our coarser appetites are appeased."

"It must be so," said Ashleigh, a little coldly.

"You do not admire the place."

"Yes—no. I don't know. I am much fatigued, and can scarcely tell."

"Breakfast will put you right. I will have it ready at once."

In a few minutes there was coffee, bread, and a substantial joint of cold venison on the board, and Jack and his father were told to fall to.

"But have you not guests coming?" asked Jack.

"We have no ceremony here," was the reply, "as they come in they will begin. And, see, here is one. Monsieur Laranche—Mr. Ashleigh and his son."

The Frenchman was small even for a Frenchman, and he made himself smaller by pinching in his waist. He wore the ordinary walking dress of his native land, with the exception of the hat; that was a broad-brimmed straw article, suitable for the climate.

"It shall be stormy yesterday," he said, in compliment to the visitor, who, of course, being English, would like to talk about the weather.

"Very rough," added Jack; "we had a narrow run for our lives."

"I hear of the story of your great swim from our good friend Wobbles," said Monsieur Laranche. "He is a brave man. Ha, ha!—so."

"Signor Pedro," said Jaundice, as a tall handsome Spaniard, smoking a cigar, swaggered in. He bowed to the visitors and sat down.

"Will you not breakfast?" asked his host.

"Anon," he replied, "when I have finished my cigar. How fares it?"

"I cannot tell."

"Nothing in the wind?"

"That I can see at present."

The Spaniard appeared to be very dissatisfied. He tossed his cigar away, and helped himself to a cup of coffee. Two more men entered, and Jaundice introduced them. One was an unmistakable Yankee, and the other of Northern Russian mould. Both had shifting eyes, and faces of doubtful cast. Jack thought he had never looked upon two more unmistakable villains.

"Mr. Jim Skipper and Niamo," said Jaundice. "One more and our party will be complete. Has anybody seen the Ogre?"

"He was coming up with us," replied Skipper, "but he stopped to give the Tiger a thrashing."

"Which he did not succeed in doing."

"No, the boy is more a monkey than a boy, and more of the wild cat than anything else. He ran up a tree after tearing out a handful of the Ogre's hair. I left our friend taking pot shots at him with a pistol. Hear him."

The report of a revolver was heard, followed by a wild shriek, but whether of pain or derision it was difficult to say.

"That's the Tiger," said the Yankee. "I'll bet he's hit."

"Done!" cried the Russian. "A ten-dollar bet."

"Done with you—quick! I hear the Ogre. Down with the dust."

The money was put down upon the table, and the next moment the entrance to the arbour was darkened by the form of the Ogre—the most diabolical thing in the form of man Jack Ashleigh or his father had ever looked upon.

Short of stature, but immensely broad and muscular, with shoulders that looked as if, Atlas-like, they might have borne up the world—his legs, bare from the knees, were models of strength; but, being bowed, were not pleasant objects; and his great splay feet, which seemed to absolutely grip the earth as he stood, reminded one of the great antediluvian monsters which science and skill have given us models of.

But the most repulsive thing about him was his face. It was not the dark skin, or the form of the features of half-caste type, that repelled one, but the look. Therein lay seven devils—cold—crafty—cruel—remorseless. It was not to be wondered at that he had obtained the name of the Ogre. It was the mildest cognomen they could have bestowed upon him.

His dress was simply a jacket and trousers of white linen—a simple attire that would have become most men, but only, in his case, seemed to add to his hideousness.

He regarded the strangers for a moment with bent brows, but gave them no sign of recognition or welcome, and sat down. Taking a revolver from his pocket he proceeded to load it. This was, evidently, the weapon he had been practising at the Tiger with.

That his companions stood in awe of him was apparent, as none addressed him until his work was completed. Returning the pistol to his pocket he helped himself to some venison and bread, and began his meal with the action of a wild beast, tearing both with his hands, and devouring the food like one famished.

"Did you hit the Tiger—eh, Ogre?" said Skipper, with a conciliatory smile.

"Malediction, no! One might as well try to hit a dragon-fly," was the reply.

"Dollars mine," said the Russian, taking them.

"What's that?" asked the Ogre. "Betting on my shooting?"

"Yes," replied the Russian. "I thought you wouldn't hit the Tiger."

"Then for your impudence you'll please to hand over half your winnings."

"But why should I?" pleaded the Russian. "You weren't here."

"Hand over."

The Ogre rose to his feet, and the Russian Niamo hastily brought out five dollars, and put them on the table. A grim smile passed over the Ogre's face as he took them up.

"The next time," he said, "I shan't wait so long. Hand out sharp when I ask for it."

"Pleasant society this," whispered Jack in his father's ear.

It was the lightest whisper possible, but the Ogre caught it, and turned to him with a frown.

"You'll not find it very pleasant if you don't take care," he said.

"I think you might be more polite to strangers," replied Jack, calmly. "We are only here for a few hours, and will not trouble you long."

"You will stay as long as I please, and go when I please," returned the Ogre.

"So that's your line—is it?" said Jack, slightly raising his eyebrows.

"That's my line!" said the Ogre, bringing his hand heavily down on the table, "and if a man here has another let him out with it."

"Father," said Jack, "give him yours and mine."

But his father did not answer him. He was leaning forward, with a fixed look and deadly pallor on his face. He was making a strong effort to conceal some awful pain.

"Father, what is the matter?"

"I don't know, Jack. I'm being torn to pieces. My God!"

He would have fallen if Jack had not caught him in his arms. His whole strength left him, his head fell forward on his breast, and he was as one dead.

"Make way there, and let me get him into the air!" cried Jack, and without ceremony he broke through the men, bearing his father with him.

Outside he saw Maggie standing by the door of the hut. As soon as she saw that something was wrong she came running down.

"What new piece of foul work is this?" she cried.

"I fear he was injured last night," replied Jack. "He has fainted."

"Bring him into the house," said Maggie; "he will be safer and better there," and the strange woman, followed by Jack with his burden, entered the hut.

CHAPTER IV.

THE OGRE'S MARK.

"THAT'S a stiffnecked young beggar," said Skipper the Yankee, as our hero disappeared; "but it's just like them Britishers —all starch and impudence."

"I'll take his stiffness out of him before he leaves here," growled the Ogre, "and set a mark on him that he won't get rid of in a hurry."

"What mark?" asked Jaundice.

"Put your heads together, and I'll tell you," said the Ogre.

The men drew up, and he whispered a few words that sent them all into fits of laughter. Jaundice was so tickled, or pretended to be so, that he rolled on the ground, and shrieked with delight.

"It's good," he cried, "and everybody will know then that he is the real stuff. Oh, dear me! you are such a humorous cuss, Ogre."

Wobbles at that moment drew nigh, coming up very much like a cur who expected to be received with a kick. The Ogre beckoned to him, and with limp limbs he rolled rather than walked up, his mouth moving, but he uttered no sound.

"Go to the forge," said the Ogre, "and light the fire. Get a good one ready, or I'll make you sit on it. Do you hear?"

"Oh! yes, Mister Ogre, I hears," replied Wobbles.

"Then obey. Off with you!"

"What a hawful life this is!" thought Wobbles, as he trotted away. "If I could only get out of it —if I could only run away, but I dursn't. What a miserable horphan I ham!"

His way lay through a shrubbery with many twists and turns in it, and he was soon out of sight of the band of ruffians, which gave him immense relief. Pausing, he wiped his flabby face with his coat sleeve, and sighed.

"If the sperrit of my loving mother is looking down on me," he muttered, "how sorry she must be for me! Three hundred pounds, three teaspoons, and a teapot all gone in a month, and me a slave to a gang of murderous willains. Oh! Wobbles—Wobbles —— Murder! who's that?"

"Massa Wobbles, dat you?" said a soft voice, and a lithe dark-skinned lad came out from the bushes. He had a handsome face, remarkably large dark eyes full of fire, well-shaped nose, and small mouth. His skin looked like polished mahogany, and his sole attire was a small white cloth about his waist, and hanging half-way down to his knees.

"Massa Wobbles, whar dat Ogre?"

"Not so loud, Tiger, or he'll hear you," replied Wobbles. "Oh! what a man he is, with the hears of a hass as we may say, he ketches everything! He's been afiring at you."

"Yes, Massa," replied the Tiger, capering with glee, "but no hittee me; bullet come quick, but me see him, and get away quicker.

"Oh! dash it—come, you know," expostulated Wobbles, "you are a hactive chap, but draw the line. You can't dodge a bullet. Come, Tiger, draw it mild."

"No hittee me," said the Tiger, emphatically. "Bullet come, and me put de thumb up to nose—so —and laugh. Ogre do a big swar."

"The haction by which you have just hexamplied your confidence in your hactivity is a wery wulgar one," said Wobbles, gravely, "and if you hindulge in 'em, you will be considered low. I never was low —it was allus the haim and hobject of my life to get into society. I was there a month, and went to the races with the noble and great, but when done out of three hundred ——. Yet I musn't talk of it. They want the forge fire lighted for some willany or the other."

"Me come and help you," said the Tiger.

"Yes, I know how you'll help, skipping all over the place; but come along."

The forge was a rough shanty in the midst of a dense mass of brushwood, and looked more like a place designed for some nefarious pursuit than for honest labour. What use a forge could be in such a place was best known to those who used it.

Wobbles and the Tiger took down a rough shutter and opened the door. Inside were all the fittings generally found in a blacksmith's shop, but they had the look of being very—very rarely used. Wobbles collected materials for a fire, and put the Tiger to work the bellows.

That boy was more like an imp than a human being—no portion of him was ever still. While he worked the bellows with his hands he kept up a fantastic dance with his legs, and when a good fire was got up and he was told to rest, he went skipping about the place like a monkey.

"I never did see such a kid," thought Wobbles, as he sat on a log smoking a pipe. "He must have got some everlasting galwanizer inside him. I'd back him agin the helectric heel. Get out of the way."

The Tiger just lightly touched the crown of Wobbles' head with his hands, and flew over him as light as a bird. Then he sprang up, caught hold of one of the beams of the roof, and drawing himself up, sat upon it, grinning and chattering.

"You do that sort o' thing a purpose to give a man a curdler, I think," said the half-terrified Wobbles. "Who was your mother?"

"Nebber see her," replied the Tiger.

"Nor your father?"

"Nebber had no fader."

"Oh! yes you had, for I knew him," said Wobbles.

The Tiger became suddenly quiet, and regarded his companion with a curious eye.

"Who was my fader?" he asked.

"A gentleman as is niver mentioned in perlite society," replied Wobbles. "Heverybody has heard on him, but nobody don't care to be introduced to him. His first name is Nick, unperlite people calls him Old Nick, but they does it behind his back."

The Tiger did not know what to make of it, and for a full half-minute was tolerably still, but the restless spirit, or whatever it was, soon set him in motion again, and he was in and out the house and over the roof, tumbling about like a cat, and getting no more harm than that feline creature proverbially does.

Several hours passed, and as there were no signs of the Ogre coming, Wobbles despatched the Tiger to see what he was doing. The active little wretch went off at a great rate, and came bounding back in a twinkling, with the intelligence that the Ogre and his chums were gambling in the arbour.

"With the stranger?" said Wobbles.

"No stranger dere," replied the Tiger, and Wobbles gave a sigh of relief.

Noon came and no signs of the Ogre, but the fire was kept up, as he might come at any moment. Wobbles, getting very hungry, despatched his will-o'-the-wisp friend for something to eat. The Tiger, with a celerity only equalled by those who obey Aladdin's lamp, brought down the remnant of the haunch of venison and some coarse bread.

"Who gave you them?" asked Wobbles.

"In at de window—out again quick," replied the Tiger; "stole him so."

"It goes agin my conscience to eat wittles thus perwided," said Wobbles, "but the wice of nature is a hoperating hinside me, and hat it we goes."

He and the Tiger picked the bone and buried it under a bush in case there should be any inquiries about it. Then they made the fire up again and waited.

Waited all through the weary afternoon—waited until night came, and Wobbles kept the fire up, and dared not leave his post. The Ogre was not the man to be trifled with.

About an hour after darkness had fallen a great shouting was heard in the distance, and Wobbles, who had been dozing by the fire, awoke in terror.

"What's that?" he cried.

"Fighting, massa," replied the Tiger, calmly "sittling de bisness ob de stranger."

"More crimes—more blood—more hawful nights with ghostesses by the dozen," muttered Wobbles, clasping his hands, "and such a young and handsome chap too! It's the work of hell, and I'll— I'll run away! Oh, that I could screw myself up to do it!"

"Somebody coming, massa," cried the Tiger, skipping up the centre beam and scuttling away into a dark corner of the roof, where he was not likely to be seen.

"It's done," gasped Wobbles, and cowered down with his hands before his eyes.

The sound of footsteps approached, and the door being kicked open, the Ogre and the rest came staggering in, bearing the form of Jack between them. He was bound seemingly with ropes, but he had not been secured without a severe struggle— the clothes of his captors were torn, and the face of the Ogre was covered with blood.

Wobbles dared not look up, and made no attempt to do so until the Ogre gave him a savage kick that rolled him over upon his back.

"Bear a hand here," said the brute, "and help us to tie him to the rack."

The rack, as the Ogre called it, was a broad board about the size of an ordinary door, with a ring intended to secure a captive, and the whole firmly fixed to the wall of the hut.

To this the men endeavoured to fix our hero, but to do this some of his present bonds were obliged to be loosened. He got his legs free, and another fearful struggle ensued.

Five strong men against a boy, and tough work for the five strong men. But for the Ogre the boy would have conquered. The muscular brute had a grip of iron, and felt the kicks he received no more than the trunk of a tree would have done.

Exhausted, Jack yielded at last, and was bound to the rack.

The Tiger looked on upon the struggle grinning, but Wobbles, aghast, cowered in the corner by the forge. When it was over the Ogre bade him blow up the fire.

"A good fire, that will heat speedily," he cried; "a roaring fire, that will make iron white."

"Ye—es," gasped Wobbles. "Oh, lor!—what are they going to do?"

"It's a pity that such a good Britisher should go about without a sign of his country," continued the Ogre with a grin. "I am going to put the Government mark on him. Off with his upper clothes—cut 'em away."

"Good," cried Jaundice; and the rest, still panting, laughed with him.

"You are slow with that fire," said the Ogre, as he rummaged among a lot of tools in a box. "Hasten —or I will put a mark on you that you shall carry to your grave."

"Better be in my grave," thought Wobbles, as he worked the bellows with a trembling hand, "than here to-night among these devils. What are they going to do?"

"I have it," cried the Ogre. "See, my comrades —THE BROAD ARROW."

"Good—brand him deep," they cried.

"I warn you," cried Jack, turning his flushed face round, "that for this night's foul work you shall live to repent."

"Boy," said the Ogre, "we have done worse, and we do not repent."

"Again I tell you pause. Brand me, and tremble."

"Blow on," cried the Ogre to Wobbles. "Up with the fire."

Between a pair of pincers he held a cast-iron Broad Arrow—the world-recognised mark for all things our Government owns. Fixing it firmly between the nippers, he thrust it into the fire.

"Work, you idle scoundrel!" the Ogre yelled. "Fire can scarce make it hot enough for him."

"Again I say to you, one and all—beware!" cried Jack.

"How shall it be, brothers?" asked the Ogre, with a sneer.

"Brand him!" they replied, and Wobbles only faintly said "Don't."

Jack heard the word, and turned a kindly look upon him.

"Of all these," he said, "you alone shall be spared."

"It is ready," said the Ogre, as he drew the brand from the fire. "Now, you accursed Britisher, beg for mercy."

"Never!" cried Jack.

"Again I say to you, beg."

"Again I say to you, beware!" replied Jack. "Monsters all, a heavy day of reckoning will come for this night's work!"

"Brand him!" they replied, and the Ogre thrust the red-hot brand between the boy's bare shoulders.

The white flesh hissed, the Ogre shrieked with laughter, and those who supported him yelled with delight; but the brave boy never flinched nor moved a muscle of his face. He was quietly collecting himself for a grand effort.

It was done—the mark was there, and this side of the grave could never be removed. The Ogre stepped back, and tossed the brand away.

"Let us re-christen him BROAD ARROW JACK," he cried.

"Henceforth," replied the boy, "it shall be my name; and when you hear it spoken, tremble in your infamy."

"Better kill him now," said Jaundice. "He is dangerous."

"Stand back!" cried Jack, as he wrenched the rack from its hold in the wall, and dashed it against the forge, where it broke into twenty pieces.

The perpetrators of the deed were aghast at this exhibition of his wondrous strength, and made in a body towards the door. Like a furious lion, angry with his bonds, Broad Arrow Jack tore off the ropes from his limbs, and, freed, looked round for somebody on whom to wreak his vengeance. Only the trembling Wobbles and the cat-like Tiger on his perch remained.

CHAPTER V.

OUT ON THE PLAIN.

BROAD ARROW JACK made one step towards Wobbles, then, remembering his promise to that horror-stricken individual, pulled up short. One glance only he cast at the Tiger, and, seeing he was but a boy, took no further notice of him.

"Who are you?" he asked, addressing the terrified Wobbles.

"A friend—indeed I am, though you wouldn't think it!" was the reply, given out through chattering teeth; "name, Wobbles—born at London—the only son of a loving mother, as doted on me——"

"I want you," said Broad Arrow Jack, cutting him short, "to guide me back to the hut of that rascal, Jaundice. I cannot very well find the way myself."

"But the tothers may—be—a lyin' in wait," suggested Wobbles.

"I ask for nothing better," replied Jack, twirling the great iron bar he grasped in his right hand; "but I do not think they will face me to-night."

"What a wery violent young man he is!" gasped Wobbles, "and only a boy, too! There'll be broken bones about if ever he becomes a man."

"Come," said Jack, pointing to the door, "light a torch, and lead the way."

"In a minute, sir," said Wobbles, shaking all over. "Oh! if there should be a scrimmage, I'm sure to get into the thick of it!"

He lighted a torch, and, with very uncertain footsteps, led the way. Jack, with sparkling eyes, and the gait of a lion, followed him; and, lastly, the Tiger, with a footstep as stealthy as the creature from whom he took his name.

It was a still night—so still that Wobbles involuntarily walked on tiptoe, as if he were in a chamber with the dead. The air was hot and oppressive; the dewless grass lay flat upon the earth; the leaves of the trees hung listless, and the very branches seemed to droop in the relaxing atmosphere. No wonder that Wobbles, born in a colder clime, and naturally of a feebler nature, should feel as if the little life left in him lay in his boots.

But if the air had been as hot as an oven—if the stillness had been the stillness of death—if all nature had been blasted around him—it would have been all one to Broad Arrow Jack.

All his thoughts and powers were concentrated on the diabolical cruelty he had just been the victim of, and what he could do in return. He cared not for the mark in itself—he loved his country too well to be ashamed of the Broad Arrow —but it was the knowledge of its being stamped upon him in such brutal mockery that drove him mad.

A boy in years, a man in form, he seemed to glow and blaze in his passion as he walked along; the torch in front seemed pale in comparison with his flashing eyes. If he could have grasped one of his torturers then the wretch would have bidden the world adieu.

But none came near him, and no rustling bush or stealthy footstep told of their presence. The hut where Jaundice lived was reached, and Jack, bidding Wobbles stand aside with a motion of his hand, opened the door, and went in.

He stood in the presence of his father and brother—seated in chairs, and propped up with pillows. A little distance away Maggie sat at work by the light of a wretched candle.

The strange appearance Jack presented drew a exclamation from his father and Cecil, and Maggie, shading her eyes with her hand, regarded him with astonishment.

"Father, Cecil, and you, dear lady," said Jack, "you may well marvel to see me thus; but foul work has been done. Did you hear nothing ere while?"

"We thought we heard sounds of fighting," replied Maggie; "but when I opened the door, and listened, all was still."

"The men, or demons—or whatever they are—"

"Call them demons," said Maggie, "and you will do them more than justice."

"These demons, then," said Jack, "hiding away in this place for what purpose I can only guess——"

"Guess at murder and rapine—at ruthless torture and slaughter of the innocent—and you will guess aright," said Maggie.

"How can they find the innocent in this wilderness?" asked Jack.

"Not far away lies the track taken by those who seek the new El Dorado," replied Maggie. "You have heard of the diamond diggings?"

"Yes, it was mentioned this morning."

"There are some who wend their way thither, and never reach the place," said Maggie; "others, returning rich and light of heart, who never find their homes."

"I understand," said Jack. "They find their way here?"

"Yes—to die!" replied Maggie, clasping her hands. "Everything here is stained with blood. If sticks and stones could speak, those here would babble tales of horror all the day long."

"And yet *you* are here!" said Jack's father.

"Yes, here until I die," she replied, passionately beating her breast. "I loved a man when his heart was fairly sound, and when his hands were white. I am a woman, and cannot leave him now, though his heart has grown as black as the shades of hell, and his hands are trebly died in blood."

"Poor woman!"

"I want no pity," she said, with a quick movement of her hand, as if to ward off sympathy. "As I have sown I reap, and will not mourn, though the harvest bring me nothing but tears and a remorse that daily rends my soul. To your story, young sir. I have interrupted you. What foul injury have you suffered?"

"When, at the end of the day," said Jack, "I left this house to breathe a little air, I strolled down into the wood, and was pounced upon by three demons. They carried me to a hut, and branded me. See here!"

He turned, and showed the blackened flesh, with the Broad Arrow spreading across his back. His father sprang to his feet, forgetting all his weakness and his injuries; and Cecil, with a cry, covered his face. Maggie's face scarcely changed—a slight knitting of the brows, and lips more closely compressed, were the only signs she gave that the sight affected her.

"Say nothing," pursued Jack; "give me no sympathy—I want none. All I need is, help to avenge this injury—this insult to me and mine. When the work was done, a great strength such as I had never known before came upon me—I burst my bonds, scared the brutes with my fury, and they fled. Tell me where I can find them?"

"How can I?" asked Maggie. "There are a hundred hiding-places here which I have only heard of—places which will defy your searching powers. They will never meet you openly again, but they will waylay you craftily, and kill you. You must away from here."

"Yes," said his father; "and we will go with you. What say you, Cecil?"

"I think with you," replied Cecil, lifting up his tearful face, "and when I am a grown man I will come back and help to avenge you."

"Bravely said!" cried Jack, putting an arm around his neck. "But I shall not wait so long, lest others rob me of my right of ridding the world of a nest of villains. Father, are you ready?"

"He will die by the way," said Maggie; "and the poor child wants a week's rest, at least."

"I could not remain here with Jack away," replied Cecil. "You have been kind to me, and I thank you; but I must go with Jack."

"I will not ask you to stay," said Maggie, "although I fear that sorrow will come of your leaving. You, sir, are in greater danger than you think."

"Madam, I could not remain here."

She urged them no more, except to take some food with them; but this they refused. The only thing Jack would accept was a cutlass which Maggie assured him had once belonged to a British sailor, and a pair of pistols but lately in the possession of a young American. Both were bound for the diggings, and never reached.

"Are you ready, father?" asked Jack.

"Ready, my son."

"Will you have no covering for your shoulders?" asked Maggie.

"No," replied Jack. "As I am I remain until my vengeance is completed. I go only to return. Tell them, when they see the Broad Arrow stamped or cut upon aught that is theirs, to tremble. They outnumber me, and are crafty; but I will meet craft with craft until I have paid back the work of this night with interest. Tell them to scatter over the wide world if they will, and I will track them. Tell them to skulk in company in the most secret hiding-place, and I will take them one by one, and those left shall not know the lost one's doom until his turn comes to share it!"

"You speak boastfully," said Maggie, a little scornfully.

"I speak prophetically," replied Jack, as he opened the door, and gazed out upon the darkness. "Even now a vision of my returning, with power to avenge, is before me. I see it—feel it! Yesterday I was but a boy—to-day I am a man, with the wrong of a lifetime upon me!"

"So young—so fierce—so terrible!" said Maggie.

"All that is fierce and terrible in me," replied Jack, "has slumbered until now. Ask my father there—ask Cecil—if e'er before they saw me tossed and torn with passion as I am this night?"

"Never before," said his father.

"Jack was ever good and gentle," said Cecil.

"Such wanton wrong and injury as this," continued Jack, indicating the brand with a motion of his shoulders, "has roused in me what might have lain dormant all my life. You, father, have oft told me the story of an ancestor who wreaked his vengeance on a false friend whose treachery shattered his domestic peace, and I see him before me now. As he was then I am to-night. Farewell, gentle lady. Thanks for your kindness. Our best wishes and pity be with you!"

"One word," she said. "You are resolved—you will carry out your vengeance?"

"If I live," he replied, "I will not falter or turn aside."

"Spare *one*," she cried, clasping her hands, "for my sake!"

"You mean he who brought me here?" returned Jack.

"Yes, yes—the man I love! Who else would I plead for here?"

"I can promise nothing to-night," said Jack.

"I know—I feel that your purpose will be carried out!" cried Maggie, sinking on her knees, and clasping Jack's hand. "But, oh! spare him! Mercy, I implore you!"

"How can I think of mercy when the blood in my veins is turned to liquid fire? No, I cannot promise."

"Mercy—mercy! Oh! for my sake, mercy!"

"Father, it is time we were gone," said Jack, and, taking Cecil in his arms, they left the hut, Maggie kneeling and clasping her head in despair.

Outside the coast was clear. Both the Tiger and Wobbles were gone. Jack, without bestowing a thought upon either, but with the visages of every man who had played a part in the cruel outrage burnt into his brain, led the way back to the plain outside the village.

CHAPTER VI.

THE OATH OF VENGEANCE.

"JACK, I must rest—only for a little while. It is the heat of the sun."

The heat of the sun does not often give the pallor of death to a face, and a pang passed through the breast of Broad Arrow Jack as he looked at his father. Two days' slow tramp across the plain, with no better food than a few roots and herbs, had told terribly upon him. With sunken cheeks, hollow eyes, and emaciated form, he was but the skeleton of the man he had been.

And Cecil, too, was wasting fast. Jack carried him all day, resting only when his father rested, ignoring heat, dust, and fatigue, and scarce lifting his eyes from his young brother's face, where the shadows of a coming change were darkening. Cecil was a handsome lad, and his well-formed features seemed to grow more beautiful as the hour of their decay grew nearer.

Poor Cecil was doomed to die. Jack knew it, although he scarce dared whisper the knowledge to himself. Grief for awhile almost shut out thoughts of his wrong, and stunted his great determination. All he sought at present was some spot where the little fellow could die in peace.

But he could not find it. His enemies were on his trail, seeking, as Maggie had warned him, to take his life by craft. Villains of their stamp have a dread of death passing that of ordinary men, and seldom run a risk by bold attack when cunning serves their turn. So these fellows came creeping on behind, watching and waiting for an opportunity to slay the brave lad.

On the morning following that night in the village, as soon as there was light enough upon the plain, he turned his face to the line of blue mountains in the distance, among which he knew he would find the diamond-seekers.

On the plain was a track, dimly defined, and this he traversed until nightfall, only diverging when a cluster of trees or bushes gave promise of food. He found enough to keep bare life within them, and that was all.

When night came he first discovered that the bloodhounds were on his trail. The air was balmy, but Cecil complained of feeling chilly, and Jack, collecting some leaves and rotten wood, after many efforts succeeded in lighting a fire. They gathered round its blaze, and were conversing in low whispers, when the report of a rifle rang out, waking up a hundred echoes over the plain.

Jack, with great promptitude, scattered the fire, and, seizing Cecil, carried him away from the sound.

"Are you hurt, Cecil?" he asked.

"No, dear Jack."

"You, father?"

"No," was the father's reply; but the brave man carried the bullet from that rifle in the fleshy part of his shoulder.

They sat down in the darkness, and watched. Nothing more was heard, and Cecil fell asleep. Neither Jack nor his father slept until dawn, when Jack just closed his eyes, to have them re-opened by the sound of a second rifle.

He sprang up, and looked around. Broken rocks, clumps of bushes, and scattered hillocks were in sight, but no living being.

A danger from an unseen source is always more terrible than one with a palpable origin, and Broad Arrow Jack felt something akin to fear that morning—not for himself, but for those with him. "If I fall," thought he, "what will become of father and Cecil? Weak, and almost helpless, they must fall into the clutches of our secret enemies, from whom we can expect no mercy."

Thrice again during that day was he—or those with him—fired at, and each time from an unexpected quarter. In vain did he exercise all his vigilance, and keep his eyes roving constantly over the landscape. Not once did he catch sight of anything more than some small wild creature—weasel, or stoat, or the like—hurrying away from the foot of the stranger.

From this he argued that those hovering around him were few in number—two or three at the outside, or perhaps only one; and, his mind reverting again and again to the Ogre, he arrived by degrees at the conclusion that his was the hand that fired these shots.

When night came for the second time they rested first by a clump of bushes, but soon after dark shifted their quarters fifty yards or so, moving as quietly as mice who know that the cat is not far distant. It was, as the two previous nights had been, very still; and shortly after they had taken up their second position Jack fancied he heard a sound like a human footfall.

Whispering a few words in Cecil's ear to the effect that he would not be long away, he crept back to the place they had left, with eyes and ears strained to catch signs of the stranger. He reached the spot, or as near to it as he could guess, and put out his hand. It touched something warm, like a man's arms, and, with a low grunt or growl, a figure sprang up, and rushed away with the speed of an arrow.

Jack drew one of his revolvers, and fired, but he missed, and a yell of derisive laughter came out of the darkness. There was no mistaking the sound of that voice—it was the Ogre.

"Demon in human form," cried Jack, "come and meet me hand to hand!"

Another yell of laughter answered him, and, although he challenged again and again after it had died away in the darkness, the foe gave no further sign.

The third day came, and the sun's light shone upon the distant mountains—apparently as far away as ever.

Jack was aware that they were making but slow progress, and he was a little disheartened at the small result of their two days' toil.

It was a hot morning—close and stifling—no wind below, and very little above. In the west were a few patches of cloud, which crept rather than sailed towards them.

Jack looked at his father, and saw a man with a hundred lines in his face, sunken cheeks, despairing eyes, and quivering hands—all strange to him a week before. His gait, his look, the broken words he uttered, all told of an absorbing racking pain within him, but he never complained.

"Father," said Jack, "you are ill. Let us rest in some cool place to-day."

"No—no!" was the reply. "On—on, Jack—away from this place. There is peace and rest among yon mountains."

"So far away!" muttered Jack. "But stay—for Cecil's sake, if not for your own."

"No, I cannot rest here. Let us go on," was Cecil's reply. "I think I can walk a little to-day. See, I am quite strong."

He was only strong enough to stagger forward half a dozen paces, and sink down upon his knees. Jack had him in his arms in a moment.

"No, Cecil," he said, "you cannot walk yet. When we reach the mountains, and you are strong again, you shall run by my side."

"When will that be?" asked Cecil, looking him quietly in the face.

BROAD-ARROW JACK.

BY THE AUTHOR OF

HANDSOME HARRY and CHEERFUL CHING-CHING.

BROAD ARROW JACK INVOKES VENGEANCE ON THE MURDERERS OF HIS FATHER AND BROTHER—HENCEFORTH HE LIVES FOR REVENGE ALONE.

No. 2.

"Soon—soon, I hope!" replied Jack, with a despairing look.

They moved on, and Jack bent over to cast some shade upon his brother, regardless of the agony of his scarred back, on which the sun rained beams of fire. Great blisters sprang up on his fair skin, and the flesh, broken by the brand, began to peel off, leaving the under and more sensitive covering exposed. But he never complained—indeed, he scarce heeded his own sufferings.

A pitiful procession this! The father first, with enfeebled gait, bent head, and clasped hands, keeping straight on, and looking up now and then at those beautiful mountains which seemed to grow more shadowy as the hours flew by; his elder son behind, naked upward from the waist, bearing in his arms the poor lad whose days were numbered.

It was near noon, although they thought that night must be at hand again, in spite of the sun not having reached the mid-heavens. The hours lagged on, when again the rifle was heard, and Jack's father, who was climbing over some pieces of broken rock, threw up his arms, and fell back heavily.

Jack was about twenty yards in the rear, and the bullet, to have struck his father, must have passed close by him—was, perhaps, aimed at him. He sprang round, but, as before, only the bushes, trees, and other common objects of the plain, could be seen.

His father demanded his first care, and, putting his brother upon his feet, he ran towards him. Cecil slowly followed.

"Father," he cried, "are you much hurt?"

Two eyes stared at him, but there was no speculation in them; two nostrils quivered for a moment, and the man lay limp and lifeless, with blood flowing from his chest. The bullet had entered at his back, and passed clean through him.

"Oh! Cecil, look here!"

But while he spoke, and ere Cecil could look, the rifle rang out from another quarter, and the sick boy leapt into the air, and came down upon his face.

With a wild cry of agony Jack raised him in his arms, and called upon him to speak; but his hands hung lifeless at his side, his face was fixed, and in this world Cecil would never speak again.

What were Jack's own wrongs to this? What was the passion of the previous night to the fury which possessed him now? The sky was red—the earth was red—his blood bubbled within his veins, and rushed and roared through his brain; he looked here and there, but saw nothing, and in his impotent fury he tore up masses of rock from the earth, and dashed them into fragments.

He cried aloud for his enemy or enemies to come forth, but no man answered him. He called them cowards, hell-hounds, and many other terms they justly deserved, and the only answer came from the vulture and eagle—so ready on the heels of death—wheeling in the air, and shrieking in anticipation of a feast.

What could he do? He could not search the wide plain. One rapid circuit revealed nothing, and, returning to the side of his brother, he beat off a pair of old and daring vultures, and, with clasped hands, renewed and strengthened his bitter oath of vengeance. What little mercy for one or more of his enemies that might have been smouldering within him was extinguished, and henceforth he lived for one thing alone—revenge!

CHAPTER VII.

BILLY BRISKET.

A LEAN lank man, with a pack upon his back, came striding through one of the gorges of the mountains that looked so blue upon the plain. He wore tight-fitting velveteen clothes upon his body, as became a man of his craft; but on his head he wore what surely pedlar never wore before—a handsome smoking-cap, with gorgeous braiding, and yellow silk tassel—the sort of thing which tremendous swells affect at home. In his hand he carried a rough stick, but nothing in the form of fire-arms or other dangerous weapons was visible.

In looks he was a simple man, with a common face, expressive of nothing in particular, and features that came under no recognised order of beauty or ugliness. You could not say that his eyes were black, brown, blue, or grey, or that his nose was Roman, Grecian, or pug, or even that his mouth was large or small. Nor could you have told his age. Some would have guessed him at twenty-five, and others at fifty, and not a few would have declined to guess his age at all. One moment he was grave, the next gay—now singing a fragment of song—anon uttering short jerky groans of despair.

There seemed to be a good deal of the chameleon in his nature, and not only his face, but his figure, apparently reflected the nature of things around him. For instance, when passing between two high rocks, his face became solemn, and his figure bowed, while in the gloom; but as soon as he emerged again into the sunlight he straightened his figure—a tall one it was—and, with a smile and song, pursued his way. He was a brisk walker, as well he might be, having little else but bone and clothes to carry with him.

"It's a long way," he muttered, as he strode along—"a long way, and one mountain is no sooner down than another comes on. Oh! my sides! Oh! my bones! Tra la la! Come, let us be happy and gay, my boy (singing); remember the world is wide; Rome wasn't built in a day, my boys"—stopping suddenly, as the shadow of a tree fell upon him. "Well, who ever said it was? Who wanted it to be built in a day, or a month, or a year; and what's the odds now? Rome *is* built, and that's enough for us. Oh, dear! what a miserable world it is! Tra la la! tra la la! tooral looral lay! Hullo! who the deuce is this?"

A bend in the gorge brought him in sight of another creature coming towards him—a tall half-naked man, as he thought he was, carrying a cutlass in his hand. The instinct of self-preservation prompted the pedlar to get behind a rock with an amount of activity rarely exhibited by anything outside the monkey tribe.

"That fellow has had a hard time of it," he muttered, peering cautiously out. What a strapping man! What a figure! What arms and limbs! What—— Good heavens! he's only a boy!"

And a boy it was—Broad Arrow Jack, with worn feet and sunburnt form—ignoring cuts, bruises, and aching bones—striding in the direction of the diamond fields. The pedlar took stock of him as he approached, and was in doubt about showing himself or not, when the question was settled for him by a large species of ant.

This little animal—popularly supposed to be the most industrious thing under the sun, although there is a little humbug about that—ventured up the leg of the pedlar's trousers, and, finding itself on new ground, tested its qualities with a bite.

The pedlar gave a groan and a skip, and rolled out of his hiding-place at the feet of Broad Arrow Jack just as he was passing by.

Jack staggered back a pace or two, and looked astonished, as well he might, at this strange apparition; but the pedlar, with a presence of mind his appearance did not give him credit for, was on his feet in a moment, and, with a turn or two of his hands, had his pack off his back, and open before the eyes of the other.

"Now, sir," he said, "what can I do for you to-day? Any cotton, tape, or needles, ink, note-paper, sealing-wax, tooth-brushes, pocket-combs, tintacks, brass-headed nails, lip-salve, ointment, or shaving-brush? Beard coming on a bit, sir, and will be as thick as a hearth-broom in a month. Let me recommend a shaving-brush. Here's a beauty, originally made for the Prince of Wales; but the noble prince went in for hair, and cast the brush upon my hands. You'll take it, I know, sir—eh?"

Broad Arrow Jack pulled up, and looked at the speaker as if he failed to grasp the meaning of his words. The pedlar spoke with great volubility, as if he was speaking something off by heart, and was in a hurry to get it over.

His open pack contained a miscellaneous lot of articles—odds and ends, bits of ribbon, old cloth, a pocket-knife or two, half a dozen combs, and a heap of other articles, with a collective value of about one and fourpence. The shaving-brush rejected by the prince bore signs of having been used—probably by the pedlar himself, who, knowing its value, would be loth to let it lie idle.

Busily sorting his stock, he continued speaking, without looking up.

"Out in the fields," he said, "you'll find a few needles and a hank of thread useful, let alone a dozen good brass buttons and a bit of old cloth or so, as rents *will* come when you least expect 'em, and a patch is no disgrace to any man. Put your own price on what you want, and I won't grumble. Eh—what's the matter?"

It was scarcely a groan he heard, but more like a stifled cry of despair. As he raised his eyes the pedlar saw a face white as a sheet, dry, quivering lips, and glassy eyes.

"Good heavens!" he cried, "you are starving!"

Broad Arrow Jack made a confirmatory sign, and the pedlar, with a haste which showed how much he valued his stock, turned his pack upside down, and shot everything upon the ground. Then, opening an inner pocket of the pack, he brought out some dried meat and a flask.

Jack was tottering on his feet, and would have fallen but for the friendly arm of the other, who supported him with one hand, unscrewed the top of the flask with his teeth, and poured some of the contents down his throat.

"There," he said, "that will pull you round a bit."

"Thanks!" replied Jack, as the colour came back to his cheeks. "You are kind ——"

"Don't talk," was the rejoinder, "until you have eaten something. Here—it is good deer's flesh; and I think I've got a ship's biscuit somewhere. Yes, I thought so."

He brought it out from his pack, wrapped up in a handkerchief, and looked at it fondly as he handed it over.

"It's the last," he said, "and I kept it for my birthday, which is next Tuesday week. Bread is scarce in these parts, and we look upon it as a grand treat."

"I won't rob you of it," said Jack.

"If you won't have it," said the pedlar, "I'll shie it away. Now, then—one—two—three—the last time of asking. Will you have it or not?"

"You are a good fellow," said Jack, and he wisely took it—and ate it.

While he was thus occupied the pedlar took stock of him, and summed up his points thus—

"Wonderful figure — wonderful strength — but pulled down a bit. Handsome, intelligent, but got some great trouble on him as hain't nothing to do with wittles and drink."

While he was thus engaged their eyes met, and Jack, seemingly quite restored, held out his hand with a smile of gratitude.

"You have shown me a kindness to-day," he said, "which I hope to repay. Your face I never can forget; but I should like to know your name?"

"Billy Brisket," was the reply, "general dealer by business—wanderer and wagabone as a matter of choice. May I ask your name?"

"Broad Arrow Jack."

"That's a rum 'un!—not a regular name, you know, is it?—what some people call a num-de-plum."

"It is my name," replied Jack. "See—it is written on my back."

The sight of the brand made Billy Brisket reel, and, tripping over his pack, he took up a sitting position on the ground.

"Good Lord!" he said, "where did you get that from?"

"What matters?" replied Jack. "Those who put it there will have to answer for it bitterly."

Billy Brisket regarded him with a keen and searching look. The result seemed to trouble him a little.

"My lad," he said, "will you tell me your story? I'll keep it to myself, if you wish it."

"It is told in a few words," replied Jack. "All I wish to reserve is, who I really am, and why I came to this country." The rest, which our readers know, he told to the pedlar.

With unflagging interest Billy Brisket listened, and gradually there settled down upon his face a deep earnestness, which looked like a powerful reflection of the look worn by Broad Arrow Jack. When the narrative was finished he got up, and began to re-arrange his pack.

"Seemingly you don't believe me," said Jack, wondering at this supposed indifference.

"I don't doubt a word of it," replied Billy Brisket. "I know the men who did it, and I know many things too awful to speak on as stands against 'em for the Judgment Day. I am only packing up, so as to be ready to start with you."

"With me?"

"Yes, my lad. I'm a-going with you, and I am going to help you through this business. I can be of service to you in more ways than one, though you mayn't think so. I haven't tramped these regions for a good seven years without finding out something—aye! something more than any man knows of! I was a-going back home now, to get somebody to help me to work out a plan. There's wealth to be got, my lad—wealth untold; and with wealth you can procure men and means to carry out anything. I needn't go home now, for I've found the friend I want—a friend worth a dozen of any men I know, boy as you are."

"But I don't understand you," said Jack, bewildered. "How can you help me? How can you give me wealth?"

The eyes of Billy Brisket twinkled like two stars as he replied—

"Come and see. Trust me, my lad."

"I will," said Jack. "My hand on it."

"And my hand on this," cried Billy Brisket—"that if I live, and you live, that lot of scoundrels shall be brought to book—they shall dearly rue their work. But, I say, won't you have a coat, or waistcoat, or something, just to keep off the heat of the sun?"

"Not yet—not yet," replied Jack. "I am ready. Which way shall we go?"

"Back by the road I came," replied Billy Brisket, "and if we step out quickly I know of a place where we can pass the night comfortably. I hope you won't mind my singing or groaning a bit now and then. I do a little of each, as I am fond of a change. Tra la la! When the wind blows—why, then the mill goes, and our hearts are light and merry. Sing hey derry down! Heigho! this is a troublesome world, and there are a lot of villains in it—confound 'em!"

CHAPTER VIII.
THE OGRE'S RETURN.

JEB JAUNDICE sat upon a log by his hut, whittling a stick, and close behind him stood Maggie, leaning against the door-post, with folded arms, and anger in her face.

"Jeb," she said, "you ought to have had no hand in this work."

"When others are in it," he replied, savagely, "how can I keep out?"

"There comes a time to all who sin when the measure of their iniquity is full," said Maggie. "Another drop, and yours will be running over."

"How could I stop the Ogre?" asked Jaundice, dashing the stick and knife upon the ground. "You know, when his mind is made up, none can turn him aside. I begged of him to let them go in peace. 'It was a mad act,' I said, 'to brand the boy. We might have killed him, and there the matter would have ended. But let him go now. He may forget or forgive us, or he may die.' 'Let him go,' I said; 'we want no more blood upon our hands.'"

"And what said the Ogre?"

"He laughed, and said his work was just begun. 'From the moment I saw that lad,' he said, 'I hated him.'"

"As the darkness hates the light, and demons turn from angels."

"The Ogre would be pleased to hear you speak of him thus."

"I care not," returned Maggie. "I do not fear him. Though you all tremble before him, his eye never meets mine."

"And yet he could crush you between his finger and thumb."

"Let him do it—let him take away my wretched life, and I will thank him!"

"What, Jaundice, mon frère!" cried Laranche, the Frenchman, as he came up the path from the wood. "A good morning! Ah, milady! So I see there shall be clouds in the domestic sky. Ah! but vat of that? The sun vill shine again, the birds shall sing, and all vill be love and peace."

Maggie neither answered him nor returned his bow, which he apparently did not notice. Throwing himself carelessly upon a rude bench, he asked if there was any news of the Ogre.

"None," replied Jaundice.

"Four whole days!" said Laranche—"four whole days! He is slow at vork."

"Or his work may be finished, and the devil got his own," said Maggie.

"Madame has lost her usual sweetness dis morning," said the Frenchman. "It is a little vinegar dat shall spoil her for the time."

"If aught had happened to the Ogre," said Jaundice, "the Tiger would have returned with the news."

"Te boy vent vith him, den?"

"The boy is always with him, or nearly so—you know that. Not that he loves the Ogre. He can't do that, unless he is fond of kicks, and blows, and being made a target of when there is nothing else to shoot at. There is no fear of any harm coming to the boy—he is as wary as a wild cat, and active as a dozen imps. Have you fed this morning?"

"No."

"Then have something. Maggie, bring us food."

"You know where to find it," was the reply.

"Te usual politeness of madame has left dis morning," said Laranche; "but it will come again, vith te return of her sweet temper. Zen ve shall all be happy."

"Hark you, sir," said Maggie, advancing, "please to remember this—in future you will please to make no reference to me in my presence, nor to give me any more of your society here than is absolutely unavoidable."

"Maggie," said Jaundice, "my friends may come to see me."

"Not here," she replied. "Go plot and plan elsewhere. Do what deeds you will—dye your souls in blood again and again—but come not near me."

She went in, and closed the door. Laranche shrugged his shoulders, and pulled up a tuft of grass.

"Madame," he said, "grows inhospitable."

"I should advise you to take her at her word," said Jaundice. "She is not to be trifled with."

"If she were my vife," said the Frenchman, "I vould tame her."

"If you were her husband," replied Jaundice, "she would tame you. But let us have something to eat. Wobbles!"

"Yes, sir," answered the voice of that valiant man, and presently he appeared, with a face whiter than usual, and his knees giving way in terror under him.

"Come here, you hound," said Jaundice, politely, "and get us something to eat."

"I'm a going, sir; but, oh! dear me, what dreadful work!"

"What is the matter with you?"

"That imp, the Tiger, has just come back. Oh, lor', what work! We shall be hanged some day. We shall be taken to the place from whence we came, and thence to be danged by the—no, I mean hanged by the neck until we are dead, and the Lord ha' mercy on your soul!"

"What is the fool talking about?" asked Jaundice, frowning.

"Two dead—the father shot in the back, and the sick boy directly afterwards. It's murderous work, and we shall all suffer for it."

"Come here," said Jaundice, collaring him by the coat, and shaking him. "Now, then, perhaps you are a little clearer. Do you feel better?"

Wobbles feebly rubbed his forehead, and stared about him; but the shaking had very little if any restorative effect upon his faculties. He was next favoured with a kick, and, as this was a failure also, Jaundice was about to proceed further with remedies of that nature, when the Ogre came stalking in.

The fatigue, and dust, and dirt of three days' travel were upon him, but he showed no signs of being worn out. On his shoulder he bore a rifle, which he grounded and held in his left hand as the others greeted him.

"What news, Ogre?" asked Jaundice.

"Well—and ill. You shall judge for yourself. Give me food first; I am famished. Well, what are you staring at?"

The latter words were addressed to Wobbles, who, in a limp attitude, was gazing at the Ogre, fascinated by a spell of horror. On hearing the question he retreated a few paces, and feebly asked—

"Was I really looking at you? Beg pardon, sir. Oh! what an awful man he is! He's not black—he's red all over!"

Wobbles, however, had sufficiently recovered to get food from the house, and place it before the others. The Ogre ate like a wolf, Jaundice simply like a hungry man, and the Frenchman with the delicacy and refinement of a polished gentleman. Wobbles was hungry, but felt that he could not eat just then in such company, and put his share into his pocket for consumption a little later on.

"Has the Tiger returned?" asked the Ogre, suddenly.

"He was here this morning. Wobbles has seen him," said Jaundice.

"It was in the middle of the night," said Wobbles. "I was just in a lovely dream, back again at my mother's side, spelling a word of two syllabubs—syllables—when in he come, and jumped on the foot of the bed. He gave me a curdler—naturally thinking of ghosts as I was when he come up—but I knowed his voice. 'Two dead and one living,' he said. 'Massa Ogre shoot two, but de oder laughs at him, and go away.' 'Two what?' I says. 'Old massa and young boy,' says he. 'Net them as was here?' says I. 'Yes,' says he——"

"I'll stop his chattering," said the Ogre, with a vengeful look. "Go and bring him here."

"As soon as he had made that communication," replied Wobbles, "he took himself off."

"Where to?"

"I don't know, sir. He come like a sprite, and he went off like a sperrit."

"Jaundice," said the Ogre, "we must hold a council. Let Wobbles summon the rest."

Wobbles was despatched, and when he was gone the Ogre drew out his knife, and savagely plunged it into the ground.

"Jaundice—Laranche," he said, "the Tiger must be got rid of—he grows dangerous. I don't understand the boy."

"Whose work shall it be?" asked Jaundice. "Draw lots, I suppose?"

"Yes," said the Ogre. "It must be done."

Skipper, Niamo, and Pedro the Spaniard shortly came lounging in, and gave the Ogre a nod in greeting. He favoured them with a sinister notice, and waved his hand as an indication that he had something to say.

"Four days ago," he began, "I left here on a piece of business that you all know. It was a mere fancy, arising out of a hatred for that British beggar whom I branded. My hatred for him may seem strange to you—perhaps I hardly understand it myself; but there it is, deep in my heart, and gathering strength every hour."

"We loathe him, too," said Pedro.

"Perhaps so," said the Ogre; "but your hatred is as nothing to mine. You marvel at it, I know; but let that pass. Years ago, before I fell in with my present pleasant company, I lived among a different class. I was born to wealth—had friends, hopes, and—loved. All I lost, and through a man I have never seen; but I care not to dwell upon the story. I only mention it because, when that branded boy and his father came into this place, I felt as if I had been brought face to face with him who wronged me."

"It may have been so," said Jaundice.

"No—no," returned the Ogre—"impossible. Oh! but for this misshapen form, and this dark skin, I might have been another man! But I care not to dwell upon that. What I am I am, and so let it rest. You know how I left you—to track those three across the plain. At first I could have shot them one by one easily; but I let them go on, knowing they must suffer, and, joy to my nature——"

"The nature of a devil!" said a woman's voice, and Maggie stood before them.

The Ogre just glanced at her, and his eyes drooped. He could not bear to look at her.

"Go on," she continued. "I have not come to disturb, but to listen. I want to know how far down in the pit of atrocity man can go."

"I followed them," said the Ogre, with a defiant gesture, meant for her alone, "hour by hour, and saw them languishing with thirst and hunger, and in mockery I fired—to alarm, not to kill. I saw a look of anxiety in his eyes—in the eyes of him I branded—and I said to myself, I will torture him through them."

"Well thought of," said Maggie, "and worthy of you!"

"It was enough for me," said the Ogre, fiercely, "that he possessed beauty—that his skin was white, and he was fair to look upon, while I am misshapen and—and——"

"Loathsome!" said Maggie, calmly.

"Loathsome, if you will," he returned. "But it is the way of you women. You cannot look beyond the colour or form of man. Had it been otherwise I should not have been the demon I am."

"It was born in you, and it will go with you beyond the grave," was the calm answer Maggie gave him.

"Do not heed her," said Jaundice. "She is half mad at all times—wholly so when the fit is on her."

"What I am is your work," said Maggie. "But let us not bandy words. Go on with your story, Ogre. Oh! how fit the name!"

"It was not until I feared that death would rob me of the pleasure of killing," resumed the Ogre, "that I took careful aim, and slew the father. While his strong son was grieving I shot the sick lad, and left him alone. You should have seen his face then. Oh! it repaid me for years of contumely—for years of pain—years of self-loathing!"

"It shall be better if you had killed the strong son," said Laranche. "Is he alive?"

"He is," replied the Ogre, with an oath. "Do what I would I could not touch him. Whenever I took aim——"

"Skulking behind some hiding-place!" said Maggie.

"Whenever I took aim," pursued the Ogre, "something always intervened between us. Now it was a bird that swooped down from somewhere, flapping its wings, at the critical moment; now it was a cloud that passed across the sun; and then it was a haze that spread across my eyesight. I could not hit him. He passed me unscathed."

"Why not have gone out, and met him hand to hand?" asked Maggie, tauntingly.

The Ogre bit his lips, but did not reply to her. Addressing the others, who had listened to him with silent but all-absorbing interest, he went on—

"At length my last shot was fired; my pouch was empty, and night came on. In the darkness I lost him, and the light of the morning revealed him not again. I turned homewards; but ere I had walked a mile a likeness of him stood before me."

"A likeness of him!" said Niamo. "Surely it was he?"

"No," said the Ogre; "it was only an ethereal outline of him—a body of light—with a flaming sword in his hand. Call it a vision, if you will—call it a fancy of my distempered brain if you will; but it was there in front of me in the day, and by my side throughout the long night. More, it spoke—not once, but, as it seems to me, a hundred thousand times—its voice never ceased."

He stopped speaking, and his strong frame trembled. His emotion had its effect upon the others—they were all pale and silent.

"And what said this spirit?" asked Maggie.

"What matters what it said," replied the Ogre, "as it was but a dream?"

"Some dreams come true," returned Maggie.

"It is a pity you let the boy go," said Pedro. "Trouble will come of it."

"Great trouble," added Niamo.

"Ah! it shall be a bad day when he meets with us," said Laranche.

Jaundice said nothing, but his bent head and fixed attitude were sufficient index to his thoughts. Wobbles—who had drawn nigh, and ensconced himself in a bush—trembled so that the branches rustled as if shaken by the wind.

"Comrades," said the Ogre, "it seems odd that a boy should be able to excite a commotion among us; but so it is. The thought of danger is new to us, as we have lived here for years in security."

"The only place on earth where you could have lived so," said Maggie.

"True," returned the Ogre, turning his face—but not his eyes—towards her. "We are outcasts—have made ourselves so, if you like. We have been driven back to the brute state by civilisation, and let us be brutes. I rejoice in it—I cast such culture as I had aside, and live, eat, and drink as a brute."

"Being brute-born," said Maggie.

"Jaundice," said the Ogre, putting a hand upon a pistol, "ask her to keep quiet."

"Maggie," said Jaundice, "go in."

She laughed lightly, but she obeyed him. As soon as she was gone the Ogre beckoned them all to draw in closer. Wobbles, in the bush, strained his ears, and caught the following—

"What shall we do?" said the Ogre. "This boy will return."

"It is not certain," returned Jaundice. "He may die—may be dead even now."

"Be not deceived," replied the Ogre. "*He will come back*—armed, perhaps, with a power to crush us. What shall we do?"

"We can only wait," said Jaundice; "and when he comes it will be time to flee."

And so said they all. Like rats with dogs outside, they preferred to remain in their hole.

"It's all werry well," thought Wobbles, in a cold tremour; "but what is to become of me?"

Again he turned his attention to the others. The Ogre was speaking.

"We must dispose of the Tiger," he was saying. "The boy, wilfully or unintentionally, may betray us. Let the first man who meets him decoy him into his house, and shoot him dead."

"Agreed," they said.

"And what of Wobbles?" asked Skipper. "He's a bit of a burden."

Conceive, if you can, the agony of Wobbles when he found himself brought on the carpet. At first he thought his life as good as gone; but the voice of Jaundice came to his relief.

"Wobbles," he said, "is a bit of a coward; but he will do us no harm. I will keep him in order, and be responsible for him."

"He's not a bad-hearted chap, after all," thought Wobbles. "Oh! dear me, how I *do* wish I could get away!"

The party broke up, and the Tiger was sought throughout the village. He was not to be found on that day, nor the next, nor the next. Days—weeks—elapsed, and nothing was seen of him.

It was a trivial incident in the main; but with the disappearance of the Tiger the men were troubled yet the more. They were ashamed of the feeling—as they were of their fear of Broad Arrow Jack—but an instinctive feeling was on them that, sooner or later, they would be called to account for the deeds instigated by the Ogre, and so freely sanctioned by themselves. And the feeling was none the less for their having no idea as to the day or the hour, or from what quarter, retribution would descend upon them.

CHAPTER IX.

THE FATAL BRAND.

IT would have been better for these men if vengeance had come upon them at once. Death—swift and sure, or even slow death with torture—would have been as nothing to the agony of apprehension they endured.

They were all strong men, accustomed to dark deeds, and possessed with as little conscience as nature will permit a man to hold.

It is a fact, and a great fact, that, sin as you may—shut your heart and ears to all admonishing sounds as sternly as you please—the inward monitor is never entirely extinguished. It is not always speaking—not always crying aloud—or we should soon place it in the category of other common sights and sounds of daily life; but it is heard when we least expect it, and when we are least prepared—in the lone watch—in the still hour of night—in the time of weakness, sorrow, and suffering.

Trumpet-tongued it spoke to these men, but it awoke no repentance—only fear. It seemed to them, one and all, as if the coming of Broad Arrow Jack among them had ripped up the past, and laid it out, in all its ghastliness, before their eyes. They shuddered as they looked; but it was the quivering of hard hearts they felt—not the movement of a softened nature.

It was strange that the threat of a boy should move them thus; but moved they were, and, although they tried to laugh it off when together, when alone the terror came back, and gathered strength with each coming. They remembered his great strength —his looks—his words—and, in their terror, magnified all a hundred times.

"He will come," they said, and for weeks these men never walked out alone, and went hither and thither, if only for a few yards, always heavily armed.

Maggie kept alive these fears, partly because it pleased her to see these hang-dog villains tortured, and partly because she believed Jack would keep his word. Again and again she urged Jeb Jaundice to fly, and he would not.

"He will come," she said, "and woe then to those on whom he lays his hand!"

"Where am I to go?" asked Jaundice. "There is not a settlement around here where one of us dare show alone. In big towns we might get protection; but here, where only small bodies have settled down, each with laws of its own, a life like mine is not safe."

"Yours is not safe here," urged Maggie.

"At least I am with those who will stand by me," he said.

"Here you are all doomed," she replied.

What Wobbles suffered volumes would fail to depict. He ate, drank, walked, talked, and slept in a state of mortal terror. As usual with a man of his nature, he concluded that he would be one of the first to get into trouble, and most likely be favoured with the most painful death.

He shut his eyes to the fact that Broad Arrow Jack had spared him, and might reasonably be expected to do so again—in fact, he had promised it—and, with an ordinary dread of death, multiplied by twelve, upon him, he skulked about day after day.

"Of course he said he would not hurt me," thought Wobbles; "but he will forget that. I'm doomed to be roasted, toasted, and branded all over. Oh! that I had taken a small beershop with the money my aged mother left me, instead of going into betting! Three hundred pounds—a teapot—but why think of it? Here I am, a doomed man!"

But weeks flew by without any signs of Jack's returning, and confidence began to return. The Ogre and Laranche went to a distant settlement to buy powder, and returned unscathed. Niamo the Russian, and Skipper the American, went out hunting and shooting, and saw no signs of the dreaded foe. Maggie lost faith in his threats, and said—

"He was but a burly boy—a braggadocio, with nothing in him. Faugh! what creatures these men are! If I had been branded—— Ah! have I indeed escaped a mark as indelible as his?"

She put this question to Jaundice, who laughed as he replied—

"Why do you trouble your mind about it? Can you alter the past?"

"God help me, no," she said, and was silent for the rest of the day.

What was that past? Too long for these pages; but enough shall be told anon to show how she came to be what she was—a despairing woman.

Skipper, the Yankee—tolerably accustomed to bunkum in his own country—was one of the first to recover, and he was almost as loud as Wobbles in declaring what he would have done if Jack had really come. At the very least he would have turned him inside out, and skinned him afterwards, to cover a drum with.

Wobbles grew so valiant in time that he pretended to make excursions with the hope of finding Broad Arrow Jack; but he took great care not to go further than the outskirts of the small cluster of huts, when he lay down, and dozed or thought an hour or two away.

Laranche and Niamo shrugged their shoulders with relief, and said little. The Spaniard drew his sombrero closer over his brows, and muttered something about "British braggers," and Jaundice fell back into his old careless indifferent strain.

The Ogre said nothing.

He alone had not changed in thought. From the day when he came from his excursion on the plain a conviction had been upon him that Jack would come back to play a return match, in which the boy would most likely prove the winner. What game it was to be, and how it was to be played, the Ogre could not tell; but he was as sure that it would be played as he was of the coming of the sun in the morn.

But he and his comrades had to live, and that gave distraction to his thoughts. The diamond fields were prosperous, and men in search of them came that way. Those with goods and chattels had to pay heavy black mail to the Ogre and his band, and those who resisted paid their lives and all they possessed.

A more reckless, lawless gang of ruffians never lived, and many a desperate contest they had with wanderers in the wilds, oft receiving ghastly wounds, and once the life of Pedro was despaired of; but he recovered—"to be saved for food for Broad Arrow Jack," the Ogre said; and all but the Ogre laughed at it as an excellent joke.

It was a strange horrible life these men led, and oft they longed to change it; but their bed was made, and they had to lie on it. To leave their home was to put themselves within the pale of justice in the shape of Lynch law.

Larauche brought home a woman once—the wife of an emigrant who was shot in an encounter with the Ogre's band—but an hour afterwards she was missing, and not discovered until the next day, when Wobbles, going to the river for water, found her body under the roots of a tree on the bank. Maggie, with her own hands, took her out, dug the grave, cursed all the brutes by whom she was surrounded, and buried her. After this Maggie reigned supreme.

So two whole years passed, and no news of Jack came—he was almost forgotten. Life went on pretty well as before—the men hunting, robbing, and gambling—Maggie living apart from all but Jaundice—Wobbles general attendant, and labouring under a general funk. And so things appeared likely to go on, when a warning of coming change arrived.

It was early morning, so early that only the dim outline of objects could be seen, and Wobbles lay awake in his particular bed, in his own particular hut, with the door barred and barricaded, as if to defy the onslaught of a park of artillery.

Wobbles often lay awake at this time, thinking. Wobbles was more than tired of his life as it was at present, and he was trying to form some plan of escape. He knew if the attempt failed his life would not be worth an old boot, for it would be considered by the band that he had a traitorous object in view, and before taking his departure it was necessary to arrange a plan with a chance of getting clear away.

He lay there thinking—thinking, with only chaos in his mind, until on this particular morning, when he was startled out of his thought by a tap at the door.

A gentle tap, such as a woodpecker gives when performing upon the hollow beech tree, or the young man with a petition to the benevolent performs upon the front door of a respectable house—not by any means the sort of tap the Ogre or any of that lot would give.

A most mysterious tap.

"Who is it?" asked Wobbles, faintly. "Come in."

He forgot all his barricading preparations when he made the request, but somebody tried the latch, and quietly pushed the door. Iron spikes were as trifles to the hair of Wobbles, and stone statues full of beaming life in comparison with his frozen face.

For two minutes he was in this blissful state, and then, his blood slowly thawing, his hair relaxed, the blood returned to his cheek, and he squeezed out a groan.

"I must have fancied it," he thought. "It's the wind."

"Tap—tap."

"Who-o-o is it?" asked Wobbles.

Something was being thrust under the door, and although the light was so dim, every nerve of Wobbles was strained to the utmost, and he could distinguish a folded paper about six inches long.

"Now, what in the name of all that's evil is this?" asked Wobbles, as the sound of departing footsteps fell upon his ear. Re-assured by the belief that the party outside was really gone, he crept out of bed, seized the paper, got into bed, and proceeded to read something which scared him more than ever he had been in his life before.

On the top was a sketch of a broad arrow, with a skull and crossbones immediately underneath. Below these the following warning—

"TO THE OGRE AND HIS BAND.

"NOTICE, UNDER THE SEAL OF BROAD ARROW JACK.

"Is hereby given, that when any or all of them shall find the above seal set upon their houses, or aught that is theirs, they will do well to repent of the past, for their fate is sealed. For them there is no hiding-place on earth—no power of man to save them. To fly will be only to meet their fate half way. To hide will be but to sacrifice the little freedom left. To hope for mercy will be in vain.

"This is no idle threat for Broad Arrow Jack has all things needful at his command. His friends, his agents, are on every side, and in giving this notice he is only carrying out a purpose long formed and settled upon by him.

"ONE BY ONE

"Shall the pitiful dastards be removed in silence, and at an hour when least expected. It may be in the day, or in the night, abroad, or at home, but the avenger shall come.

"Villains, let your dark souls tremble when the brand of Broad Arrow Jack is on your doors."

* * * * *

"This," gasped Wobbles, as he lay back quite flabby with fear, "is about the pleasantest thing I've met with in this pleasant life. Oh, I'm done for! Come, roast or toast—boil or bake me, and let me get it over."

CHAPTER X.

THE OGRE IS WARNED.

WOBBLES, as in duty bound, resolved to lay the extraordinary missive he had received before his superior, Jeb Jaundice, but the sun was well up before he could summon up courage to leave the shelter of his hut, and the intervening ground between his own place and that of his lord and master was verily a vale of terror to him.

Every bush, every tree, had its secret foe lurking behind it in his vivid imagination; and half a dozen times at least, when a wild cat or a bird, or some small animal, crossed his path, he fell upon his knees, and begged his life at the hand of his visionary foe, until the silence, and the absence of any violence, restored the little confidence he generally possessed.

When he presented himself at the door of Jeb Jaundice he had lost the power of speech for the time, and, instead of knocking as a sane person would have done, he fell against the door, and gave notice with his head of his arrival.

Jaundice opened the door, and Wobbles fell into his arms.

"What the deuce is the matter with the man?" cried Jaundice. "Here, stand up, will you? There you are. Now what's the row?"

Wobbles held out the paper, and Jaundice took it. He was a rapid reader, and speedily absorbed its contents. His face was of ashen hue as he turned towards the interior of the hut and called for Maggie. She came to his side, but little changed since the days when Jack and his friends took shelter with her.

"See here, Maggie," said Jaundice.

She glanced over it, but not a muscle of her face moved.

"Well," she said.

"You call it well," replied Jaundice. "Do you despise this threat?"

"No," she said; "but I have looked for it these many months past. I knew it would come. It has haunted me by day, and filled my dreams at night. I saw the fiery spirit in the boy, and knew he was not of common mould. You had a hand in the mad work, and must be content to bear the consequences."

Jaundice did not reply, but walked away, putting his hat over his brows like a man in a furious passion. He expected that she would at least have shewn some anxiety for his safety, as she had hitherto done, in spite of her bitter railings at him. He felt he had lost her love at last, and, although he had treated it so lightly and scoffingly for years, he felt its loss now.

"It would have been better to have killed the boy," he muttered, as he strode along. "But the Ogre was for torture. He would have branded him from head to heel ere he had done with him. What mighty strength for a lad! What is it now? Two years must have made a man of him. What has he been doing? How and when is he coming, and what form will his vengeance take?"

It was the very vagueness of the danger, combined with the certainty of there being cause for apprehension, that made this murderous villain tremble. He had a hundred crimes upon his head, a life of infa to answer for, and death had a thousand terrors to him unknown to those who live honourable and noble lives.

He called his boon comrades together, and under a tree on the bank of the stream, where many a murderous scheme had been hatched and worked out, the cruel desperadoes gathered together.

There they were. Pedro, the Spaniard, with his swarthy face tinged with yellow; Skipper, the Yankee, with his long loose limbs, lantern jaws, and leaden eye, chewing tobacco, and whittling a stick with affected indifference; Laranche, the Frenchman, in an elegant attitude, with one hand upon his hip, and the other twirling his long black moustache; Niamo, the Russian, stolid of nature, but ever and anon furtively biting his nether lip; and lastly the Ogre, brown, brawny, and ferocious, but a little cowed withal.

Jaundice read the message, and when it was finished there was silence for awhile; the five men looked here and there—anywhere but at each other.

"I guess," said Skipper, at last, "that's a bit of bunkum."

"I hope you may find it so," returned the Ogre. "I have a different opinion."

"Is it not a little veak to be afraid of vun small boy?" asked Laranche.

"If we knew what our danger really was," said Jaundice, "we might face it, and if need be—die."

"It is not the boy alone I fear," said the Ogre, gloomily; "rest assured that he will come back with a power to carry out his threat. He was born to command, and men will follow him as the sheep follows an Eastern shepherd. I never knew fear until I saw him."

"When he comes," said Niamo, "let us fight him."

"When will he come?" asked the Ogre.

"I don't know."

"How will he come?"

"I don't know."

"Therein lies our danger," returned the Ogre, and then there was another silence.

It is a well known fact that men of brutal dispositions are the greatest cowards when their own safety is in actual peril, and that they bear suffering but indifferently. The ruffian who beats and robs old men and women howls under half a dozen cuts of the lash, receiving not a tenth of the torture he has inflicted on his victim—the wife-beater is the first to give in at a stand-up fight with a man his equal; and, last but not least, boys who torture helpless and defenceless animals dance about and howl under the lightest punishment. Cruelty is indeed twin brother to cowardice.

This band of ruffians, who had hitherto lived by robbing and slaying others weaker than themselves, shuddered at a threat full of unknown terror. Could they have found their foe, they might have fought. Could they have seen him, and known him to be their superior in power, they would have begged for mercy—all but the Ogre, for whatever his fears were, no thought of that entered his head; but their avenger was unseen, his strength unknown, and the shadow of coming punishment was in consequence trebly dark.

"We must alter one thing," said Jaundice; "we live too far apart. My house is big enough—let us live together."

Selfish fear prompted the offer, and the others knew its worth, but they gladly accepted it. Henceforth, for individual safety, it would be better to cling together.

But in this they reckoned without their hostess. When they went in a body to the hut, and Jaundice told her of his offer, she refused to admit one of them.

"I am tied body and soul to one of you," she said, "but I will have none of the rest."

"Come—come," said the Ogre, advancing, "you must not be inhospitable."

"The first man," cried Maggie, taking up a hatchet, "who crosses my threshold I will strike dead."

"And she will do it," said Jaundice; "she is a devil."

"You have made me so," she replied, "and must make the best of your work."

"Ah!" said Laranche, drawing in his breath, "if I vas only blessed vith vun so fair I vould teach her how to be gentle."

Maggie cast a glance of contempt at him, and retreating, closed the door, and put up a bar behind it. The men looked at each other in doubt, not knowing what to do.

"It is the only hut that will hold us all," said Skipper.

"Let us then build another," suggested Laranche.

"Good morning, gentlemen," cried a mild voice behind them, "anything in my way to-day—any cotton, needles, tape, buttons, sealing wax, or notepaper? I've got some of the patent indelible ink that the Sultan of Turkey uses for his love letters, and the Great Mogul of Seringapatam wrote sonnets to the Three Graces with, only a dollar a bottle. Any braces, straps, buckles, belts, neckties, knives, razors, purses—anything in my way to-day?"

The men all turned on hearing the voice, but none betrayed any great surprise. Jaundice hailed the speaker by name.

"Hullo, Billy Brisket," he cried, "what are you doing here?"

"Picking up a living, sir," replied the pedlar, humbly, "or rather an existence, for living it aint, seeing as how I often tramp a hundred miles to earn a dollar, and then in the end get robbed of it."

"Ha, ha! robbed," roared the listeners. "Who would rob you, Billy?"

"Lots of gent'emen as aint so honourable as you are," replied Billy. "They takes advantage of my being a funky sort of chap, born so, and therefore not accountable, and they ought to be kinder. I sold Black Stodger—you know Black Stodger—him as keeps the shanty in the Fern Tree Gulley——"

"Yes, we know him," they said.

"A great rascal—a sorry rascal," continued Billy

Brisket, shaking his head sorrowfully. "'What's the price of these braces?' he says. 'Three dollars,' says I. 'All right,' says he, and takes the braces. 'Now pay me,' says I. 'No,' says he, 'we'll play poker for the money.' 'But I can't play poker,' says I—'I never gamble.' 'Then,' says he, 'we'll fight for it.' But you know, gentlemen, that I can't fight, being born funky; so I plays poker—a game as I never played before, and Black Stodger wins the price of the braces, and brings me in ten dollars in debt."

This story amused the listeners, and they all laughed—even the Ogre, who exhibited his rows of ivory teeth, and gave vent to his feeling in several short barks, which was the nearest thing to a laugh he could do. Billy Brisket, while speaking, pulled off his pack and opened it, exhibiting a variety of articles, bearing a very strong resemblance to those he had shown Broad Arrow Jack two years before.

"You don't seem to drive a very brisk trade," said Jaundice. "It's three years since I saw you, and I'll swear you had that bottle of ink then. I noticed the torn label, and that chip in the neck of the bottle."

"Ink," said Billy Brisket, rather hastily, "isn't a thing much required."

"And you had three packets of needles too, and that bit of striped cloth."

"See now how hard it is to live," said the pedlar, looking up with tears in his eyes. "I walk here and there—fifty, a hundred miles at a time, and have to beg a crust of bread and a drop of water to keep body and soul together. If I sell anything they rob me, unless I happen to meet with honourable gentlemen like you, who buy and pay like gentlemen."

"Except on the last occasion, Billy," said Jaundice, with a short laugh.

"That was only your fun," replied the pedlar. "But I will close my pack and show you the things by and by. I want to stop here for a day or two if you please, gentlemen, as I'm weary and footsore, and I've not spoken to a living creature for days. I'm lonesome and miserable, and I hopes you won't turn me away," and Billy Brisket, overcome by the thoughts of his lone condition, lifted up his voice and wept.

"Can he stop?" asked Jaundice, addressing the Ogre.

"What matters?" replied the Ogre, indifferently.

"Oh, thank you sir," said Billy Brisket, taking this answer for a permission to stay; "may you never want home and friends, gentlemen, and may you never be so poor as I am!"

"While here," said the Ogre, "make yourself useful. We are going to build a hut large enough for all, and, as cutting up material is rough work, I think we had better pull down the old cribs. Off with that pack, and come and help me with mine."

"I've got so used to the pack," replied Billy, with a wriggle, "that I should be quite lost without it. It's part of myself. I should feel the loss of it like a limb."

The Ogre nodded his head to intimate that he might do as he liked, and led the way to his hut. The rest followed, keeping tolerably close together.

A short walk brought them in view of the hut. Something on the door caught the Ogre's eye, and uttering a deep oath he staggered back.

"Dear me," said Billy Brisket, "what a curious sign you've got upon your door—a broad arrow! I declare. It is about the funniest sign for a public house I ever knew. Quite original—quite."

But the sign, branded deep into the Ogre's door, was none of his own making. It was the work of an unknown hand—the warning promised to him and his fellows. He, as the chief offender, was wanted first.

CHAPTER XI.

THE OGRE IS TAKEN.

"YOU always were a jocular gentleman," said Billy Brisket, shaking his head at the brawny ruffian, "with very great originality. I remember a little joke you played on me——"

"Silence," cried the Ogre, savagely, "unless you want me to knock the life out of you. Stand back, will you? Comrades—you see this?"

Yes, they saw it, and both looked and felt very uncomfortable. The brand was deep and bold, and recently done. Jaundice put his hand upon it, and found the wood was scarcely cold.

"Ogre," he said, "he who did this has but just left his work. He would be alone, and surely we are not afraid of one—man or boy."

"No," replied the Ogre, rousing himself from a fit of meditation, "I am ready."

They looked about for some indication of footsteps, but found none. Nothing more than a smouldering fire at the back of the Ogre's hut. Whoever had placed the brand had done his work boldly.

The ground was soft all round, but there was not the least trace of any footsteps—not a stone displaced—not a twig broken—not an inch of moss or grass crushed. A spirit would have come and gone, and left as much trace as Broad Arrow Jack or those who had branded the door for him had done.

Billy Brisket forebore to ask any questions, and kept very much in the back ground while the search was going on. The eye of the Ogre was full of malevolence, and it would have been risky work saying aught to rouse him. Billy, being such a funky fellow, was careful not to excite his ire.

"Wait here a while," said the Ogre, suddenly, and kicking open the door of his hut, went in.

It was a rude structure, very inferior to that of Jaundice, with only one small opening, which served as a window. This had a shutter over it, and when the door—hung to swing to—closed, he was in complete darkness. There was another door at the back, usually kept bolted and barred, and very seldom used. Through a chink of this there came one ray of light.

The party outside sat down upon some logs scattered about, and Billy Brisket took up a position opposite the brand on the door, surveying it with much curiosity.

"It's an odd-looking thing," he said, "but I don't see why there is all this fuss about it. Somebody having a lark, I reckon."

Nobody replied to him. They were all silent and gloomy, but the curiosity of Billy Brisket was not to be checked, and he went on—

"I know you are all good-natured gentlemen, and won't mind telling me all about it. Who made the mark?"

"How should we know?" replied Jaundice, savagely.

"I ask, sir," replied the pedlar, softly, "because I think I can tell you something."

It is impossible to describe the face of Billy Brisket as he spoke these words. The measure of its innocence was full. A babe in arms was not more guileless in looks than he.

"What have you to tell?" asked two or three.

"Not much—perhaps nothing," said Billy. "Do you think a young fellow did this?"

Every eye was upon him in a moment, but they only looked on innocence.

"A young man with an arrow on his back?" pursued Billy.

Jaundice sprang up and grasped him by the collar of his coat with both hands.

"You know something," he said, "something that you ought to have told before. Out with it, or I'll throttle you."

"Oh, don't sir!—please sir!" gasped Billy, falling on his knees. "Don't drop upon a poor beggar like me. Oh, have mercy upon a wretched man as never made a dollar in his life without being robbed of it the next minute!"

"Well, what do you mean?"

"I—I met a young fellow—a gigantic young fellow—marked with an arrow, and—and I've only just thought of it. Oh, don't sir—please, sir!"

"Where did you meet with him?" asked Jaundice.

"Out on the plain, to the south."

"Was he alone?"

"No, sir—there were quite two hundred men with him, and he had me brought before him and asked me all sorts of questions, which I couldn't answer. Oh, please, sir!"

"Don't bawl in that way. I am not going to hurt you—go on!"

Billy Brisket, while speaking, kept his eye upon Jaundice, but his ears seemed to devote their attention to the Ogre's hut. If the listeners had been less occupied with his story they must have noticed the remarkable appearance he presented.

"What were his questions" asked Jaundice.

"Oh, about you and the others, and I told him that I had not seen you for three years. Then he told me that he was an old friend of yours, and that you would be very glad to see him; but I was not to tell you he was coming, as he intended it to be a pleasant surprise for you, and I never thought he could be other than a friend until——"

"That's enough," interrupted Jaundice, savagely. "Comrades, we must get away at all risks. Open the door and tell the Ogre he is wanted."

The Russian went to the door. He got no answer, and thrust it open. "Ogre," he said, "here is news for you—we must fly at once."

There was no answer, and he went in, holding the door open with his hand. One glance he cast around, and then uttered a shout of dismay and surprise.

The hut was empty—the Ogre was gone.

CHAPTER XII.

BILLY BRISKET AND WOBBLES.

"DIABLO," muttered Pedro, as he strode to the door, "what fiend's work is this?"

"He has left by the back door!" cried Jaundice.

"How shall that be?" hissed Laranche. "It is *bolted and barred!*"

So it was, and amazement and dismay was in every face. They had seen him go in—there could be no doubt of it, and he had not left by the door he entered—that they could swear. Had he left by the chimney? But no, again—it was scarcely wide enough to give passage to a child.

Again, why should he leave, and make no sign?

And if taken away by force, how was it that no sound of a struggle reached his friends? The Ogre was not likely to tamely submit to a foe, or to be carried away without calling upon his friends for help. But even supposing he had been conquered and carried silently off, by what means had he been removed from the hut?

Of all who stood there only one had upon his face a look of quietude, and that was Billy Brisket, and he, without a muscle moving, looked calmly on. There might have been a quiet twinkle in his eye, but it was of the very quietest order, and without close observation could not have been seen.

"He's gone," said Skipper, "but how the tarnation he did it I don't know."

"Is there a cellar to this house?" asked Billy Brisket, calmly—" a place where he kept his wine and that sort of thing?"

"That's a pretty question to ask, confound you," replied Jaundice. "Look here, mates, there's something more than earthly in this. That was not a boy who was here two years ago."

"Who shall it be then?" asked Laranche.

"The arch-fiend himself come to tempt us to our ruin."

All men have a spice of superstition in their nature, and the friends of Jaundice were disposed to have faith in his suggestion—the more so, as it seemed impossible to have captured and carried away the Ogre otherwise than by supernatural means. Their faces grew pale, and with one common instinct they began to move away, Billy Brisket, with his expressionless face, bringing up the rear.

"Come into the arbour," said Jaundice, suddenly. "Something must be done."

This was the place where the breakfast was spread on the morning Jack and his father breakfasted there. It was but little changed, the table and chairs were there, and the men sat down. Wobbles, who had been loitering about somewhere, came in at the same time, and looked round at their lowering faces in dismay. Billy Brisket made him a respectful bow.

"Hullo!" said Wobbles, "you here—turned up again with some of your muck?"

"A poor man must get a living somehow, sir," said Billy, respectfully. "Don't be hard on me."

A coward is invariably a bully, and Wobbles was a tremendous one. Frowning on the pedlar, he told him that they wanted no beggar there.

"No indeed," said Jaundice; "we have something to talk over. Take him away, Wobbles."

"Here, get along with you," said Wobbles, giving Billy a kick. "Sharp's the word. Hout you go!"

"Don't kick a poor man, sir," said Billy, so softly that his voice sounded like a whisper; but Wobbles went at him again.

"There's another kick—and another," he said, administering them vigorously. "Now, tramp, cut along. I'm a-goin' to see you out of the village."

"Can't I stop one night?" asked Billy.

"No, you can't."

"An hour?"

"Not a minute."

Billy Brisket looked round at the rest, appealingly, but their faces were turned from him. He was left to the mercy of Wobbles.

It was a fine opportunity for the funky one, and he enjoyed it amazingly. He had been kicked about and cuffed for years, and here at last was a man whom he could kick and cuff to his heart's content. As Billy moved away with a mournful face he rushed at him, and gave him a fourth kick.

"I ask you," said Billy, appealingly, "not to be hard on a weak, helpless, hungry man."

"Oh, blow your weakness! dash your helplessness, and jigger your happetite!" replied the remorseless Wobbles. "I don't orfen get a treat like this, and I'm goin' to enjoy myself. There's another."

Billy took it quietly enough, and had Wobbles been one atom less the fool than he was he would have suspected that something lay beneath this calm exterior; but he was as big an ass as one could hope to find in a month of Sundays, and Wobbles went on with his fun.

"Chaps like you," he said, "aint fit for nothing but kicking. You are such cowardly beggars. You've got no pluck. Come, move on quicker! Oh, you won't! Then there's another—and another."

Immovable, meek, and mild, Billy Brisket walked on, receiving kick after kick, until he was well out of the sight of the arbour—then he turned round and faced his persecutor with a look that caused that valiant man to shrink into his boots.

"Your name," he said, "is Wobbles, I believe?"

"Never you mind my name," replied Wobbles, with a faint show of keeping up his courage; "it aint no business of yourn."

"Mr. Wobbles," said Billy, "I'll trouble you to take off your coat."

"My coat! wot for?"

"You've insulted a gentleman, and I'm a going to have a round or two with you," replied Billy. "Don't move, don't attempt to cry out for help, or I'll knock your two optics into one. Off with your coat!"

"You are going to take a mean badwantage of the habsence of friends," said Wobbles, whose face rivalled the lily in its whiteness.

"I am going to take the nonsense out of you," replied Billy Brisket, removing his pack, and keeping a very expressive eye fixed upon the wretched Wobbles.

"I niver could see any good in fighting," said Wobbles, "but some people are allus at it. They niver can see anything in a joke, and if you only gives 'em a playful kick, in a kind of lark, they shows their teeth, and bites instead of larfing."

Billy Brisket paid no heed to this very reasonable explanation of his late conduct, but persistently ignoring the humorous side of the business, removed his coat, and got himself ready for fighting, with a very serious air.

"Will you get ready?" he asked Wobbles again.

"Well, you see I'm willing for to do it," replied Wobbles, with an argumentative air, "but I don't see what good can come of knocking each other about. I've been thinking ever since we met that we was born to be friendly, and I ses to myself, ses I, 'Here's a chap as is fond of a lark, and will take a little kick as such, and so ——'"

What more he would have said in his defence was cut short by Billy Brisket, who suddenly pounced upon him, seized him by the throat, and shook him until his teeth rattled like the bones of a nigger troupe. When half his life had been shaken out of him Billy let go his throat, and taking his nose between his finger and thumb, dragged him round in a circle, until his gasps for mercy had faded away into low groans of agony. Finally he turned him round, and gave him a kick equal in power and precision of application to all those he himself had been favoured with.

This piece of work being done he let him go, and Wobbles sank to the earth in a dying attitude, rolling his eyes in agony.

"Ca-atch—me—having—a—a lark agen," he gasped, "unless I knows the party to be friendly."

"You made a mistake," returned Billy Brisket, with a fierceness totally at variance with the mild demeanour he had shown in the village, "and but for my orders I would have killed you, you beggar! Do you know who I am?"

"William Brisket, Esquire," replied Wobbles, in his softest tones.

"More than that," said the pedlar. "I am Captain Brisket, for I've a good score or two of good men under me, and I've a colonel who is the best and bravest fellow going. Get up!"

"Another kick and I shall hexpire," said Wobbles, imploringly.

"But I am not going to kick," said Billy Brisket. "I am going to enlist you in my troop. Get up, and I'll see if I can make a man of you."

"I shall never make a soldier," said Wobbles, as he slowly rose.

"You will make as good food for powder and lead as a much better man," said Billy Brisket. "You come with me. I want a servant, and you shall be mine. But don't try any tricks, or I'll give you such a dose that this morning's business shall be to it as the prick of a pin to the kick of a horse. You hear?"

Wobbles was cowed completely, and abjectly signified that he heard, and wished to obey.

"Now," said Billy Brisket, "we will away to the colonel. You know him."

"Indeed no, sir, Captain Brisket," replied Wobbles.

"Surely," said Brisket, "you have not forgotten Broad Arrow Jack."

"Oh, lor'!" gasped Wobbles, and, as a dog follows his master, he followed in the footsteps of Billy Brisket, who jauntily wended his way over the plain.

CHAPTER XIII.

THE FLIGHT OF JAUNDICE.

NIGHT had fallen upon the village, and the band of dismayed ruffians had formed no settled plan for flight or defence against the enemy they had made for themselves—Broad Arrow Jack. To turn away might be to rush into the hands of him they hoped to avoid, and as for defence how could they do anything in that direction without having some idea of the power they had to contend with?

And of this they knew nothing, except that it was great and mysterious, strong enough to remove the strongest of their band as if he had been a stick or a straw, from their very midst in broad daylight, silently.

The idea of constructing a hut was given up. There was no time for that or anything, as a day or an hour might seal their fate. For the present they all resolved to camp in the arbour—it was as safe as any other place. Jaundice alone proposed to return home.

"I shall at least be near enough to help you if I hear a sound," he said.

They raised no objection to his leaving them, and the only additional anxiety they had arose from the absence of Wobbles, who, of course, did not show up again that day. Not that they cared for Wobbles personally, or, indeed, for each other; but the second disappearance they could not help putting down to the power that removed the Ogre.

Jaundice had a project for himself in his head when he proposed to live at home, and it was this, to fly alone, and leave the rest behind. In the dusk of the evening he laid the plan before his wife.

"Maggie," he said, drawing up to her side, and speaking so softly and kindly that her eyes opened with contemptuous surprise. Experience had taught her that whenever, during the past few years, he spoke in that way he had some selfish end in view— "Maggie, you have made many sacrifices for me during your life."

"You mean," she answered, coldly, "that I have sacrificed life itself."

"Well, we won't bandy words, Maggie," he returned; "say that it is your life. But much as you have done I want you to do but one thing more, and then I swear I will be devoted and loving to you for the remainder of my days."

"It is not much to promise," she said; "your days are numbered."

"Perhaps," he said, affecting to laugh, but he licked his dry lips, and glanced round the gloomy room with feverish apprehension. "At least, I am alive now, and while there is life there is hope. We have raised the devil among us, and I am going to fly."

"You wish to go alone?" said Maggie.

"Yes, and if I reach any place on the coast I will send for you," he replied, "and we will fly across the sea to some distant spot, away from such hellish men as have been the curse of my life and yours, and live in peace."

"Peace can never come to us on earth," she said; "nor will you change any more than the Ethiopian can cast his skin, or the leopard his spots. Why did you not fly without a word to me?"

"Because I love you still."

"As the wild horse loves shackles round its limbs," said Maggie, "No, Jeb; it was not love, but fear. You have left me before, and, like a bloodhound, I have tracked you. I am an outcast from all who loved me once. It is your work—you have made a monster out of a woman, and, Frankenstein-like, it will be with you till you die."

Broad-Arrow Jack.

"DEAR ME!" SAID BILLY BRISKET; "WHAT A CURIOUS SIGN YOU'VE GOT UPON YOUR DOOR—A BROAD ARROW, I DECLARE!"

"Maggie, you are hard upon me, and mistrust me too much," he pleaded.

"I trusted you too much once," she said; "but now I know you, and trust no more. You feared that I should come upon your trail, and be a guide to your foe. Come, is not that true?"

He hung his head, and made no reply. Maggie uttered a short sharp laugh of triumph.

"See what an open book you are to me!" she said. "Had I known you as well years ago I should have been a happy woman now Have you no fear of leaving me alone with those brutes outside?"

"Why should I?" he asked. "They all fear you to a man."

"Oh, yes!" she replied, with a smile. "They know that I have claws. But go, Jeb, as you wish it."

"With your free consent?" he asked.

"With my free consent," she replied.

"And you will not follow me—at least, for a while?"

"I promise nothing," she said, "except that, if you live, we shall meet again."

And with this he was obliged to be content. He was at liberty to go as he willed—to leave his old companions and her behind; but she would not say what her movements were likely to be—only that he might be sure she would, if she desired, find him again.

He, indeed, felt something like Frankenstein as he looked upon the creature he had made out of a beautiful and once loving woman, and he would have given half his chance of escape to have seen her lying dead at his feet; but the blow he dare not strike himself—he was too deeply dyed already. With her conditions he prepared for flight.

He packed a small case with food, and filled a flask from a small keg of coarse brandy. These he strapped round his waist, and put a powder flask and some lead into his pockets. His rifle was already loaded, but he examined it carefully, put a fresh cap on, and pressed it down close to the nipple.

"My life may depend upon this charge," he thought.

It was close on midnight by the time his preparations were completed, and, opening the front door quietly, he listened. The murmur of voices in the arbour at the rear came round to him, and he knew that his movements were not suspected. Maggie stood close behind him, and, turning to her, he whispered—

"Good-bye. Kiss me, Maggie; we may never meet again."

"Fear not," she replied. "I feel that this is not our final parting."

"Won't you kiss me, Maggie?"

"You may kiss me, if you will," she replied, holding up her face. "I cannot return it. I have taken an oath."

He touched her cheek with his lips, laid a hand for a moment on her shoulder, and crept away. Maggie, standing by the door, watched his form until it was lost in the gloom, then covered her face with her hands, and sank down upon a fixed seat by the door, and when, after long hours, the morning light came gliding through the trees, she was sitting there still, with her cheeks bedewed with tears.

It was Laranche who came round and found her. He was going to the spring that bubbled up before the hut for water. He paused before her, and gave her a polite bow.

"Ah! madame," he said, "you have a love for the blessed part of the day. The early morning is so pure. It always makes me think of my home and childhood."

"You are facetious, monsieur," replied Maggie.

"No," he said; "it shall be a true sentiment. Vere is the good Jaundice?"

"He is dead," replied Maggie.

"Ah—so!" cried the startled Frenchman. "Dead! It is sudden!"

"Yes," she replied; "I buried him last night, All through the darkness I have been toiling at his grave."

"And vere," asked the Frenchman, with his old coolness, "shall your devoted husband be buried?"

"Where you will never find him," replied Maggie, and made a motion of her hand to inform him that she had no more to say.

Laranche knew her too well to press her further, and went back with the story to his wondering companions. Skipper, the American, hit upon the truth.

"The fellow's bolted," he said, "and this is a dodge to keep us in the dark."

They went up and hammered lustily at the back door. They got no answer, and broke in. The hut was empty. Maggie, too, was gone.

CHAPTER XIV.

BROAD ARROW JACK AND HIS MEN.

CLOSE under the shadow of a grove of trees lay some twenty men, taking refuge from the mid-day heat, and just behind them were a number of horses picketted, enjoying great heaps of grass which had been torn up from the open plain, and brought thither by their masters.

The appearance of the men, without reference to the air of concealment upon all, was peculiar. Their dress was Mexican, and the materials of the best. Their short jackets were literally loaded with gold lace, and the arms they bore were for the most part elaborately inlaid with gold and silver. Each man had a sword, pistols, and rifle.

But their dress of velvet jacket, short breeches, heavy boots, and gorgeous sashes and scarves could not conceal the fact that none of these men were Mexican-born. They were British to a man. Tall, powerful, daring-looking fellows, such as our country fills its army and navy with, and sends out to be pioneers in newly discovered lands.

They were clustered in groups, for the most part smoking in silence, but a few were conversing in whispers, and glancing occasionally towards a portion of a tent at the end of the grove, just discernible through the trees. Two men a little apart from the rest will give us a clue to the nature of the conversation of the whole.

"I'll tell you what, Nat," said one—a man about forty, with a thick dark beard up to his eyes, and hair thick as a lion's mane, "the work was beautifully done, and I wouldn't have had a grip like it on me for the love of Polly Simpkins."

"Who is Polly Simpkins?" asked the other—a fair-haired, broad-shouldered fellow about thirty. "You've always got some girl or the other in your head, Tom Larkins."

"Polly aint a living creetur," replied the other. "She's an ideal I've formed of what a woman ought to be, and I've never found one like her yet. But never mind Polly, bless her heart! The colonel's on the 'tarpee,' as the French says. Isn't he a buster?"

"And I'm told he's not eighteen," said the other dropping his voice. "Billy Brisket says so."

"You mean Captain Brisket, Nat Green."

"It comes natural to call him Billy," replied the other, laughing. "He is such a jolly good fellow, such a plucky man, and would die for the colonel."

"So would I," replied Tom Larkins, "although I don't know why. He don't say much to us, and we are all working for him in the dark. It's a case of 'Do as I tell you, and ax no questions,' but as we've all swore to it we must do it."

"I do it with pleasure," returned Nat Green, stroking his fair beard. "He holds me to him, and I can no more get away than a needle can leave a magnet."

"It aint his dress—is it?" said Tom.

"Well, no," replied Nat, "seeing that he wears nothing but a pair of canvas trousers and boots. He is not ashamed of that broad arrow on his back —that's certain."

"Who put it there, Nat?"

"I don't know, but I think it's got something to do with the work we have in hand. But don't let us go prying into secrets which don't concern us. Here we are, with good pay, splendid dresses, lots of fun, and if we are puzzled a bit what's the odds?"

"He must have an enormous lot of tin somewhere. Where do it come from?"

"I don't know, and I don't care."

"No more do I."

A silence followed, and Nat Green's pipe being out, he filled it again, and lighted it from his friend's. The subject of their conversation seemed too fascinating to be resisted, and Nat soon resumed it.

Suddenly Tom Larkins's hat was tilted over his eyes, his hair rumpled, and somebody chuckled in his ears.

"Dash it, what now?" he growled, and, righting his cap, he looked up and beheld a veritable imp of a nigger dancing before him. It was the Tiger, unchanged in form or feature.

"Yah! Massa Green," he said, "steal on you quick, knock 'um hat ober."

"Don't you know the orders?" growled Nat Green, looking about for something to throw at him. "Silence in the camp."

"Who make de row—who swar den?" asked the Tiger, dodging a lump of earth Nat threw at him. Massa Broad Arrow Jack know dat I am silent. Come dis way, go dat way like shadow—neber a sound."

"Quiet enough when you are at work," said Nat, "but a rowdy at play. Come here."

"You take me for big fool," replied the Tiger, grinning. "You come here, and catchee me."

"That would be a good game to try, certainly," replied Nat.

"Just think wot a family of 'em would be," said Tom Larkins, watching the antics of the Tiger, who twisted, turned, skipped this way and that, and was never still for a moment, "nothing safe for him, nobody, as one may say, sacred to him. Yesterday, just as Jim Blathers was a-putting of a choice morsel of buffaler tongue into his mouth, a thing he'd saved for a relish like, this chap takes it, and bolts up a tree like a flash of lightning, and perches hisself on the top branch and eats it. But you mustn't do nothing to him."

"No, the colonel is too fond of him, Tom."

"And he's devoted body and soul to the colonel. If anybody touched the colonel when he was nigh he'd fly at him, and tear his eyes out like a wild cat."

"So he would. Hush! here's the colonel himself."

And then there came striding through the trees the gigantic form of their leader, Broad Arrow Jack. Two years had given him height, and hard toil of some sort had bestowed upon him muscles that lay up like ropes upon his arms. He wore no visible covering, but a pair of sailor's trousers and boots. In his belt a pair of pistols rested, and a cutlass hung by his side.

His face was wondrously handsome, and a strange fascination lay in the depths of his dark blue eyes, as he turned them towards the two men, who rose and bowed respectfully. The Tiger ceased his antics, and remained in a fixed attitude, with his head bent down, and his hands clasped before him, like a slave awaiting orders. The other men, scattered around, all ceased smoking and talking, and got upon their feet. In years a boy, in looks a man, in strength a giant—Broad Arrow Jack was lord and master of them all.

"Has Brisket returned?" asked he, addressing Nat Green.

"Haven't seen him, colonel," was the reply.

"He was in de village, massa," said the Tiger, without looking up, "talking soft to de lot ob rascals."

"Why does he loiter?" muttered Jack, impatiently, "there is other work to be done. Tell him when he returns," he added aloud, "to come once to me. Let all be ready to start."

"Yes, sir," replied the men, and Jack turned h footsteps towards his tent, whither we will follo him.

Under the canvas lay the Ogre bound hand an foot, with a faint line on each side of his mouth where a gag had recently been. Fear and fury struggled for the mastery in his evil countenance as Jack entered.

The scar upon our hero's back stood out bold and clear, for while the sun darkened his skin it whitened the work of the Ogre, and brought it out in bold relief. An indelible mark, never to be lost on this side of the grave.

The furniture of the tent consisted of a table and camp-stool, and on the latter Broad Arrow Jack took his seat, glancing down upon the Ogre with a look of satisfaction.

"I ask you again," said the Ogre, after a silence, "to tell me what my fate is to be?"

"And I tell you again that I will not tell you now," replied Broad Arrow Jack. "Think of all you would do in my place—that perchance may help you."

"You are not a man or boy—you are a demon," hissed the Ogre.

"I am what you and your fellows made me," replied Jack. "Think you such deeds as yours can go unpunished? I come not as the avenger of my wrongs alone, or of my murdered father and brother's untimely death, which was your work, but of the wrongs of hundreds. I know your story —I know all that you have done for years. If there is any among your list of crimes which you have forgotten, ask me, and I will refresh your memory."

"This is mere braggadocio," said the Ogre.

"Is it?" replied Broad Arrow Jack. "Let me give you reason to think otherwise. Five years ago, on a summer's night, a man was crossing yonder plain. He was alone and weary, and, meeting you, asked for shelter. You spoke fairly to him, and bade him come to your hut. Quietly and unseen by your fellow-knaves, you took him there, and learnt how he had been toiling in the diamond fields with fair success, and was now homeward bound with the means to give his wife and children, whom he had left in poverty, bread for the rest of their days. Who spoke kindly to him and bade him godspeed one moment, and stabbed him to the heart the next?"

"I swear that he insulted me before I struck a blow," said the Ogre, whose dark face was covered with perspiration. "I swear it."

"You lie," said Jack. "He was dead ere he knew how trebly damned was the villain who called himself his friend. But let me tell you more. I knew his name, where his wife and children were left, and that which you have robbed him of shall be sent to them with his sad story."

"You must find the diamonds first," said the Ogre, with a grin.

Broad Arrow Jack took off his belt, and opening a leather pocket inside, drew out a packet.

"See here," he said, spreading the contents before the eyes of the maddened Ogre; "do you know them?"

"Are you of this world?" cried the swarthy ruffian

"I am like you—flesh and blood," replied Broad Arrow Jack, restoring the diamonds to his belt; "but things passing strange have come to aid me in my plan of vengeance."

"It is manly to kill," said the Ogre; "slay me."

"No," replied Jack, "your time has not yet

come. When I have gathered the rest you shall suffer together. I could have taken you all, easily but I do my work in mystery, knowing that all the tortures I can inflict would not equal what those rascals suffer in their agony of fear. They fear me as they fear death—who comes at an hour no man knows of, but comes when he will."

The sound of footsteps drew his attention to the mouth of the tent, and Billy Brisket stood before him. The face of Broad Arrow Jack beamed with a smile of welcome. No other man on earth could chase away the shadow resting there.

"Ah, Brisket," he said; "welcome. I have been anxious about you!"

"It's all right," replied the pedlar, taking off his pack and tossing it aside. "I got clear without much trouble, and have brought in a recruit. Hallo, come up there!"

Wobbles, so limp that it was a wonder he could stand upon his feet at all, came tottering up, and stood before the young giant, who gazed at him quietly, and apparently without much interest.

"So," said Jack, "you have come to fight in a good cause?"

"Yes, sir," replied Wobbles, rolling his eyes about, and not much assisted towards composure by meeting the glance of the Ogre. "Oh, yes, sir!"

"You enter the service willingly?"

"I'm hoverjoyed to do so," replied Wobbles, following out the teaching he had received from Billy Brisket on his way thither. Broad Arrow Jack waved his hand, and Billy Brisket pointed to a tree, bidding him sit under it and move if he dare.

"If hever I get hout of this," thought Wobbles, as he sat down, "I'll have a cut and run for Old England again. Casual wards is paradises to games of this description."

He sat a good hour before Billy Brisket came out of the tent, and with a whistle summoned the Tiger, who came tumbling down from a tree, and went hurriedly into his master's tent. He was there but a few moments before he came bounding out, and sped away with the speed of the wind.

"If I could run like that," thought Wobbles, "I'd bolt; but——"

"Get up, sir!"

"Yes, sir."

"Can you ride?" asked Billy Brisket, who had advanced upon him.

"I don't think I've been on a horse since I had threepennorth at Hampstead one Sunday," replied Wobbles, reflectively.

"I ask you the question," returned Brisket, carelessly, "because we are going to start directly, and you, to keep up with us, must ride. There is only one horse—we call him 'old Joss'—you can have. He's a good 'un to go, but he's vicious, and the other men don't like him. He's got a knack of chucking people off, and beating them with his hoofs or biting them in the fleshy parts of their bodies. Last Tuesday he pounded a man to a pulp, and then made a meal of him."

"But what am I to do with a brute like that?" asked Wobbles, aghast.

"Why, ride him, to be sure," replied Billy. "You'll get no other."

If any one can picture the feelings of Wobbles at this moment they had better do so, as it is quite out of my power to describe them. A quiet horse would have given him what he called a "curdler," but the prospect of being on the back of a vicious, biting, kicking brute was a hundred perils and fifty forms of suffering rolled into one.

Whether the story told of the horse by Billy Brisket was true or not we are not going to say, but shortly after the whole camp was in motion, and several of the men came up and asked Wobbles if if he was going to ride "old Joss," evidently taking an interest in that animal and his new rider. On receiving a reply in the affirmative, they shook Wobbles by the hand, and bade him good bye.

"It's hard," said Tom Larkins, "to get that hoss as soon as you've jined, for a man ought to have a run for his life; but cheer up—he mayn't do nothing wuss than break a rib or two, or take a bit out of one of your legs. Bear up, old man."

CHAPTER XV.
OLD JOSS.

THERE was no fuss or noise in the breaking up of the camp. Such words of command as were given passed from mouth to mouth in an under tone, but most of the movements were guided by signals. Broad Arrow Jack's tent was struck, rolled into a small compass, and put upon a horse. The Ogre, Mazeppa-like, was bound upon another, and with a guard of twelve mounted men, headed by our hero, led the van.

The horse Jack rode was a powerful roan, with bone and muscle enough to have carried one of the ancient knights in armour, and in sober truth a good horse was needed to carry that commanding form, which sat astride the beast with perfect ease and grace.

As Jack commanded men so he commanded beasts. The horse which carried the Ogre had neither bit, bridle, rein, nor halter—nothing, in fact, of the ordinary style of thing to guide it; but it kept by the side of the young giant, turning to the right or left, halting, or going on in obedience to the slightest movement of his hand.

Billy Brisket, or Captain Brisket, as he called himself, did not move on with his colonel, but remained behind in charge of the rest of the men, or he would not have probably indulged in the little bit of fun he got up at the expense of Wobbles.

As soon as his leader, who struck out across the plain in the direction he had traversed with his father and Cecil, was well away in the distance, a sensible change took place in the demeanour of the men. They talked louder, laughed merrier, and in a general way did many things to prove the old adage about the absence of the cat tempting the mice to play.

"Bring forth the wild horse," cried Billy Brisket, striking an attitude, "and let the valiant Wobbles mount."

"If you wouldn't mind," said Wobbles, hoarsely, "I should prefer walking."

"Walk!" returned Billy Brisket. "Never—produce the wild horse."

Half a dozen men, with ropes in their hands, disappeared and dived in among the tethered horses with the air of having a desperate task in hand. They shouted—crying "Woa," "Stand still there," "Mind his heels," "Take care of his teeth," and many other things addressed to the wild horse and to each other, and Wobbles listened in mute terror, wondering what would become of him when once in the power of this untamed steed, who was a terror even to these valiant men.

With much apparent difficulty they brought out the famous horse, old Joss, a tall bony steed with a mane and tail that would have touched the heart of an undertaker. Such a gaunt ugly brute has seldom blessed the eyes of man.

The age of this animal was difficult to guess at, but any man who knew a horse's head from his tail would have put him down as going on for forty. Billy Brisket said he was ninety-eight, but there were some matters in which the said Billy could not be entirely trusted.

As the history of old Joss is of some little importance, to account for his conduct hereafter to be related, I may as well give a brief account of it here. It may serve perhaps to amuse as well as to enlighten our readers.

Old Joss was born in a travelling circus, while on a tour in the West of England. His mother was the famous mare that played Black Bess in the thrilling adventures of Dick Turpin, and was considered to do the death scene to perfection, and his father was the celebrated horse that would ring a bell for his dinner, say grace before he partook of it, drink out of a bottle, walk lame when wanted to, walk in perfect time, and carry a full-sized man by the belt about the ring.

With such gifted parents, old Joss, when a very young Joss, came out strong, as might be expected. He soon acquired all the tricks of his father and mother, and was only excluded from Dick Turpin on account of his sex. He had plenty of pluck, amazing intelligence, and soon became a star among the performing horses in the world. There was not a known trick of his fellow-horses which he could not do.

It is unnecessary to fully detail his performances here. Some of his acquirements will be shown as our story proceeds, and it only remains for us to account for his appearance in the wild tract of country where we find him.

He performed many, many years in the towns of England, Ireland, Scotland, and Wales, so often indeed that his tricks became too well known to draw money, and in his old days his owner sold him to an American, who shipped him for New York.

The vessel encountered rough weather, and getting her rigging knocked about until it was little better than useless, was driven far out of her course, and finally wrecked upon a reef. Every living creature on board but old Joss was drowned, and that sensible creature having a deck stable, was thrown into the sea, and with its fore feet in a mass of wreck, reached the shore, and took its way up country.

Around its neck was a large brass plate, medal-shaped, which it always wore, and this proclaimed everything concerning it but its age. That, for prudential reasons, was concealed from the American purchaser.

All that need be said further is, that one day old Joss, with his brass plate round his neck, strolled into the camp of Broad Arrow Jack, and became a willing prisoner, behaving like a quiet sensible horse for awhile, but eventually revealing one by one all his accomplishments, which was a never-failing source of amusement to the men.

This then was the steed on which Wobbles was to distinguish himself, and the men now brought him forth, so shackled and bound by ropes, that the wildest of wild steeds might, if so placed, have dismally failed at an attempt to get a clear kick at anything or anybody.

Wobbles was not a good judge of a horse. Half an hour's experience on one of the galvanised corpses which tumble about Hampstead-heath for ninepence an hour can scarcely qualify a man to grasp the points of "the friend of man," and when he looked on old Joss, ever so many hands high, with bones enough to construct an antediluvian monster out of, and saw all the shackles, which would not have been put about this frantic creature unless actually necessary, he turned sick, and sank in a heap upon the ground.

"It's murder," he groaned, "no man can ride him. He's a being hung."

"The colonel's orders were for you to break him in," replied Billy Brisket. "We've all tried and failed."

"He's more likely to smash me," groaned Wobbles, looking at the feet of old Joss, swollen by age and tribulation to the size of quartern loaves.

"Anyhow get up, and see who is master," suggested Billy Brisket.

"I'm willing for to give in," said Wobbles; "he's free and hearty to have the best of it."

"If you don't get up," was Billy's reply, "you must be put up."

"And tied on," said Tom Larkins.

"Or screwed on," suggested Nat Green. "A screw or so would make the riding safer.

"You have your choice," said Billy Brisket. "If you are screwed on he'll roll over you; if you aint you can only fall off, and it may be, not very much hurt."

"I think perhaps I had better get up," said Wobbles, who was not certain that these violent and reckless men might put the screws through a tender part of his body.

They gave him a leg up, and put the reins into his hand. Old Joss, who had been taught that it was the proper thing to show spirit with a rider, made a feeble effort to stand upright, but his fore feet were too much for him, and he came down again with a crash that made the earth tremble, and brought the eyes of Wobbles to his cheek-bones.

"Cast off the shackles!" cried Billy. "Let the noble rider have fair play."

"Don't be in a hurry," pleaded Wobbles; "I'm hardly in the saddle yet."

But the reckless monsters of the prairie, as Wobbles in his heart called them, were remorseless; they cast off the bonds of the mighty brute, and left Wobbles and his steed to settle any disputes.

A dispute arose at once.

The memory of old Joss had grown hazy with years, and memories of his early days always cropped up whenever anybody got upon his back. It may also be that the music of musicians mostly numbered with the dead resounded again in his ears.

What it was nobody knew, but whenever he was favoured with a rider he at once began an entertainment more amusing to the lookers on than to the individual who participated in it. Wobbles and he went at it at once.

First he knelt as a salutation to an imaginary audience.

Then he got up and kicked out behind, to express his joy at finding himself in good company.

Then he began to waltz, with very little of the grace of former years, his movements being a series of convulsive jerks that made Wobbles fly off at different angles, and necessitated a firm grasp upon the mane; and, forgetting that he was in a grove, with trees tolerably thick, old Joss banged his body against this trunk and that trunk, occasionally giving the legs of Wobbles an ugly nip, until he had got through the allotted amount of dancing. At the end he tried to bow upon his knees, in recognition of fancied applause, but fell upon his nose, and Wobbles fell off upon his head.

"Now look here," said Wobbles, addressing the convulsed spectators, on his back, "I think you'll backnowledge that he's come off wictor, and I gives in."

"It was the colonel's orders," said Billy Brisket, "that you wasn't to give in. Put him up again."

Not only had Wobbles to be assisted up, but old Joss also, for that invaluable and fiery horse, having fallen upon his nose, fell into musing o'er the happy days for ever fled, and was in no hurry to get up again. Tom Larkins gave him a gentle reminder in his ribs that brought him back to passing events, and after a series of struggles he got upright once more, and sneezed over the prostrate Wobbles.

"Put him up again," said Billy Brisket, pointing to the fallen horse-breaker.

Wobbles dared make no complaint—he read determination in the eyes of all, and once more he was tossed into the saddle. Old Joss, unconscious of having ever distinguished himself, was preparing to travel the old road over again, but Billy touched him behind with his riding whip, which happened to be the signal for Black Bess to die, and accordingly he fell down in a heap, and once more introduced Wobbles to the dust.

"Of all the brutes," gasped Wobbles. "Keep him off me. Don't let him roll."

"He's giving in," cried Billy Brisket—"he feels he's got his master. Rouse him up."

But old Joss would not be roused. He knew that the proper thing to be done was to carry him out of the ring. He had seen his mother do the trick a hundred times, and he was not to be induced to rise until he at least had been carried a few yards.

"You've killed him," said Billy Brisket. "You've been too much even for his stout heart."

For a moment the heart of Wobbles swelled with pride. Had he indeed proved to be a horse-tamer? He got upon his feet and looked round with the elation of a victor, but old Joss disappointed him again. Having probably dreamt that he had been carried out of the circus, he made a grand effort, and struggling up, capered about with the elegance old men afflicted with acute rheumatism display, when, under the influence of potent liquors, they attempt an Irish jig.

"Your work is not yet done," said Billy Brisket. "Up again, old man."

Wobbles groaned, and was assisted into the saddle. Old Joss, concluding that the performance was over, and the company moving away to another destination, bent forward as if drawing a van, and started off at a shambling trot, jerking Wobbles up and down like one of those wooden balls we see in the shops of the filter-maker, dancing on the top of a jet of water.

CHAPTER XVI.

LOST LEON.

IT may easily be understood that Broad Arrow Jack took no part in anything humorous: but he was wise enough to know that, however willing these men were to serve him—and more willing men never lived—they could not be brought to his sombre state of mind.

They had no wrongs to avenge; they simply served a noble leader, who drew them towards him by the irresistible fascination of a commanding spirit. His noble form—his proud fiery eye—his deep-toned musical voice—all played a part in subduing these men, some of them the wildest spirits the world ever shone upon.

For the present we reserve all details of the gathering of the band, and how, in a little over two years, Jack had grown powerful in that wild uncultivated land. That Billy Brisket had a hand in it was certain; but what he did, and how he did it, he kept from the men, and, as they were well content to await a time for a revelation of the great secret, we hope our readers will be the same.

Jack heard the laughter behind him, but heeded it not. All his attention was concentrated on the Ogre, whose malevolent eyes looked at him now and then, only to drop again. There was something in the face of Jack he could not look upon.

"It is not fair," he said, after a mile or two of ground had been covered, "to cut a man's flesh up with cords. See how I am bound."

"Give him more freedom," said Jack to his men. "Stand still, Sue."

The mare which carried the Ogre became like a statue, and some of the most painful cords were loosened; but those round the waist and ankles were left. The Ogre breathed a little more freely.

"I only wish to hold you secure," said Jack. "Your punishment is yet to come."

"What is it?" asked the Ogre.

"Wait and see," was the answer. "Forward all!"

The second party were speedily left behind, and with the fading away of the noise they made a silence came, broken only by the noise of the hoofs of the horses, their occasional neighing, and the rattle of arms.

Sternly, with his face to the front, Jack rode on, his body-guard—the more sober of his followers—riding as silently behind him.

So they rode on for a good two hours, and then a form was seen by one of the men coming fast upon their track. Jack called for a halt, and the Tiger came bounding up to his side.

Still keeping an eye upon his prisoner, Jack drew aside, and held a whispered conference with the swarthy-skinned boy, who had as much of the wild beast as anything else in his composition. What he had to say was quickly said, and he was off back on the way he came.

"I think," said one of the men, "if the devil is to be found in any human form, there is a bit of him there."

"No—only the demon of mischief," replied another. "There is good in the wild lad."

"Silence!" cried their leader, and once more the men were dumb.

But not for long. A few minutes' ride brought another form in view—as slender almost as the Tiger's, but not gifted with his activity—toiling painfully on. The dress he wore was Spanish, and at the first sight Jack thought it was a boy; but, on a nearer approach, he saw lines of care which are never scored on the face of youth, be its sorrows deep as the sea.

The features were small, and perfectly formed; the eyes dark, and full of light—defying fatigue, as it were—and the small white hand grasped a riding-whip, which was fretfully employed in cutting off the tops of tender plants as the stranger moved slowly along.

He looked back as the tramp of steeds reached him, and when Jack rode up, paused, and respectfully saluted. Jack reined up his horse, and looked at him curiously.

"Whither are you going?" he asked.

"I know not," replied the stranger, in a low tone. "I have lost my way."

"You are a strange figure to find here," rejoined Broad Arrow Jack. "Hard work and you have ever been strangers."

"And yet I have toiled in my way," was the reply, "and but for being wrecked on the coast might have now been with those I love. But pass on, I can find my way."

"Nay," said Jack, softening in his manner, "I cannot think of leaving you. You will perish in this wilderness. Have you no companions from the wreck?"

"No; I alone was saved."

"And I alone survive," thought Jack, and he was drawn towards the stranger by the power of sympathy.

"There is something in our stories akin," he said. "You had better go with us."

"If you would have me," replied the stranger, casting down his eyes. "I shall be but an incumbrance to you."

"A very small one," said Jack. "Your name, sir?"

"Call me Lost Leon," said the stranger, "and let me keep my other."

"Again we have a thing in common," replied Jack. "I keep my name concealed. We shall be friends, I know. Can you use a weapon?"

"The small sword and the pistol—no more," said Lost Leon.

"Here, take this pistol," said Jack; "shoot at yonder white stone."

The delicate stranger took the weapon, and after a steady aim fired. The stone was broken into a dozen pieces.

"Good," said Jack; "you will do. Here, take the other—you will require them. Spring up behind. We have not far to go ere we halt for the night. My good horse will make light of you. Give me your hand."

Lost Leon held out a small brown palm, and as the mighty hand of Jack closed over it seemed to be lost. Lightly and nimbly the delicate form sprang up behind him—in a side-saddle position.

"We are going but a little way," he said, "and this will do."

Jack pressed his knees against his horse, and the noble creature, heedless of its additional burden, trotted forward, and never halted until the banks of a stream were reached, and here the word to halt was given.

The tent was pitched, and the Ogre, as before, placed beneath it. One of his hands was released, and food was given him, but while he ate Broad Arrow Jack never left his side. The meal over the swarthy villain allowed his bonds to be put on again without resistance, awed, as it seemed, by the presence of Broad Arrow Jack.

When darkness came a rude lamp was lighted and hung up in the tent, and Jack sat by the Ogre until midnight, when one of the men came in to take his turn at watching, but his leader told him to go back to his rest.

"I want no sleep to-night," he said. "Where is the stranger?"

"Lying under the shade of a rock apart from us all," was the reply.

"Has he been in any way communicative?"

"He has not spoken to us."

"Bid him come here."

In a few seconds the stranger entered, and stood before Broad Arrow Jack with his back to the Ogre.

"What would you with me?" he asked, in the same low tone.

"Only a little conversation with you," replied Broad Arrow Jack. "I want to have you as a friend. You have the tongue and manner of people of gentle blood."

"Yes," said Lost Leon, "but what I was I can never be again. All that was worth having in this life I have lost."

"You speak bitterly, and must have known sorrow."

"Almost more than I could bear; but—you—you have none."

A sad smile passed over our hero's face.

"I have," he said, "a sorrow and a wrong, both too deep and bitter ever to be forgotten. See there!"

He pointed at the Ogre, who was watchfully awake, and Lost Leon turned to look at him, this time placing his back to the light.

"See there," said Jack, "one of earth's demons—man only in form."

"I was once like other men," replied the Ogre, "until my wrongs made me what I am."

"Your wrongs!" said Jack. "What were they but the wrongs bred out of evil passions foiled, and unworthy schemes frustrated. In the country beyond the sea you were only less vile than here because strong laws held you back."

"You guess at that," said the Ogre.

"No," replied Broad Arrow Jack. "I know you now," and stepping forward he knelt down by the Ogre's side, and whispered something in his ear.

A short cry of panic escaped the dark villain's lips, and heaving up he sought to break his bonds; but they held him fast.

"Who are you?" he cried. "Are you more than mortal that you can taunt me thus?"

"Who I am," replied Jack. "You shall know before the end. Leon——"

"Call me Lost Leon," interposed the stranger. "Never speak of me otherwise than as lost."

"Lost Leon, be it then. See here—one of a nest of vipers that I will scotch first, then kill. Will you join me in this good work?"

"With heart and hand."

"Swear then, as all who aid me have sworn to do my bidding without question—to go here or stay there as I direct; to do all things—even to take life at any word.

For a moment Lost Leon hesitated, then the clear voice rang out—

"I swear."

"Enough," said Broad Arrow Jack; "you are my brother."

"Am I awake or dreaming?" muttered the Ogre. "That voice—I know it, but whose is it? Am I haunted by the shadows of the past? Is this death, and am I in the world beyond the grave surrounded by the shadows of those I wronged come to deal out measure for measure? What is my fate?"

Drops of agony rolled from his brow, and his mighty chest upheaved with the convulsion of a heartfelt fear. He had known the power of dread many times before, but never aught like this.

The hour, the scene, the stillness of night, the feebly-flickering camp-fire outside, the mighty form of the conqueror, the familiar voice as it seemed to him of Lost Leon, all aided in fixing upon him that deadly fear. But he did not pray. Words of appeal to the all-ruling Power had long been strange to his lips. He might have lisped them in his childhood, but had ne'er spoken them in youth or manhood.

The memory of a hundred dark crimes came back to him, peopling the tent with the faces and forms of those long since dust. Many a cry for mercy lifted to his adder ears echoed around, mingled with the shrieks of the weak and the curses of the strong who had fallen victims to his relentless hand.

Oh, what a harvest of agony it was! Every seed sown in his iniquitous life was bearing a hundred fold.

He lay with a volcano in him for many hours, long after Lost Leon had left the tent, and, at the first streak of day, fell into a fitful sleep, but only to dream of horrors to which his waking visions were light indeed.

But not for long he slept. The footfall of horses, the voices of men shouting aroused him, and after a meal—he could eat even them, so much animal lay in his nature—he was replaced upon the back of Sue, and the cavalcade, silent and stern, pursued its way.

With the light he lost half his fear, and he was a cunning wolf again. In secrecy he tested his bonds, and found one yielding. Hope that hangs around the vilest brought back the fire to his eye. The bare chance of escape gave him new life, and hardened him once more.

"If I get free," he muttered, "I will have revenge for this. Let me have this proud boy for one hour in my power, and, for aught I care, a thousand demons may rack me for ages."

CHAPTER XVII.

PEDRO SNARED.

WHEN the fact of the flight of Jaundice had become fully apparent to those he had left behind him in the village, each man cursed him bitterly for a coward and a traitor, and, at the instigation of Laranche, the Frenchman, they one and all took a solemn oath to deal with him as such if ever he crossed their path.

As a preliminary and earnest of their kind intentions they wrecked his house, made firewood of his furniture, and finally pulled down the hut, and burnt it, too. This acted as a little relief to their feelings, and, putting him away from their thoughts they began to think about themselves.

It has been said that there is honour among thieves. So there is, but precious little. With them honour and self-interest go together, and, when the sacrifice of self-interest is demanded at the shrine of honour, they invariably decline to do so, but offer up honour to self-interest, as the form of sacrifice most congenial to their feelings.

When the remaining members of the band set to think over the flight of Jaundice, they saw—or thought they saw—that he had made good his escape by it, and there entered into their heads the idea of doing what he had apparently so successfully done.

Pedro, the Spaniard, was the first to entertain and the first to resolve to put it into execution, and, accordingly, the very next night he stole away while his companions slept, and bent his steps towards a little settlement he knew of about twenty miles away.

As he crept through the trees he paused to listen, as it was quite possible that he might be followed; but the only sound he heard was a slight rustling in the branches overhead—no doubt caused by the slight breeze blowing at the time. A very slight breeze it must have been, as he could not feel it on his fevered face.

"Once away," he muttered, "I will give up this accursed life, and live like an honest man."

What good resolutions we make at the time of trouble, and how we break them when all is right again! Pedro was much the same as the best or worst of us, and his resolutions were not worth a straw, as time will show.

When clear of the wood he had a look at the stars, took his bearings, and struck out across the plain with the stealthy footsteps of a cat and restless eyes, looking here and there for signs of danger. The mysterious way in which the Ogre had been taken off naturally imposed upon him the belief that Broad Arrow Jack had more than mortal means at his command.

The slightest noise startled him, and each minute brought a new terror, which only faded away with the arrival of another. The crackling of a twig— a stone rolling beneath his tread—the note of a night bird—the movement made by some small animal—together or in succession—kept his nerves constantly on the strain.

"Accursed be the hour we saw him!" he muttered, as he paused to wipe his brow. "Accursed be the Ogre for his mad folly! Accursed be everything but—myself!"

"Whee—woe!" shrieked a voice in his ear, and something flapped heavily against his back.

In the fury of fear he turned and struck out with his knife. But he only chopped the empty air—no living thing was near.

What was it!

"If you are mortal," he cried, "come forth and meet me."

A dead silence reigned. The earth was as still as the cloudless sky above.

"This is hellish!" muttered the Spaniard. "I, who have never believed in aught but what I saw, am being punished for my unbelief. The saints protect me!"

He moved on with a faltering step, with the knife in his hand—more from instinct than from an idea of making efficient use of it—with eyes that gleamed in the darkness. Presently came the cry again.

"Whee—woe!"—a most unearthly shriek, which no words can give a fair impression of. It might have been the despairing cry of a lost soul. Once more he was struck—this time in the breast.

He fell back, and sank upon his knees. "Holy Mother," he cried, "have mercy on a sinful child! Spare me—spare me!"

"Ha—ha!" laughed a shrill voice, and a form or a shadow flitted rapidly past him.

Pedro fell upon his face. "I am lost!" he cried— "lost!" and unconsciousness came to relieve him from his misery.

How long he lay there he never knew, nor could he tell the hour when he awoke to find his hands tied behind him and his eyes tightly bound. A number of people were moving about him, and voices that appeared familiar to him reached his ears.

"Time to move forward," said one. "Put the prisoner on a horse."

"Can't he have old Joss?" asked another voice, speaking very faintly.

"No, certainly not. No other man must mount that fiery steed until you have tamed him."

"Tame be jiggered," answered the previous speaker. "You can't tame a horse that is full of antics, and would just as soon walk on his head as his feet. I've been off his back so orfen that I'm a reglar mass of bruises——"

"Silence!" cried the other voice. "Mount the prisoner, and advance."

"May I speak?" asked Pedro.

"Yes," was the reply; "but be brief—our time is short."

"In whose power am I?"

"Broad Arrow Jack's," was the reply, and Pedro shuddered.

"Why am I blindfolded?" he asked. "At least let me have light."

"No," was the reply; "you will have but one more short look upon the light in this world. When you stand face to face with your accuser."

"Am I speaking with Broad Arrow Jack?"

"No."

"Let me free," pleaded the Spaniard, "and I will tell you of hidden wealth, and how to snare the others. I was not so guilty as the rest, and I will help your chief with his just vengeance."

"A foolish offer," replied the other, "seeing that we hold already what you propose to give. In vain will your comrades fly—they are in a net. In vain have you hidden your plunder—every coin and every jewel will be unearthed when our noble leader thinks fit."

"Some will escape you," said Pedro, with a laugh.

"You are thinking of the box of ancient diamonds you sank in the stream, and now lies chained to the roots of the old willow," whispered the voice in his ear. "You chose the spot, knowing your comrades avoided it since the wife of one your victims sought refuge from your violence there. Poor fool!"

"Where gained you my secret?" asked Pedro in despair.

"What matters?—we know everything," was the reply. "Forward."

Pedro felt himself lifted up and put astride a horse. A rope was passed under the belly, and his ankles secured with skilfully tied knots. Somebody took the head of the horse, and the tramp of twenty moving steeds fell upon the prisoner's ears.

"Lost," he muttered—"lost! Holy Mother, have mercy upon me!"

Of course it is very easily guessed into whose hands he had fallen, but how he came there must remain a secret for the present. It was not chance, but skill; and Billy Brisket, who was the speaker, spoke truly when he said the band of miserable men were in a net from which there was no escape.

The men surrounded the prisoner, and Billy Brisket and Wobbles rode about fifty yards in the rear—Billy Brisket on a splendid mare, and Wobbles on the wonderful old Joss.

It was all very well for scoffers and scorners to talk to him about taming that fiery steed, but what man in the world could have done it? Old Joss had the hide of an elephant, and the obstinacy of a mule. When he made up his mind to do a thing he did it, and you might as well have licked a wooden horse—neither whip nor spur made the least impression upon him.

If he had gone through his performance in a regular manner it would not have mattered so much, but Wobbles never knew what he was going to do. Sometimes it was walking, sometimes a simulation of death, or something else equally aggravating, but his favourite notion was to try to stand on his head.

Whether he had ever done such a thing or whether he had a new inspiration upon him it is not quite clear, but the performance from a performing point of view was not a success. It is true that Wobbles always rolled down his neck, and came a flopper on the ground, but as this feat was quite outside the intention of old Joss he cannot be given any credit for it. Wobbles had serious notions of strapping himself sometimes to the saddle, but as old Joss occasionally rolled—in agony—a feat he used to perform in a graphic representation of the Battle of Waterloo, where he was supposed to be shot—the idea was given up as dangerous.

On this occasion he appeared to be in a sober frame of mind, and Wobbles was in consequence rather happy than otherwise. As he kept in the saddle now sometimes for five minutes at a time without any accident, he was beginning to think he was a horseman—not exactly of the first water, perhaps, but a little above the average.

But his joy was ever brief-lived. The sobriety of old Joss was all a sham. In a quarter of an hour his genius was coming out again, and down he went like a shot, apparently stone dead. Wobbles went off like a stone out of a catapult, and lay spreadeagled half a dozen yards away.

"Blister the brute!—burn him!" he groaned. "Who would have thought of that?"

"Come and rouse him," said Billy Brisket, with a face as grave as a judge. "Don't put up with his nonsense; take it out of him."

"I've tried everything," said Wobbles, brushing the dust off his clothes; "but I've only had a day or so to work upon him. Get up, you bladder-hocked brute! Get up, you fiddle-headed beast!"

But old Joss would not get up until he had been carried a few yards—out of the ring in his imagination—and two of the men were signalled to come back and give a helping hand. They each took a fore-leg, and with Wobbles and Billy Brisket pushing in the rear, they got the old wretch over six or seven feet of ground. Then he got up as lively as a kitten, and kicked out so suddenly behind that Wobbles had a narrow escape of having his brains dashed out.

"Oh, you beauty!" he said. "You hanimal!"

With assistance he got up again, and with the exception of a couple of waltzes, and one pretence that he was going to roll—but didn't—old Joss behaved in the most creditable manner for the next mile or so. It is true Wobbles fell off twice when he thought the old brute was going to do something. The very thought of these antics made him limp. But such trifles can scarcely be put into the list of the casualties of the day.

The route taken was past the village again, but with a skilful knowledge of the landscape the men wended their way so as not to reveal themselves. Old Joss, for some reason or the other, showed a tendency to wander in that direction, but when Billy Brisket gave him a real taste of the whip—such as Wobbles dare not administer—he prudently changed his mind, and went the right way like a well-conducted horse.

The whole day passed without their seeing a living creature. They travelled over what appeared to have been once a tolerably-frequented road. There were faint tracks of wheels upon it still, but weeds and moss had freely grown, and man for months, at least, had not ridden there.

Billy Brisket seemed to know the road well, and whenever his men paused where the trace of it was almost obliterated, he directed them on their course without hesitation.

At nightfall they halted as they entered the first mountain gorge, and camped on the very spot where he had first met with Broad Arrow Jack.

Pedro had not spoken since the morning, and when they halted he only asked if somebody would make a cigarette, and put it between his teeth. This office Billy Brisket did, telling him to make the most of it, as it was the last he would get for many days to come.

As it was with the Ogre so it was with the Spaniard. The very uncertainty of the fate in store for him gave reins to his imagination, and created a hundred forms of torture, and pictured all sorts of violent and lingering deaths.

With his cigarette between his teeth, and his back to the rock, Pedro sat brooding until near midnight. There was little noise in the camp, although there was more merriment than those who attended upon Broad Arrow Jack displayed. Nobody spoke to him, and, apparently, nobody was near him. At last he rolled slowly over, to see if he was alone, and immediately his shoulders touched those of another man.

A silent guard sat on either side of him. He felt the net was close around him.

It was a little past midnight when the clang of horses' feet fell upon his ears, and the whole camp was aroused.

Pedro heard the rifles cocked, and the voice of the leader giving the word to stand close.

But friends, not foes, were at hand. It was Broad Arrow Jack and his men, covered with the dust of a hasty ride. Their horses were flecked with foam.

"What now, my chief?" cried Billy Brisket.

"Bad news," replied Broad Arrow Jack. "The Ogre has escaped."

"The Ogre escaped!" thought Pedro, with a start of joy. "Then there is hope for me—the Ogre lives!"

"Abandon all foolish hope," said a voice in his ear. "The Ogre has escaped only to be captured again. Every mesh of the net is sound."

CHAPTER XVIII.

BROAD ARROW JACK'S HOME.

"ESCAPED!" said Billy Brisket, aghast. "How did he manage that?"

"Come aside with me," replied Jack, "and I will tell you."

"Let me look to my prisoner first," was Brisket's reply.

"Who is that?"

"Pedro, the Spaniard."

"One of the smaller fry; but he must be held secure. Send him on to Black Rock."

"At once?"

"Yes," said Jack, and Billy Brisket gave orders for the removal of Pedro to Black Rock, of which more anon.

As he was returning to the side of his chief he caught sight of Lost Leon, and seeing he was a stranger scrutinised him carefully by the light of the camp-fire, which had been lighted for cooking purposes.

Lost Leon bore the scrutiny with an unmoved face, seemingly indifferent to the puzzled look upon Billy Brisket's face.

"Who is that, I wonder? I've seen him before," muttered Billy, and put the question to his chief.

"The same fancy had caught me," replied Jack, "but I cannot call to mind who it is. What matters? He has taken the oath, and is bound to us for ever. Stop now; we are alone."

"Now about the Ogre."

"Yes, the Ogre. Late this afternoon we halted by the Red Creek, and pitched the tent. He, bound as usual, as I thought, was laid down there, and I remained with him, carelessly drawing my pistols from my belt, and placing them upon the table. For half an hour I was engaged in arranging matters which I will tell you of later on, and then, hearing a noise without, I went forth to see how it was, and found Lost Leon quarreling with one of the men."

"Lost Leon is the stranger."

"Yes, Brisket."

"I don't like the looks of that stranger," muttered Billy. "Perhaps he had a hand in—but go on, my chief; let me hear all before I begin to judge."

"The quarrel had arisen from some little foolish joke on the part of Maddox. He is as strong as a bull, you know, and in a spirit of fun took the stranger up by the waist and held him in the air. Lost Leon resented with passionate fury, and drawing a dagger, would have stabbed him, if others had not interfered and held him back. Even then he only waited to be free to avenge what he considered to be an insult, and my presence alone had a soothing effect upon him. I made Maddox apologise, and, having smoothed matters, was returning to my tent, when the Ogre, free of every bond, sprang out with my pistols in his hands. One he aimed at me and fired, but, as you know, it was a waste of powder. I shall not die until my work is done."

"Ay, it is so," returned Billy, nodding his head, "you are as good as shot-proof."

"Having fired, he sprang upon the back of Sue, who, I need not tell you, always grazes untethered. Stooping down he gave a most unearthly shriek in her ear, and the mare startled, leaped up, and tore madly away. I whistled as I have often done, but the shriek must have deafened her, for she heeded it not, but went away straight over the plain. Our first confusion over, those who had rifles handy fired, and others rushing to their steeds mounted and rode in pursuit; but Sue was the fleetest of them all, and speedily disappeared in the dusky distance.

"As he rode away," said Jack, in conclusion, "the Ogre turned and fired the second pistol, but the distance was so great that the bullet fell short. I saw a little cloud of dust it raised ten yards in front of me."

"But why did you not follow in pursuit yourself, my chief?"

"Because it would be a waste of time. He cannot escape entirely except he slay himself, and that he will never do. He has no real control over Sue, as she had neither bridle nor rein, and he must eventually go where she will, or take to his feet. I do not think he will do the latter, and Sue, I feel sure, will bring him back again. Now, the only point is where will she go. To Black Rock, I think, and thither I must go, to be prepared to receive him."

"You will go on then?"

"At once, and you, with the men you have left, must ride hard to the pickets, and put them on the alert. You had better ride westward, as Jaundice has taken that direction."

"Am I to bring him back?"

"Not yet," replied Broad Arrow Jack. "He can be taken at any time, but keep upon his trail. I want him to believe himself to be free—to exult in his supposed escape. Watch him, then; if he repents and seeks a better life—if not, you know what you have to do."

"He will never change."

"I do not think he will—he is too deeply dyed."

"Shall I go alone?" asked Billy Brisket.

"Can you trust that cowardly fool?"

"I have him in my power. He no more dare disobey me than he dare mount yon precipice and throw himself into the valley below."

"Then take him with you," said Broad Arrow Jack, "as he might prove to be a burden to me. Farewell, then, till we meet again."

"Are you going at once, my chief? Will you have no rest?"

"None," replied our hero.

"Or food?"

"Give some to my men. I have need of none. We must be at Black Rock before the dawn."

"But you are weary."

"Brisket," said Broad Arrow Jack, "fatigue and I are strangers. I can shake it off as the dust. Farewell! you know your work. Give my men something to eat, and bid them be ready in ten minutes to follow me."

In a little over the time he mentioned the men had partaken of a hasty meal, the horses had been given a little water, and just tasted the green refreshing grass. Then he rode on with his followers, and sight and sound of him were speedily lost in the gloom of the night.

"A proud spirit—a great spirit," muttered Billy Brisket. "Who would not follow such a leader to death? Come, I like this work—it is worthy of a man. Now, my noble Romans," this he said to such of his followers as remained—nine in number, "I dare say you would like a little sleep."

"If we can get it," said one.

"Then get it you shall to-morrow night," replied Billy Brisket, "for this night you must away. The devil is loose, and the outpickets must be warned."

He told them off, each man to a different point of the compass, all but Wobbles, and in a short space of time he and that valiant hero were left alone. Wobbles, who had been in mortal fear of being sent on dangerous duty, was beginning to breathe freely when Billy Brisket pulled him up short.

"Wobbles, my friend," he said, "for you and me I have reserved the most dangerous duty of all. You will have an opportunity to distinguish yourself."

"I don't want it," replied Wobbles, suppressing a groan. "This isn't at all in my line. I'm not a fighting man, and I wasn't a fighting boy. It's much better in my hopinion to lie down than to be knocked down."

"If you lie down here you will in all probability never get up again," said Billy. "So brace yourself up; we are going after your old master."

"Not Jeb Jaundice?" exclaimed Wobbles, aghast.

"That's the man and no other," rejoined Brisket, "and you'll have to bring him back dead or alive. If he kills you, why there's an end of it; you will have done your best, and nobody can grumble. If you fail you will have to suffer the penalty of Broad Arrow Jack's law."

"What is that?" asked Wobbles, faintly.

Billy Brisket did not reply in words, but he took the two ends of his handkerchief and held them up like a rope, and made a curious noise in his throat, as if he had a difficulty in breathing. The illustration was perfect, and Wobbles understood.

"This," he muttered, "is a go of goes. Anyhow I can't get out of it. Jeb Jaundice will double me up like a daily paper. Oh! my sainted mother, why did you save up three hundred pounds, and why didn't you pawn them spoons and teapot, and leave me a penniless horphan? I shouldn't then have gone into society, and got mixed up in the most blessed of all blessed messes as ever a chap got into."

"Haste there—haste!" cried Billy Brisket. "Bring forth the wild Joss."

"I'm a coming with him," replied Wobbles, as he rolled up the grazing cord on his trembling arm. "Woa there, you brute."

The brute, as he called old Joss, seeing that his night's rest was about to be disturbed, was not in the most pleasant of humours, and running with his head down at Wobbles, tried to butt him like a goat. Wobbles dodged him skilfully, and laying hold of his mane, tried to mount.

But this old Joss was determined to resist to the utmost, and began a fancy dance that would have made the fortune of a circus if he had only thought of it in his earlier days. Wobbles was hustled here and there until he was quite out of breath, and would have been worsted in the struggle if Billy Brisket had not come to the rescue.

The hand he laid upon the bridle told that noble horse he had a man at him who was not to be trifled with, and, as old Joss was a horse of good reasoning powers at such times, he gave in, and stood as quietly as a lamb.

"Now," said Billy, "mount—will you?"

"Give me time," gasped Wobbles. "I aint a hacrobat. Stop a minute—I'm on the wrong side. That's it! Ugh! hold him a minute—don't give him his head until I'm properly settled down!"

It was very wrong of Billy Brisket to let the old horse go before Wobbles was quite settled, and very unfeeling of him to laugh when the animal gave an original sort of buck-jump into the air, and came down with his fore-feet spread out at different points of the compass. A struggle ensued,

BROAD ARROW JACK.

and it was doubtful if he would not roll over; but he got right at last, and set off in a deliberate high-stepping trot, bringing his feet down heavily, and shaking the hapless Wobbles like a jelly at every step.

"We may be attacked on the way," said Billy Brisket, as they went down the gorge, "and if it is by anybody whom we do not want, we had better bolt."

"Bolt?" said Wobbles, savagely. "How?"

"Put spurs to old Joss, and you will find the Arab steed nothing to him. All he wants is a little management—with that he hasn't his equal living."

Wobbles did not reply, but he ventured to think that old Joss was the only one of his breed. If such another existed, poison was too good for him.

"Two years in a coal-cart would do him good," he muttered; "and when wore out at that he might have a few years in a late 'bus, then a go at night cab work, and arter that be sold to a knacker, who would doctor him up for a fair. Then, I think, his nonsense would be taken out of him. If I ever live to see him through it I shall die happy."

As if in derision of him and his thoughts, old Joss neighed, and kicked out one hind-leg, finishing off with a sneeze that brought the nose of Wobbles between his ears. Then he seemed to be suddenly inspired with a desire to show his paces, and broke into a violent, remorseless, bone-shaking, jelly-making trot.

Meanwhile Broad Arrow Jack rode through long defiles in the mountains, pausing now and then at a spring to wash out the mouth of his horse—an example followed by his men—keeping on his way through the semi-darkness with the boldness of one thoroughly well acquainted with the road. It was a wild beautiful country, with great crags on either side towering to the sky, and great forests in places running up from the base to the summit.

Birds and beasts abounded, and scarce a step was taken without some four-footed or winged creature being startled by the invasion of their home. Twice a tiger crossed their path, switching his long tail angrily; but a stentorian shout from Broad Arrow Jack sent him scared away.

The hiss of the snake—the snarl of the wolf—the deep growl of more dangerous beasts—accompanied the brave band as it rode fearlessly along, one only showing slight signs of nervousness, and that was Lost Leon; and his fear was not cowardice in the true sense of the word—only the weakness of a frail frame.

In ordinary danger Lost Leon would probably be as brave as any one. Proof of his spirit had been given in the way he resented the practical joking of Maddox—a burly fellow, who could have crushed every bone in his body without much effort.

Silence was maintained until their path led them into a wood growing in a valley between two great hills. Here Broad Arrow Jack pulled up, and, dismounting, bade his followers do the same. This step was necessary, as the branches grew low for some distance, but in about half an hour they arrived at a spot where the trees had been cleared away, and a tolerably plain road made. Here Jack remounted and rode forward briskly, his men tailing off behind him.

Suddenly their road was barred by a dozen mounted men, and a challenge rung out—

"Who goes there?"

"The avenger," replied Broad Arrow Jack.

"The pass-word?"

"The Brand of the Brave."

"Dismount!" rang out, and the new comers gathered round the young giant, asking for news.

"None as yet," he answered, "but a stranger will be here to-morrow. Sue will bring him. Let him ride free by, even to our house. Away all of you—hide—every man, all but Lost Leon, and he will come with me. A torch there!"

One was lighted instantly, and handed to him.

By its light he saw Lost Leon regarding him with apprehension.

"Fear not, stranger," he said, "you are one of us. No harm shall come to you."

"I was foolish to think of it for a moment," replied Lost Leon, smiling. "I will follow you whithersoever you go."

"Bravely said," cried Jack, and waving his hand to the men they rode off to the right and left. "Now on to Black Rock, my mountain home."

"Have you a home here?" asked Lost Leon.

"Ay!" cried Broad Arrow Jack, turning on his companion two flashing eyes. "Such a home as the kings of the earth might be proud of—such a home as must have known a king indeed."

"How came it yours?" asked Lost Leon.

"Thereby hangs a tale," replied Broad Arrow Jack. "Let us go to it. The dawn is nigh."

CHAPTER XIX.
BLACK ROCK.

LOST LEON was full of wonder, and his eyes strained ahead to catch a glimpse of the home Jack had spoken of. The dawn was at hand, and broke as they left the wood behind them and came into view of the strangest, and perhaps the most beautiful scene eyes of mortal had ever looked upon.

Well might the fragile stranger utter a cry of joy and astonishment. Above him towered a mountain, with great crags and jutting rocks, intermingling with luxuriant verdure and groups of noble trees. At the foot ran a stream clear as crystal, with a pebbly bottom, where lay the dark forms of the trout, and chub, and dace, watching for the food which came with the sunlight. Silvery eels peeped from beneath great stones, or wound their sinuous way through the water, turning, twisting, bending with wonderful grace, and on the banks there grew wild flowers in profusion, unfolding their leaves in the first warmth of the morning.

The mountain was of circular form, like the crater of a great volcano, and had been one most likely in the ages so far back that one can only express the time in figures—a conception of it is impossible; but there were rents in it in places, and through one of them a golden shaft streamed down, and kissed the roof of the house Broad Arrow Jack had called his own.

It was on the other side of the stream, and at first escaped Lost Leon's eyes, impressed with the majesty of the great mountain beyond, but when he saw it another cry rushed to his lips, and, half uttered, halted there.

Let me, if I can, describe that home. A building a hundred feet or more in length and seventy high, built of many-coloured stones, with a great porch fantastically carved, with figures of serpents and birds and beasts entwined. About the porch three great pinnacles, so delicately formed that it seemed as if a breath would blow them away; to the left and right a cluster of lesser pinnacles, each varying in design.

The face of the place was one mass of fretwork of stone, cut in perfect taste, with the powerful execution of the ancients. Trees, flowers, and living things had all been called in to play their part in ornamentation, and skilful hands had woven, as it were, coloured stones into a resemblance of the object represented, and the eyes of the birds and beasts sparkled with a dazzling brilliancy, which puzzled Lost Leon more than all else. By the porch the glittering was dazzling.

"Is it not a home for a king?" asked Broad Arrow Jack.

"I cannot understand it. It does not seem to be real," replied Lost Leon. "Who are you?—what are you?"

"What you see me—a boy in years, a man in sorrow," he replied. "Think not that I built you

Broad-Arrow Jack.

A CRY OF MORTAL TERROR ESCAPED JEB JAUNDICE AS HE LOOKED DOWN INTO THE VALLEY—THEN ALL WAS DARKNESS.

NO. 4.

place. It was made by men whose dust has long been lost in the earth—by men who may not have known the value of things they worked with. See those glittering eyes, each a rare diamond, cut and polished with an art which our boasted civilisation cannot rival. And up above, where the trees and flowers grow thickest, lies the spot where those jewels were found, the bed from whence the puny baubles men seek in yonder diamond fields have drifted down."

"Can it be true?"

"You shall see and judge for yourself, Lost Leon. Once on a time—heaven alone knows when—the water rushed down by the spot I name into the stream below, bringing with it the diamonds by the thousand perchance. The lesser passed on to be washed out in yon distant plain. You may have heard of it. Men have been toiling there for years."

"I know—I know," replied Lost Leon, softly.

"The greater diamonds remained behind," Broad Arrow Jack went on, "at least so I judge—and the cunning men of old traced them to their source, dammed up the waterfall, turned it from its course, and reaped a harvest such as the world seldom sees."

"It is a strange tale."

"But true. Behold the proof. That house was created by those who prospered here. How old it is I cannot tell. It wears well, for no great storms assail it. They spend their fury on the mountain tops, and only the refreshing rain comes down, falling gently in this windless place—only the gentlest breezes, and those but rarely, come down here. It might be the abode of Peace."

"I can scarcely believe I look upon a man," said Lost Leon. "How learnt you of this place?"

"Through one of noble, generous heart."

"A man of gentle blood?"

"Yes," replied Broad Arrow Jack; "but not as the world judges it. Poor in pocket, poor in name, he found this place, and terrified he kept his secret, knowing how men would wrangle and fight for it. Rivers of blood perchance might flow, and he said nothing, until he heard the story of my wrongs. Then he said, 'It is yours; take it; use it as you will,' and by its means I have brought my band of faithful men together."

"But can you trust them? Are they more than mortal?"

"No, but I hold them in a double bond—self-interest and love for me. The latter is the stronger, and I fear them not. Of all you see here I take no more when my work is done. The original noble giver takes but little—he wants it not; the rest is yours."

"But this task of yours—what is it?" asked Lost Leon.

"To avenge the death of those I loved."

"But how?"

"That is my secret—ask no more," replied Broad Arrow Jack, and lightly touching his horse with the spur he rode across a shallow part of the stream.

Lost Leon followed, and the pair reined up at the porch. Broad Arrow Jack took the reins, and fastened them to a stone ring worked in the solid masonry, then signalled his companion to enter. Lost Leon obeyed, and entered a great hall with walls and floors of pure white marble, curiously wrought in harmony with the exterior.

The light came from openings, or rather perforations, near the roof, and gave that subdued effect one finds in old abbeys and cathedrals. In the centre was a lantern of beautifully carved wood, with stone cups for oil and wick. Otherwise, the hall was bare of all but a great bundle of woollen materials in the corner.

"Here," said Broad Arrow Jack, "my men sleep. On either side are numerous rooms devoted to various purposes, the storage of firearms, provisions, and so on, brought up from the settlements by my trusty agents."

"All of whom you trust?"

"To a man. Already one has died rather than reveal my secret. A band of roysterers, mad with drink, asked him where he came from. He refused to tell—they shot him, and, as he lay bleeding on the ground, tried to worm out his story. Dying he refused. Outside we have raised a stone to his memory."

"Will you not avenge him?" asked Lost Leon.

"It was done," he replied. "I left my men to do that, and all who shared in that are silent now."

A sadness came over him as he spoke, and moving forward he opened a door to the left, revealing a small chamber with three sides of solid stone, and a fourth of beautiful tracery, through which the light came from the outside.

"This," he said, "is my own chamber. From it I can see all who approach without being seen. There is a similar one within. Will you have that, or would you prefer the society of the men? They are rough, but sterling and honest."

"If you will permit me," replied Lost Leon in a low voice, "I would rather be alone."

"So be it," replied Jack, "here is your chamber. You will find another door on the other side leading to a passage which will guide you to another entrance. You can come and go at will."

"Suppose I attempt to betray you?" said Lost Leon, with a smile.

"To whom?" asked Broad Arrow Jack—"to the diamond-seekers, who have no law or order? To the distant band of settlers, whom I could scatter at will? No, I do not fear you—or fear your heart. You are bound to me as others are."

"You speak confidently."

"I read the eyes of those who serve me. The eyes are books that never lie."

"And in yours," said Lost Leon, looking full at him, "I read a purpose that nothing less than death can turn aside. Oh! that I might ask——"

"What?" said Broad Arrow Jack, as Lost Leon paused.

"No, not now, at a more fitting time," replied Lost Leon, and entering his chamber, he softly closed the door behind him.

"A strange being," thought Broad Arrow Jack, as he lounged upon a pile of rugs, which formed his couch by night, and resting place by day. "I cannot understand him. But what matters? Does he understand me? Is it not enough that he is bound to me as the others are?" and, stretching himself out, our hero succumbed to the fatigue he had lately endured, and fell into a sound sleep.

CHAPTER XX.
HOOKEY SETTLEMENT.

IT is just possible that some of my readers have not heard of Hookey Settlement, and more than probable that a very few of them are personally acquainted with it, and quite certain that one visit to it would have been enough for my young friends, one and all.

Hookey Settlement began bad, and is bad to this day. If you want to be ripped, gouged, stabbed, shot, or put out of the world by any of the many methods designed by man, go to Hookey Settlement, and you will get it done with a promptitude and despatch rarely equalled, and surely never surpassed.

The founder of this abode of brotherhood was a Yankee, who had made the place of his birth, and several other places where he ought to have died, a little too hot for him, and he, hearing of the diamond fields, bent his steps thither, determined to reap the fruits of other people's labour, like the good, honest, downright, murderous villain he undoubtedly was.

But on his way thither he fell in with another Yankee, making his way to the fields with a van-load of whiskey, his intention being to open a drinking booth, with real stimulating poison at a diamond a glass, or two, or even three, if anybody was fool enough to stump out to that extent.

Now, the name of the Yankee first named was Jereboam Bounce, and he was a keen man, and wise in many ways. He had an eye to business, had Jereboam, and when he came across a hole big enough to put his head or hand in, his hand or head was thrust in accordingly.

He was also one of those men who recognise a good thing when it is thrown in his way. Providential gifts he called them, and looking upon his fellow-countryman with a van-load of whiskey with an appreciative eye, he saw in him a gift from the gods, and accordingly took an early opportunity when he was surveying the landscape ahead to shoot him down.

The proprietor of the whiskey fell, but not being quite dead he out with his own weapon and let fly at Jereboam, who, turning quickly, presented his profile to the view of the other and had the bridge of his nose shot away.

Jereboam, indignant at having his beauty spoiled, finished his foe with a second shot, and thinking him unworthy of the rites of burial, drove off with the van-load of whiskey, and left him to the crows, vultures, or any other carrion creature disposed to make a meal of him.

Resolved upon living an honest life, Jereboam Bounce built a shanty about twenty miles from Peaceful Village, the abode of the Ogre and his friends, and started a drinking booth for travellers going to and fro.

Drink draws as well as carrion. Men came unto Jereboam and drank freely, but so well was his shanty conducted that on an average not more than two people were killed outright in a week, and the number of those wounded might almost be counted on your fingers.

Congenial society gathered around him—other shanties rose about him, communication with a town on the coast was established, and Hookey Settlement prospered.

How it prospered is nobody's business. It was a better place than Peaceful Village. The men of Hookey were rowdies and rough, but they had no organised system of murder. They only shot a man down when they got a fair chance, and if he had anything about him—why—they took it.

Gambling was the principal trade carried on, and those who kept the market going were men going out to the diamond fields with a little money, or those returning with a little fortune. In either case to enter Hookey Settlement was to leave all tin behind. When cleaned out the loser was expected to leave quietly, and if he did not one of the brethren picked a quarrel with him, and either shot or stabbed him, according to the fancy of the moment.

I hope I have not dwelt too long upon the description of this delightful place, but the temptation to give a fair idea of it overcame me, and I set it down. Let me now proceed with my story.

It was morning, and Jereboam Bounce stood by his door inhaling the pure air. The face of Jereboam was flushed, and the eye of Jereboam was troubled, for he, the said Jereboam, had been very drunk overnight, and was in a feverish state, and while very drunk he had been pretty well cleaned out by a stranger who arrived at the Settlement two days before.

A stranger in a residential sense, but known unto Jereboam as an occasional visitor, and his name was Jeb Jaundice.

That worthy turned up with the look of having travelled all night, and announced his intention of stopping at Hookey Settlement for a few hours. He was told that he was welcome, and asked to play. He played for two days, and cleaned out Jereboam as he had never been cleaned out before.

Had it been done by an ordinary traveller Jereboam Bounce would not have cared a fig—he would have got it back somehow; but Jeb Jaundice belonged to a gang whose very name was a terror, and it was dangerous work playing any tricks upon him. Hence the troubles of the cleaned-out Jereboam.

"If the cussed skunk was any other chap I'd do for him in bed," he muttered, as he glared at the landscape malevolently; "but it's risky—that lot is too powerful, and too unscrupulous. They ain got no sense of what is right and fair."

It will be seen that Jereboam knew nothing Broad Arrow Jack having fallen upon Peaceful Village, or he would have piped another tune. In unhappy ignorance of the break-up there he cursed his hard luck, and cowered before Jeb Jaundice.

"He is a cussed skunk!" he said aloud, again.

"Who is a cussed skunk?" asked a voice behind, and Jeb Jaundice, a little pale, but otherwise all right, came out, and leant against the other doorpost.

Jereboam extracted a feeble smile from somewhere, and put it about his mouth. He hardly knew what else to do.

Jeb looked at him sternly.

"That's the way," he said, "with you half-and-half men. You never lose half a dozen dollars without howling and cursing."

"Half a dozen dollars!" said Jereboam. "Come, that's cutting it down. I've lost nearly a pint of uncut diamonds—the fruit of long years of honest and industrious trading."

"Win them back again," said Jeb Jaundice. "Put down your stake, and I'm at you again."

"I've got nothing but the whiskey and the shanty to put down," said Jereboam.

"Stake them, and I'm on."

"Done."

There and then the cards were produced, and they sat upon the ground to play. As an assistant to a clear head Jereboam brought out half a pint of whiskey in a battered pewter pot (only a week before a man had been knocked on the head with it), but Jeb Jaundice had a jug of water.

As the game proceeded the inhabitants of the other sheds or shanties—a dozen in number perhaps —came out one by one, and gathered round.

At first luck fluctuated, bearing a little in favour of Jereboam, but as time wore on the cards became his foes again, and the fate of Jereboam was as good as sealed. The whiskey and shanty were going—going—almost gone in an hour.

He played desperately, and he drank rashly. The pewter pot was replenished, the colour deepened in his cheeks, and his eyes slowly came forth from their caverns, and stood out like marbles. Jeb Jaundice preserved an unmoved face.

The lookers-on were silent, but their looks spoke. Ruin was bearing down upon Hookey Settlement, for with Jereboam all would fall.

They, too, held Jeb Jaundice in awe. They knew who he was, and who were his friends, and those friends might know of his being there, and if he were missing would make troublesome inquiries concerning him. Had they but known the truth their minds would have been much easier.

The game was at its close. The last tub of whiskey was gone, and the shanty itself was the final stake.

Jeb Jaundice was dealing the cards, smoothly and skilfully, watched by wary eyes, when a voice made players and lookers-on start.

"Good morning, gentlemen. Any knives, scissors, ink, pens, paste or powder, needles, thread, cotton, tape, or buttons, sealing-wax, note paper? You all write occasionally to the dear ones at home, I am sure, gentlemen. Anything at all in my way?"

It was Billy Brisket, with apron, smoking cap, slippers, and pack—the humble pedlar all over—a meek, humble, inoffensive man from head to heel.

"Any thing in my way?" he asked, softly. "Gun caps, wads, neckties, or——"

"Can't you see we are busy?" cried Jeb Jaundice, frowning at him. "What are you skulking about here for?"

"Oh, not skulking, gentlemen, I assure you," replied Billy Brisket, with a gentle smile. "I am only a poor devil, trying to make a crust of bread by honest trading. Business is bad, indeed. I was down your way the other day, Mr. Jaundice, and nobody bought a button of me."

Jaundice frowned at him, as an indication that he wished him to remain silent about what he saw and heard there.

Billy made a slight sign of acquiescence, and turned to Jereboam Bounce.

"Enterprising as usual, sir," he said. "I hope your usual good luck is attending upon you."

It must have taken seven devils at least to get up the expression which came over Jereboam's face as he swore a frightful oath. Taking out a pistol he cocked it, with the intention of finishing off the meek and inoffensive Billy, but that wary gentleman got behind one of the company.

"Don't, sir; please, sir," he said, "if you've had bad luck. Thanks. I always bring good luck to those I am fond of. Go on with the game, dear Mr. Bounce, and don't waste powder and shot on such a worthless creature as I am."

Not being able to get a clean shot at him, Jereboam Bounce put up his weapon, and resumed the game. Billy Brisket proved to be a speaker of truth—the luck had changed.

Every card was a friend to Jereboam, and, with a rapidity truly startling, he won game after game, until the whiskey and the shanty were his own again, and he was pulling back the other valuables he had lost the day before.

"I stop now," cried Jeb Jaundice. "I want something to eat."

"Play on—play on!" said Jereboam.

"No," returned Jaundice. "I won in two lots, and I'll lose in two lots. Give me something to eat, and I'm with you again."

"Right!" cried the Yankee; "but, hallo! mister, where are *you* going?"

"I was going on, sir," replied Billy, meekly. "I don't see any chance of doing business here."

"Stop, and keep my luck going. I'll buy your pack, if you like."

"You had better stop," added Jeb Jaundice. "I have something to say to you."

"Very well, gentlemen. Of course your word is law," returned Billy, and, with a look of deep humility, he took a seat upon his pack, and awaited further orders.

CHAPTER XXI.
ONE FOR JEB.

AS a little refreshment was needed all round, Jereboam Bounce brought out a table, and spread a coarse but substantial meal upon it. Food was never charged for at his establishment, but he made it up in drink—that was sold at about twenty times its value.

The men all paid for their drink—most of them indulging in raw spirits—but Billy Brisket was desired to drink and eat free of expense.

"You came and changed my luck," said Jereboam, "and you may liquor up out of a bucket, if you like."

This Billy Brisket, with great self-denial, declined to do, but took a little in a tea-cup without a handle—the only piece of earthenware the establishment could boast of—and half of his moderate allowance he tossed upon the ground when nobody was looking. Billy had work in hand which required a cool head, and he was wisely abstemious.

Bad as things were with him, he made no further effort to sell, and the men of Hookey not being inclined to purchase, business in that direction fell through, but the more serious dealing was speedily resumed.

Jereboam Bounce had so much faith in the good luck waiting on him through Billy Brisket that he made him come and sit close by his side, making him as comfortable as possible with a very characteristic promise.

"If I win," he said, "I'll make you as drunk as a one-eyed fiddler; but if you've deceived me, darned if I don't give you ten yards' start and take a pot shot at you!"

"But I can't make luck," pleaded Billy.

"You *must* make it!" was the consistent reply. "You brought it here—you put it on me—and if you don't want to get away from business into the other world you keep the pot a bilin'—d'ye hear?"

"Oh! yes—I hear," replied Billy Brisket, calmly. "Go in and win."

The spell, however, had been broken by the meal, and luck for a while went the other way. Jeb Jaundice was exultant, and Jereboam furious. Taking out his revolver, he put it on the ground before him.

"Now, you see that," he said. "I calls it Biting Bob. The barrel's straight, the powder's good, and the bullet's heavy. If you don't want the weight o' that bullet to be added to yourn, come out with some luck, you blighted pedlar!"

"Go on," said Billy, smoothly. "The turn of luck will come."

So Jereboam did go on, and, as the prophet had said, the luck veered round, and Jeb's ill-gotten gains went back rapidly. The Yankee was jubilant, and blessed Billy with a fervour only found among the sons of that young but free and enlightened country in which the sun is everlastingly rising, and never setting.

"Good cuss!" he said, among other things which cannot and shall not be put into print—"rip-and-tear old hoss! Out with the luck! May I be split up into fiddle-strings if I don't give you the run o' my shop for a month!"

But the luck fluctuated, as luck will, and evening found the gamblers still at it, with the spectators still in full enjoyment of a well-spent day. The current of fortune had borne Jereboam Bounce onward, and Jeb Jaundice was within a shade of being cleaned out.

He said nothing; but he looked a little, and thought much. If ever he had felt any friendship for Billy Brisket—which is very doubtful—it was scattered to the winds, and the absorbing desire of his heart at the moment was to have that individual slain by inches, beginning with his toes, and ending with his face.

The last card was played as the sun went down, and Jeb Jaundice was as poor, barring his clothes, as when he came into the world. Preserving a calm exterior, he rose to his feet, and asked Jereboam to stand a drink for old acquaintance sake.

"For I am going further on," he said, "to see some old friends."

"If you please, sir," said Billy Brisket, humbly, "may I ask which way you are going?"

"Westward," replied Jaundice.

"That is my way, sir," said Billy, "and, as I'm a timid nervous man, perhaps you wouldn't mind my going with you."

Jeb Jaundice was surprised, and the men of Hookey staggered. They had read the face of the ruined gambler, and had been debating in their minds the possibility of his giving them a treat by falling on the pedlar, and performing one or more rowdy feats upon him. If he only did a bit of gouging it would be something, but more than one entertained a hope that Billy might lose his nose or one of his ears in addition.

Just for a moment there entered into the heart of Bounce a desire to warn the man who had brought him such good luck, but there came the remembrance of his promise to entertain Billy

Brisket for a month. The spirit of economy was upon him, and he decided to let him go. Jaundice would, no doubt, put him comfortably to rest, and that would shut out the possibility of his making any future claim, or, in other words, endeavouring to trade on the gratitude of Jereboam.

Jeb Jaundice, with murder in his heart, spoke softly, and, in polite phraseology, said how happy he should be to have the society of Billy Brisket. He was always so very polite when in his most treacherous mood.

The pair set forth together when night came on. It was not quite dark, for the heavens were filled with stars, which gave a weird light to the earth, and enabled them to keep the rough road without much trouble.

They were silent, these two men. The brains of both were busy, each working out an imaginary accomplishment of a set purpose—each watchful and wary of every movement of the other.

It never entered into the head of Jeb Jaundice to conceive that Billy Brisket would attack him, but he thought it possible he might be only foxing, and really design to make his escape under the cover of the gloom of night, and, therefore, he never moved his eyes from him.

The hands of Jeb Jaundice were in his pockets; one hand grasped a pistol, and the other a bowie knife. The hands of Billy Brisket were behind his back, supporting his pack apparently, but in those hands was a fine strong rope with a running noose in it.

Thus they kept, Jeb eagerly striding forward, so as to get so far away that no cry could reach the Hookey Settlement. He wanted a place where he could vent his fury upon what he imagined to be a helpless man.

Did he really believe the pedlar had anything to do with his ill-luck? Did he for a moment entertain a conviction that any man could in any way influence those pieces of pasteboard without touching them?

It is not easy to say. Men who profess to believe nothing are generally saturated with petty superstitions, and Jeb Jaundice may have believed Billy Brisket had wronged him.

At any rate he had lost his all, and black murder was in his heart. For awhile he forgot all else, even his terror of Broad Arrow Jack, and all he wanted was a fitting spot to do his foul work in.

The road led them to a clump of trees. As the dark mass grew out of the gloom Jeb Jaundice saw he had found the place he wanted. It would be easy to cut him down, to kill him, and drag his body a short distance from the little frequented path. Birds and beasts would soon find out the slain, and do all the undertaking work that was needed there.

Both men involuntarily paused at the entrance of the wood. The moment of the day had come to each, although each knew not what lay in the breast of the other.

Billy Brisket might suspect—and probaby did—but he did no more.

For the first time since they left the settlement he spoke. Looking into the dark depths of the wood he said—

"That's a horrible-looking place!"

"It's only a little bit of wood," replied Jeb Jaundice, carelessly.

"To me it looks like a grave," rejoined the pedlar.

Jeb Jaundice started, and shuddered. This man, so soon to be his victim, had assuredly a presentiment upon him. A grave! Well, it was dark enough for anything.

"What an odd fancy!" he said, laughing harshly. "Go on, my good feller."

"I am afraid," said Billy, drawing back. "You lead the way."

But Jeb Jaundice did not want to do that—he wished to have his man in front, and bade him go on.

"We can't walk together," he said, "the path is too narrow. Go on; d'ye hear?"

The tone told Billy Brisket that he must either obey or close with his man. To obey he saw now would be to meet with his own death, and his only chance lay in bold attack. He was preparing for a rush when a friend came most unexpectedly to his aid.

A shooting star of great magnitude shot across the sky, leaving a train of fire behind it.

It was so bright that Jeb Jaundice saw his shadow as clearly as if a full moon had suddenly leapt into the heaven. Startled he turned to see from whence the brilliancy came, and the next moment the cord was dropped over his head, drawn tight, and his arms made fast.

"One word," said Billy Brisket, as he tripped him up, and neatly deposited him on his back, " only a whisper, and it is your last!"

How changed he was! The soft-spoken trembling pedlar had become a man of stern purpose. There was command in his voice and in his attitude, under which his grotesque dress was buried. It seemed to Jeb Jaundice that one Billy Brisket had disappeared, and another of totally different nature come in his place.

Surprise did away with all resistance, and without a struggle he allowed his arms to be bound. While performing this business Billy Brisket changed again to another character.

"There," he said, "trussed and ready for market—like a goose—a wild goose that could not see the snare, or more like an ass, perhaps, that went into the pound to nibble grass, and was very much astonished when somebody shut the gate. 'Tra, la, la! A frog he would a wooing go—heigh ho, Sir Rowley!—whether his wife was willing or no—with a rowley powley.' There, I think you will do now, and I hope you are comfortable."

As men would act themselves so they think others will act, and Jeb Jaundice felt as though his last hour had come.

"If you are going to kill me," he groaned, "let it be done quickly; but I never wronged you, and why should you take my life?"

"You never wronged me," replied Brisket, "but you have wronged others."

"Let others avenge themselves," said Jeb Jaundice.

"Just so," said Billy Brisket, "and I am going to hand you over to one who will deal with you justly."

"Who is that?"

"That," said Billy Brisket, "you will shortly see."

In a moment the awful truth flashed upon the wretched man.

"Don't tell me," he cried, "that you are working for Broad Arrow Jack!"

"Him and no other," replied Billy Brisket, coolly; " so meditate on what is coming, and be as happy as you can."

The terror Jeb Jaundice felt at first sank into insignificance in comparison to the deadly fear the prospect of meeting with our hero inspired. He writhed in his bonds—he begged, he implored to be let free. He promised amendment, he vowed he would go away, and live alone like a wild beast in the wilderness, and in solitude repent of his sins. For the sake of his wife—the woman he had brought down to misery and despair—he asked for mercy; he promised to be a slave to him who held him; to give him wealth—a wealth Jeb Jaundice himself did not possess—if he only had his freedom.

"I would rather die at once," he cried. "If you will do nothing else, kill me."

"No—no," replied Billy Brisket, "that is not my work. I am not a public executioner. Say no more, my friend."

"At least, tell me my fate."

"That is only known to Broad Arrow Jack" was the reply, and taking a whistle from his pocket the pedlar blew twice upon it.

A tramp of horses' feet and the voice of a man fell upon the ears of Jeb Jaundice, made trebly acute by terror. He even knew the voice, and hailed Wobbles as he came up on the back of old Joss, leading Billy Brisket's horse by the rein.

"You too!" he cried—"you in league with my enemies! Oh, for an hour of freedom, and I would teach you a lesson, you miserable cur!"

"Go it," replied Wobbles, in a despairing tone, "say it's me. You've arranged it between you I suppose, that I am to blame. It's a hartful dodge got up to drive a hinnercent chap stark staring mad. And it all come of a frugal mother saving up three hundred pounds for me to go into society with, which led up to backing wrong horses ——"

Old Joss, who had been listening very attentively to this harangue, had now enough of it, and signified his intention to cut it short by gathering himself together in preparation for one of his buck jumps. The experienced Wobbles knowing what was coming, rolled off at once, coming down to the ground in a most undignified heap.

"Get up," said Billy Brisket, "and help me to put this Jaundice chap on my horse."

"Wouldn't he ride heasier on old Joss?" mildly suggested Wobbles. "I don't mind walking; I rather like it."

Billy made no reply, but taking Jeb Jaundice by the head, nodded for Wobbles to take the heels, and between them they got him into a sitting position on the horse. He made not the slightest demur to this proceeding, and the pedlar taking the bridle led away his horse, with the prisoner huddled up, body bent, and head down on his breast, miserably brooding.

"Follow as quickly as you can," said Billy Brisket, "and make for the Black Rock."

CHAPTER XXII.

SUE AND THE OGRE.

BROAD ARROW JACK had not been long sleeping when one of his men came and tapped lightly at the door. In an instant he was upon his feet, awake and on the alert.

"Who is there?" he cried.

"Maddox, chief," was the reply.

"Come in!"

Maddox, big, brawny, and muscular, entered the room, doffing his hat as he did so. Broad Arrow Jack, with a gesture, bade him speak.

"Sue is coming home, chief," he said.

"Which way?"

"Up by the Golden Pass."

"Alone?"

"No, my chief, she bears a burden."

"Good," said Broad Arrow Jack, with glistening eyes. "Let no man show himself, I alone will relieve Sue of what she bears."

"Would it not be better for some of us to be near?" asked Maddox, hesitating. "He is armed, and——"

"Maddox," said Broad Arrow Jack, proudly, "have you forgotten who and what I am?"

"No, my chief."

"Then go and rest assured no harm will come to me until my work is done—then come what will it matters not. Go prepare one of the inner chambers for a guest. I will invite him in."

Maddox bowed and left the room, and as the inner chambers have been mentioned we will give a slight sketch of how they were situated, and what part they played in this wonderful mansion.

There were three sets of apartments, divided by two passages, the outer two lighted through the stone tracery before described, and the rest either dimly lighted from above, or without any light at all, the walls and doors fitting to a nicety.

The interior room running up the middle of the building, and divided into two sets of five each by the great entrance hall, were cells in fact, and appeared to have been used as such once upon a time for in one a skeleton had been found, and when an attempt was made to move it the bones crumbled beneath the touch.

Many and many a year must have passed since flesh covered those bones and the breath of life gave them motion. This, we may state, was the only relic of once living creatures found in the place.

There were cellars too, but these had only been explored by Broad Arrow Jack and Billy Brisket. What they contained nobody knew. The men were forbidden to enter therein, and although there was neither lock nor key to bar their way none of Jack's followers thought of disobeying him.

The penalty of disobedience was—death.

To break the oath of the band was to become an enemy to it—a traitor to the cause of the leader—and enemies and traitors were marked men. Jack had never had cause to punish a man yet, but all knew he would most assuredly do so if offence was committed.

"Be true to me," he said, "and I will be true to you. Obey me, and you shall have a princely reward. Turn against me, and I number you with those who have wronged me."

They heard and heeded, and as time passed he gained their love and devotion, in addition to their fear. In the strongest bonds which held men together he held them fast.

As he crossed the hall to go out several of the men entered by the porch. Drawing up, they stood quietly with uncovered heads until he had passed. This was no enforced discipline of his, but a self-imposed recognition of the commanding power of his presence.

And of a truth he was a noble youth, the like of which is not seen in every generation. Had he lived in the days of chivalry he would have been the hero of the lists, and a god in the battle-field. Majestic in form, dauntless in spirit, handsome as Apollo, he was favoured beyond the lot of mortal man.

The Golden Pass was the way he came with Lost Leon, one of the few entrances into that great cup-like valley. Crossing the river he entered the wood, walked a little way, then knelt and listened.

Yes, the sound of a horse approaching at an easy trot was plainly distinguishable. Sue, with her burden, was coming home.

That burden was, of course, the Ogre.

Without bit and bridle, he was at the mercy of his steed, but, as Jack had thought, he preferred going whither she willed to trusting to his own feet. How could he suspect the mare would play a part to bring him to confusion?

The strong muscular ruffian sat on the steed like a Centaur, watchfully enough, but hugging to himself the belief that Sue was taking him away from all enemies. The land was strange to him, but whither it was leading him he cared not, so that it led him away from Broad Arrow Jack.

The wood was so silent that he could not dream of the presence of a foe—here, at least, he felt himself secure, and in his exultation laughed aloud.

But that laugh was turned to a shriek of frenzy as the one he most dreaded sprang out from the trees, leapt up, and seized him by the throat.

"Fool!" cried Jack, "to think you could escape me."

"You are not mortal," was the Ogre's answer, as Jack released him and pinioned his arms with the grasp of a vice, "and that horse is thy foul fiend."

In response to this Sue kicked up her heels and galloped off. Broad Arrow Jack raised the Ogre, and holding him by the arms behind, bade him move forward.

What was the spell which caused this one time undaunted scoundrel to obey like a child? Whatever it was he obeyed him like a child, until they reached the outer part of the wood, and then with a sudden effort he sought to wrench himself free.

But Broad Arrow Jack held him tight, and raising him in the air dashed him down with a force that threatened to break every bone in his body. Bewildered, aghast, he lay there groaning, while Jack removed the brace of pistols he had in his belt.

"I may as well reclaim my own," he said. "Now, up with you, and go on."

All the pluck was shaken out of the brute, and quivering like a beaten horse, he rose up and crawled on ahead. The mansion came in sight, and he saw it, but the beauty and novelty of it made no impression upon him. He had no thought save for that terrible foe behind him.

"Here is the ford," said Jack. "Cross the river."

Unhesitatingly he stepped in, and with a momentary idea of ending his life there and then, looked up and down as if seeking a deep place into which to plunge and end his misery. But Jack understood the action, and bade him go on.

"You cannot drown," he said; "the fate I have designed for you will be yours."

Only one more spark of resistance did the Ogre show. On the opposite bank he paused and turned round. Jack, without warning, struck him in the chest, and he went to the earth as if he had been shot.

"I am master here, and I will be obeyed," were the words which rung in his ears.

This completed the victory—the Ogre was cowed. He entered the house which Jack, for a reason, had called Black Rock, and in the hall was commanded to stand still. Still trembling from the shock of his last fall he stood quiet, while Jack, with a shout, summoned his men.

They came trooping in—a hundred good men, at least—and, forming in a circle, gazed wonder-stricken at their chief and his prize.

"See here, all of you," said Broad Arrow Jack, "this is the beast who brands boys, and slays the weak and helpless. Look at the man who slew my suffering father and younger brother. Stay— no violence!"

They would have torn him to pieces, but Jack warned them off. For the present the Ogre must live.

"Place him in a chamber," he said, "and guard him well. Larkins and Green, look to him. And think not," he added, turning to the Ogre, "to get free again. Were I to turn from this door, and give you a week to get away, I could hold up my hand and bring you back."

The Ogre believed him, and Jack was not boasting. The chance of escape from the net he had spread were very small indeed. Far and wide its meshes lay.

Broad Arrow Jack went back to his own apartment, and when Tom Larkins touched the Ogre on the shoulder, he looked up like a man in a dream. One hurried glance he cast around, and then, in obedience to the beckoning finger of his gaoler, went meekly to his cell.

CHAPTER XXIII.

WOBBLES ACQUIRES A LITTLE PROPERTY.

WHEN Billy Brisket bade Wobbles mount his horse and follow him, he had evidently forgotten the various gifts of that glorious animal, and how his little bursts of genius made mounting and following rather a difficult business.

On that night old Joss was in a very contrary mood. He neither wanted Wobbles to mount, nor had he the slightest intention of following the other horse if he could possibly avoid it. Accordingly, as soon as his fearless rider put one foot into the stirrup, with the intention of getting into the saddle, he commenced a series of sideway skips of a most discomposing nature.

As old Joss skipped Wobbles hopped after him, with a heart full of anathemas, and yet with words of honey on his lips.

"Steady, good old man," he said; "don't chuck your best friend on his back. Other people are down enough on me without you coming out with perwersities. Woa, then, beauty—woa then, you hanimal. Here, dash it—jigger it, don't keep me in this hattitude—can't you hear the stitches agoin'? Good old Joss—fine old boy. Oh! jigger it."

As he was on the point of dropping down exhausted, old Joss kindly stooped, and made a pretence of allowing him to get into the saddle. Wobbles got his leg over his back, and then—up he went—three feet into the air, and sent the valiant one over his head.

Wobbles came down, spread out like a flying squirrel, and although his breathing organs were a little disarranged he was otherwise not much hurt. Fury made him bold, and rising he seized old Joss by the mane, and shook his head, until the teeth of that miserable steed rattled again.

This so confounded his knavish tricks that he gave in, and standing quiet allowed Wobbles to remount, and when he felt the weight of his rider in the saddle set out at a steady old trot, following, as Wobbles hoped, in the wake of the other horse.

Billy Brisket had disappeared, and was too far ahead in the wood for the sound of his horse's hoofs to reach the ears of Wobbles, but the latter, believing there was only one path in the wood, rode forward, trusting to the sagacity of old Joss.

Heaps of stories have been told about travellers, who, having lost their way, trusted in the sagacity of their horses, and, according to the stories, had always come out all right. Wobbles in his youth had read many of them, and he followed the teaching therein conveyed.

He gave old Joss his head, and let him go wherever he pleased.

That sagacious brute gave vent to a chuckle, turning it off into a sort of cough at the finish, and with a perverse spirit full upon him, doggedly set to work to find out some way of going astray, and it is hardly necessary to say he found it.

At a certain point, about half-way through the wood, the path divided, and, although old Joss knew full well his brother steed had gone to the right, he turned to the left, and lost himself as soon as he conveniently could.

He lost himself so effectually that he and his master were in the wood all night—Wobbles in a state of mind impossible to realise, unless one could get into his skin—and when the morning came the old brute trotted into the plain again, full in sight of Hookey Settlement.

Wobbles knew the place, and would f in have ridden on; but old Joss thought the place might have good bait and livery stables, and, getting th bit between his teeth, bore down upon it.

Experience and sagacity led him to the abode Jereboam Bounce, and, arriving before the door, h intimated to Wobbles that it was a place to stop by kicking up behind, thereby inducing the bol equestrian to fall off. The shout of execration h uttered brought Jereboam to the door.

"Hallo!" he cried. "What brings you here?"

"This —— hanimal," replied Wobbles, with a vicious glare at old Joss, whose demeanour now was that of a well-conducted guileless beast. "I shouldn't have come without him."

"It's nigh two year since you was here," said the Yankee. "'Bout that, aint it?"

"Yes; I don't often leave home."

"All well up there?"

"Pretty well," said Wobbles, hesitating to speak of matters which might get him into trouble. "I never saw them look better."

"No?" said Jereboam. "Ah! they are nice free and easy children up there. I say, what will you take for your hoss?"

The cheeks of Wobbles glowed with pleasure. An offer for old Joss! Who would have dreamt of it? Jereboam, too, evidently fancied him.

"Two hundred dollars," he said, boldly.

Not a muscle of the face of Jereboam moved; but, calmly surveying the bony old beggar, he asked—

"What's his age?"

"Rising six," replied Wobbles.

"Sixty, you mean," said Jereboam Bounce, drily. "I was an old man at hoss-dealing afore you had cut a tooth. Now, look here. I'll stake ten dollars and a pint of whiskey ag'in that animal, and we'll play for him. I want something to do. All the others have gone away to hunt, and I feel dull and lonely. Come now—are you on?"

"Yes," said Wobbles, recklessly, and Jereboam went in to get the cards.

Fatigue, suffering, and agony over being parted from Billy Brisket, had sent Wobbles to the lowest depths of misery. It mattered little to him what he did. He had no great love for old Joss, and, indifferent to the fact of the horse not being his own, he was prepared to gamble for him.

In five minutes old Joss was lost to him, and Jereboam Bounce, elated with success, asked Wobbles to have a drink.

"You'll want a stimerlant to walk home on," he said, "and a thimbleful of whiskey is the thing."

They had a drink together, both watching old Joss as he blundered from one tuft of grass to another, tearing it up with his old teeth, and mumbling over the welcome food like an old man. Wobbles was rather sorry to part with him, for he was the only horse he had ever ridden since his boyhood's days, and although he was a little eccentric, he was not vicious. Wobbles had fallen often, but never had a bone broken, nor had he ever been bitten, trampled on, or kicked, as he had feared. No, he and Joss were very good friends on the whole, and it seemed a pity to part company just as they were getting used to each other.

"I suppose," said Jereboam Bounce, "that he is pretty quiet."

"He's a lamb," replied Wobbles, fervently—"a hangel of a horse."

"He is black enough for something else," rejoined the Yankee. "I think I'll try him."

"Now for some of his hantics," thought Wobbles, but old Joss justified his being called a lamb, and allowed Jereboam to mount without demur.

"Come up," said the Yankee, digging his heels into him. "Forrard, old man!"

Old Joss showed a deal of white in his left eye, but he started at a trot, and allowed himself to be ridden up and down two or three times.

"Well," said Jereboam, pulling up, "he aint a bad 'un, although he's bony. I aint sorry as I've speckerlated on him."

These words, eulogistic of the noble steed, were the last Jereboam Bounce spoke on earth, for old Joss concentrated himself for a grand effort, and kicked up behind as Wobbles had never seen him kick before.

Jereboam Bounce went up into the air like a rocket, turned over, and came down like a stick. His head and the earth collided, and his bounce was at an end.

With his head under his chest, and his legs and arms anyhow and nohow, he lay. Wobbles, aghast, looked at him, and old Joss, blooming with success, looked at him, and so the three remained for a full minute or more.

"Get up, old man," said Wobbles, in a feeble whisper. "I hope you aint hurt."

But the attitude and stillness of the fallen man were unmistakeable.

Wobbles did not expect an answer—knew, in short, he would not get one.

"I say," he said, turning to old Joss, and speaking to him as he would to a fellow-man, "you've done it now. You will get into trouble for this."

The answer the fiery animal gave was characteristic and expressive. Turning his back upon Wobbles he gave one whisk of his tail, and went on nibbling the grass with an air of sweet contentment.

"What's to be done now?" thought Wobbles. "I wish somebody had been here to stand by me. They'll say I killed him; and yet—who is to say anything now? I've done nothing, and if I go away who's to say anything? I wonder if—if—he's got any money in his pocket. It's no use to him, and if I don't have it somebody else will. But fust let me compose his limbs into a heasy hattitude."

He composed them so that he could get at his pockets, and then began to turn them inside out. The search was more profitable than he expected—disclosing to his eager view half a dozen paper packets of diamonds among other things—the proceeds of many a day's villainy.

"Diamonds!" he cried—"real diamonds—worth—how much?—thousands perhaps—thousands. Me, Wobbles, worth thousands! Ha—ha! Wobbles rich—ho—ho! Shade of my sainted mother, hover around your loving son, and help him to find his way back to the old country! I could swear I found 'em in the diamond fields, and I could sell 'em there. Come, old man, we'll be off."

But the old man, old Joss, was not inclined to leave there in company. Kicking his heels up gently h suddenly set off at a lumbering trot, and despite the cries, threats, and expostulations of Wobbles, kept on his way, and was speedily lost in the distance.

Wobbles sat down, and fairly cried with rage and vexation. Tired and worn out he could still have made some shift with riding, but walk he could not until he had had some rest. Next to rest he needed refreshment, and as the latter at least could be had he entered the shanty of the departed Jereboam, and helped himself to food and drink he found there.

He was in full swing with a very plentiful meal when the sound of voices and footsteps fell upon his ear, and he had barely opened the door of a cupboard, and shut himself in when several men entered together, and called for Jereboam Bounce by name.

"Where are their heyes?" thought Wobbles. "He aint fifty yards from the door."

The next moment one of the new arrivals saw the dead man, and drew the attention of the rest. They moved to the door, but went no further.

"It's no use," said one; "it's all over with Jereboam—look at his pockets. Whoever did it have got what we've come for, but I think if we are smart we can pick up the trail, and settle 'em."

"But first," said another, "let us have a look over the crib, and see if there is anything else worth taking."

"I'm as good as a dead man," thought Wobbles, as he sank down in a heap. "Farewell to everybody. Oh! lor, here they come. If my mother hadn't left me anything I should never have come to this. Why couldn't she spend it, the miserable old miser? She ought to have known better than to bring her only child into a mess like this."

CHAPTER XXIV.

AN UNBELIEVING TRIO.

"AH! it shall seem that we go out one by one—we make promises—we take oaths, and we break them," and Laranche, the Frenchman, shrugged his shoulders in a very expressive manner.

He was speaking to Jim Skipper and Niamo—the

trio sitting on the bank of the river with their rifles on the ground, but handy in case of emergency. Niamo took up a handful of stones, and casting them into the river, watched the eddies in silence. Skipper opened his big bowie knife, and pared his nails.

"It's come to this," he said, "every man for himself. Pedro has escaped, Jaundice has escaped, and the Ogre's gone goodness knows where. I'm inlined to think the whole thing is a dodge."

"A what?" asked Niamo, looking up.

"A dodge," replied Skipper, fiercely, "a plot, a plan—a plant between the Ogre, Pedro, and Jaundice, and that wild cat of a wife of his. I don't think that there is such a being as Broad Arrow Jack—at least, not about here."

"But remember the brand upon the Ogre's door," said Niamo.

"Ah, tat brand of te Broad Arrow," said Laranche.

"Couldn't any fool have put it there?" asked the Yankee, savagely. "Now, I'll just give you my reason for saying that I think we've all been done. Look here, we've all made a little money—somehow —ain't we?"

Yes, they had made money, and they admitted it with a smile.

"And when we took our share," pursued Skipper, "of whatever came—in our way—no man was fool enough to carry it about with him, but he put it away in some quiet place only known to himself— didn't he?"

"I should think so," growled Niamo, with a coarse laugh.

"It was not right to put temptation in a brother's way," said Laranche, apologetically.

"But some of our brothers found out where mine was," said Skipper, thrusting his knife up to the handle into the ground with a fierce imprecation. "Yes, by George, they took every dollar, and left me this, thinking I would be such a blarmed fool as to be took in.

He drew a sheet of paper from his breast, opened it, and spread it out before the eyes of the others. On the top was a Broad Arrow, and below was written—

"Your ill-gotten gains have been taken from you, and will be devoted to the alleviation of suffering caused by murderous scoundrels like yourself. Anon he who took it will call for you. Be ready to meet your fate.—BROAD ARROW JACK."

"All bunkum," he said; "Jaundice wrote this. He was good at a dozen hands, you know. What do you think of it?"

But neither the Russian nor the Frenchman were thinking of Skipper's lost wealth so much as they were of certain valuables they had in snug places. They looked at each other with very white faces, until an impulse seized them both, and springing to their feet they rushed off in opposite directions, leaving him alone.

In a few seconds the Yankee heard a cry from the Russian's lips, speedily followed by another from the Frenchman, and the two men came tearing back, foaming at the mouth. Laranche made straight at Skipper, and seized that astonished worthy by the throat.

"Give me back my gold and jewels," he cried, "my hard-vorked for gains—my treasures—my life —te only ting I've lived for—give tem back!"

"And mine too," growled the Russian, turning up his left foot, and giving his knife a turn or two on the bottom of his shoe. "That or your life!"

Skipper was the most muscular man of the two, but Laranche was like a wild cat, and his fingers claws. With a tenacious grip he held on until the face of the Yankee became crimson, and his tongue was protruding from his mouth. The strength of the Frenchman was, however, fortunately expended, and letting go he fell back upon the ground, and lay there panting.

For a moment Skipper seemed inclined to resent this unlooked-for attack with his knife, which he had left sticking in the ground; but as he drew it out a grim smile passed over his face, and he gave up the idea.

"You pair of fools!" he said. "Do you think I should rob you first, and then tell you of it? Could I not have skeddadled with the lot of it if I had found it?"

"My yellow gold—my bright diamonds!" moaned the Frenchman.

"The accursed thieves!" said Niamo. "You are right, Skipper. Other hands than yours have robbed us."

"Yes; and the Ogre is at the head of it," replied Skipper. "Come, I see no fear now. Let us make tracks from this place. We shall find 'em not far away, making merry with our stuff. But I will cut short the fun of any one of them, meet them where I may."

And the other two believed they had been grossly deceived by their old comrades, and called to mind many instances of the cunning of Jaundice and the Ogre, who had always assumed a superiority over the rest, and been most closely bound together. Pedro also had been of a taciturn nature, and that was charged to his account as cunning to conceal the deep plot existing. Wobbles they regarded as simply the tool of Jaundice.

So the three wiseacres put their heads together, and, after some discussion, settled upon the direction the Ogre and his confederates must have taken, and arranged to go the next morning on their trail.

Then, more easy in their minds than they had been for many a day—notwithstanding the loss of all they held dear—they lay down in the house of Jeb Jaundice, and slept.

How long he remained undisturbed Jim Skipper never really knew, but it appeared to him to be but a few minutes from the time he closed his eyes when he found himself awake, in the grasp of a strong pair of arms, and a voice whispered in his ear—

"One word, and you are a dead man!"

He could not have spoken if he had wished, for the unbelief of the day was scattered, and he knew, although he could see nothing, that he was in the grasp of Broad Arrow Jack. Another pair of hands put a handkerchief over his eyes, and he was carried out.

The strong arms bore him, as if he had been a child, rapidly away, and, by the branches that occasionally brushed against him, he knew that he was being borne through the wood. Suddenly it entered into his head that he was being carried to the forge.

"Spare me!" he cried.

"Silence, on your life!" was the answer.

He heard a door open, felt a hot flame upon his cheek, and *knew* he had guessed aright. He also knew he was going to be branded, and what had seemed such excellent sport when practised upon another had a thousand terrors to him now that it was about to be performed upon himself.

"It was not me who marked you!" he gasped "I was only a tool in the hands of others."

"Silence!" was the only answer he received, and his bearers tossed him upon the floor. Hands were laid upon his arms and legs, and he was held stretched out, with his face upward.

No brand of iron could have given him the torture apprehension did. Blindfolded he could not see—only hear voices speaking in an under-tone, and the working of the bellows, and feel the warmth of the blaze. The moments dragged so that, although he was not there a minute before Broad Arrow Jack began his work, it seemed to him an hour or more.

And Broad Arrow Jack's work was this.

Kneeling down beside the prostrate man he quickly and skilfully tattooed upon his forehead a broad arrow—a painless operation in reality, but made painful by the fears of Skipper, who moaned and groaned, and implored mercy to be shown him. Such is the power of fancy that this raw-boned and ordinarily strong-nerved man, having the surroundings in his mind's eye, believed he was being scarred by a red-hot weapon, and being marked again and again until he felt the fire was burning into his brain.

The operation over he was cast into a corner, and bidden to lie still, and in mortal terror he obeyed, listening to the slight sounds made by those in the hut moving to and fro.

Presently he heard the voice of Laranche, begging for mercy, and putting the blame on the rest, as Skipper had done. The Yankee was much edified by hearing himself referred to as being an especial promoter of the original crime, and a denial was on his lips, but it was stopped by a hand being put over his mouth.

Laranche underwent the same ordeal as his confederate had done, but as it proceeded he realised its nature, and became quieter. When it was over he was placed by the side of Skipper.

Another pause, broken only by the slight movements made by those at work in the hut, and Niamo was heard pursuing the same tactics as the others had done. He was innocent; he had been rather friendly disposed towards Jack—had tried to spare him, in fact—but numbers carried the day against him— Laranche and Skipper being especially persistent in their desires to brand a noble English lad, &c., &c. But it was all cast to the winds; he was marked also, and placed beside Laranche.

There the three villains lay, each afraid to move, lest some punishment should befall them. The hut was still as death, and the fire gradually died down into a dull red light, scarcely giving any warmth. At last Laranche made a slight movement and raised his hand. It was unchecked. He touched the handkerchief without hindrance; he dragged it off, and looked about him.

The hut was empty of all save himself and his two comrades.

"Gone!" he said. "Up, and open your eyes! The coast is clear. Ha! Skipper, shall you be here?"

"Yes," replied the Yankee, sullenly. "We are all here, it seems, and a nice prank has been played upon us. Blow up the fire."

The Frenchman complied, and as the light fell upon him each man saw that the other had a broad arrow tattooed on his forehead—a mark they would carry with them through life.

"Sacre," hissed the Frenchman, "this shall be a good joke of this big boy; but a hat will hide it— we have our lives."

The others said nothing, but the prospect seemed to be very unpleasant. Still their lives were spared, and they had not expected that.

"It is something to have it all over," said Laranche, but the next moment his eye fell upon a paper nailed upon the wall, and he read—

"I have but set my mark upon you. When the hour of retribution comes I will claim you.—BROAD ARROW JACK."

CHAPTER XXV.

JAUNDICE BROUGHT IN.

THE vast circle of great black rocks surrounding the house of Broad Arrow Jack stood out bold and clear against the early morning sky as the young hero came forth to breathe the invigorating air. He was alone, and, crossing the stream with hasty strides, he entered the forest, keeping awhile to the main path until he came to a large tree, with the Broad Arrow cut into its bark.

There he paused, and sat down upon the wide-spreading roots, holding his head between his hands. What his thoughts were no movement of his body revealed; but there he sat still as a statue, until the rustle of some scattered leaves aroused him, and, looking up, he saw the Tiger before him.

"Ha!" he said. "You here?"

"Yes, massa," replied the boy, making an obeisance, and keeping his eyes fixed upon the ground. "Me come all de night."

"Good boy!" said Jack, and touched him kindly on the shoulder.

The Tiger raised his eyes, and showed them full of gladness. "Massa," he said, "I lib and die fo you."

"Your news, Tiger."

"Three bad man with mark here," said the Tiger, touching his forehead, "gone 'way from de village. Massa Brisket, with Massa Jaundice, coming dis way. Also bring dese paper stuffs out from Massa Ogre's hut, in de roof."

He drew a pocket-book from his girdle, and handed it, with a low bow, to his master. Jack took it, and, without looking at the contents, questioned him further.

"Have you left my message where I told you?"

"In de east, sir, and in de norf," replied the Tiger; "but go to de oder places to-day."

"Can you do it? Are you not worn-out?"

"Neber tired," replied the Tiger. "If hungry find plenty food; if sleepy, get into de tree, on de branch—just close de eye, and off again. Oh! massa, you am de fust dat speak kind word to de poor Tiger, and he neber forget."

"You have been faithful to me," said Jack, "and shall have your reward anon. For the present there is more work to do—so away."

The Tiger saluted, and was gone in a moment. Jack opened the pocket-book, and spread the contents before him. The light had now descended into the valley. Showers of gold fell through the trees, and lay in patches on the earth; the air was filled with the odours thrown out by grateful flowers; night had struck its tent, and left, to give place to another day.

At first Jack glanced but carelessly at the papers, but as he read on his face changed, and an expression of deep interest settled upon it. He read rapidly, tossing over paper after paper with a deepening excitement until he came to the end. Then he put them all back carefully, and rose to his feet.

"So," he said, "I am not avenging my own wrongs only. This brute is—well—no stranger to me. Ah! how often have I heard my father breathe his name coupled with a curse! Strange that he did not know him, but he was suffering when they met. The Ogre, he must have known, and in pure malice have added to the debt he owed. Oh! monster, villain, dog, I have you now.

"Shall I kill him?" he asked of the air—"shall I cut short his hellish life? No, for with death comes rest, and why should he rest while I am living with the burden of my wrongs? No, Ogre, as you choose to call yourself, the first taken, you shall be the last to die. For the rest they may perish at any time. Ha, what have we here?"

The tramp of a horse, and the voice of a man, singing, "Tra-la-la—tra-la-la! When the wind blows then the mill goes, and our hearts are light and merry! Steady, my friend, don't swear, for hey derry down, when a man frowns he's— Won't you be quiet? Then I will gag you."

"But I am in torture," said a second voice. "You might as well put me on a gridiron at once."

"I would if you were a saint," was the reply, "but as you are a devil I shall leave the cooking of you until the proper time."

"That's Billy Brisket," thought Broad Arrow Jack, and stepping out into the middle of the path he confronted that worthy leading a horse. with a man strapped upon his back.

"Hi, noble chief!" cried Billy Brisket, "here is another bird in the net."

"Who is it?"

"Jeb Jaundice, gambler, wife-beater and general scoundrel."

"Cut his bonds," said Jack, and a few slashes with a knife put the prisoner on his feet.

He was stiff and sore, for he had ridden thus for more than twenty-four hours, with very little rest, and no food to speak of, but he tried to put on an air of indifference as he stood face to face with the proud boy.

"You know me," said Jack.

"Ay, I do," he replied carelessly, "and I think your joke a good one."

"The last you will ever appreciate," replied our hero. "Come here."

Jeb Jaundice made an effort to stand his ground, but he nevertheless advanced, and stood within a few feet of Jack. Billy Brisket sat down upon the ground, and leant his back against a tree.

"Brisket," said our hero, "you are worn out. Go and rest."

"Well, I won't say no," replied Billy, "for I've not closed my eyes these two nights. But watch him," he added in a whisper; "he is a slippery customer."

Even while he spoke Jeb Jaundice was casting his eyes about him, and speculating on the chances of getting away.

Jack took him by the arm, and the strong man winced under his grasp.

"The devil take you!" he said. "You need not crush a man's arm to pulp."

"No, but I will crush your soul to powder," replied Jack. "Brisket, leave us."

Billy made a profound bow, and retired with the feeble but hasty steps of a man worn out, and anxious to get to rest. Jack and Jeb Jaundice were left together.

"So," said Jack, looking into the eyes of his shrinking prisoner, "you are here; come to meet the doom set apart for you."

"I did not come of my own free will," replied Jaundice. "But being here I beg of you to hear me."

"Speak on."

"You and yours were wronged—injured terribly!" said Jaundice, clasping his hands appealingly. "But from the first to the last it was the Ogre's work."

"Why do you pause? Go on," said Jack.

"I appealed to him in vain to have mercy upon you," said Jeb. "Indeed I did. Heaven bear me witness, I would have spared you!"

"And yet, when the fell work began at the Ogre's bidding, it was your voice that cried 'good!' and your hands that tore away the clothes I wore, your voice that bade them kill me when the torture was over. Why lie and quibble when all that took place on that night is printed in letters of fire on my brain?"

"I was but a tool," muttered Jaundice.

"A willing tool in that and other crimes. Was it not your hand that clove in the head of an aged emigrant with an axe, and in mockery bound his two children together, and cast them into the stream? Was it not you who, when they came to the surface, shrieking for mercy, cast a stone, bidding them hold their squalling. Oh, remorseless scoundrel!—hellish villain!—and yet you would whine and ask for mercy from me now."

"All this was before you came," said Jeb Jaundice, sullenly. "But who has told you I know not, as no man witnessed their drowning."

"So you fancied," returned Jack, "but one witness lives—to hang you if need be for your crimes. Not that I mean to hang you, as I have a more fitting fate in store. Come."

"I will not go!" shrieked Jaundice, throwing himself upon the ground. "I cannot bear torture—will not bear it. Help!—help! Murder! Help!"

"You cry to the wind alone," replied Jack, lifting him by the collar. "All this is useless. You add to your agony, and waste my time."

"I will not leave this place!" cried Jaundice winding about him like a snake, and holding on with the tenacity of despair. "Kill me now if you wish, but I will not be tortured. Oh, heaven, is there nobody to save me? Help!"

Jack seized him by the arms, and, forcing him back, bent his body into a bow, then, with a sudden twist, wrenched himself free, and pinioned Jaundice behind.

"Will you go in peace?" he asked.

"Ay, where you will!" gasped Jaundice; "but no torture—no torture! I cannot bear it."

"Follow me," said Jack, releasing him, "and remember, escape is impossible. Give me further trouble, and you shall rue it bitterly."

Jeb Jaundice, trembling with abject fear, followed him quietly. A brave man under ordinary circumstances, he was cowed before the wondrous spirit of Broad Arrow Jack.

Without once looking back to see if he was followed, our hero turned into a narrow path, where the thick moss and patches of long grass showed it was but little frequented, and kept on for a mile or more. This brought him to the outskirts of the wood, at right angles with the palace wherein he lived. Here the landscape suddenly changed: fine trees, rare plants, and rich foliage gave way to rugged rocks rising up in precipitous recesses to the height of many hundred feet.

"Follow steadily," said Jack, speaking to Jaundice without turning, "and unless you have a good head don't look down."

Then he began the ascent up a path where nature had been aided a little by man—winding about round and over great masses of rock, along narrow ledges, up treacherous slopes, until the toil of half an hour brought them to the summit.

Then Jack paused and waited for Jaundice, who was picking his way with as much care as he would have done with the promise of a long and happy life before him. It is true there came a whisper urging him to throw himself from the rocks, but then came the thought, "What follows death?" And he kept on.

Some will say he ought to have fled. Surely he would have had a chance of life if he had turned at the foot of the hill, and plunged into the wood. Perhaps he would have had; but he could neither turn nor flee, he could only follow; an irresistible fascination led him on.

At length he stood on the hill top, with Jack facing him. There was a curious light in the eyes of the young giant—a light of triumph Jaundice thought—and it brought him trembling to his knees.

"Mercy!" he cried, "I am not fit to die!"

"You are not fit to live," replied Jack, "and why should I spare you?" "Whom in all your wretched life have you ever spared? Look, man, upon the fair scene before you—a Paradise! Think you this earth was made for such monsters as you are?"

"Only spare me."

"Look, I say, and drink in the beauty cast on all things by the glorious sun. Hear you that?—the song of birds. Listen to their voices hailing another day. Look on it, I say, and drink in what light you can, for darkness will soon be upon you."

Jaundice, powerless in his terror, could only grovel and feebly beg for mercy. Darkness at hand! Ah, that must mean the darkness of death—awful—horrible—terrible to him.

He might have faced death swift and sure if it had come upon him without warning, but he had seen the grim shadow so long before him—growing more hideous every day—that he trembled before it as a child might have done in the presence of some hideous monster.

A more pitiable object than Jeb Jaundice stretched out on the ground, clawing it in his agony, was never seen among men.

"Come," said Jack, raising him, "you are losing

Broad-Arrow Jack.

NO. 5.

THE RAPIER ENTERED THE SPANIARD'S BREAST AND HE FELL BACKWARDS INTO THE CHASM—A SHEER FIVE HUNDRED FEET.

time. Will you not have one look at this fair valley?"

"Mercy—mercy!" cried the wretch, with his eyes fixed upon him.

"I have sworn an oath, and I will keep it," said Jack.

Then he grasped Jeb Jaundice by the waist, and raised him like a toy in the air. Jeb looked upon the valley, and a wild shriek, with the peculiar ring in it which mortal terror gives, escaped his lips, and all was darkness.

He had fainted.

Jack did not cast him down, but with a strange smile upon his face, laid him on the turf, and stood awhile regarding him, with arms folded.

"Not yet—not yet," he said. "Death swift and sure should be the lot of the good. As a cat plays with a mouse so I will play with you, until the time comes. What cowards these brutes are!—taking the life of others so freely, clinging to their own so basely."

Turning away he walked to a mound, about thirty feet high, a little distance off. That it was artificial there could be little doubt, as its shape was that of a perfect cone, but many a century had rolled away since the hand of man first piled it up.

Grass grew thickly at its base, concealing a trap-door let into the earth. A massive door, bound with a dull metal that was not iron for it had no rust, and covered with cabalistic characters. At this door Broad Arrow Jack knocked thrice.

A few seconds only elapsed before his call was responded to by a stunted deformed creature of the negro type—a dull-eyed, heavy, sullen monster of a man—if indeed he was a man at all.

He did not look at Jack, although he made him an obeisance, but stood, with face averted, awaiting orders.

"Caliban," said Jack, "you see a man lying yonder, take him, and keep him until I shall come again."

Caliban made some reply in a deep guttural tone, in words which were only a strange jumble of incomprehensible sounds, but he understood his commands, and that was enough for Broad Arrow Jack.

Without another look at Caliban or Jeb Jaundice he strode to the edge of the precipice, and careless of following the regular path, dropped from rock to rock, until he reached the bottom, then plunged into the wood, and disappeared.

Caliban lost little time in obeying his master. He only stayed to watch his descent, and to dance uncouthly two or three times around the insensible man. This done he took him in his arms, and with a yell that a triumphant demon might have uttered, plunged into the earth. The trap-door closed with a dull, sullen sound, and Jeb Jaundice was lost to the light of day.

But barely was he gone when a slight figure sprang up from the shelter of a rock hard by, and rushing to the trap-door knelt, listening—then, with sudden fury sought to tear it from its socket, and, failing, gave vent to a low wail of despair. It was Lost Leon, who, lying on the turf, with hands tightly clasped, gave vent to a passionate flow of words.

"Oh! why did I not do my best? I am weak, but I might have done something; but now, who can save him? Whither has he gone? What devilish hiding place is this? It is just, that he should suffer, and yet, shall I be his judge?—I who —— but away with all memories of the past! Let him rot there if his conqueror wills it—and yet, how can I live and know he is being tortured? Fool that I am to think of him—but can I ever forget? No—no, never—I will save him yet."

CHAPTER XXVI.

WOBBLES AGAIN DISTINGUISHES HIMSELF.

A LITTLE while ago, we left our friend Wobbles in a very painful position—shut up in a cupboard with what he conceived to be a tremendous host of bloodthirsty villains seeking his blood, and the mental state he was in could only be fairly realised by another Wobbles in another cupboard, with another band of desperadoes approaching the door; therefore we will not attempt to describe it.

The fact is, there were only three men outside, and they were three friends, or rather acquaintances, of long standing—Niamo, Laranche, and Skipper, who, that morning meeting with the men of Hookey Settlement out hunting, thought it would be a fine opportunity to drop down upon Jereboam Bounce, and take stock of his worldly possessions.

Having been deprived of their little all, they were going in for his, to begin the world anew with, and it had been arranged between them, to prevent any future dispute about the possession of the said property, it would be better if they relieved the above-mentioned Jereboam from all worldly care—in other words, they decided to cut his throat.

"One more or less shall be no vorse," said Laranche.

"No worse—we can't be worse," returned Niamo, and Skipper confirmed this assertion with an oath of true western flavour.

Believing Jereboam to be at home they made straight for his house, passing his dead carcase within fifty yards without noticing it, and entering into the place of refreshment for man and beast, as described in a previous chapter. There they searched for what they found not, eventually coming to the cupboard wherein Wobbles was confined.

On opening the door the light fell upon what they at first took to be the corpse of their old follower and attendant, for Wobbles lay pale, fixed, and helpless. But the discovery excited no great emotion in their hearts. Skipper merely remarking as he was about to close the door again—

"So, Bounce did for Wobbles; but what the darnation brought the fool here? He never had a dollar to speckerlate with."

To this Wobbles unexpectedly replied—

"Oh! yes, indeed I had. My sainted mother left me three hundred pounds, and ——"

"Ah!" exclaimed Laranche; "shall it be so? Is not of the dead my friend? Vell, come out, and tell us about Jereboam."

"Jereboam," replied Wobbles—he now fully recognised his old friends, and gathered courage from their peaceful demeanour—"is gone aloft."

Laranche looked at the rafters of the hut as if he expected to find him there. Wobbles hastened to explain more fully.

"He's left this wicked world—he's downright dead and defunct."

The trio looked at him a little bewildered, although they knew Jereboam was dead. They thought he was out of his mind; and they had good reason for thinking so. No lunatic under the sun, moon, and stars ever looked wilder or more wretched than he.

"You don't seem to believe me," he said.

"I shall believe when I come to understand," replied Laranche.

"Come out and have a look at him," said Wobbles.

He led them forth, and introduced them to all that was left of Jereboam Bounce; and the sight seemed to make them all uncommonly quiet.

"Who did it?" asked Skipper at last.

Wobbles was on the point of telling the truth, but changed his mind.

"Broad Arrow Jack," he said.

The bare mention of that name made them all start and look round. Wobbles had his cue now, and went on.

"He took him up in his arms," he said, "tossed

him into the air as if he had been a—a—cork out of one of his own bottles, and down he came on his head, and never spoke again. See if his neck aint broken."

They examined him, and found it was so. This made them more thoughtful than before. They pulled their hats right over their noses, and looked at each other dismally.

"When shall this be done?" asked Laranche, pointing to the dead man.

"Half an hour ago."

"And how came you here?"

"Broad Arrow Jack brought me to—to—see fair play. But, there, it's as much as my life is worth to tell you any more. He'll be back directly, and it will be better for you to clear out."

"Which way is he gone?" asked Niamo.

"I don't know."

"Which way will he come back? Is he alone?" asked Skipper, boldly.

"No," replied Wobbles; "he's got at least fifty men with him, and—but look here," continued he, as an idea came to his fertile brain, "it wouldn't do for you to be found here, and it won't do for me to leave, as *he* told me not to leave. So I've got a way out for all."

"Out with it!" said Laranche, impatiently.

"He's only coming back to bury the body," continued Wobbles, "and when that is done he is going back to the mountains—you see 'em over there—then you will have clear tracks t'other way. Now, suppose you get into the cupboard where I was, and keep quiet till he's gone."

"But if he should find us there?"

"He won't," returned Wobbles. "He'll only say to me, 'Seen anybody?' 'No,' says I, and then off he will go. Get in; it will be all right."

"But let me ask you a question," said Skipper. "How is it you are with him safe, while ——"

"Don't ask questions now," said Wobbles, hurriedly. "I'll tell you all by-and-bye. I am not going away with him. In with you. I hear him coming."

He heard nothing, and they heard nothing; but they fancied they did, and dashed into the house like rabbits into a burrow, and, without further thought, they stowed themselves in the cupboard.

"You'll find it rather warm and close," said Wobbles, as he was closing the door; "but don't mind that. I'll let you out as soon as he's gone. Here he comes with his men. What grand fellows they are! Keep quiet, if you value your lives; and be everlastingly thankful to me for the kindness I've shown you to-day."

Wobbles closed the door, scarcely able to repress a chuckle. Then, to make all secure, he quietly proceeded to barricade it with a beam, fixed like a stay between the door and the rough counter. While this was in position it was almost impossible for the door to be got open.

In addition he piled up every object he could find—so quietly that the men inside had no suspicion of the nature of his work until a barrel, badly placed, slipped and fell. The noise it made aroused a suspicion within, and somebody knocked at the door.

"All right," said Wobbles, calmly; "I've got you safe enough. Hammer away. If you stifle yourselves there, all the better!"

"Open!" cried a muffled voice, and the door creaked beneath the pressure of the men within; but the door was strong, and the barricade held firm. Wobbles laughed aloud; a furious yell within answered him, and a knife was thrust through one of the upper panels.

"This won't do," said Wobbles, and, taking up a hammer from the counter, he broke the point off. "Spoilt that tool, at all events. I say, you chaps inside there?"

"Yes, you cur," cried Laranche, from within.

"I only want to tell you something before I go," roared Wobbles. "I settled that chap outside and I've got his tin! Yah!"

They answered him with a united curse, and Wobbles, unable to tear himself away without a few more words, went on.

"You are a bold lot, aint you," he said, "and a wonderful knowing lot, to let a hass like me take you in? I'm just a-going to make your box a little tighter, and then I'm hoff. Don't use violent language—it's low; and no amount of it will blow the door down. Oh! dear me, what a treat this is! I never knowed what real enjoyment was before. If my sainted mother is a-looking on I'll bet she's a-larfing fit to bust!"

He was looking about for nails while thus soliloquising, and he found half a dozen good long ones, just suited to his purpose. These he drove through the door with a coolness really wonderful, when his natural cowardice is considered. Having completed this task, he made his final address.

"You chaps have been reg'lar took in," he said. "Years ago me and Broad Harrow Jack swore a oath to awenge our hinjuries. Did you think I was going to forgive them kicks as you give me? —reg'lar lifters some of 'em was—and I've hopped about for days together. But I took a hoath, and I've kep' it. The wrongs of the sufferin' Wobbles ham awenged."

Then he took himself off, and with a corky step quite unlike his usual slouching tread, he turned his face to the mountains, leaving these men stifling in the atmosphere of a cupboard now ten times fouler than the Black Hole of Calcutta was in its palmiest days.

Pent-up they could not exert their strength. In vain they strove to burst the door—in vain they hacked it with their knives, cutting and wounding themselves in their fury and agony. They knew no pain but the torture of finding themselves shut up living in a coffin.

In their fear they had not contemplated the horrors of that confinement.

So let us leave them, to shriek and struggle in impotent fear and fury, suffering even as they had made others suffer, avenging on each other the crimes of years.

CHAPTER XXVII.

THE OGRE IN HIS PRISON.

READER, did you ever look upon a wild beast newly caged? If you have travelled no further than the limits of our island you have not, but you may see some brute brought over the sea turned for the first time into a new prison-house, and if you recall that you will have some faint notion of the Ogre when first he was cast into his den.

Alone, and away from the influence of Broad Arrow Jack's presence, something of his old audacity and ferocity returned. Rapidly he felt his way round the dark dungeon, and having traced its limits to a prison of some twenty feet square, all of cold, hard stone, he began to blaspheme, and to beat with his fists upon the wall, as if a blow from any living man could have caused them even to quiver on their strong foundation.

This gave him a little relief, and he sat down to think, and while he thought a faint light, coming from he knew not where, dimly illumined his dungeon.

That light had been always there—as it is in so many places where darkness is assumed to dwell—and its coming on him was only his eyesight getting accustomed to the place.

He had something of the cat in his nature as he had of the wolf—a great deal of the latter, I may say—and ere long he could see the outline of the door, through which he had been thrust, and make out the walls were plain and bare. The ceiling he could not see—it was lost in impenetrable gloom above.

For hours he sat, revolving in his mind the past, the present, and a probable future—not with sorrow —not with repentance, but with frenzied, hopeless despair. He cursed, as foul men foiled or thwarted in their base aims only can curse, breathing out such language as only willing pupils of the archfiend can utter.

He was galled at the thought of his late terror, at his yielding to the influence of a boy. He asked himself if he had been mad drunk or asleep that he did not stand up and resist it, and in a spirit of bravado he got upon his feet, and shouted for Broad Arrow Jack to come, and in a struggle for life and death give him an opportunity to re-assert his manhood.

"How could I be such a fool?" he cried. "I, who until I met this vengeful boy, never knew fear? I have been unmanned by some secret subtle power—the power of a magician or of poison. Oh! that I was free again, with a hundred men around me, with only these bare arms to defend myself— see if I would quail. Halloa there! you baby ruffian, come here—I defy you," and once more he beat the door with his fists until the blood ran down

Then came partial exhaustion, and with it cunning. Why should he cry out in this way, warning them of his fury, when if he was silent they might trust themselves in his cell? And if there was a dozen of them he would grapple with one, and hold on to his throat until they beat out his life.

"Yes," he muttered, "that shall be my task—one last life. Give me that, oh! fiends, and then make me your slave to all eternity. Hark! a footstep."

It came and passed, while he crouched by the door, ready to pounce upon his jailor if one should enter. But he was disappointed, and in his reckless madness rose, and struggled with an imaginary foe.

So he wore himself out, and presently sank down and fell into a deep sleep. When he awoke he found a loaf of bread and some water beside him. His jailor had stealthily come and gone while he slept.

This increased his passion, and another useless paroxysm ensued. After it he ate his bread and drank his water, not that he cared for either, but to keep his strength ready for the hour of need.

"It was a chance," he said; "they knew not that I slept. The next time I will be ready."

Long he paced his den like a restless beast. Footsteps passed the door, voices spoke outside, but nobody came. He tried to find a lock, but the fastenings were all outside—there was not even the head of a screw or bolt to grasp.

"I will not sleep," he muttered, as he paced to and fro. "No, for what are hours and days to me? Have I not seen the sun rise and set four times, and never closed my eyes in sleep, and can I not do it again? He does not mean to starve me— food will be brought again—by himself perhaps. Then his life or—mine. Hear me, foul spirits, who have been the guardians and guides of my life, I swear it!"

How the time crawled! He paced for a day at least—so it seemed to him, and no living creature came. The voices and footfalls became fewer and farther between, and eventually ceased altogether.

"Night again is here," he said; "I may expect them now."

Again he crouched, with eyes that shone like stars in the darkness. The lust of blood was blazing in his veins—the appetite for cruelty was gnawing at his heart. Oh! for a life—a life!—some living creature to hold fast in deadly grip, and to have the music of a shriek for help, and a despairing appeal for mercy in his ears.

"Mercy!" he hissed. "What have mercy and I in common? Who was ever merciful to me, even when— But I dare not think of that time. I had some manhood then. Now what am I? Oh, will he never come?"

And then he lay, until he thought day and night must have come and gone, and the stillness remained unbroken. He could bear no more, and, rising, he again paced to and fro.

"I will not sleep—I will *not* sleep," he kept muttering. "He must come anon."

He crossed his dungeon, and touched something with his foot. He stooped, and raised it. Another loaf of bread, and his pitcher refilled.

"What is this?" he cried, aghast. "Who has come and left me like a shadow—or have I slept? I swear I have not. These eyes of mine have never closed, and yet man or fiend has been here—or am I going mad?"

He asked this question aloud, and an echo came from above. "Mad," it said, and he clasped his head with his hands to still his throbbing brain.

"I will not go mad," he said—"why should I? No, let me hold fast to my own idea, and I cannot. Another life—another life! Give me that, then let reason go when it will. These are tricks to juggle me into a belief of this boy having supernatural powers, but I am not so easily deceived. There is no such thing. There is nothing beyond this world. I laugh at it—I scorn it—I defy all that can be brought against me. See, I am calm through it all—my pulse is steady—my brow is cool. Fool, cease your pranks and come or send a man to fight me."

Bent on keeping awake to assuage his thirst for murder, he walked up and down, calming himself as well as he could by diverting his mind as far as possible from the present, and thinking of congenial scenes of the past. Possessed of an iron will, he bent down his agitation and became himself again.

Suddenly he paused. A stone beneath his feet had shaken. Slightly, it is true, but enough to tell him it was not fast like the rest. Hope sprang into his heart.

"If nothing but earth beneath," he muttered, as he trod backwards and forwards to find it again, "I will burrow my way out like a mole."

It was some time before he found it again, as in his haste he got out of its track, and wandered all over his cell; but he came upon it again at last, and, kneeling down, tried it with his hands.

Yes, it was loose, but still closely fitting, and defied his efforts to raise it. In his efforts to lift it from its place he dragged the skin from his finger tips, and split his nails, but he returned again and to the assault. With the prospect of life and liberty he cared for no physical pain.

And yet the task seemed hopeless. The stone rocked and rocked, but never budged from its resting place, and a long—long spell of toil brought him only defeat. Again wild passion took possession of him, and as he had beaten on the door, so he beat upon that stone.

As his huge fists rose and fell like hammers upon a blacksmith's anvil, it gave forth a hollow sound unnoticed by him at first; but as it grew louder and louder, it reached his ears, and he paused.

Was the sound above or below? He dealt the stone a blow that split it in two, and an unmistakable rumbling came from beneath.

What lay there?

It might be only another and a deeper prisonhouse, but it might also be the path to freedom. The place was old, and had been built in the ages when men were fond of secret passages and mysterious subways to be used in the time of trouble, or to carry out some foul purpose—murder, rapine, or what not—and this might be one of them.

Inspired by the thought he struck the stone again and again, utterly regardless of his bruised and bleeding hands. It split here—split there, and then suddenly collapsed, and fell in fragments.

The Ogre listened intently, thinking they had fallen to some great depth, but all was silent. Whither then had these fragments gone? He could not answer the question.

A careful examination of the opening with his hands showed that no staircase or steps were connected with it, and here he was foiled again. It appeared to be only the entrance to a fathomless abyss, and dare he launch himself into that? No. But dare he stay where he was? Again, no.

"It can only end in death," he muttered, "and that will be better than the infernal torture of the past few hours. Here goes, for life or death."

He let himself down until he hung by his hands, and holding on by sheer strength groped about with his feet in search of something to rest upon. There was nought but the empty air.

"I will go back," he muttered, as a sudden terror of the awful nature of his position came upon him— but, no; his strength was gone in the new fear, and he had no power to raise himself an inch.

"Oh, horror!" he cried. "And is this to be the end? Am I doomed to fall into the hell poets and priests speak of? Am I in the jaws of death? Oh! for another hour of life—half an hour—a minute! Help!—you murderous fools! Help! You can bring me bread—come and save my life!"

CHAPTER XXVIII.

CALIBAN AND JAUNDICE.

LET us leave one scoundrel reaping a just reward of his infamy, and turn our attention to another, Jeb Jaundice, whom we left in charge of the hideous Caliban.

When Jaundice awoke from his insensibility he found himself in a dome-shaped apartment, lighted up by a huge oil lamp hanging from the centre. In circumference the place was about sixty feet, and was perfectly formed of smooth well-worked stone. On one side was a table covered with a cloth, and having on it some bread and wine. Seated by it, and partaking of that simple fare, was Caliban.

No nightmare was ever more horrible to man than this vision was to Jeb Jaundice; and, although he tried to persuade himself it was only a vision, the feeling which ever attends reality would not permit him to do so.

It was real enough—the room—the table—Caliban —all terribly and horribly real.

Caliban made a sign to him to come and eat, but he would as soon have sat down to a feast with a cannibal as with him there; and although he tried to hide his loathing under a polite bow, as he refused, it was unmistakeable even to Caliban.

The monster was indignant, and rose with such a fearful look upon his face that Jeb Jaundice hastened to the table, and signified he was willing to eat, drink, and be as merry as he could.

Caliban smiled, showing a score or so of tusks that would have been quite in harmony with the jaws of a wild boar, and, drawing a stool from under the table, signalled to Jaundice to sit down.

"You are very kind," said Jaundice. "Do you speak English?"

Caliban evidently understood it, for he nodded, but he made no reply.

"You understand what I say," said Jeb Jaundice. "Am I a prisoner?"

Another nod.

"Who brought me here—Broad Arrow Jack?"

A third nod, and the exhibition of an additional tusk or two.

"I see. Then he did not throw me over the precipice. Which would have been a mercy," he added to himself. "Anything but this!"

Caliban made a noise probably intended for a laugh; but to Jaundice it sounded like the gurgling of a choking man. He hastily took a glass of wine as a deadly sickness came over him.

"So I am a prisoner, and you are my gaoler?" asked Jaundice.

Again he got an affirmative answer.

"Where is this place? Near where I lost my wits?"

No answer.

"You are not to tell?"

"No," said Caliban, with a nod.

"At least you can tell me how long I am to stay?"

A nod in the affirmative.

"A week, perhaps?" asked Jaundice, with affected carelessness.

Caliban smiled sarcastically, and took a little wine.

"A month?"

Caliban swallowed his wine, and cackled. The sound was horrible.

"A year—two—not while I live? Oh! God—not that!"

"Yes and yes," said Caliban with sundry nods, and Jeb Jaundice felt the icy coldness of unutterable horror at his heart.

"But it is not always thus? You have daylight sometimes?"

"No—no!"

"You hear me, and nod. Why do you not speak? Is it some freak to make my horror greater? Only the deaf are dumb."

Caliban suddenly thrust forward his face, and opened wide his huge jaws. Jeb Jaundice looked, and saw the cause of his silence—*his tongue was gone!*

"Awful—oh! unbearable misery!" cried Jeb Jaundice. Then it dawned upon him that he might, by expressing sympathy with Caliban, make a friend of him, and so lead up, perchance, to an escape.

"Poor fellow—poor fellow!" he said, trying to pat him as he would a dog; but Caliban drew back with a contemptuous cackle, and let him know that game would not do. Jeb fell upon the bread—being very hungry—and was silent until the keen edge of his appetite was removed.

He was getting accustomed to his position—or perhaps I ought to say, getting bold enough to look at it—and, with the absence of the fear of immediate death, his old cunning came back. Better wait awhile. This monster might be made a friend.

Caliban having finished his meal with the draining of the wine-bottle, got upon his feet, and, to the terrified amazement of Jaundice, favoured him with an uncouth dance that would have made the fortune of any man acting as demon in a pantomime. It was not without a certain grace; but the hideous contortions of his face, and the twisting of his misshapen limbs, made it very demoniacal.

At the termination of this performance Caliban drew the attention of Jeb Jaundice to something on the other side which he had not noticed before. It was a splendid little lathe, fitted up for the cutting and polishing of diamonds and other stones. On one side was a small heap of jewels—as they came from the earth—on the other a number cut and polished to a high pitch of perfection.

"What, in the name of all that is wonderful, is this?" asked Jaundice.

Caliban cackled, kicked up his heels, and carried his chair over to the lathe. Signalling to Jeb Jaundice to bring his stool Jeb obeyed, and was told to sit down and work the treadle. He did so, and Caliban went to work upon a fine diamond, that Jeb Jaundice knew would, at home, be worth many thousands of pounds.

What the whole heap was worth he would not have undertaken to say without a pencil and paper to work it out. At the very least there was a fortune for a nobleman.

"All Broad Arrow Jack's?" he asked.

Caliban nodded, and gave him a dig in the ribs with his elbow, which nearly knocked him off his stool, as a hint to keep quiet. After that Jeb Jaundice asked no more questions while the work was in progress.

That Caliban was a splendid workman a mere novice would have seen, but Jeb Jaundice was no novice, having had the handling of many diamonds in his time, and he saw the work of the monster was perfect.

"They would give their ears to have him in some of the workshops of Europe," he thought. "He is not a workman, but a genius."

It was a relief for Jeb Jaundice to have something to do, and something to look at, apart from Caliban; but after the first hour a weary feeling of monotony came, and he began to feel how terrible was the life before him. How long would he be able to bear it? A week, he felt sure, would kill him. But he under-estimated the power of endurance which men, as a rule, possess. Some have lingered for years in worse places than he was in.

At last the work ceased, and Caliban brought out another bottle of wine, which he calmly finished in two draughts, without offering his prisoner any, and once more he indulged himself with a dance—ten times more uncouth and horrifying than the one Jeb Jaundice had looked upon before.

Jaundice tried to look away, but there was a fascination in the brute that kept them face to face, and not a single step was lost to the looker-on.

"He seems to be dancing himself into a frenzy," thought Jaundice. "What next will he do?"

The answer came almost immediately. Caliban, having finished dancing, brought out from a box some manacles, which he put upon the wrists and ankles of the prisoner, and, finally, with a chain, secured them to his own wrist.

There was no bed but the bare floor, and Caliban, having extinguished the lamp, lay, or, rather, fell, down just where he was, and seemed to sleep immediately.

Jaundice had no resource but to lie down too, and side-by-side with the monster he passed such a night as he had never known before. All his previously experienced horror and suffering sank into insignificance beside it.

CHAPTER XXIX.
A BROAD ARROW FEAST.

"THE chief gives a feast to-night," said Tom Larkins.

"That's good," replied Nat Green; "we want a little brushing up occasionally. A good laugh is a fine thing for a man."

"I wonder, Nat, if we shall ever see *him* with a smile?"

"Never, I fancy. The sort of smile we should like to see is gone from him for ever."

"I hope not," said Tom, thoughtfully. "Such a handsome chap, too! Put him in fine-fitting togs, and where would you see a swell like him?"

"Not here, although we have some good-looking fellows amongst us," replied Nat, giving his head a knowing twist.

"Ah!" said Tom, laughing, "I see, old fellow, you are a bit of a puppy still."

"So I am. But I can tell you there was a time, and not two years ago, when bright eyes beamed upon me, and pretty faces flushed when we met. But no matter, the time will come again."

Nat gave a few finishing touches to the bridle he was cleaning, and sauntered away, sighing. Tom, with an amused face, looked after him.

"Nat thinks that gal of his is breaking her heart for him," he said; "as if she hasn't had a dozen sweethearts since. There is only one true woman in the world, and that's my Polly."

As Polly was purely an ideal character, Tom Larkins's opinion of women was none of the best. He shouldered a saddle he had been repairing, and entered the great hall, where a number of men were engaged in fixing up three long tables with planks and tressels.

Lost Leon, leaning against the wall, was looking on with an indifferent air. Tom put the saddle in a corner out of the way, and joined him.

"You don't seem to be brisker," he said. "I never did see such a dull chap. Come, wake up, we are going to be merry to-night."

"You will never see me merry," replied Lost Leon.

"Why not?" argued Tom. "Suppose you have had trouble of the past put it into your pipe and smoke it, and make the best of the present. By the way, you don't smoke?"

"No."

"Nor drink, unless it's water or tea. Come now, Mister Leon, you can't expect to have a light heart on that stuff. You must try some of the liquor the chief gives us on these occasions."

"Your chief seems to possess a magic wand. How can he obtain good liquor here?" asked Lost Leon.

"Has it brought over by his convoys. Bless you, we want for nothing.

"How many men has he in his pay?"

"I don't know. Thousands perhaps—I can't tell," replied Tom.

"Scarcely so many, I should think," said Lost Leon. "This thinly populated country would not supply so many."

"And do you think he stops here?" said Tom, with contempt. "Why, there's not a week passes without his having a score or more letters from over the sea."

"How does he get them?"

"His trusty postmen bring them. We have fifty men who cling to a horse like a leech, and ride day and night, sleeping, when they want to sleep, in the saddle."

"Impossible!"

"You may not believe it, but it is true. With the vast wealth at his command he can do anything. You don't seem to like it."

"Oh! I—I was thinking," replied Lost Leon, confusedly. "But is not this a terrible power for one man to hold? So young, too, with all his hot blood in full play."

"He's cool enough when need be," said Tom. "What he's set his mind on he'll do, even if it was to walk straight through yonder mountain."

Lost Leon made no reply to this, and shortly after went out with an air of great dejection on him. A number of men were leading strings of horses to the river for a drink and a paddle in the shallow ford. Among them was old Joss, who had come home in the night, and looked as fresh as paint.

Without heeding an invitation to help with the watering, Lost Leon crossed the ford, and plunged into the forest. Turning aside from the path, he sought a retired spot, and there cast himself upon the ground, quivering with something more than bodily pain.

"Great Father of Mercies," he cried, as he clutched the turf with his hands, "let me but save his life, and then take mine, and give me rest."

For a long, long time he lay there, occasionally breaking out into sobs and tears and prayers, until the first shades of evening fell. Then rising, he sauntered slowly back, and found the great hall illuminated.

The tables were all full of men, laughing and talking. At the head of the centre one sat Broad Arrow Jack, with Billy Brisket on his right—no longer in the garb of a pedlar, but gorgeously and wonderfully dressed in a suit of green velvet, elaborately trimmed with gold. On the left of Jack was a chair, which Lost Leon instinctively knew was reserved for him.

"Would I were worthy of it," he said, as he advanced. "He so good, so noble, so brave, while I—well, I am what I am."

"Ha! welcome, my friend," said Jack. "You are late."

"I have been wandering in the woods, and lost myself," said Lost Leon.

"You would have to go far to lose yourself from me and mine," rejoined our hero. "I could bring you back from ten days' wandering with ease."

"So far?" asked Lost Leon, quickly.

"And farther. Now drink, and be merry."

"You drink nothing yourself."

"No, merriment and I have parted company for awhile."

"Let me then be sober with you," urged Lost Leon. "I too find it hard to make merry. The springs of sorrow are ever bubbling from my heart."

"There is nothing like making merry," said Billy Brisket, who had been making very merry indeed. "I should like life—to be—one long—unbrokensh tooral-looral chorus."

"Would not that in time become monotonous?" asked his chief.

"Not a bit of it," replied Billy, pulling his hat over his left eye. "I could tooral looral all the day and all the night. Come, sing to me the good old song of—of—how many yearsh? oh, forty!—the good old song of 'Forty Yearsh Ago.'"

"That's right, Mister Brisket," said one of the men, "tip us a song."

"Who are you calling Misty Brishket?" asked Billy, getting upon his feet, and glaring at the offender. "Don't you know my proper name?"

"Yes, sir, Captain Brisket," returned the man, quite aghast at Billy's unexpected wrath.

"Captain be bothered! I'm a colonel! I promote myself, to-night, Colonel Brisket of—of—the First Broad Arrow Jack Rifles. Who's that laughing?"

"I don't think anybody was laughing," replied Jack.

"Oh, yes, there was laughing," said Billy, getting more dignified every moment, "and I'll have the man brought forward, then off with his head, and so much for laughing. Drag the miscreant to my feet!"

Billy was terribly in earnest, and in his then condition nothing less than the life-blood of somebody would have appeased him, if an interruption had not come in the form of the Tiger, who came bounding in like a sprite, and stood before his master.

"Well, Tiger," said Jack, "do you bring me news?"

"Not much, massa; but I got Massa Wobbles," replied the Tiger.

"Got him; where from?"

"I missed him the other night," said Billy; "thought he had bolted, and had made up my mind to shoot the traitor. Ha! I remember, I have been laughed at. I must have blood!"

"Presently," said Jack, "when I have finished my business with the Tiger."

"The business of my noble chief," replied Colonel Brisket, gravely, "goes before everything."

"That is right," said Jack, laying a hand upon his shoulder. "Now, Tiger, where did you find Wobbles?"

"On him back, massa, groaning wif a pain bout him somewhar."

"Where is he now?"

"Coming along, massa; here he am."

"Bring him here."

Wobbles was just entering the hall, looking the very picture of woe.

For thirty-six hours he had tasted nothing but roots, which, however "nourishing to niggers," as he said, were not very sustaining to a man accustomed to the luxuries of life. The Tiger, who went here, there, and everywhere, with the swiftness of the swallow, found him wandering helpless upon the plain, and brought him in.

He was amazed to find himself in such a place in the presence of so many men, and he was commencing an apologetic address to the company generally when the Tiger took him by the arm, and led him up to the chief.

"Where have you been?" asked Jack.

"Noble chief," said Wobbles, faintly, "if you would only let me have a peck and a drink afore I begin, I have a pile to tell. Noble chief, I have awenged you! But give me a peck and a drink, or I shall go off!"

"Give him food and wine," said Jack, and, leaning back in his chair, he remained silent and grave while Wobbles fed.

And how he did feed to be sure. Never fainthearted where the struggle was with food alone, he now displayed astonishing consumptive powers, disposing of everything they put before him, until the voice of repletion cried "Hold!—enough!"

Then came his story.

He had, so he said, and our readers know how much truth there was in what he said, met with Laranche, Niamo, and Skipper, and, burning with zeal in the good cause of his noble chief, had slain them one and all.

"We fought," he said, "for five hours with sticks, having no other weapons, and I run 'em all over the prairie, until they took refuge in the house of Jereboam Bounce, as is a party as may be known to you, sir. Jereboam came out to take their part, and I settled him. If you doubts me there is his corpse to prove it."

"Whether he is dead or alive matters little to me," said Jack. "It is with the others whom I am concerned. Are you sure they are dead?"

"As door-posts," replied Wobbles, "for, after I settled Jereboam, I went in and settled them. You'll find their bodies in a cupboard behind the bar."

"This is a strange story," said our hero. "What do you think of it, Brisket?"

"I think," replied Billy, "that it is what life ought to be, all tooral-looral. Wobbles, my friend, you are a confounded liar!"

"Now this is very hard," said Wobbles, appealing to the company generally. "When a man does a good thing give him credit for it."

"Understand me," broke in Jack, impetuously, "if you have done this you are no better than an interfering fool! No hand but mine should have silenced one of them. I will inquire into this; and if you have told me a falsehood I'll get your hide tanned, for you will need to have it tough."

"Respected chief——"

"No more; go. Take your seat at one of the lower tables, and come no more near me until I send for you. Tiger."

"Yes, massa."

"Are you ready to go again?"

"Yes, massa."

"Away then to Hookey Settlement, and bring me word if these men are alive or dead. If dead return at once; if alive you know your work among the outposts."

"Yes, massa."

As Wobbles, dismayed and disheartened, turned to leave, his eyes fell upon Lost Leon, and with a start of surprise he staggered back. Our hero was talking in a low tone to Brisket, and did not perceive the action. Lost Leon remarked, and rose—

"Come out," he said.

"Oh, yes! Out where?" asked Wobbles.

"Into the open air. I have something to say to you," was the reply.

"I'm a-coming; but, I say, what does it mean? Am I——"

"Come," said Lost Leon, clutching him by the arm—"come out, you fool!"

The men had returned to their drinking, and the pair went out without much notice.

As soon as they got clear of the hall Lost Leon seized Wobbles by the hair of the head, and knocked his cranium against one of the pillars of the portico with such violence that he fancied all creation had turned to stars."

"Come now," he said, "none o' that. I never did nothing to you."

"You had better not!" hissed Lost Leon. "You had better put your head into a lion's mouth than do aught against me. You know who I am."

"Well, considering that I've known you ever since I——"

"Silence!—enough. A fool's eyes oft beat the vision of the wisest. Now, understand me, I am here for a purpose of my own, and I will not be thwarted. Keep my secret, and you will come to no harm; attempt to betray me, and I will rend the skin from your bones like a wild cat!"

"Very much like a wild cat," groaned Wobbles. "I've no doubt you can come it strong, but I aint a-going to say nothing. Only it do seem hard that wheresomever I goes, and whatsoever I does, I seem to raise up parties against me. I wish I had never had a sainted mother, then I couldn't have got into a confounded hole like this!"

"You had better not return to the board to-night," said Lost Leon, "or you will be letting out secrets in your cups."

"I don't want to go. I'm knocked up, and want sleep."

"Lie down here then, under the portico. The night is warm, and you won't come to any harm."

"I don't care if I do," muttered Wobbles, as he stretched out his limbs; "but whenever I dies I mean to have it cut with my mother, for the mess she put me in with that blessed three hundred pounds."

He was speedily asleep, and then Lost Leon returned to the hall, and resumed his seat. The noise in the hall was very great; at least half a dozen men were singing, and all the rest were talking—very few were listening.

It was only once in a way that Broad Arrow Jack permitted these bouts, as it would have been a false policy to hold too tight a hand over the men; but he was always present to prevent anything like a riot. At the first sound of a quarrel he was on the spot, and his commanding presence acted like oil upon the troubled waters.

Billy Brisket had fallen asleep, and was muttering something about "cotton, tape, needles, buttons, or any other article, gentlemen?" and Broad Arrow Jack was moodily mapping out something upon the table.

Suddenly Tom Larkins, pale and trembling, stood before him.

"What now?" asked Jack.

"My chief—the Ogre!" gasped Tom. "I went just now to see if all was well, and by the secret passage reached his cell.

"Go on—quick!" said Jack. "I know what is coming, but tell me all."

"I listened for his breathing or his curses, and he was free with both; but all was silent. I struck a light. The cell was empty. There was a stone gone from the floor."

"No more just now," said Jack. "I will go with you to see what has been done."

"May I come with you?" asked Lost Leon.

"Aye, if you will," replied our hero. "But the others can be left to their drinking. I had not dreamt of this. But the villain has only met with another flash of hope! He can never escape me!"

CHAPTER XXX.

WHITHER GONE.

"SEE here, noble chief," said Tom Larkins, holding the lantern over a hole in the middle of the Ogre's cell. "He went this way."

"Lower the light, and let me see what lies below."

Tom Larkins tied his handkerchief to the lantern, and lowered it into the opening. At the bottom, on a heap of rotten rubbish and the dust of ages, lay the broken fragments of the stone broken by the Ogre, and a distinct impression of his feet as he dropped down.

Yes, he dropped at last, after half an hour of the most awful torture it was possible to conceive, holding on until the skin of his finger tips burst, and he fell, leaving a bloody impression of his grip behind him.

Only a matter of eight inches or so, nothing more, and when he realised the fact he cursed his stupidity with a terrible bitterness, instead of being thankful, as a man one iota less the demon than he was would have been; but all such good sentiment had been dead in him for many years.

Of the way he took more anon. For the present, I must remain with my hero, who was not a little vexed at the good fortune which had befallen his prisoner; but he preserved an unmoved countenance, and, taking the lantern from Tom Larkins, bade him return to the hall.

"Say nothing," he said, "until I return, and give you leave."

"I am dumb, my chief," replied Larkins.

"Dare you follow me, Lost Leon?" asked Jack, when Larkins was gone. "We may have a perilous way to travel. I know something of the secret way under this wondrous place. The builders of it fairly honeycombed one side of the mountain.

"It is yours to command," replied Lost Leon. "I have but to obey."

"Nay, you go willingly and freely with me, or not at all."

"I go freely."

"First, then, let us look to the lamp. Just trimmed, and good for five hours or more. It will do. I will bear it until good fortune guides us to the Ogre. Then you must hold it while I secure him.

He sprang down, lantern in hand, and Lost Leon lightly and nimbly followed him. The ground seemed to have been strewn with rusted ferns and leaves—long, long ago, as the outlines of many still remained, but the moment they were touched they crumbled to dust. The footfalls of Jack and Lost Leon fell silently, and at every stride a cloud of fine pungent dust arose, which was almost stifling.

"Here," said Jack, as they moved along a passage about twenty feet wide, "the wind has never come. Phew! I shall be choked. Let us proceed quietly. Hold the light lower. Thank you, I have his trail now."

The huge feet had left a track that even a policeman might have followed. Wandering in the darkness, he had groped his way, blundering from side to side, and feeling along the smooth stone walls, where his broad fingers had brushed away the fine dust.

In some places he appeared to have turned back a little, as if despairing of escape, but only for a short distance. In half a dozen strides he had changed his mind.

The passage was long, and sloped gradually upwards for about ten times the length of the building, Jack judged, when a door for a moment barred their way. It was fastened on the outer side.

"Stand back," said Broad Arrow Jack. "Now, keep the light up."

He ran at the door, and thrust his foot against it with tremendous force, bursting it outwards with a sound that found a dozen echoes in the passage behind. Darkness still, for it was night; but had it been day he could have seen without the aid of a lamp, for a flight of steps led straight to the upper air.

They followed them, and came out among a clump of bushes which alone concealed the entrance. There was little or no attempt to hide it from observation.

"The very simplicity of this place deceived me," said Jack. "I have passed by these bushes fifty times, and never suspected that they concealed anything. For the present I fear he is clear away. We will rejoin our friends."

"Will you not pursue at once?" asked Lost Leon, in surprise.

"No; it will be time enough to-morrow," he replied, carelessly. "Go where he may I will find him again, and bring him home—fear not!"

"And yet methinks you keep your prisoners loosely," said Lost Leon.

"Indeed! But how know you I have more?"

"Oh! well enough—at least I guess so. Now I am but an idler, doing nothing for my bread. Make me one of your gaolers."

"You!" exclaimed Jack. "What power would you have to detain them?"

"At least I would keep a faithful watch."

"Be it so," said Jack, after a little thought. "I have another prisoner with one gaoler, who is as good as ten when he is sober; but there are times when he drinks. It would be as well to have another with him."

"Yes—yes!" There was a little eagerness in Lost Leon's voice which Jack ought to have noticed, but he did not.

"It will necessitate your living almost entirely away from the light of day."

"I care not."

"Then come to me to-morrow, and I will take you to your charge. Now we will return, and keep our friends company until daylight. Then I begin work in earnest. With the rising sun an enemy dies!"

"So—so soon?" stammered Lost Leon, and again there was something in his voice and manner which Jack ought to have observed, but it passed by him unheeded.

"At daylight; and I call you to witness that what I do is fair and honest. Do you know the great cleft on the summit of the southern hill, crossed by a huge trunk of a tree, which serves as a bridge?"

"I have seen it," said the listener, softly.

"Be there early, and hide among the bushes. See and hear everything, but move not. You understand me?"

"Yes," said Lost Leon—and his voice sounded scarcely above a whisper.

"Enough."

They went back to the hut, and on entering Jack stumbled over the sleeping Wobbles, on whom he bestowed a hearty kick for being in the way.

Wobbles merely muttered something about his sainted mother, and slept on as soundly as ever, quite overcome with fatigue and his evening meal.

Billy Brisket was gone, whither nobody knew, but in a little while he returned, sober and clear-headed. He had been down to the stream, and cooled his head with a plentiful supply of cold water. It was clear enough, but ached abominably; and, of course, he vowed he would drink no more.

"It's perdition," he said, "and I would take the pledge if I thought I could keep it. Life is one long life of unbroken misery. Oh, my head!"

"Never mind your head," said Jack. "The Ogre has escaped again!"

All thoughts of his head went in a moment, and his whole self was concentrated on the news he heard.

"Escaped!"

"Yes, but not so loud. Better keep it to ourselves. Only Tom Larkins knows it, and he can be trusted. There was a passage from his cell to the outside, and he discovered it."

"Phew! How long has he been gone?"

"Some hours I should think. Every step I took raised a cloud of dust—his must have done the same, but when I passed through the dust he raised had settled down."

"When next you catch him kill him at once and have done with it."

"No, I will keep him in terror until the last. To-morrow I begin."

"With whom?"

"Pedro the Spaniard. You promised him to see the light once more before he died."

"I did."

"Your word shall be kept. Bring him to the Southern Bridge at dawn, and leave him there."

"Will you fight him?"

"Of course; I will not slay him in cold blood. He shall have a chance for his life; so shall they all when their time comes. Ha! Lost Leon, you look brighter."

"Yes," he said. "A little while ago I had a pain about my heart, and I have been relieved of it."

CHAPTER XXXI.

ONE.

FROM the hour of his capture Pedro the Spaniard had never seen the light. Placed in a cell where the faintest trace of it never came he passed many, many weary hours, haunted by the words which were whispered in his ears—

"You will have but one more short look upon the light in this world—when you look upon the face of your accuser."

And who was his accuser he asked himself a thousand times—foolishly asked it, seeing that there was but one answer—

"Broad Arrow Jack."

And when he did face him—what then? Torture and death—perhaps a slow and lingering death, such as savages love to bestow upon their foes. He dare not think of it, and yet it haunted his waking and sleeping hours.

He had a gaoler, who came and went in the darkness, and gave him food. Sometimes he heard his footfall, but oft he came without a sound. But he never spoke in reply to such questions as Pedro ventured to put.

The time was long and weary, but utter despair did not take possession of him, as he lived. Every hour, every day, gave him a better chance of escape. It might be the purpose of Broad Arrow Jack to terrify him only, and after an imprisonment set him free.

Or he might relent.

Vain hope!—vain desire! And the time came at last for the terrible awakening.

He heard the door open for the twentieth time or so since his confinement, and thought it was only the usual gaoler bringing him his meal; but he thought the footstep was different, and, to his amazement, he spoke.

"Pedro, the Spaniard."

"Here," he answered.

"Advance."

He stepped forward, and immediately his arms were pinioned.

"No resistance," said the voice; "it is useless. Steady now, while I bind and blindfold you."

"Where am I going?" asked the prisoner.

"To look upon the light of day, and meet your accuser."

"Holy saints, protect me!"

"What weapon can you use best?" was next asked him.

"The rapier. I was a master of fence in Spain," he replied. "But why ask me that? What weapon can I use bound as I am?"

"You will be set free when before your accuser."

"And will he fight me fairly?"

"Yes."

"With the rapier?"

"If you wish it."

"I do," said Pedro, drawing himself up. "But if I am victorious?"

"You are free to go where you will."

"I am satisfied," said Pedro. "Let me look upon the light."

It was many years since he had handled the rapier, but in his earlier days he was renowned among his countrymen for his skill. If his right hand had not forgotten its cunning he would make short work of this Broad Arrow Jack, for what could he know of the art of fencing?

His guide took him by the arm, and led him

forth through a passage into the open air. He heard a murmur of voices, and one man asked him if he should come to dig his grave.

"Silence!" said Pedro's guide, sternly. "The chief brooks no jest when serious work is on hand."

The offender apologised, and the guide led his prisoner on, leaving the murmur of voices behind him, through the stream, over broken ground, and then up, up a rough path, long and wearying.

Pedro felt the warmth of the sun and the fresh morning breeze upon his face—both grateful to him after his confinement in the close, dark cell.

"May I see now?" he asked.

"Not yet," was the reply. "Keep quiet. He who will remove the bandage will presently be here. I see he is coming. Farewell, my friend, I hope you bear me no malice."

"A curse upon you!" muttered Pedro.

"Well," said the guide, philosophically, "I suppose I must take that as there's nothing else to get. But I fancy your curse and blessing are about the same value. Adieu!"

His footsteps rapidly retreated, and Pedro was left alone a minute or so, ere he heard a steady firm footstep approaching. The bonds of his arms were severed, his bandage pulled off, and he looked upon the light, standing face to face with his accuser—Broad Arrow Jack.

Our hero had a pair of rapiers under his arm, which Pedro's appreciative eye saw were of the finest make. He took in everything before him—the tall, splendid form of Jack—the sloping mountain side—the great rent spanned by the rude bridge formed of one vast trunk of a tree—the undulating land beyond—the rising sun—all he saw, and grasped the many details of the scene in the moment which elapsed before our hero spoke.

"You know me?" he said.

"Yes," replied Pedro, with a shudder, "I do."

"And you guess why I am here?"

"You have weapons, and I suppose you mean fighting," said Pedro, with assumed indifference.

"So," said Jack. "Now, make your choice, for only one of us must leave this spot alive."

In spite of his faith in his swordmanship, the heart of Pedro shrank within him. He made one last effort to turn Jack from his purpose.

"Why should you kill me?" he asked; "your life was spared."

"Is it not just you should die?" asked Jack. "Have you not, by the laws of any and every country under the sun, forfeited your life a hundred times?"

"I suppose so," said Pedro; "but there was little or no law here."

"I have established one," rejoined Jack. "I am the avenger of my own wrongs and the wrongs of others. Make your choice, and speedily, for I have work before me to-day which must be done."

"You are confident," said Pedro, scornfully.

"I am. I feel I shall conquer you."

"Perhaps you do not know I was a teacher of fence." It was Pedro's last effort to save himself by intimidating his foe, and it failed.

"I too have some knowledge of it," replied Jack, quietly. "Some years ago I took lessons from one of the first masters—Poictiers."

"He was an impostor," growled Pedro; "he knew nothing of the art."

"That shall be proved now by the performance of his pupil—are you ready."

"In a moment," replied Pedro.

He made tremendous preparations with a twofold object—to gain time, and to impress Jack with a notion of his superiority. He tried his weapon—swished it to and fro—bent it almost double—balanced it, and so on, with all the little antics of professors of fencing.

"Ready."

Their rapiers crossed, and Pedro turned cold. The first touch told him he had need of all his skill and energy to come off victor. Calm, immovable, Jack stood in an easy graceful attitude, while Pedro went through a series of assaults—well enough in their way, but feeble in their result with him. A turn of the wrist this way or that way was enough to put aside the Spaniard's weapon.

As thrust succeeded thrust without any result his heart beat quicker, and his brow grew darker. Who and what was this boy who held him so easily at bay, as man had ne'er held him before?

But it was not all skill—strength, courage, and a firm belief in being the victor helped Broad Arrow Jack in the encounter. They fenced him round and about, as it were, so securely, that if there had been two Pedros instead of one the result would have been pretty much the same.

The rapiers twirled and flashed in the sunlight as Pedro, getting hot and angry, increased the rapidity of the assault. He thrust here and there, feinted, and indulged in every trick he knew—all —all in vain.

Calm and immovable as a rock, Jack received the assault, and, gradually working round, brought Pedro with his back to the bridge.

Then our hero pressed on.

Abandoning defence, he began to attack with great force and skill. The Spaniard, grinding his teeth with fury, had no resource but to retreat or die.

Back, step-by-step, he went, until he felt himself upon the rugged bridge. Jack pressed on furiously, and pushed him inch by inch into the centre.

"Spaniard," he cried, "prepare to die. Beneath you is your grave."

"May the light of day be——"

"Silence," cried Jack. "Blaspheme no more."

The rapier lunged forward, and entered the Spaniard's breast. He tossed up his arms, gave one short gasping groan, and fell over into the chasm five hundred feet down.

Twice his body turned, then plunged head first into a dark hollow, and disappeared.

"One," said Jack, and tossed the rapier after him. "He has a grave a king might be proud of. No foot of man has ever trodden there. Lost Leon!"

Pale and quivering, Lost Leon came out of a hiding place among some bushes, and stood before the avenger.

"Did he die in fair fight?"

"Yes," said Lost Leon.

"Was it just he should die?"

"He has had an undeserved honourable death."

"So shall all perish," said Jack, "when their time comes."

"Is that to be the grave of all your enemies?" asked Lost Leon, looking down with a shudder into the awful chasm.

"No," he replied, "I will not pollute any spot on earth with so much villainy. Each shall die a different death, and I will scatter their bones far and wide."

"I tremble as I look upon you."

"Fear not, Lost Leon," said Jack, "I will never harm you."

"Not if I give you cause?"

"But you will never give me cause. I read in your eyes that you are attached to me."

"Ay, yes," said Lost Leon, "but sometimes we sin against our will."

"If you do that I will forgive you. Now, come with me, and begin your duties as gaoler. I am going to leave a prisoner—one, Jeb Jaundice, an arrant knave—under your care for a few days, as I have something to do for a short time away from here."

"Trust me," said Lost Leon, in a low voice, "and kill me if I betray your trust."

CHAPTER XXXII.
LOST LEON'S TRUST.

THE prison-house of Jeb Jaundice was not far away, and Broad Arrow Jack, accompanied by Lost Leon, were soon standing by the trap-door, on which the former gave the signal of three knocks.

Caliban—blear-eyed, uncouth, and horrible-speedily answered, and Jack, drawing him aside—said a few words. Caliban looked at Lost Leon carelessly, and, with a bow, acquiesced in what his chief desired.

"He is dumb," said Jack, as he rejoined the newly appointed gaoler, "and not very amiable in aspect, but you need not fear him. He is very harmless. If you tire of his company, as I am sure you will, set him to work at diamond-cutting. You will find interest in his skill."

"Shall I see the prisoner?" asked Lost Leon.

"He will be with you night and day. Farewell, and keep your trust."

"If I fail slay me," was Lost Leon's answer, and they parted, Broad Arrow Jack returning towards the palace, which looked like a pretty toy in the deep valley below.

Caliban, grinning mightily over some joke he had to himself, signalled to Lost Leon to follow him, and, raising the trap-door, led the way downwards to the underground passage. The door closed behind them, and Lost Leon felt a huge paw laid upon his shoulder.

"Ugh, the monster!" he muttered, and drew back.

Caliban tightened his grasp, and half-led, half-dragged his companion along the dark passage, until he came to the other door, which led into the apartment. This he thrust open, and gave a view of the interior.

Jeb Jaundice was seated at the lathe, examining some stones Caliban had been at work upon. The noise made by the approach of the two gaolers caused him to turn round. He greeted Caliban with affected warmth.

"Ha! my poor dumb friend," he said, "so soon returned. What news of the great and noble chief? Ha! two of you—another prisoner?"

"No," replied Lost Leon softly, "I am another gaoler."

"That voice!" said Jaundice, springing up, "I should know it. Am I dreaming? Maggie!"

"Hush!" whispered his wife—for she and Lost Leon were one, "I have come to save you."

Caliban, who had closed the door the moment he and his companion had entered the room, and crossed over to his lathe, neither noticed this greeting nor heard the words which passed. Caliban had been drinking heavily overnight, and was a little dull that morning.

"My good, my noble, my loving Maggie!" said Jeb Jaundice, still speaking softly, and trembling like a leaf. "Oh, that I had ten lives to repay this devotion!"

"I would have none of them," replied Maggie. "One life of yours has been enough for me."

"So cold still—so unforgetting."

"I am here," said Maggie, coldly, "not because I am true to you, but because I am true to myself. It is woman's nature to forgive an injury if she cannot forget it, and to die if need be for the man she professes to love. Shall I be less than a woman?"

"You have ever been more than woman."

"So smooth of speech, Jeb Jaundice. Ah, you will die with a falsehood on your lips! Say that you love me."

"I hold you in my heart dearer than life itself."

"Say that, if ever you get free, you will be true to me in all things, loving, gentle, and kind, as you were the first day I gave up my life to you."

"I will be all that to you."

"Tell me that no other face or voice of woman shall have any allurement or charm for you—that I, and I alone, shall reign within your heart."

"It shall be so until I die."

"Hypocrite and liar!" hissed Maggie.

Jeb Jaundice started back, and cast a look of apprehension at Caliban, but that blear-eyed monster was busy with his jewels.

"That's just like you, Maggie," he whined. "You never will believe me."

"I believed you once, and you deceived me. Can I ever believe you?"

"I see how it is," said Jaundice. "You have come in masquerade to triumph over me, to mock me! You hell-cat, whose mistress are you now?"

She sprang back as if stabbed, and glared at him like a tigress.

In a moment the passion died away, and she was calm again.

"Even that" she said—"even that I will bear Jeb Jaundice."

"Yes," he said, sullenly.

"I will set you free from here if you obey me. Come, sit by the table. Will he listen?" pointing to Caliban.

"He is busy, and will not trouble us."

Maggie sat down, and Jeb took a seat beside her. He tried to put his arm about her, but she thrust him off.

"You fool!" she said. "Your folly will spoil all. See now."

Caliban turned round from the lathe, and grinn and nodded at Maggie, showing every tooth in head. He evidently had a very excellent jo Maggie nodded back again, and he resumed work.

"What is the matter with that fellow?" asked Jeb Jaundice.

"The monster has a better instinct than better men," replied Maggie, calmly. "He guesses I am a woman. But I have no fear. I have both steel and powder and poison, a stiletto, a pistol, and some of the drug you have used in the old times."

"I remember," replied Jeb Jaundice, shivering.

"See here," said Maggie, producing a packet from her bosom. "You know it. Is there enough to send a man to sleep?"

"For a week," replied Jaundice, "if ever he wakes again."

"I will poison no man," said Maggie, preparing to cast it down.

"It will not poison," hurriedly whispered Jaundice.

"You swear it?"

"Yes."

"For once, Jeb Jaundice, I will believe you. Now for my plan, formed since I came here. Yon monster seems to have taken a fancy to me."

"And no wonder, Maggie, for you are beautiful still."

What a look it was she gave him! If he had been vulnerable to contempt it would have slain him.

"That door closes with a spring," she said. "Where is the key?"

"He keeps it in his breast, with others."

"Good! Now heed me, Jeb Jaundice. There is no time to lose. Broad Arrow Jack has left by this time, and will be absent about two days. This will give you a start. Make the best use of it."

"Aye! I will—when I am free."

"Be patient for a few hours, and you shall be so. This monster drinks, I believe?"

"Heavily, and yet sleeps as lightly as a dog," replied Jeb Jaundice.

"We will woo him to his drink," she said, and went over to Caliban.

The dumb man was busy polishing a stone fit for a queen's coronet, and was gloating over it with the ravenous glare of a miser; but he put it aside when Maggie went up to him and laid a hand upon his shoulder.

How the brute grinned! He was undoubtedly

Broad-Arrow Jack.

BROAD ARROW JACK SEIZED LAVANCHE BY THE COLLAR, SWUNG HIM OVER THE PRECIPICE, AND THERE HE DANGLED BETWEEN HEAVEN AND EARTH.

NO. 6.

aware of Maggie's sex, and his bloodshot eyes were full of what some men call love.

She made a sign that she wanted something to drink.

He put away his work, and brought out a bottle from under the table where Jeb Jaundice and his wife had sat. He also produced two horns, and was about to fill them, when Maggie pointed to Jaundice.

Caliban looked at his prisoner, and shook his head. Such good wine was not to be thrown away on him. Then he filled the horns—his own with a powder in it, quietly placed there by Maggie while he was looking at Jeb Jaundice.

Prior to drinking, the uncouth brute went through one of his dances, and made an effort to get his arm around Maggie's waist; but she drew back with a forced laugh, and began to dance by herself.

This pleased Caliban, and the pair performed a sort of savage Irish jig, to the amused amazement of Jeb Jaundice.

"She is a wonderful woman!" he muttered to himself. "Such strength of purpose—such will! I wonder whether she really loves me, and, if she does not, will she ever love me again?"

As regards the latter question, he might as well have asked if the sea would give up its dead at his bidding. Maggie might, in the truth and strength of her womanhood, serve him again and again, but she could never love him more.

When Caliban was tired of dancing he drank his liquor, and while he drank Maggie tossed half hers under the table. Caliban refilled his horn, and tossed it off.

"How long?" asked Maggie, smiling at Caliban, but addressing her husband.

"In five minutes or less," he answered.

Caliban looked from one to the other, wondering what their words meant. There appeared to be no understanding between them, and as he did not exactly catch what they said, he troubled himself no more about the matter.

"Drink and dance," said Maggie, to the brute, and in a few seconds the pair were off again.

Little by little the steps of Caliban got slower, and a peculiar glaze overspead his eyes. He seemed to be going rapidly blind. But he danced on, uttering peculiar noises in his throat, which were no doubt compliments to Maggie strangled at their birth.

Suddenly, and without further warning, he pulled up, and fell to the ground as if shot—all of a heap, with his head under his chest.

"You have killed him," cried Maggie.

"Not a bit of it," replied Jeb, coolly. "Listen, can't you hear him breathing? Now then, the keys. You'll find them in his breast."

While Maggie searched, Jeb coolly and quickly transferred to his pocket most of the valuables from the bench. His knavery was uppermost through all.

The keys were found, and Maggie, with no other thought than to save the life of Jeb Jaundice, gave no heed to the jewels, but hurried to the door, and at the second attempt found the key to fit it.

"Now, away," she said—"quick!"

They went out, and the door of itself closed behind them. In a few seconds they were standing in the open air.

"Do not pause for leave taking," said Maggie, "but fly at once. Take a westerly direction, for I see a cloud of dust in the east—Broad Arrow Jack and his men are travelling there."

"Won't you come too?" he asked.

"No," replied Maggie, "two will excite observation."

"Just so," he said, coolly. "Well, good-bye, dearest."

"Good-bye, Jeb."

"One kiss, Maggie."

"For mere form sake, Jeb?"

"No, Maggie," he replied, with sudden earnestness, "for love."

"For fleeting love," she said—"love out of a moment's gratitude."

"Good-bye," he said, kissing her; "we may meet again."

"When the world is old and gray, and the fires of the sun are cold," returned Maggie. "But begone. Make the best of your freedom."

He turned away and sped over the rocks, running for awhile like a hare doubling on its pursuers. Maggie watched him until he disappeared behind some trees.

"It is done," she said, as she turned towards the palace. "Now to meet justice, and receive my due. Farewell, Jeb! you and I, in this world, will never meet again."

CHAPTER XXXIII.

A DOUBLE DISAPPOINTMENT.

FOUR days later Broad Arrow Jack, Billy Brisket, and about fifty men, were returning homeward across the plain, after a fruitless search for the Ogre. The young chief was gloomy, for the result upset what was looked upon as a certainty.

The trail was clear at first, and it led to a vast plain, which afforded no food, and no known shelter to man. He was on foot, and his pursuers mounted. His re-capture seemed inevitable. Spreading out in a long line they went in pursuit for two whole days, and caught no sight of him.

It was absurd to suppose he had outdistanced them; he must, therefore, have doubled back, or hidden away in some place which their eyes had failed to detect.

"Say that he had three hours' start," said Billy Brisket, with a savage glance around him, "he could not have got far away enough to escape us. If he went to the right or the left it would lead him again to the hills, and there every pass is guarded. To return is to get into the jaws of the lion again."

"I fear he has escaped," replied Jack, gloomily.

"Escaped!"

"Not with his life; but he may have fallen down one of the numerous crevices among the rocks—some of them are of great depth."

"If that is the case there is an end of him," said Billy.

"But that will not suffice for me," said Jack, earnestly. "By my hand alone he must die for me to be satisfied."

"That is a matter of opinion," said Billy; "for my part I should bother no more about him. The villain is dead—must be. You know, if he were alive, we should find him without trouble."

"Well, we shall see. He may be found yet. But on my return I will clear off another from the list."

"Jeb Jaundice?"

"Yes."

"And a good riddance."

"I intended to reserve him for the last but one; but these rascals are like eels. It requires an iron hand to hold them."

"And when all is done, what then?" asked Billy Brisket.

"Why, you and I, old friend, will part," replied Jack, sorrowfully.

"Part!—and why?"

"You can go into the world, and make the best of your remaining years. What is your age?"

"Say forty."

"Ah, then, Brisket, you may look forward to

thirty years of such a life as you love. You have wealth——"

"So have you, and youth to boot. Come, my chief, you are hipped to-day. This little hitch has upset you, but it is nothing. Here, I will sing 'Tra-la-la;' and yet, now that I try, I find I am out of voice. We are both sad, my chief."

They rode on for awhile in silence, Billy Brisket with a most dejected face. He was, as I have said, a very mirror of a man, reflecting the feelings of those who were near him, particularly when they had so much influence as Broad Arrow Jack, whose power over the pedlar was immense.

From the first moment they met Billy gave up himself and all he had to him, as freely as he would have given a crust of bread to a starving wretch in the street. He had not even a thought or a wish apart from his welfare.

"Whatever it is I can't tell," Billy used to say to himself; "but there it is. I am as much his slave as if I had bound myself to him for life—more so—for I am a willing one, and rather like it."

As they neared the house, tired, dusty, and very much out of temper at the result of their fruitless search, Jack perceived a figure standing on one of the rocks, apparently watching for their coming. As he drew nearer he saw it was Lost Leon—or Maggie.

She came down swiftly, and presented herself before him with folded hands across her breast. Jack waved his hand in greeting, and said—

"So soon tired of your trust?"

"I am not here for that," she said. "May I speak with you alone?"

"Yes. Go forward, my men, I will follow you."

Led by Brisket they crossed the brow of the hill, and descended a rugged path, their trusty steeds walking with the ease and confidence of mountain goats. Jack dismounted, and took a seat upon a bank of earth. Maggie stood before him.

"Come, friend," said Jack, "won't you sit down? You look tired and worn."

"I am worn body and soul," she said. "Oh! kill me—kill me!"

"Kill you, indeed!" said Jack, "why should I do so?"

"I have broken my trust. Jeb Jaundice is free, and far away."

For a few moments Jack seemed incapable of grasping the meaning of these words, but as their full purpose grew upon him, a cloud black as night settled on his brow.

"Who freed him?" he asked.

"I—I alone."

"What share had Caliban in it?"

"None. I drugged him, and left him prisoner, but he has torn his way out like a wild beast, and fled."

"He, at least, was afraid to face me You are bolder," said Jack, drily.

"I am bold in my desire to die."

"You repent of this broken trust then?"

"No, if it were needful, I would do it again," was the reply.

Jack scarce knew what to make of the being before him. She had acted and spoken like a mad person, yet was perfectly calm and collected.

"Have you forgotten your oath?" he asked.

"No."

"To obey me in all things—to be true to me alone even unto death."

"Yes, I knew all; yet I betrayed you, for I had an oath much older than the one I gave to you."

"I do not understand you. To whom was it given?"

"To Jeb Jaundice—long, long years ago. That I would not break. Through all I have been true to him."

"I know you now," cried Jack, taking her gently by the arm. "Oh! how blind we have all been not to see through this thin disguise!"

"Kill me!" said Maggie, kneeling, "and I will bless you as you deal the blow."

"No—no!" said Jack. "I could never strike a woman—nay, more, I do not even reproach you, for I find in you a true heart that a king might clasp to his breast, and be proud to call his own. Women like you are the leaven of the world. But you must away at once."

"Oh! so good—so kind!" said Maggie, weeping; "so noble!"

"My kingdom ends where such civilisation as this part of the world can boast of begins," said Jack. "I myself will guide you to the frontier, and bestow upon you enough to place you above want."

"A prince in goodness!" said Maggie. "But do not turn me away. If you spare my life, let me live by you as your slave."

"No—no!" he said. "No women slaves for me!"

"You say you will take me back to civilisation. What can I do there? No—no! let me live here, or kill me!"

"It cannot be," said Jack, calmly. "You must go. Await me here, and I will fetch a horse, and then we will ride to the frontier together. You have betrayed me. I forgive you; but we must part."

He left her, and when she was alone she fell into a passion of weeping, which seemed to rend her very soul; but long ere he returned she was calm again. He found her standing like a statue awaiting him.

"See here," he said. "I have a good horse. It will carry you to the world's end, if need be."

"If my grave lay there, I would test him," she said, and from that time to the moment of parting she spoke no more.

With a halt now and then for an hour or so, they rode on for thirty-five hours—over plains, through valleys and woods—challenged now and then by armed men, who sprang up like spectres from the earth, and seemed to be wakeful day and night. At night Jack gave them the password, but in the day the sight of him was sufficient.

Of all he made inquiries in an under-tone, and received from them replies which plainly irritated him; but to Maggie he said nothing. He rode on a few paces in front, with his eyes fixed straight before him, and never turned to look at her.

Poor broken wretch! She was to be pitied. Trampled upon, insulted, neglected, the qualities of a sterling woman yet remained in her. A faded, crushed flower, there was fragrance in her still.

As they rode on she was thinking—wondering what would have been her lot if she had found years ago one to love like him who rode before her, in the place of the cold heartless brute who had wrecked her life, and ruined her peace.

"But why think of it?" she moaned within herself. "It never can be now. The past is irrevocable."

It was early dawn when they reached the spot for parting. From a great hill they looked down upon the smoke of many huts and houses, where the toilers at the diamond-diggings dwelt, a broad river running in their midst. Already the toilers were rising to labour, and many, like ants, were moving to and fro.

Jack held out his hand, and as their palms met he pressed a small packet upon her.

"Take it," he said; "you will find it enough for moderate wants."

"I have but one want and wish," she said—"to die."

She raised his hand to her lips, and the next moment they were parted in this world—for ever. He turned his horse, and rode homeward, ne'er looking back; but he carried with him the memory of two dark despairing eyes, in whose depths lay the love, remorse, and agony of a great soul, tossed and torn by conflicting emotions.

CHAPTER XXXIV.

LARANCHE.

ON returning to the palace Jack found the Tiger awaiting him. That active messenger had been there twenty-four hours, and had been devoting his time to tormenting Wobbles in an impish fashion, that went far to derange the little intellect the vicissitudes of life had left that valiant man.

"Which," he said, when the Tiger bonnetted him for the eleventh time, "if I only had one clutch at you somewheres about the throat I'd forgive everybody, even my sainted mother. Just one grab is all I ask."

That being denied him he took to shying stones at the Tiger, until he gave Maddox the benefit of one in the ribs, and had to flee for his life into the great hall, where he called upon the men there to protect him.

"I am not going to hurt him," said Maddox; "only to duck him. Hand the beggar over."

"Don't do it," pleaded Wobbles. "He's got murder in his heye."

But they did hand him over, and the burly Maddox was carrying him out, holding him by the waist, when Broad Arrow Jack appeared. At the sight of the chief Maddox immediately dropped him, and Wobbles made tracks over the ford into the wood, where he passed the rest of the day in solitude and trembling.

The Tiger, always on the alert, immediately presented himself before his chief, and waited to be spoken to.

"Well, Tiger, have you been to Hookey Settlement?"

"Yes, massa."

"Are the men I sent you to find dead or alive?"

"Alive, massa; but bery much chop bout de skin. Massa Laranche reg'lar ripped up bout de back, and bery ill."

"He is lying there?"

"Yes, massa."

"And the other two——"

"One gone one way—one de oder. Massa Skipper am trabelling up dis way—creep, creep in de night, skulk, skulk in de day."

"How were they saved? Who rescued them?"

"De men ob de settlement come back just as dey was bout to chaw each oder up. Hear de rumpuss in de cupboard, and let dem out. I hear dem talk it ober, and laugh like good un, massa."

"Good Tiger," said Jack, approvingly; "what should I do without you?"

The Tiger looked up, his eyes sparkling like diamonds.

"Massa say kind words," he said, "and Tiger bery happy."

"Away then, boy, and follow Niamo. Dodge him—drive him in. You understand?"

"Yes, massa," replied the Tiger. "Skip up in de dark—slap so—dis way, dat way—just as I gib it to Massa Pedro lying down among de brislers dere."

"How knew you that?" asked Jack.

"Been down to look at him, massa," replied the Tiger. "Tumble down some ob de way, but not bery much hurt. Climb dis way dat way coming back, and bery near break my neck."

"You will do it some day if you are not careful—but away with you. A wonderful creature!" he added, as the Tiger went away. "The eye of a hawk, and the activity of a cat and monkey combined. Something in the Darwinian theory, I fancy that boy is a connecting link. Now for Skipper, the Yankee!"

He went back to procure a rifle, pistols, and bowie knife, three classes of arms Skipper was pretty well sure to be furnished with, and then sought out Billy Brisket, who was telling off some men to send for supplies.

"That work," said Jack, "can rest for a day or two. I want those men to go to the western plain, and beat up my game to the Pine wood by the Three Springs. There is but one bird, Skipper the Yankee; get him into the wood by the day after to-morrow, and leave him there."

"It shall be done, chief," replied Billy Brisket, as coolly as if he had been told to get a head of game for supper."

"You must ride," said Jack. "I will go on foot, as I have a call to make by the way. Stay! I had better have Sue, to ride out of the mountain range, or I may be late. Where is she?"

"Grazing in the fern gully."

"Good. I will seek her. And you, Brisket, start at once; there is no time to be lost."

They shook hands, the men saluted, and Jack went in search of Sue. In ten minutes, without bustle or excitement, Billy Brisket, with a score of men, started to beat up the game.

Meanwhile Jack had found Sue—she came to his first call—and on her bare back was riding swiftly towards the plain.

He reached it shortly before dark, and, leaping from the back of his steed, dismissed her with a pat, and the word—

"Home."

Without hesitation she set off on the backward route at a smart gallop, and the clatter of her hoofs speedily died away in the distance.

Jack took a short rest, and with a glance at the stars for a guide strode swiftly over the open plain.

He passed through Peaceful Village, silent and deserted, pausing once to look upon the ruins of Jeb Jaundice's hut, and conjuring up Maggie as he had first seen her standing by the door, with a curious, wild, untameable look upon her face, and then wended his way to Hookey Settlement.

The great spirit of that place, Jereboam Bounce, was at rest. That very day they had buried him. Two drunken men dug his grave; four, very much the worse for liquor, carried him there, and one of the chief mourners, very far gone, fell in upon the body, and had a very narrow escape of being buried also. The ceremony over, the whole party returned to the hotel, and did their best to lessen the stock of spirituous liquors and tobacco, while Laranche, stretched helplessly upon a bed of sickness, vainly cried out for a drop of water.

Affliction sore had fallen on the Frenchman. He was ornamented with at least half a dozen ugly wounds, and the struggle in the cupboard had left him no clothes to speak of. He was in a very bad way, was Laranche; and he took his bad way very badly.

What were his chief thoughts? Repentance over the past? No. Hope for the future? No, unless it was that he looked forward to the pleasure of meeting Wobbles one day, and having a settlement with him in a quiet corner. Such a meeting would be very bad for Wobbles.

He lay in a side room, where he could, through the half-open door, command a view of part of the bar. For hours and hours he had watched the others drinking, gambling, smoking, swearing—doing, in short, anything but heed him—and his sufferings were quite equal to a second-rate martyrdom.

He swore a little in five languages, and a great deal in one—his own. Rise he could not, for arms and legs were stiff and helpless with just-closing wounds; and so the day passed, and as night came on the company in the bar succumbed to whiskey, and went down one by one.

They lay like logs—these brutes; and he lay like a mummy endowed with life. There was an old eight-day clock which Jereboam had picked up cheap from an emigrant (he knocked the original owner on the head, and brought it home, to keep his memory green), and this dear old thing—wound up by Jereboam an hour or so before he died—ticked loudly and sedately in the stillness.

To Laranche it seemed to mock him, and he would have given something to have had one blow at its face with the poker; but it kept on, "Tick! tick!" hour after hour, until he gave up swearing from sheer exhaustion, and lay still like the rest.

A parching thirst consumed him, and he was beginning to grow delirious, when he heard somebody moving in the bar. Again he was going to cry out for water, but he caught sight of a moving figure, and the words froze upon his lips.

It was Broad Arrow Jack, who, stepping lightly over the drunken ruffians, entered the room, and stood before Laranche.

"Mercy—mercy!" he groaned.

"Even as you have shown it," replied our hero. "But fear not, I will not kill you now; I do not fight with sick men. I come to tell you that a month hence I shall require you to meet me."

"I will come where you will," gasped Laranche.

"No, I will come where you would fain not see me. Be it where it may, I will be there. This is the tenth of May, on the tenth of June make up your worldly account. What can I give you now?"

"Water—water!" gasped Larauche.

Jack went out, and speedily returned with a pitcher full. Laranche drank greedily, and sank back like one relieved of intense pain, but he uttered no thanks.

"Remember," said Jack, "the tenth of June. Think not to escape me. I have set my seal upon you. Repent and beware!"

And then he was gone, and Laranche uttered a wild cry of despair. Was it true he had but one short month to live? Thirty-one days' apprehension worse than death! It would have been easier for him to die at once than to have a day to look forward to when death would come.

He had inflicted much torture on men, women, and children in his time, but all that he had given was small compared to what he himself suffered. He knew, he felt he was in the net—there was no escape, and he must die.

Yet a month had been promised him. A month was a long time—his wounds might heal, and he, with care and cunning, might get far away. Yes, there was hope still, but so feeble and flickering that it only made darker the darkness of his fears.

CHAPTER XXXV.

TWO.

CROUCHING behind a bush lay Skipper the Yankee, a bowie knife in his teeth and a rifle in his hand. All through a long and terrible day he had been conscious of a circle closing around him.

He saw the first man at sunrise approaching on horseback, and a wild fear drove him in the opposite direction. Two hours later he saw another man approaching, so like the other that it might have been the same. Then he turned to the right, and saw another—to the left another, and by degrees made out a circle of about a score of well-mounted men.

They were in no hurry, but advanced slowly, and at noon coolly picketed their steeds and filled their pipes. One alone kept in motion, and he rode round from man to man, pausing before each, and making signs towards the spot where Skipper lay.

A little beyond the western side of the circle was a small wood, the same where Jack and his men camped when they first captured the Ogre. Skipper looked at this spot, and thought what a fool he was not to have sought refuge there when first he saw his danger.

And while he blessed his stupidity the circle opened out into a horse-shoe shape, with the wood for a base, and began to move steadily down. Here was the very chance he wanted, and, laughing in his sleeve, he crept, snake-like, towards the proffered shelter.

"I thought the darned skunks were down upon me," he muttered; "but what is their game? That long chap—as seems tarnation familiar to me—sartainly pinted almost down my throat. Who the stars is he?"

The individual alluded to was Billy Brisket, but in the gorgeous uniform he had exchanged for his pedlar's dress it was not easy to recognise him. It was his action that was familiar to Skipper more than his form, which, excepting height and breadth, was completely changed.

Brisket had long marked down his prey, and having once got an eye on him, was not likely to entirely lose him. Very sharp eyes had the expedlar, with experience to tell him how to use them.

"Close in—close in!" he said to the men as they neared the wood; "we've got a bird. There he goes, in among the bushes, fancying, like the fool he is, nobody saw him. Keep a sharp watch, men, until the captain comes."

The two ends of the horse-shoe united quickly, and the circle was again complete.

Jim Skipper was hand and foot in the net.

But he knew it not, and, lying under some bushes, chuckled as he thought over the cunning retreat he had made—a safe one, he fancied, as he lay there for two hours, and no sound of pursuers fell upon his ears.

"As soon as the night comes," he muttered, "I'll be out of this, and get clear off. It won't do to risk open ground while there is daylight.

He was not quite certain whither he was going, but the necessity for getting out of that country was sufficiently apparent to show him that going in some direction was imperative, and his mind turned as the minds of more than one of his old comrades had done, to the diamond fields. There was a multitude of men there, and if he took another name and shaved his face clean, who was to find him?

Lying on the ground against your will is a monotonous proceeding, and if ever Jim Skipper felt truly grateful for anything in his life he was grateful for the darkness when it came.

Creeping out, he went towards the outskirts of the wood, feeling his way carefully lest he should slip upon a rotten branch or fall over anything, and so give a clue to his whereabouts to anybody watching for him. Not that he thought there was the least fear of that, these strangers being there by pure accident, he considered, and no doubt had gone on their way. Only it was just as well to be careful.

The thick foliage overhead gave him a peep of the stars here and there, but presently a great gap showed him he was nearing the plain. A few moments more, and he would know whether a clear path lay before him or one blocked with foes.

His heart beat fast—he could hear it—and in his blasphemous fashion cursed the very sound that proclaimed life was in him. He was afraid that somebody or something—he knew not who or what—would hear it, and pounce upon him.

The plain at last, and not a sound save the cry of some night bird afar singing a mournful song to its mate. Above, the broad sky, studded with stars—below, the dimly lighted earth, cold and still.

He was alone, as he had been a thousand times before when bent upon some villainy. Then he was untroubled, careless of all things, except the object he had in view. Now he was seeking only to save his own life, and yet he trembled, and cold drops of dew gathered round the tattooed broad arrow on his forehead.

"This is a cursed life," he muttered. "Once let me get out of it, that's all, and see if ever I leave bricks and mortar and somebody to see that a man aint hunted to death."

You see the idea of being hunted haunted him

dimly still, although all was so silent about him. He could not see, but he felt, as blind men feel, that other life was near.

The feeling was a true one.

He had advanced about fifty yards into the plain when a man rose from the earth with a rattle of arms and cried—"Back!"

Mr. James Skipper went back at once with a rapidity of movement only found in those who have some strong stimulus to exertion, and entered the wood with such haste that he ran against a tree violently, and brought himself down upon his back.

On his back he breathed a long list of suppressed curses, which relieved him; upon his feet again he debated.

"That chap was on the look-out," he muttered; "but he mayn't have been on the look-out for me. But where was the tothers? Nobody seemed anigh him. Perhaps he was alone. Guess I'll go and try another line."

He worked his way out at right angles, and again came in view of the plain. It was as quiet as it was upon his last visit, and, bent almost double, he crept out upon it, and covered quite a hundred yards before somebody laid a hand upon his shoulder.

"Back!" cried another voice, and he was swung round, and pushed towards the wood.

The effect of this second check to his very laudable desire to get away was to make Mr. James Skipper damp all over with mortal terror. He shook like a leaf, and his teeth played like castanets to the music of some strong language wrung from him by the startling nature of his position.

He did not run against a tree this time, but he sat down at the foot of one and ruminated.

"Guess it warn't the same chap," he muttered; "can't be, unless he cut round quick, and come on me by luck. I'll try another pint o' the compass."

For the third and last time he made an effort to escape from the wood; but he fared even worse. Barely had he got clear of the tree before he received a violent blow in the chest, which sent him staggering back into a sitting position, and in the dim light he saw the outline of a tall powerful man.

"Back!" he heard again. "In vain you attempt to escape. Your hour is near!"

"What's the—the—tarnation game?" he asked.

"The game," was the reply, "is a serious one—the stakes, life and death!"

"I only want to know who are the players?" muttered Skipper.

"Yourself and Broad Arrow Jack!" replied the other, and disappeared—melting away, to all appearance, like a shadow.

"It's no use," muttered Skipper. "I've run off the track, and I'm going to etarnal smash. Anyhow I hope I'll be killed outright."

He never moved from his seat all that night, awaiting sullenly whatever fate might befall him. When the morning broke he was sitting with his head bent down upon his chest, and his eyes on the ground, hopelessly despairing.

A footstep fell upon his ear, but he did not raise his eyes. The avenger might deal the blow at once, if he willed, only let him deal it swiftly and surely.

"James Skipper," said a musical voice, deep-toned as a bell, "look up. We are alone."

He had no need to look up to know whose voice it was, but he obeyed, and saw the form of Broad Arrow Jack within half a dozen paces of him.

"You see me?" said Jack.

"Yes," was the surly reply.

"And know me?"

"Only as you call yourself by the name of Broad Arrow Jack."

"At least you know why I am here?"

"'Taint difficult to guess; but go to work. You've got a pile of men to help you, and 'taint much of a job to kill a worn-out half-starved brute like me."

"Drink some of this," said Jack, tossing a flask towards him. "I do not fight with the sick; and as for my men, they have left. I am alone."

Skipper emptied the flask, tossed it back without thanks, and said—"Gammon!"

"What do you mean?" asked Jack.

"About your men. They are only skulking about here somewhere, in case I should show fight."

"You are an unbelieving fool," rejoined our hero. "See you yon cloud of dust in the horizon? They are homeward bound. Alone I come to avenge myself—not in cold and cruel slaughter, but in fair fight, as man to man. I am armed as you are—pistols, bowie, and rifle. Take your choice of weapons, and let us begin."

"So," drawled Skipper, half doubting the absence of the men, yet reading truth and honour in Jack's eyes, "you want me to make my choice?"

"I do."

"Then," said Skipper, rising, "I guess I'll have the rifle, for I'm no hand with the pistols, and the bowie aint good for anything but a scrimmage, when you slash about ginerally, and land in somebody at every dig. The rifle, I says, and shots at fifty yards until one goes over."

CHAPTER XXXVI.
RUN FOR IT.

"AGREED," said Jack. "Are you loaded?"

"No, I aint," replied Skipper, "as I didn't think I'd want it."

"Load while I measure the ground," said Jack.

Skipper smiled—a disagreeable smile of cunning. His rifle *was* loaded, and as Jack turned to pace the ground he cocked it quietly.

Not so quietly, however, as to escape Jack's ears. Quick as lightning he sprang aside half a dozen yards, and a bullet went shrieking by.

"It was an accident!" yelled Skipper.

"You liar!" returned our hero. "You have had your shot, and I will now have mine. Pace the ground yourself."

"I won't!" cried Skipper. "Don't be hard on me. Give me life—only another day! Keep me as a slave, and I'll swear to do whatever you may wish. Kill me if I don't!"

"I tell you," said Jack, striding up to him, and quietly removing the pistols and bowie from his belt, "you will have no mercy from me. You have had your shot, and I will have mine. Run for it. Base and treacherous as you have been, I will not fire until you have marked fifty paces. Go!"

"And if you miss me?"

"You may go your own way free, as far as I am concerned, for ever."

"You swear it?"

"No, I promise. If that is not enough you will get no more."

Skipper drew himself up to run for dear life—at least there was a chance of it. Fifty paces was a long way, especially if a man took long strides, and his legs were a trifle longer than the average lower limbs of men.

Jack, with his rifle resting easily on his arm, stood ready. The Yankee looked at his calm face and bright clear eye, and the prospect of escape grew dim. He turned sick and faint, and staggered forward a couple of paces.

"'Taint fair," he said; "I swear it was an accident."

"Don't perjure your soul with your last breath," replied Jack, sternly. "Go on; at fifty paces take your last look of earth and sky."

"It's murder," gasped Skipper. "You aint got the right you aint——"

"Either you or I must mark the ground," said Jack.

"Once more I ask for mercy."

"Go on—there is none from me. I am immovable."

Suddenly Skipper swung round, and went off at a great pace. His legs were long, and he ran like a greyhound, covering the ground with huge strides.

"Lord have marcy on me!" he muttered; "send his barrel may be bent, or no bullet in it, or fill his eyes with dust, so that he can't see straight. Marcy —marcy! I aint fit to die!"

In his easy attitude Jack watched his flight, counting the steps taken up to forty; then he put the rifle to his shoulder, covered his man, and as Skipper's feet were taking the fiftieth stride fired.

The Yankee pulled up, gave a terrific bound into the air, turned half over, and pitched on his head.

Jack came up, turned him upon his side, and looked at his face. A look of surprise and pain was fading quickly from it. In a few moments it was gone, the jaw fell, and the placidity of death smoothed his features, and made them look fairer than they had ever done in life.

As a living being he had been repulsive—evil passions were ever uppermost, marring all. In death he was a well-featured man enough, with large grey eyes, aquiline nose, well cut firm mouth, and square powerful jaw.

"Had I not slain him I should never have known him," said Jack. "When death comes in the devil departs out of a man, and leaves him as God made him."

Laying down his rifle, Jack raised the dead man, and bore him back to the wood. There between two trees a shallow grave had been dug, and into it the avenger laid him and the rifle. He covered the body with earth, trod it well down to keep beasts of prey from it, and with his bowie knife cut upon the bark of the nearest tree the initials "J. S." and beneath them a broad arrow. This done, he went back for his rifle, and shouldering it, walked sadly back towards his home in the mountains.

* * * * * *

Bands of loafers are as plentiful as blackberries in a young country. By a young country I mean a land where a new era of civilisation is setting in. As for an absolutely young country, I don't believe there is such a thing. This old earth of ours has been turned over and over, bringing up fresh crops of humanity, and, as a natural result of turning over, improving in production; but the young sprouts are always a little wild and vicious, and until the roots have taken firm hold, and the leaves have grown strong, there is a little confusion, and a great deal of uncertainty as to what the crop will really be.

To return. Bands of loafers are always to be found in a young country, and on the day Jim Skipper met with his merited fate there were three of the class wandering through a mountain gorge, in a dinnerless condition, and without an idea where a dinner was to come from.

They had left the diggings, having found hard work and a sound thrashing, bestowed upon them by the court of Judge Lynch for petty peculations, disagree with them. They were, in short, travelling for the benefit of their health, and, if possible, to he replenishment of their pockets.

Three Englishmen they were, I am sorry to say, originally members of the class who do anything but work at home, and have an extensive acquaintance with the police authorities. Born thieves, they lived thieves, and promised to die members of the same profession.

"I'm precious hungry," said one—a red-headed fellow with a squint. "I don't know as ever I felt so 'oller afore."

"And I," said another, "have some idea what a sausage skin when left alone in the world may feel. At home we allus had something, for if you was on the mill you got your toke reg'lar, although they only just gives you enough to keep you dancing on the werge of starwation without lettin' you die under it."

Suddenly the third cried out—

"Here's a cove a-coming."

And then they all got into the shadow of a rock, and fixed their eyes on the cove alluded to, wondering if he had anything about him which could be applied to gastronomical purposes.

"He's a rum-looking chap," said the man with the squint. "He aint got no hat."

"Nor a coat."

"Blowed if he's got even a shirt!"

"He's wuss off than we are."

Then they looked at the fragments of doubtful linen sorrow and trouble had left them, and their bosoms swelled with pride.

"Nothing to be got there," said the man with the squint.

"Don't you be in a hurry," said number two. "He may have got hisself up on the cadging lay, and be a rolling in wealth, and have his two trousers pockets full o' broken wittles."

"Lord send he's got something!" was the prayer of them all, and again they crouched, and waited until he drew nearer.

It was Broad Arrow Jack, homeward bound, stern and silent, and in no humour to be interfered with. But that the three gentlemen knew nothing about, and, as he drew level with them, they rushed out, and the man with a squint, being desirous of producing a dramatic effect, cried out—

"Stand and deliver! Wittles, drink, or tin! Shell out!"

Jack looked at the fusty wretches, haggard, wan, and dirty, and made them a sign to let him pass, but they barred his way.

"We must have wittles," muttered the man who squinted, his eye taking an extra turn in the wrong direction, and making him look more villainous than ever.

"Fools!" said Jack, with a frown. "Are you all mad?"

"Well-nigh," said one. "We aint had any toke to speak of for a week or thereabouts—leastways, it seems so to me."

"I have no time to throw away on such hang-dog men as you," said Jack. "Clear the path!"

"Wittles, drink, or tin!" muttered the squinting spokesman of the party.

Scorning to use his weapons on such creatures, Jack sought only to terrify them, and, stooping down, he took up a huge piece of rock, and raised it above his head.

"Clear the way!" he cried.

They cleared the way by staggering back against the rocky sides of the pass, astounded at such an exhibition of strength.

The squinting man went down flat, and lay gasping.

Jack hurled the huge weapon against the rock above their heads, dashing it into a hundred pieces, which showered down upon them, inflicting half a score or so respectable bruises. Then he passed on his way.

"What a cove!" said the squinter. "Who is he?"

"Don't know," replied one of the others. "I never seed the like o' him. You was too wiolent, Conky, at fust, and too funky when you seed he wouldn't stand it."

"Not more funky than you, Curler."

"Yes you was. Wasn't he, Pigeon?"

Pigeon, who represented number three of the party, opened his mouth, and gave reply—

"You was both precious done—you was Never did I see sech in my life."

"Which you was brave—wasn't you?" asked Conky, sarcastically.

"Well, I stood my ground until you ran back," replied Pigeon, "and then I come back to keep you company."

"Who's game to go and ask him to tip us something?"

It was Curler's suggestion, and Conky favoured him with an answer.

"I will," he said, "for I don't think he's got real wenom in him. If he had he could have gave us one about the ribs that would have been all the wittles and drink we should ever want."

"Go it," urged Curler and Pigeon, and Conky went upon his mission.

He ran fast, and speedily overtook Jack, who heard, but did not heed his footstep. Having got within professional begging distance Conky began his tale of woe.

"If your honour will only tip us a trifle we'll be wery thankful. We are all hard-working men, with wives and families all down with the measles, and haged fathers in the hinfirmary—dash it! No. I don't mean as we've got 'em here. We left 'em t'other side of the sea——"

"What do you want?" asked Jack, turning so suddenly that Conky backed over a stone, and vented the rest of his part of the conversation in a sitting position.

"Wittles and drink," he said. "We are all starving."

"Is that true?"

"S'help me! I aint tasted nothing since last Monday morning, when I gave my youngest kid the last crust in the cupboard, and came out blinded with tears—that is—no—I did once do it."

"You look hungry," interrupted Jack. "If you and your companions really want food follow me."

Conky beckoned to the Curler and Pigeon, and in a hoarse whisper imparted this glad tidings to them, and the trio followed meekly and respectfully in the wake of Broad Arrow Jack, who led them over hills, and through valleys and woods, until their weary bodies were well-nigh exhausted, when Black Rock and all its wonders appeared before them.

The men were outside engaged in cleaning various things, harness, cooking utensils, and so on, and Billy Brisket was lying on his back upon the grass smoking a cigar. He jumped up and saluted his chief, and the men paused in their labour, saluted, and remained at the attention.

"Is it done?" whispered Brisket.

"Yes," replied Jack, "number two has paid the penalty."

"Good," said Brisket. "But who may these be?"

He looked at Conky, Curler, and Pigeon, with no friendly eye, and they put on the expression of perturbed innocence, so common among professional cadgers, when regarded by inquisitive spectators.

"I found them starving," said Jack. "Give them food, and then dispose of them as you will."

He passed in, and Billy Brisket beckoned to one of the men to bring him a camp stool, on which he sat with a magisterial air.

"Come here you three," he said, "closer, and let me have a look at you."

The way the three unfortunates approached was a sight—they were as shy as cock sparrows who have doubts of a brick trap.

"Ha! I thought so," said Billy, after a moment's inspection. "Your names are Conky, Curler, and Pigeon—petty filchers, thieves, and vagabonds."

"You've got our names right, sir," said Conky, "but s'help me, it must be some of our family as is guilty of all them things aforesaid at the conclusion. Pigeon's got a cousin as have been no end of trouble to his family—aint you, Pigeon?"

"He's got a nateral liking for police-courts, and aint never happy unless he's afore the beak," replied the truthful Pigeon. "It breaks my heart, it do, to think on him."

"You are very much like that same cousin who stole my boots at the fields, and sent me about in slippers," said Billy; "and I'll swear it was you," turning to the startled Conky, "who took my hat. You've got it on now, and a filthy state you've made it in. Here, one of you take it off."

One of the men jerked off Conky's hat, and Billy bade him see if his initials were not in the lining.

"Yes," said the man, "two capital B's."

"Perhaps you know me now," said Billy.

"But you can't be the pedlar chap," said Conky.

"Yes I am, and before I obey the orders of the chief I'll—I'll deal with you on my own account. I swore, at the time you robbed me, that I would give you all a licking if ever I got a chance. Somebody fetch my slippers."

They were speedily brought to him—Conky, Pigeon, and Curler, wondering what was coming.

"These slippers have worn well," murmured Billy, "now stretch 'em one by one across the camp stool. That's it—the squint-eyed one first."

As soon as the expostulating Conky was got into position, Billy used the slipper with such discretion and energy that the recipient yelled and howled most frightfully. The Curler and Pigeon looked on, damp and limp with apprehension.

The Pigeon suffered next, and took the first half-dozen blows like a man. The seventh drew tears, the eighth extracted a howl, and the ninth brought forth an appeal for mercy; but full three score did he receive ere he was let loose to assuage the pain with rubbing.

Curler gave them some trouble before he was got into the proper angle; but when he was duly fixed Billy gave him three score for his original crime, and ten for the unnecessary bother he had given. Curler took each blow very ill, and shed tears.

"Now, when you want any more," said Billy, "you have only to ask for 'em, or to go prigging something. Give 'em all they like to eat now, and set 'em work to do."

The precious trio were desired to sit down, which they did a little sideways, choosing soft spots on the ground to rest upon. Curler went in for mud; but a little damp was better than the discomfort a hard place would have entailed. Food was brought, and they ate ravenously.

Just as they finished, Wobbles returned from the wood with some sticks for the cooking fire. No sooner did he behold the strangers than his jaw and the bundle he carried fell.

"Well, I'm jiggered," said Conky, "if here aint old Wobbles! How are ye my 'arty pal?"

"Stand off!" cried Wobbles. "I don't know how you came here, and I don't want to know. I've done with you, and your low society. It was my ruin, combined with the mistake of a sainted mother; and I won't have any more of it!"

"Come, don't shunt old pals," replied Conky. "Many and many is the spree we've had together, and, since weve jined company agen, let us be friendly. I should have thought you'd have been glad to see us, and proud to find we didn't cut you, for if ever there was a chap as cut up cursed bad it was you."

CHAPTER XXXVII.

A DISCOVERY.

WOBBLES uttered a despairing groan, and rolled his eyes skywards. For a long time past all sorts of evils had been gathering round him, and not the least of them was the latest arrival of old friends.

It may be that Wobbles was a fool, but every fool has a bit of the rogue in him, and there were dark pages in the Wobbles history which would not bear the light of day. Nevertheless, he sought to ignore the past.

"You can go your way, and I'll go mine," he said. "If we did meet occasionally and have a friendly glass at a public, that aint no reason why you should, just as I am getting into a good position, much loved and respected by those around me, come and fix yourself on me."

The eye of Conky glittered, and Curler and Pigeon exchanged bitter smiles. This exhibition of false friendship on the part of Wobbles roused the cynical portion of their amiable disposition.

Conky looked around. The men had all disappeared, and their voices were heard in the great hall, where they were gathering round the board. Now was the time to take the nonsense out of Wobbles, and he made a signal to the Pigeon, who laid hold of the legs of Wobbles and dragged him down.

"S'help me," hissed Conky, in his ear, "the likes of you aint fit to live, cutting them as stood by you in byegone years."

"Who's a cutting of you?" whined Wobbles; "I never see such chaps. When I gets up a lark to see if your friendship's true, you gets hold o' my legs and brings me down enough to bust a party."

"Look you now," said Conky, "what I'm going to say I mean, and Pigeon and Curler means it too —don't yer?"

The two gentlemen addressed affirmed this with an oath of great strength. Pigeon being, perhaps, a trifle the more fervent; but he was a child of impulse, and never did things by halves.

"So now," continued Conky, "you hears us, and mind us, unless you want us to blab about that little ob of the widder's till— "

"Don't," pleaded Wobbles.

"Oh, you mean cuss!" growled Conky, glowing like a turnip lantern with virtuous indignation, "to go and rob a poor woman as got a livin as one may say in pennorths. A poor creeter that was obliged to mix up bloaters with bacca, tea, firewood, and general chandlery, to pay the rates and taxes of the oppressor."

"Come, I like that," said Wobbles. "If I did take the till, who got wot was in it?"

"And did you think," asked Conky, sternly, "that even for a moment men like me and Curler and Pigeon was goin' to let you thrive on willany of that sort? Not if we knowed it."

"But you spent the money," said Wobbles, "and when I asked you for only a tanner the Pigeon give me a kick as lamed me for a month."

"I thought of that poor widder, and couldn't hold myself no longer," replied the Pigeon. "A man of feelin' draws the line somewheres."

"You was allus drawing lines," grumbled Wobbles.

"There was another job," continued Conky, "as I never thinks on without being cold all over. That poor little innercent boy as was going for change for 'arf a crown, while his father and mother were at home a-sittin' afore the fire, and not even dreaming of the wolves as roam about seekin' wot little kids with 'arf-crowns they may devour. Who shoved that kid in the gutter, and knocked the 'arf-crown out of his little hand? Oh, what willainy!"

"Didn't you pick it up," asked Wobbles, "and swear you hadn't seen it, and didn't I find all of you in the public changing it? Come now."

"Did you ever hear the like o' that afore, Pigeon?"

Pigeon had evidently never heard the like, he was so fervent in his declaration that such audacious assertions were utterly strange to him.

"And what do you think of it, Curler?"

Curler declared it "chilled his witals" to listen to it. "Men aint got no conscience now-a-days," he added, "nor no remorse."

"But let us bury the past," said Conky, graciously, "and come to the present. Who is that young chap with the mark on his back?"

"Broad Arrow Jack," replied Wobbles.

"What is he doing here with all these men?" was the next question.

Wobbles, after a moment's reflection, told what he knew of our hero's story, only leaving out his part of the life in Peaceful Village, and boldly asserting that he had been with Jack for years, as one of his principal friends and counsellors.

Strange to say the listeners believed him. A thorough-paced scoundrel, who lives by lying and deceit, is not easily imposed upon, but they are sometimes easily taken in.

"And how is this kept up?" asked Curler.

"Eh?" asked Wobbles.

"This kept up—this place—these men, with their welwet clothes and fine weppings?"

"All the cellars underground," replied Wobbles, "are chock-full of suvrins. Ah! you may stare, but 'tis so. This place was once the palace of a king, and when a great war came on he gathered all the gold of the people together, and put it into the cellars; then he sent out the people to fight, and got 'em all killed, and wery happy he would have lived if he hadn't taken the small-pox, and died in hagony."

"Oh! come," said the three listeners, "draw it mild!"

"Captain Brisket, the party as—hem!—had a little game of slipper with you, told me so, and I believe him."

This was true. Brisket, in one of his lightest moments, had favoured Wobbles with this entertaining story. It was believed by him, and, after a moment's hesitation, by the trio also.

"You see," argued Wobbles, "a man must have something to keep up a place like this, for you've got all you want to eat, and there's everything of the best, and he never goes out anywheres—except on the awenging bis'ness; and I *know* that all them sparkling things on the front there is diamonds. Ah! you may stare—it's a fact! And I know, too, that there must be pecks of jewels about the place, as well as the gold."

Conky, Curler, and Pigeon went into a short trance, and came out of it with wild visions of future wealth for themselves. With so much gold, and so many jewels, the little they required would scarce be missed.

"Who keeps the keys o' them cellars?" asked Conky.

"The chief," replied Wobbles, "but t'other day *I found a duplicate to one on 'em!*"

The others gasped, and tried to speak; but words failed them. Wobbles, with a curious look upon his face, went on—

"Yes, I found the key, and when the chief was away I went down into the cellar, and there was gold in great bags piled up just like bags of flour in a mill."

"Didn't you open one on 'em?"

"Yes, I did; and I ran my hand into the lovely coins; and you never felt anything like it. Oh! it was scrumptious!"

"Of course you didn't take none?"

"Not one."

"Which was werry right and honest," said Conky, virtuously. "Look at a man's property, if you like; but don't touch it."

Pigeon said that was the way for a man to act, and Curler declared he would slay his own father if ever he suspected him of touching a penny.

"Of course you kep' the key?" said Conky, carelessly.

"Yes," replied Wobbles, producing an old-fashioned piece of ironwork very much like a tuning-fork.

"That's a skewrious key," said Conky.

"Yes, it is."

"And it opens the cellar door?"

"It do."

"Them bags, if put up neat, must be a pretty sight?"

"They *are* werry pretty," replied Wobbles.

"But I suppose you wouldn't like to show 'em to us?"

"I don't think I dare," said Wobbles, hesitating.

"Come now," said Conky, encouragingly, "be a man. Act kind to an old pal. Give us a peep— only a peep! There's nothing like a lot o' sacks well put up—they look so pretty! I'm fond of seein' them in a mill. My father was a miller."

"He spent nearly all his life *on* the mill," said Pigeon, softly.

"In the mill," returned Conky, with a frown. "Between being in and on a mill there is a wast difference. But, I say, Wobbles, you will give us a peep."

"Perhaps I may some day."

"No, don't put it orf, or you may be sorry you didn't act kind with old pals. Let it be to-day."

"Couldn't go near the place in daylight," said Wobbles.

"To-night then, arter dark."

"Well, to-night, then," said Wobbles; "and if you aint kicked out of the place afore be here about midnight."

"We will," they all answered, in a hushed whisper, and their hearts beat rapidly as they thought— well, no matter what. Time will tell.

"I will leave you now," said Wobbles, rising, "as it won't do to be seen too much together. Remember, at the midnight hour."

"We will be here," they said, in thrilling chorus, and Wobbles left them.

He hurried round to the back of the palace, and then, in a cool sequestered spot, he threw himself down upon one knee in a tragic attitude.

"Wengeance!" he hissed. "It shall be mine! Shall hanythink turn me aside from the path of justice? Never! For, have I not sworn a hoath? Conky, Curler, and Pigeon—tre-emble! I'm on yer!"

CHAPTER XXXVIII.
NIAMO.

THAT evening a convoy of men and horses, the former walking, and the latter bearing great packs upon their backs, arrived at the palace, and a lively scene ensued. Conky and his friends were set to work by Brisket, and in the course of their labours were favoured with a sight of the interior of the aforesaid packs, which found much favour in their eyes.

No end of good things came to light—flour, meat, coffee, tea, wine, fruit, and a hundred other luxuries and requisites for the band, all of which Wobbles informed them had been especially shipped over the sea for Broad Arrow Jack.

"He's got a reglar fleet o' wessels," he said, "going backards and forrards to all parts of the world. He could, if he liked, have all the luxuries of the uniwerse, but he draws it mild until his wengeance is accomplished."

Then, under his breath, he added—

"As I do. Wery little wittles and drink shall pass my lips until I have these three villains in the toils. Ha—ha!"

"What are you laughing at?" asked Pigeon.

"Look alive there, you skulking scoundrels!" bawled Billy Brisket. "Remember this—there is a bit of leather on the slipper yet."

The effect of this was to rouse them up like ants stirred with a stick. They ran to and fro with bales and parcels, and spoke no more until their work was done. The men of the convoy went in to eat, and the others lay about the grass smoking.

Billy Brisket tossed some tobacco to the trio of thieves, for which they expressed their gratitude in the most abject terms, wriggling after the manner of mendicants who had received a liberal donation.

"You fellows being here," said Billy, "may stop here, but you must work, and do as you are told. Don't try any of your old tricks, or you will get into trouble."

"Oh! no, sir, it's fur from my thoughts," said Conky, and Pigeon and Curler said the same.

"By the way," continued Billy, lightly, as he was turning to go, "don't roam too far from the palace, as everybody found a half a mile away, and unable to give the passwords, is instantly shot."

A slight sinking was observable in all three as they received this intimation, but they all averred that nothing would tempt them to roam at all.

"All right," said Billy, "I thought I would tell you, so that you might not complain if you found yourselves walking about with an ounce of lead inside you."

"Not so heasy as we thought," said Pigeon, when they were alone.

"Not quite," said the other two, and sadness o'erspread their intelligent countenances.

They made themselves cigarettes with bits of paper, not having a pipe of any sort, and were inhaling the fragrant weed, when the Tiger came leaping across the ford, and dashed by them into the palace.

The boy was covered with dust, except about the feet, which had been washed on his way across the river, and he showed signs of having come a long way at a great pace.

He made straight for the door of Broad Arrow Jack's apartment, and knocked.

"Come in!" cried our hero, and the boy entered, and stood just within the door.

"Ha! Tiger, back again?"

"Yes, massa."

"You have been following Niamo?"

"Yes, massa."

"Well?"

"He hab made him lilly hut in de middle ob a cave, down whar de riber fall down de big stone."

"By the cataract, Tiger?"

"Yes, massa, and dere he lib, jes' peeping out in de day, and goin' bout at night to put down de lines for fish, and de oder tings dat he hab to eat. Him look bery bad, and jump wheneber he hear a lilly noise."

"And I'll warrant you have been playing some tricks on him."

The Tiger grinned tremendously, and looked slily at Jack as he replied—

"Me jes' trow stone dis way, dat way, sometime, and in de night, when he come out ob de cabe, gib him one slap on de chest, dat make him screech like de fox wif him leg in de trap. It bery funny, massa."

"Yes, but be careful. You may get into trouble some day."

"No, massa, neber. Me much too quick—quicker dan de bullet from de gun. Neber catch me, massa."

"I hope not. Now, Tiger, which is the shortest way to the cataract?"

"Ober de split hill, and down by de big white wall, but massa neber trabel dat way."

"No, Tiger; I am not exactly a cat."

"Me go dat way, massa."

"Yes, you rascal; but which is the next best way?"

"Round by de red rocks, massa. Me show de way."

"When will you be ready?"

"Now, massa."

"No, no. I won't kill a willing horse. Come in two hours. I know you don't need much rest, but you must have a little."

"Better go at once, massa. Me quite ready."

"No, Tiger. You hear what I say, and you know I like to be obeyed."

"Yes, massa."

Two hours later Tiger was in the room again, and found Broad Arrow Jack armed with rifle, cutlass, and pistols, ready to start. A small bundle of food and drink was slung about his waist; another was ready for the Tiger, who tied it round his neck and declared himself ready.

"Go out and see if the coast is clear," said Jack.

The Tiger departed and returned like a sprite, reporting all outside quiet, with a bright moon shining. The strange master and servant went out together, the Tiger skipping a few paces in front, as Shakespeare's Puck might have done.

Across the stream to the wood, and as soon as they were within its shades a deep voice rang out—

"Who goes there?"
"The avenger."
"The pass word!"
"Justice."
"Pass on, and all's well."

Again forward, guided by the broken light of the moon falling through the foliage, another hundred yards, when again they were challenged as before, or rather Jack was challenged, for in each case the Tiger, with his catlike footstep, passed the sentry unheeded.

This strange boy seemed to have the power of gliding over objects without sound—not even the breaking of a twig betrayed his whereabouts, and whenever he disappeared, as he often did in his restlessness, Jack simply kept straight on, and made no attempt to find him.

He came and went as he willed. Now and then Jack got a little out of the path, but in a few moments the Tiger was back by his side to guide him, and so all through the night they travelled in the direction where the doomed Niamo skulked within a cave, crouching like a wild beast who knows the hunter is on his trail.

CHAPTER XXXIX.

NIAMO IN HIS DEN.

THERE is something very romantic in the idea of living in a cave—free of all the trammels of society, hunting, eating, and sleeping when we will, and paying rent and taxes to no man. To boys especially this life of barbarous freedom has many charms; and, given a dry cave and a good even climate, it would not be so very bad; but, lacking these, such an existence would be scarcely bearable.

Now Niamo, the Russian, had taken up his abode in a cavern furnished with every discomfort. The floor was soft, and the roof a filter for the ground above. Reptiles loved the place, and came in swarms, seemingly indifferent to his presence. He killed them by scores, but the more he slew the more they increased and multiplied in numbers.

Nothing less than a mortal dread of Broad Arrow Jack would have kept him there. The discomforts of his residence were partly forgotten in the fear he felt, and for days he lived on, making the best of surrounding circumstances.

He gathered leaves and sticks, and made himself a dry bed, which was promptly taken possession of by swarms of noxious reptiles and insects, who, no doubt, conceived the whole thing was arranged for their especial benefit; but Niamo was not troubled—he was beginning to feel even a sense of pleasure in their companionship.

Like all other men, he could not bear to be utterly alone.

And yet it was his intention to live alone there, say for two years, and by that time Jack would probably have given him up, and, having wreaked his vengeance on the rest, left the place. Slow of thought, as became his birth, he had fashioned that plan in his mind, and with dogged resolve prepared to carry it out.

"He will never think of looking for me here," he said, and laughed in his heart as he thought how much cleverer he was than his brethren.

It was hard work getting food, but he did it. He made snares and set them at sunset, returning at early dawn to see if good fortune smiled on him—which it generally did. He gathered herbs and roots, bruised them into a pulp, and ate them with the raw flesh of such small animals that he snared. He dare not make a fire, although he had the means; nor dare he use the pistols he carried in his belt, as either might be the means of revealing his whereabouts to the watchful eyes he dreaded.

So for seven long days he lived, or rather dragged on a miserable existence. Time passed so slowly that he dared not think of the many months he had resolved to spend there.

By day he lay about the mouth of the cave, sleeping when he could, and idly whittling sticks, or making snares of withies when awake. A man with a mind one degree less sluggish would indubitably have gone mad.

His great consolation was—he was safe. That held him up through the miseries of his daily life.

Niamo was never a very handsome man—indeed, stern critics of human beauty would have called him confoundedly ugly—but he had something of the man in him until he went to live as a beast, and it was astounding how brutish his appearance speedily became.

Not even the clothes of civilisation could hide it—a mangy lot, it is true, but clothes still—and yet you could not tell where it was, for matted hair and a dirty face do not of necessity make a brute of a man. No, it was not these alone—the whole man was sinking to the level of a hunted wild beast.

He seldom spoke aloud, and when he did he spoke no other words than these—"I am safe here."

This was his one absorbing idea, and he dwelt upon it, until the words came parrot-like from his tongue.

But on the morning of the eighth day his sense of security was scattered to the winds. He had been out in the dark wood, waiting for the dawn, to examine his snares; and, having taken advantage of the earliest light to do that work, he returned home with a brace of rabbits on his shoulder.

He reached the cave, stood before its mouth, and, looking up, started back trembling.

There in the soft clay was a broad arrow deeply cut.

The blood rushed to his head, and the tattooed mark upon his forehead stood out bold and clear. For a moment he felt as if he must swoon, but the feeling passed, and he turned to flee.

"Halt!" cried a loud voice, and Broad Arrow Jack stood before him.

"So," he said, quietly, "you thought, Niamo, that hiding here would save you?"

The Russian opened his lips to speak, but his tongue clave to his mouth, and no words came forth.

"Vain hope," said Jack, "as you see. The sands of your life are nearly run. This day is to be your last."

As the others had begged for mercy so begged he, but Jack checked him.

"No," he said. "I am the instrument of justice, and cannot heed your prayers. That which I have to do must be done. Pedro is dead, Skipper is dead, and the hour for Larauche to die is named. Why should you be spared? You are armed with pistols, I see. Are they loaded?"

"Yes—no. I don't know," said Niamo.

"Examine them."

"Is it, then, to be a duel?" asked the Russian.

"Yes," replied Jack, "and for that purpose I set my mark upon you. Skipper, by his treachery, foiled my object, and compelled me to shoot him like a dog. You, if you will, shall die like a man."

"Your mark," faltered Niamo, touching his forehead, "do you mean this?"

"Yes, that is mine, as you know. Can you guess why I put it there?"

"No; unless——"

"Ah, I see you understand. Are your weapons loaded?"

"Yes, but the caps are damp and useless."

"Here are others—dry and good. At ten paces."

Even as the others had hoped so Niamo hoped. He was a good shot, and, at least, had as good a chance as his opponent.

He drew himself together, and took up the attitude of a practised duellist, standing sideways, and presenting as little as possible of his body to his opponent.

Broad-Arrow Jack.

A HUGE BRANCH OF A TREE LAY NEAR.—BROAD ARROW JACK USED IT AS A BATTERING RAM AND IN WENT THE DOOR.

NO. 7.

Jack paced the ground backwards ten paces, and stood still.

"Shall I," he asked, "give the word, or you?"

"I," said Niamo, eagerly. "At the word three fire."

"As you will," said Jack, carelessly.

There was an unusual light in the deep sunken eyes of Niamo as he received this advantage. Once more he examined his pistol, and carefully pressed the cap down upon the nipple.

"Are you ready?" he said.

"Yes," replied Jack.

Niamo looked Jack full in the face for the first time.

All the nerve of the man was concentrated by the one great effort he had to make.

"One!" he said.

A finger of each was put upon the trigger.

Niamo's lip quivered.

Jack was as cool and easy as he would have been standing alone.

"Two!"

The weapons were raised a few inches. Niamo's breath came quickly through his lips.

"Three!" he shrieked, and fired.

Jack winced slightly as the bullet from the Russian's weapon cut the skin of his shoulder, then took a quick aim, and pulled the trigger.

For a moment it appeared as if he had missed his mark, for the Russian stood upright, slightly rocking on his feet. But his eyes were suddenly glazed, his whole body relaxed, and he fell in a heap, with his face upon the ground.

Jack, pale but firm, advanced, and turned him over.

In the centre of the broad arrow upon the Russian's forehead was a small round hole—there the bullet had entered, and pierced his brain.

"Three," said Jack. "Half of my task is done. Is it wrong to have slain him thus? I cannot think it, for he has taken the lives of many by cunning and in secrecy, while I have killed him in fair fight. He has died the death of a man. Have I been less than just?"

He looked down upon the mass of clay from whence the life had fled, pondering awhile; then, taking it up in his arms, laid it within the cave.

Then, coming forth, he climbed up the face of the clayey cliff, and, choosing a spot, cut a strong stick, pressed it in, and made a deep hole for blasting. He emptied his powder-flask into it, rammed it well in, and drawing from his pocket a slow match fixed it in its place.

Finally he filled up the hollow with small stones and clay, pressing each one firmly into its place, and lighting the match dropped down to the ground, and withdrew to a distance to await the explosion.

It came in a minute or so. There was not much noise—a saloon-pistol would have made as much—but the face of the cliff split up, and a great mass came tumbling down over the mouth of the cave, hiding it from sight.

"He was but a brute," said Jack, as he turned away, "but I have given him the tomb of a king. It is his, and his alone. While the world lasts no other man may share it. No hireling sexton's spade shall disturb his bones. Alone he lies, even as the others lie. To each and all there shall be a grave of solitude. I have sworn it!"

CHAPTER XL.

WOBBLES THE AWENGER.

WHEN three gentlemen like Conky, Curler, and Pigeon, covet their neighbours' goods, they exert all their energies to obtain them. Wobbles had spoken of bags of gold—luscious bags of gold—bursting with sovereigns, and is it to be wondered at that these petty pilferers should have felt their desires get the better of the feeble spark of honesty which lingers even in the vilest breast?

Bags of gold!

Think of it ye youngsters with limited pocket money—ponder over it as you feel in your trousers' pockets for the shilling which vanished at least a week ago, and conceive how nice it would be if you found that some fairy had been kind and good enough to put a little linen bag full of yellow boys in its place.

A moderate-sized bag will hold a hundred sovereigns.

An ordinary sovereign will buy two hundred and forty penny tarts.

Multiply that by a hundred, and you will realise the amount of brief pleasure and dyspeptic agony you can get out of a bag of gold.

Now, Conky, Curler, and Pigeon had long been without pocket-money. They had not treated the world very kindly, perhaps; but the world had been hard upon them, the inhabitants thereof being much more liberal with kicks than halfpence to the trio, and therefore bags of gold were dear to them.

How they longed for the hour for Wobbles to lead them into those wondrous cellars—how they watched the waning day and blessed the sun for moving so slowly, and how rejoiced they were when it set at last, and the great rocks grew dim and misty in the gloom!

They were all together outside the palace, seated on the ground in a state of feverish excitement. The place was very quiet. Most of the men were sleeping, and the few who were awake lay on their backs in the great hall, smoking. There was no wind; the trees were as quiet as the rocks, and the only sound heard came from the stream as it curled and eddied over the stones.

"I hope he will come soon," said Conky, as he cast his antagonistic eyes upon the evening star. "Wobbles oughtn't to keep us waiting when there is such a shine on."

"Here he comes," said Curler; and they all held their breath.

Wobbles came out, apparently calm; but the fires of vengeance were burning within him. Had he not sworn an oath, and should he not keep it? Was he to be always trampled in the dust, and were his enemies ever to prevail? Certainly not. The hour of Wobbles' triumph was at hand.

"Now, you chaps," he said, in a whisper, "you must be werry careful, and come as quiet as you can."

"Mice shall be rampageous hanimals to us," said Pigeon.

"Our shadders will make more noise," said Curler.

"You had better take off your boots," suggested Wobbles. "It won't hurt you to walk without 'em."

They took off their boots readily—for what were boots when bags of gold were in question? Wobbles put them all in a row on a piece of rock near the edge of the stream—a proceeding which rather astonished Conky.

"What is that for?" he asked.

"Better leave 'em there," replied Wobbles. "The Boots will think you put 'em out to clean."

"Have you got a Boots?" asked Conky.

"Lots of 'em," replied Wobbles, lightly. "Now, come along! but leave your hats here, too."

"Why?"

"You will find it hot—the passages are close. Also them wisps o' things you call handkerchers."

They had no objection, and their hats and handkerchiefs were placed with the boots. Wobbles looked the very soul of triumphant cunning.

"Now," he said, "have the goodness to foller me."

In Indian file they went, Wobbles taking his cue from robbers he had seen upon the stage, and walking on the tips of his toes, the others following in the same fashion—all intensely cunning in look and action, but Wobbles the most cunning of them all.

He did not enter by the portico, but went round to the back of the house, where he showed his friends a small doorway ready open to receive them.

"Henter!" he said.

"It seems to be hawful dark," said Conky, peeping in.

"Like the cattlecombs at Kensal-green," said Curler.

"You can't expect the place to be hilluminated for you," replied Wobbles tartly; "if you are afraid to go in stop where you are, and be jiggered to you."

"Don't get so hexasperated over nothing," said Conky; "we aint a-going to funk it. Are there any steps?"

"Heleven," replied Wobbles.

He did not know the exact number, and gave this at a guess. As there happened to be thirteen Conky got a fall, and the others above him. Wobbles checked some violent utterances by assuring them that anything above a whisper would most assuredly be overheard.

He closed the door and struck a light with the good old-fashioned match that will strike anywhere regardless of a particular box, and lighted a dark lantern, which revealed a long passage chilly as a tomb.

"Go on," said Wobbles, "second door to the right."

They went on, Conky first, and found the second door to the right—a solid iron-bound door, standing half open.

"Is this the place?" asked Conky, pausing.

"That's the place," replied Wobbles.

"They don't seem to take much care of the gold."

"I've just unlocked the door," replied Wobbles. "Go in."

Conky entered—Curler and Pigeon followed him. The rays of the dark lantern were suddenly turned the other way.

"Here, show us a light!" cried Conky. "We can't see no bags of gold."

"Ha—ha! ho—ho!" yelled Wobbles, in demoniacal triumph. "Perish all of you, my henemies!"

He banged the door, and bolted it. Conky, Curler, and Pigeon uttered a simultaneous shriek, uncommonly like the cry of a cat in a trap, and made a general dash at the door.

Hard and fast.

Conky knocked the skin off his nose, Curler gave himself a black eye, and Pigeon made unto himself certain stars in the depths of his eyeballs, but the door stood firm. They were prisoners.

"What is it?" shrieked Conky, tumbling about in the darkness. "Ham it a dream? Is it real, or isn't it? Curler, are you there?"

"Yes."

"And you, Pigeon?"

"Yes, and wish I wasn't."

"Then it's all true!" cried Conky, clasping his hands in despair, "and Wobbles have done us. But perhaps he have only shut us up for a joke. It must be a joklar heffort on his part. It can't be nothing else. Oh! yes, it is a joke. Wobbles was allus a funny feller."

But neither Curler nor Pigeon answered him. The joke, if indeed it existed, was a very serious one—a practical effort on the part of the genius Wobbles which would most probably end in their all being slowly starved to death. They appreciated the performance, but could not enjoy it.

"You see," continued Conky, "it must be a joke. No man could think of shutting us up serus."

"Men think of rum things," replied Pigeon, savagely, "as you thought to-day. Do you remember suggesting that we should cut Wobbles' throat as soon as we found where the gold was, and make off with as much of it as we could carry?"

"I was only a-joking," said Conky.

"He overheard you, I think," replied Pigeon, "and this is joke for joke, and look here, as you begun this joking business first me and Curler don't mean to starve if we can help it. If no wittles don't come in a few hours, and if Wobbles really means to starve us I'm blowed if me and Curler won't turn cannibals, and eat you."

"That," said Conky, laughing feebly, "is about the best joke of the lot."

"I hope you'll find it so," replied Pigeon, calmly, "but I means it serus, and as I'm getting sharp-set already you jest think over your sins, and smooth matters—then you will take cutting up more kindly."

"Perhaps you won't find it so easy," muttered Conky, as he drew out his knife and opened it. "If any man lays a hand on me I'll finish him."

Meanwhile the cunning Wobbles had beat a retreat to the outside of the building, where he put out his lantern, and thrust it into his breast.

"I have haccomplished my hoath," he said, and went to the hall, where he found a number of the men drinking and smoking.

Nat Green was among them, and by the light of the lamp he noticed the extraordinary paleness of the avenger's face.

"What's up, Wobbles?" he asked.

"I've had a kind o' turn," replied Wobbles.

"A turn—how?"

"You remember them three chaps as was brought in to-day."

"Yes," said Nat, and more than one curious face was turned upon Wobbles—"three thievish-looking rascals."

"Well," said Wobbles, "they will never thieve any more."

"Hallo! how's that?"

"They've all chucked theirselves into the river," said Wobbles, deliberately. "I see 'em do it."

"Oh, come now," said Nat, "that won't do."

"Won't wash at all," said some of the men.

"If you won't believe me," replied Wobbles, "you must have the hevidence of your senses. I was a-coming up here when I see 'em all take off their boots and hats and neckties, put 'em down in a row, then hembrace each other like brothers as was parting for hever, and go head-fust into the river."

"It's an odd story," said Nat.

"Come and look at their boots, hats, and neckties," said Wobbles.

Nat was puzzled, and the others also, and they went out in a body.

There, sure enough, were the articles of apparel Wobbles had named.

"You see," he said, "it's true enough. I haven't deceived you in any way."

"Yes," said Nat, "these are the boots and the hats and the neckties, but it doesn't follow that the men are in the river."

"But I see 'em go in all head-fust," urged Wobbles.

"Very likely," replied Nat; "but, nevertheless, I fancy the chief will look into this business. I twigged you fellows together, and it was easy to recognise you were old friends."

"That's it!" cried Wobbles, despairing. "Go it. Be down on me as was hever hinoffensive. Say that I chucked 'em in the river. Do what you like—say what you like. Go it! Everybody's down on me!"

"I'm not down on you," said Nat; "but if that lot of beggars pitched themselves into the river I'm the Great Mogul of Tartary!"

"Then you don't believe me?"

"No, I don't. In short, you are a liar!"

Wobbles groaned. A conviction of the truth came upon him. In his exceeding cunning he had over-reached himself.

CHAPTER XLI.

CALIBAN AND HIS CHIEF.

WHEN Broad Arrow Jack learnt from the lips of Maggie of the escape of Jaundice he gave no thought of Caliban, nor of the wealth he had in his charge. Maggie, as we know, was ignorant of her husband's theft, and could, therefore, make no allusion to it. Had she known of it, Jeb Jaundice would never have been allowed to leave with his ill-gotten gains.

But he was gone, and for nearly twenty-four hours the dumb diamond-polisher lay in a state of stupefaction. Then reason and knowledge returned, and the memory of recent events came upon him with terrible force.

At first he only thought of the escape of the prisoner, and that was enough to turn him into a wild beast; but one glance at his bench told him that he had lost more than the man who had been left in his charge. Then his fury became demoniacal.

Whenever he was under the influence of any emotion Caliban danced, and all his uncouth actions were powerfully expressive of the nature of the chords touched within him. There was murder in every movement—the promise of remorseless cruelty in every twist and turn of his huge mis-shapen limbs. He understood all.

This hideous brute, with true brutish instincts, had known from the first moment he met Maggie that she was a woman.

Her disguise did not deceive him, although it was so successful in imposing upon so many men very much higher in the scale of humanity, and, knowing her, Caliban fell in love.

It may seem incredible, but it is, nevertheless, true that Caliban not only loved, but fancied he was loved in return. Maggie smiled so sweetly upon him, and was so indifferent to the prisoner, Jeb Jaundice, he could not think otherwise.

But now he saw how he had been fooled, and in addition to the anger, arising from being outwitted in his capacity of gaoler, he had the mortification of finding in his prisoner—as he believed—a successful rival.

Therefore Caliban danced a dance full of vengeful fury.

When it was over he went out in search of his chief, but Jack was away, and did not return for three days.

All through the daylight Caliban lay upon a high rock watching for his coming back, and at last he came, bringing with him the three men, Conky, Curler, and Pigeon.

Caliban followed Jack into the hall, and knocked at his door. He was desired to enter, and presented himself before his chief.

"Well," said Jack, "and what brings you here? What do you want?"

The dumb man intimated that he wished Jack to come out with him.

"Where to? Is it to your den? It is needless. I know your prisoner has escaped."

"But that is not all," the expressive eyes of Caliban replied.

Jack guessed the truth, and a terrible frown overspread his face.

"You have been robbed," he said.

Caliban made a despairing gesture, and threw himself upon his knees. He expected nothing less than immediate death. It was the penalty promised him when Jeb Jaundice was placed in his hands.

Drawing his cutlass Jack raised it, and for a moment it seemed as if he would strike, but he sheathed it again, and turned away.

"No," he said, "I cannot kill you. Go, and let me never see your face again!"

A great cry came from Caliban—a prayer not to be cast off. No words could be more expressive, but Jack was firm.

"No," he said, "I can never trust you again. By dawn to-morrow you must be gone. After then you will be treated as an enemy. You understand?"

He understood, and the bright pleading look in his eyes died away to the sullen fire of dogged resolve. Yes, he would go to find the man and woman who had deceived him, and wreak his vengeance upon them. Then he would return, to ask no better fate than to die by the hand of his chief.

Jack had no more to say—he did not even look at his uncouth servitor again—and Caliban went out with his eyes fixed straight before him. He paid a brief visit to his late home, where he gathered a few necessaries together, and turned his steps over the plain, following, by a curious instinct, in the track Jeb Jaundice had taken.

Meanwhile Jack sent for Billy Brisket, and imparted to him the story of this double loss, which made Billy very hot and furious—the more so as it was a painful fact that the prisoner had succeeded in eluding the vigilant search of all the scouts despatched to find him.

"The dog—the hound!" said Billy. "To think that he should get away with his life, and fortune to boot! Tra, la, la! Oh! confound him! When the mill blows, then the wind goes—I'm all upside down!"

"I do not see how he is to escape, or the Ogre either," replied Jack. "Our circle is complete—every avenue is watched."

"True; but it seems odd we have found no trace of him."

"None at all?"

"None."

"To-morrow we will take up the pursuit again."

So it was arranged; but in the middle of the night a horseman, covered with dust, and riding a panting steed, came up through the forest. He was challenged as he came, and gave the pass-words. He was one of them, and at the palace asked for the chief.

"He is sleeping," said the guard.

"I have news of importance," was the reply.

"Will it not wait till the morning?"

"No; and, if you value your life, let me pass, or rouse him, and say that I—Hans Breimich—am here."

It was dangerous to delay the transmission of a message so pressing, and Jack was aroused. Half a dozen torches were lighted, and he and the messenger stood face to face.

"What brings you here, Hans?" he asked.

"Sad news, my chief. The German band at the Granite Pass have turned traitors."

"Indeed!" said Jack, calmly, "Then they shall be punished. But you were of that band—how is it you are not with them?"

"Because I have been true to you, chief," was the proud reply. "I was asked to join them, but I declined, and they were debating how to kill me when I mounted my horse and fled. They chased me many miles, but my horse outstripped theirs, and I am here."

"You have done well. Why have your countrymen revolted?"

Hans paused, and looked at the men around. He had something to communicate which was not for their ears. Taking a torch in his hand, Jack bade the German follow him to his own apartment. Then he thrust the light into an iron ring in the wall, and bade Hans go on.

"Two nights ago," said Hans, "I was on duty in the pass when I saw two men skulking by. I gave the alarm, and instantly they were surrounded and captured. I saw we had gained a prize—they were the two men described to us as the Ogre and Jeb Jaundice."

Jack started, and looked up with more interest than he had hitherto shown. This news was unexpected, and he bade Hans proceed.

"They yielded without fighting," he said, "and were apparently resigned to the capture. Jeb Jaundice was quite gay with the men, and told them the story of his imprisonment and escape from here. Whether that story was true or not I cannot tell."

"What was his story?"

"He said he was imprisoned in a secret chamber where you kept your wealth—described by him as the wealth of a nation. From thence he escaped, first slaying his goalers, and stowing about his person your most valuable jewels. These, he declared, are safely hidden in a place known only to himself."

"He robbed me of much," said Jack, but his plunder is not so great as he would have you think."

"Be that as it may, the men believed him, and, as I think, during my absence he promised them an immediate share. So they told me, and when I lifted up my voice against the traitorous project then dawning, I was told to wait as long as I liked for your promise—they had something better in hand. Jaundice had also given them some jewels, as earnest of what was to come."

"And with that they let him and his companion go?"

"My chief, they have gone with them, and messengers have been sent to beat up recruits. 'We will gather men around us,' said the Ogre, 'and teach this saucy boy a lesson that shall go deeper into his memory than that brand upon his back.'"

Jack paced to and fro with quick footsteps. This was news of startling import indeed. Some of his plans threatened to be thwarted by the disaffection of these traitorous Germans.

"Hans—Hans," he said, "you told me your men were true!"

"True while they had an interest in your cause," replied Hans. "I warned you they were mercenary."

"So you did."

"And while they had your promise only before them they were firm. The sight of ready wealth was too much for them. It was a monotonous life, my chief."

"It was," replied Jack, eyeing him keenly. "You were tired of it."

"Oh! no. I could never weary in your service."

"You profess well. But to return to your false friends. Whither have they gone?"

"They are making for the coast, my chief," replied Hans, looking down.

Jack paused in his walking, and fixed his eyes upon the German. The man seemed to shrink under his gaze.

"Hans, you are lying."

"My chief, I—I lie to you!"

"Yes, to me."

Jack went to the door and threw it open, "Without there," he cried, "a guard of honour for a traitor."

A dozen men rushed into the room and surrounded the trembling Hans. He turned a livid face towards Jack, but his eyes quickly fell.

"Search him," said our hero.

"My chief I have nothing, I swear it," he cried. "Search him."

It was quickly done, and half a score rare jewels were laid before Jack, who turned them over and examined them carefully.

"These," he said, "I think, are mine."

"I fled with them," said Hans. "I—I was obliged to take my share to—to—get away with the jews, and——"

"Enough, you have been bold in coming here," interrupted Jack; "but weak in thinking you had the power to deceive. Comrades, he is a traitor. You know how to deal with him."

Hans threw himself upon his knees, and shrieked for help. "I am guilty," he yelled; "but if my life is spared, I will confess all."

"I never trust a second time," was Jack's reply; "remove him."

They carried him out, writhing in mortal fear, and bore him into the wood. For awhile his shrieks echoed in the night air; but, ere long, the steady tramp of returning men was the only sound that broke the stillness, and Hans the traitor was dangling lifeless from a tree.

CHAPTER XLII.
THE TENTH OF JUNE.

THE spirit of lawlessness increased in the land. Throughout all the vast country in which our story is laid the evil passions of men ran rampant. The wrongs of Broad Arrow Jack had long been imperfectly known—vague rumours and positive assertions twisted and turned the story into many shapes. Some said he had been maimed and scarred by his enemies until his appearance was too revolting for him to appear in public, while others were equally certain that he had never been injured at all.

"He is a rowdy," they said, "with a lie upon his lips, who, while pretending to avenge his wrongs, lives by plunder and murder.

But, divided as they were as to the justness of his cause, and the honour of his conduct, they were one as to the power he possessed, for in every quarter there were bands of men well armed, well mounted, and bearing on their garments the crest of their chief—the Broad Arrow, worked in gold.

No act of lawlessnes had ever been committed by these men, but the people doubted, and whispers were abroad of their being like the Thugs in India— base and treacherous—doing their work stealthily and surely.

It is astonishing how people hold to wrong ideas. The tenacity they display in keeping a grasp upon falsehood and error is perfectly marvellous, and this idea of Broad Arrow Jack having once got into their minds took root and flourished. The squatter in his hut, the diamond-seeker in the fields, the hunter on the plains, learnt to look upon our hero as a scoundrel of the first water.

Perhaps the idea gathered strength from his not having been seen by others than his men—and some of these could not boast of having been in his presence, but their fellows had—and at the time of the escape of the Ogre and Jeb Jaundice there were many ready to take up arms against the brave young fellow if a leader could be found.

"Who is this fellow?" said some, "to come here with all the idle vagabonds of the earth, to shut up the mountain-passes, parade the plains, and challenge us as we come and go, saying—go here, or go there. Who is he? What is he?"

None could tell, but ignorance and fear continued to fan the flame of dislike, and when it was known that an antagonistic party was being established, men who had idle hands began to inquire their way to it, and to flock thither.

This power was the Ogre. With a nucleus of men formed of the traitorous Germans, he began his task of opposition. His old bravado and dogged courage came back with freedom and power, and, having established himself in a secure camp among the hills, he sent out his messengers.

And this was the substance of the message they carried—

"This Broad Arrow Jack is nothing more than a brigand. By means of reckless crimes and cunning he has acquired vast wealth, and lives in kingly splendour at a place he calls Black Rock. Come and root him out! The work will pay you well— there is loot for thousands! A bold and fearless leader calls you!"

The agents were successful, and men began to flock in. Within a week the Ogre had more than a hundred black sheep in his flock—good murderous scoundrels—ripe for anything so that it paid

Efforts were also made to corrupt some more of Jack's men; but the return of one agent with the intelligence that he had seen a brother agent introduced to a piece of rope, and elevated to the branch of a tree, checked their energies in that direction.

The home of the Ogre was almost impregnable. It was formed on a small piece of table-land, with precipitous cliffs on every side except one, where a narrow path wound up from the valley below. At the summit it was only wide enough to admit of two men going abreast; and here rough earthworks were thrown up, and covers made for riflemen, who could easily decimate a strong assaulting party. As a place simply for defence it was secure.

The one thing needful in case of attack was provisions—a fact recognised by the Ogre, and his first act was to get in such stores as he could obtain by means of the chase or plunder—he was not particular which.

"Take everything that comes in your way," he said to his ferocious followers, "and say it is wanted for Broad Arrow Jack."

Far and wide plundering was carried on; but all they obtained gave them few comforts. They had no tents, scarce a change of clothing, and only the roughest food.

The Ogre, Jeb Jaundice, and all the men slept upon the ground, and ate and drank like brutes.

The life suited the Ogre in his present mood. Jeb Jaundice was tired of it from the beginning; but he stood in awe of his leader, and said nothing. Every day he cursed the hour that threw them together again, and sighed for an opportunity to leave him and his surroundings.

It was strange they should meet; but, in making his escape from Black Rock, their chosen paths crossed, and they met. Jaundice, in a fit of indiscretion, told of the prize he had secured, and was called upon to share it with the other.

Had he dared he would have refused; but the Ogre was not to be trifled with, and, the spoil being divided, they travelled on together until they fell into the hands of the treacherous Germans. How Jaundice worked upon them we know.

At first he only hoped to be allowed to escape, but the Ogre saw a prospect of carrying out a cherished dream, and, ignoring the entreaties of Jeb, he began his task, gathering men about him as already described.

He was a good general, and for nearly three weeks his haunt remained undiscovered. Finally, however, the trusty agents of our hero found out his retreat, and carried the report to their chief.

Jack gave orders for a hundred men to be ready in two days, equipped and provisioned for a week's service. Meanwhile he had an intermediate task to perform.

The tenth of June—the birthday of Laranche—was at hand.

CHAPTER XLIII.

THE FATAL DAY.

THE ninth of June came, and Laranche was still lying at the store of the late Jereboam Bounce, ill more in mind than body. The men of Hookey Settlement were not unkind to him, but they were but rough nurses, and poor administrators of consolation at the best, and Laranche progressed but slowly.

There was one man who was more attentive than the rest, and it was to him that the Frenchman confided the story of the wrongs of Broad Arrow Jack, and how he had so far avenged them. This man was an Englishman, named Trimmer—a reckless, careless dog, who apparently never troubled himself about the past, present, or future. The story amused him—he laughed at the notion of a number of men being terrified by the threats of one, who, in years at least, was little more than a boy.

"But," said Laranche, "you shall laugh anoder vay ven you shall see dis boy. He is a giant, he is impregnable, you can neider shoot, nor stab, nor kill him. He shall be more dan mortal. I swear it."

"I'd like to give him the lie," replied Trimmer. "Let me have a shot at him at ten paces with a pistol, or sixty with a rifle, and I will show to you how to end him and your funk together."

Laranche shook his head, and sighed.

"You do not know," he said; "you talk about the impossible."

"I've heard a deal about him," said Trimmer, "but not in the light you put him. He's got a lot of men at his back, and goes about marauding."

"No—no!"

"But I say it is so."

"You talk idly," said Laranche. "Who has he robbed—who but me and my comrades have suffered by him? He left us when we branded him, without a sou, and now, see—he comes back with wealth and power. Ah! it is not like life—it is not real. He is more than man."

"I once read a story about a chap as sold himself for vengeance," said Trimmer, reflectively—"sold himself to the old 'un, but of course I didn't believe it. The devil need not buy them—they are only too ready to give themselves up to him."

"Something in dat, friend Trimmer, but he may buy some people."

"So he may, and this Broad Arrow Jack chap may be one of them."

"He is great—he is terrible!" cried Laranche, with sudden terror, "and to-morrow he will come for me."

"Why wait for him? Cut and run for it," suggested Trimmer.

"Where to?" asked Laranche, with a haggard look.

"Oh, anywhere!" said Trimmer. "Clear out and hide."

"Useless—all useless," replied Laranche, despairingly. "I know it is so; I feel it. I have that within me which cannot lie, and it says, 'Flee if it shall please you; but, go where you will, this avenger shall find and slay you.'"

"It's odd," returned Trimmer; "but I think funk is a great friend to him. I don't want to mix myself up in another man's quarrels, but, if you like, I'll stand by you until this birthday of yours is over, and if he really shows himself I'll have a go in at him."

"He will kill you."

"In that case there will be an end of me and my pilgrimage in this world. It won't matter much. I never did any good, and never shall. Kicked out of school, turned away from home, I apprenticed myself to the vagabond trade, and became a master of the business before my teens were out."

"Ah, it is good of you," replied Laranche. "But vat shall you do ven he vill come? He is a giant; he is proof against shot, and laughs at steel. Ah! vat shall you do?"

"I have a plan," said Trimmer—"a very good one. Suppose you bolt, as I said, and I'll get into bed with a six-shooter and bowie ready. The moment he enters I'll let fly at him, and chance the rest."

A faint ray of hope dawned on the Frenchman's face. The plan at least offered a chance of escape. He embraced it.

"It is kind—it is good of you," he said. "At dark I will crawl away as I can, and you shall take my place. You shall be kept in my memory green——"

"All right," said Trimmer, indifferently; "it will be something for me to do. You had better get into my clothes, and I'll put on yours, ready to clear out if it comes to a bolt."

Laranche got out of bed, and, gaining strength from hope and excitement, dressed himself in Trimmer's garments, and Trimmer put on those of the Frenchman.

The latter were rather foppishly cut, and on the figure of Trimmer, which was of the burly order, looked inexpressibly ridiculous.

Shortly after the night set in Larauche stole forth like a wary fox stealing from a wood when the hounds are nigh. All was dark, and the only noise that broke the stillness of the night came from one of the Hookey settlers, who, in drunken solitude, was singing, or rather howling, the burden of a sentimental song.

He chose the north star for a guide, and moved on out of the settlement with the stealthy footstep of a cat. Once a small animal, or something light of tread, went by him, but that was all. Unseen, unheard, as he hoped, he got clear away, and once on the plain increased his pace to a trot.

All thoughts of his recent illness died away. The dim prospect of escape gave him strength, and all the night long he kept on, pausing but once to drink and lave his face in a brook faintly glimmering in the starlight.

Towards dawn he came to a rising ground, broken in places, so that he had carefully to pick his way. It was strange to him, and had, as far as he could see, no beaten path, but he kept on. Any road was better than none, so that it but led away from the place he had recently left.

As he progressed slowly upwards a stone occasionally slipped, and rolled down into the plain, some of the larger ones falling with a noise which echoed far away. The ear of one practised in following a human trail would have wanted no better guide.

Larauche did not believe he was followed. He could not see how any man could have traced him in the darkness; but the sound of the falling stones made him tremble, and increased his caution so that he felt his way inch by inch, testing each fragment of rock before he put his foot upon it.

His progress was necessarily slow, and tremendously laborious. It soon began to tell terribly upon him, and every minute or so he was obliged to pause and rest.

"Ah! it shall be terrible," he muttered. "Anoder night like dis and I should die. Ah! vat is dat?"

A stone rolling below as others had done; with him the dread thought that he was followed after all came over him, and the chilly dew of fear burst out upon his forehead.

He was sitting down when the portentous sound came upon his ear, and his first impulse was to get upon his feet and fly madly on; but his limbs, weakened by sickness and fatigue, refused to move, and kept him on the spot.

What was death to what he endured then?

All the agony that fear can give was his, and presently there came to him the sound of stealthy footsteps. Somebody was coming up.

But who was it?

He would have been glad to believe it to be nothing worse than some beast of the forest, or some or lintry plunderer coming in search of prey, but he knew it was neither of them. Something told him it was Broad Arrow Jack.

Up—up came the footsteps to within fifty yards of him, and then ceased. Bending forward with staring eyes he tried to catch a glimpse of the much dreaded form, but the darkest hour—that just before the dawn—was on the earth, and he could see nothing but the profoundest gloom.

He dared not—could not move, and there he sat until the first flash of sunlight dispersed the stars, and gave outline to the things on earth. He was watching the sky when it came, and as we turn in lonely places expecting to look upon some dreaded form, so he turned and bent his eyes below.

Too true. His heart had not lied to him. There was the tall majestic form of Broad Arrow Jack coming slowly upwards towards him, and bounding down on his homeward way was the swift-footed Tiger, who had been our hero's guide throughout the night.

When Larauche left the village Jack and the Tiger, who had arrived in the vicinity some hours before, left it too, with scarce a dozen paces between them, the Tiger, close up to the doomed man, holding one end of a thin cord, with which he guided his master, who held the other.

So they journeyed, and never once was the wondrous Tiger at fault. With the eyes of his namesake he kept the quarry in view, and ne'er left it until the dawn released him, and then in obedience to a sign from Jack he sped away.

Larauche could not speak, but he made an effort to flee. Rising, he ran forward a few paces, and found himself upon the edge of a yawning gulf, which ran to the right and left. On both sides the ground was too broken for him to travel fast—with Jack behind him there was no escape. He had fallen into a trap of his own seeking.

"Mon Dieu!" he said, "how shall I be saved?"

The cry was too late—his doom was sealed. Broad Arrow Jack advanced, seized him by the collar, swung him over the precipice, and, kneeling down, held him dangling there.

CHAPTER XLIV.

MR. TRIMMER'S QUEST.

MR. TRIMMER lay in the Frenchman's bed, watching and waiting patiently for the coming of Broad Arrow Jack. Accustomed to take all things philosophically, he was not at all irritated as hour after hour passed and nobody appeared. On the contrary he became more easy and comfortable under the conviction that each moment brought him nearer to the time when they should meet.

"All I want is one shot at him," he thought; "if I miss, then let him bring me down."

He had no animosity against Jack, having never seen him; but the extraordinary surroundings of our hero, his wrongs, his mysterious power, his revenge upon his enemies, raised him above the common run of men, and Mr. Trimmer desired to have a shot at him as a bold hunter longs to bring down a strange animal he hears of.

But the night passed, and Trimmer was still waiting for him who never came. At last he arose, gave himself a wash, carelessly tied a necktie round his throat, and went to the door.

The gray light of morning lit up the plain; but, far as the eye could see, no living thing was moving. The scattered huts of the settlement were quiet; even the vocal gentleman had given in shortly before sunrise, and gone to sleep with his head in a bag of nails and a broken bottle comfortably arranged under his spine. Trimmer was impressed with the beauty of the hour, and for a moment the picture of his childhood's home rose dimly before him, but he thrust it back into the storehouse of his memory, and lounged coolly and carelessly up the settlement.

"I guess," he said, "as this Broad Arrow Jack would not come to me, I'll go to him; but which way? Some say he is to be found in the east, and others in the west. A pretty wide difference between them two points of the compass—couldn't well have wider. I don't know which way to go. When in doubt, toss up."

He took an old battered penny from his pocket, kept by him for that purpose of gambling. "Head is west, tails east," he said, and sent it spinning in the air.

It came down on its edge, and stuck in a damp place in an upright position. Mr. Trimmer regarded it with a thoughtful eye.

"You were always a knowing cuss," he said, shaking his head at it. "No mint ever forged a copper that could take you in my beauty. You know the rig of 'em as they pass, and unless you are in a mind to aggravate me you go wrong; but when you go down yourself, how cunning you are!

Nobody could ever tell your ring. Speak up, and tell me what you mean by getting perversely on your edge like that?"

He tilted his hat over his left ear, and thought out the important question. The answer came to him in something under ten minutes.

"I've got it," he said; "this Broad Arrow boy is to be found neither east nor west. It's either north or south. So up you go again. Heads for north, and tails for south."

The coin came down flat with the head uppermost, but striking a small pebble, it skipped up, and turning over, presented the other side to the eyes of its master.

"Oh! you artful beggar," growled Trimmer, nonplussed; "perhaps you wouldn't mind letting me know what game this is. You've done me and you know it. It's very clever, but it puts me in a fix. I can't tell what point of the compass to work in. Blarm you for a beggarly copper! You do anything like this again, and I'll promote another to your place; and, mind you, I'll take good care you never deceive another man, for I'll chuck you into the river. See if I don't."

Putting the coin into his pocket, he shut his eyes, turned round twice, and went straight on. Without a guide he was obliged to trust entirely to chance.

Chance stood his friend.

He had not travelled far before he saw a slight figure approaching him at a great rate, and presently he saw that it was a negro boy, whom he had seen two or three times before, and knew as the Tiger, living in Peaceful Village. Here was an opportunity for obtaining information, and Mr. Trimmer embraced it.

"Hallo! you imp, come here!" he cried.

The imp fearlessly approached within a half-dozen paces, where he pulled up grinning.

"Dat you, Massa Trimmy?" he said; "how bout de tail ob Massa Nibble horse dat you cut off in spite?"

"What do you mean?" asked Trimmer, slightly flushing. "Who says I did it? Come now, out with it, and let me know the party."

"In de night you come," replied the Tiger, "sneak, sneaking up, wif big knife in your hand, gib one great slash, get de tail off, tie big stone to him, and drop him in de riber."

"I'll have your life if you go about telling them lies," cried Trimmer.

"No lies, Massa Trimmy, all de trufe," said the Tiger, shaking his head.

"Who see me do it?"

"Me did, massa, wif de one eye dat I nober close, me see you do it."

Trimmer's face was a spectacle. For a few moments he seemed to be struggling with a very sour gooseberry, but he got it down at last, and resumed his ordinary calm exterior.

"Well, Tiger," he said, "I don't deny it to you, seeing as it's no use; but you keep quiet, or I'll riddle you. D'ye hear?"

The Tiger nodded coolly and contemptuously. He had no fear of being riddled by anybody.

"Can you tell me where to find this chap they are all talking about? Broad Arrow Jack."

The Tiger nodded his head and laughed.

"Yes, massa," he said; "but me not going to do it."

"Oh, yes, you will!"

"No, massa, agin orders dat am; you wish to see him, me lead you dere."

"All right, lead on."

"Hab de eye blindfolded first," said the Tiger.

"Oh! come, that's gammon, you'll be up to some trick."

The Tiger became very demure, and looked as if he and tricks had ever been strangers.

"Massa Trimmy," he said—"Massa Broad Arrow Jack am my massa. and it am him orders dat all be blindfolded dat come to de camp."

"Then it aint far away?" replied Trimmer.

The boy looked at him with indescribable cunning, and winked his right eye.

"Wedder de way be short or long," he said, "you know it when you got dere."

"You're a promising chick," said Trimmer; "but here, tie my eyes up. Anything for a novelty; but if any of my old chums come along and see me being led by a nigger, they'll think I've gone right off my head at last."

"Me lead you out ob de way ob eberybody," said the Tiger.

Mr. Trimmer then submitted himself to the hands of the Tiger, who blindfolded him so skilfully that there was no chance of his getting a peep of the ground even. The next moment Trimmer felt his brace of pistols whisked out of his belt.

"Hallo, you imp!" he roared, "what are you doing?"

"Massa Trimmy," said the Tiger, firmly, "don't touch de handkercher, please, or me must fire at you. Keep de hand down and come quietly--den you am safe; up wif eben a lilly finger, and you will hab one ob your own bullets in your back."

"Well, this is a neat fix," growled Trimmer; "fancy me being took in in this way."

"And yet you am so bery cleber," said the Tiger sarcastically.

"I'll never think so again," replied Trimmer; "from this hour I sets myself down as the darndest fool that ever wore a pair of bad boots—go on, I'll follow."

"No, Massa Trimmer," said the Tiger, gently, "you first, me just behind, so dat I hab clean shoot when you come any ob your tricks. A lilly more to de right, den straight on."

With his hands in his pockets, Mr. Trimmer moved forward. Fate had brought him into a very humiliating position—one, in fact, he could not fight against without coming out second best, and he bore it as he had born many other ups and downs in life.

The Tiger was quiet, cool, and determined. Ever on the alert he guided his prisoner with the sound of his voice, keeping him on the even ground, and clear of all obstacles. Surely a stranger pair were never looked upon.

But although the Tiger was grave, he had a practical joke in hand, and instead of making for Black Rock, he guided Trimmer back by the way he came—up to the very place he started from, skilfully keeping him clear of the hut. The hour was late, but the settlers were still asleep, and the Tiger was able to carry out his little plot successfully.

"You must be tired, massa," he cried, "sit down."

"I don't know that I'm particularly tired," replied Trimmer, "but I should like something to drink."

"Me get it den," replied the Tiger.

He sped away without a sound, and flew rapidly over the plain, leaving Trimmer by himself. There he sat for awhile wondering what had become of his cunning companion, and debating within himself what would be the result if he removed the handkerchief. Finally he decided it was not worth the risk, as the Tiger might be foxing near, and sat still.

"May be," he thought, "I'm already in the camp of this Broad Arrow Jack, and this imp have gone to fetch him. If so, everything is uncommonly quiet."

How long he would have sat there it is difficult to say, for he endured half an hour of it with perfect philosophy, but an interruption came in the form of the settler who had been exceedingly drunk over night, and awaking somewhat feverish, came out to get a little fresh air.

When he saw Trimmer squatted in the middle of the rough road, with his eyes blindfolded, he thought that he was blessed with a novel form of delirium tremens, and began to curse his luck which never would allow him to keep drunk for more than a onth at a time without bringing on him a lot o disagreeable visions, and divers aches and pains. Trimmer heard his curses, and spoke—

"Who is that?" he asked.

"Me, Bob Porter," replied the settler.

"Bob Porter!" exclaimed Trimmer, "why, who brought you here?"

"That's good," said Bob, "do you think I want to lie in bed all day?"

"Lie in bed—what bed? Does he give you beds?"

"He—who?" asked Bob Porter. "You've gone off your head, old man."

"Where's the Tiger?" asked Trimmer.

"I aint seen no tigers—no lions, and no helephants," replied Bob Porter—"nothing but a jackass sitting in the middle of the road with a handkerchief over his eyes, like a kid playing blind-man's buff."

Trimmer's eyes were opened, and snatching off the handkerchief, he beheld the familiar home of his manhood. He neither cursed nor swore, but a faint smile flickered about his mouth as he got upon his feet.

"That boy is a clever cuss," he said; "but when next we meet I'll put something about his head and eyes as shall last him as long as he lives."

"You seem to have been done somehow," said Bob Porter.

"I've been done anyhow and everyhow," replied Trimmer; "but I'll take it out of Broad Arrow Jack when I meets him. You see if I don't."

And while the words were on his lips the noise of horses came upon his ear. Turning, he beheld about fifty horsemen approaching.

"Who the tarnation is this?" he asked.

"May be it's Broad Arrow Jack," replied Bob Porter, "and now's your time to go in for him."

CHAPTER XLV.

THE LAST OF LARANCHE.

SWINGING to and fro in the grasp of Broad Arrow Jack, Laranche looked upon the last scene he was ever to see on earth. He would have cried out, but his tongue clave to his mouth, and he could only hear and not answer the words of the avenger.

"Cowardly, treacherous, remorseless dog! think of the past and repent! Not for myself alone do I hold you here. This is but a fitting climax to a long list of crimes. But for one deed of yours, I would have given you the same chance as others for their lives. I would have met you in fair fight, but think of the sailor boy who came to seek his brother in the diamond-fields. He crossed your path. You remember him?"

Laranche could only groan. He had no words at command.

"If you had not come here by the decree of fate," pursued Jack, "I would have dragged you to a place as good for my purpose. I had designed, arranged everything, but you of your own free will have come hither. Here is your harvest field—here in a few brief moments you will reap all you have sown for years."

Again the Frenchman groaned, and he strove to raise his arms appealingly, but his strength was gone, and they sank lifeless by his side.

"But to the story of the sailor boy," said Jack, "who seven years ago came, as I said, to seek his brother. He was an orphan, but had rich friends who would have taken care of him. He preferred an independent life, even as his brother had done, and came here to seek him. You met him on his way, spoke kindly to him, lured him with soft words, and as he slept by your side upon the hills plundered him. The act of theft aroused him, and with true courage in his young heart he sprang upon you and cast you down. The struggle was long, although it was boy to man, and you were bruised and beaten as a dog, like you should have been. At last you conquered and got him helpless and bound. What did you do then?"

At last Laranche found his tongue, and answered—

"It is all false! I never knew the boy!"

"He wore a ring," said Jack, "which you dragged from his finger, breaking the flesh in your cruel haste. The work of plunder done, you dragged him to such a precipice as this, swung him over, and left him hanging there—living food for carrion birds."

"Hear me—it shall not be true!" groaned Laranche. "Nay, hear me!"

"That ring," said Jack, "I found among other of your ill-gotten gains brought to me by my trusty messenger, the Tiger, who was an eye-witness to your crime, as he has been to many others. His restless wild spirit kept him ever on the trail of one or the other of you and your villainous comrades. I had wrongs enough of my own to put right, without this; but such are the wondrous ways of fate. Edmund Maurice, my old schoolfellow, murdered cruelly—unseen, as you thought—is to be avenged by me!"

"It is not true! Hear me, and you shall see it!" shrieked Laranche.

"What he must have suffered you now know for the first time," said Jack. "Look down upon your grave, and think of it."

"It is all a lie!" said Laranche. "I never shall see de boy!"

Jack's mouth compressed, and, looking down into the face of the Frenchman, he made another appeal to him.

"I beseech you," he said, "to confess all! Die not with a falsehood on your tongue!"

"If I confess," cried Laranche, "shall you give me my life?"

"You have confessed to me," replied Jack. "It is enough."

"And you will spare me?"

"No!"

A wild shriek rang out from the doomed man's lips, and, gathering his strength anew, he clutched wildly at the face of the rock. His wild despair—his frantic efforts—were horrible to look upon, and Jack, with a sickening heart, felt something like compunction dawning in his breast. Was it worth while to kill this wretched brute—would it not be better to let him live? But while he debated within his mind the collar of the Frenchman's coat gave way, and he fell.

The rock was not quite perpendicular at the top, but sloped precipitously, and Laranche, instead of falling clear, slid down the face of it at a tremendous pace.

No more awful sight than his mad efforts to save himself was ever seen. He clawed, he bit, as he slid down—now head first, now feet first—until he came with a thud upon a huge stone half imbedded in the cliff. It gave way with his weight, but not before he had grasped it with the death-grip of despair, and together he and the stone bounded into the air.

Once they turned together, and then struck the ground fifty feet below, Laranche undermost, with all that was human in form and spirit crushed out of him.

So died Laranche—as cruel a murderer as ever lived on earth. Of his earlier history we have given only a brief glimpse; but the fate he met with was well merited—a hundred dark crimes lay upon his soul.

All that Jack told him and others of their crimes was true, as also was the declaration that he avenged others as well as himself.

He would, no doubt, have dealt more mercifully with them if the dark catalogue of their deeds had never been unfolded to him; but many and many an evening, while his plans were ripening, he had listened to the stories of the Tiger—told with an unmistakable air of truth—until his blood ran swiftly with hate, and all the passionate fires lighted by his wrongs blazed up with treble fury.

Such as are necessary for the purpose of my story I have told; but there were many others of terrible purport told in the twilight by the Tiger which equalled anything revealed in these pages in atrocity and utter remorselessness.

Often, in his first days at Black Rock, Jack longed to rush out at once, and deal death and destruction to the band of brutes in Peaceful Village; but the prudent counsels of Billy Brisket restrained him.

"Make all sure," he said. "Get your net well spread before you frighten your fish."

Billy Brisket was a business man, and arranged all matters of supplies. Jack alone reserved to himself the right of choosing the men; but there was little picking or choosing in it. He accepted all comers, and moulded most of them to his will. The only exception was found in the Germans who had betrayed his cause by following the Ogre and Jaundice.

It may be thought that all these preparations were unnecessary to crush half a dozen men—and certainly they would have been for the most part superfluous if it had been the purpose of Jack merely to kill; but mere slaughter was not in his designs. Pedro, Skipper, and Niamo had each and all been treated with fairness. It was as much as they could expect, and more than they deserved, to be treated according to the code of honour of the day.

Many a nobly-born man has brought the same fate upon himself by a word or a look—a fate truly undeserved and revolting. Duelling, as it was practised some fifty years ago, was simply polite murder. The young and inexperienced were often called out by old and practised hands, and shot down with as much coolness and deliberation as a crack shot shows at Hurlingham with a pigeon.

That was one business, and Broad Arrow Jack's another. At home our laws would have punished the wrongdoers; but, in the primitive land I write of, men at that time had to be their own judge, jury, and executioner.

To return. So well did Billy Brisket arrange things that every want of the band was supplied. A trusty agent disposed of the stones sent to him—some of them in the rough, and others cut by Caliban—and in return sent all that was needed on to Black Rock, and from thence other supplies were despatched to the various bands of men guarding the mountain passes or patrolling the plains.

Of the actual amount of the resources at the command of our hero it is unnecessary to say more at present than that they were more than ample, and freely given by Billy Brisket.

Once Jack spoke his thanks in no measured terms; but Billy declared he would run away if ever he heard the like again. The subject was, therefore, dropped; but the deep sense of his obligation was ever upon our hero. The simple honest pedlar was, in his thoughts, the dearest of friends, and the only one he had now left on earth.

As for the pedlar, he was so bound up in Jack that he had not one selfish thought apart from him. To live with him, and to die for him if need be, was all he asked; and his enthusiasm went a great way towards increasing that of the men.

Jack's wrongs were his wrongs—Jack's wants his wants—and all he hoped for was that the day would come when Jack would have a joy to share with him, too; but from the hour that Cecil died he had never felt the sweet emotion of happiness, or tasted aught but the contents of the cup of sorrow—and that he had drained to the dregs.

What was to come out of their present life the pedlar could not tell. He could only wait and hope, doing his best for the brave youth, aiding him in all things, giving up all to his cause with a generosity the world has seldom seen.

CHAPTER XLVI.
SPECTRES.

WOBBLES was scarcely the man to execute a diabolical deed without some qualms of conscience, and as soon as he had time to reflect upon the consequences of shutting up three men in a dark dungeon, without food or water, his mind became troubled, and he repented of the evil he had done.

Not for the deed itself, however, but for the consequences entailed upon himself. These men would die, and if nothing worse came of it Wobbles would have been free from care; but when people are starved to death, or have their throats cut, or are shot, it is their invariable custom to haunt the author of the deed, and make life a burden to him or her, as the case may be.

Wobbles was convinced of this. From his earliest infancy he was imbued with the idea that murderers always went about with fear in their hearts, a scowl on their faces, and the shadow of the slain in constant attendance.

Of course he did not number among the villains such slaughterers as ignorant doctors, dealers in bad whiskey, and manufacturers of cheap confectionery. Nor did he include the tradesmen who, reckless of all consequences, adulterate right and left—give pure fat for butter, birch-broom for tea, and ruined water for milk. If he had, how many would have escaped haunting?

But having shut them up he must either leave them there or open their prison doors. The first entailed a haunted life—the second would surely bring him trouble. Conky, Curler, and Pigeon were men of venomous dispositions, and were sure to take the trick played upon them in no amiable spirit.

All night long Wobbles debated within himself what to do, but could come to no settled idea. He was in doubt up to noon, and then conscience gained the victory.

"Better let 'em out," he thought, "and tell 'em it was a lark. Wonder whether they'll believe me? Some people might think being shut up in a damp cellar for twelve hours rather serious."

Undoubtedly they would, especially Conky, Curler, and Pigeon, who were the last men in the world to find any enjoyment in being imprisoned, even if they had been on the best of terms in their confinement, which they were not, as we all know.

Still Wobbles had great faith in his powers of persuasion, and thought he could incline them to think he had only been indulging in a harmless bit of fun, and wended his way to the cellars, where he halted before the door, and knocked.

"How are you, old chaps?" he asked. "All right inside there?"

A low rumbling sound alone answered him. That was but the echo of the noise he made upon the door.

"I say," he cried again, "I've had enough of my lark; I've come to let you out. We've all been larfing fit to split about it, and everybody hopes as you won't take it rough. We are allus up to some lark here."

Again he got no reply, and as a dreadful thought came upon him the hair of his head stood stiffly up.

"They're all dead," he gasped; "died in the night!"

It was an awful idea, and already he felt their shadows gathering around him. He would have turned and run, but his limbs refused to move, and he sank limp and helpless against the door.

"Just like people of that sort," he groaned; "to go and die right out of spite, when I was only having a bit of fun. But perhaps they aint dead, only waiting against the door to have a wenomous rush at me. They can't be dead. No man could be so perwerse as to die in twelve hours. I say, come now, speak up, and I'll let you out. D'ye hear?"

"It's too bad," he muttered, after waiting in vain

'or a reply; "I'm sure they are there. I'll unlock the door and bolt."

Having left the upper door of the passage open there was light enough for him to see what he was doing, but his hand trembled frightfully, and it was some time before he could get the key into the lock.

Prior to turning it he made one more appeal to Conky, Curler, and Pigeon, to come forward, and act fair and manly.

"When a man has a bit of a lark," he said, "you shouldn't take it too serus. People as lives here allus takes larks as meant as sich. Don't be spiteful, but come out and have your dinner. It's just ready smoking 'ot, with a hodour sweet enough to take the hanimosity hout of any man."

But the perverse creatures would not answer, and at last in a sort of frenzy he turned the lock, opened the door, and ran.

He reached the outer air, and paused for the sound of footsteps, but none reached him. The passage was silent, save for the slight creaking of the prison door.

"They are all dead," groaned Wobbles, aghast, "and I'm a haunted man. Oh! Wobbles—Wobbles, you hidiot, why did you hever swear a hoath? Wengeance aint in your line; you ought to have left it to your Broad Arrow Jacks and sich-like parties, as would take the wisit of a ghost rather friendly than totherwise."

He was in a wretched state, and walked away with his head bent down, and an air of general dejection. Suddenly he ran against Nat Green, who was lounging about, smoking a pipe.

"Hullo! Wobbles," he cried, "what cheer? White as a ghost—eh?"

"Why do you speak of ghosts?" asked Wobbles, in hollow tones. "Aren't the harrows of conscience enough without the wiperish stings of sich as those? Go thy way, and spare a broken man."

"You've got into a bad state," said Nat.

"It don't matter much to you," replied Wobbles, regarding him with an eye that reminded Nat of a gimlet. "Leave me—leave me to remorse!"

"Here, come," said Nat, "don't go on in this awful way. Tell me what's up. Confide in me as a friend."

"Friend!" echoed Wobbles, "the word is 'ollow mockery. I have no friends. Henceforth I lives alone—no, not alone, but severed from my feller man by—by remorse!"

"I see you have need of advice," rejoined Nat. "Again I say—confide in me."

"If I could only trust you," groaned Wobbles, "but by so doing I places my life in your hands."

"It will be in safe keeping," said Nat. "Out with it, whatever it is."

With many roundabout wanderings, and heaps of excuses for his crime, on the ground of its being founded on mirth, Wobbles told him all. Nat listened very gravely, and appeared to be quite overcome with grief when the story concluded.

"I am sorry for you," he said, grasping Wobbles by the hand; "but I would not be you for worlds."

"Oh, you wouldn't," replied Wobbles, faintly. "Why not, old chap?"

"Because all your wust fears will be confirmed. Your life will become a burden and a curse."

"Oh, will it?"

"Yes. Did you ever hear the story of Baron Blucher?"

"Was that the chap as fought Wellington on the field of Waterloo?"

"No; the Blucher there was the duke's friend. The one I speak of was a fourth cousin—a sad feller, given to murder and all sorts of villainy. He had his own way for years—ate, drank, and slept after his murders like a child, laughed at ghosts, but the day of retribution came."

"Oh, did it?" said Wobbles, with a wan look; "and served him right. But he did his serus—mine was a harmless bit of a joke."

"So he said in the end," replied Nat, regarding Wobbles with much tender compassion; "but the ghosts had their joke in their turn. It came about this way. The hour was midnight."

"Yes," said Wobbles, "they allus come at midnight. Why can't they come in the daytime?"

"They prefer darkness," replied Nat. "But hear the story of Blucher. The hour was midnight, the sky was full of ink-black clouds, there was lightning and thunder in the air, and Blucher, in his lone chamber on the summit of the loftiest tower of his castle, sat by the table, on which a large cotton candle burned dim and low. The corners of the turret were enveloped in gloom."

"Awful!" said Wobbles, shuddering. "Was he alone?"

"Have I not told you so? He was alone in his iniquity, and for the first time in his life his hardened mind was troubled, and yet he knew not why. He never thought of his crimes, but laid his gloom at the door of biliousness, and cursed the weakness that led him to have pork chops for supper.

"There was a lull in the storm," continued Nat, after an impressive pause, "and the big bell booming the midnight hour fell upon his ear. In his bitterness and biliousness he swore at the bell for tolling, and registered an oath that he would have it down on the morrow. Alas, that morrow for him was never to dawn!"

"Oh! wasn't it?" said Wobbles. "Why didn't it?"

"Hear the story," replied Nat. "The bell ceased and the candle, which had hitherto, with all its weakness, given a respectable yellow light, burnt blue, and a chill air swept like an ice-blast through the room. Baron Blucher tried to swear at the cold, but his tongue froze to the roof of his mouth, and he could not utter a word."

"It's a pity he swore," said Wobbles. "It's enough to rile 'em."

"Rile who?"

"The sperrits."

"I never said any spirits came, but you have rightly guessed what followed. As soon as the candle had sunk to the proper shade of blue a ghastly figure appeared at each corner of the room and, with a gliding motion, bore right down upon him."

"Horrible!" ejaculated Wobbles.

"He was in a fix," said Nat. "A bold man would have faced a single ghost, but this artful lot had so arranged matters that, turn where he would, there was one ever behind him. That settled him, bold as he was, and he sank in a huddled heap upon the floor.

"What followed," continued Nat, taking the horrified Wobbles by the button-hole, "can only be guessed at. The people of the castle heard shrieks cries, and groans—rising high above the storm—and rushed up the turret. But their way was barred—the staircase was full of spirits, that, with a wave of the hand, sent them staggering back. 'Your master is doomed!' cried weird voices. 'He has long been accursed, and must die!'

"So, having done all that could reasonably be expected from hired servants they went down into the great hall, and spread the banquetting-board with all the contents of the larder. 'For,' said they, 'Blucher is done for, and won't want anything to-morrow. Let us be merry.' They were not only merry but very festive, and before cock crow every man was dead drunk, and every woman very much knocked up, and they all slept until the heat of day, when some awoke, and, remembering the events of the preceding night, grew bold in the daytime, and prepared for a visit to the turret.

"They went up softly, turned the handle of the door, and the foremost peeped in. 'Horror!' he cried, and fell upon the flat of his back. The second stepped over him and took a look also 'Horror!' he said, too, and fell upon the previous

Broad-Arrow Jack.

ALL THAT HAS EVER HAPPENED AT PUBLIC EXECUTIONS PALES BEFORE THE STORY OF THE WAY THE TWO MISSIONARIES DIED.

NO. 8.

party as heavily as he could. A third advanced, and thrust his head in at the door. He did not cry 'Horror!' but simply said, 'Where the d—— is he?' and nobody could tell. Baron Blucher was gone!"

"Gone!" said Wobbles.

"Yes; and from that hour has never been seen or heard of. Rewards were offered, the engines of the law and the help of private and public detectives pressed into the service, but all failed, and it was only reasonable to expect them to do so. Detectives are very fallible in dealing with the creatures of this world—how can we expect them to follow that which lies beyond the grave?"

"I wonder what became of the baron?" said Wobbles, thoughtfully.

"Ah, therein lies the terrible mystery!" sighed Nat. "It is so difficult for us to fathom the ways of ghosts. They have always something new for every fresh victim. You never know when to have them."

"But they always know when to have you," groaned Wobbles.

"Yes, indeed, they do," said Nat, "and then, I say again, I would not be you upon any consideration. I don't give you a week to live."

"And yet it was only a joke," said Wobbles—"only a joke, I assure you, Mr. Green. I ses to myself, ses I, 'This place is wery dull,' I ses, 'there is no fun goin' on,' I ses, 'and let us have a lark,' I ses. And I was goin' to tell you all about it when I showed you them hats and boots by the side of the river, but you went away in sich a hurry. But you'll stand by me. You'll be my friend, won't you?"

"That I will," replied Nat, warmly. "I'll stand by you through thick and thin. Rely upon me, old boy."

CHAPTER XLVII.
THREE SPECTRES MAKE A MISTAKE.

WHEN a man promises to act as the friend of another, he ought to keep his word. Nat Green was therefore in honour bound to stand by Wobbles, and see him through the trouble he had brought upon himself.

And now let us see how he stood by him.

It will be remembered that he had never from the first believed in the suicide of the three strangers.

The story was wild, improbable, very weak, and fully worthy of Wobbles, who with his asinine capacity thought his idiotic plot would be swallowed head and tail. Nat Green did not swallow it, but set about to find out what had become of Conky, Curler, and Pigeon.

He discovered their whereabouts by accident. Passing by the entrance to the cellar or dungeons, or what you may please to think them, the noise of one or more persons hammering upon a door reached his ears. Following the sound, he came to the spot where the trio were confined.

The thickness of the door was very great, and all he could do was to exchange a few broken sentences with those inside, but such fragments as "You let me out," "Be the worse for you," and the name of Wobbles reached him. From those he drew a conclusion that he had come upon the three missing men, and proceeded to set them free.

This he did easily, having been a locksmith once upon a time. The lock was, as most old locks were, of simple construction, and with a bent piece of stiffish wire it was expeditiously turned back, and Conky, Curler, and Pigeon were released.

They came out like raging bulls, thinking it was Wobbles they had to deal with, and rushed straight upon him, meditating vengeance. Two skilful blows which laid Curler and Pigeon in the dust brought unto them a sense of their error, and Conky, who had prudently allowed his comrades to lead the van in the attack, apologised in the name of all, and peace was restored.

"But for me," said Nat, "you would have been starved to death, and now that I have saved you I think you ought to do as I tell you for a day or two."

They all swore that they would obey no other man but him while they breathed on earth, and then lifting up their voices together they asked for something to eat.

"We've been in there a week," said Conky, "and never tasted bit or sup."

"You've only been there five or six hours," replied Nat; "so lads, none of your gammon. But, however, come with me—I'll give you something to eat, and you must keep quiet in the place where I put you until to-night."

At the back of the palace stood the stabling for the horses, rough but strong wooden huts run up more for use than ornament. Nat stowed the three friends there in an empty loft, and fetched some food and drink for them.

While they ate and drank he unfolded his simple plan to them, which was a design upon the peace and happiness of Wobbles. Conky, Curler, and Pigeon were to visit him as spectres, and scare him out of his senses.

"Which will be a fitting punishment for him," said Nat, "after his base attempt upon your lives. About midnight I will come for you, and show you where he sleeps."

"But about your chief?" said the prudent Conky—"how will he take it if Wobbles kicks up a shindy?"

"The chief is away," replied Nat, "and is not expected for a day or two. Now keep quiet for the rest of the day. Nobody will come here, and you are as secure from observation as if you were already dead and buried."

He left them, and, closing the entrance door, locked it, and carried away the key. Nat was a sort of comptroller of the stables, and could do pretty much as he liked there. That day the horses were all out grazing, and nobody was about. Everything looked well for his little joke.

Left to themselves the precious trio remained silent for awhile. They were all thinking, and, strange to say, their thoughts were all on the same tack. The light in the loft was dim, as it came only in scattered rays through chinks and holes, yet they could see each other's faces, and as their eyes met a cunning leer dawned upon one and all.

"Good sort of chap that," said Conky.

"Unkimmon," replied Curler. "But *that* ought not to stand in the way."

"No," said Conky.

"No," said the Pigeon.

And then there was another silence.

"Wobbles didn't show us where the money bags are," said Conky, breaking it.

"No," returned the Pigeon, "but they *are* here somewheres."

"Yes," said Conky.

"In course," said the Pigeon, "or how is this place kept up?"

"Ah! that's it."

And once more they became silent and meditative.

"Conky," said the Pigeon suddenly, "what's your move? Out with it."

"Do you think this chap knows where it is?" said Conky.

"Oh! he wouldn't split on his chief—the wrong sort."

"In course he is. But if we got him down, tied him with a rope, and swore we would cut his throat unless he told, he might reveal it."

"Yes, that would do," said Curler, approvingly.

"It's fust-rate," assented the Pigeon.

"And when he had told," pursued Conky, "we could get hold of a good lump of it, settle this chap —he's good-natured, but it won't do to let him stand in our way—and then clear out."

"Good!" said Curler.

"Splendiferous!" said the Pigeon.

"Everybody but him thinks we are dead, I fancy, and if we do the trick bright and spry I don't see how we are even to be suspected."

"But where do you think the money's kept?"

"In my opinion in the chief's room. That's where I should keep it if I was a chief."

"It's reasonable to think so," said Pigeon. "All we have to do is to get there."

"You know the place?"

"Yes, Wobbles showed it to me."

In this way they spent the day, discussing their precious plot, and making arrangements to meet every likely hitch or difficulty they could think of. Not once did they speak of their intended murder of Nat Green in any way than as something disagreeable which must be done for their welfare. As for being grateful to him for having saved their lives they never even thought of it.

The day was very long to them, as they were naturally impatient to begin the task they had arranged for themselves, but it came to an end at last, and with the midnight hour Nat Green arrived.

He brought a lantern with him, just to light them out of the loft. Conky, who had a constitutional dislike to light at any time, kept back from its rays with his hands behind his back. In those hands he held a rope, which he had found in the loft, ready to bind Nat as soon as an opportunity offered.

"Now, you fellows," said Nat, as he put the lantern down, "must remember that you are no longer solid bodies but spirits, and the least noise you make will be quite out of character. You will find the ground rather damp, but I reckon that a little dew won't hurt you."

Conky said the dew always freshened him up, and made reference to the many happy nights he had passed on the seats of the Green Park, and that of St. James's, when he had the good luck to escape the vigilance of the park-keeper, whose duty it was to clear out all spooning couples, vagabonds, and other odds and ends, when darkness fell.

"It cuts into the marrer at first," he said, "but you gets used to it."

"All right, then, if you don't mind damp feet. Come along."

"Ready, sir," replied Conky. "But who is that in the corner?"

Nat, all unsuspecting, turned.

Conky made a sign, and all three fell upon him. Conky got the rope over his arms, Curler clung round his legs, and Pigeon, being the weakest of the three, took the lightest part of the work, and held his mouth.

Nat was taken aback—the attack was so unexpected—but he struggled fiercely, and the four went staggering all about the loft. The lantern was kicked over and extinguished, leaving them in complete darkness.

"Hold on there!" growled Conky. "If he gets loose now we are done for."

"I've got him," gasped Curler. "But be quick and shove a bit of rope about his legs."

It was done, and Nat was made helpless. They threw him down, and Conky, kneeling on his chest, bade Pigeon free his mouth.

"Holler once," he said fiercely to Nat, "and you will never holler again!"

"You are a precious lot of rascals!" said Nat, coolly. "What are you going to do?"

"That you will see presently."

"Rob and murder me, I suppose."

"You aint worth robbing," said Conky, disdainfully. "It's the chief's stuff we wants."

"Oh, that's it, is it?"

"Yes, and you must tell us where it is."

"Must I?"

"Yes, and we will have it out of you."

"You will be clever fellows if you get out of me what was never in me."

"What do you mean by that?"

"I don't know anything about it."

"That's a lie!"

"And that's polite. But go on. What more do you want?"

"Nothing," said Conky; "but you tell us, wil' you? It's in the chief's room, aint it?"

"Where else should it be?" replied Nat.

"I told you so," said Conky, to his friends. "Gag him, Pigeon. Now, mind this, young fellow; if you've deceived us we'll come back and settle with you."

"You won't find the money loose," said Nat. "There are such things as secret springs and underground store-houses. Some of 'em in the left-hand corner of the room—you understand."

"Well, you are a good-natured chap," said Conky, delighted. "I said so, and my mates knows it. I've got quite a friendly feeling for you."

"The consciousness of having your friendship would support me through any trouble," said Nat.

"I hope it will," returned Conky. "Now you must be gagged—in a friendly way, of course. You needn't mind it; but business is business, you know, and a man as only half does it can't expect to get on. Don't choke him outright, Pigeon; but make him safe."

Pigeon, without much tenderness, fixed a piece of stick prepared for the occasion in Ned's mouth, and tied it tightly with a piece of string round his head.

After testing his bonds carefully, to see if they were secure, the three knaves stole softly down, and, with cautious steps, made for the portico of the palace.

Apparently nobody was about. There was a light burning dimly in the hall, which was empty, and, creeping in, they stole towards the chief's door.

It stood ajar. Fortune favoured them.

More, a light was burning in the room also—it being a custom to keep one there, so as to be ready for the chief when he returned.

They went in, and Conky pulled the door to behind him. It closed with a click, which fell unheeded on their ears. All their minds were wrapped in the thought of golden money-bags.

"In the left-hand corner," said Conky.

Thither they went, Curler carrying the light. They looked and felt about for a long time, but found nothing.

"I don't see no knob," said Conky. "This is the left-hand corner."

"Perhaps he's a left-handed chap, and meant the right," suggested Pigeon.

It was not a brilliant idea, but it was better than none. They tried the right-hand corner, then the other corner, then went over the floor, turned Jack's simple couch upside down, and yet found no knob nor anything like a secret spring.

"It's my opinion," said Conky, at last, wiping off the perspiration of disappointment from his face, "that we've been gammoned."

"Looks like it," said Pigeon and Curler together.

"Then I proposes we go back and settle the deceitful warmint."

"So we will," they said.

But the return was not so easy. The door was closed, and, as far as they could see, had no interior means of opening it.

They searched all over it, assisting their labours with a mighty lot of swearing. They pushed with all their might, but it stood like a rock. All their efforts were thrown away. They were caged.

When the truth came upon them in all its ghastliness they became limp, and sank in a body on the floor, speechless and helpless. There was only one thing they could think of, and that was the return of Broad Arrow Jack.

And when he did return—what then?

Aye! there was the rub—the fearful rub! Better for them had they never been released from the dungeon below—better by far to have died by inches than to meet the wrath of Broad Arrow Jack!

CHAPTER XLVIII.

THE MARCH.

PERHAPS in all the history of the human race there were never three prisoners less anxious for the coming of their gaoler into the cell than were Conky, Curler, and Pigeon.

Look at it as you may they were in a dreadful fix, for mind you it mattered very little who came. The bare fact of their being in Broad Arrow Jack's private apartment was sufficient to condemn them. With only one object could they possibly be there.

"It was all your fault," groaned Conky. "There never were two such chaps as you, Curler and Pigeon, for getting other parties into a mess."

"Oh! come now, that's too good," returned Pigeon. "Who first spoke about tying up that good-natured chap and robbing the place?"

"I didn't," said Conky, with an obstinate look.

"Oh! now didn't he, Curler? You heard him."

Curler reflected for a moment undecided which way to vote. Of the two, Conky was the stronger man and he gained the day.

"No, Pigeon," said Curler, "he never opened his lips about it. You was the first to name it, and you reglar led us both away."

The face of Pigeon betokened the utmost amazement. Anything so cool and heartless he had never met with in his life before. He stared from one to the other like a man in a dream.

"You was allus a blunderer," pursued Curler, "and if ever I mix myself up again with anything you do, hang me!"

"Oh! you are a precious pair," said Pigeon, grinding his teeth.

He said no more, and the others were not at all disposed for conversation. In gloom and silence the caged blackbirds passed the night.

And not only the night, but the greater part of the next day, trembling at the sound of every footstep, and dying by anticipation the thousand deaths which the poet tells us falls to every coward.

But at last he who was most dreaded came. The door was opened, and Broad Arrow Jack entered. At first he did not see the three trembling wretches in the corner, and sat down by the table with a thoughtful look upon his face. Pigeon, with a low groan, attracted his attention, and then he saw them.

"Oh! mercy, sir," gasped Pigeon. "We was a strolling about when we came at this place, and the door shut, and we was kep here——"

Jack arose, and without uttering a word, took Conky and Pigeon by the collar, and dragged them like two bundles of straw through the big hall, down the steps of the portico, and then with a jerk sent them flying a dozen yards or so, throwing them over and over like well-hit skittles.

Returning, he took up Curler, who was too limp to fly, and taking him by the waistcoat and nape of the neck he carried him out too, and sent him travelling down the steps like a shot out of a gun. Conky and Pigeon were just getting upon their feet, when Curler came up against them with the force of a rocket, and down they went again.

Jack, without taking any further notice of them, retired, and the precious trio, after lying quietly for a minute or so, sat up and looked at each other.

"Might ha' been worse—mightn't it?" said Conky.

"Much worse," said the other two.

But their troubles were not yet over. Barely had they got upon their feet when Nat Green appeared. He came sauntering up in a cool easy fashion, and called upon them to halt.

"If any of you beggars move," he said, "I'll bring you down."

"Which we wouldn't move for worlds," murmured Conky.

"Fall in, shoulder to shoulder," said Nat.

They fell in, rather wondering what was coming.

"Right about face!"

They performed this military movement, marvelling yet the more.

"Stand steady!"

Then he stepped back a pace or two did Nat, and, with a rush, bestowed such a kick upon Conky as that worthy individual, albeit he had received many kicks, had never known the like before. It as near as possible turned him clean over, and gave him a general idea that the world had come to an end, and he was wandering wildly about a revolving sky.

Curler and Pigeon looked upon their fallen comrade, and shuddered. But they moved not, a kick was bad, but a bullet was worse, and prudence chained them to the spot.

The next to fall was Curler, and as he received his salutation he uttered a short sharp cry, very much like the squeak of a rat, and curled up on the ground he became a cushion for Pigeon when his turn came. Pigeon, when afterwards describing the kick he received, said he never thought of it without somehow calling to mind the battle of Waterloo and a cannon-ball.

"The next time," said Nat, when he had finished his business, "you play any tricks upon me, look out for something more than this."

He left them, and in due time they got into a sitting position.

"Might ha' been worse," said Conky again.

"Much worse," the others said, and then they spoke of something to eat. Accustomed to the buffets of the cold hard world, they took hard knocks and kicks lightly.

They got what they required from one of the men, and shortly after they had finished their meal the sound of a trumpet awoke a hundred echoes among the hills.

"What's that?" asked Conky, addressing one of the men who happened to be near.

"The call to arms" he answered, "we are going away from here."

In a few minutes men on horseback came in from all quarters, and those who were about the house saddled their steeds, and then all fell in with the order and precision of a cavalry regiment.

The last to appear was Wobbles on Old Joss, and as that noble steed was treating himself to a walk, his rider's attention was fully occupied in keeping his seat. He saw nothing of his old friends until close beside them, when, catching sight of the three men whom he believed to be dead, his every limb relaxed, and he fell off.

There are three living things which seldom come to much harm through a fall—a child, a drunken man, and a born fool. Wobbles was one of these, and he was not at all injured by his tumble. He was only staggered by the unexpected vision before him.

"Oh! come now, dash it!" he said, "don't come bothering a fellow in daylight. Night's your time, if at all. Come now—"

"It's all right," said Conky, "we aint ghostesses at all. We was let out of the trap as you put us in."

"Then you aint dead?" said Wobbles, faintly.

"No."

"You are sure of it?"

"Certain, although I shouldn't mind if I was," said Conky, gloomily.

"Then I think I'll get up," said Wobbles. "Oh, what a lark it's been all round!"

"Glad you think so," said Pigeon. "We aint got much of a larf out of it."

The appearance of Jack and Billy Brisket, the latter in his gorgeous uniform, and both armed with swords and pistols, cut short the conversation. Two splendid horses were led forward, which they mounted; and as Billy Brisket got into the saddle his eye fell upon the unmounted trio.

"Hallo!" he said, "these fellows must go with us. We shall want some cooks and general servants in camp. I suppose you have no objection, Jack."

"Not at all," replied our hero. "Only, let them keep out of my way."

"Of course they cannot walk," said Billy. "Are there any horses they can have, Green?"

"There is only old Fireworks in the paddock," replied Nat.

"Will he carry double? These fellows are not very heavy."

"Oh, yes, he'll manage."

"That will do, then," said Billy, with a humorous twinkle in his eye. "Wobbles can take one up behind him. Joss will make light of him."

"He'll never stand it," said Wobbles.

"Bring out Fireworks," said Billy Brisket. "Haste, there is no time to lose."

Nat Green went for Fireworks, and speedily brought him back, ready saddled for Conky and Curler, who regarded him as malefactors look upon a public executioner.

Neither of them had ever been astride a quadruped in their lives.

Fireworks was a tall, raw-boned, hollow-backed horse, with an immense fiddle-head, and a great patch of white in his eyes. At the best he was an ugly brute; but what little beauty he might have boasted of perished when his previous owner, in a humorous, drunken fit, cut off his tail, leaving only a stump about two inches long.

This stump was very flexible, and Fireworks had the power of working it as if it were on a pivot. You could just get a crupper over it, and if Fireworks did not object the crupper remained, but when he was disposed to get rid of it he turned the stump once and was free.

Between Fireworks and old Joss there existed an undying animosity, which would have ended in the death of one or the other if age had not impaired the kicking powers of both, but as far as they could express their feelings towards each other they did with hearty good will. Whenever they were left alone together they ran at each other like bulls. If one went down the other fell over him, and the breath of the pair was, as a rule, knocked out of their bodies. It was quite half an hour before they could get up again.

Once, when old Joss was musing over the past, Fireworks crept softly up, and, having taken his bearings properly, he let fly with his heels, and caught old Joss under the fifth rib, leaving a proof-print of his heels upon the old performer's skin.

That kick Joss never forgot or forgave, and it was the one fervent wish of his old age to return it with interest. But the task was difficult. Fireworks was a horse of frivolous mind—had never studied life—and did not even know what a circus was like. He never meditated, and in vain did old Joss lie in wait and sneakabout. Fireworks was not to be done—he was ever on the alert and ready.

As Nat Green led him up for Conky and Curler, old Joss uttered a loud snort of defiance, which had such an effect upon Pigeon—who was scrambling up behind Wobbles—that he went right over the other side, and stood upon his head, balanced to a nicety for a moment, and then went over on his back with a smack like what we frequently hear in a butcher's shop.

Friendly hands raised him, and helped him into his seat, with the assurance that if he did that sort of thing more than twice a day he might hurt himself.

Conky and Curler were of opinion that walking suited them best; but Billy Brisket sternly bade them mount, and slowly and laboriously they got into the saddle—Conky in front, and Curler behind.

"Forward!" cried Jack, and his willing horse dashed across the stream, followed by others, with a mighty lot of splashing and snorting, leaving Fireworks and old Joss, with their double burdens, to bring up the rear.

CHAPTER XLIX.
NOBLE HORSEMEN.

THERE are many living things which have an antipathy to cold water. The feeling is often found in even the most intelligent form of bipeds; but no living biped or quadruped ever had a greater dislike to the pure liquid outwardly applied than Fireworks and old Joss.

Instead of following the gay cavalcade they pulled up on the banks of the stream, and regarded it with the utmost aversion. Old Joss felt the water with his fore-feet as little trembling boys do with their hands, and shook his head as much as to say that it would not do. Fireworks did not seem inclined to touch the water at all.

"Come up!" cried Wobbles, who, compared with his companions, was a noble horseman. "You can't stop here."

He gave him a sounding whack upon the ribs; but he might as well have smitten a towel-horse. Feeling in old Joss was almost dead. Instead of moving forward, as requested, he turned a leaden eye upon Fireworks, and, perceiving that he was gazing meditatively upon the water, conceived that now or never was the time to kick him.

With this evil object in his mind he commenced a slow and cautious advance upon his foe, to the alarm of Wobbles, who begged of Conky to get along, or "murder would come of it."

"Hit your horse over the head," he said. "He'll go on then."

"Not if I knows it," replied the cautious Conky. "It will only make him wicious."

"They'll be at each other in a moment," groaned Wobbles. "Oh! here we go!"

The subtle Fireworks was no more to be taken in than heretofore. He saw old Joss advancing, and at the proper moment turned and faced him. Two terrific snorts were exchanged, and then they ran full tilt at each other, bearing upon their backs four of the most unwilling knights ever seen in the lists or out of them.

The shock was terrific, but neither horse nor horsemen fell. Pigeon simply slid down to the tail of old Joss, and by holding hard on the crupper of the saddle kept there. Old Joss himself staggered into the stream, and feeling he had fought enough for the day, turned and trotted over.

Fireworks, bent upon further hostilities, followed, calling upon old Joss by snorts to turn and fight. Old Joss, with other snorts, said it was not quite convenient just then, and kept on.

It was a grand chase.

Old Joss stimulated by fear, and Fireworks by murderous intentions, went on at a tremendous pace, nearly six miles an hour, I should think, apparently regardless of their double burdens. They crossed the river, dashed into the wood, where the beaten track preserved them from going astray.

The four riders had a hard time of it, especially Pigeon, who was not astride his horse, but lay on the rump in the attitude of the shipwrecked mariner in the circus, who, despairing of life, yet swims manfully on the tail of the frantic steed. Pigeon only swam with his legs, as his hands never let go of the pommel of the saddle.

Conky and Curler on the back of Fireworks were shaken to the right and left, dashed against each other, tossed up and down, and generally knocked about. How they kept on travelled on, Conky with a black eye, given him by the head of Fireworks, and Curler with a blue nose, bestowed upon him by the cranium of Conky.

On—on through the forest the wild steeds and the riders went. Old Joss having a blind side frequently ran against trees, and so barked the legs of Wobbles that if he had found the bone bare he would not have been surprised.

In vain did he rein up the steed—the bit had no more effect upon the leather jaws of old Joss than a packthread would have had upon a pig. As for expostulations, Wobbles might as well have asked the tide of the sea to pull up for him.

Old Joss was past his prime, but there was life in the old dog yet, and the way he lifted those quartern-loaf feet of his we must rank among the great deeds of the animal creation. In vain did Fireworks pursue, the twenty-five clear feet between them he could not reduce.

Perhaps Fireworks was a little embarrased by the two individuals upon his back, who were sometimes together and sometimes apart, now both clinging to his ribs, now one on his neck and the other on his tail. In addition to this they kept up a broken series of remonstrances, mingled with bitter revilings, which took the following form, the words in parenthesis representing as nearly as possible the music of their teeth :

" Woa—a there (clicketty, click); stop, old orse (click, click—clicketty, click); go steady, old ma—an (click, click, click); heasy does it, you infernal bru—ute (clicketty, clicketty, clicketty, click); once hoff, ketch me ever getting on again (click, click—clicketty click); oh, my sides—oh, my ribs! you shambling bag of bones (clicketty, click—click, click); I wish I had you at the knacker's—oh! (clicketty—click, click, click)."

The most gallant man of the lot was, as I have said, Wobbles. He and Joss were old friends, and he had acquired just sufficient of the art of horsemanship to stick on. In an attitude that would have done credit to a Cockney on Hampstead Heath he rode on, toes well out and well up, body back, hat over his eyes, and elbows squared in the fashion some people adopt at the dinner table. Proud of his horsemanship he looked with pity on his fellows, yet enjoyed their discomfort exceedingly, and if his legs had escaped the knocking about before alluded to he would have been perfectly happy.

On—on—under the great trees, with no signs of flagging in the old horse in front, and no diminution in the revengeful determination of the other in the rear. On—on—under the shade of the forest, and so to the more open ground in the passes between the mountains.

Here the ground grew rougher, and the quartern loaves of old Joss frequently got into dangerous quarters. He was more than once upon his nose, and several times upon his haunches, but he never really fell. It seemed as if some little cherub had taken him in charge, and shielded him from all harm.

But the watchfulness of cherubs, like the energies of man, have a limit, and the cherub of old Joss, if indeed he had one, at last deserted him, like a cold and cruel cherub, in the stoniest of stony places.

Left to his own desires, and with nothing worse than his own energies to help him, he went down at once with such a smash that any other horse would have had every bone in his body pulverised; but it did not hurt him, bless you. He lay as calmly as a colt asleep.

But Wobbles and Pigeon fared badly. Both were thrown, and as they approached mother earth looked very much like bats flying. When they met the earth they lay still, with all the life for the time shaken out of them.

Fireworks was close behind, and being unable to stop himself went over him. The legs of Fireworks by the way, were very hard to move, but when once they got in action they were like an express train, and took a deal of pulling up. Nothing less than a brake all over him could have been of any service. So he went in straight for old Joss, and Conky and Curler joined the other noble horsemen.

The horses were the first to recover, and having had enough of warfare for the day, they cocked as much tail as they had, as a sign of truce, and diverted their energies to the little bunches of grass between the stones. Of the men Wobbles was foremost on the road to recovery. He had been thrown so often that he was in a measure hardened to it.

He got upon his feet and shook himself like a dog. Then he felt all over his body to see if his bones were all right, and finding no great damage done, gave Pigeon a helping hand and examined him. Nobody was seriously hurt, and presently they were all on their feet.

"This sort of thing is allus happening to horsemen," said Wobbles, with assumed cheerfulness. "Life in the saddle is wery much like life out of it—all ups and downs, and shakes and knocks and bruises. Let us be bold and manly. Ketch the horses, and on again."

But talking of catching a horse is one thing and doing it another. Fireworks and old Joss were in a skittish mood, and showed an amount of dodging power far beyond that possessed by any ordinary horse over four years old.

Playfully they waited until the hand of the pursuer was almost on the bridle, then, with a jerk and a snort, they were off and away, kicking up their heels with joy. In vain did the four bold riders try all they knew to circumvent them—Fireworks and old Joss defied all their efforts, and at the end of an hour's chase were yet free.

"This is nice," said Wobbles, sitting down in despair. "Every minute them chaps ahead is further and further away, and here we are without wittles and friendless—left in a country where I don't think there is even a wild potatoe to be got for love or money."

"Let us go back," suggested Conky.

"Not if I knows it," replied Wobbles. "There are twenty of the best men left in charge of the palace, and their orders are to shoot everybody who shows before the chief returns. Oh! we are in for it—starwation, misery, and crows to pick your bones. Oh! that I had never had a sainted mother, with a turn of mind for saving up sixpences and shillings for an only son! I might now be doing well in some trade, and living the life of a happy man."

CHAPTER L.
LOOKING BACK.

WHEN Broad Arrow Jack halted for the night a full moon was shining in the sky. Thirty miles of ground had been covered, and a rest was needed by the horses and men. As far as he was concerned he could have gone on. Fatigue had little power over his muscular frame, and now that he was, as he believed, on the way to execute upon his foes the last act of vengeance, his nerves were strung up to a pitch that would have enabled him to bear and survive the hardships of a dozen ordinary men. But he was alone in his might; the rest lacked his powers of endurance, and for their sake he halted on the plain.

The men ate and slept. Jack ate a little, but slept not. On the bare ground, with his head resting on his arm, he lay, listening to the tethered horses cropping the coarse grass and plants within their reach, and to the hoot of the owl as it winged its lumbering flight, with his mind wandering back to events of but a few years ago, and yet which now seemed to be so far—far away.

How long ago it appeared since he left his home in England—a grand old home, too, where a long line of his forefathers dwelt, and dealt out noble generous hospitality.

In that mansion used to be
Free-hearted hospitality;
The fires up the chimney roared—
The stranger feasted at the board;
But like the skel'ton at the feast
That warning timepiece never ceased,
For ever—never:
Never—for ever.

Moment by moment the old clock on the stairs had ticked the time away, and the glory of his house was gone. Of all who had borne his name he alone remained—branded, and walking the earth half-naked, with the furious thirst for vengeance raging in him—bent upon slaughter, living a wild, romantic, unnatural life, which, at times, he fancied could not be real, but a passing dream.

"And what will be the end?" he said, half aloud. "My work done, whither shall I go?—what shall I do? Shall I ever accomplish the purpose that first brought me to this land?"

"Awake still, my chief?" said a voice near him.

"Yes, Brisket," he replied. "I am more than usually restless to-night."

"I grieve to hear it. You are young, and may bear this superhuman fatigue for a time, but the breakdown will assuredly come at last."

"I suppose so. But do not remain here. You have need of rest."

"No," replied Brisket, sitting down beside him. "Your restlessness is, like other things, reflected in me. Heigho! I am thinking of the old country to-night."

"England?"

"Yes, not that I have much to think of. I am only a poor beggar, so lowly that I never even heard my great grandfather mentioned. Now you, I know, can go back and back until you want fifty greats at least to the furthest off grandfather."

"Yes," said Jack, sadly, "I can go back a long way; but what of that, if it is to end here?"

"But it won't. You will go back to old England, and resume your family name, whatever it is."

"I will tell you, if you like, Brisket."

"No—not now. Keep to the old programme. I want nothing better."

"Well, be it so," said Jack. "If I complete my work you shall know all. If I fall, I am the last of my race, and the name will perish."

"I am not the last of the Briskets," said Billy, reflectively, "nor is there a likelihood of a last Brisket being on earth. No sooner does a Brisket marry than he finds himself surrounded by a dozen children—mostly boys—who, as soon as they can think, dwell upon matrimony, and perpetrate it as soon as circumstances permit. The Briskets increase and multiply amazingly."

"Were you ever married?" asked Jack.

"Me? No—not quite, but very nearly," replied Billy, making a wry face. "It was that which sent me here. I was fond of her, and would have made her a good husband."

"I am sure you would."

"Thanky! Yes, I would have done my best to render her happy; but she preferred Scroggles, and she had him. I went to the church to see her married, tossed her a bunch of flowers as big as your head as she was leaving the church, sold out my horse and van, and came over here to drown my grief and make a fortune."

"And you have done both, I trust?" said Jack.

"One is all right," replied Brisket, scraping his chin with his finger and thumb; "but I don't know as I've quite forgot her. When the heart's fixed, years don't change it. I never close my eyes at night without wishing she may be happy."

"Brisket," said Jack, warmly, "you are a noble fellow. Every hour shows me more clearly how truly great you are."

"Oh! I aint all honey—I've never took to Scroggles. When he was first sticking up to her I waited on him and we fought. Scroggles got the best of it, being a head over me, and having the shoulders of an ox. By the way he was a butcher, and how a woman could take to a man with an odour of suet continually hovering around him I don't know, but she did it. Heigho!"

A silence followed, both Jack and Brisket dwelling on their respective pasts. The former was the first to speak.

"It has often been on my lips, Brisket," he said, "to give you my history. A marvellously strange one, I assure you. Once powerful and rich, the idleness, indifference, and extravagance of successive generations brought us down. But we were still honoured and respected when a foul fiend in the form of a man worked our ruin and his own."

"You refer to the Ogre."

"Yes, vile as he is, coarse and loathsome to the eye, that man was once respected too. He had kings of India for his forefathers, many of them handsome and noble. The mind must have fashioned his body and made it what it is."

"Mind goes a great way in that direction."

"Yes, but no more of the story at present. You shall know all soon. I have been thinking of what I have done of late to-night, and wondering how far I am justified in carrying out my vengeance. I think—I do not know—that perhaps I might have spared some of the lesser wretches if their full history had been kept from me. But it is too late for regret. Jaundice and the Ogre alone remain, and for them, as far as I have dealings with them, there shall be no mercy."

"The others earned their fate a hundred times over," said Brisket. "They are dead and gone. Think no more of them. I wonder where the Tiger is?"

"He will catch us up—the boy is unerring on the trail."

"And Wobbles and that lot are far behind."

Jack made no response to this. He was not particularly anxious about Wobbles or the other gentlemen with whom he was travelling. Billy Brisket finding he was disposed to be quiet, said no more, but went back to his old sweetheart in his thoughts, until sleep closed his eyes.

He was awakened by a noise and confusion in the camp, and starting up found it was daylight. Jack was marshalling the men together, and among them Billy recognised Wobbles and the others who had just arrived covered with dust and worn down by fatigue.

Fireworks and old Joss were with them, fresh as May rosebuds, and as playful as young elephants. Old Joss, who had arrived at the conclusion that in the last skirmish he had got the best of it, was particularly skittish.

Conky and Curler had each registered a solemn oath that nothing would induce them to cross Fireworks again, and when the camp was put in motion they walked, taking it in turns to lead that gallant steed. Pigeon also declined to mount, but Wobbles with a scornful laugh sprang into the saddle, and bade old Joss "come up."

He came up with a walk, and then came down in the dying scene in "Dick Turpin," and if Wobbles had not rolled out of the way Joss would have crushed the life out of him. But he was more than usually gracious that morning, and, getting upon his feet again, allowed Wobbles to resume his seat.

By this time the main body were well on their way, and Wobbles again urged old Joss to use the limbs he was blessed with. Right well did that priceless animal obey, and, with a snort of contempt addressed to Fireworks, went off at a heavy gallop.

"Keep straight on," cried Wobbles, at parting, "and leave your horse to guide you. And mind you take care of him, as he is a particular favourite of the chief."

"A nice thing to take care of him," said Conky, eyeing Fireworks viciously; "what had we better do?"

"Foller," said Conky.

"Foller," assented Pigeon.

And follow they did, sadly enough, leading old Fireworks, who, in the absence of old Joss, seemed to lose his fiery spirit, and crawled along like a donkey who has no object in life beyond getting a sand-cart up a hill.

CHAPTER LI.

A VISION.

THE Ogre and Jaundice were very active meanwhile—the Ogre particularly so—and every effort was made to strengthen their position and increase their allies.

They could give little, but they promised much. Men accepted their promises and believed their story, and each day saw fresh recruits of the idle, the lawless, and the adventurous.

Rapidly the body was organised. Each man had his work apportioned to him—some to hunt, some to cook, some to repair clothes and clean arms, and others to camp and scout duty.

A few of the most daring were told off to go here and there, plundering, keeping up the falsehood started at first, and doing it all in the name of Broad Arrow Jack, bringing thereby opprobrium on our hero's name.

Ill news flies fast and falsehood speedily takes root.

By the time Jack was expected by the Ogre there was not a lone hut or a village from there to the coast where his name was not reviled and cursed.

"All goes well," said the Ogre. "Yet a little time and all the country will come out to crush him, and you and I, Jaundice, will be called the saviours of the people."

"You are more sure of the matter than I am," replied Jaundice, gloomily. "I felt from the first that we were doomed men. Why not have got clear away when we had the chance?"

"Bah!" exclaimed the Ogre. "It sickens me to hear you. Come forward and look down upon the valley. See, every pass is guarded by men as wild and furious as Eastern fanatics, believing what I have taught them, that Broad Arrow Jack spares none within his power. The picture of his torture-chamber which I gave to the men last night roused some of them to madness. 'Lead us to this hell-hound!' they cried, 'and let us nail him to a tree!' Oh, how sweetly they absorbed it all—taking it in as a babe imbibes its mother's milk!"

"Yes, that is all very well, I say again," returned Jaundice, "but wait until he appears upon the scene, and you will find all things changed. He has a strange power of attraction which no man can resist. You and I have felt it."

"It was a foolish weakness—past, and gone for ever," said the Ogre.

"No—no! It was the power of a great presence, nothing more or less. He is our superior, and we shall fall by his hand."

"You are a coward, Jaundice!"

"I am not. Look here. You are proud of this position, of its strength, of those you have gathered about you. I see in this place nothing more than a self-made trap, and look on the men as so many creatures who will one day turn and rend us."

The Ogre turned from him impatiently and went back to his tent, from whence he could look down upon the only path that led up to the table land. But Jaundice was always full of his fears, and the Ogre had his own; still he was superior to his companion in this. He kept them to himself.

While Broad Arrow Jack was far away he was bold and full of hope, but when the news came that he was steadily advancing, the thermometer of the Ogre's courage began to go slowly down.

He fought against it, laughing at Jaundice for possessing the same feeling; but when he laughed the loudest he feared the most, and little by little began to think it would have been wiser to have gone away when an opportunity offered itself. He felt how unwise he had been, after the above recorded interview with Jaundice, more than ever.

Stretched upon his rude couch of skins, he lay with his head upon his hand, gazing at the glorious panorama of mountain, plain, and valley lying before him, heedless of its beauty, which few spots on the earth could rival.

On his heart there lay a shadow which had been gathering for days, which the bright sky could not lighten, and as he lay with his eyes fixed upon the horizon from whence he knew his enemy would come, a small cloud arose.

Why should he liken it to Broad Arrow Jack?

There was nothing in it formidable at first, only a white ball of mist, but it had a fascination for him, and he never took his eyes from it.

Up it came, changing from white to dun colour, from dun to brown, from brown to black, swelling out and overspreading the heavens, until it shut out the sun, and blurred the tints of the fair landscape.

The air was hot and still, and save for the rattle of arms, as some of his men moved to and fro, the Ogre heard nothing until from the great black cloud there leapt out a fork of fire, and thunder rolled and echoed among the mountains.

The first shot fired, the heavenly warfare went on fast and furiously. Here and there darted the all-withering flames, rocks were rent, trees blasted, and two men, hurrying up the cliff for shelter, were slain.

The Ogre saw them fall, and as they lay with their faces uppermost he saw in them a likeness to Jaundice and himself, although there was no more real resemblance than there is between men of different nations and colour. Both the slain men were pure Germans, with flaxen hair and small even features. Yet the Ogre traced in them a likeness to Jaundice and himself.

He could not move—that power had left him. A waking nightmare, more horrible than anything which dreams can bring, was upon him. He had seen a few such storms, but never one that awed him. Lightning and thunder had hitherto been only natural phenomena. Now they were forerunners of a doom to come.

The rain came down heavily, descending as from a water-spout. Rivulets were created, and sluggish streams suddenly sprang into turbid life. Dry valleys became watercourses, and cascades leaped from beds hard and dry with the drought of months.

The earth smoked with mist, and in the vapour the Ogre saw the shadows of the dead arise—accusing men, women, and children, slain in his brutal lust of plunder and blood—each with the face towards him, dimly defined, yet so clearly seen by the inner vision of his blackened soul.

And so he lay throughout the storm, unharmed in body by the elements, but scathed, and rent, and torn by the fires of a conscience fanned by fear. Anon the clouds broke, the moon came out, the cascades ceased, and the turbid streams slowly settled down; but the peace that came to them came not to him, and all night long the grim spectre of an approaching death was by his side.

How lightly we in health and strength talk of death—how little we, who live tolerably decent lives, know what the man soaked through and through with crime feels at its approach! Surely the dark terrible dread has a meaning! It cannot be in us without a purpose. If there is naught beyond the grave why this dread of death?

"I am a fool! I am a child!" cried the Ogre, springing up. "Where is my manhood? I had it once. Hallo, Jaundice, where are you?"

"Here," said Jaundice.

He was drenched to the skin—during the storm not having left the spot where he parted from the Ogre. There was a wild look in his eye like that which comes to a man who has seen some terrible sight.

The Ogre glared at him savagely.

"Have you been drinking?" he asked.

"No—no!" replied Jaundice, "but I have seen something."

"Well, so have I—a storm—a terrible storm!" said the Ogre.

"It was not that. When it began I saw a figure in the valley—the figure of a woman. I knew it at once—it was my wife."

"Well, what of that?" asked the Ogre, impatiently. "You don't suppose she will ever leave you?"

"At first," pursued Jaundice, without regarding the interruption, "I thought she was alone; but I soon perceived there was another figure close behind her—a more clumsy figure—the figure of Caliban."

"Your late gaoler?" said the Ogre, carelessly.

"Yes, on they came up the path to the summit of the rock, and paused before the mouth of your tent."

"I did not see them," said the Ogre, with a surprised look.

"Hear me, and do not marvel," replied Jaundice. "Caliban passed into the tent, and my wife came on to within a pace or two of me; then, raising her head, she showed me a ghastly wound in her throat, pointed towards your tent, and disappeared."

"Great heavens!" exclaimed the Ogre.

"If you can interpret dreams, tell me what it all means?" said Jaundice.

"I cannot," replied the Ogre; "but I will swear that Caliban never came near me."

CHAPTER LII.
A BATTERING RAM.

ON the third night after starting the Tiger joined the band upon the march. He brought very little news—none of any importance to my story.

Jack bade him prepare for being sent upon a dangerous mission on the morrow, and dismissed him for the night. He passed the intervening time between then and the morning in skipping about like a sprite.

It was not until noon that Jack fully decided upon sending him upon the errand he mentioned. It was truly a dangerous one, being neither less nor more than a visit to the Ogre's haunt, to ascertain his strength, and how he had fortified his position.

"Do not run into useless peril," he said to the Tiger.

"What dat, massa?" asked Tiger "I neber hear ob him."

"Danger is peril. Do not let them get hold of you, or give them the chance to kill you."

The Tiger laughed merrily, exhibiting thirty-two splendid teeth—even as a model in a dentist's window.

"Neber fear, massa," he said. "I larf at de lot, be blow to 'em."

"At night, then," said Jack, "you start. Choose your own time, and come back as soon as you can. We are travelling in a straight line; you cannot miss us."

"All right, massa. Nebor miss you wedder you go straight or crokum."

As he had a few hours to spare the Tiger employed them in making little expeditions into the country on either side. Rest was fatigue to his restless nature, and just prior to the resumption of their journey at noon he came back and reported a discovery he had made.

"A hut," massa," he said, "wif men looking trough long bit ob brass wif glass at de end ob it—taking de spy ob you."

"Indeed," said Jack, "a telescope bent on me Lead the way, Tiger. I must look into this."

Without a word to the men, and merely telling Brisket he was going for a short stroll, he followed the Tiger, who, taking advantage of broken ground, led him up so cunningly that he came upon the hut in question and the men, without being perceived, until he was within fifty yards of them.

There were six men in all. Four immediately turned tail; the fifth, a little podgy man, very much like Sancho Panza, tumbled all in a heap against the hut, and the sixth rushed in and closed the door.

"Odd!" thought Jack. "These fellows must have heard of me. Open here, will you?"

He thundered upon the door with his fist, and in reply the fellow inside sent a bullet through the panel.

Jack, with an angry frown, made a rush, and endeavoured to break down the door. The bolts and bars were too strong, and resisted him.

A second shot was fired, and, doubly angry at this treatment—as undeserved as it was unexpected—Jack looked about him for something to force a passage into the hut. A huge branch of a tree lay near, and, taking it up in his arms, he held it like a battering ram, and charged.

The door went down like a thing of paper, and the Sancho Panza fellow outside fainted clean away.

The man inside was made of sterner stuff, and, with his rifle clubbed, aimed a blow at Jack's head. Jack sprang forward, and, with one turn, wrenched it from his hand.

The man drew his bowie knife, and Jack dealt him a blow that laid him helpless and breathless at his feet.

He dragged him outside, took the remaining arms he had, and asked him what he meant by firing upon a peaceful stranger.

"You are no stranger to me—at least, in name," was the sullen reply, as soon as he could speak.

"Well, suppose I am not. But did I ever harm you?"

"Not in myself. But is a murdered brother no harm? You killed mine."

"Who is your brother?"

"Stephen Hardacre. I am Daniel Hardacre."

"I know him not. I have never even heard of him."

"Did you not send your men to plunder his little farm, to take away such flocks and herds as he had? Did you not command them to leave his little garden a wilderness, and was it not done—and well done?"

"I am amazed!" said Jack. "I do not understand you."

This was but one of the Ogre's deeds, or rather a deed instigated by him; and Daniel Hardacre, in bitterness of spirit, told a story of plunder and incendiarism as brutal as ever was perpetrated by anything in the form of man. Jack listened calmly to all that was said, and bore the reproaches, boldly heaped on him, unmoved.

"I have been traduced," he said, "and you have all been led astray. This was the work of an enemy of mine. I have neither the need nor desire for plunder."

"So you may tell me," was the doubting reply.

"Come to my men, and be convinced. Who is this poor fellow?"

He pointed to the Sancho individual, who had not shut his mouth or blinked his eyes since Jack rammed the door in. Daniel Hardacre said—

"He has suffered also. He had a wife—she is dead. He had land—it is laid waste; he is homeless, friendless, and forlorn."

"And this," said Jack, "is laid to my charge?"

"All, and much more," was the reply.

"Come and see how you have been blinded," said Jack, "and learn who are the real authors of these crimes."

"Woe to him," said Hardacre, "if ever we should meet! If you are deceiving me may you be accursed."

"Fear not," replied Jack, "but follow me."

Hardacre went back with him and Sancho too. A look at the men who followed our hero shook his doubts—an hour spent with them scattered all mistrust. He learnt Jack's story, and from that hour became one of his most devoted followers.

"All the country is deceived," he said; "they

are led away by a lie. Let me be your missionary, and preach the truth to them. I will raise such a nest of hornets that the authors of these falsehoods shall curse the day they breathed them."

"Go," said Jack; "but send all recruits to me."

"It shall be done," replied Hardacre.

And so he and Sancho went forth together, and began their preaching, with what success we shall presently see.

This was the first intimation Jack received of the nature of the warfare raised against him, but in a few hours he heard much more. One of his scouts came riding in with the intelligence that all the country had risen against him. Even the men were deserting the diamond-fields to do battle against the "brigand, Broad Arrow Jack."

"It is a reglar scare, chief," the man said, "and all the crimes of the last ten years are laid to your charge."

"I see," said Jack, turning to Brisket, "I shall want two armies—one to preach the truth, and the other to practise warfare."

"How many men do you think are against us?" asked Brisket, addressing the scout.

"They will soon be numbered by thousands," replied the man, and the countenance of Brisket fell.

CHAPTER LIII.
MR. TRIMMER GETS INTO TROUBLE.

BROAD ARROW JACK had laid out a certain road by which he meant to reach the Ogre in his stronghold; but, ere he advanced, he found difficulties arising in every direction. Every little pass was guarded, every point of vantage taken possession of, and in the two following days he and his men had at least a dozen skirmishes with the outposts of the foe.

In all these he was victorious.

But as the defeated men fell back they served to swell the ranks of those who guarded the places in the rear, and soon it dawned upon our hero that the task he had set himself would require all his energies, all his tact, all that he could bring into the field, to ensure success.

He was not fighting against his enemies alone, but against the wild panic of a people. On every side—at wide distances apart, it is true—settlements had been formed, and vast bodies of emigrants had come over the sea, some to till the land, some to seek wealth in the diamond fields, and others to trade and play the part of mediums between the old world and the new nation then forming.

Among these people, most of them unlettered, ignorant men, the wild panic ran.

Broad Arrow Jack was a brigand.

He was a murderer, a thief, a ravisher of women, a plunderer of the poor. A hundred ruined homes bore witness, so they said, to his diabolical outrages.

The agents, appointed and self-chosen, of the Ogre increased and multiplied on every side.

Like a great tidal wave the fear of the brave lad swept over the land. In far-off settlements, where only the birds could apparently have whispered his name, he was spoken of as a spoiler and a blood-stained monster. Lots were drawn for men, who for the sake of the rest should go to help the great and noble Ogre, who called himself Captain Ogre, to stamp out this pest from the land.

They took with them money, goods, arms, ammunition, and horses to help the so-called saviour of the people, and as Jack was marching on, so these small bodies of men were, like rivulets, bearing down to swell the joint stream against him.

And, as he advanced, the power against him became more and more apparent. He met little knots of men at every turn, some of whom had the hardihood to show fight, only to be beaten and take refuge in flight. Others fled without a blow; but in every case they bent their footsteps or turned their horses' heads towards the home of the Ogre in the mountains.

One night, when Jack and his men were resting, he called Billy Brisket over to him, and a long and earnest consultation took place.

"It will never do," said Brisket, "to risk the possibility of a failure."

"Failure!" replied Jack, peevishly. "I cannot—will not fail!"

"Well, you know best; but you are only mortal. I reckon now that the odds are ten to one against us, and they are daily growing greater."

"Then we must not pause."

"Steady, my lad," said Billy. "We have been met with cunning, and let us give cunning in return."

"I will have nothing but what is open."

"Very well—don't," said Brisket, calmly; "but I suppose you can wait a little, and do nothing?"

"I have waited years; and a few days will not matter to me."

"Then wait, and leave the management of this business to me. If I understand you aright, you have no ill-feeling against these men so blindly mad against you?"

"None."

"And your only purpose is to secure the Ogre and Jaundice?"

"Alive. Bring them dead, and my purpose will not be accomplished."

"Very good," said Brisket. "To-morrow you shall pitch your tent in a place where you can defy these scattered bands of men, and bide your time until I shall bring up a power to crush them."

"If bloodshed can be avoided, let it be so; but those who stand between me and those villains do so at their peril."

"They shall be warned," said Brisket.

The details of their encampment were then discussed, and before dawn the band was weakened of a dozen men, who were sent forth on various errands —some to bring up stores, others to the seaport with messages for agents there, and the rest to the various bands of men guarding certain outlets where they were no longer wanted.

And on the morrow they came in sight of the Ogre's home, standing out boldly about seven miles distant, and on a well-chosen spot Broad Arrow Jack pitched his tent.

A rough entrenchment was thrown up, and the outposts of the Ogre, alarmed, fell back to the shelter of a narrow pass which a dozen men ought to have held against a regiment.

And there they rested seven days, Jack keeping for the most part within his tent, and only coming forth to look at the stronghold of his enemy, as if he feared it would be, by some mischance, moved away.

But there it was, and in mockery of his foe the Ogre had hoisted a rough flag of canvas, with a broad arrow cut out in black, and stitched upon it. By the aid of a glass Jack could see it, and it made him smile.

"A little while," he said, "and you shall haul your colours down."

Each day brought strength to the Broad Arrow camp. The Tiger, so true upon the trail, was one of the first to come in, and he was sent forth to seek and guide thither those who were doubtful of the road. He brought in many, including Conky, Curler, and Pigeon, who had been living, so they said, for days on grass and the bark of trees. Old Joss brought in Wobbles without help.

One morning the Tiger brought in a stranger—a cool, collected stranger, who carried pistols in his belt, and seemed to be very intimate with the young and cat-like negro. Jack was informed of his arrival, with a request from the stranger for a short interview.

Jack was surprised at the request, but he bade him be shown in, and accordingly Mr. Trimmer came lounging in, with a calm face and searching eyes.

"How d'ye do?" he said, coolly, and taking a seat upon the table began to whistle.

Jack, without moving a muscle of his face, made a sign for Mr. Trimmer to leave the table, and take up a more respectful position. Mr. Trimmer merely produced a cake of tobacco from his pocket, cut a huge plug from it, and tucked it carefully into his left cheek.

"I'm glad to see you," he said, "for I've been in search of you for weeks. You didn't come that night."

"What night?" asked Jack.

"When I got into the Frenchman's bed, intending to have a pot shot at you when you came to skeer him. You wouldn't have skeered me, I can tell you."

"Oh, indeed!"

"No," said Mr. Trimmer, thoughtfully shaking his head, "you wouldn't have skeered me a bit—you wouldn't. I never was skeered in all my life, and I don't mean to be."

"Indeed!" said Jack again, so quietly that Mr. Trimmer ought to have paused before going further; but Mr. Trimmer was a gentleman supremely satisfied with himself, and he went on.

"When I heard Laranche talk of bolting I larfed," he said; "when he told me why we he was going to bolt I larfed. It amoosed me to find a full-grown man skeered by a boy."

"And you consider me a boy?" asked Jack—oh! so quietly!

"Not a common boy," replied Mr Trimmer—"sartinly not; but I'm clawed, and skewered, and biled, and frizzed if you are a man!"

"But, suppose I prove myself equal to a man, what would you think then?"

"I might call you a man."

"Get off this table, then."

"What for?"

"In the first place, it is a folding one," replied Jack, "made to be packed in a small compass, and not calculated to bear the weight of your pig's carcase; and, in the second place, I object to a stranger coming into my place and acting as if it were his own."

"Oh! you object to that, do you?"

"Yes, most certainly."

"Well, whether you do or not," said Mr. Trimmer, jauntily, "here I sits, and if you puts a finger on me I'll bring you down as sure as my name is what it is!"

"You are bold."

"I aint easily skeered."

"You are also rude."

"I was born without manners, and I shall die so; but I stands the ground as I took up when I wasn't fifteen, and I says every man has a right to do as he likes."

"Precisely," said Jack.

What followed had better be put into Mr. Trimmer's own words, spoken afterwards by him to a select audience of admiring listeners.

"He come on me," he said, "like a rocket, or a thunderstone, or a cannon ball—anything but like a mortial being—and, afore I knowed what was up, I see all creation spinning about like a top, and the table went to eternal smash; then the ground hit my head hard, and I went up in the air like an ingy-rubby ball; then I seemed to have got on the end of something which I arterwards found to be his arm, and I was chucked and jerked about anyhow and everywhere—h'isted up one moment, and flopped down the next with such a souse that I reckoned myself all apple squash in no time, and when it was all over I found myself doubled up like a blessed hedgehog who had got all his prickles put the wrong way about, and felt as if I'd been half toasted, to let me know what real grilling was. My coat-collar was gone, all the shirt as he had left me hung like a frill round my neck, and you could have put all the breath left in my body into a thimble, and had room for a marble arterwards. 'I gives in,' I ses—'I'm skeered;' and, if ever I spoke the truth in all my lying life, I spoke it then."

And in this way was Mr. Trimmer subdued, and became one of the most devoted and all-admiring followers of my hero, Broad Arrow Jack.

CHAPTER LIV.

A MESSENGER RECEIVED.

"TRIMMER!"

"Yes, sir," replied the defeated one, as he stood before his master on the second day after his defeat.

"You know the Ogre?"

"Yes, sir, I've seen him many a time—and a low-bred ugly customer he is."

"I want you to go with a flag of truce, and bear a message to him," said Jack.

"That's an ugly business, going into the lion's den when he's hard up," thought Trimmer; but he merely said in reply, "I'm on, sir."

"You had better take two or three men with you," said Jack.

"Very good, sir," replied Trimmer.

"Choose those you would wish to accompany you."

"Which do you feel you can spare best?" asked Trimmer, with the face of a man going out to a quiet tea.

"Take whom you will," said Jack. "This is my message—I am anxious to avoid useless bloodshed, and I challenge Jaundice and the Ogre to single or double combat. I will fight them alone or together, with any weapon or weapons they may choose, in any place, at any hour, provided there are fitting arrangements made for fair play. If I fall by the hand of one or both, my men shall be at once withdrawn, and they shall go where they will."

"All right, sir," said Trimmer. "Can you let me have a rag to take with me, as the little linen I had when I came got into trouble when you and I collided?"

"Brisket shall give you a white handkerchief," replied Jack, and Trimmer—whose collarless coat was buttoned close up round his throat—bowed with marvellous politeness, and retired.

He had a stroll round the camp, with the object of finding four of the most useless men, and settled upon Wobbles, Conky, Curler, and the Pigeon. Having gathered them together, he told them that they were to accompany him to the den of the enemy.

They one and all mildly demurred; but Trimmer was firm.

"It's the chief's orders," he said, "and them as don't like to obey 'em are to dance on nothing, with some carefully-combed and spun hemp about their throttles."

So they yielded to his persuasive voice and went, in fear and trembling, the calm Trimmer leading the way, with a white handkerchief tied on the top of a stick, and a short black pipe in his mouth, smoking like a penny steamboat's funnel.

The whole camp gave them a cheer and many encouraging words as they went forth; but no amount of cheering or hopeful words could have put strength into the limp legs of the quartette who followed in his wake.

"We are all doomed men!" groaned Wobbles. "The Ogre is a man as will think nothing of skinning us."

"Can't we bolt?" asked Conky.

The question reached the ears of Mr. Trimmer, who, turning his head over his shoulder, replied—

"The first man as makes a rearward movement will be shot like a skunk. Here, come forward, the lot of you, so that I may keep an eye on you."

Broad-Arrow Jack.

"HOW CAN YOU EXPECT MERCY?" SAID JACK.—"YOU DESERTED FROM MY RANKS, JOINED MY ENEMIES, AND ATTEMPTED MY LIFE!"

NO. 9.

He drove them thenceforth, and in a short time they were in the lines of the enemy, who, failing at first to see the flag of truce, let fly at them, and drilled a hole through the hat of Wobbles. Fortunately no other mischief was done, and after a little parleying the party was allowed to enter the pass.

They were gone fifteen hours, and returned shortly before noon the next day. Trimmer had his head tied up, and all the others limped in a way that spoke of soreness in some influential part of their anatomy.

A little pale, but otherwise unchanged, Mr. Trimmer presented himself before his leader in his tent, and saluted.

"Well," said Jack, "what said they?"

"Not much, chief," replied Trimmer, calmly, "but they did a great deal. I was took with the rest before the Ogre, and as soon as I saw him I knew he meant mischief. He and the t'other chap had been drinking, and they was jest in the humour for anything—they was.

"'Who are you?' ses the Ogre.

"'Ambassador from his highness Broad Arrow Jack,' I ses, and then I gave your message. He hears it, and looks at the other chap, and laughs.

"'Good idea that,' he ses.

"'Werry,' replied the other, and he laughs too, but he was so drunk that he fell off his stool, and lay there reglar helpless.

"The Ogre calls in some people then, and whispers a few words in their ears. They laughs, and tells us to come out. We went out, and they seizes the chaps I took with me, and larrups 'em, until I thought they would have been flayed alive. Then they tries to larrup me, but I stood up agin it, and so they gets me down, and the Ogre coming out, he tells 'em to cut off my ears."

"To cut off your ears?" cried Jack.

"Yes, and they does it, slick and right away. I must wear a thick handkerchief or a big wig all the rest of my days," and taking off his handkerchief he showed the horrible wounds left by the diabolical mutilation.

Jack rose, and paced to and fro with agitated steps. His grief and rage overpowered him for the time, and he could not speak, but he found his tongue at last.

"Trimmer," he said, holding out his hand, "forgive me. If I had dreamt of such an atrocity I would rather have died than sent you."

"Don't mention it," replied Trimmer, as he warmly grasped the hand of his chief. "It aint your fault, and I mean to play the return rubber by-and-bye. T'other chaps would be glad of a pot of ointment if you've got such a thing."

"They shall be seen to," said Jack, with a wave of his hand. "But oh! what scoundrels these men are! Trimmer, you shall be bitterly avenged."

"Don't think of me," replied Trimmer. "I've lived too long among kicks and blows to feel sore at any rub I get. Still, I must say, I should like to have kept my ears. They are always useful, and sometimes ornamental. Mine weren't particularly ornamental, but I took 'em with the rest of things I've got about me, and didn't grumble. Shall I take another message back?"

"No, thank you, Trimmer; you are a brave man, and I cannot spare you."

"Anyhow," said Trimmer, as he lounged out, "I'm ready for anything or anybody when you wants me."

CHAPTER LV.

TWO MISSIONARIES COME TO GRIEF.

A FEW days passed without any event of imtance. Both sides were, however, busy with preparations for the coming struggle, which, for such a place and among such people, promised to be of serious import.

The affair of the flag of truce excited much indignation among the Broad Arrow men, and Trimmer, as he deserved, came in for much sympathy. Conky, Curler, Pigeon, and Wobbles were left, however, to take care of themselves.

The general opinion was that "a licking could not possibly do any one of them harm, and might do them a little good."

"And yet," said Wobbles, bitterly, when he heard of the hardness of the people's hearts, "they calls this a lovely world, overflowing with brotherly love, and all manner of sich like stuff. Henceforth I lives alone—a sort of 'ermit, for I knows the world and despises it."

"It seems to me," said Conky, gloomily, squinting at the sky, "that some men are born downright unfortunate. Do what they may, they never holds a trump; my life have been a long string of unvarying deuces. Perhaps if I'd fallen into better company, I might have been better off."

On this, Curler, Pigeon, and Wobbles bristled up, all looking very much like dung-hill cocks, who are disposed to forget innumerable thrashings and have one more go in.

Wobbles took the lead.

"If," he said, "you had fallen into better company, how long do you think a low warmint like you would have stopped there?"

To this the somewhat staggered Conky made no reply, and Curler emboldened came forward.

"When I 'ears a thing like you," he said, "a talking of better company, I feels a rising in me as can't be stopped, for if ever there was a chap in this world as rose through the people he met with, it was you."

"Draw it mild," said Conky, softly. Brave as he was, he generally, to use a turfy phrase, "cut it" when multitudes rose up against him.

"You draws it mild," said Pigeon, fancying he was on safe ground; "you never was nothing better than a bonnet to a speeler, or a duck's egg to a leery gander, afore we took you up. And now when you find you are gettin' on in the world there's no holdin' you in."

"Who's gettin' on in the world?" asked Conky, for the want of something better to say.

"All of us—a little," replied Wobbles, placing his hand upon his breast, where a certain bag reposed, and held fast the wealth of the once contumacious Jereboam Bounce. "Who knows, now that we've got a start in life, but we may go home to the old country and be all lord mayors?"

"I wouldn't go home for that," said Conky, in disgust. "If I went in for anything I'd be a poor-law guardian."

"Wot for?" asked Curler.

"Because then I should have people to deal with as can't say nuffin do what you may. They comes for relief, and you gives it to 'em if you like, and if you don't they goes without it. Lor', if once I sit on a poor-law board won't I be down on them as comes a gammonin'? I once took relief from four different parishes, and should have gone on but for you, Pigeon."

"Yes, I know," said Pigeon, sadly, "we was doing well; but my saying I was second cousin to the beadle was our ruin. He was a proud man—he wouldn't stand it; and having devoted two days to henquiries he bowled us out, and we was done."

Of similar touching memories of the past they talked for many hours, thereby relieving themselves from the monotony of a sick couch, for all had been so mauled and beaten that for many days perambulation was impossible.

They had sinned, it is true, but they had suffered much, and if they had suffered more I dare say it would only have been just.

A break in the quietude of the camp came at last. A party bearing a flag of truce arrived, and stood without the earthworks of the Broad Arrow camp. It was composed of five men, strong muscular fellows, all heavily armed. They sought, they said, an interview with Jack.

"Don't go," was Brisket's advice; "they mean treachery."

"Ask them to come here," replied Jack; "I do not fear them."

They were bidden to enter within the camp, but this they declined.

"We cannot trust ourselves with brigands," they said.

Jack immediately gave orders for them to be surrounded, and his active men performed this manoeuvre with great rapidity. The truce party were called upon to lay down their arms and they did so.

"We have come into the net," said their leader, "and we must die like men."

Jack came forth, and told them they would not die.

"Declare your purpose," he said, "and go."

"We can declare it," replied the leader, "and die. Our object was to slay you!"

"And why?" asked our hero, calmly.

"You ask this in the face of our wrecked homes," said the leader, bitterly, "of our slaughtered little ones. and our wives, who, thank God, are now no more."

"The hellish work was not mine!" said Jack.

"Whose then?" asked the leader, fiercely.

"The man you serve or his agents," replied Jack. "Right well has he covered himself in his outrages. I have never harmed you or yours."

"So you say."

"So I swear. But brought you no message from the demon who has blinded you?"

"Only this," replied the leader; "that if you are given up to him your men may leave here unharmed."

"He is too kind," said Jack, quietly. "And by what power does he send such an impudent message to me?"

"By the power of his strength! Those who serve him are closing in around you. In a few days escape will be impossible."

"Why, then, did you not wait?"

"Because our wrongs are too great," replied the leader, passionately. "But eight days ago you or those who serve you came upon us in the night and fixed a broad arrow upon the door. I thought it was some jest; but on the next night you came to rouse us from a peaceful sleep, and deal death, dishonour, and ruin around us. Oh! villain—cursed villain—how can you ask us why we could not wait until it was too late for us to deal out vengeance ourselves?"

He was a tall, fine man, with a vigorous expressive face, and as he poured out the story of his wrongs the veins in his forehead stood up like cords. The others, in a more subdued form, expressed a similar emotion.

"Blind—all blind!" said Jack. "Have you all suffered?"

"All," replied the leader. "But why do you mock us? You know how you have worked, and with what success."

"Nay," said Jack, proudly, "I am innocent of all you accuse me of. This hand of mine has never done a foul deed, or taken life, save in what I consider to be a just retaliation for my wrongs. Your ruined homesteads, your slaughtered children, and all else are the work of the Ogre, Jaundice, and a chosen few, who keep their secret well, and laugh as they gull you."

"I have only your word for this," said the man.

"Go back," replied Jack, "and give the Ogre this message—tell him to lie, and murder, and plunder, and make fools of the noble and honourable, with all the art he can use—tell him to call hordes of the cunning, the foolish, and the weak together—tell him to shut himself up where he may—even in the bowels of the earth—and all shall be in vain! He is doomed—he and all who, knowing him as he is, willingly serve him."

"Go I back alone?" asked the leader.

"No—all of you," returned Jack. "I kill neither the helpless nor the foolish. Back to the master you, in your folly, serve; tell him what I say, and leave him."

"If all you say is true," said the man, "it is our duty to serve you."

"Nay," said Jack, "I want none of you—I will not have you. There are sufficient stout hearts here who know how to work my will when the time shall come."

"And yet ——"

"No more!" said Jack, sternly. "Begone! You have taken the word of the first knave you met, and helped to blacken my name. It is enough—I will have none of you. Lead them forth, and send them back to their *noble* master."

Doubting and troubled, the men were led to the outside of the camp, and sent back to the stronghold of the Ogre, where they delivered the message boldly to the man it was intended for.

He and Jaundice were drinking, as usual, when they came, and as the man who had been spokesman throughout gave his return message the features of the swarthy villain grew black with rage.

But he spoke smoothly—declared the leniency of Jack was but a blind to lure all honest men over to him—and the five settlers, scarce knowing what to think, went to rest.

And while they slept an armed force came suddenly upon them, gagged and bound them, and bore them away. The next morning five shapeless masses of humanity lay at the base of the great cliff, and the carrion birds came from far and near to hold high revelry on their bones.

"We must have no doubting men here," said the Ogre to Jaundice. "Disaffection grows, and ought to be, at the first sign of its coming, stamped out like a disease."

"But have you no thought of those ghastly objects lying below there?" asked Jaundice, shivering.

"None," said the Ogre.

"I looked upon them this morning," continued Jaundice. "I was drawn thither in spite of myself, and, looking down, I saw a flock of carrion crows busy with *those we put there*. Great power above us, it was awful!"

"You have no nerve," said the Ogre, contemptuously.

"I am not all brute even yet," said Jaundice, as he walked away.

The Ogre looked after him with a dangerous light in his evil eyes. "I see," he said, "it all rests upon myself. Disaffection, cowardice, and all else must be stamped out, if need be, even in you."

It was only an hour afterwards when a messenger came with the intelligence that two men were wandering among the outposts, preaching the goodness, honour, and truthfulness of Broad Arrow Jack. Men were listening and wondering, the Ogre was told, and more than one believed.

"Secure those men," said the Ogre, "and bring them hither."

In a dozen hours they were secured and brought. Sancho and Hardacre were in the presence of a remorseless judge.

"You have been preaching against me," said the Ogre.

"Yes," replied Hardacre, calmly, "and I have said nothing but the truth."

"And not half the truth," added Sancho.

"Take them in the night," said the Ogre to his select followers, and hang them within the sight of the branded young fool who dares to pursue me."

And in the night they took the two missionaries, gagged and bound, and hung them up on the branches of a spreading tree, and left them to die.

Untutored hands did the work of the common hangman, and, with ill-adjusted cords around their throats, the two unfortunate men struggled long for their lives.

All that has ever happened at public executions pales before the story of the way they died. One man—a follower of the Ogre—was told off to see they did not escape, and he was found at early morn held fast to the place spell-bound by the horrors he had looked upon.

He was discovered by Broad Arrow Jack—who was walking about alone, regardless of the risk he ran—who, seeing the two forms he well remembered, dangling lifeless, fell upon the wretch, and seized him by the throat.

"Whose work is this?" he asked.

"Not mine!" gasped the man. "I had no hand in it."

"But you know who did the deed," said Jack. "Speak, or I will choke the life out of your wretched carcase!"

"We only obeyed Captain Ogre," was the reply. "We hanged them, and they died hard. I am sorry. I would not look upon such another scene to save my own life."

"Died hard! Tell me all."

"They were pulled up, and left to my care. All night long, as it seems to me, they kicked and groaned and gasped, and by the light of the moon I could see their wild eyes staring! Oh, spare me! It was horrible!"

And the man, a poor ignorant brutal creature at the best, covered his face with his hands, and shuddered.

"And you," said Jack, "could look on such a scene, and not cut them down."

"I never thought of it," replied the man, and Jack, with a bitter word, kicked him from him.

"Surely," he said, as he stood before the two dead men, "the measure of that monster is more than full. This day, if my arm can wreak its vengeance, the Ogre shall be no more!"

He brought up a number of his men to look upon the scene, and to bear record of the deed. Then the two victims of the Ogre's cruelty were taken gently down, and buried in a grave, with no other headstone than the tree on which they died.

CHAPTER LVI.

MAGGIE AND CALIBAN.

THE great diamond fields were in full swing, and there was work for all. The majority of those who assembled there laboured in search of the precious gems which the world holds so dear; but there were many—and they were for the most part the more prudent—who worked in other ways.

Some were hewers of wood and drawers of water, others baked and brewed. Many administered to the inborn love for amusement, and not a few gambled, stole, cheated, and went on an evil way, which in many cases was, if at all sweet, remarkably short.

Among those who catered for the diggers in the way of amusement was a woman, who sang nightly at one of the shanties which the speculative mind of an enterprising gentleman had set up. It was a music-hall in embryo, an opera company in the bud; but most of the people who performed there had bloomed long ago, and were in the sear and yellow leaf of existence.

The woman in question was no longer young—the hand of Time lay heavy on her, and a face, once beautiful as the dawn of a spring morning, was faded and wan; but there was the outline of her past treasure left, and this, with the remnant of a once sweet voice, made her an immense favourite with the earth-stained toilers who came to the wooden hut at night, to find some relaxation from their arduous labour.

Whenever she appeared they rose *en masse*, and hailed her with a shout. When her song was over they cast money upon the stage, and flung their hats to the ceiling. They swore by her—they, in their rough way, wrote letters enclosing gifts, and left them at the door of the place. They made her offers of marriage, and more than one quarrel arose as to who was eventually to be the happy man.

She heard all—received all, but gave answer to none. The money was sent away to be hoarded, not for her own use, but for one more worthless; and alone she lived, close to the scene of her triumphs, stealing to and fro, and speaking to no man.

And this was Maggie Jaundice, who, true as only a woman can be, yet clung to the man she loved in her girlhood, and toiled for his benefit. "If he should escape," she said, "he shall have enough in another land to keep him honest."

She did not want him for herself—she had no wish to live with him again, but the love once fixed in the strong clay of a woman's soul could never be uprooted, but rather grew and flourished in that most congenial soil. Is the old distich true?—

"A woman, a dog, and a walnut tree.
The more ye lick 'em the better they be."

Surely that was written by some coarse hound who had no gentleness in his breast, but ate, and drank, and swore, and trod upon the weak and helpless. Ah! a woman wants no beating. If she remain good under that she will be something better with kindness.

I am not going to dwell upon Maggie's life in the diamond fields—my intelligent readers can easily imagine what that was. Monotonous, but not utterly miserable. She had a purpose in her life, and that always keeps us from utter misery.

One night she was singing her best to the all-admiring diggers. It was a simple song—one she had known in her childhood, without one line in it to suit the palate of those who love coarseness, without one word in it to draw a laugh from the reprobate mind; but these men, half brutes as most were, listened, and felt some long-hidden spring within them drawn to the surface. In some it broke forth in tears.

She saw her power and gathered strength from it. Her eyes wandered from one row of attentive faces to another, until, in a far corner, they looked upon—

Caliban.

Yes, there was the monster who had once played gaoler to her husband, sitting with his eyes fixed upon her with a look no woman, especially one worldly wise, could ever mistake.

She shuddered, paused in the midst of her song, and turned as if to go.

The proprietor of the place, who acted as chairman, asked her in a hurried voice if she was ill, and held up his glass for her to drink from.

She put it aside with a motion of her hand, and went on with her song, forcing out mechanically the notes which hitherto had rolled out spontaneously.

The song ended, the applause rang out, the gifts were tossed upon the stage and gathered up, and she went back to the rough dressing-room.

Thither the proprietor presently came to ask her what ailed her.

"It was nothing," she said, "merely an odd fancy. I am sometimes nervous. Will you lend me your revolver?"

"What for?"

"To protect myself. There are many strangers in the fields just now, and some, I fear, are rather rough. Some may seek to rob me."

The man said nothing more, but gave her the revolver, and Maggie left. As she got outside she saw an uncouth figure waiting for her. It was Caliban.

Pretending she did not see him she moved on, but he put himself before her, and in the light of the moon began one of his uncouth dances—horrible in its fantastic movements and meaning. He told the story of his love as plain as others ever told it in words.

She looked around. The field was clear of all but themselves. Those not in the music-hall were at rest.

"Stand back!" she cried, drawing her revolver, and presenting it at him.

He laughed in *his* way, which was awful to hear, and stood aside. She walked boldly past him to a small hut erected for her, went in, and closed the door.

Caliban came up, and lay down like a dog in front of it.

She heard him settle down with his weight against the door, and put all she could into a barricade to keep him out; but she might have spared herself the trouble. Caliban had no idea of forcing his way in—at present.

In the depths of his savage brain there lay the desire to win and woo her if possible, but with it there rested the resolve never to part from her again.

CHAPTER LVII.
SENTRY DUTY.

WHEN Wobbles formed part of Trimmer's escort it was an extremely fortunate thing for him that neither the Ogre nor Jaundice recognised their old companion. Had either done so, Wobbles would not have escaped with a simple thrashing.

But both were the worse for drink, and in the five men they only saw so many emissaries from the enemy's camp. It was only because Trimmer was the leader of the party that he was doomed to suffer more seriously.

Apparently he took his injuries very quietly, but no man ever lost his ears yet without feeling the loss keenly, and in the depths of Trimmer's bosom great fires of wrath were burning.

But he kept them down, and not even the smoke of his internal furnace was allowed to escape. Looking seriously, he went about his work unchanged, save in the appearance given him by the handkerchief which he now wore continually round his head.

It was only when alone that his face showed what he felt.

Then the placidity faded out, and in its place there came a look of stern resolve. He would examine his arms carefully, sharpen his bowie, and hack in the air at an imaginary foe.

"If it wasn't going ag'in the chief," he muttered again and again, "I'd go up and settle 'em both. There's a way of doing everything if you only set your mind to it. But I'm bound—I am. The chief claims 'em for himself."

One of his favourite duties was sentry work. Trimmer liked that, as it brought him close to the foe, and whenever he got a shot at one of them, that man went under. Five men in three days fell by his hand, and after that the outposts of the Ogre became exceedingly wary.

Jack knew nothing of this, or perhaps he would have stopped it at the first. At length, however, it reached his ears, and he sent for Trimmer.

"What is this you have been doing?" he said. "You have disobeyed orders."

"Yes," replied Trimmer; "but I've only brought down such men as I've marked. They all had a hand in this," pointing to the place where his ear had been.

"I grant it is pardonable," said Jack; "but it must not be. While here you must act according to orders. If you wish to carry out a private object you must leave."

"It's hard to bear," said Trimmer.

"So it is," replied our hero; "but you bear it like a man. I am proud of such men as you are."

"That is enough," cried Trimmer; "henceforth I live for you alone."

He went on sentry no more, for fear as he said of "being tempted," and Wobbles was appointed to his post.

The first night the valiant one went on duty he was placed in a hollow in the rock, with instructions to keep his eye upon the narrow path running towards the foe, and to give the alarm and fire into the air if a foe appeared in sight.

The moon was at her full, and the scene before him was almost, as the saying goes, as bright as day. A rabbit scuttling across the road could have been seen plainly.

Darkness had great terrors for Wobbles, but he would have preferred it, for he recognised the fact that if he could see an enemy, that enemy would have a fair chance of seeing him. The hollow in the rock was a shallow one, and was for concealment a delusion and a snare.

He lay crouching there for awhile, his eyes fixed ahead, and scarcely daring to move. The silence was unbroken for an hour or more, and then a footstep in the rear startled him.

Cowering low down, so that his chin almost touched the earth, he looked in the direction of the sound, and beheld two forms approaching.

One a woman and the other a man.

The woman appeared to be hurrying away from the man, and turned half a dozen times in a hundred yards to warn him off. The man stopped, but expressed his defiance in an uncouth dance.

"By Jingo!" thought Wobbles, "I knows 'em both. It's Maggie Jaundice and that underground brute, Caliban. "What are they doing here?"

"Maggie was too much absorbed in beating a retreat from him to have eyes for aught else, and pulled up within half a dozen yards of Wobbles, to turn once more, and hold up her hand threateningly. A bowie knife gleamed in the moonlight, and Wobbles turned cold.

"They are all alike here," he said, "all a-thirsting for blood, and that woman is as bad as any of 'em. She allers was. I wouldn't have a Mrs. Wobbles like her for all the mint-money of old England."

"Stand back!" cried Maggie, hoarsely. Voice and attitude both told of a fatiguing journey. "If you come within reach of my arm I will strike you dead, as I live!"

Caliban gave vent to some of his hideous cackling, and danced in derision, but he kept his distance. Maggie was weary and worn, but she had the substitute for strength—courage—in her still.

She passed on, and Caliban came up. He saw Wobbles and paused. The grimly humorous expression of face with which he had followed Maggie changed to one of intense ferocity.

In a moment his strong arms were around the sentinel, who in gasping tones cried out for mercy.

Mercy he never would have had if Caliban had not speedily recognised him, and, with a contemptuous cackle, he threw him down upon the ground. Caliban in the first instance had evidently mistaken him for another.

"It's only a lark of yourn, I knows," murmured Wobbles; "but it's a rough 'un, and don't come quite as sich to them as has to bear it. A man aint made of glass, I knows, but at the same time he aint all cast iron."

Caliban, who had been looking up the pass after Maggie never heeded Wobbles until she disappeared. Then he turned and signed to him that he wanted something to eat.

It so happened that Wobbles, with a view to a most probable appetite, had brought some meat and bread with him. This he handed to Caliban, who bolted it whole like a famished wolf.

Then he signalled for drink, and Wobbles produced a flask full of wine. Caliban put it to his lips, and never took it away while a drop remained.

"Of course," muttered Wobbles to himself. "Go it. Never mind me or my property. Nobody ever did, leastways when they knowed I had it; but just now I happens to have a little about me as nobody knows of, or they would be round me like a pack of ravishing wolves. Hallo! what now?"

Caliban was upon his feet, making signs for Wobbles to take off his coat. The garment of the dumb man was in a very bad condition, and he desired an exchange.

Wobbles turned pale, for within the lining of that coat was stitched the wealth he inherited through the death of Jereboam Bounce.

"I can't part with that," he said, in quavering tones.

Caliban imperiously signalled to him to hand it over at once.

"It's a birthday keepsake," pleaded Wobbles, "made for me by a mother who have gone aloft, which, with all her herrors in screwing up for me, she was of kindly 'art, and I loves her memory. Take my boots and my hat, but spare me my coat."

But Caliban was bent upon having the coat, and intimated nothing else would do. A desperate feeling came to the rescue of Wobbles. He felt very much like an old hen about to be robbed of her young, and was almost as plucky.

"You can't and shan't have it," he said, backing, and mechanically cocking his rifle. "I'd rather blow your brains out. Stand back."

Caliban, with a defiant grunt, rushed on him, and Wobbles, in the fear of losing his treasure, fired. The dumb monster staggered back, and fell.

Wobbles fled.

He ran like a deer, shrieking for help, until he ran against Nat Green, who with a dozen men were rushing towards the spot from whence the noise of the gun proceeded.

"Hallo—hallo!" cried Nat, "what's up?"

"The henemy—the henemy," gasped Wobbles, "coming up strong. I've shot one of 'em."

"Then he put his nose into the muzzle of your gun," replied Green, with a contemptuous laugh. "Here, let us see who is coming."

"They are led by Caliban," said Wobbles. "If you see him shoot him down."

His fear of the dumb monster was intense. He had made an enemy of him for life, and knew he would get no mercy from him. He had heard many a story of the dumb man's rancour when once his evil passions were aroused, and he had good cause to tremble.

They went back to the spot, Wobbles keeping well in the rear, and found—nobody. Caliban was gone.

"I thought," said Nat Green, "it was all your fancy."

"Perhaps that pool of blood is fancy," said Wobbles. "I shot him, and he fell there."

That somebody had been shot was certain. A great patch of blood yet warm and moist lay upon the hard ground, and a little further there were large dabs, showing the way the wounded man had taken. He was still upon the trail of Maggie.

"You've hit somebody," said Green, seriously, "and if it is Caliban I'm downright truly sorry for you. Keep out of his clutches, for when roused he is a very demon of a fellow."

"I did what was my duty," replied Wobbles, with a shudder; "but seeing as I've done it I hopes the chief will act honourable, and see that I'm well guarded. A man ought not to be murdered for doing his duty."

"Of course not," said Nat Green, "and if Caliban shows, I for one will shoot him down. But still I don't see how he came to be fighting on the side of the enemy."

CHAPTER LVIII.

THE PUNISHMENT OF CALIBAN.

"JEB JAUNDICE, awake!"

Jeb Jaundice turned feverishly upon his rough couch, half opened his eyes, and muttered a curse in his sleep.

"Jeb Jaundice, it is I—Maggie, your wife."

He awoke then, and sat up staring. Before him was his wife, with the light of the morning streaming through the entrance to his tent full upon her face. In the white light she looked more like a spectre than a human being. He took her for the former.

"Spare me," he cried—"spare me. As you were loving in life haunt me not in death."

"Fear not," replied Maggie, coldly; "I have had too much of you in life to trouble you when once I am quiet in my grave."

"Then I look upon you living?"

"Yes, touch me, and be convinced."

Jeb Jaundice, assured of being in the presence of an earthly visitant, laughed as he laid a hand upon her arm.

"Yes," he said, "it is my own dear Maggie. What has brought you here?"

"I come to ask for your protection."

"Indeed," he said. "I thought you were quite capable of taking care of yourself."

It was a brutal answer, and she winced under it, but she made no reference to it as she proceeded.

"Jeb Jaundice," she said, "admit at least that I have done enough to entitle me to your protection."

"If you need it you shall have it," he said. "I am glad you are here, Maggie. I have thought a hundred times of you, and if you will only forget and forgive the past we may be happy together."

"What mad idea have you in your head now?" she asked. "Have I not forgiven? But how can I forget? Is it in my power to shut the doors of the mind, and let nothing that is there come forth?"

"At least," he said, "you can try to forget."

"Jeb," she answered, "say no more. There are some things I would do for you, and others I would not. I would toil day and night, risk my own life—nay, lose it for your sake; but to be what I was once, a fond wife again—never. You have set up the barrier against that. Friends only henceforth, Jeb, while we live. I was a friend to you in your trouble at Blackrock—be a friend to me. I saved you from the power of that monster, Caliban. Save me from him now."

"Save you from Caliban! What has he to do with you?"

"He haunts me, follows me everywhere with a horrible love. I feel as if some loathsome beast had set his heart upon me."

"Where is he?"

"Not far behind me," replied Maggie, "he is sure to keep near me. Like a bloodhound he has followed me from the diamond-fields to here."

"And have you walked the whole way?"

"Yes, see how thin I am—look at these almost fleshless hands," replied Maggie, "and here are my eyes deep sunk within their caverns. Oh! Jeb Jaundice, were it not so deadly a sin to take life, how gladly would I take mine!"

He was sorry for her—as sorry as a man of his stamp could be, and rising, he went to the corner of the tent, and brought out some bread and brandy.

"You are starving," he said; "eat and drink."

She ate and drank sparingly, and presently sat down upon the ground. Jeb Jaundice sat down beside her.

"Maggie," he said, "is your resolution irrevocable?"

"Yes," she said, "for it would come to that sooner or later. But leave me to rest. I am so worn that I can scarcely move."

"Nay, lie down, Maggie, and let me watch beside you," he said.

A faint smile flitted across her features as she made a gesture of dissent.

"Ah!" she said, "you are kind now, but your heart is a hard polished piece of steel, and the breath of love soon passes from its surface. No, Jeb, I do not need so close a guardian. Go without and watch there if you will."

"It is hard," he said, "not to be trusted."

And in a feeble way he felt himself to be an injured man. He went out, closed the tent carefully, and paced slowly up and down, thinking.

Was he really sorry for the past? He thought he was, and for the time he was a repentant man. The return of his wife, worn and wretched as she looked, had aroused a feeble representation of the love he bore her at first within him. And he had loved her once—as such men love—and sworn by her. She had been away from him for a time, and come back almost as something new.

"If we could only get away from this accursed place," he muttered, "and hide somewhere far over the sea, I think I might, if I was kind, win her back again. In the main she is as true as steel. But how can I leave? I am in a net, or two nets—one spun by a revengeful foe, the other of my own making."

Then he wondered how Maggie had learnt of his whereabouts, but that was solved afterwards by her telling him that the story of the struggle going on was the great theme in the diamond-fields, and the topic of every-day conversation, and from one there she had received directions as to the road to take.

He played the sentry for an hour or so, until a commotion he heard attracted his attention. Looking down he beheld the figure of Caliban being escorted and led up the rock by some of the Ogre's followers.

It was an unfortunate thing for Caliban that he should arrive at a time when Jeb Jaundice was thinking kindly of his wife, and particularly unfortunate that he should come a sort of wild fantastic suitor.

For the first time for many a year Jeb Jaundice felt indignant and jealous on account of his wife.

He had once suspected her being attached to Broad Arrow Jack, but that was more in mockery than aught else. Now he felt furious to think that even a monster like Caliban should look with a tender eye upon the woman he had so long and systematically neglected.

The way up was tedious, and a good ten minutes would elapse before the party would arrive at the table-land. He utilised these ten minutes in a conference with the Ogre, who had passed a feverish night, and was in no very amiable mood.

"Who's there?" he asked, as Jeb entered the tent.

"Me—Jeb," was the reply. "I want you to give me your help in a matter."

"I am not inclined to help any one just now. What is it?"

Jeb Jaundice gave a rapid account of the story told by Maggie, and the Ogre shrieked with laughter.

"Serve her right," he cried. "She might have had other lovers more comely, but she despised them all, and now she has one who will stick to her like a leech."

Jeb Jaundice frowned. Among other lovers she might have had the Ogre no doubt, but she had openly reviled him long ago. Jeb was anxious to say something to that effect, but prudence forbade him.

"But I do not mean to have this fellow following my wife," he said.

"How will you stop it?"

"May I deal with him as I like?"

"Yes, I care not; the fellow is nothing to me," and turning over, the Ogre went to sleep again.

A smile—a cruel smile—came into the face of Jaundice.

As he left his leader's tent, outside he met Caliban and his escort. Caliban had a wound in his shoulder, still bleeding.

"Ha! my friend," said Jaundice, "things turn about in this world; a little while ago I was your prisoner—now you are mine. Where did you find him?" he added, addressing the men.

"He came to the outpost this morning, and gave himself up. He made signs that he wanted to come here. We understood him to mean that you or Captain Ogre knew him."

"Aye!" said Jaundice, drily, "we both know him. He was the willing tool of Broad Arrow Jack. He was kept to torture the weak and helpless, to kill or maim, as it suited the whim of his master."

The eyes of Caliban protested against this, but he made no other sign. Jaundice held a whispered consultation with the men, and, when it was over, they led Caliban to a rude hut, standing at the far end of the table land.

Then, without his offering resistance, Caliban was bound, and stretched upon the ground. Some of the men looked pale, and it seemed as if they were engaged in some unpleasant task. Jaundice read their looks, and urged them on to some deed he had in view.

"Remember," he said, "it is only justice. As he has done to others, so you do to him."

"If, sir," said one of the men, hesitating, "you would spare us, we shall be glad."

"Go then," said Jaundice, " and leave him to me."

They went out quickly enough, and Jaundice was left with his prisoner. The men haited outside for a moment, until a short horrible cry of pain reached their ears. Then they turned and ran.

In a few minutes, Jaundice also came forth, and he too was ghastly pale. Some hours later he stood before his wife.

"Maggie," he said, "be no longer in fear of Caliban."

"How so?" she added.

"Come and see him."

He led the way, and she followed him to the hut. Jeb Jaundice threw open the door, and Caliban came crawling forth. He turned his face to Maggie, and she staggered back.

"Great God!" she cried, "he is blind."

"Yes," said Jeb Jaundice, "my hand did it. You can easily avoid him now."

"Oh! say you did it not for me," she cried. "I would not blind the meanest thing on earth to spare myself an age of pain. Poor, poor fellow!"

She put a hand upon his shoulder, and the poor mutilated creature lay down at her feet, and whined like a dog. She understood him then. He had not pursued her as men, calling themselves noble and better, would have done. He had only followed her as a devoted dumb animal might have done. It was all clear; his sightless eyes spoke plainer than e'er they had done before.

Woman's breast is the home of pity. The meanest, poorest, plainest creature, if suffering, can touch the chords, and bring out the music of woman's tender compassion. Caliban was an ugly, misshapen monster of a man, blind, dumb, and repulsive to look upon, but Maggie pitied h'm, and all that was revolting in his face and form was forgotten.

"Caliban," she said, " I grieve more deeply than I can express in words. I am the cause of your second great misfortune. Forgive me."

The sightless head bowed down, and the huge hand held up as if he begged of her not to think of him. She laid one of her small brown hands upon his arm.

"You will find it hard," she said, "to wend your way along the road. Come, I will be your friend and guide, and you shall be my faithful watchdog."

Hot tears rained down the face of Caliban, and the muscles around his mouth quivered. All that was good and pure in him—and the meanest of us have the little spark which keeps up our kindred with holy things—was touched. He would be her dog, that quivering face said, and no dog could be more faithful than he.

Whether it was the contrast afforded by Caliban, or the light of compassion which will beautify most faces, or both, it matters not. Be the cause what it may, Maggie seemed in the eyes of Jeb Jaundice to grow young and beautiful again.

The tide of passion came back with full force, sweeping along the barren coast of his hard nature, splitting up the great rock of indifference which had stood so long between him and her.

"Maggie," he said, in trembling tones, "surely you will never prefer the friendship of that —— creature to my love?"

"Your what?" she asked.

"My love."

"Jeb Jaundice, the only love you ever had was the love I gave—you have none of your own. Had you loved me we never could have come to this. False to me in a hundred ways, I have clung to you, not to gain from you that which you have not to give, but to be true to myself. I loved you, I gave my heart, and can never take it back; but I will not be the toy of any man, even if he holds the keys of my soul."

"You are unkind, Maggie. I swear I love you."

She laughed harshly, and turned to go.

"Farewell, Jeb," she said, "it is better I should leave you, or you will perjure your soul the more. If ever you have need of money, here on this paper you will find the address of a man who has charge of a little money I have made for you."

"But what do you mean, Maggie?" he asked; "you toil for me, slave for me, risk your life for me and say you love me, and yet you will not stay by my side. I do not understand you."

"You never did," she replied. "If you had, you might have now been a happy prosperous man."

"And will you leave me?"

"Most surely I will."

"And shall we never meet again?"

"That I cannot tell. Time will answer your question. Give me the password."

"Once more, Maggie——"

"No more; you know me. The torture of the rack would never induce me to change my mind. I am going. What is the password?"

"Revenge!" he said, gloomily.

She waved her hand to him, and taking off her scarf she bound it round the arm of Caliban, leaving a loose end to hold by.

"I can guide you now," she said, and, without another look at her husband, she moved away.

He watched her down the narrow path, saw her enter the valley, stopped here and there by watchful sentries, and so into a great rift in the mountains, when she disappeared.

"Without one glance back," groaned Jaundice. "I have indeed lost her now. What a fool's trick it was to blind that brute, and yet I thought it would have pleased her to find herself free from him, without his being slain! Maggie always had an aversion to taking life. What a woman she is— what depth of soul—what strength of purpose—and if"—he paused and looked up at a cloud flying athwart the sky—"if I had known—but I did not, and I am a doomed wretched man—without hope in this world or the next!"

CHAPTER LIX.

A FORAGING EXPEDITION.

AFTER that night when Wobbles encountered Caliban he showed a great distaste for sentry duty, volunteering to do any amount of camp work, menial or otherwise, if Nat Green would only find a more suitable man to fill his place.

He might have spared himself the trouble, for it had already been decided to keep him in the camp. Broad Arrow Jack declared him to be worse than useless, and bade Billy Brisket send him out no more.

There was also an idea afloat that Wobbles was just as likely to let fly at a friend as a foe, if one should visit him when he was on duty—an opinion derived from the various confused accounts he, in the course of two days, gave about that midnight adventure of his.

"It is my belief," said Nat, "that Caliban—if it was him—was only coming in a friendly way, and being let fly at, has very naturally cleared off— crawled into a hole like a rat, perhaps to die."

So it was decided to put Wobbles to other labour. But Nat Green kept him for several days in suspense, declaring it was the intention of the chief to give Wobbles the most dangerous post, so that he might be able to fully cover himself with honour and glory.

"But I don't want to be covered with anything of the sort," pleaded Wobbles. "Anbody can have the honour and glory—I'll give it to 'em."

"But the eyes of all are on you," urged Nat.

"Let 'em take 'em off again," replied Wobbles.

"I don't think they will," said Nat, with a sad shake of the head.

"What a thing it is to have had a sainted mother!" groaned Wobbles, when he was left alone. "She must have known that she was working for my ruin. I wish I'd never had a mother. Another night like that will kill me."

He suffered much until Nat Green kindly released him by appointing him to more suitable work. Forage was needed, and some of the men were despatched to a plain to cut grass. Others were wanted to tie it into bundles and bring it to the camp; and what better men than Conky, Curler, Pigeon, and Wobbles for such an agricultural pursuit could be found?

"You had better ride Fireworks and old Joss down," said Nat, calmly, "just as you rode them before, and bring back as much as the horses will carry at night."

"Wouldn't it be better to have stronger horses?" suggested Conky. "Fireworks and old Joss are gettin' past their work, and ought to have rest. I hates cruelty to hanimals."

Curler said he loathed it, and Pigeon told a story of his grandfather, who devoted a considerable fortune and a long life to looking up people who ill-treated their cattle.

Nat Green cut him short at an interesting point, where the grandfather was at a meeting in Exeter Hall, receiving a piece of plate subscribed for by the friends of humanity.

"You will get away at once," he said. "It is the chief's orders, and you are to ride. Disobedience here is punished with death."

Left to themselves, the quartette were very sad. Horsemanship was not at all to their taste, especially when such eccentric steeds had to be ridden.

"I wonder why these horses can't be friendly?" said Conky, with a savage frown.

"They never will," replied Wobbles.

"I've got it!" cried Conky, after a painful pause.

"Well, what is it?"

"You and Pigeon go forrard on old Joss, and me and Curler will foller. If they don't see each other them hanimals will be quiet."

"I wish I was sure of that," said Wobbles. "Howsomever, let's be off, or the chief may be down on us; and when he does—oh, my eye!"

Old Joss and Fireworks were duly captured, and Wobbles and Pigeon were hoisted upon the back of old Joss, surrounded by a circle of admiring men, who were looking forward to some of the circus tricks and the usual fun.

But old Joss disappointed them.

He was in an excellent humour that morning, and, not having been out for days, was full of spirits. The way he lifted his feet at starting excited the admiration of all beholders.

He went off so suddenly that Pigeon, who was not quite settled in his seat, knocked his chin against the head of Wobbles, and bit his tongue. He saved himself from a fall by throwing his arms around the neck of his companion.

"I say!" gasped Wobbles. "Come, none o' that. You'll have us both off."

"I aint a-goin', if I can help it," hissed Pigeon, whose grip was strong enough to promise Wobbles suffocation. "Pull him up."

"Can't," said Wobbles. "Let go, you murderous villain!"

Pigeon considerately loosened his grasp a little; but his position was one of great peril. The trot of old Joss was trying at any time, but on this occasion it was positively awful.

He lifted his hoofs about five feet in the air, and brought them down again with a sound like carpet-beating. He also snorted, cocked his ears, and now and then at odd times hoisted that part of his frame Pigeon sat upon in a jerky sort of way that would have tried the temper, if not the skill, of the best jockey in Europe.

"We are comin' orf!" cried Pigeon, suddenly, as he went over, after one of the above-named jerks, to an angle of forty-five degrees.

Fortunately Wobbles went the other way, and the balance of horsemanship was preserved. Getting upon smooth ground, old Joss settled into a more easy trot, and the two noble riders righted themselves.

"I say!" whispered Pigeon.

"Well?" asked Wobbles.

"We are out of sight of the camp now. Shall e get off and walk?"

"When he stops."

"Can't you pull him up?"

"Can't you see that I'm trying?"

Indeed he was, and any other horse would have had half his head cut off by the bit; but it would have taken a steam-saw to get through the jaws of the dear old animal, and Wobbles tugged in vain.

"Where he gets his sperrit from I don't know," gasped Wobbles, as old Joss gave another rearward twist.

"I wish his sperrit lay at the tother end, and you had it all," was the reply of Pigeon, who had risen so high in the air that his heels had left their mark half-way up the haunches of the steed.

"He don't seem to be giving in at all," said Wobbles, as they went round a corner like an express train.

"Suppose he's gone mad?" said Pigeon, and then he began to debate within himself what would be the result of sliding off behind.

He glanced at the hind legs of old Joss, and shuddered; for the magnificent action that animal displayed, as he threw out his hoofs quite three feet to the rear, with a curly upward turn, suggested a violent kick in the ribs and an untimely death.

"Can't be done," he groaned. "I'm on him until he stops. Woa, there!"

"You hold your tongue," said Wobbles, exasperated—"a-bullying a horse as you know nothink about. He won't stand it."

"I only said 'Woa!' and surely a man can say that? Hallo! where is he going now?"

"It seems to me," replied Wobbles, in thrilling tones "that there is a kind o' stone wall, and he's a-going to try to jump it."

Nothing in response to this could Pigeon offer. From head to foot he was as cold as ice.

The "stone wall" was only a pile of loose stones, formerly part of a rough shanty erected by some travellers. The roof had been taken off and burnt long ago, and the rude walls had gradually fallen to pieces. Only one portion, about sixteen feet long and five high, remained, and this old Joss was going straight at, bent upon getting over or through it.

He arrived at the spot, and rose like a bird at it.

His fore legs got over, but the infirmity of old age remained with the others, and they were left behind. A few of the top stones were knocked off, but the others remained, and there he was, with head on one side and tail on the other.

"He's done it now," said Wobbles.

"Yes, let us get off and help him over."

Easier said than done. As soon as they made signs of dismounting old Joss began to plunge about violently, and there was a prospect of their all coming down together on the top of an ugly pile of remorseless stones.

"Better keep still," said Pigeon; "perhaps he is only stopping for breath."

So they sat still, and old Joss apparently went to sleep, making sundry noises, not unlike those made by a man when he falls asleep in a chair with a back just high enough to support half his spine.

"He sleeps," said Wobbles, in a most thrilling whisper.

"He doth," returned Pigeon, also carried away a little by the tragic nature of the situation. "Now's our time or niver."

"Let me get off first, as I'm in front," suggested Wobbles.

"No," said Pigeon, "the man behind ought to be the first."

Neither cared somehow to be left alone on the back of the "sleeping beauty," and while discussing the subject old Joss showed symptoms of coming back to life. As soon as they were quiet he went off again.

"There's nothing to be done," said Wobbles, "but to sit here and wait for whatever turns up."

What did turn up we shall presently see.

Meanwhile Conky and Curler had, with the aid of Fireworks, given a little amusement to the Broad Arrow men. When the enemy of old Joss was brought forward it unfortunately happened that he caught a brief glimpse of old Joss going off at a furious pace in the distance, and forthwith there came upon him a burning desire to pursue and overtake him. The spirit which excites men to contest races and so on was upon him, and Fireworks was resolved to out-trot his enemy or die.

He started just as Conky got one foot in the stirrup, turned him over right on his head, and knocked down Curler, who was holding the bridle. Half a dozen men rushed at him, who held him as well as they could, and in hurried tones bade the prostrated ones mount at once and be off and away.

Conky, who in a confused way was studying mental astronomy, was heard to say that he wanted the life of something, and Curler, lying rolled up like a ball, bade them go away and let him die in peace.

"Get up," said Nat Green. "Sharp—the chief is coming."

The terror of that name was enough, and the two wretched vagabonds got upon their feet, and approached the skittish Fireworks—with the dejected looks of men going to the scaffold.

"Quick!" cried Nat. "I hear the chief's voice, asking why you are not gone."

"Give us a hand," said Conky.

They gave him twenty, and put him into the saddle. More friendly hands put Curler up, but in their haste with his face to the stumpy tail of the impatient Fireworks.

"I can't ride this way!" he shrieked.

"No time to alter it now," cried Nat. "Hold on to the crupper. Let go!"

They let go, and Fireworks, with a snort like a whale blowing, bounded forward, and went in pursuit of old Joss, ignoring the agonising cries of the two men who bestrode him.

Horsemanship is seldom acquired except by men who begin in their infancy and practise it up to manhood. Even with that advantage it is doubtful if any two men in the world could have ridden back to back with comfort.

Conky and Curler were but children of the saddle, and Curler had, in addition to general inexperience, the further disadvantage of riding with his face to the tail—and such a tail as it was! It was more like a cabbage stump than the article usually found in the rear of a horse.

The eyes of Curler, as he clung to the crupper, were fixed upon that tail, just as the tight-rope dancer keeps his eye on a certain spot, and thus preserves his balance—thereby was Curler, in all probability, saved from a horrible fall.

And yet it was not to preserve his balance that Curler fixed his eyes upon that stump. His great anxiety was for the crupper, which threatened each moment to come off; and if it did?

What then?

He had visions of flying in the air, holding on to the extreme end of the crupper, as Cutty Sark clung to the tail of Tam O'Shanter's horse, and he had fears that the crupper might show the weakness of that same tail, and come clean off.

Again, what then?

Broken bones, bruised limbs, shattered body—perhaps death itself.

And all this hung upon the stump of a tail!

Curler had some idea of grasping the tip, and keeping the crupper on, but there was not enough to hold by.

Finding this idea of no value, he gave up all ideas together, and abandoned himself to the most blank despair.

On over the rough and almost untrodden ground, into hollows and over big stones, round corners, up hills and down dales went Fireworks, resolved upon overtaking old Joss, and eventually gaining the victory.

To the credit of Fireworks, it must be stated that when he started he had no more malevolent object than to overtake and pass his ancient enemy, but it must be remembered that he was but a poor, weak, frail creature, extremely liable to be overcome by the temptation of the moment.

If he had not been tempted he would not have fallen.

But——

On turning a corner he came into view of old Joss astride the stone wall, deep in the thick of a refreshing sleep. It was not at all necessary for the purposes of recognition for him to see the head of his foe, a long acquaintance had made him familiar with every line of that graceful form, and, foreshortened or backshortened, if you like, as old Joss was, he knew him.

The ready wit of Fireworks grasped the situation, and in it he beheld the chance of a lifetime. If he and Joss lived, as was probable, another fifty years, Joss might never get himself into a similar position.

The eyes of Fireworks brightened, the stump of his tail went up an inch too high, and off went the crupper. Curler clinging to it, with the grip of the well-known drowning mariner, went off also, and dangled about the haunches of the old horse like a bathing dress in a high wind, and Conky clung to the mane, uttering shrieks of despair.

Wobbles and Pigeon also awoke to the awful peril of the hour. The first said—"here's the wild helephant a-coming again;" and the second, between his teeth, hissed "d—— him."

Old Joss also awoke from a sweet refreshing slumber—such as only infants, old horses, and men who have drunk seven sorts of Bass's pale ale at different public-houses can understand—to feel by instinct, for he could not see, that his old foe was near.

Alive to his danger he was getting the sinews of his legs into working order for a scramble over the wall, when Fireworks assailed him like a battering ram.

The effect was tremendous.

His head went down, and his other part was twisted high in the air, and turned clean over. Wobbles and Pigeon travelled for some time through space, and then met in a sprawling condition. Side by side in some land that was new to them—a brilliant bright land, all fireworks, and spinning trees, and revolving skies, and no end of wonders known to those who are suddenly transported thereto.

Fireworks was victorious.

But he did not come off scathless.

That very cunning old horse had reckoned without the stone wall. He did not even get a glimpse of it.

His impetuosity, which had more of youth than old age in it, carried him bang against this remnant of the shanty and over it, and he and his riders went together. Curler, still clinging to the crupper, had an idea that he had got into a stonemason's yard when all the stock and trade was being blown about by a high wind.

Conky went down with Fireworks, and for full ten minutes was where Moses was when he put the light out; but on coming back to consciousness he found himself hanging over the lower branch of a tree like something to dry, and beneath sat Curler, in a Whittington attitude, listening to distant bells which apparently did not promise him anything satisfactory.

At a little distance was old Joss, with his four legs in the air. Half buried in the stones Fireworks lay snorting his triumph, and far away Wobbles and Pigeon sat side by side, making curious jerky motions to the world in general, like inferior specimens of waxwork in want of oil, and short of a cogwheel or two in their mechanical arrangements.

"Well, I'm blessed—'ere's 'orsemanship," said Conky; "if ever I seed the like—'Ampstead 'Eath is a fool to it."

CHAPTER LX.

A SPY.

BILLY BRISKET had been one of the spectators at the start of old Joss and Fireworks—but a distant one. His tent was pitched upon a piece of rising ground, from whence he could command a full view of the camp, and it was from its interior that he looked upon the departure of the two famous horses.

The sight gave a relish to the cigar he was smoking, and as Fireworks, bearing his strange burden, disappeared, Billy lay down on his back and laughed until his sides ached.

"Talk of shooting and hanging rascals like those," he said; "why, it is a merciful proceeding. Those four vagabonds die every day of their lives!"

As his cigar was getting low he took out another, and, lighting it from the end of the first, lay back upon the rug, he slept on, and speculated upon the finish of that day's performance. My readers know what it was; but as Billy did not, he amused himself for half an hour in conjuring up all sorts of probabilities and possibilities.

From these he was aroused by a shadow falling upon the patch of light cast into the tent by the sun. Looking up he beheld Trimmer.

"Anything up, Trimmer?"

"Caught a spy, sir," answered Trimmer, laconically.

Trimmer's face was a little flushed, and there was blood upon the sleeve of his coat.

He had, apparently, not secured the spy without a struggle.

"Where is he?" asked Brisket.

"Got him outside, sir. Here, you, come and show yourself."

The spy, a hang-dog looking villain, with his arms tightly bound behind him, came forward and stood in the mouth of the tent. Billy Brisket eyed him up and down, and fancied that he had seen him before.

"Hallo, friend!" he said, "what brought you here?"

The man compressed his lips with a determined air and made no reply.

"You will find a little confession beneficial," added Billy. "Who sent you?"

"Wasn't sent," replied the man, sullenly; "came of my own accord."

"Did you, indeed? Trimmer, what was he doing?"

"Sneaking round the chief's tent like a dog in search of a bone."

"Well," said Billy, "I have no doubt the chief will pick one with him. Bring him along, Trimmer. I fancy I have seen you before, my friend."

"I will swear I never set eyes on you until to-day!" replied the man, warmly.

"You are too energetic, my friend. Now I know I have seen you."

"It is your fancy."

"No, no; but where it is I cannot tell just now. I shall remember presently."

Jack was not in his tent when the party arrived there, but he came in shortly after, and greeted Brisket as he always did, warmly. Trimmer, in return for his salutation, got a friendly nod, and the prisoner was speedily favoured with a searching look.

"A spy, chief," said Brisket.

"Once an old friend—or supposed to be so," said Jack.

"No, sir, you are mistaken!" cried the spy. "I swear you are!"

"Brisket," said Jack, "have you forgotten Baron Steinnitz?"

"By Jingo," cried Billy, slapping his thigh, "I thought I knew him."

"I swear," said the prisoner, "that I never was a baron!"

"You called yourself one at all events," said Jack, "and you once held a position of trust at Black Rock, but only kept it a few days. You have cut off your beard, and altered yourself in every possible way, but I know you."

"Mercy!—mercy!" cried the prisoner, sinking on his knees.

"You ask for mercy," said Jack—"how can you expect it? First you robbed me, then you join my enemies, and spy upon me to work my ruin."

"I came to ask pardon for my past faults," pleaded the prisoner.

"How was he found?" asked Jack.

"I came upon him lying behind your tent, chief," replied Trimmer.

"Has he been searched?"

"No."

"Search him."

The brown face of the prisoner turned a deep sallow, and the look of a man who has lost all hope came over him.

Trimmer rapidly and skilfully turned his pockets out, and produced a variety of articles, among them a small metal ball, about the size of a walnut.

Jack took it in his hand, and examined it.

Steinnitz smiled faintly as if he had, in the midst of his trouble, found something amusing.

"You were always a clever fellow," said Jack—"full of invention if I remember rightly. Tell me what this is?"

"I can tell you what it would be."

"Well, go on."

"Your death. It was my purpose to have blown you and this tent to atoms! Fortunately, you were away when I came. I am sorry."

"You were employed to do this?"

"Yes."

"By whom?"

"Why do you ask when you know it can only be one."

"The Ogre."

"Yes. I was wandering about starving when I heard he had taken up arms against you. I went to him with this idea, and he accepted it. I made that infernal machine in two days."

"You are clever; the workmanship is perfect. So, this would have killed me?"

"Yes, if I had thrown it at you with moderate force. I advise you now not to press it too hard. There will be little of any of us left if it goes off."

"It shall not be used—at present," said Jack, putting it carefully down. "But tell me why you conceived my destruction—you wronged me, but I pardoned you?"

"I work for pay, as I must live," was the sullen reply. "Now hang me. I have failed, and must pay the penalty."

"Nay," said Jack, "I want not your life. It is of little value to me."

"You pardon me?"

"Yes, on one condition."

"I accept it, whatever it is."

"Go back to the Ogre, and tell him you have succeeded."

"Yes, and when he finds out the truth he will hang me. It is only putting off the day."

"Not at all. Come back here, and you shall be protected."

"I'll do it," said Steinnitz. "I'll give him a detailed story of my triumph."

"Tell him the camp is disordered."

"Ah, yes! I know your object now. If he believes me he will come out to attack—you will be prepared, and Captain Ogre will find himself in trouble."

"You were always a clever fellow," said Jack. "Go and do your work. Deceive me at your peril."

"To work with you is the best game I can play," replied the prisoner. "I always had an affection for the strongest side."

"Take him outside the camp," said Jack, "and set him free."

Trimmer cut his bonds, and the two went out together. Trimmer looked a little vexed, and presently explained the cause of it.

"I hoped," he said, "to have had the pleasure of hanging you. I never went in for being public executioner, but I think I could have worked you off."

"I am very much obliged to you," said Steinnitz, with more politeness than might have been expected of him.

"You call yourself a baron—don't you?" said Trimmer, sternly.

"I do. I am the head of a very old family."

"If you are the head, what, in the name of the piper that played afore Moses, is the tail like?" asked Trimmer.

"Better look for it and see," returned Steinnitz, suavely.

"You are a scientific chap—aint you?" pursued Trimmer.

"Yes, a little."

"And you made that busted think out of your own 'ead?"

"Yes, I did."

"Now don't it strike you as being a mean sort of thing for to kill a man without giving him a chance?"

"Not at all."

"Perhaps it's your only way of fighting."

"What do you mean?"

"Perhaps you can't use the bowie or pistol," said Trimmer.

"If I had occasion to do so I would have a try."

"Would you now?" asked Trimmer, eagerly.

"Yes, I would."

"And when you come back will you have a go in with me?"

"What for?"

"Never mind what for. Will you or will you not?"

No. 10.

BROAD-ARROW JACK.

BY THE AUTHOR OF

HANDSOME HARRY and CHEERFUL CHING-CHING:

OUT OF THE DARKNESS A MAN WITH A LONG KNIFE IN HIS HAND SPRANG UPON BROAD ARROW JACK.

"Well, I don't mind obliging you if I have nothing better to do."

"Your hand on it," said Trimmer, extending his palm.

"Here's mine," said Steinnitz.

"It's to be a reglar rip and tear fight—no quarter asked for or given?"

"That's about it. It will suit me," said the other."

Trimmer put a hand upon his shoulder, and looked affectionately into his face.

"Lord send you back soon," he said; "then what a treat we will have together!"

"I shall look forward with pleasure to our meeting," said Steinnitz.

"Farewell, old man, and don't be longer than you can help."

Steinnitz took off his hat, and bowed with mock politeness.

"I shall never rest," he said, "until our happy meeting comes about."

"You won't disappoint me?"

"It would break my heart to do so—believe me."

He swaggered off, and Trimmer, with a thoughtful face, stood watching him until he was gone. Then he turned, and walked slowly back to the camp.

"It was hard work," he muttered, "to keep my hands off him, but as he's coming back it won't matter. Only fancy trying to blow up the chief! Well, if I had known it at the time he would have been on his back now. If he don't come back sharp I shall bile over."

CHAPTER LXI.

FALLING INTO THE SNARE.

BARON STEINNITZ, as he chose to call himself, lost no time in returning to the presence of his employer, the Ogre, whom he found engaged in making a rough map of the country. Jaundice stood just behind him, with his eyes fixed ahead, as if his thoughts were far away.

"Ha!" said the Ogre; "you have returned?"

"Yes."

"And have you succeeded?"

"Admirably. Broad Arrow Jack lies dead, and his people are in confusion."

"Retreating?"

"No; for at present they scarce know what to do," said Steinnitz.

"Is grief or fear the ruling emotion?"

"Grief. They have no fear. They laugh at you, and say you will never venture from your stronghold."

"You hear that, Jaundice?" said the Ogre, turning to his companion.

"Eh—what? I was not listening," said Jaundice.

"You never are listening now," muttered the Ogre. "What is the matter with you? Can't you get that wife of yours out of your head?"

"No, I cannot," replied Jaundice, shortly.

"There was a time when she troubled it very little," sneered the Ogre.

"If you and I are to be friends, drop that subject once and for all."

"Ha! Do you ride the high horse?"

"In that country—yes. I am in no humour to be chaffed about the woman who calls herself my wife," returned Jaundice.

The Ogre's face grew black, but he said no more on the subject, and renewed his conversation with Steinnitz.

"Did this fellow suffer? Was he killed outright, I mean?"

"No, he was much mangled; but he lived an hour."

"An hour? Too short a time; but it was better than nothing," said the Ogre. "You shall be well rewarded—when we get to Black Rock."

Steinnitz bowed, and, as the Ogre returned to his map, concluded the interview was at an end. He passed out, and Jaundice followed him.

"Hi! Steinnitz," he said, "come here."

Steinnitz followed him to a safe distance from the tent, so that nothing could be overheard."

"You are a handy fellow," pursued Jaundice.

"Some consider me so," was the calm reply.

"And you are not troubled with a conscience?" said Jaundice.

"If I am, it troubles me only in my sleep. I dream a bit."

"Do you?" said Jaundice, with a shudder. "So do I—sometimes; but dreams are nothing. They have no real connection with the past, present, or future."

"I would not be so very sure of that," returned Steinnitz.

"Pooh! I am certain of it," said Jaundice; "and there is nothing in them, even if you dream your dreams half a dozen times over, as I have done of late."

"Ah!" said Steinnitz, "you are a brave man to pass over repeated dreams so lightly."

"Do you believe in them?" asked Jaundice, with an apprehensive look in his hollow eyes.

"I must believe in what my experience tells me is true."

"Your experience?"

"Yes. I have more than once dreamt a dream thrice, and it has always come true," replied Steinnitz; "but what of that? Yours may not."

"I hope not," said Jaundice, with a shudder.

"Is this all you have to say to me?" asked Steinnitz, after a pause.

"No. You have served us well in this business—will you serve me personally in another?"

"If it pays me."

"I will pay you well for it. You know my wife?"

"Yes, I have seen her. She is a wonderfully handsome woman."

"You need not comment upon her beauty," said Jaundice, that is a thing of the past."

"I thought it palpably present," replied Steinnitz, "but that is not my affair. She is your wife, and you have a right to think different."

"Oh! of course. Well, it is of her I would speak. She is no longer my wife."

"Indeed!"

"No, only in name. She has dishonoured my name, and must die!"

Not a muscle in the listener's face moved, only his eyes showed that the idea of the name of Jaundice being dishonoured amused him.

"Does your conscience stand between you and the murder of a woman?"

Steinnitz answered readily—

"Not at all—why should it? There are too many of them about."

"Then," hissed Jaundice, "go and kill that hag who calls herself my wife."

"I have heard," said Steinnitz, "that she was no common wife to you."

"What you have heard and what I know are two different things," said Jaundice. "She has left me."

"With another man?"

For a moment Jaundice paused, but he found the answer.

"Yes," he said, "with another man."

"To me," said Steinnitz, "that seems incredible."

"What matters whether it is true or not? Will you do my bidding?"

"Yes. Where shall I find her?"

"She travelled in the direction of yon giant peak; she is in one of the valleys there. Go and find her."

"I will," said Steinnitz; "and the price?"

"Half what I possess in the world, whatever it is," replied Jaundice.

"Done."

And so they parted.

Steinnitz towards the peak pointed out by his employer, and Jaundice to his tent, where he lay brooding until sundown. Then with the darkness came a revulsion of feeling, and he repented of having sent the desperate brutal Steinnitz on such an errand.

"I was wrong," he said; "she is but a woman, and might have relented, and we might have known happiness together again. Now, if he does his fell work, what hope have I left? Oh! Heaven grant he may fail. Success will make all here and elsewhere unbearable darkness to me. Oh! misery, is there a hound on earth so lost as I am?"

Meanwhile Steinnitz went forth in doubt as to which of the things he should do. Attempt to carry out the commission of Jaundice, or seek the safety of Jack's camp.

"I don't want to kill the woman," he muttered, "for I rather admire her; neither do I want to run the risk of meeting the Ogre again. How can I fully trust any man? This Broad Arrow Jack may finish me off after all if I return. I know what I will do. I'll go and shoot the fellow who has run off with pretty Maggie, and perhaps then she will run off with me. Why not? Take me all round there are many worse-looking fellows than I am. Of course there are—ahem! rather."

CHAPTER LXII.

IN THE HANDS OF THE ENEMY.

AS a day and a night elapsed without the four horsemen bringing in any forage, the Tiger was despatched in search of them. Scarcely had he been despatched when old Joss walking lame came in, and he was followed by Fireworks, who in the pride of comparative youth endeavoured to conceal under a jaunty air a pair of broken knees, and a wide gash across the bridge of his nose.

"Now I wonder what these two critters have been doing?" said Trimmer, to Nat Green.

"Perhaps they've killed that lot outright," was the reply.

"Oh no, none of them will be killed in that way. I know enough of the stars to say that much. If you put 'em all into a full water butt and screwed on the lid they wouldn't take any harm in a month. Nothing less than a rope will settle 'em. They'll follow in due time."

Mr. Trimmer said this in happy ignorance of what had befallen the four horsemen, which I will now proceed to explain.

The horses were the first to fully recover, and old Fireworks, content with another brilliant victory, went off to graze, followed at a respectful distance by old Joss, who was planning in his mind a scheme of vengeance that would fully wipe out the stain he had received.

His mind naturally ran upon brick walls, and all he wanted Fireworks to do was to get astride one and fall asleep in his turn. If he would only do that old Joss had a plan for giving him such a Roland for his Oliver that he would never snort defiance again.

But alas! there were no more stone walls, and if there had been, Fireworks was not likely to put himself into the position old Joss required. Not he. If not quite so wise as old Joss he was not fool enough to do a thing of that nature.

The two animals found plenty of food, but the digestion of old Joss was quite ruined by the way that stumpy tail of Fireworks displayed itself. It was astounding to see the amount of triumph it expressed, cocked perfectly upright, and occasionally wagging, as its owner thought, over his great feat. The sight was gall and wormwood, and old Joss was quite bilious.

At last he lay down and went to sleep, and dreamt, very likely of the days of his youth, of the exciting scenes in the circus, and the applauding multitude. From this he was aroused by somebody falling over him, and awaking he found darkness around and heard the voice of Conky.

"What was it?" asked that individual in a thrilling whisper. "It was warm and smooth, and about the size of a rippypotamus."

"Where is it?" asked three other voices, in agony.

"Just atwixt us," said Conky.

Old Joss thought it was time to get upon his feet, and accordingly began the series of movements attendant upon that exertion. The struggle was not more than a minute in duration, but the noise he made scared the four hapless wanderers, and they fled in every direction.

It was curious that none of them conceived it to be the old horse; but the fact was, he was like no other animal. Breathing and getting up with him was such a tremendous affair, and brought from him so many sounds—doubly and trebly horrible in the middle of the night—that wiser and braver men than the quartette referred to might have been scared.

His lying down too was unique in its way, reminding one of the shooting of a cartload of stones, bones, or general rubbish, as he did not double up like a common quadruped, but kept his legs quite stiff, and fell sideways with a crash—like a towel horse. Fireworks, with more of his early elasticity left in him, could get down very comfortably, by first sitting on his haunches and relaxing the sinews of his forelegs, by which means he got upon his nose, and into a position suitable for slumber.

Having spent half his life in running away from one thing and another, Wobbles was very active on his legs, and despite the darkness skimmed over the ground like a swallow, easily outstripping his companions, who, in their frenzy, dodged about here and there, and covered no ground to speak of.

How long Wobbles would have kept on can only be guessed, for in the zenith of his flight and the strength of his running he joined company with a tree for a moment and scattered the little wit fear had left him.

Then he caved in.

"I don't care," he muttered, as he lay upon his back, inspecting the multitude of shooting stars visible to him in the sky. "They may come and finish me off as soon as they like. If my mother had done her duty she would have strangled me at my birth, but she was a blessed selfish old cuss, nursing and coddling me so that she might have the pleasure of screwing up for me afterwards. She was a trying old woman."

Tribulation had made him reckless and Wobbles did not care what became of him. He lay on his back, ignoring passing hours, until daylight came; and even then, like the sluggard we read about in our infancy, he declined to get up.

The daylight, however, he saw but imperfectly, for in his meeting with the tree he had received two tremendous black eyes, which had swollen enormously in the night, and left him only two little slits to see out of. Through these he presently saw about a dozen men advancing towards him.

They were strangers to Wobbles; but he did not care—he was on his back, and intended to remain there for the rest of his days. If anybody objected to his keeping that position they might pick him up and carry him away. Personally he was resolved to do nothing.

The men came up and looked at him, and, as he lay quiet, they thought he was dead.

"Poor chap!" said one; "he's been murdered."

"No doubt," said another, "and robbed."

"Perhaps."

"Let's see if he has got anything about him."

One knelt down and was going to unbutton his

coat, when Wobbles, remembering what he had there, woke up.

"Get out!" he said.

"Why the warmint's alive!" cried the man, staggering back.

Then they all gathered round, and one man asked him who he was.

"A horphan," replied Wobbles, surlily.

"Well, Mister Orphan, what are you doing there?"

"Nothin'."

"Then get up and do something at once," said the man.

"Shan't!"

"You are a cheeky one," said the man.

"No, I aint," replied Wobbles; "I'm only a desperate one. I am tired of my life. Go thy way, friend, and leave me here to die."

The men held a whispered consultation, and speedily arrived at the conclusion that Wobbles had either been maltreated, and had all his senses knocked out of him, or he was a confirmed lunatic.

They were followers of the Ogre, out in search of provisions, and one of their standing orders was to bring in all suspicious-looking persons they might encounter. Wobbles was a suspicious-looking individual, and they decided to take him in.

"You must go with us," said the leader of the party.

"I won't!" replied Wobbles.

They pricked him once and he said "Oh!" They pricked him a second time and he swore. They pricked him yet a third time and he got up in a hurry.

"What are you doin' of?" he asked.

The question was rather late, but they were good enough to answer him—

"Prodding you to make you get up."

"Why can't you leave a man alone to die in peace?" was the next question Wobbles put.

Again they answered him—

"We've got orders to take in all the likes o' you."

"Where to?"

"That you will presently see."

Feeling it quite useless to kick against the pricks, Wobbles went, and pursuing a roundabout course, to avoid the camp of Broad Arrow Jack, they travelled all day and at night brought him to the stronghold of the Ogre.

He had been there before—had Wobbles—and he knew it, although it was dark when he arrived. But he did not care; he was tired of life, and was—so he fancied—quite prepared to die.

"If they will only do it easy, and not torture me, I don't care," he said.

That was all very well. Wobbles no more really wanted to die than the old man in the fable, who implored Death to come to him, and, when he put in an appearance, politely asked him to call another day.

Wobbles was put in the hut where Caliban lost his sight, and two men kept guard over him. They kept an eye upon his movements by the aid of a lantern swinging from the ceiling.

In the middle of the night there was a commotion outside, as if the whole camp were moving, and several men came in and out, holding whispered conferences with the two men on guard. The substance of one of them reached the ears of Wobbles.

"March at once?" said one of the guard.

"Yes."

"Isn't that rather sudden?"

"Rather; but the captain intends to attack just before daylight."

"Yes, he will have an easy job of it now that Broad Arrow Jack is dead."

Wobbles started, and a question was on his lips; but he held back and listened for more.

"I never heard the whole story," said the previous speaker. "How was it brought about? Who killed the villain?"

"One of his own followers."

"And when was it done?"

"Three days ago."

"Three days ago!" thought Wobbles. "That's a lie or a mistake. I saw him alive and well two days ago. What is the game?"

When left alone with his guard he proceeded to add to the information he had received by inquiries.

"Excuse me, gentlemen—ahem!" he said; "but did I understand as Broad Arrow Jack is dead?"

"Yes—the villain has met with his reward at last."

"Well, as to his being a villain that is an open question; but let me ask you why you call him one?"

"He is a brigand—a murderer and a destroyer of homes."

"Oh, indeed!" said Wobbles; "and may I ask how long he's been in that way?"

"Years."

"Oh! years, has he? And who has he robbed and plundered?"

"Scores of people."

"And who says he did it?"

"Our noble leader, Captain Ogre."

"Oh!" said Wobbles, drily—"Captain Ogre is a noble leader—is he?"

"The noblest of leaders. Do you know him?"

"I," said Wobbles, "have knowed him for years."

"Why, then, do you ask the question?"

"Just because I do know, and a more arrant warmint never hopped about on two legs."

"Beware," said the man, "what ye say may be reported to our leader."

"Do it," said Wobbles, recklessly. "I don't speak from hearsay—you do. I aint gammoned by a warmint—you are. Ain't there another with him, Jeb Jaundice?"

"Yes."

"He's a beauty," said Wobbles. "We was friends in the old country, and when I came into my estate, left me by an aged mother, who, whatever her failings, had a love for her only child, robbed me of it, he did—led me into the wildest speculations on the turf. I made a book with him once, and if there hadn't been a race—if no horses started—or if all went in and won, I was bound to be the loser. Oh! he's warmint number two, and as sich put him down in the catalogue."

"Is this true?" asked the two men as they looked at each other.

"True," cried Wobbles; and then he told them of the old life of Peaceful Village, only varying from the truth when he described himself as a saint in the midst of hosts of devils; and how often he had risked his own life to save that of some hapless victim who had fallen into the toils of the villains, his masters.

Then he went on to state what he knew of Broad Arrow Jack, and again what he said was pretty correct, except that which concerned himself.

"He's fond of horses and men as can ride," he said, "and it's the way I sticks on to a unbroken horse of his as pleases him; that is why he made me a sort of first lieutenant of his corpse."

What more he said, or how he piled up the agony, need not be put down here. He gained the confidence of the two men, and through them the good opinion of many others. The whole of the men left to guard the table land, about forty in number, became his friends.

All the rest had gone with the Ogre and Jeb Jaundice to attack the supposed disordered camp of Broad Arrow Jack.

"Our best game," said Wobbles, addressing the men about, "is to side with Broad Arrow Jack. He is sure to defeat the Ogre, and, if we keep him out of here, will capture him. When Jack, my friend, sees what we have done in his good cause he will reward us all. He has more wealth than half a dozen kings; the front of his country house is covered all over with diamonds.

CHAPTER LXIII.

THE OGRE'S ATTACK.

AT the head of a large body of men, Jeb Jaundice and the Ogre rode towards the camp of Broad Arrow Jack.

So confident were they of victory—so sure of having only a disorganised foe to defeat—that they took no pains to send an advance guard to detect ambush, but rode on, gaily laughing and chatting, as they would have done at a pleasure excursion.

And good reason had they for mirth.

Broad Arrow Jack, their dreaded foe, they believed to be dead, and all the vast wealth which had helped him so powerfully was as good as theirs. When the men of the camp were all murdered or routed, the watchword was to be—

"Back to Black Rock."

"And there," said the Ogre, "we will have such a snug little retreat as no other part of the world knows of. We will have our merry companions—our wine—our women. We will laugh at all laws, except our own, and play such a game as the father of all evil might himself be proud of."

"I wonder if Maggie would come," said Jaundice, gloomily.

"Maggie is dead ere this," replied the Ogre. "Steinnitz is not the man to fail. Consider yourself a widower, and make preparations for another bridal feast. I will be your parson, and you shall be mine. Rare fun we will have, my boy."

"Perhaps."

"Croaking and groaning again, now that we have as good as the whole of the world before us. Bah! you make me ill to think of you. I blush as I look upon you."

"I am not all devil yet."

"So you think; but let me tell you, Jeb Jaundice, that if you are not all devil now you were a few years ago. I can call to mind things you did which no *man* could have done."

"I remember them well."

"I am glad you do; so no more whining, if you please. Our life will be short, I dare say; but let us make hay while the sun is here. The clouds will come quickly enough."

"And envelope us in darkness for ever," said Jaundice.

"Well, so be it; I care not. For we will laugh and sing and dance the hours away. Ha, ha! Jeb Jaundice, what bright days have come upon us!"

"You must have been drinking early this morning," said Jaundice.

"Oh, yes. Not of the cup of alcohol though. Only water, I assure you, at present. But in my heart there is a little fountain of happiness, and in the air a bird that sings of wealth and jollity, and freedom—true freedom, untrammelled days and nights, monarchs of all around us."

"The crowns we wear would make any head uneasy."

"Except ours," cried the Ogre, slapping him on the back. "Come, Jeb, be cheerful—without drink if you can, with drink if you cannot. You have a flask by your side—empty it."

"It is empty," replied Jaundice, "and I might as well have drunk so much water; but see, we have outridden the men."

"We will walk with them," said the Ogre. "I feel as if my limbs would be the better for stretching. Turn the horses loose."

"We may want them again."

"No; we shall find a host of them in the camp of the dead boy."

"You are more confident of success than I am."

"How so?"

"Suppose Steinnitz has lied."

"Oh, no!" said the Ogre, taken a little aback—"that is impossible."

"Why, he is a born rascal, and therefore a liar!"

"You are hipped, my friend. Turn the horses loose."

"There goes mine."

They let go the bridles, and the horses, glad of freedom, bounded away.

The Ogre, confident as ever, strode on, followed a few paces behind by Jaundice.

So on for a couple of hours. In the meantime a small body of men had overtaken the Ogre, and formed a body-guard.

Jeb Jaundice dropped behind to bring up the other men.

The foremost party reached a deep glade in the wood, and were, as they calculated, close upon the camp of their foes.

The Ogre, still heedless, strode on, looking neither to the right nor left.

"Halt!"

It was not the voice of the Ogre which spoke, but his men pulled up. The Ogre raised his head, and uttered a shriek of fury and despair.

Broad Arrow Jack stood before him.

"Well met," said the young hero. "Steinnitz was true to his trust."

"The scoundrel has betrayed me!" hissed the Ogre.

"Paid agents change their masters sometimes," said Jack. "But yield, villain! You are in my power."

"Never!" cried the Ogre. "Rather yield yourself. You are alone, and I have four hundred men at my back."

"What care I?" cried Jack, drawing his sword. "Again I say, yield!"

The Ogre drew his weapon, and the blades crossed, flashing in the broken sunlight streaming through the trees.

The men in the rear seemed to be incapable of giving assistance, until the Ogre, finding himself hard pressed, cried out—

"Help!—help! you fools!" he cried. "At him! Surround him! Cut him down!"

The men thus urged gathered strength from their numbers, and came forward in the shape of a crescent. Jack saw his peril, and pressed furiously on.

"At him!" yelled the Ogre, as if he were urging dogs on to a wild beast. "Tear him!—rend him! and you shall have a rich reward! I hear the others coming. He is in our power now. Forward, Jeb Jaundice, we have the lion here!"

It was not a lion he at all cared to face longer than he could, for, as his men closed in, he suddenly turned and ran.

Jack could not follow, as there were a dozen swords and pistols pointed at his breast.

Quick of thought and action he resolved upon retreat. With one slash to the right and another to the left he cleared a path, and left two men dead upon the ground. Active as a deer, he bounded away, and called aloud for his men.

The crashing of bushes soon told of their advance, and the Ogre's men, in spite of his curses and entreaties, fled. The Broad Arrow men, led by Jack, came on, and made sad havoc among the followers of the Ogre. Twenty were slain and thirty made prisoners. The others were scattered in every direction, and the Ogre and Jeb Jaundice, without attendants, were flying towards their stronghold.

"A curse upon the folly that tempted me to send our horses away!" said the Ogre.

"I said it was wrong at the time," replied Jaundice.

"You have said everything was wrong for days," sneered the Ogre, "and you would be a poor prophet if you were not right once in a way. Haste, or they will overtake us! I hear them coming. Our men will get back by the various passes, and we will rally, and make amends for this defeat."

"A curse upon that Steinnitz!"

"All I ask is to have him one minute in my grasp," said the Ogre—"one minute, no more. I would squeeze his lying throat a bit, I'll warrant you!"

"I hear them coming."

"Yes, here, by this path—it is the shortest—I know it well. They will go by the other. Run, Jeb Jaundice, if you would escape that devil we raised to haunt us."

They both ran well, being muscular men and accustomed to a hardy life, and soon outstripped their pursuers, who, being doubtful of the way, got into a bit of a maze, from which even Jack was unable to extricate them. Billy Brisket would have been a sure guide, but he was away in search of the Wobbles foraging party, not one of whom had returned.

Jack was wise enough not to leave his camp too far in the rear, being uncertain what forces the Ogre might yet have at his command, and, having lost trace of those he sought, returned.

The Tiger was away with Brisket, or he would have been invaluable; but when the pair returned, bringing with them the forlorn Conky, Curler, and Pigeon, the boy was at once despatched to the Ogre's stronghold, to see what was doing there.

Meanwhile, the Ogre and Jeb Jaundice had reached the narrow upward path, and toiled slowly and laboriously towards the summit. They were much blown by their recent exertions, and looked like two hunted wolves returning to their lair.

Here at least they felt sure they were free from immediate danger; but lo! as they neared the top, a voice came unto them—

"Pull up you two, or I'll let fly into the thick of yer."

They looked up, and beheld Wobbles, with a sash round his waist, another about his shoulders, and a large assortment of weapons stuck all over him.

They were too surprised to speak, and stood quite still.

"In the hold days," pursued the valiant one, "you had your way. In the new days I'm going to have mine. You've had your bit of fun here. I'm master. Cut it—vanish—slope—hook it, or *my* men shall blow you bang into the hair!"

"What in the name of a legion of devils is the meaning of this?" asked the Ogre, in a state of helpless rage.

"I don't know, how should I?" replied Jaundice.

"The meaning is this," said Wobbles; "your men have bowled you out, and are now my men. They've had enough of you, and they've taken to me. I don't bully 'em, and swear and tell 'em lies. I'm a friend as well as a captain, and they've swore a hoath as big as your head—and that's a tidy size—to die under my banner. Up with it, my lads, and let him see it!"

In prompt response to his words a flag ran up the pole, where formerly the Ogre flew his waving banner, and, opening to the breeze, displayed a rude caricature of a woman's head.

"In case you shouldn't recognise it," said Wobbles, "I tell you that the picture upon yon is the nearest thing to my sainted mother that I can get out of charcoal. The men have heard of her wertues, and finding them reduplicated in me, they have, as I said, swore a hoath. Now I gives you two wagabones and outcasts just ten seconds to clear out, and if you don't go then, reckon that you will be buried by bits."

"This must be some joke," said the Ogre.

"Is it?" said Wobbles. "Now, my lads, show 'em a dozen rifle muzzles, and give a serus touch to the picter."

The rifles and heads of the men appeared over the breast of the earthwork at the summit of the pass. Both the Ogre and Jaundice were convinced that Wobbles was perfectly serious.

"Well?" said the former.

"Well?" said the latter.

"I suppose we must."

"We cannot force the pass."

"And if we do, what good will it give us?"

"Then let us retreat."

"And be sharp, or Broad Arrow Jack will be up this way."

Accordingly they turned and retraced their steps. As they went down the voice of Wobbles came after them.

"If it wasn't for having lived with you so long," he said, "I would have let into you at once, but for the sake of old times I lets you off now. Only in the future, if you walues your precious lives, shun Wobbles the awenger."

CHAPTER LXIV.
CAPTAIN WOBBLES.

"I WONDER," said Conky, "what can have become of Wobbles?"

"He's got into trouble somewheres," returned Curler.

"It's the lot o' some people to be in trouble," remarked Pigeon; "but they brings it on themselves, and oughtn't to grumble."

He was in a moralising mood, and would have gone on to a considerable length if Conky had not cut him short with the pointed inquiry as to who "appointed him to preach?"

"Can't a man open his mouth serus without being insulted by being called a parson?" asked Pigeon, a little huffed.

"I didn't go so far as that," said Conky. "I didn't mean to downright insult you, Pigeon; but I hates the moral dodge, and you knows it."

"Some of your family was in the line," put in Curler.

"But it never paid," returned Conky. "Besides it's low, and never ought to be taken up except all other games have failed. Whatsomever your game is, play it open and manly."

Coming from such lips, these words had a deep import, and Curler and Pigeon were much impressed. Pigeon was quite grieved to think he had so far forgotten what was due to his manhood as to become moral.

"I know it aint what you might expect of me," he said, penitently; "but most men is likely to have slips of the tongue. I didn't mean to preach, and, if I had a brother as come that sort of thing, I'd knock him on the head, and do my feller-man a service."

"But as to Wobbles—where is he?"

This question was discussed, but no satisfactory conclusion arrived at. Nor could they ascertain from anybody in the camp what had become of him. Even the Tiger was at fault, and could give no clue.

The idea of any of these gentlemen having an affection for Wobbles was, of course, absurd; but they were keenly anxious to know what had become of him, as he was, in a measure, their friend and supporter in the camp. Apart from Wobbles there was not one sympathetic heart around them.

The men would neither eat, drink, nor sleep near them, and the trio lived apart from their fellowman, for the most part spending their time in gloomy reminiscences of the past and dismal prognostications of the future.

It was not until two days had elapsed that the fate of Wobbles was ascertained. The Tiger, sent to the Ogre's stronghold to reconnoitre the movements of the enemy, returned with a letter from Wobbles, written on the fly-leaf of a book, and addressed to Broad Arrow Jack. Here is the precious epistle verbatim:—

"TO THE MOST NOBIL ERO, BROADE HARRER JACK, FROM HIS DEWOTED SERWENT AND OBLEEGED FOLLERER, CAPTING WOBBLES.

"Dare Ser,—Sinse larst we met, when ole Josh and fireworks come it strong over a stone wall, and ni shoke the ole of hus to bits, i fel in with a parti has brote me hup here, and I conwerted em to the trooth for awl the lies the Hoger tole, let alone Jeb Jaunders, ho is a reglar warmint—and the wai he made hup that book on the races, wen i stode to lose everything, and coudent win nothin, come out as you mite, wood ha' told hany man wot he was maid of—i come hup hear, got round the men, and wen the Hoger and Jeb showed hup we give 'em ten seconds, for hold frendship's sake, to git clare away, or ime blode if I woodent have maid bits of em, and now thare gone, and I, as capting hof a nobil band, holds the plase, and means to stick to it ontil I has horders from you, my sperior, and then ime willing for to turn hout.—So no more from yure umbel serwent,

"CAPTING WOBBLES."

"It is a curious letter," said Jack, turning it over. "I scarcely know what it means. What is your opinion, Brisket?"

Billy Brisket read it carefully, and, like a wise man of old, interpreted it.

"He has got possession of the Ogre's den," he said, "and, with the aid of some friends, keeps it."

"And where is the Ogre?"

"Gone away, the letter says."

"Where to?"

"That we are not told."

"I must go up at once, Brisket. You keep watch here."

"You go alone?"

"Yes. Why not?"

"There are many enemies abroad still."

Jack smiled quietly.

"Enemies!" he said. "I have only two, and nothing would please me better than to meet them together."

"Your courage alone," said Brisket "will carry you through anything."

With only his cutlass and pistols Jack set forth, guided by the Tiger, who, in about three hours, brought him to the foot of the table land. Wobbles saw him coming, and the flag, bearing the dim portrait of the departed Mrs. Wobbles, was hoisted in his honour.

Nor did the courtesy of the great self-elected captain stop here. Armed at all points, and politely carrying his hat in his hand, he came down to greet the great chief.

Jack felt there was something intensely absurd in the whole affair, but Wobbles had done him a real service, and he received him gravely.

"I have your letter," he said, "and have come to learn more than can be expressed on paper."

"Afore we proceeds, sir," said Wobbles, "may I ax a great favour of you?"

"Yes—go on."

"When you meets them as is brave and bold you ginerally shakes 'em by the hand."

"What then?"

"Well," said Wobbles, with a smile of triumph, "I think I have come out pretty strong this time, and if it aint asking too much, may I—just one shake——"

"Oh! with pleasure," said Jack, holding out his hand.

Wobbles grasped it hard and held it for a moment near his breast as he bowed. Then he sighed, and released it.

"Noble chief," he said, "I'm now stimerlated to do something as will open the eyes of them as don't believe in me. Give your orders for anything you like—I'm ready with a supply. All I ax is that somebody else may ride old Joss, as the movements of that hanimal are sometimes confusing. If Wellington had rode him at Waterloo, I'll bet Napoleon would have doubled the British army into a cocked hat."

"You shall have your wish; but tell me all that has occurred, so that I may understand the situation."

Wobbles told him all that had transpired, and Jack listened gravely. He was glad that Wobbles had not fired on the two scoundrels, as he desired to settle with them himself, and told him, on no account, if ever so much provoked, to take their lives. Wobbles vowed he would sacrifice his own rather than do it, and at the time he meant it.

As it was necessary to take precautions to prevent the escape of the two villains, Jack returned at once to the encampment, instructing Wobbles tohold the place which had so opportunely fallen into his possession. He fully understood the innate cowardice of Wobbles, but here again he showed his wondrous power.

"Keep it in my name," he said, "and I will rank you among my friends."

Wobbles was quite six inches taller when the chief was gone, and really felt as bold as a man need be. If the Ogre and Jaundice had turned up then at the head of a body of men, he would have fought them bravely.

But as nobody turned up he confined himself to making certain martial preparations, and issuing orders from the Ogre's tent which he now made his own. No stage baron or king was ever more bold and grandiloquent than he.

Fortunately he had a number of simple-minded men, who knew nothing of his antecedents, to deal with, and they, taking the manner for the man, obeyed him readily.

Among other things he ordered a new earthwork to be erected—so carefully planned that every bullet fired from it, if perfectly directed, would take effect upon the one already made, and be of immense service to an assaulting foe. He also established a drill, founded on his having once seen the trooping of colours at the Horse Guards, and forced his men into all sorts of military shapes and figures, which, if carried out on the battle-field, would have ensured the destruction of every man jack of them.

"There is nothing like discipline," thought Wobbles, as he lay back in his tent, after his day's labour. "It improves the men, and gives 'em confidence in their leader, only I'm bothered if I can see the use of it. When we gets into haction I hopes as they won't so mix themselves up as they did to-day. What ho! there."

The sentry who had been pacing up and down the side of the tent answered the call, and stood at the "attention" conceived by Wobbles, with his rifle sloped and his right hand against his cheek.

"Wine there," said Wobbles, frowning at him.

"Ain't got none, sir," replied the man; "but there's a keg of brandy."

"Ha! it is so," said Wobbles. "Then bring forth the brandy."

"It's covered over with a cloth, and forms your piller," said the man. "Captain Ogre allus slept on it."

"Did he?" returned Wobbles. "It was a noble thought, and worthy of him. Where is the goblet?"

"The what, sir?"

"The goblet. Something to drink out of."

"You will find a tin mug in the corner, sir."

"It is well," said Wobbles. "Depart."

The man returned to his post, and Wobbles, having found the keg of brandy and the tin mug, filled himself a bumper.

"The hodour of this," he said, as he sniffed it, "aint wery good, but let us hope as the taste is better."

It was cheap fiery brandy, and made him blink as he swallowed it.

It also brought on a fit of coughing.

"Wha—at—ho—how—there!" he cried again.

The sentry once more presented himself before him.

"Wa-ater," gasped Wobbles.

"Aint got any up here, sir."

"What, don't you drink it?"

"Not if we can help it, sir."

"And what do you wash in?"

"When we think of washing, and it aint orfen," replied the candid sentry, "we goes down below and gets it over."

"Well, mind this," said Wobbles, "some water must be got up at once. I'm a temperance man, and I means to keep you sober."

A look of dismay overspread the sentry's face, but he did not venture to expostulate. Wobbles growing hardened to the liquor, sipped it, and went on.

"Drunkenness," he said, "is a wice as won't suit me. When a man gets too much into his brains he swallers that which robs away his mouth—no, robs away his head—no, what is—— Sentry, what saith our friend William Shakespeare on that head?"

"Don't know, sir," replied the sentry, who in the old country had been a humble tiller of the soil, and a great consumer of greens and bacon; "never heerd of him, sir."

"Not heerd of Shakespeare?" exclaimed Wobbles, aghast. "Really such horrible incomprehensible ignorance must be washed down."

He washed it down with the rest of the contents of the tin mug, and as soon as it got well into his system he became exceedingly grave and thoughtful.

"Sentry," he said, "had'st thou ever a mother?"

"Yes, sir."

"Did she love thee?"

"She give I a good lickin' sometimes," replied the man, with a grin.

"Hear me, and be not frivolous," pursued Wobbles. "Is that mother of yours alive or dead?"

"Dead, sir."

"When did she die?—in what place?" asked Wobbles.

"Workus," was the brief reply.

"Did she leave you anything?"

"Eh, sir?"

"Did she leave you any property—a tea service—a teapot—a little money screwed up in sixpences, or anything of that sort?"

"No, sir."

"You are sure?"

"She never left I a brass farden, and the guardians made I pay for the funeral," was the reply.

"She was a kind mother!" sighed Wobbles. "Bless her name! If she had left you anything it would have been your ruin. Sentry, you may go."

"Yes, sir."

"Yet stay. One question more. Did you ever try to go into society?"

"I paid into the King's Head Sick Club, but the secretary chap runned away with the money."

"That was not my meaning; but no matter. Did you ever make a book?"

"What book, sir?"

"Did you ever bet on horse-races? Were you ever on the turf?"

"I never even seed a race in all my life."

"Oh, happy man!" said Wobbles, regarding him with a heavy eye, "hear and heed one who has passed through the furnace of life, and know all about it. If ever you have an aged mother, and catch her screwing up sixpences for you p'ison her, and save yourself a lifetime of misery. And if ever you make a rush at society don't begin in a public-house, where men talk horses all the day long, and lunch off quarters of pork pie, and are allus ready to show you how to win money, although they haven't a blessed sixpence of their own. Shun all bookmakers, tipsters, sporting landlords, and ladies who will imbibe two half-quarters of gin running. Do this, sentry, and you'll live and die a happy man."

CHAPTER LXV.

A MESSAGE FROM JEB JAUNDICE.

HAVING concluded his lecture Wobbles dismissed the sentry, and lay back to reflect upon his greatness. His attitude would have been worthy of Alexander the Great or Napoleon, taking their ease after one of their victories.

"After all," he mused, "that mother wasn't so bad, for, out of her indiscretion greatness has grown. I am a leader of an army—small, but still an army. Ahem! is Captain Wobbles strong enough? Ought it not to be General Wobbles, C.B.? By the way, what does C.B. mean?—something about Cold Baths, I suspect. If so, they won't suit me. Cold baths—I hate 'em!"

No doubt he did, as he came of an unwashed race. After a little thought C.B. was rejected, and he decided to simply assume the grade of general.

The strangest part of the business was his men believed in him.

His bounce carried them away from the first, and the brief visit paid by Broad Arrow Jack confirmed them in their faith.

"Hold the table land until you hear from me," was the substance of Jack's parting words.

The little experience of camp-life he had had taught him the necessity of keeping up a strict watch, and his men were told off in couples to guard the path, and relieve each other throughout the night.

"And if thou seest anything greater than a rabbit," said Wobbles, as he instructed them in their duty, "blaze away, and blow it to Jericho."

It was about the middle watch, and Wobbles was in the heart of a sweet sleep, when a rifle was fired by one of the men on duty, which made him leap off his couch like a madman.

"My horse!" he cried, "my kingdom for a horse! Here, what's the row? Keep 'em off until I'm ready! Fall in, there! Fours right and left; make a firm square, with your general in the middle to protect you!"

And rushing out of the tent he tripped over one of the pegs, and pitched upon his valiant nose. He could have shrieked for help, but, remembering what was due from a man of his rank, he made a powerful effort, and kept silent.

"Let me be firm," he thought, "for on my courage the lives and safety of my troops depend. Ho, there! who fired the gun?"

"I did, sir," replied one of the sentries, advancing out of the darkness. "Some fellow crept up, and shied a stone at us, and ran down the path again. Smith fired, but missed him. The stone fell here, I think—yes, I have it, sir. There is a paper round it."

"This," said Wobbles, as he took it, "may be a message from the enemy, desiring to capitulate."

It did not matter in the least, that, as far as he knew, there was no enemy to capitulate. He only said what he conceived to be the proper thing under the circumstances. Hast thou a light, sentry?"

"No, sir."

"Excuse me, but—ahem!—would it not sound better if you addressed me as general?"

"Yes, general."

"Thank you. Yes, it does sound better—more euphonious as the learned people say. Besides, if strangers are near, they are not likely to take any liberties with me. Rank ought to be, and must be, respected. You understand that, sentry?"

"Yes, general."

"You are a wise man—a clever man. Good night."

He returned to his tent, and having shut himself in procured a light, and entered upon an examination of the document which had arrived so mysteriously.

It was a piece of paper about six inches square, and on it was written the following message—

"You, Wobbles, give up this place, and we will not harm you, but if you stand out against it we will come and take it, and flay you alive. We shall have men enough to do that to-morrow.—JEB JAUNDICE."

"All brag and bounce," said Wobbles, coolly. "I know if you could take it you would have come at once, and made it very warm for me. Villain, I defy thee—ha—ha! I scorn your threats—I de—fe—y thee."

He was quite right in looking upon the threats of Jeb Jaundice as so much bunkum. Both he and the Ogre were in a fix, without a friend to aid them, nd were skulking in a small cave at the base of the liff, waiting for daylight to show them some route to escape by.

The loss of their position and power was so sudden and complete that neither of them could fairly realise it. The Ogre, crouching in the darkness, and awaiting the return of Jeb Jaundice, was in a state bordering on madness.

Could he have sold his worthless soul, as some men in fables are said to have done, he would have parted with it, for one hour's power to kill, and maim, and torture whom he wished. Wobbles, whom he had hitherto regarded with contempt, would have had his full share of suffering.

"Such a pitiful cur—such a crawling hound," he muttered, "to have the audacity to defy us. Ha! Jeb, is that you?"

The sound of a soft footstep passed near as he put the question, but no voice vouchsafed a reply. Ready to take alarm at everything, the Ogre drew his knife, and stooping down endeavoured to see who it was.

He lay at the mouth of the cave, and in front of him the great hills stood out boldly against the faintly illuminated sky. The darkness of the valley, however, shut out all objects then from view.

"It was some small beast prowling," he muttered, and he stretched himself out at full length.

The moment he drew his eyes from the valley a hand smote him on the face, and a shrill voice cried—

"Hoo—hoo! Massa Ogre, found you out."

"That accursed Tiger!" cried the Ogre, springing up. "Come here, you whelp, and let me get a shot at you."

"Dat bery likely. Oh! no, me off to Massa Jack wif news about you."

The Ogre drew a pistol, and fired in the direction of the voice, but a shriek of laughter, dying quickly away in the distance, told him he had missed his mark.

"We must not linger here a moment," said the Ogre. "Where is that crawling hound, Jaundice?"

In his frame of mind everybody came in for a complimentary term, and when Jeb Jaundice did turn up, only a few minutes afterwards, he was staggered by the way in which his companion in trouble addressed him.

It is not necessary to put into print what he said—my readers must draw on their imagination for it. Jeb Jaundice remonstrated. If he had not been afraid of him he would have answered in a like manner.

"Don't speak to a man like that," he said. "Remember we are old pals."

"I remember nothing except that I was always your master and always will be," returned the Ogre.

"Pals!—what do you mean by calling me your pal?"

"Well, but wasn't we friendly in a way?" mildly urged Jaundice.

"We were so far friends as suited my book—nothing more. You were but a puny rascal at the best. A wife-beater is never more than half a man."

The face of Jeb Jaundice spoke volumes, but his tongue said nothing.

"Please to remember," continued the Ogre, "I am one of those masters who like to be obeyed, and will be obeyed, or I will know the reason why."

"The word master is rather harsh to use between you and me."

"It is a word that I intend to use and act upon. I am off at once, you can follow me."

"Follow you?"

"Yes, in your proper place—master and man. I had my valet once, and why should I not have him again?"

"This is surely some joke."

"I never joke," replied the Ogre. "Come, we will away."

"But why this haste?"

"That is my affair," returned the Ogre. "There may be a need of going, or it may be but a whim of mine. But it is enough that I am going, and you must follow."

"Well, lead on," said Jeb Jaundice, sullenly; "I will follow."

"You are wise," said the Ogre, as he strode forth from the cave.

"I'll not put up with this," thought Jeb Jaundice, as he went after him. "Some mad devil has taken possession of him. I'll shoot him down. No, I won't; I'll betray him to Broad Arrow Jack, who perhaps in return will spare my life. A good thought, and it only remains to find a way to do it."

CHAPTER LXVI.

THE FATE OF CALIBAN.

MAGGIE was bent upon returning for the time to the life in the diamond-fields, where she would have an opportunity to make money, and be tolerably secure from any attack her enemies might make upon her.

She and Jeb were now parted for ever.

The gulf between them had been wide for many years, but the affection of woman had bridged it over. Now the bridge was shattered, and all the king's horses and all the king's men would never build it up again.

She could never harm him, nor aid in doing him harm, but she felt she could do no more for him, and thenceforth determined to live alone.

It was strange, but true, that now she had really severed from the man whom she had loved so truly, a feeling of desolation came upon her—a feeling she had never really known before; and as she wandered on, followed by the uncouth Caliban, the hot tears at intervals ran down her cheeks.

Few women could have borne the position, with all its attendant horrors, but she had led a rough life from early womanhood, and her nerves were steeled to danger. She had no fears such as women might naturally feel under the circumstances.

A day and a night she travelled, and while she slept Caliban watched with his ears like a faithful hound, and resumed the journey in the morning without showing any signs of fatigue. Even food he refused to partake of, as their stock was scanty, although Maggie urged him to do so.

She laid her small hand lightly on his broad shoulder, and thanked him.

The sightless eyes flashed forth a dim light, which had its origin in his soul, and taking her fingers lightly he raised them to his lips with as much grace and more real tenderness than a knight of old would have done.

"A strange creature!" mused Maggie. "And to some so loathsome—to me once so, but now no more so than a faithful dog. Poor Caliban!"

Towards evening they were walking through a narrow pass, which opened into a high plain, commanding a distant view of the diamond fields. Maggie was hurrying on, with as much speed as the condition of her companion permitted of, as she hoped, by travelling all night, to reach the fields by the morning.

Several times she had seen bodies of men in the distance, and had hidden until they passed out of sight. Not that she feared them much, but they might prove troublesome, and delay her on her way. In the pass now she saw one man, standing before her as if to bar her way.

One man was nothing for her to fear, and she continued advancing until they were within a few feet of each other. Then he called upon her to halt.

"A word with you, Mrs. Jaundice," he said; "or shall I call you sweet Maggie?"

"Call me nothing,' she replied, "and let me pass. I do not know you."

"No; but women forget men easily. You have seen me once, and do not even remember my face. I looked once upon you, and your image is graven on my heart. Madam, I come with a message for you."

"Say from whom, and end this fooling," she said.

"I come from your husband," replied he; "and my name is Steinnitz."

"Well, your message."

"It is not exactly a message, but a commission. I am to kill you!"

Maggie shuddered, and for the first time felt fear within her.

"To kill me?" she faltered.

"Yes, to slay you as cruelly as I can," replied Steinnitz.

"But, surely, you lie. Bad as Jeb Jaundice is he would never desire to kill me."

"Jeb Jaundice," said Steinnitz, "is but a man. He loved you, and you have grown cold and false to him."

"Cold I am, for the chill waters of his cruelty have quenched the fire of love. False I am not, and your tongue lies for him!"

"Madam," said Steinnitz, "I but bring a message from him. I know nothing of its truth. For that which he asserts to be true he bids me kill you!"

"And will you do it?"

"Not if you wish to live."

"I am not fit to die, and therefore would yet live on," she said. "Let me pass."

"Thou shalt live, but on one condition," said Steinnitz.

"What is it?"

"Madam, I love——"

"Go on," she said, as he paused. "Is it a love for another that softens your heart towards me?"

"No," he said, "I love you."

Caliban, who had up to this time been an attentive listener to what was passing, now uttered a low cry—unheeded, however, by Maggie or Steinnitz—and, crouching down, crept towards the latter.

Steinnitz did not even see him, and continued—

"You are startled, I see," he said, "and have a look that with some men would pass for virtuous indignation. With me it only goes down for good acting."

"Indeed!" she said, calmly; "and what do you propose?"

"Why should I say more?" he said. "Men who love desire the object of that love."

Caliban, crouching like a tiger, crept towards him, feeling his way silently along the ground.

"And you can think," said Maggie, "that I, having loved once, can ever love again?"

"I would fain hope so. Gratitude for having spared your life ought to do something."

"Gratitude, you murderous hound—you base hireling of the basest man that ever damned the life of woman. Shall I be thankful to be spared for a deeper hell than sudden death can give me? Come to your work; but, see, I am armed, and you shall not do my husband's bidding as easily as you think."

"Put up that toothpick," said Steinnitz, coolly drawing a little nearer. "It would only be a waste of energy on your part. I smile at such things as that. Nay, you shall have your choice of any weapon I wear, if, after I have reasoned with you, you still reject me."

"I'll hear no reason—there is no need of it," she said.

"Then listen to another power!" he cried, suddenly springing forward, and, throwing his arms around her. "Ha, my pretty bird, you are caged! One kiss, now, as an earnest of happiness to come."

"Help, Caliban!—help!" cried Maggie, struggling violently.

Steinnitz had forgotten him, but as Maggie cried out an arm was thrown round his throat, and his head was drawn back until every bone in his neck cracked.

The scoundrel, half choked, let go his hold, and Maggie, succumbing to fatigue and horror, fainted.

Steinnitz got his head round, and the two men closed. Caliban was unarmed, but his powerful grip was not to be shaken off. Steinnitz, with his arms down, could not get at his weapons. He was a prisoner, and powerless.

Then came the struggle for a fall, and Caliban considering he was blind, held his own wonderfully well; but Steinnitz had every advantage, and, driving him back over a stone, cast him down heavily.

The head of the faithful hound, or man—or what you will—was dashed upon the corner of a rock, and the blood spirted out a foot on either side of him. Half dead, half dazed, he still held on.

Steinnitz strove to get free, but the great horny fingers were locked behind his back, and ten times the power he had at his disposal would not have set him free.

Once, twice, thrice, Steinnitz slowly raised the head of his antagonist, and dashed it down again, and each time the life-blood came more freely forth. But still the faithful hound held on.

Caliban made great efforts to get his foe undermost, but his blindness and the injuries he had received hindered him. Steinnitz kept him down, but could not unclasp those iron arms.

And in the midst of this Maggie came back to life, and, rising, looked upon the horrible scene. It was like a nightmare to her—the blood—the ghastly looks of Caliban—the fiendish ferocity of Steinnitz, and, overwhelmed with horror, she fled, shrieking.

Steinnitz heard her cries, and knew that he was losing that he had risked his life for. His fury almost drove him mad.

"Let go—let go!" he cried, dashing the head of the fast-dying Caliban upon the rock.

But a short cry of defiance was all the answer given him.

Fast the life ebbed out, but even coming death could not relax that grasp, nor death itself, for when the fire of life died out of that savage breast the horny knotty fingers were locked as fast as ever.

The living and the dead were bound together.

What Steinnitz felt when he realised his position no words can tell; but as the darkness came the air was filled with his cries and shrieks, and no man heard or heeded him.

CHAPTER LXVII.

WHITHER GONE?

TWO weeks passed by, and Broad Arrow Jack still remained in his camp, unable to tell which way to go, for the Ogre and Jeb Jaundice had again most unaccountably disappeared.

The Tiger took back the intelligence of their whereabouts when they were in the cave, and Jack was there in the morning with a band of men to capture them; but, as we know, they had left, and all trace of them half a mile from the spot lost.

Messengers were sent in every direction to the diamond-fields, and to the various posts held by Jack's men. Odds and ends of their disbanded followers were brought in and questioned, everything done in short that could be done, but all in vain. The Ogre and Jeb Jaundice had once more got clear away.

"The devil favours his own, Brisket," said Jack, "but I will have them yet."

"Oh, yes," said Billy, "we shall get them, but it's a long job."

"Come, Brisket, you ought not to despair."

"I don't; all I say is, that it's a long job—confound 'em."

Billy Brisket was cleaning his rifle as he made

this remark, and he gave the barrel a vigorous polish, and putting it together, placed it in a corner of the tent.

"I hate grumblers," he said, squatting down on the ground, "and I never, if I can help it, grumble at anything, but lately I've set my heart upon seeing old England again, and that is why I think things are so slow, I suppose."

"Why not go, Brisket?"

"And leave you?"

"Yes, why should I selfishly demand the sacrifice of your life, and all you have to further my ends? I give up all."

"Not if I know it," said Brisket, smiting the ground energetically with his fist. "What! let them warmints get off scot-free? No, my lad, your heart is not more set on punishing them than mine is. If I went to England without you I should not rest. As for being selfish, look here, my lad, I'm proud to know you, proud to give up all I have to you, and thank you for being so much to a childless man."

"Well, Brisket," said Jack, "we will say no more about it then, but do our best to bring these villains to book."

"And I won't grumble any more, if it takes ten years to do it."

"You are a good fellow, Brisket."

"And you are the noblest fellow that ever broke bread."

Here ended the conversation, and Billy Brisket went out to look after some duty of the day. Messengers during the morning came riding in from various parts, and all brought the same tale. Neither the Ogre nor Jaundice had been seen.

They also reported that the tone of the country was in some places doubtful. The Ogre had lost the majority of his partisans, but still many hardheaded ones declined to be convinced, and held out that Jack might be all that was represented. But none were disposed to take up arms. Those who had fought for the Ogre were seeking their homes, and the others were not disposed to leave them. This left matters very much as they were before.

Jack was very gloomy, and the sadness of his face deepened. It was principally at night that he felt the shadow of sorrow, and oft, when all but the sentries were asleep, he would go out and sit by one of the camp-fires brooding until the morning light sent him back to his tent.

On one of these occasions, about fifteen days after the disappearance of the Ogre, he was sitting in this way, with his eyes fixed upon the glowing embers of the burning wood, when out of the darkness a man with a long knife in his hand sprang upon him.

Jack would have been struck down but for his natural quickness of eye, and that saved him. The gleam of the blade flashed before him—his arm went up, and he caught the would-be murderer by the throat.

The man was strong, and, Jack being in a recumbent position, the odds were against him; but his powerful arms kept his assailant at bay until the noise of the struggle brought men to his assistance. The man's arms were bound, and he was placed before Jack, who desired that the fire might be stirred up, so that a light might fall upon his face.

When the flame flashed up Jack saw a man of forty or so, with a haggard face, fixed in expression, save the eyes, which moved restlessly to and fro, like those of some wild beast, fresh caged, but not yet tamed. The man was a stranger to him.

"What brings you here on such an errand?" asked Jack.

"Vengeance!" replied the man.

"How have I wronged you?"

"Three nights ago," said the man, "I returned from the fields, where I had been tending sick cattle, and found naught but the bodies of my wife and child, and the smoking ruins of my house. The door had been wrenched from its hinges, and on it I found the broad arrow—your sign."

"No—not mine."

"Yes, indeed!" said the man, smiling bitterly. "Your story is well known to me; but I do not care to bandy words with you. Do your worst. What in the name of heaven have I to live for?"

"My poor fellow," said Jack, "believe me, my enemies have done this. I have never wronged man or woman. Set him free."

The man stared.

They cast off his bonds and Jack bade them give him his knife again.

"Go," he said, "or, if you have no home, find one here. I will be a friend to you, seeing that my enemies have brought ruin upon you."

"But I do not understand you."

"My men will explain. But let me ask where lies your home?"

The man pointed out the way, and Jack saw that it was almost in a line with Black Rock.

"The fools," he said, "are going inland. They cannot escape me now."

Half a dozen rough riders were at once called out and sent in different directions. The Tiger, too, was despatched to bring what news he could, and Jack, with new life instilled into him, passed some time in arranging for a speedy departure.

But the days wore on, and the men one after the other returned with the tidings growing too familiar, that neither the Ogre nor Jaundice could be found.

The last to come in was the Tiger, weary for once and footsore.

"Massa," he said, "I reckon dey am not bout dis country, or I must hab seen dem."

"Whither are they gone?" asked Jack, and echo answered "Whither?"

CHAPTER LXVIII.

MR. TRIMMER HAS IT OUT WITH STEINNITZ.

SOME articles were wanted from the stores established in the diamond-fields, and Trimmer with a dozen men was despatched to obtain them.

An expedition of this sort suited the disposition of Mr. Trimmer, whose ears, having got nearly well, no longer troubled him, and, barring the eccentric appearance given him by the handkerchief tied close to his head, there was nothing in his looks to shut him out from congenial society.

The society which Trimmer loved was not over and above particular, for if once it had commenced weeding out on account of absent ears, noses, and eyes, at least two-thirds of its members would have been obliged to make tracks.

In his heart Trimmer was a gambler. He thought cards the most beautiful of books, and the rattle of the dice was perfect music in his ears. There was little or no gambling in Jack's camp, and the time oft hung heavy on his hands.

Therefore he rejoiced over being sent to the diamond-fields, for then he could at least have a few hours of uninterrupted felicity, and more, if good luck favoured him in the setting out.

His way led him through the pass where Caliban and Steinnitz fought out their deadly fight, and there he found two arms severed from a body, and, pitched behind a rock, they found the rest of Caliban.

The men knew who it was, although Trimmer did not, and they asked leave to bury him. Trimmer bottled his impatience to get at the cards and dice, and smoked a pipe while they did the last office for the dead man.

There was much surmise as to how the dumb diamond-polisher came by his death, but the truth was not hit upon. How could they hit upon any connection between him and Steinnitz?

Arrived at the fields Trimmer hired a shanty for

BROAD-ARROW JACK.

BY THE AUTHOR OF

HANDSOME HARRY and CHEERFUL CHING-CHING.

"YONDER IS MORE OF THE OGRE'S FOUL WORK," SAID BROAD ARROW JACK—"LET US RIDE THITHER."

No. 11.

his men, and evening having set in he walked to a familiar gambling saloon, where he hoped to find good company.

To his astonishment he found it empty of all except the proprietor, a tall scowling fellow, sitting on the top of a barrel, smoking an enormous cheroot.

"Hullo, Whiffler," said Trimmer, "what means this cursed empty hall? Has everybody swore off gambling?"

"It aint that exactly," replied Mr. Whiffler, "but they've swore on to singing."

"Swore on to singing?"

"Yes. A woman as used to be here at the music-hall, and drew wonderful, has come back, and sent everybody mad. There aint much in her looks now, for she's oldish, but that she's been a downright fust-rate one any one can see."

"That's Jeb Jaundice's wife, I expect," said Mr. Trimmer.

"Right you are. Afore she went away she used to sing a kind o' sentimental ditty, such as women and children like, but this time she's giving them what some calls despairing songs. I don't know anything about 'em. I go by what they tells me. All singing is much the same in my ears."

"Except the music of chinking gold," said Trimmer, facetiously digging him in the ribs.

"Ah! there you have me," said Whiffler; "gold is the only thing that strikes fire out of a man like me. I loves it—I lives on it, and I should like to sleep on it, if I had enough and it made a softer bed. But about this woman. She's turned the men right orf their heads, and drove 'em mad. Some of 'em actually shed tears."

"Nonsense."

"It's a fact, and they aint ashamed of it. Oh! its a precious go—this infernal mouthing, robbing me of my business and my rights."

"Is she singing to-night?"

"Yes, listen. Hear that hullabaloo. She's just come on."

"I'll run over and see her."

"If you get in you'll be lucky."

"Anyhow I'll try."

"Have one game of poker before you go."

"No, another time."

It was a great temptation to resist, but the curiosity of Mr. Trimmer was aroused, and could only be satisfied by looking upon the enthusiasm of Maggie's supporters. Hurrying out he ran down to the hall, and asked the man at the door what was the price of admission.

"A dollar," was the reply, "but I don't think there is room."

"I can squeeze myself in anywhere," he replied, and putting down the money, he passed through the narrow dorway and entered the hall.

It was crowded from end to end, and every man was breathless and still. Maggie was singing a portion of the dying scene in "La Traviata," and every note thrilled through the rugged listeners.

Her voice must have been excellent indeed when she was young, and even now it was far beyond what we usually hear in the concert-rooms of London. It had all the power and richness possessed by some of our famous prima donnas, and only lacking the unceasing training which those professionals indulge in.

Trimmer listened, and tried to preserve his coolness and indifference, but could not. When a woman—be she old or young—pours out her soul in song or words, man must listen. The roughest—although he scarce knows why—finds himself drawn towards her

The song ceased, and the silence continued until after Maggie had left the stage. Then the spell broke, and the shaky building trembled with the applause.

Trimmer regained some of his coolness, and took a look about him.

Many of the spectators he knew by sight, and a few were, to his knowledge, rough and hardened ruffians; but one and all seemed to be changed and softened down.

"It's a rum go," thought Trimmer. "What a woman can do if she likes—twist and turn the best of us like a bit of string!"

His eyes, having scanned those in front, were next directed to those behind, and close to him he beheld the last man he would have thought of—Steinnitz.

"I'm darned!" he said. "What is he doing here?"

For the time being Steinnitz was engaged in dwelling upon the beauty of Maggie's song, with his eyes raised to the ceiling, and the rapt look upon his face of a man whose whole mind and body are absorbed in one thought.

He remained thus while Mr. Trimmer worked his way over to his side, and gave him a friendly dig in the ribs. Then he awoke with a start, and became aware of Trimmer's presence.

"Well met!" said the latter. "I've come over here expecting to have a bit of a fling with the bones; but everybody's here, and I've nothing to do."

"Well, I can't give you anything to do," replied Steinnitz, tartly.

"Oh, yes; come out and let us have a bit of fun together. Where's your knife and poppers?"

"Haven't got them."

"That's a pity; but we will play for a choice of mine."

"I don't want to play," returned Steinnitz. "This woman sings again in half an hour."

"You will be able to come back by that time, or you will never hear her sing on airth again. Come on, or I'll shoot you where you stand."

Steinnitz knew that his very presence there was a risk to himself. He had come in late, under cover of the general excitement, and purposed stealing away again as soon as the singing was over.

There were several inhabitants of the diamond-fields who had old scores to settle with him, and would have done it, too, if they had known he was there.

"Don't kick up a row," he said, hurriedly.

"Then come out," replied Trimmer.

Steinnitz paused no longer, and they went out together, Trimmer holding him tightly by the arm, and keeping him a little in front, in case he should try any bolting tricks. He also held a pistol ready to use if such an emergency should arise.

"Where are you going?" asked Steinnitz.

"To Whiffler's rooms," replied Trimmer.

"I can't go there."

"Why not?"

"I'm a marked man there. I was falsely accused of playing with loaded dice."

"Oh, indeed! That's awkward in a general way; but you need have no fear. There isn't a creature in the place to-night except Whiffler, and he won't hurt you unless I tell him to."

"But what are you going to do?"

"Come and see."

The face of Steinnitz became very dogged as he yielded to the persuasive voice of the charmer, and together they went into Whiffler's place, and found him still upon the barrel, finishing off his big cigar.

He seemed a little surprised, and, no doubt, was, but he did not get off his barrel, or say a word. It was Trimmer who spoke.

"Whiffler," he said, "you know Steinnitz?"

"Remember him well, and I wonder he has the cheek to come back here."

"He didn't come—I brought him. We are going to play a little game."

"So—then don't let him use his own dice."

"We will use yours, Whiffler."

"What's the stakes?" asked Whiffler, as he got off the barrel and opened a cupboard where there were dice and cards enough for fifty players.

"I am going to play him for his life and mine," replied Trimmer.

"Eh?" said Whiffler, looking round.

"His life and mine are the stakes," said Trimmer, "nothing more, and nothing less. It's too much trouble to fight this weather. It's too hot. The man who gets the worst of two throws out of three will have to stand up and take what the other can give him out of one of those pistol barrels."

"But how do I know the dice are fair?" asked Steinnitz, turning pale.

"Naturally you think they won't be," said Trimmer; "but let him choose his box, and I'll choose mine. That's fair, aint it?"

"Straight and true."

"But if I win shall I go away free?"

"Whiffler will see to that—won't you, old man?"

"I'll go outside the fields with you, and see you clear away; and I don't think there is a man about who will attempt to stop me."

This was quite true. Whiffler was a terror to most of the men about there, and allowed to go to and fro at all times and seasons without molestation. Steinnitz either was, or appeared to be, satisfied.

He chose his box, and Trimmer chose his. They sat down at a table, and Whiffler lounged against the wall, watching the play.

"You first," said Trimmer, and Steinnitz threw.

"Sixes!" he cried.

"Good," said Trimmer, coolly shaking the box. "Aces as I live. One to you."

Steinnitz smiled, and the paleness began to leave his face. He threw again.

"Six and four," he cried—"ten!"

"You are in luck," said Trimmer, as he rattled the box. "Now then, you bone devils, if ever you did a man a good turn do it now."

He threw them out, and they fell—six and five. Steinnitz uttered an oath, but Trimmer checked him.

"You can't have it all your own way, and if you swear at the bones they will play an ugly trick. My turn now. Here goes."

The dice fell upon the table—a four and one—a poor throw. The spirits of Steinnitz again rose.

"It's a poor throw," he said, "that can't beat that."

"You have to do it. Chuck away," said Trimmer.

Steinnitz took his turn, shaking and flourishing the box about. At last he threw, and looked at the dice. A terrible pallor came over his countenance. He looked upon two deuces.

"The bones run in couples to-night," said Trimmer, calmly, "you've lost by a point. Whiffler, can I finish the business here?"

"Sartinly, you've used the room, and I want to have some share in the fun."

"Stand up!" said Trimmer to Steinnitz.

"It's murder," gasped the wretched man.

"No it aint, for I gave you a good run for your money. It's a fairer business than you tried on with Broad Arrow Jack. Stand up, I say!"

"I won't."

"Shut the door, Whiffler. That's it; push the table away. I'll shoot him as he is."

"Mercy!" cried Steinnitz.

"Mercy to you. What for?"

"But I'll not be killed this way," cried Steinnitz, rushing towards him.

Trimmer stepped back a pace, took a quick aim, and fired.

Steinnitz pulled up suddenly, and, for the fraction of a second, stood upright, quivering. Then he fell forward upon his face, and lay still.

"Dead, I'll bet a dollar," said Whiffler.

"I swore I would do it," said Trimmer. "What shall we do with him?"

"Shove him out of the window. The patrol will be round presently and find him."

"But won't they suspect you?"

"Of course they will, and they have done a dozen times before, but suspicion can't hang a man like me. Bear a hand. The gal have finished her singing, and the boys are coming here."

Trimmer gave a hand, and all that was left of Steinnitz was quickly dropped out of the window into the dark street.

Two minutes afterwards the room was full of gamblers, and the coolest of them all was Trimmer, notwithstanding that he had a run of luck against him.

CHAPTER LXIX.

REBELLION.

CONKY, Curler, and Pigeon, being rather an incumbrance to the Broad Arrow camp, were despatched, with Fireworks and old Joss, to take up their abode with Wobbles, and wandered about for the best part of two days, subject to all the tricks those eccentric animals were wont to indulge in.

Old Joss, for instance, died after the manner of Black Bess no less than eleven times in the first five hours; and furthermore, did, on sundry and divers occasions, waltz about in a fashion which, however graceful, was decidedly embarrassing to those who had charge of him.

Conky led Fireworks, who was tractable enough in some things, but given to snorting and cocking his stumpy tail at old Joss. He also challenged him to combat by lifting his hind legs alternately in a contemptuous manner, and likewise, in a horsey way, referred to his great triumph over his enemy, which appears to be rather mean, when the nature of that triumph is considered.

"I never did see sich a blessed old brute as this is!" said Curler, as old Joss, suddenly remembering that he used once upon a time to walk round the ring on his hind legs, essayed to do so once again. "What's he up to now?"

"'Ang on the 'alter," suggested Conky, "and keep his 'ed down."

"If you was to go on forrard with yourn," said Pigeon, "ourn would be quiet enough."

"I aint a going on alone in this country," said Conky, decidedly.

"Then get behind a bit, and don't exzite our hanimal."

They tried this, but Fireworks had too much spirit to follow a defeated foe, and with half a dozen stiff-legged bounds, which lifted Conky off the ground, got in front again, and, in defiance, curled his tail over his back until it looked like a meat hook.

"If Mister Green hadn't told us we should be hanged if we lost 'em," said Curler, "I'm blessed if I wodldn't turn 'em off, and let 'em run wild!"

"I've an idea," said Pigeon, suddenly.

"You've had 'em afore, and they wasn't much use," said Conky.

"But this is a good 'un."

"Hout with it."

"Let's blindfold 'em. If they can't see each other they won't be so rampageous."

"It aint bad," said Conky. "We can only try it."

So the two horses were blindfolded, and the result of the great experiment was that they both lay down, and refused to get up until the bandages were taken off. When this was done they arose by degrees, and moved off more frisky than ever.

But the great feat of all was getting up the narrow steep path which led to the fortress governed by the energetic Wobbles. Here was a task which would have tried the energies of a horse in prime condition, and how these two fossilised specimens of quadrupeds were to be got up neither Conky, Curler, nor Pigeon knew.

"I think," said Conky, "that we had better go on, and see if they'll foller."

"Let's tie 'em head and tail together, and drag 'em up."

This was Pigeon's suggestion, and Curler shut him up by asking him how long it was since he took to nigger's work."

Wobbles, from above, looked down upon his old friends, and not being at all desirous of their company, was at first induced to treat them as enemies, and order his men to fire upon them; but second thoughts told him that they might be bearers of a message for him from their chief, and he gave orders for them to be admitted to his presence "when they got up."

Then he mixed himself a little brandy and water, filled his pipe, and, taking up a position where he could command a view of the ascent, prepared to enjoy himself.

Old Joss made the first start. He used to go up one side and down the other of a double flight of stairs when he was a public favourite, and he went gallantly at his work. Fireworks, not to be outdone, followed, but they stopped or fell down so often that the whole afternoon was gone when horses and men lay blown and exhausted upon the summit of the table land.

"We're hup," was the exclamation of Conky, as he sank limp and breathless upon the ground.

Neither Curler nor Pigeon said anything, for they could not, and Wobbles was too lofty to make any remark. He simply regarded them as barons of old (on the stage) used to regard their serfs.

The two horses did not get up until near sunset, when they staggered to their feet, and put themselves out to grass, on a spot where there was a fair supply of that luxurious vegetation.

Meanwhile Conky, Curler, and Pigeon had, to use a homely phrase, "put their feet in it," by assuming a familiarity with Wobbles.

It was Conky who began it, shortly after he got his breath, and was still upon his back.

"I say, Wobbles," he said, "give us a hand up—will you, old man?"

"Who are you Wobblesing of?" asked the general, sternly.

"Why you, in course. There aint another Wobbles about—is there?"

"Here I command, and am spoken to as General Wobbles."

Conky, Curler, and Pigeon laughed consumedly, and appeared to be quite overcome.

"Gineral Wobbles!" said Conky. "Oh! my sides. What next?"

"You'll find it no joke," said Wobbles; "so no check. Silence!"

"Silence yourself," said Conky. "Who are you?"

"Ah! who is he?" asked Curler.

"Who?" softly echoed Pigeon. He did not like to be behind his comrades, but he did not intend to wholly commit himself until he knew the exact position.

"I've told you once," said Wobbles, as he walked away, "so beware!"

When he was gone the trio exchanged glances of astonishment, with a dash of humour in their composition. Conky was perhaps the most edified.

"I think," he said, "we shall have some fun here."

"We shall," said Curler.

"Lots," remarked Pigeon, although he was not quite certain about it.

"He seems to have got a tent here like a swell," said Conky.

"Let's wisit him," suggested Curler, facetiously.

Wobbles had retired inside, and when the humorous friends went thither, with an air of assumed gentility, they found him in conference with one of his men.

Conky swaggered in, and sat down. Curler swaggered in, but stood up, and Pigeon went in rather meekly, and kept his feet also, standing very near the means of exit.

"You are intruding," said Wobbles, imitating the coolness of his chief.

Conky laughed, Curler sneered, and Pigeon rubbed his nose thoughtfully.

"This is intrusion," said Wobbles, putting it in another form.

"Oh! let us hend this jiggered nonsense," said Conky, impatiently. "Here, what can you give us to heat and drink?"

"Sentry," said Wobbles, "thou hearest?"

"Yes, general."

"And understandest?"

"Yes, general."

"Go and do your duty."

He saluted, and hastened out. Wobbles looked up in a meditative manner, as if he was alone, and had some deep problem to work out.

"I say, old man," said Conky, "give us something to drink."

"Were you addressing of me?" asked Wobbles, fixing an eye upon him that ought to have made a colander of his head, but somehow didn't.

"In course I was."

"Are you aweer," asked Wobbles, with the calmness only worn by true greatness, "that this is open re-bel-li-on?"

"Did you ever see the sich like?" asked Conky, addressing his friends. "Aint it good?"

"Unkimmon," replied Curler, "only it wants washing down."

"So it do. Mr. Wobbles, where do you keep the liquor?"

"Halt!" cried Wobbles, springing up—"fall in—right about face—all fours—I mean fours—seize the caitiffs, and bear them hence."

"What's the meaning of this?" asked Conky, as he found himself and friends in the grasp of half a dozen men.

"It means this," replied Wobbles, "that I, in the name of the great Broad Arrow Jack, am master here, and that you have rebel-li-ed against his authority, and will be shot to-morrow morning at sunrise."

CHAPTER LXX.

AT BLACK ROCK.

IT will be remembered by those who have perused this story that a small detachment of men was left in charge of Black Rock, wherein there lay, or was supposed to lie, the vast treasure which enabled Broad Arrow Jack to carry on his plans.

Where that treasure was none of the men knew, but there was sufficient wealth scattered about to have repaid the trouble of gathering. The precious stones in the ornamental walls alone were worth a large sum.

For many days not a thought of wrong entered the heads of any of them. They went about in the pursuit of their various duties, watching faithfully and well over the place left in their charge, but as the time passed the influence of Jack began to wane, and dark thoughts entered the minds of the little band.

Yet no man spoke.

Each conceived that the lust of wealth was on him alone, and strove to beat it under. Some were successful in their efforts to do right, others every hour fell further and further away from the path of honour.

There was one man named Craddock, who in times past had been one of the most enthusiastic supporters of Broad Arrow Jack, and he loved him still, but the second love which entered his breast—the love of wealth—fought with the first, and gained the victory.

He was a big square-set man, with shoulders that looked as though they could have held a house upon them—a tall handsome man, with a dark swarthy face. He was half English, half Spanish—having had for a father a captain of an English merchant vessel, who married a Spanish woman whom he met with on one of his numerous voyages.

A hot-blooded man when up—a determined man when he chose—Craddock was, of all others there, the most dangerous when led away by thoughts disloyal to his noble chief.

But he was led away.

Not without a big fight—for the man would go away into the woods, and struggle with the right and wrong within him, until great beads of perspiration fell from his forehead, and groans came from his quivering lips. But wrong triumphed in the end, and, once the scale fairly turned, there was no going back for Craddock.

"I'll have what I can," he said, "and get away."

There was also another man, whose name was Steyne, and he, too, had a struggle within himself to do right, and lost the battle. He and Craddock fought it out the same day, and, meeting shortly afterwards, read each other's faces correctly.

"Craddock," said Steyne, "what are you thinking of?"

"What are *you* thinking of?" was Craddock's reply.

"Nothing in particular—only that it was rather lonely here."

"And dull."

"And nothing to do."

Then there was a pause. The two men filled their pipes, lighted them, and began to smoke, keeping their eyes upon each other.

"Speak out, Steyne," said Craddock.

"You first—you are the elder."

"Then let me ask you if you are going to stop here?"

"No, I aint."

"And you won't go away empty-handed?"

"Not if I can help it. Will you?"

"No."

"Then it only remains for us to decide what we shall fill our hands with."

Another pause—both men smoking thoughtfully this time, with their eyes on the ground.

"There's lots to be got," said Craddock, softly—"lots that is just under our noses; but there is more to be got that we've never set eyes on."

"So there is," returned Steyne; "but where is it kept?"

"That is what we must find out. Have you any idea?"

"Not the least, and I see by your face you have not."

"That we must now proceed to find out."

"But how about the rest? We cannot trust them."

"No," said Craddock, decidedly; "they must be kept in the dark."

These two men went back, and kept aloof from their companions, using all their leisure time in prowling about Black Rock, and searching here and there for the wealth they felt certain was lying there; and, while they prowled, the eyes of others having half-developed thoughts similar to their own were upon them.

"I say," said Craddock, two days afterwards, "we shall have to be very careful. This morning, as I was round at the back, I saw Dixon sneaking after me."

"I can't turn without having somebody about me like my shadow," said Steyne.

"I fancy some of these people may turn out troublesome."

"No doubt they will."

A silence, and both very thoughtful indeed.

"It would be a good thing if the lot were away," said Craddock, suddenly.

"So it would—if, being away, they would hold their tongues."

"But they won't do that, Steyne."

"Oh, no."

"Speak up, Steyne—say what had best be done," said Craddock.

"No, I won't," replied the other, "for I don't like conspiring. It never comes to any good; but you do the best you can for our cause, and I'll do the same. And if anybody should die or be missing, we won't talk about it."

"I understand you. Your hand upon it," said Craddock.

"'Tis here—the thing is as good as done."

That very night, one of the men acting as sentry was killed. He was found by his comrades stabbed in the back, and nothing was left whereby the murderer might be traced. Craddock and Steyne were very doubtful indeed, but did not go near each other.

The work once begun went on rapidly. Ere the day was out another man was missing, and search being made for him, he was found behind the house with his head battered in.

"Who did this?" was the general question, and no man apparently could answer it. A growing distrust of each other set in. Only two men in the whole place trusted each other, and their names were Craddock and Steyne.

Another morn brought another tale of horror. Two men on duty had been killed—one stabbed, and the other struck down as before.

"Who is the murderer?" was asked all round, and all declared their innocence. No two men could be more fervent in their oaths, asserting their innocence than Craddock and Steyne.

"He puts a good face on it," said Craddock, looking at Steyne.

"Craddock is a friend to be proud of," thought Steyne, and they became more closely allied than ever.

That night no man cared to go on duty, but it was mooted—"If the chief comes and finds no man to challenge him we shall all be shot."

"Let us draw lots," said one.

They drew them, and the duty fell on two young fellows, one barely twenty, and both full of the hopes and aspirations of youth.

They went out and never returned. In the morning, as they did not come in, those who were left went in a body to find them. One they discovered lying on his face with blood trickling from his side, the other lay under a tree with his clothes torn, and the signs of a great struggle upon him. He had at least a dozen wounds in various parts of his body, and had evidently fought bravely for his life.

The band was now considerably thinned, and the panic among those remaining increased. Only Craddock and Steyne preserved anything like a calm exterior.

"You are a plucky fellow," said Craddock to Steyne as they were returning.

"There's a little of the true grit about you," returned Steyne.

They shook hands, exchanged smiles, and went home rejoicing.

I do not want to dwell upon this tale of horror, or to pile up the agony in describing what the doomed band felt as their numbers rapidly thinned.

One by one they were slain, some in the woods, some at home, until only Craddock, Steyne, and another remained.

This third man was a grizzled old trapper, who had lived in lonely places by the year together. He knew little of fear when it came in the ordinary course, but the startling events which had come about at Black Rock shook his nerves, and taught him what it was to dread death.

But he was a plucky old man, and would not shirk his work. There was a duty to be done, and somebody must do it. "One at least," he said, "ought to guard the pass in case the chief should come."

"One at least," said Craddock and Steyne together, "but who shall do it?"

"Draw lots as before," said the old man.

They were drawn, and the trapper had to go forth. He stood in the porch in the twilight, buckling his belt about him with all the coolness of a man going upon an ordinary hunting expedition.

Craddock and Steyne lay close by him smoking, and regarding the trapper with the look of interest people bestow upon men who are doomed to die.

"I reckon," said the old trapper, looking up at the sky, "we shall have it rough to-night."

"May be," replied Craddock. "But you surely aint afraid of the weather?"

"I am afraid o' nothing that I can see and hear," said the old man; "but when there's that about which I can't grasp I get puzzled and shaky like. I don't understand these murders as have been going on."

"I think," said Craddock, "that we must be reg'larly hemmed in by enemies, who are going to take us one by one."

"Appears so," returned the trapper. "But you take it coolly."

"I don't see any use in doing otherwise. If we are to die let us die like men."

"Just so. And you, Steyne, appear rather to enjoy it."

"I aint in a mortal funk like some people," said Steyne.

"There aint been no more than natural funk showed by any here," said the trapper, bending his brows. "Here we've been penned in like sheep with a duty to do, and we've all done it. I've seen many odd things, and people being picked off is nothing new to me. But I do say that this b'isness is a puzzle to me—so are you!"

"We?" said Craddock and Steyne.

"Yes, you. It appears to me that you are so cool that you must know all about it, but I can't prove it. If I could I'd shoot you like a couple of rats as you sit there—yes, I would!"

"You are a little cheeky, seeing we are two to one," said Craddock.

"Small odds, if what I fancy is true," said the trapper; "but I aint a-goin' to shoot any man down for fancy. I did it once, and found I was in the wrong, and put away one of the best friends I ever had."

"Well, we are friendly with you—aint we?" asked Steyne.

"It aint much, one way or t'other," replied the trapper; "but all I've got to say is this—if anybody oemes a-nigh me to-night—come one—come two—I'll shoot 'em down first, and ax who they are afterwards!"

Having uttered this warning—plainly directed at the two men—he shouldered his rifle, and, with a long swinging step, strode away.

"He's been an ugly customer in his time," said Craddock.

"So he has," replied Steyne; "but we are ugly customers, too."

They did not exchange another word, but, drawing away from each other, they lay down as if to sleep.

An hour later a terrific thunderstorm burst over the valley.

It was a rare occurrence to have such a storm in the valley, and, as invariably happens, all the more terrible for its rarity.

It was not the sort of night to be out in—much less the night for the enactment of a bloody, cruel deed; and yet a bloody cruel deed was done.

The vivid lightning, showing up the river, trees, and general objects around almost as bright as day, also revealed the old trapper lying on his face, shot through the heart. The report of the weapon which slew him had been lost in the roar of the aërial artillery.

CHAPTER LXXI.

BEWILDERMENT.

WITH the sun the storm passed over, and only the fallen trees, the hundred cataracts and thousand rills running down the slopes, remained to tell the story of its coming. Craddock and Steyne lay upon the same spots they had retired to the night before, not having apparently moved.

"Been roughish," said Steyne, "as—as—ahem!—the old trapper said."

"Yes," replied Craddock, "he was right—he was a good judge of the weather—ahem!"

"Has—he—he—come back?" asked Steyne.

"I—haven't seen him."

"He ought to be back—you know."

"No, I don't know—anything about him," replied Craddock, tartly.

Steyne put a finger upon his nose, and looked cunning.

"Nothing at all," he said. "Oh, no!"

"I really don't. If he doesn't come in soon I think we ought to look for him."

"I don't mind, Craddock, if you don't. Let's look for him now."

"Why should I mind? I have not harmed the old man."

"Not at all," said Steyne, with a repetition of his sly look.

Craddock was a little huffed, although he hardly knew why, but the jocular strain Steyne was indulging in seemed rather to jar upon his feelings.

He was a little sulky as they went out to look for the old trapper.

They knew the spot where he would be found—living or dead.

That he was not living we know, and dead they found him.

Neither man seemed to be very awe-stricken as they looked upon him. With death in a score forms they were familiar, but surely now one or the other ought to have betrayed emotion.

"This is the last of those who stood in our way," said Craddock, turning the dead man over. "You aimed well, Steyne."

"I aimed? You mean that you did," replied Steyne.

"Me! I never left the palace last night."

"Nor I."

"Steyne, don't lie."

"If there is a lie in it, Craddock, it is yours."

"I do not lie. I never left my couch last night."

"Then who killed him?"

"I don't know, Steyne."

Both the men were puzzled and their usual composure was gone.

If neither of them lied, who had killed the trapper?

"I did not see you do it," said Craddock, "but as you killed the rest I——"

"I killed the rest?"

"Yes, you. Who else would have done it?"

"Why you."

"I swear I did not touch a man!"

"Now, Craddock, there is no need to gammon me——"

"I am not gammoning; it is perfectly true. I never put a finger on one of them."

His fervour carried conviction to Steyne, and Steyne's amazement assured Craddock that he was innocent too!

"We arranged it all," said the latter; "but if we have not killed them who has?"

"I can't tell."

"No more can I."

Their jocularity and lightness of heart were gone. Both had been very easy of mind, as each thought his comrade was doing all the foul work as a matter of choice. Now that the truth was known they trembled.

What was the mystery?

Who had slain their companions one by one?

Was all the baseness and treachery they contemplated known to some power above mortal men? And were they, as an especial act of vengeance, reserved unto the last for a doom more terrible than all?

They were so bewildered that they thought nothing fairly out—so terror-stricken they knew not whither to turn. Whether to fly or remain where they were they could not tell.

"It was an evil hour," said Craddock, "when we meditated treachery against our chief. No good could come of it."

"Evil has sprung out of it," said Steyne. "We are both doomed and accursed! But do not let us part. Whatever the danger let us face it together."

"It shall be so," replied Craddock, and their hands closed upon it.

Fear bound them together in a bond stronger than common friendship.

CHAPTER LXXII.
THE TRAIL OF THE OGRE.

"HASTE, Brisket! We have no time to lose. The men will come up by-and-bye."

Broad Arrow Jack pressed his knees against his horse's side, and the noble animal bounded forward willingly in response. When sympathy exists between the steed and his rider neither whip nor spur is needed.

Billy Brisket, who was neither so good nor so fearless a rider as his chief, was a little careful of his neck, and guided his horse in and out the rough places, but, on the whole he stuck manfully to the saddle, and rode fairly well.

"Ten years' tramping on foot has rather spoiled my horsemanship," he said, as he came up with his leader.

Jack had suddenly reined up, and turned his face to the north.

"What is that?" he said, pointing to a dark cloud in the horizon.

"Storm coming."

"No, it changes too rapidly. That is a great fire."

"More of the Ogre's foul work. Let us ride thither."

"Here are some of your foremost men coming up."

Jack only waited to bid the men, who came in hot haste on the trail of their impetuous leader, to wait there for his return, and he and Brisket set forward in the direction of the fire.

An hour's ride brought them to the spot, where they found a farm and a score of stacks burning, while a man and his wife and half a dozen children looked on stupefied.

As Jack reined up the clatter of his horse's hoofs drew their eyes towards him, but not one spoke a word.

"Whose work is this?" asked Jack.

The man took off his hat, rubbed his forehead, but seemed unable to reply.

Jack put the question again, and the woman found her tongue.

"That demon, Broad Arrow Jack, did this," she said.

"Indeed," said our hero. "Who told you so?"

"We have seen him."

"What was he like?"

"A swarthy villain—half devil—half nigger. He came upon us with a dozen men, demanded money and food, had both—then, in wanton mischief, fired our home. We are ruined, and must starve."

"So," thought Jack, "he is gathering men together again. The scotched snake will yet give me some trouble to kill."

"The man who wrecked your home," he said, aloud, "was not what he called himself. I am Broad Arrow Jack. See here, I shall bear that which gave me the name to the grave. This was done in wanton devilry by the brute whose hand has ruined you. He is rightly named the Ogre."

"The Ogre of Peaceful Village?" said the man, suddenly waking up.

"Yes."

"Ah, would that I had known it! All his men should not have saved him. By his hand my only brother died. I came here and prospered. He was toiling in misery and poverty at home. I sent for him and he came. Crossing the great plain between my home and the sea he encountered the wretch you name, who robbed him of his all, and sent him here with a dozen wounds to die. Oh, would that I had known it to-night!"

"But why did you not kill him as it was?" asked Jack.

"See here," replied the man, pointing to his wife and children. "I might have failed, and they would have suffered. But had I known who he was I think I might have forgotten even them in my wrath."

"I am in pursuit of him. Which way did he go?" asked Jack.

"I scarce marked his retreat, but I heard him name a place?"

"Do you remember?"

"No; but perhaps you do, Mary."

"Black Rock was the name," she said.

"Black Rock!" exclaimed Jack, starting. "He is bold, I think. And when men are bold they are sometimes successful. But surely it was mere boasting—a blind to our friends here. He thought they would associate Black Rock with my name."

"Who knows it is your place?" said the man.

"Half the country by this time. We have been burdened with traitors of late."

"Yes, it is so—and yet I cannot think he would be so bold. He is cunning, and would scarce tell of the way he was going."

"It was not the Ogre who spoke, but a tall, dark, dissipated-looking man who was with him. He called him Jaundice. This man mentioned Black Rock, and the Ogre cursed him for a fool," said the man.

"He has gone thither," said Jack. "And now, friend, what will you do?"

The man who was addressed looked up, and shook his head sorrowfully.

"Sit here and starve," he said. "All that I have will soon be ashes."

"Nay, that is scarcely worthy of a man. Will you work?"

"My fingers to the bone if I can get work to do," was the reply.

"Give him a note to Warren," said Jack to Brisket. "He will find him something. Let him buy a claim for him."

Billy Brisket wrote a short note with a pencil on a leaf he tore out of his pocket-book, and gave it to the man.

"Mr. Warren is our agent at the diamond-fields," he explained. "You have only to ask for him by name, and any one will guide you thither."

"Thank you," said the man, "you give me new hope. But oh, my home! The work of twelve long years turned to ashes in the night. If you get that monster in your power grind him to powder."

"It will go hard with him when next my hand is laid upon him," replied Jack. "Farewell, my friend, I have something to do."

He shook hands with the man and his wife, turned his horse's head, and galloped back. Billy Brisket was soon in his wake, a little unsteady in the saddle, but riding pluckily.

CHAPTER LXXIII.

A BARRIER.

GOING to Black Rock!

The notion was worthy of the Ogre, who was perhaps as desperate a man as the sun shone on. Beaten out of his own stronghold he was going to the camping-ground of the victorious general.

And such a camping-ground as it was!

The wealth of a score of princes lay there, hidden away in a place only known to Brisket and Broad Arrow Jack. Hidden away so well that few men with a clear year before them would have found it; but luck often favours fools and worthless men, and if——

The very thought made Jack give his gallant horse a pressure with his knees, harder and more imperative than usual. It leaped forward, and took him to where he had left his men full ten minutes before Billy Brisket and his animal could get over the ground.

All the men had arrived, Nat Green and Trimmer being in command during the absence of the two leaders. Jack merely said he was going to Black Rock, and although the surprise was general, none ventured to show it. When Brisket came up they all went forward, with Jack as usual in the van.

Nat Green and Trimmer rode side by side, and the following colloquy took place between these gentlemen—

"Going to Black Rock!" said the first.

"Yes, odd, aint it?" remarked the second.

"Given up the business, and going to retire?"

"Hardly likely, yet looks like it."

"A little, but *he* don't look like it."

"Then he's foiled, and going back to meditate."

"Yes, that's it, and a rest won't do us any harm."

"Not a bit. I wonder what will become of Wobbles and his lot?"

"I dare say he has forgotten them. Close up here—forward, my lads, and keep as near to the chief as you can."

Jack, having given his steed a rest, was riding forward hurriedly again, anxious to overtake the Ogre before he reached Black Rock. He was not more than seven or eight hours in advance, and by taking a narrow path he knew of, he would, if he rode hard, be able to intercept his cunning foe.

The position of Black Rock has been explained before, but in case it may have escaped my readers I will briefly describe it again.

Black Rock lay in the depths of a huge basin. On every side rose enormous hills, sloping for the the most part precipitously, but dotted about were passes, five in number, by which the palace might be reached.

By no other way could horses go, and the particular pass Jack was making for was known to himself and men as the Needle pass, owing to its extreme narrowness. Three men abreast or one horse completely blocked it.

If it could be gained much time would be saved. The better part of a day's journey would be spared them, and as it was, as he believed, only known to a few of his faithful followers and himself, he had little fear of finding it defended. A dozen men well armed could have held it against five hundred men; in short none but madmen would have attempted to force it if its passage had been disputed.

Jack rode fast, being by far the best mounted. Billy Brisket and the others were soon left behind, in spite of their efforts to keep pace with their chief. Once the ex-pedlar called upon him to stop for a moment, but he only waved his hand in dissent, and rode on.

"He'll go in for them single-handed, and lose the game," said Billy Brisket in despair, "but you can't stop him when his blood is up."

"I reckon that when he comes to the push," said Trimmer, "and the game begins, he'll throw something close on sixes"

"You are a bit of a gambler—aint you?" said Brisket, turning in his saddle.

"Rather, and shall be till I die. I never hear the rattle of the bones or see a pack of cards dealt without turning cold all over. Then in a moment the blood rushes back, and I go in white I have a sou."

"You gambled when you were sent to the fields?"

"Yes," replied Trimmer, quietly. "I won one game—the game of red. Do you know it?"

"No, never heard of it."

"I played a man for his life or mine—and won it."

"And then?"

"As he had lost his life I took it. It was that German fellow who tried to blow up the chief."

"And you shot him?"

"Clean. Then I went in for the other game, and luck went dead against me. I lost everything; I haven't a sou. What is more I did not pay for the fodder."

"You lost the chief's money?"

"I did."

"You will get into trouble for that," said Brisket.

"Well, if he is what I take him to be he will put one game against the other, and cry quits. If he won't, let him shoot me, and I won't growl. All I ask is that he will do it himself."

"Why should he?"

"To oblige me," said Trimmer. "All I ask is to die by the hand of a *man*, and he's one if there is such a thing on airth."

"You're an odd fellow."

"Always was. But look here, don't tell the chief about that money."

"Why not?"

"Because I will tell him myself."

"About the best thing you can do," returned Brisket.

Meanwhile Jack rode on apace for three hours or thereabouts, and then paused by the banks of a small stream, where he washed the feet of his horse, allowed it to drink a little, and turned it loose for half an hour among the rich grass. He laved his own face, drank a small quantity of the clear liquid, and lay upon the bank, brooding.

Events seemed to be turning against him, and the fear of being foiled after all was gathering in his bosom. He began to think that he had been too confident of the power he possessed, too certain of the working of his plans. The idea of the Ogre escaping him made his blood boil, and, like the Malay in "running a muck" among his brethren, he "saw red."

What! should the monster who branded him, and slew his father and brother, go scot free, to work more devilry and misery in the world? Was he after all to come out triumphant? Surely it could never be.

His steed refreshed, he mounted again, and looking back saw a cloud of dust, which told of the advance of his followers; but, without waiting, he caused his horse to swim the stream and rode on.

Late in the day the ground grew rougher, and the great hills which had been lying in the distance for many hours stood out boldly and brilliantly in the light of the setting sun. Jack was compelled to proceed with more caution, and wisely left the pace to the judgment of the horse.

Dropping the reins on the neck of his steed, he fell a-thinking of the past, present, and to come, and woke not from his trance until the sun went down and the moon came up red and full.

Then he drew rein, and looked about him. At his right was a tall rock, sugar-loafed shape, which he knew was near the Needle pass. Only once had his horse been there before, and now it had brought him right.

"Good fellow," he said, patting its neck, and the intelligent beast neighed joyously in response.

"If men were but as faithful as brutes," said Jack, "how different the world would be! Here is the pass. Stay, it is not there, and yet it should be straight before me. Let me look again. The sugar-loaf rock to the right, the stunted oaks to the left, here the pass with its high rocky walls should be, and *yet it is not here*. What is the meaning of this?"

Descending from the saddle, he walked over a mass of broken stones, and took a closer view of the spot. Where the pass should have been was a piled-up mass of broken rock.

"I see," said Jack, "cleverly and wisely done. He has blasted the rocks, and closed the pass."

It was a bitter blow, and Jack felt it keenly, but he would not admit it even to himself. Springing into the saddle, he turned back and rode until he met his men.

"We will halt for the night," he said, "and go on to the Fern Gully."

"That is quite a day further round," said Brisket.

"If it were a week we must go. The Needle Pass is closed."

"Closed—how?"

"The Ogre has blasted the cliff, and nothing less nimble than a cat could climb the ruin he has made."

"I reckon," said Billy, as he rolled himself up in his rug, and lay down to sleep, "that our troubles are not yet over. The enemy has the cunning of a wolf, and Dame Fortune gives him a helping hand."

CHAPTER LXXIV.

DOOMED TO DIE.

IT was night, and, in their condemned cell, Conky, Curler, and Pigeon tremblingly awaited their coming fate.

As their prison-house was of the lightest order of structure, Wobbles had taken care to have them secured with a good strong rope, placed so discreetly round their respective necks that if they indulged in much freedom of action one was very likely to choke the other, and very probably himself also.

Their hands were also secured behind their backs, and their legs tied together, so that their liberty was fully restricted; and as they sat on the floor, with their backs to the wooden wall, and the light of a feeble lamp upon their faces, three more dejected broken-down specimens of humanity were never yet gathered together under one roof.

"Can't you keep still?" said Conky, for the fifth time, as Curler, affected by the damp, indulged in an involuntary sneeze. "Another tug like that and you will choke me."

"Can I help sneezing?" asked Curler; "you are the most unreasonable chap I ever met."

"No I aint, you ought to hold off sneezes just now."

"So I would if I could."

"No you wouldn't, you would work up a sneeze to spite me—wouldn't he, Pigeon?"

Pigeon replied to the effect that in all the course of his existence in this revolving globe of ours he had never known a man so much given to sneezing at inopportune moments as Curler, and expressed a wish that the next time he so far forgot what was due to his fellow-man he would sneeze his head off.

"You were allus a sneak, Pigeon," said Curler, with a sneer. "You never was the party to come forrard manly, but waited ontil yer see which way the wind blowed afore you stepped in."

"There aint a breath of hair to-night," replied Pigeon. "Everything is as quiet as a country churchyard."

"Now just you look here," said Conky, who was on the other side of Curler, the unfortunate sneezer being in the middle, "that's a nice thing to talk about just now—a churchyard. What do you mean by it, you low-bred aggravatin' warmint?"

"Yes," said Curler, "what do you mean by it—you—you—kangaroo?"

"I didn't mean nothin'. I used the word churchyard as a similar," pleaded Pigeon. "How sharp you both are. I think you might be kinder to a poor harmless chap, as you are goin' to be shot in the morning."

"If I could only have one punch at your head," hissed Conky, grinding his teeth, "I'd shatter it like a cracked coker-nut!"

His wrath was none the less for his being obliged to vent it in a stiff position, without moving any muscles but those in his expressive countenance.

The running noose about the necks of the trio was exceedingly dangerous. It was the work of a man who had been a sailor, and for that clever arrangement Wobbles promoted him to the post of corporal, and gave him a man to command.

"I'm all wrong to-night," sighed Pigeon. "But do you think Wobbles will really shoot us?"

"I don't know," replied Curler, a convulsive shivering setting in all over his body. "He seems to have changed. His friendship for us seems in a way to be null and void."

"You should have been kinder to him from the first," said Conky.

"Me! Now, come, that's cool," returned Curler. "Wasn't you the first to show your teeth?"

"Me?" exclaimed Conky, quite overcome. "You hear that, Pigeon?"

"Yes, I hear it," said Pigeon.

"And don't you wonder that the roof don't fall in when such lying is going about?"

"No, I don't!" said Pigeon, rebelliously, "seeing that I don't know it was a lie."

"I'd like to be free for five minutes," growled Conky, "I'd ax no more."

"But what's the good of quarrelling?" said Curler, "as we all are in a fix, and I don't see no way out of it unless Wobbles can be softened down."

"If we get up a petition," suggested Curler, but Conky cut him short.

"Get up a balloon!" he said. "Where's pen and ink?—where's paper? Who's to write, and who's to take it when it is written? If you haven't got nothing better than that to bring forrard go to sleep."

"We shall all be asleep directly," said Pigeon, gloomily, "in the last sleep. I wonder how a chap feels when he's smit by a bullet?"

"I'd let you know how a man feels when he's kicked if I got the chance," said the irate Conky. "Shut up! I hear footsteps."

"Perhaps it's a chaplain coming," suggested Conky. "If so we ought to try to soften him down. Let's sing a hymn."

"I don't know no hymn!" snarled Conky.

"I knows one werse of 'All in Jordan,'" said Pigeon.

"Then give it mouth," said Conky, and Pigeon, through his nose, began—

"I have got a father in the promised land,
I have got a mother in the promised land,
Oh, how he-appy I shall be to go there too."

There was something in this refrain which touched Conky on a tender place, and in a voice like the groan of an ungreased handsaw he bade Pigeon shut up.

"Look soapy," he said, hurriedly. "Here's the chaplain."

The chaplain, however, turned out to be Wobbles himself, who came in with a guard of two, with rifles cocked.

Bombastes Furioso himself was small beer in comparison to our courageous friend.

He swaggered in with a sword by his side—a rusty affair, picked up by one of his men—and this, getting between his legs a little, marred the dignity of his arrival by precipitating him forward nearl upon his nose. Recovering his equilibrium he cocked his hat over his left eye, and frowned upon his captives.

Sweeter humility than their countenances expressed was never seen. Pigeon, who had often perambulated the streets of London on the "decayed tradesman lay," was, perhaps, the most striking; but both Conky and Curler did credit to the art of humbug.

"So," said Wobbles, "thou art here, and in my power."

It was quite unnecessary for him to say anything of the sort, seeing he was acquainting them with a fact already too painfully impressed upon their minds, but his whole conduct now was founded on ancient high life as he had seen it upon the stage, and he would not abate one jot or tittle of his imaginary magnificence. In his mind's eye an audience was ever near, looking on.

"Yes, Mr. Wob—gineral, we are here," said Conky.

"A little bit cramped, but otherwise comfortable," added Pigeon, in a conciliatory tone.

"Thou art caitiffs and traitors to a man," returned Wobbles, waving his hand loftily, "and thou shalt die."

"But wot have we done, mister—gineral?" asked Conky."

"Thou hast been rebellious in a camp where rebellion is the foreshunner—shorefunner—no, forerunner of death, and thou art doomed," said Wobbles.

"I know that appericences are agin us," said Conky, whose face was the colour of a sheet of the *Times* before it is printed, "but don't let 'em guide you to wrong conclusions, or you may be sorry."

"Worry sorry," added Curler.

"And it's no use being sorry," said Pigeon, "when it's all over, and we—we—have—jined the departed."

"If we've done anything much out of the line of honour," said Conky, "we're everlastingly and blessedly sorry, and we can't say no more. Nothing could grieve me more than to offend you, gineral."

"And thinkest thou that words which putter no barsnips—butter no snarspips—parsnips, will turn me aside?" asked Wobbles, with a sarcastic smile. "No—no! Guard, are the prisoners safe—examine their bonds."

One of the men brought the light, and the other having examined the ropes, pronounced them to be quite secure.

"It is enough," said Wobbles. "Leave us for awhile. I would fain be alone with the prisoners, but be within call in case any of them should be taken ill—ahem!"

The guard retired, and Wobbles fronted his prisoners with folded arms, frowning as only the great and powerful can when within their strongholds, and in a position to frown without restraint.

"Hark ye," he said, "I am here to recall the past, so that ye may not question the justice of your sentence."

"But surely," said Conky, "you'll never carry it out?"

"To-morrow's sun, or rather the sun that is just coming up shall shine upon your speechless corpsers. Not a word. Hear me.

"Long years ago," he said, holding up a finger, "there was a youth, to whom all that is fair in life is fresh, who had just come into a little property which a misguided mother left him. He was young, guileless, and without stain, up to none of the moves of life, and as ready to be taken in as a che-ild. That boy was me."

"You was innercent then, gineral," said Conky.

"A reglar lamb," said Curler.

"So fresh that the wery hair was perfumed with your innercence," said Conky.

"So it was. But no matter, let it pass," said Wobbles, not intending, however, to let anything pass if he could help it. "The little property went.

Fust the lions came, and had a gorge, and when there was wery little but bones left the wolves came and picked 'em. Thou wert the wolves."

"We was bound to get a livin'," murmured Conky, "or we wouldn't have done it. A hundred times we've talked about paying over the little we got back to you. It warn't much, but it hung on my neck like a millstone."

Curler assured Wobbles he was quite bowed down, and Pigeon declared his sleep had been broken ever since.

"Wain words, wain words—I can't swaller 'em," said Wobbles. "Thou must die. Not, as I have said, by the rifle. I will not perlute the barrels of my noble men with your blood. No, a sterner, longer, more terrible, awful, horrible fate is in store for ye."

"Oh! come," said Conky, "you musn't go too far. Have mercy upon old pals."

"Never!"

"Spare us and receive a blessin'," said Curler.

"Never, jigger your blessin'!"

"Let me go, and I'll never come a-nigh you agin," said Pigeon.

"Never!" cried Wobbles. "Ha—ha! ne-ever! In the tide of ewents in mortal life everything comes round, and my turn is here. The dawn is at hand, tremble—prepare! Farewell—farewell! Guard!"

"Yes, general."

"You can come in now," said Wobbles, "and remain with the prisoners throughout the night. At dawn bring them forth."

"Yes, general."

Wobbles, without another look at the prisoners, strode out with the gait of an ass in a lion's skin, and closed the door behind him.

"I'd like to have his (something internal) and cook it for him, I would!" growled Conky, and both Curler and Pigeon's cheeks were bedewed with tears.

"I wonder what he is going to do?" said Conky, after a pause. "Guard, can you tell us?"

The guard did not answer except by a sign to intimate that conversation between them was forbidden.

"He aint a man—he's a demon!" groaned Conky; "and if I ever—but, no, I shan't. He'll settle us as sure as fate!"

CHAPTER LXXV.
A TRIO OF MAZEPPAS.

"THE only question is," said Wobbles, pacing to and fro, "how to get 'em down again?"

Before him were old Joss and Fireworks engaged in getting a precarious living out of the rather scanty vegetation on the high land wherein they now dwelt. Looking at them no man or woman could have conceived how deep was the rivalry and deadly the hatred which existed between them.

But in the new land they seemed to have signed a truce.

Why it was is almost an open question. The scanty pasturage may have had something to do with it. Their food being less stimulating than what they usually got, their fiery spirits may thereby have been subdued. But, be the cause what it may, there they were, more like cronies than deadly enemies, eating the grass of poverty with sweet content, at peace with each other and all horsekind.

"The question is," said Wobbles again, "how to get 'em down?"

It was a great question, and one which a royal artilleryman might have failed to solve. Men of the artillery service with good horses will ride up and down anything not absolutely upright, but with animals like old Joss and Fireworks skill and judgment were thrown away. Their movements were entirely guided by the mysterious hand of fate.

"How to get 'em down?" said Wobbles for the third time. "Who-ho! Gregg, come hither!"

Gregg was one of the men to whom Wobbles

had given a lecture upon the folly of having mothers, especially those who got their sons into trouble by leaving them the hard scrapings of years. He was a simple-minded man was Gregg, with a little knowledge of the cultivation of land and a fixed idea that to cultivate the mind was in a way working against Providence.

Thus it came about his mind was not cultivated at all, but was a garden wherein the weeds of confused thought grew apart, and wild briars of stolid ignorance flourished exceedingly.

"Gregg, my follower and henchman, come hither."

"Yes, general," said Gregg, advancing and saluting."

"You—ahem!—have been accustomed to horses?" said Wobbles.

"I druv a team nine year, general," replied Gregg.

It may be mentioned, by the way, that Gregg used to drive his team sitting on the shafts in a state of sound repose. Had the horses under his charge been one whit less intelligent than they were he and they would have been dead long ago.

"And where didst thou drive thy team?" asked Wobbles.

"At whoam," replied Gregg. "There be no teams here."

"'Tis well," said Wobbles. "Thou art the man I want. I, too, have been accustomed to horses, but not of your sort. Mine were fiery barbaric steeds, that went prancing about the park—high-sperrited things, you know."

"Yes, general," said Gregg, implicitly believing him.

"Now, look at those animals," said Wobbles, pointing to the two rivals.

Gregg turned his face towards them, but, as far as his looks went, they had not the least interest in his eyes.

A wooden figure turning on a pivot would have had as much expression.

"What do you think of them?" asked Wobbles.

"Old uns, general."

"Well, yes, they are at least well into their prime. Now, do you think you could get them down into the valley?"

"Dunno, general. It be rather steep."

"The steepness is the difficulty, Gregg. But, say, will you take 'em down?"

"I'll ha' a try, general."

Had he been the possessor of one more grain of wisdom than lay in his noddle he would have seen the peril of the task, and shunned it, but it was his ignorance which gave him what served for bravery, and Wobbles looked at him with admiration.

"Thou art a brave man," he said, "and you shall be promoted—ahem!—one day. Get them down, brave Gregg."

Gregg got a rope, and, dividing it into two, made up a couple of rough halters. These he fixed on the two steeds, and tying the head of Fireworks to the tail of old Joss, he mounted the latter, sideways, and began the descent.

As a matter of choice he would have ridden Fireworks, but in that case he could not have tethered old Joss to his companion. No rope would have remained ten seconds on the tail of the former.

"Come hither—woa—hold up!" cried Gregg, as old Joss slid down twenty feet or so in a sitting position, dragging old Fireworks on his head.

"Gregg is a brave man," thought Wobbles, as he looked at him; "but he will never see the light of another day."

In all probability he would not if he had been any other man. In a saddle in a proper position he would have gone off a dozen times in as many seconds; but, sitting huddled up, he was as safe as a sack of oats, and came out of every trial triumphant.

Those two horses got down very much after the fashion of those who indulge in the Canadian fun called "toboggin"—they slid the whole way, and only fell when they got on to the level of the valley, where they both went down in a heap, and Gregg, rolling over backwards, hit the ground with his head with a sound like half a postman's knock.

"Come hither; woa, Smiler," he said.

The blow drove away the present, brought back the past, and he thought for the moment that he was with his old team.

From this dream he slowly awoke, and, surveying the two prostrate beasts, wondered what he ought next to do.

Fortunately he remembered his instructions only told him to get them down, and not a word was said about his picking them up, so he left them there, and returned to his commanding officer.

"Thou hast done well," said Wobbles.

"I got un doon, and left un there," replied Gregg, with a brevity born of modesty.

"It is enough," said Wobbles, "I will remember thee."

A few minutes later Conky, Curler, and Pigeon were summoned to their doom. All were so limp that if the neck rope had not been removed they would have strangled each other. Every half-dozen steps the guard had to prop up one or the other.

They were led into the presence of Wobbles, whose tender nature would have yielded to the imploring looks of his old friends, if he had not fortified himself with drink. He was, however, about three parts drunk, and his heart was adamant.

"Art thou ready for thy doom?" he asked.

"If you are really serus ——" began Conky.

"Serus," interposed Wobbles, "the tides of the tidal ocean should not turn me aside—the thunders of the mountains, and the clattercacks—cattleracks —I mean cataracts should not move me. I have sent for thee to know if thou hast a message for home. If so I will deliver it."

Whatever messages they might have had to send did not come to hand at the moment, and the appalled trio remained silent, save with their teeth, which chattered horribly.

"It struck me this morning," continued Wobbles, regarding them with the eye of a defunct codfish, "that thou mightst have some relations who would sigh for thee, when thou wert far away—ahem! under the green sod—or perchance thy bones whitening in the forest. Say—hast thou any?"

"I haven't got none," said Conky, surlily.

"I've got a huncle somewheres," said Curler, "but as he aint been heard of these ten years, and changes his name twice a week, you might have some trouble to find him."

Despair gave Curler strength, and he spoke in his old ribald tone. Wobbles regarded him sternly.

"It is no time to jest," he said; "what sayest thou, Pigeon?"

"Nuffin," said Pigeon, shortly.

"But surely thou hast a mother—most people have a mother once in their lives," said Wobbles.

"I don't know whether I have or not," said Pigeon. "I haven't seen, or heard, or thought of her since I was a kid, and if I knowed where she was I wouldn't send her nuffin."

"Is this kind—is this affectionate?" asked Wobbles.

Pigeon felt goaded, and in a loud voice asked Wobbles what he meant with his "gammon." Wobbles rose, and, standing tolerably upright, made a signal to the guard.

"Bear them to the valley," he said, "and bring forth the wild horses."

"I will not shoot thee,'" he said, to the prisoners; "that death were too honourable for traitors. Hinch by hinch on 'orseback shalt thou die. Prepare their bonds, and let us send them to their doom."

"Wot are you going to do?" asked Conky.

Broad-Arrow Jack.

NO. 12.

LIKE TWO OVER-RIPE PIPPINS THE MEN CAME DOWN AND EXPOSED TO VIEW THE INTERESTING FACES OF CURLER AND CONKEY.

"Bind ye to the horses, and send ye on to the wilderness," replied Wobbles.

The three prisoners became more limp than ever; the prospect was truly horrible. Their legs doubled up, and they fell.

"Carry them down," said Wobbles.

A difficult task, seeing all were bound together, but they were half-carried—half-dragged into the valley, where the two fiery steeds were still lying.

All the followers of Wobbles were there, looking on for the most part with very solemn faces. Wobbles was the gravest of them all. There was even a tear in his eye, but to be just he must punish the rebels. On public grounds, and for the safety and well-being of the place he commanded, he could not spare them.

"The only question is which can carry two?" said Wobbles. "Gregg, my brave follower, which is the strongest beast?"

"T' chap wi' de stumpy tail be that, general," said Gregg; "he got a little more sperrit, general."

"Get him up, and bind on two," said Wobbles, "the prisoner Conky, and his companion in infamy, Curler."

They got up Fireworks, but short commons, and the terrific descent combined had taken all the pluck out of him—a quieter animal never stood in a sheepfold.

First they laid Conky across his back, and bound him fast—arms round the neck, and feet under the belly. Curler was put up next. His arms were bound to Conky's arms, and his legs to Conky's legs.

"Are they se—ecure?" asked Wobbles.

"They won't come off for a month," replied Gregg.

"Good, put the other upon old Joss," said Wobbles.

It took a vast amount of labour and a little time to get old Joss up, but it was done, and Pigeon, bereft almost of life by fear, was so bound that escape without friendly aid was impossible. Not one of the trio begged for mercy. They were tongue-tied, spell-bound by the horror of their position.

"Set the steeds free—cast off the wild horses," said Wobbles, "and let them away—away to the mountain's brow."

Sundry slaps, pinches, and cries of encouragement were given for full ten minutes without either of the steeds moving. Old Joss was the first to respond; a faint light returning to his eye, he seemed to remember something, and working round like a rocking-horse, he set off at a slow trot.

Pigeon shrieked, and this aroused Fireworks, who, seeing his enemy on the move, went in pursuit of him. Conky and Curler yelled, and the triple voices, acting in the place of whip and spur, stimulated the animals into motion. Old Joss snorted, Fireworks replied, and increasing the pace they bore away their burdens, as Wobbles said, "into the barren wilderness."

CHAPTER LXXVI.

IN POSSESSION.

AS the day advanced the terror of Craddock and Steyne deepened. Each hour brought them nearer to the night, and as all their comrades had been slain in the darkness they had good reason to dread its coming.

Once Steyne suggested flight, but Craddock only shook his head in reply. Flight, he thought, was useless.

"But we can't be worse off," said Steyne.

"Or better," replied Craddock. "Here we are like rats in a cage, and we can only await our coming fate with as much courage as we can muster."

"Do you mean to say that I am afraid?" asked Steyne.

"*I* am," replied Craddock, candidly, "because those who have smitten our comrades down are invisible. A curse upon the day I entered the service of this mysterious being whom we call chief."

"It is bad for us," returned Steyne, with a gloomy frown, "but we were both down on our luck, and were glad of anything. Besides, if you had not suggested this business we should now be all right. It is our own fault."

"I suggested it?"

"Well, don't let us quarrel. Say that we made it up between us, and there let it rest. We entered into a speculation and failed."

"But we can't go on in this way—walking about like another pair of Siamese twins."

"For the present don't let us part."

They kept by each other throughout the day, and, when the night came, sat down in the shadow of the porch to watch for the foe both feared would come. They dared not shut themselves in the palace, as that would cut off all chance of flight.

Silently they lay hour after hour, watching the moon as she rose up behind the trees and sailed over their heads, until the palace was hidden in the shadow of the great mountain behind.

"No enemy yet," whispered Craddock.

"No, thank heaven!" replied Steyne, and hope came and warmed their hearts. Perhaps after all they were not doomed like the rest.

But why were they spared?

Both knew how worthy they were of death, and this somewhat lessened the hope of being saved. Still they clung to it, and their excitement softening down they yielded to fatigue, and fell asleep.

In the early morning light two figures came creeping up the steps of the porch as silently as leopards stealing on their prey. The sleeping men heard them not, nor knew their peril, until each had a strong hand on his throat.

They awoke.

One glimpse of the rosy hue of morning, and then——

But why dwell upon the brutal deed? It was soon over, and the Ogre and Jaundice, panting and red-handed, went down to the brook to wash their fevered faces and clear away the awful stains.

"That clears them all off, I think," said the Ogre, as he knelt down by the water-side.

"It doesn't seem as if it would come out this time," said Jaundice fretfully. "See here."

"Your hands are clean enough," replied the Ogre.

"You tell me so," returned Jaundice, with a wild look in his eyes, "but I am not blind, and I can see it still. See here upon the thumb and forefinger and here on the palm. Deep—deep red, as bright as the sun setting on a misty eve."

"You are a pitiful cur," said the Ogre, "with all the fear of a woman."

"I cannot help it," returned Jaundice, with a haggard look. "I am weary of myself, of my life, of everything. I am like a drunkard, who knows strong drink is killing him, and yet must drink it or die. I am drunk with crime—my soul is on fire with the lust of blood, and I must do such deeds as these or die."

"You *dare* not die," sneered the Ogre, "because you have in you a fragment of the old woman's faith in the future."

"It is not faith, but certainty," said Jaundice. "You and I will live for ages to rue the work of our few years so woefully misspent here. Come, I am ready; I will wash no more. The stain may stay."

"Hark ye!" said the Ogre, planting himself before Jaundice, "I don't know whether you are fooling me, or whether you have gone mad with fear. Which it is doesn't matter to me, but I will have no more of it."

"You must have it if I will it so," replied Jaundice.

"What! do you defy me?"

"Yes, you and all living things!" cried Jaundice. "Here, plant that reeking knife in my heart, and I "'t thank you. In the great future there can be no greater hell than I know now. Strike, Ogre! you have doubly dyed and damned my soul—complete your work, and kill the body!"

"I do not want to hurt you," replied the Ogre. "You talk idly. You were a knave years before I knew you."

"Yes," said Jaundice—"a petty knave, who practised tricks to get money, but guiltless of bloodshedding. It was through you I first took life, and you have made me what I am."

"You would have developed in any soil," said the Ogre. "It was in you; so no more of this folly. You have been deprived of your drink of late, and have run down. Come, help to hide our work, and then the palace shall furnish us with all we need, if I think aright."

"I'll not touch the men."

"Why not?"

"I will have no more of it. Let those who have rallied round you again, believing you to be the avenger of their wrongs, come and see what you and I can do."

"Are you mad?"

"Almost. I have little sane thought left in me. Oh! it was a good thought of yours to spread ruin abroad, and appoint yourself as its avenger! The great demon himself could not have shown more cunning."

"I did it in mockery," replied the Ogre; "and you at one time thought it an excellent jest. I think so still. Go and bring our faithful followers, and, since you will not touch these quiet things of clay, I will put them from your sight ere you return, when you shall have a bumper, and we shall be merry again."

Jaundice, without answering, crossed the ford, and struck into the forest, pausing now and then to look at his hands and shudder. In his mind's eye the stains were still there.

"I will keep you," said the Ogre, looking after him a little while, "until I no longer have need of you; and then, friend Jaundice, you shall have your will—you shall be put to rest!"

He went up the steps into the hall, where he found a couple of strong halters, used for the horses. Fastening one to each of the dead men, he dragged them down to the side of a deep pool at the bend of the stream. In this, with heavy stones strongly attached, he sank them, and returned to the palace, as if he had performed some ordinary labour.

"Give me but three clear days," he muttered, standing before the rich porch with folded arms, "and the treasure that is in you I will find. That done, I will show this land a clean pair of heels. Hark! I hear the men coming. Good, faithful, blind asses, every one!"

Jaundice and the men—about thirty in number—were soon upon the scene. Blind men, as the Ogre said; but not all so blind as they pretended to be. His flock, for the most part, were sheep; but he had among them wolves in sheep's clothing.

"Welcome," said the Ogre, "to the home of the brigand, Broad Arrow Jack! Sit down outside while I and Mr. Jaundice search within for food."

There were stores in plenty—ship biscuit, preserved meats, wine, and fruit—and they all were soon merry. Jaundice drank deeply, and became something like his former self; but he could not wash those stains away.

"Still here!" the Ogre heard him mutter, as he held his hand up to the light—"a deeper and deeper red! They go down to my soul. How, then, can water on the surface wash them away?"

"Drink, Jaundice," he said. "Here's to the confusion of our enemies, and life, prosperity, and happiness to us all!"

"Life," cried Jaundice, with a wild laugh, "I do not want; prosperity and happiness can never be mine nor yours. Already I see the end coming—the black cloud of a shameful death is rising above yon hill tops!"

"Drink!" said the Ogre.

"Give me a bottle," said Jaundice, "and alone in some spot I will seek oblivion."

He snatched the bottle from the Ogre's hand, and, rising, walked away. The men regarded him curiously, and exchanged glances of surprise.

"Poor fellow!" said the Ogre. "He has never been himself since Broad Arrow Jack robbed him of his all. He suffered much—his home destroyed; his children slain; his wife—well, she is far away, and, I devoutly hope, dead!"

He sighed, and put on an expression of deep sympathy for his suffering friend. On the whole, it was not bad acting; but he and sympathy had long been strangers, and they did not harmonise very well together.

A little later he went in search of Jeb Jaundice, and found him lying at the foot of a tree, in a sudden sleep. Here, now, was an opportunity to kill him, and for a moment the desire was upon the Ogre.

"No—no!" he said. "It would be risky, and perhaps spoil all. First to get riches—then to get rid of my followers, and when you and I, dear Jeb, are far away and alone, I will free myself of you and your puny fears for ever!"

On returning to the palace he found the men examining the outside with curious eyes, and some with their knives were endeavouring to pick out the jewels which glistened here and there.

"Good work, my men," he said; "out with them, and put them together. The spoil, if, indeed, it is not as I think, worthless, shall be divided."

"This," said one of the men, picking out a brilliant, "is a real stone. No Brummagem stuff ever shone in this way."

"Great news, indeed," said the Ogre. "But put all into a common treasury, and place it in my charge for the present. By-and-bye it shall be distributed."

He appointed two of the men to act as receivers, and the others, inspired with the love of plunder, smashed the beautiful fretwork to get at the gleaming jewels.

Ere half the day was over the lower part of the palace was a ruin.

Meanwhile the Ogre had been exploring the inside with very wonderful results, which must be related in a future chapter.

CHAPTER LXXVII.

A WILD RIDE.

ON, on up the mountain pass went the wild steeds, old Joss and Fireworks, with their quivering agonised burdens. On, on at the rate of two miles and a furlong an hour, or thereabouts, over rough plains and across patches of level sward they went.

The feelings of the three sufferers can only be feebly described.

They had all seen Mazeppa at the circus, and visions of wolves, eagles, vultures, and other uncanny things which love the flesh of man, floated before them—starvation, thirst, and, finally, death, formed the only prospect ahead.

Old Joss was at home. That intelligent brute, carrying his memory back to his early days, brought up a vision of his mother bearing the above-mentioned Mazeppa to his doom, and all he wanted was the ring, the sawdust, and the brass band, to have made his happiness complete.

He knew how helpless his burden was, and rejoiced thereat.

Neither bit nor bridle curbed his fiery spirit. He was free.

Fireworks was free too, and the joy which cometh of complete liberty was upon him.

Side by side the pair went, rejoicing in their freedom.

They turned down a pass which led into the wood where the encounter between the Ogre and Jack took place, old Joss slightly ahead, and leading. Fireworks for once gave way to him, as he appeared to know the country, and to have some definite idea of his destination.

There in an open glade the two great animals halted to rest, and partook of food side by side—all their personal animosity being softened down by their having a common enemy in their power.

The three travellers were much shaken, and had suffered prodigiously. Conky, for instance, had bitten his tongue twice while indulging in a groan, and that member being much swollen, his articulation was rather imperfect.

"If ever I get hole Wobs," he said, "I—bab—livery."

"Who'd have thought he'd got the wenom in him?" said Curler. "It's all up with us. If we has ten mile more of this I shal! get under the brute's belly, and then he'll mash me with his feet."

"It's all a dream," said Pigeon. "I don't believe I'm awake. I can't——"

"They're orf agen!" cried Conky, every hair of his head and face bristling like the brush attached to a hairdresser's machinery.

"He's giddy!" cried Curler, alluding to old Joss.

But, no! An animal with his powerful brain is seldom giddy. He was only indulging in a waltz to express his satisfaction, and owing to his recent exertions the waltz was a little more stilty and jerky than usual.

Fireworks looked on first with approval, then with amazement, and finally with envy. What old Joss could do he could do—that he was open to bet upon, and put everything he had in the world on it, down to the stump of his tail—and, at length, he too began to twirl.

Not being used to such exercise it affected his head, and his waltz soon became a wild stagger. Had he not run against several trees he must have fallen. Finally, a stiffish knock on the head brought him round, and looking about him he found old Joss was gone.

His keen eye glistened, and bending his head down he listened. The heavy thud of the feet of old Joss as they fell reached his ears, and he started off in pursuit.

On, on through the forest, under noble trees, whose branches spanned a hundred feet, and whose trunks were as substantial as the waist of a Dutchman. On, on through mossy dells, and across purling brooks. On, on; now in a patch of sunlight—now in sweet cooling shade, the steeds and their burden flew.

Conky, Curler, and Pigeon would dearly have liked a little conversation on their sufferings, but if one of them opened his mouth it closed again instantly with a click like that of a spring lock. With such jolting control over their jaws was impossible.

What was the ride like?

Well, it was like anything but a ride. Perhaps crossing the channel on the top of a barrel in a short choppy sea would be the nearest thing to it, but even that lacked the most agonising part of the journey—the sensation of being shaken from head to heel every time one of the feet of the fiery steeds rose and fell.

Away—away, out of the wood into the open plain, o'er which a black cloud hung—a remorseless black cloud, that had apparently been waiting for their arrival, for as soon as they got under it down came the rain copiously, generously washing the trio as they had never been washed before, not even during their occasional stay at the Government houses in Pentonville and Coldbath Fields.

Perhaps this was the greatest trial of all, and as the cold cruel water crept over their quivering frames they groaned aloud, and cursed the day they saw the light. Yet even this misery brought an abundant blessing. Some of the water found its way into their mouths, and cooled their parched tongues.

Old Joss and Fireworks revelled in the storm. They kicked and pranced, and snorted in their joy, and when it was over they sought out a pool of water about three feet deep, and lay down in it in a state of perfect bliss.

The water was up to the heads of the riders, and grim death seemed near. They shrieked aloud, and implored of their steeds to move on, but they shrieked to the winds and begged of horses of stone. Until their own time neither of them would move.

When they did get up both indulged in a shake on the principle of a water dog. The bonds of Curler were slightly loosened, and he went over to the side of the brute that bore him, and took up the attitude of the Indian of the circus, who is going to do the daring feat of picking up a cocked hat from the sawdust with his teeth.

"I'm done for now," he groaned, and his legs tightened with the grip of despair.

On—on over the plain, pursued by a wild turkey, whose path they crossed, and whose curiosity they aroused. His curious "gobble gobble" lent new terror to the scene, and the six eyes of the three men stood out of their heads a good inch or more.

The plain was passed, and the noise of rushing waters fell upon the ears of the riders, and by-and-bye they saw close by a cataract falling from a gap in a great hill, and winding away in a rapidly running stream. Into this stream old Joss plunged and Fireworks followed him.

The water was much deeper than those noble steeds anticipated, and both in an instant were carried off their feet, and borne away, whirling and twirling, occasionally coming against each other with a mighty thud. But both were brass pots, and very little harm came of it. Conky had his legs nipped once, but he was cold with horror, and all minor feelings were dead within him.

Down—down the fast flowing stream, past tall trees, which waved their arms in mockery on the banks; past high rocks, that frowned upon them, and bade them go on to death; past smooth slopes crowned with rich woods, where the leaves rustled with a sound like laughter.

Down—down, amid the hiss of water and through a thousand eddies, until they came to a spot where the stream suddenly narrowed to the width of a few feet, and rushed between two tall rocks. Old Joss foremost, went sideways into the gap, and was immediately jammed hard and fast. Fireworks was with him instantly, and there were horses and men fixed between two walls, sixty feet high, held firm by tons of rushing water.

It rose and fell in its mocking joy, now over the horses, now retreating, until they were almost dry and suspended in mid air, but anon coming back with a rush that threatened to pulverise every bone in their bodies.

The noise of the waters was like unto the howls of legions of demons. It hissed, it shrieked, it roared, it foamed, it leaped, it bounded as a wild beast. Confusion itself was there—chaos could have brought no greater horror to the trio of petty knaves, who looked, for the tenth time at least that day, upon death.

They breathed only at intervals, and then in short gasps. The utmost caution was necessary, as the water had an ugly trick of coming straight at their mouths as soon as they opened them, and it was only by watching their opportunity with a caution which deadly fear sometimes brings, that they were able to take in sufficient of the vital fluid to keep life within them.

No mortal hand could drag them from their perilous position.

Suppose old Joss had been released, he would have been swept onward, and just below was another cataract, where the water leaped into the air with the sweep of a rainbow, and pitched upon the land again sixty feet below.

Old Joss was tough, but a fall like that was a little too much even for him.

Here were perils which the original Mazeppa never faced, and what can save them now? Wobbles, thou art indeed avenged!

CHAPTER LXXVIII.

THE OGRE'S SEARCH.

THE construction of Black Rock has in a previous chapter been explained in a rough fashion. It was only necessary then to give an outline of the place, and it will probably be remembered by most of those who have followed the narrative throughout; but, in case there should be some who have either not read or forgotten what they have read, I give a brief description of it again.

The construction, as far as form went, was simple. In the centre was a great hall, and on either side three lines of rooms. Two passages ran from end to end, having on one side an outer set of apartments, and between them the inner, where, as previously explained, little or no light penetrated.

There were no windows in the place, but in the outer apartments the light permeated through the fine stone-work, giving that subdued look to them which we find in old abbeys and places of that description.

The Ogre went to work in a systematic fashion.

First he took the outer rooms, and examined them one by one. In that nearest the hall on the right-hand side, facing the entrance, he discovered large stores of food—all sorts of preserved things, brought from over the sea, and intended to be used when the ordinary supplies of the chase fell short. He and his men could stand a siege for twelve months in such a place—if only there was drink to be had.

This he discovered in an adjoining apartment. There were wines of all descriptions, carefully stowed away in roughly-constructed bins; spirits in jars, and even beer in barrels—an amazing assemblage of good liquors.

"The money spent upon getting these things here," thought the Ogre, "must have been very great. The wealth of this boy must have been enormous. Fortune has not only smiled upon him, but folded him to her breast. But where *is* that wealth?"

He was anxious to find it, but before leaving he took stock of the wines. There were champagnes, ports, sherries, and clarets in profusion. One particular bin was labelled, "Broad Arrow Jack's White Claret." At this the Ogre laughed.

"The boy drinks the stuff fit for him," he said. "Claret—pah! the stuff for babes and men who want to be poisoned! I'll have none of it. The 'white claret,' as he calls it, shall wait until Broad Arrow Jack comes here again. But will he ever come? Not if I can keep him out."

"Jaundice must be kept out of this place," he muttered, as he helped himself to some spirits out of a stone jar, "or I shall have a mad brute running amuck among my plans. The door appears to have no fastening. Let me have a look at it."

The door he had found ajar, and the mystery to him was, how the men left in charge of the place had escaped the temptation of drinking of the best. But he knew not that he was on the side of the palace where the men never came. Their stores were on the other side, and even in Jack's absence no man ever presumed to tread there.

They were kept from intruding partly by honesty, and partly by reverence for their chief, but principally by fear.

The palace was a mysterious place, and a hundred stories had been kept afloat among the men concerning the many pitfalls for those who trod carelessly in strange places. Billy Brisket had at first been the means of circulating these reports, and, once afloat, voluntary assistants kept them up.

There was a little truth in these as in most reports. The palace *was* a mysterious place, and there were many pitfalls, if you knew how to get into them.

The examination of the door revealed to the Ogre the fact that it closed by a spring, but how that spring worked all his examination—extending over half an hour—failed to discover. He was obliged to leave the door as he had found it—open to any one who came.

The next apartment was full of odds and ends—empty bottles, sacks, and so on—cast aside as being of use no longer. But his cunning would not allow him to pass it by. He knew that some men were wise enough to have an open hiding-place for that they most valued, and Jack *might* possibly have chosen to hide under this rubbish the great means he undoubtedly had at his command.

But the Ogre found nothing.

Hot and dusty, after turning over the rubbish, he went back to the wine stores for another drink before pursuing his search. Two empty rooms gave him only disappointment, but the third was more satisfactory in its revelation.

It contained a lot of plate, solid gold and silver, ranged round on stone shelves, fixed on the sides of the apartment. The first glance revealed that it was very valuable in itself, but of little use to the Ogre. As he contemplated a final solitary retreat, this mass of metal was of little use to him. What he wanted, and what he knew was there, was something more compact—in short, diamonds.

So he wandered on from room to room, all open, and in many cases without a lock of any description. Some contained articles of use—some arms and ammunition, others saddles, bridles, and other equestrian requisites. So he skirted one end of the building, and found not what he sought.

The middle apartment, of which he had had some little experience, were left for the time. He wanted a lamp, and somebody with him to explore them. He shuddered as he thought of the days he spent in one of these dungeons, and dared not go alone.

Jack's own room was closed, and the bare fact of its being made secure, led him to believe what he sought lay there. He could just make out the outline of the door, but all his attempts to open it were thrown away. But he was not disheartened — he understood the art of blasting, and in due time that door would be brought down.

Pausing in his search he went out to the men, who he found had gathered round the stables, where a score of horses were living a life of idleness. This was a great discovery, and the possibility of making the animals his friends, when he had done with the others, entered the active brain of the Ogre.

Why should he not make pack-horses of them, and bear away what he had already discovered, in addition to what he hoped to find? It would be a heavy task, a superhuman one to get them over the track of wild country between there and the coast, but he had superhuman strength, and might be able to do it.

He gave his instructions for the horses to be well cared for and exercised, and went in search of Jaundice. He found him sitting under a tree, undergoing all the agreeable sensations which come in the brain from a heavy attack of strong drink. His eyes were dull, his mouth dry, and parched, and his hands shook like those of one with the palsy.

"Ha! Jaundice," he said, slapping him on the back, "the dog has bitten you very severely. Have a hair of him."

Jaundice took the flask tendered him, and after two failures, got it to his mouth, and drank a draught that might have killed him had he possessed a constitution a whit less strong. The fire liquid ran through his body, and gave him that fictitious strength which only wards off death, to make his final coming a thousand times more terrible."

"I am better now," he said. "What a cursed feeling it is!"

"But when it can be cured in this way what matters?" said the Ogre. "I have been examining the home Dame Fortune gave to this proud boy."

"And what have you found?"

"Nothing—a few drinking cups, some food, arms, and ammunition, but nothing more."

"It was a wild idea—a foolish one to come here. Why not have got away at once? I had a dream just now."

"A dream? Well, so had I," returned the Ogre, "but what it was who cares? Dreams have no more substance than the rack which skims across a summer sky. Up, man, and forget it. I want you to help me to complete my search."

"I cannot move just yet," said Jaundice. "More drink."

"You cannot last this way," replied the Ogre, as he gave him the flask. "You are going the wrong side of the post, friend Jaundice."

"I have never been on the right side since I was a babe in arms," returned Jaundice. "As soon as I could think at all I set out steadily on the road to the devil."

"And when we have found him," said the Ogre, with a hoarse laugh, "we shall not find him so bad as we have been led to think."

"You are strong yet, and speak mockingly," said Jaundice. "Wait until you get into my state. Give me another drop. I am getting as cold as a stone."

"Empty the flask," said the Ogre, "but stop there for awhile."

Jaundice did so, and with a shake declared he was ready. Together they returned to the palace.

"How can this be closed?" asked the Ogre, halting under the portico.

To all appearances outside there was no door, but inside they found, hoisted high up above the entrance, a solid mass of masonry, suspended on strong chains, worked with pulleys on either side. The Ogre tried its working, and found it went up and down as easily as an ordinary portcullis. A smile of satisfaction stole over his face.

"In case of siege," he said, "we shall be tolerably secure. I think I will put it down now in case of accidents. Take the other side, Jeb."

Between them they got down the mass, and without artillery no living man could force his way in.

"A limited garrison, even like ourselves," said the Ogre, "is enough to guard this place. I have studied part of that wing. Let us now try the next."

In arrangement it was much the same as the others, but having been devoted to the men in the service of Broad Arrow Jack they found nothing to repay them for their trouble. The cells in the interior now alone remained.

"To examine these," said the Ogre, "we must proceed with great care. First, to get a light."

"No, first to have some more drink," returned Jeb Jaundice.

"Nay, man, a little food would be better," urged the Ogre.

"Food," said Jeb Jaundice, shuddering, "I loathe it! No; drink—drink—nore drink, or I must die!"

"It will soon be all over with him at this rate," thought the Ogre; "but I must keep him up while I can. Come into the hall, and I will fetch you a little."

Jeb sat down upon the stone flags, and remained with his head down until the Ogre returned with his flask refilled. Jeb Jaundice put it to his lips, and kept it there while a drop remained.

"It gives me new life," he said. "It is new life."

"The life that ends in death, I swear!" said the Ogre.

A roar outside drew his attention from his companion, and as he ran towards one of the rooms to peep through one of the holes in the tracery the report of a score or so of rifles reached him. Shouts, oaths, and cries for mercy followed, and well he knew what they portended.

"Broad Arrow Jack," he said, "is on the scene. I have shut up my garrison just in time."

CHAPTER LXXIX
OUTSIDE THE PALACE.

THE noise and confusion outside the palace arose from a meeting between Broad Arrow Jack's men and the supporters of the Ogre. Jack himself was not with his followers when the attack began, having lingered a few paces behind with the Tiger, to whom he was giving a few instructions.

"Go to the table-land," he said, "and bid Wobbles come hither with those he has under his command. You had better be his guide. That done, speed on to the outposts, and bid them all come in with as much haste as they can."

"Yes, massa," was all the Tiger said, and was off like an arrow.

Meanwhile Brisket had led the men on towards the palace, and arriving at the foot found a number of men gathered on the opposite bank. A rush to arms was made, and Billy was favoured with a volley which laid two of his men low.

A yell of fury escaped the lips of the remainder, and plunging into the stream they dashed over. The Ogre's men tried to make a stand, but they could just as well have stood up against the rush of a torrent.

They were broken and scattered in every direction, and being killed in detail when Jack appeared upon the scene.

"Hold, there!" he said. "No more bloodshed. These men are but tools of the Ogre. Where is he?"

The closed porch of the palace gave him all the answer he needed, and with a bitter heart he turned away. As he did so a rifle sent forth its flame through the fretwork of the wall, and the bullet whizzed past Jack.

"A close shave," he said, coolly; "but you fire in vain. You can neither destroy me nor save yourself."

The Ogre heard his words, and fired again. The ground was ploughed up by the bullet, but Jack remained unharmed. He really seemed to bear a charmed life.

But remaining there was, to say the least, imprudent, and Jack drew his men away under cover. The wounded of both friend and foe were taken to the stables, where they were laid upon beds of coarse grass, and their wounds examined by Brisket and Jack.

Two were serious, and the men could not be expected to recover.

They were very quiet, and appeared to suffer no pain, but internal bleeding was doing its work, and ere the sun set they were gone.

Both men were good men and true, and had served Jack well. As he bent over the men his eyes filled with tears, and the hand he put upon them was as tender as that of a woman.

"I am sorry to part with you," he said; "but I think you know it must be."

"Yes, chief," said one, a tall bronzed young fellow. He spoke quietly enough, and showed no fear of death. "We can't all expect to get off scot-free when there is fighting about."

"Is there anything I can do, Harrison, for those you leave behind?" asked Jack.

"I leave nobody behind," he replied, "unless its Polly Grooves. She lives at Titherton, and her father keeps the inn there. I was fond of Polly, and she sent me here; and yet I think she loved me. But when a girl is a coquette she goes dead against her own feelings."

"You would send her a message?" said Jack.

"Yes, chief."

"She shall have it. I may not be able to deliver it myself, but it shall be sent. I will write it on my tablets, and it won't be forgotten."

"Tell her," said Harrison, turning his fast dimming eyes away to conceal his emotion, "that since I came over the sea I've thought of her a'most night and day, and that I died blessing her."

"It shall be done."

"And now, chief, if you'll give me one shake of the hand I'll trouble you no more."

"Give me your hand. And now, Mason, let me have yours."

The other man held out his hand, and Jack sat down between them.

"Have you any message to send, Mason?"

A spasm of pain crossed the man's face, and it was full a minute ere he replied.

"Chief," he said, "there are some things which a man keeps to himself all his life, and I've had my secret to keep."

"If you would keep it still, do," said Jack.

"No, I can speak now. I was married, but my wife was not true to me. It was her ruin and mine, for the scoundrel left her long ago. Now, if she could be found—but it would be troubling you."

"No, a few pounds will secure agents who will find her."

"If she is poor there's a bit of money in the lining of my jacket as may be of service to her. Let her have it without knowing who it comes from. I don't want to make a song of my forgiveness."

"You are a good man," said Jack, "and I am sorry to lose you."

"Oh, I can die!" replied the man.

"For comes he slow, or comes he fast,
It is but Death that comes at last."

"I was fond of poetry once, and so was she. We used to read it together by our own fireside; but I'll not think of it now. I've got a bit of a rough life to turn over afore I die. Thank you, chief, for all your kindness, and good-bye."

Jack shook hands again with both, and left them. In another hour both had left their sorrows and troubles behind them.

It was not the first time by many that he had looked upon such scenes. During the past year many good men had died in his cause, and died without repining, and now, as he walked towards the wood, he pondered within himself, wondering how far he was justified in using so much good material for his own private ends.

Of late he had had many sad hours, and many doubts and fears.

When first he began to carry out his scheme of vengeance, finding all things to his hand, he was confident of success. The possibility of failing in any one instance never even dawned upon him.

To a certain extent he was successful, but the crowning point of his work had yet to be carried out, and labour as he might it always seemed to be frustrated at the moment of apparent success.

Perhaps the way he expressed his fears to Brisket will place the matter more clearly before our readers. The ex-pedlar, with a big cheroot in his mouth, sat under the shade of a tree amusing himself by pelting a small snake with stones. The reptile was very spiteful, but fortunately not venomous. It hissed, and curled itself up defiantly ready for a spring as Jack came up and with an impatient movement thrust it aside with his foot.

"You have spoilt my fun," said Billy. "I was just seeing what the little beggar was made of."

"Brisket," said Jack, throwing himself down beside him, "here we are again—foiled."

"But the birds are caged," said Brisket."

"Caged in a cage with a hundred outlets perhaps, of which we know nothing."

"Well—yes. It may be so, for except in a pantomimic scene I never saw anything like that place for traps and doors and curious openings and outlets. Still they may not find them."

"Some evil genius guides and defends them," said Jack, gloomily.

"And therefore sooner or later will let them in," replied Brisket, cheerily. "The end must come, for see how all the strength, gathered round them by falsehood, has crumbled to pieces."

"What have you done with the prisoners?" asked Jack.

"I gave them the choice of serving us or going about their business. We cannot be bothered with prisoners, you know."

"No, I suppose not. How many joined?"

"About half. The rest marched away."

"With their arms?"

"Not if I know it," said Brisket.

"You have done well," said Jack, "but now as to the Ogre and Jaundice. How are we to get at them?"

"Not very easily—in fact, not at all while their provisions last, unless we get some other aid."

"They can live there for months."

"True—if we let them, but I think we can get them out in a fortnight."

"How?"

"Just listen a moment. I'll whisper it."

Jack bent down his head, and Billy Brisket, leaning forward, whispered half a dozen words in his ear.

"Will that do?" he asked, aloud.

"It will," replied Jack, "if it can be carried out."

"Leave it to me, and meanwhile let every avenue be guarded. The secret passages cannot extend more than half a mile from the palace, and a circle of watchful men will cut off their chance of escape, if, indeed, they have any."

"To-night or to-morrow, at the latest," said Jack "the outposts will be coming in. We shall then have plenty of men. But what if those scoundrels discover our secret riches?"

"They won't do that while a drop of brandy remains," replied Billy, with a confident nod. "You could not have a better hiding place. Cellars and iron safes are as nothing to the frail prison-house which holds your wealth."

"Yours, Brisket."

"No, yours—or yours and mine if you insist upon it. Now, cheer up when I am away, and look for my speedy return. All I want is half a dozen men, and as many horses."

"Take whom you will."

"No, I will take none from here. You are going to release Wobbles from his charge."

"Yes."

"Then I will ride round that way with the horses and take him and his men."

"Good. Farewell, Brisket, and come back soon."

"I'll be back like a swaller," said Brisket, "and here comes a man with my horse. I ordered him on spec half an hour ago."

Billy climbed into the saddle, and having lighted another cheroot, rode off as boldly as a huntsman, although he was admittedly a bad horseman, and sometimes in imminent peril of parting with the saddle when at a full gallop; but quiet, quaint Billy Brisket was not troubled much with fear of any description, and he would have ridden at a brook or a five-barred gate, if either had been in his way, as coolly as the leader of a field of fox-hunters.

"It's time enough to grumble and growl when you fail," was a motto of his. "Go in and see what you can do, or you will never know what you are capable of."

Jack sat alone, musing sadly, and occasionally speaking aloud, under the impression that he was alone. But just above, lying full length on one of the lower branches of the tree, and concealed by the foliage, were two men, eagerly watching his every action, and listening to every sound.

"When all is over," Jack muttered, "what then? Shall I—can I take the vast fortune Brisket—good, generous Brisket—gives me, and resume my time-honoured name? To gain wealth, for that we came. It was the great object of my father's life, and he, I know, would have me fulfil it; and yet shall I be happy? Can I ever know what it is to feel the heart throbbing with joy? No, it can never be!"

It was pitiful to see one so young and noble borne down with grief and care, but for the time he was so, and as he buried his face in his hands his strong frame shook with emotion.

But the storm passed quickly and he was his iron self again, and with a proud step was walking away when one of the men in the tree gave vent to a short sharp cough.

"That's just like you," said the other in a whisper. "Blow yer for a blessed himage!"

"Can I help a cold in my chest?" asked the other. "Aint I had enough suffering in cold water to be chilled for life?"

"Hold your jaw—do! He's coming back."

Jack had heard the sounds of whispering, and was returning in a casual sort of way, with his eyes and ears engaged in active service. He had no idea of the precise spot from whence the sounds proceeded, and it is probable the men would have escaped detection, if the individual who had not coughed had not slipped partially down and displayed a pair of ill-formed legs to view.

"Who's there?" asked Jack.

"We are done for!" gasped one of the men, and he who had slipped off made frantic efforts to regain his perch.

"Let me help you down," said Jack, coolly, as he took hold of the end of the branch, and shook it violently. Like two over-ripe pippins the two men came down, and exposed to view the interesting countenances of Curler and Conky.

CHAPTER LXXX.
A LIVING WEDGE.

"AND pray what are you doing here?" asked Jack, sternly. "I thought you were with Wobbles."

"We had a little difference with him, sir," replied Conky, "and he sent us back again."

"And you immediately played the spy on me," said Jack. "Do you know the penalty?"

"The spy, sir?—oh! no, sir. I'll take an alphadaver that I never dreamt of such a thing. Did I, Curler?"

"I don't know what you've dreamt of," replied Curler. "All I knows is, that I'd sooner die than spy upon anybody. It's low and it's mean it is, and that I can't abear."

"Why were you in hiding?"

"Well, sir," said Conky, "there's nothing like the truth. Captain Brisket have been rather 'ard on us now and then, and we see him a-coming, and we got up this tree. Then we sat down, and we was kep so long a-waiting that we both fell asleep."

"And listened to the conversation between Captain Brisket and myself?"

Conky put himself into an attitude appropriate for a fervent oath.

"S'help me," he said, "I never heerd a word, and Curler knows it."

"Not a blessed syllable," said Curler; "we was both fast asleep."

"Fortunately there was nothing for you to hear," said Jack, coolly, "or I would have hanged you on suspicion."

Conky and Curler shuddered, and the former hoped that "sich a noble gintleman would not go and string up two poor friendless coves without a fair trial."

"And where is your precious companion?" asked Jack. "Spying elsewhere?"

"No, sir, we left him with the horses."

"What horses?"

"Fireworks and old Joss, sir, which old Joss, sir, is wedged up atween two rocks about fourteen feet from the ground. The water as come on after the storm having gone down, and left him high and dry, and Fireworks is a-standing on the left bed of the river, and bleating like a lamb. He seemed to be wery sorry for his old henemy, and to have forgiven him in his 'art—don't he, Curler?"

"Judging by the present feeling of them horses you might take 'em for twins," replied Curler. "I never seed a prettier picture."

"And you want help to get the old horse down?"

"Yes, sir."

"Stay here, and I will send you some, and when you return here report yourself to me."

Jack left them, and the two petty knaves exchanged a few words of congratulation at having got so well and speedily out of what at first promised to be an ugly fix. They were still congratulating themselves when Nat Green, followed by a man carrying an axe and a coil of rope, appeared.

"Well, you two scurvy villains have turned up again?" said Nat.

"We've come agin our will—we don't want to introode," replied Conky, tearfully; "but being tied on, and the old horses bent on coming home, we was bound for to do it."

As these words wanted some explanation Nat asked for it, and Conky out with the whole story, which he dare not tell Jack, as he scarcely knew how he would take the accusation of rebellion.

"Which rebel we didn't," said Conky, "being loyal and true. But Wobbles was that bumptious that he wanted yer to live on your marrer bones. 'A cat may look at a king,' I ses. 'No, he mayn't,' ses Wobbles; 'but the king may kick the cat to the d——!' and then he had us Mazeppared."

"And so the old horse got himself fixed up in a watercourse," said Nat.

"Regular jammed," replied Conky. "Wasn't he, Curler?"

"Squeezed as tight as a pig in a box," replied Curler.

"And the rush of that water," continued Conky, "was terremenjuous. I niver had sich a rinsing in all my life. It went up and down and in and out our clothes as if we was sewers and being flushed."

"The comparison is not a bad one said Nat.

"I thought it was all up," Conky went on, "for we was quite choked, and garpsing in sich a way that we only breathed in little bits. Then the water went like magic, and Fireworks hung on to the ropes round old Joss with his teeth until they broke. That set one on us free, and so, as the water had gone down to a foot or so, we was tolerably safe, but that weak we all lay in a heap for a good half hour. At last we was all free but old Joss, who was 'igh above our 'eds like a livin' 'ighgate archway."

"How long is that ago? When did you leave him?"

"Hearly this morning; and, having a recollection of the way, we came on, telling Pigeon to keep a eye on the cattle in case anything happened to 'em."

"You should have ridden on with Fireworks," said Nat.

"So I would, sir," replied Conky, "but he wouldn't come. I niver did see sich a change in a hoss. It's the most tracting thing I ever see, and brought tears into my eye. Didn't it, Curler?"

"I see 'em rollin' down your cheeks like gunshots," replied Curler.

All this time they were walking on at a brisk

pace, for, apart from every other consideration, the eccentricities of old Joss made him a favourite, and Nat Green was anxious to save him.

"Any other horse," he said, "would have been killed outright, but old Joss has ceased to be flesh and bone. He is all leather and steel. Nothing hurts him."

It was a good four miles to the gully, and over the broken ground an hour was spent in getting over that distance. Arriving there Nat Green looked upon such a scene as his eyes had never beheld before.

High up, between the two tall rocks, still damp with the water which had rushed by on the previous night in such a copious stream, was old Joss, fixed head on one side, and stern on the other, with his legs hanging helplessly down. He was still alive, but that was all that could be said of him.

Even his hardy nature was giving way under the peculiarly painful nature of his position.

Close under him stood Fireworks, head and tail down, and weeping the tears of repentance, or cold from exposure. All thoughts of rivalry were dead within him. His old rival's life was fast ebbing away, and Fireworks was almost heart-broken.

Close by stood Pigeon, so clean-looking about the face, and so well washed all over, that Nat scarcely knew him.

Pigeon was in low spirits, too, and rather, as Conky expressed it, "cranky."

"You aint been any time, have you?" he said. "Why didn't you keep away altogether? Have you brought any wittles?"

"What do you want with victuals?" asked Nat.

"To eat 'em, to be sure," replied Pigeon. "I don't want nuffin to drink, as I believe I've got a gallon o' water about me still. All I axes for is something to eat, as I feels fit to polish off a bag of tenpenny nails."

"Old Joss is the first consideration," said Nat. "Let me see. How is it to be done? Hum! Oh, I have it! We will get a rope under his haunches, and go up to the top of the rock. There we can haul him up, and let him fall upon his head. That is his only chance of being saved."

"And that's a poor one," said Conky. "For, if he comes down with a run, he'll smash hisself to bits."

"Not he," said Nat, confidently. "Here, take this end and climb up, while I pass the other end under him. Look smart, there."

"Which I aint used to climbing up stone walls," said Conky, as he began the ascent. "I say, Curler, keep a heye on the bottom in case I comes down with a run."

"Keep a heye on yourself," replied Curler.

"The way of the world," muttered Conky, dismally. "When a man's in clover he's got no end of friends, but in the time of triberlation they cuts him to a man."

He made the ascent, however, without accident, and Nat Green, having passed under old Joss, clambered up the other side, and in this way the rope was got under the belly of that noble steed.

"All hands here!" cried Nat, and Curler, and Pigeon, and the man had to make the ascent, too. Curler was the only one who had a fall, which was looked upon as a retribution; and even his was hardly a fall—he only slipped and grazed his hands, knees, and nose in a rapid downward flight. As neither threats nor persuasion could induce him to make the ascent again, they did without him.

"Now, then!" cried Nat. "A long pull, a strong pull, and all together! Ready there!"

Why was it that no warning was given to Fireworks, who, in his deep grief, was not conscious of the efforts being made on behalf of his friend? It was hardly fair, for old Joss, suddenly released, came down with a rush, floored the sympathetic Fireworks, and fell upon him, and both lay senseless.

It was a good half-hour before they could be brought round; but the extraordinary vitality of the two quadrupeds at last asserted itself, and once more they stood upon their feet.

Old Joss, in horse language, apologised for having fallen upon Fireworks, and begged for pardon. Fireworks, with horsey snorts, declined to forgive the outrage, and took up the old stand-point of a bitter foe.

"Take them home," said Nat; "and don't any of you try to ride them. Both the horses want rest."

"I aint likely to get on 'em on my own account," said Curler; "for I think I've had enough of 'em to last me a lifetime."

"I'd just as soon get on the back of a mad bull," said Conky, as he led old Joss away. "Come on, you two, with the tother, and let us have a little rest somewheres. We want it."

CHAPTER LXXXI.
INSIDE THE PALACE.

"JEB JAUNDICE, we must watch by turns," said the Ogre, "as we can't tell what this boy may be up to. I fancy he will go in for blowing out the front of the place."

"Let him bring it down, and crush out my life, and I'll thank him for it," muttered Jaundice.

"No, you won't," returned the Ogre, coolly. "You want to live."

"I do not."

"Oh, yes, you do; because you dare not die! Ha! ha!"

"You are making merry at my expense," said Jaundice, frowning.

"Well, so I am, because you are very amusing," said the Ogre. "Drunk, you are all brag; sober, you are all funk. You want to live, yet have nothing worth living for—you want to die, yet dare not face death."

"Go on!" said Jaundice. "You will go too far presently!"

"How so?"

"I carry weapons," said Jaundice.

"Yes; but you will never use them on me."

"Do not be too sure of that."

"I am sure of it; for, look you, Jeb—you *dare* not kill me!"

"Not dare?"

"No, for that would leave you alone here; and alone you dare not be."

"I do not care to be alone."

"I say you dare not—without drink. Try it. The night is coming on, and, as I have something to do in the way of exploration, sit here in this hall."

"No—no!" said Jeb Jaundice, shuddering. "It is true—I dare not be alone. I am brought to such an awful pass."

"Drink less, and you will be all right again."

"It is not the drink. I take that to drown the horrors of my life," said Jeb, with a gesture of wild despair. "And to think of what my life might have been, and what it is! Maggie, with her passionate love and true womanhood, would have made me happy."

"If you had not been a brute," said the Ogre, calmly; "but, being a brute—all gross and sensual—you ruined her peace, and created a hell for yourself."

"It is true; but what are you making for yourself?"

"It is already made," said the Ogre.

"You are laughing—you sneer at conscience."

"Granted," said the Ogre, "but I do not in my heart deny its existence. It is with me, as with you, but I fight against it—won't have it, and so walk free, except now and then when it bears me down to a pit, so dark that the blackest night on earth is noonday compared to it."

"Then you are sick too," said Jeb Jaundice, with a laugh, which had more of misery than mirth in it.

"Yes, sick unto death at times, and laugh as I

may at the prospect of the future, I cannot hide my eyes from the faint vision of its possibility. But who cares—you or I? No—no, Jeb! Here, drink, man, a bumper, and then again to search for the wealth of this cub."

"Suppose it has been removed?"

"We shall find it here. Drink to our success in good fiery brandy."

"Ay, brandy—brandy!" said Jeb, hoarsely, as he took the glass with a trembling hand; "it gives me new life.

They drank enough to poison two ordinary men, and once again Jeb Jaundice was full of life and spirits. He talked and laughed—he even sang, but the Ogre remained the same. What he had taken had not apparently affected him.

First taking a peep at the outside, where all was clear, the Ogre lit a lantern, and returned to his search for the hidden wealth. He went at it systematically, taking each apartment in its turn, and examining it thoroughly. In this way he had examined all the outer rooms and several of the dark cells. In none of them he found anything more than the goblets and other pieces of plate which have been already alluded to.

In the dark cells and cellars lay his great hope of finding what he sought.

He wanted to leave Jeb as watchman, but that worthy gentleman demurred. Even in his cups he preferred company.

"It is not safe, I tell you," said the Ogre, impatiently. "Stay here in this room; there is light enough for a child who has been scared by an ignorant nurse."

"I'll try," muttered Jeb, "but I'll not promise."

Turning into the left wing the Ogre entered one of the cells—cold, dank, damp as a well. This was his old prison-house, and the opening he had made still remained. He did not recognise the place until he saw this, and then a shudder ran through his frame.

The mortal agony he had endured while he hung there was not likely to fade from his memory while he lived.

"Ah!" he said, holding the lantern down, and peering into the darkness below, "you are but a simple passage, and yet I made a hell of you, and peopled you with raging devils, thirsting to bear me to my torment. It is an illustration of the fears of men, and I'll have no more of them. If I remember rightly, as I crept into the outer world that night, thinking and caring only to get once again into the light, I thought the moon was the sun, and forgot myself when I blessed the stars."

He spoke the last words aloud, and "forgot myself" softly echoed up and down, sounding like the whispering of spirits.

Pausing he held up the light, half fearing to see some horrible form repeating his words with mocking lips. The next moment he laughed at his childishness.

The echoing of his laughter was truly horrible, and was so long dying away that he had great difficulty in persuading himself of its being an earthly sound. With compressed lips he moved on, his foot falling noiselessly on the dust of centuries gathered on the floor.

The wall was bare for a long way, but he came upon a door at last, made of wood, but strongly bound with some metal. Putting down the lantern he tested the metal with his knife, the point of which left a white shining trail behind it.

"Silver!" he said, and what he called the "accursed echo" went on repeating "Silver—silver!" until it faded away into the faintest sound, so light that it might have been the whisper of a fairy.

It was beautiful, imperious, and awe-inspiring, and the Ogre in his hardness yielded to its influence. Coarse in body, depraved in soul, defiant in spirit, there were chords in him which could be touched, and make him feel the weakness of his vaunting and the poorness of his boasted strength.

Such chords were touched now.

He stood still, listening to the hushed murmurings of the subterranean ways, scarce knowing what to think of the awe within his hardened breast. Memories of the past—dim visions of the future—floated upon him. As we dream and think of things, with the murmuring of a distant ocean in our ears, so thought he.

Back into the past in a moment, and ere that moment had passed away he was going on into the future, into the great unknown. And, lo! in the midst of a mass of uncertain vision, there suddenly loomed out a lone figure, hurrying over a wide plain, which had no bounds but the sky, and no light but that which came from one lone star.

Hurrying on the figure went, as if it sought some haven of rest, but the more it hurried the further off that haven seemed to be.

The plain extended to an infinite distance in the mind's eye, growing more barren every step, and the one star began to pale.

It faded and died, and the lone figure, weary in pursuit of rest, lay down to die. And in the darkness beasts crept up, and huge birds wheeled in the air, screaming, all scenting their prey, and eager to have the life-blood of the lone man, who, with hands clasped above his head, grovelled on the cold earth in the agony of one hopelessly cast out from all light and life for ever.

All this come and gone in a moment, and the Ogre was awake again, standing in the passage with the last faintest echo dying in his ears.

"I am growing old and foolish," he thought, shaking himself. "I have ceased to be a man. To work—to work! for something tells me I shall find what I have sought so long."

He passed the light over the door. All the visible fastenings were bolts and bars, and all on the outside. The first drew back to his touch smoothly and easily.

He could have laughed with joy, for he fancied this was an assurance of its having been recently used. But he forgot the dust of many years lying thick under his feet.

He put his hand upon the second bolt, but as he drew it back a fearful shriek rang through the place.

"Help—help!"

The echoes took it up, and the Ogre staggered back with a hundred shrieks in his ears.

"What is it?" he cried, wildly.

"Help—help!" yelled the voice again, and the echoes, ever on the alert, repeated it jubilantly again and again.

The Ogre, half-mad with a terror new to him, rushed forward, and in his haste, trod upon the lantern. His heavy foot crushed the horn and light, and he was in complete darkness.

For the third time came the cry "Help—help!" and with it there was the sound of a heavy body falling. A moan followed, the echoes bandied the cries and moans backwards and forwards for a while, then all was still.

"What does it mean?" thought the Ogre, as his trembling hand passed over his brow to wipe away the perspiration gathered there. "Is this place the abode of what I have never believed in—spirits accursed?"

Only the word accursed was taken up by the echoes, and as it was whispered in his ears he felt it was addressed to him—"Accursed—accursed!"

"And it is true!" he cried. "I have done enough to make a lasting hell for a dozen men!" and staggering forward he fell upon his face and lay as one dead.

CHAPTER LXXXII.

BIG BEN.

IT is quite unnecessary to make any secret of the project Billy Brisket had in his head. It was neither more nor less than to purchase a piece of artillery which one Richard Skewball had in his possession.

Richard Skewball was a great man at the diamond fields. He had a dancing booth, a drinking bar, and a gambling saloon. He throve, did Richard, in a commercial sense, and as he throve he got more into the habit of getting drunk every day of his prosperous life, until at last no man ever found the said Richard sober.

He was proud of two things—his wife and an old field gun—and how that wife came into his possession he was always relating, but how he got the gun he never would reveal.

"I married Sal," he would say, "three weeks arter I met her in a tuppeny omnibus. She had on a pink bonnet that fetched me, and knocked my two eyes into one. I looked at her—she looked at me. 'A fine day, miss,' I ses. 'It is, sir,' said she. 'And which way are you going?' I axes. 'With the omnibus,' she ses, looking as soft as you please. 'But arter you leave the omnibus?' I ses, with a cheerful kind o' leer as I was given to in them days. 'I'm only out for a walk, and it don't much matter,' ses she. 'Then come along, I ses; 'I've got a bun in my pocket, and let us go into the park and feed the ducks;' so we went, and she showed her lily white hand as she chucked the bits in; and, at last, I couldn't stand it no longer, and, giving her a squeedge, I ses, 'When shall it be?' 'When you likes,' says she. So I has the banns put up, and we was married as pleasant as ever could be, barring her old father, who turned up unexpected at the last moment a little beery, and taking the font for a drinking fountain, kicked up a row because there wasn't a cup to drink out of, and accused the beadle of stealing it. However, I got my Sal, and we come over the sea together. But don't ax me where I got that gun from, as I won't reweal it to mortal man."

The aforesaid Richard Skewball was seated outside his dancing booth, chewing the cud of tobacco, mingling its flavour with the juice of the more ordinary cud of sweet and bitter fancies. The hour was early, and all his customers were away digging and delving and washing, and blessing or swearing, according to the luck that turned up.

Sal was indoors, getting the dinner ready, and Richard, not anticipating visitors, kept his eyes on the ground until a voice hailed him.

"What cheer, Richard?"

Raising his eyes he looked upon Billy Brisket, attended by a pale-faced man, who had the shade of a dying swagger on him. This was Wobbles, whom he did not know, but being acquainted with Billy he hailed him by name.

"Hallo, Brisket, what cheer to you! Where have you been all these long days and nights, and years?"

"I've been up and down in most places," replied Billy, "and latterly I've been with a friend known as Broad Arrow Jack."

"Then, if I was you," returned Richard Skewball, "I wouldn't say anything about it here, as some people haven't got friendly ideas about him."

"Some people are asses," said Billy, "and don't know why they hate a man, or why they like him. Broad Arrow Jack is one of the noblest fellows that ever lived. But that's neither here nor there."

"I suppose not," said Richard. "Well, what have you come for?—a ticket for the dance to-night? If so, all's taken. I couldn't sell another. As it is the people who are coming will have to be jammed in, and spin on the same spot like teetotums. Move about they won't be able to."

"I've done with dancing years ago," said Billy.

"What I want to know is, have you got Big Ben still?"

"I should think so. I fired him yesterday, it being the missus's birthday, and that blessed eldest boy o' mine run in front of it just as I put the poker to it, and there aint a blessed hair left all over his head. If he hadn't stood with his back to it he would have been blinded."

"He was always a venturesome boy," said Billy.

"There aint his like in these parts," replied Richard Skewball, proudly. "He's rising nine, and he's got his bowie like a man. He's stuck up Jerry Parson's son over a game of odd and even t'other night, gave him one in the calf of the leg, and you bet he wins every time he plays now."

"He's a promising boy, I know," said Billy. "But about this gun. Do you want to sell it?"

"No, I don't," said Richard; "and, if I did, I dursn't face Sal arter I'd parted with it. How are we to keep her birthday without it?"

"That's true," replied Billy, looking a little nonplussed. "But look here. If you won't sell it, will you lend it—for a consideration—say, two pound a day? Come, that's handsome."

"What do you want it for?"

"To keep the birthday of Broad Arrow Jack," replied Billy, readily. "It's coming off in about a week, and we want a royal salute for the occasion."

"I don't know anything about this Broad Arrow Jack, except what I've heard," replied Richard Skewball; "but I knows you, and I knows you to be as straight as a gun. If you'll say Broad Arrow Jack is straight, I'll take your word against the lot."

"Take my word for it, then," said Billy. "He's the noblest, best, and bravest lad—except your little chap—that was ever looked on."

"In that case I'm on, if the missus is," said Richard. "Who's your friend?"

"Captain Wobbles, chief gunner to our great chief, Broad Arrow Jack," said Billy, with a curious look in his left eye.

Wobbles turned white, and was palpably faint; but he said nothing.

"And he'll fire Big Ben, I suppose?" said Richard Skewball.

"Yes, that will be his office."

"Then, if the missus will let you have him, I will give Captain Wobbles a few instructions before he takes him away. But about this two pound a day. Is there any gammon in it?"

"Not a bit—our chief could pay ten, if need be; but I think two pounds enough."

"Then come in and see the missus. Hallo, Sal!"

"Well, what do you want?" asked a female voice, with more tartness in it than most people are particularly fond of.

"Here's a gentleman come to borrer Big Ben."

"Then he can't have it!"

"But come out first, my chick of chicks, and see who it is."

Mrs. Richard Skewball—a stout buxom woman, with the sort of eye that makes a railway porter polite without thinking of coppers—came out from a side room, wiping her hands upon her apron. As soon as she saw Billy Brisket she ran up and greeted him with a hearty kiss.

"What, Billy, old man!" she said. "It's glad I am to see you!"

"Just like her!" said Richard Skewball, quite overcome with admiration. "No nonsense—open and free; hearty or t'otherwise—a kiss or a scratch! She was fond of you, Billy, in the old days."

"Because he's an honest man," said Sal, "and, knowing I liked him, never came any puppyish nonsense. So it's you who wants Big Ben—is it?"

"Yes," said Billy; "for a week or two. Your birthday is just over, and it won't be wanted just yet."

"Take it and welcome!" said Sal.

Broad-Arrow Jack.

The ogre crept under the hammock and Broad Arrow Jack was at his mercy.

NO. 13.

"At two pound a day," put in Richard, with a business air.

"Who talks of two pound a day?" asked Sal. "Not you, Dick, I should think, to old Billy Brisket, who saved your life!"

"But the money aint to come out of him," urged Richard.

"Never mind who it is to come out of," said Sal. "If Billy Brisket wants Big Ben let him have it."

"Old Ben will be in good hands," said Billy. "Captain Wobbles is an experienced artilleryman, and knows how to manage it."

"Oh, of course!" said Wobbles; but to himself he groaned—"I never let sich a thing off in my life; and, having got old Joss off my hands, I'm fixed up with something that will blow my brains out!"

"Won't you have something to eat?" said Sal, on hospitable thoughts intent. "There's some cold mutton in the larder—enough for a snack. Dinner will be ready in a couple of hours; but you want something, I know."

"Mutton," said Richard, "is a heavy price just now. You can't get a bone—and a well-picked one—under a dollar."

"Bring out that mutton at once," said Sal, sharply.

Richard gave a slight skip, as if he had on previous occasions been stimulated with something stronger or more persuasive than words, and hastened to put the cold mutton before his guests. It was a leg bone, and there was not much meat on it, but he regarded it with a loving eye, and as Billy took out his knife bade it a tender adieu.

"I'm fond of cold mutton," said Billy. "The fat, with lots of pepper and salt, is unkimmon nice. Where's the pepper, Dick?"

"Pepper," said Richard, "is frightfully dear just now."

"Get out the pepper," said Sal, and Dick, knowing it was a question of pepper for him or his guest, fetched it with the promptitude and despatch of a West-end waiter.

Wobbles and Billy ate their fill. After the meal was over they went round to the back of the booth to have a look at the gun. It was a small field piece, mounted on two wheels, with the usual fixings, and, apparently, in a good serviceable condition.

"He will carry shot?" said Billy.

"I've never tried him," returned Richard Skewball. "But I've no doubt he'll carry anything. He's a beauty!"

"No doubt," returned Billy. "Well, Mrs. Skewball——"

"Don't Mrs. Skewball me. Call me Sal, as you did in the old days when you came round with your pack," said she. "A little familiarity from a true man like you won't put Dick's collar up."

"Not at all," returned Dick, heartily; "but I don't let any body else come out in that way."

"No more do I," said his wife, coolly. "I know how to stop impudence without your assistance."

"Of course you do, dear."

"Then don't talk nonsense. Now, Billy, you can have the gun. Have you far to take it?"

"Some miles."

"But you will never get it over the ground."

"I've a score or so men to help," replied Billy. "We shall fix a couple of stout ropes on him, and get him along."

"And mind you bring him back safe."

"In the hands of Captain Wobbles," said Billy, "he will have all the care and attention of a child."

"Oh, I'll look arter it!" said Wobbles, with a dismal twitching about the corners of his mouth.

"Afore you take him away," said Richard Skewball, in a whisper to Wobbles, "I've just this to say. When you fire him use a long poker, and don't stand behind him."

"What for?" asked Wobbles.

"Never mind," replied Richard Skewball, mysteriously. "It aint in me to say anything against Big Ben, but when you fire him remember my words, and act upon them."

"I will," said Wobbles, with a savage frown.

Billy took a whistle from his pocket and sounded it. In a few seconds the men he had spoken of came in.

A couple of strong ropes were fixed to Big Ben, and Billy bade Wobbles mount.

"Get on the top of it," he said, "and mind you keep it out of the ruts. You are responsible for it."

"Is it loaded now?" asked Wobbles, faintly.

"Let me see," said Richard Skewball, musing—"is it? Yes—no. I don't know. I see my Dick ramming something into it this morning, and it might have been powder."

"But suppose it goes off?" said Wobbles.

"In that case," replied Richard, "you'll find that a buck-jumping horse is nothing to him."

"Forward, there!" cried Billy. "We have no time to lose. Farewell, Dick! You shall hear of us shortly."

"And don't mind the missus," whispered Dick. "It's a joking way she's got of larfing at that two-pun' a day."

"You shall have it replied Billy, softly. "Good-bye, Sal. I never saw a woman wear like you. Younger and fresher than ever."

"As fresh as when we met in the omnibus," said Dick.

Then they all laughed, and Billy ran after the party with the gun, and looked with an eye of satisfaction on the suffering Wobbles, who, astride the cold metal, sat with his eye upon the touch-hole, as if he expected it to send forth an eruption equal to that occasionally displayed by Vesuvius.

CHAPTER LXXXIII.
CAGED BY A MADMAN.

A MAN possessed with such an iron constitution as the Ogre could boast of was not likely to lie long in a state of insensibility arising from a mental cause. The shock of fear passed rapidly away, and he was soon awake again to the horror of his position.

The light was out, and the darkness around him profound. No sound but his own breathing broke the stillness.

"Who gave that cry, and what has happened?" was the question he asked himself.

As if in mockery of him a peal of wild laughter came rushing down upon him, echoing and rocking as before. The hair of the man who believed in neither God nor devil was lifted up.

"Is this life, or am I dreaming?" he muttered. Then bracing himself up, he cried—" Whoever you are, stand forth and show yourself. If of this world I defy you—if of another I defy you still."

"See then," cried a voice, "they come—they come—marching on—yet never leaving me—ever moving but ever before my eyes—tramp—tramp—yes, I see and hear you, but halt, I cry—halt, there, and in the name of all the fiends get you gone."

"I know that voice," muttered the Ogre, "and could tell it easily enough but for these accursed echoes."

"A thousand headless men!" shrieked the voice again, "and marching too—tramp—tramp. Oh! get you away, for I cannot look upon you. But now I shut my eyes you are with me still. Away—away—or this brain of mine will burst!"

"Why, it's Jeb Jaundice," muttered the Ogre, "been drinking himself into a mad state, I suppose. What a fool I have been! Let me get a light and go and stop his mouth."

He groped about, and having found the lamp, lighted it with flint and steel which he carried; then hurrying back to the opening by which he had descended, he came upon Jeb Jaundice, standing with an axe uplifted in his hand.

"What, Jeb, old fellow," he said, soothingly—"what new joke is this?"

"Stand back!" cried Jeb, tossing his dishevelled hair into his eyes which seemed afire. "Stand back, you headless leader of a thousand headless men! Stand back, or I'll cleave your skull in two!"

"That's nonsense," said the Ogre, affecting to laugh; "if a man is headless, how can you cleave his skull?"

"At all events I'll cleave yours," said Jeb. Stand back!"

"I must settle him at once," thought the Ogre, feeling in his belt for a pistol; "he has become dangerous."

But Jeb saw the action, and quick as lightning he tossed the axe he bore up through the opening, and sprang after it. The Ogre fired, but the bullet sped harmless up to the roof of the cell, and flattened there.

"Ha, ha!" shrieked Jeb. "Now you have shot your arrow, show your head, and let me cleave it. You must return sooner or later—so come at once; but if you do not, I can watch and wait—I can watch and wait. Hear that—is not that good metal to cleave a skull with?"

He rang the axe upon the hard stones, and the sound it made told it was good metal indeed, but the noise was not at all musical in the Ogre's ears.

"Here's a confounded fix!" he muttered. "Caged by a madman, without food or drink, and a lamp that will be out in two hours! I wonder how long the fit will last?"

He spoke the last words aloud, and Jeb readily answered him.

"For ever!" he said. "I can stop here for ever, and I shall cleave your head at last."

"But, Jeb, hear me!"

"I *do* hear you," replied Jeb. "Who says I do not?"

"Nobody. But let us reason about this business. Do you know me?"

"Oh, yes!" said Jeb, with a laugh; "I know you very well—too well!"

"Who am I?"

"You are the headless king of a headless race of devils," replied Jeb Jaundice, with a madman's laugh. "Know you! I should think I do!"

"But I am not the person you speak of. I am the Ogre, my old friend."

"You are not the Ogre, and he never was my friend," was the prompt reply.

"I am the Ogre—indeed I am!"

"My good man," said Jeb, with the calmness of one who was thoroughly convinced of being in the right, and was not to be led away by mere argument, "you are *not* the Ogre—he went to the devil a thousand years ago!"

"You are mistaken—you have been misinformed," said the Ogre, who had a hard struggle with his passion to keep it down.

"Am I?" said Jeb. "Then tell me that my eyes lied. I *saw* him carried away. He was put into a boat and sailed away with the arch demon over a sea of blood to a land of fire."

"Mad as he can be!" muttered the Ogre. "I can only remain quiet, and perhaps he will go away or fall asleep."

What it cost him to keep still for the next half-hour he alone could tell; but he did it, and never moved an inch. The watcher above was quiet, too.

"Jeb!" said the Ogre, speaking low, to see if he was still there and awake.

"Well," answered Jeb, calmly, "what do you want?"

"I thought you were asleep, and was afraid of disturbing you."

"You would not have disturbed me, as I never sleep! It is a thousand years since I closed my eyes. I never shut them even for a moment."

"That is odd. You must be a wonderful man," said the Ogre.

"I am a wonderful man—a very wonderful man!" returned Jeb, complacently. "I am as strong as an ox, and never either eat, drink, or sleep!"

"I am proud of having such a man for my friend," said the Ogre.

"Well you may be," was the reply.

"And I am sure your friendship will be of immense advantage to me."

"So it will," said Jeb, as quietly as ever—"when you get it!"

"I should like to have your friendship," said the Ogre. "May I come up?"

"You may try," replied Jeb; "but, if you do, I'll cleave your skull!"

"You jest, old friend."

"Do I? Then I shall crack a joke and your head together. Ha! ha!"

"Is he mad?" thought the Ogre, clasping his head with both his hands. "Or am I mad—or is this some trickery of his to scare me away? Perhaps he has discovered the treasure. I'll go upon the other tack. Jeb Jaundice!"

"Yes?"

"It is time this foolery ceased. I am coming up."

"All right!" replied Jeb; "I am ready for you. You will soon be out of your misery!"

And Jeb playfully tapped the axe upon the hard pavement, to intimate that it was ready, too. Passion for the moment made all dark around the Ogre.

"I'll not be humbugged," he muttered. "It may be all boastful nonsense. Here goes!"

He leaped up, and grasped the edge of the opening; but the next instant he saw the axe gleam in the darkness above, and let go again.

"He means it," he growled, as he drew back and wiped the perspiration from his forehead, "and I'm done for."

The lamp was getting low and opening the door he trimmed the wick with his fingers. Even this was observed and commented upon by the watchful madman.

"When that lamp goes out," he said, "you will be done for. In the darkness you will be lost, for being headless you cannot see without a light. I can see anywhere."

"You cannot see in the dark any more than I can," said the Ogre, savagely.

"Put out the light and see," returned Jeb Jaundice. "In the gloom I will come upon you like a shadow, and then where will your skull be?"

"Where it is now," said the Ogre, tauntingly. "For what can you do—such a shallow-pated madman?"

"Who says I am a madman?" asked Jeb Jaundice, fiercely.

"I do," replied the Ogre, who had another pistol in reserve, and had it ready to let fly as soon as Jeb dropped down, if he were mad enough to do so.

"Oh! *you*?" said Jeb, calmly. "Then it doesn't matter, for nobody heeds the words of a headless ass."

"Oh! yes, they do," said the Ogre, "there are a lot of people here laughing at you."

"If *I* hear them laughing," said Jeb, "I'll come down, but I won't take your word for it. You are such a liar."

"So are you," said the Ogre.

"Ah! that's what *you* say, but your words don't count."

It was no use trying. Jeb would not be drawn down, and the lamp was getting low. As the prospect of being down there in the dark was very unpleasant the Ogre was at his wit's end.

What could he do?

Try his chance again at getting up through the opening.

No, it was too risky. If there had been a flight of stairs he might have done it with a rush, but having to pull himself up by sheer strength he would for several seconds be at the mercy of the madman above.

Should he try another shot at him?

Again no, for beyond the charge in his remaining pistol he had no ammunition, and if he fired and missed he would be worse off than ever.

Then came the thought of retreat.

Why not leave by the way he had traversed when he escaped from captivity? Abandon the place and Jeb, and the prospect of plunder for the time at least? He thought he might go out for a time at least, obtain food, and return. Jeb Jaundice, in his mad state, would keep on watching until he was exhausted, and he might abandon his idea, and leave his post.

Yes, that was the better thought, and taking up the lantern, he said—

"Well, Jeb, as you won't let me come up I am going for a stroll, but I shall come back again shortly."

"Whenever you come," replied Jeb Jaundice, "I shall be ready for you."

The Ogre, with another muttered imprecation on his head, stole away, and with ease traced his way along the secret passage to the spot by which he had escaped.

He reached it, and one glance wrung from him a groan of despair. It was choked up with stones and rubbish. Busy hands had stopped it up as they stop the hole of a fox.

He was caged indeed.

And how low the lamp was getting! He trimmed the wick, but it gave no better light, the oil was almost exhausted.

"I'll go back," he said, "in the dark. Perhaps I can do that secretly which I cannot do openly."

So he put out the light, and hid the lantern in his breast. Like a cat he crept stealthily back, listening for some sound to tell him when he reached his destination. He heard one.

"So you have come again," suddenly cried Jeb, above him, "and in the dark. Well it matters not to me for I can see you. I told you so. Ha, ha!"

CHAPTER LXXXIV.

THAT BOY OF SKEWBALL'S.

AS the cavalcade, of which Wobbles formed so prominent a part, wound along the narrow road leading through the diamond fields, the eyes of the workers, who were digging, washing, and examining, were often turned towards them with a sort of curious inquiry.

But very seldom anybody spoke, and then only a few words were exchanged, the dialogue taking a form similar to the following—

"That Skewball's gun?"

"Yes," replied Billy Brisket.

"Surely not the Big Ben?"

"Ay so."

"Hev he sold it?"

"Not quite perhaps."

"What will his gal do without it on her next birthday?"

"Oh! we shall be back with it before then."

"And whither going then?"

"To keep my birthday," Billy Brisket replied. "Get on, lads."

The diggers were too busy to stop long, and the removal of the gun excited no feeling but that of curiosity in any breast until they were quite clear and well out upon the half-formed road.

Barely had they got a mile upon their way when a boy with a shock head of air, wild devil-may-care eyes, and ragged clothing, came bounding towards them. He ran like a deer, and when he came up with the party he was no more out of breath than the arrival I have likened him to would be after a playful canter over a hundred yards of green sward.

"Hallo, look hyar," he cried. "Whar you going to take that gun to?"

"It's Skewball's lad aint it?" asked Billy Brisket.

"I reckon it air," replied the boy. "Who says I aint? You let that gun alone."

"No—no, my lad," said Billy "your father haf lent it to me, and I'm going to fire it on my birth day."

"And I want to fire it now on my birthday," replied the boy. "That's what I loaded it for this morning."

"Loaded! is it?" said Wobbles, rolling off like a ball off a housetop. I knew it—I felt it; hinstinctively I knowed the powder was there."

"Look here, my lad," said Billy, regarding that boy of Skewball's with an expression which said 'I am not going to have any nonsense.' "You can't fire that gun."

"Why not?"

"Because you would bring a swarm of people about us, wondering what was up."

"Then why wasn't it kep at home until I fired it?" asked the sweet youth. "I had only gone round for a few mates to come and see me do it."

"Your mates," said Billy Brisket, "will be disappointed for once in a way."

"Then I aint to set it off?"

"No, you aint."

"All right," said the boy, sullenly, and, plunging into some bushes, disappeared.

"Now, Captain Wobbles," said Billy Brisket, "mount your steed again."

"Oh, but look at it—quite bloated with gunpowder!" pleaded Wobbles. "It aint right to risk a man's life on a thing like that."

"It aint half so rampageous as old Joss," replied Billy.

"Whatsomever the failings of old Joss, may be," said Wobbles, "he wasn't at all likely to bust, and this harticle is."

"Are you going to get up?" asked Billy, advancing a step or two.

"Well, but when?"

"Oh, if you want help I'll give it yer," said Billy, and as the help he promised threatened to be of a very stimulating description, Wobbles hastily got up again, and with a calculating eye as to the part of it most likely to be affected by the bursting, sat as close to the muzzle as possible.

"Jes like a boy," he groaned within himself—"a preparing of pitfalls for the hinnocent. Dash him! I wish somebody had rammed his head into the muzzle, and blown him to Putney Bridge!"

In his position Wobbles was the last of the party, for the gun brought up the rear, and, of course, travelled with its muzzle pointed behind. The men who drew it along had their backs to the noble captain, and thereby escaped witnessing the agony of his countenance.

At every jolt in the road his heart leapt into his mouth, and occasionally he implored the men, for the sake of their lives, to pick out soft places.

"Guns," he said, "when they go off, swing round ginerally, and I shouldn't like to see you hurt."

"Guns," said Billy Brisket, from the front, "don't go off unless you put a match to the touch-hole. Gunpowder is not detonating powder."

"I don't know what you mean," said Wobbles. "If there's anything wuss than gunpowder about it's nothing to me. There you are again, in another rut. I never did see sich men."

At length they came to better land, where the green sward grew between the trees, and the cool breeze rustled through the leaves, and fanned their heated faces.

Wobbles felt better, and a sweet smile of ease played about his mouth.

But here, when he thought all danger past, his greatest peril came, for out of the trees there suddenly stepped a youthful form—the form of Skewball's boy—who with a nimble tread jumped lightly on the limber of the gun.

The men heard not his footstep, nor felt the additional weight, for he was a bony young villain, without any superflous flesh about him, and weighed very little more than a feather pillow.

As for Wobbles, his instincts were again at work, and he knew what was coming, but he could no more have spoken a word of remonstrance, or called for help than a man forty fathoms under the sea, he was that spellbound with horror, was poor Wobbles.

That boy of Skewball's took a box of matches out of his pocket, and struck one on the breach of the gun.

"Who said I wasn't to fire it horf?" he asked, sternly, and thrust in the fuse."

Now, if Wobbles had kept his seat, no great harm would have come of it; but, in his hurry to dismount, he got in front of the muzzle, and was blown, as he thought, over about ten miles of country.

But the fact was the charge was not a very heavy one that boy of Skewball's having obtained it by petty purloinings from his father's stock; there was only enough to blow Wobbles about ten yards from the muzzle, and there he lay, blinking like an owl, and instinctively anathematising the aged parent whose frugal habits had brought him so much misery and ruin.

The sweet Skewball youth, having kept his word, disappeared with the rapidity with which he came, and no eye but that of Wobbles looked upon him.

"What on earth induced you to fire that gun?" asked Billy.

"Me!" exclaimed Wobbles. "Is it likely I should do it?"

"But you have done it."

"It was the boy."

"What boy?"

"That boy of Skewball's."

"Oh! nonsense!" said Billy. "Get up. You are not hurt, are you?"

"I don't know," replied Wobbles, feebly; "but I think I've got a round shot somewheres."

"Well, the gun can carry both of you," said Billy, quietly. "Put him on. A shot more or less won't hurt him."

Wobbles was too much shaken to argue any point used. Limp and wretched he was put upon the gun again. Then, for the first time, his own particular followers began to have doubts of him, and to whisper among themselves.

CHAPTER LXXXV.

BLOWING UP THE PORCH.

A SERIES of delays are a great tax upon a man's patience, and Broad Arrow Jack, twenty-four hours after the departure of Billy Brisket, became impatient of the delay.

His chief follower and officer was now Trimmer, who still wore the handkerchief bound about his head, although his wounds had long since healed; but, as he said, "the sting remained." A man going about the world without ears is likely to come under more public notice than is quite agreeable.

"And if anybody in the future should ax me why I keep my head tied up," he said, "I shall say that I've got a perpetual cold that wants a deal of taking care on."

He was a cool card; but that did not prove him to be devoid of feeling. Many men show more than they feel, and others feel more than they show. Trimmer was one of the latter, and never made a wry face or uttered a word without cause for doing so.

To him Jack entrusted the command of the sentries by day, and looked after the same himself by night. Trimmer wanted him to change about, as the night was the hardest work; but Jack was rather peremptory in the matter.

"It is for me to arrange," he said, "and you to obey."

"Just so, sir," replied Trimmer, and as he went out from the presence of his chief he held communion with himself—"work getting a little trying for the youngster. No wonder. He's had enough to break a dozen down. No man I know could have borne it."

He mounted his horse and struck out for one of the narrow passes, guarded by a dozen men, to see how they were getting on, and on the way he came to a small pool of water, smooth and still as glass. The sight of it brought an idea into his head.

"Mister John Trimmer," he said, "looking-glasses are scarce here, and you haven't seen yourself since they made a roundhead of you. Here's a chance for you to see how far they've spiled your beauty. Woa, nag! stand still. You shall have a drink when your master's little fit of vanity is over."

First tying his horse to a tree, he went over to the pool, knelt down, took off his handkerchief, and looked in.

The contemplation of himself was long and steady. When it was over, he drew his head up, and sat down upon the bank.

"Well, Mister Trimmer," he said, "who would think the loss of a pair of ears would make such a difference? You were a good-looking chap once—there were gals about who were proud to know you; but now—well, if you show without this handkerchief you'll get pelted, you will. It was a good trick —by old Belzebub it was the act of an accursed demon, and if I had him here, with my hand upon his throat, it would take half a dozen horses to drag me off."

In a moment he was like a volcano, then cool again. Loosing the rein of his steed, he led it to the water.

"Drink!" he said, "and may the pool never be smooth again, unless it can reflect a prettier sight than I am."

The horse drank, and he remounted and rode sorrowfully away, with the reins hanging loosely down. Then he aroused himself, and became erect once more.

"What matters?" he said. "The heart of a man doesn't lie in his ears, and I am stout and strong. Forward my gallant nag," and shaking the reins, and pressing his knees into the sides of his horse, he urged it on, and rode through the forest at a furious pace.

He was back in the presence of his chief, and gave in his report before nightfall. "All's well," he said, "every avenue's guarded."

"But how long will it be ere Brisket returns?" was Jack's question.

"He cannot possibly be here under a week," replied Trimmer.

"And a week I cannot wait," said Jack.

"But you must, unless ——"

"Unless what?"

"You blast some portion of the palace, and make a breach."

"I do not understand blasting," said Jack.

"No more do I," replied Trimmer, coolly, "but all men must have a beginning, and I am willingly to try."

"We will try together. I know this much—you must drill a hole, put in the charge, ram it well home, and fix a slow match. In theory I have it, but not in practice."

"Well, having it in theory is better than not having it at all."

"It must be done, to-night, and at dawn we will fire the shot. Have a dozen men ready to guard the breach when made. I alone will enter."

"Alone, chief? That will be odds against you— two to one."

"Odds are of no moment when such fires as I have are raging within me."

"Well, chief, you shall be obeyed. I'll have the men here." But he added to himself, "I'm darned if you shall go alone. I reckon I'll be close handy when there are blows about."

It was a wild scheme, born out of impatience, but when one of Jack's nature gets a thing into his head it was next to doing it.

As soon as it was dark he and Trimmer went softly up the stairs of the porch, and kneeling down, listened.

All was quiet within.

They had with them two excellent chisels, a mallet and an augur, some prepared powder and a roughly constructed fuse to finish the work.

Now this fuse was the work of Jack and Trimmer, and consisted simply of a piece of string dipped in water and rolled in gunpowder. Not a bad thing if used at once, but apt to get dry quickly, and become dangerous.

But neither of them thought of this. The fuse was laid aside, and having chosen a spot, they began their work.

Chip—chip a dozen times, and then a pause.

"Do you hear them moving, Trimmer?"

"I hear nothing, chief."

Jack went on slowly but surely cutting a hole through the stone just in the centre of the porch. He worked hard, striking with wonderful correctness when the light he had to guide him is considered. In a little while he gave way to Trimmer.

"Cut straight and deep," he said.

"As straight and deep as if I were ploughing a hole in the heart of one of them," replied Trimmer.

He worked well in his turn, and after awhile both listened.

"No sound inside," said Trimmer.

"We shall take them by surprise," replied Jack.

So they went on turn and turn about until the stone was cut through to a mass of softish clay underneath.

A considerable quantity of this was scooped out, and the fragments of stone cut off put in at the bottom to form a bed for the powder.

This, in quantity about four pounds, was laid in with one end of the fuse in its centre and the other end brought outside. Then the square-cut hole was filled up with pieces of stone and clay, and rammed tight home with the handle of the mallet.

"I guess that is a very pretty piece of work," said Trimmer.

"Go down to the men, and bid them be ready. Do not let them come too near."

"But about yourself, chief?"

"I will look to my own safety."

Trimmer went down, and in a whisper bade the men get ready to rush up and guard the expected breach. His next care was to see what his chief was doing.

He was sitting quietly waiting for the dawn.

And the men sat down too. Their wait was not to be a long one, for the task of preparation had occupied the better part of the night. Already some of the stars in the east were growing pale.

"You know your duty," said Trimmer, to the men. "As soon as the breach is made, rush up, and let no one come out. Don't shout, but knock them down, and make them prisoners. The chief and I are going to see what is inside."

By-and-bye the light grew stronger, and Jack was seen to rise, and hold up his hand as a signal for them to be at the attention. Long watching had made them drowsy, but a little shaking put them right again. They were all on the alert.

Jack struck a match, and shielding it for a moment from the light morning breeze, applied it to the fuse.

In a moment there was a great glare, and a crash, like a peal of thunder when close overhead. The front of the palace seemed to rise, and divide into a hundred pieces, and then fell.

Broad Arrow Jack came staggering down a few paces, then great masses of masonry rolled upon him, and he fell.

"The fuse was dry," shrieked Trimmer, "and the chief is crushed to death. Stand by, my men, he is dead. I want to see them who are within on my own account. Death to the Ogre!"

And with excitement he ran towards the ruins, leaped over them like a madman, and rushed through the breach.

CHAPTER LXXXVI.

IN WHICH CONKY, CURLER, AND PIGEON DISTINGUISH THEMSELVES.

THE noise of the explosion was heard far and wide around by all the men, among others Conky, Curler, and Pigeon, who were reposing in one of the haylofts, taking out of bundles of grass the rest they needed after their recent terrible exertions.

Not that their repose was entirely satisfactory, for in it they rode their wild ride over again, and were jammed a hundred times, at least, between rocks a thousand feet high; and Pigeon, who was a particularly good hand at diabolical dreaming, dreamt he was up among the stars, suspended in space, with nothing but the tail of Fireworks to hold by.

But the dreams of all suddenly came to an end with the explosion, and springing up they knocked their heads together, and staggered about the loft like drunken men.

"What now?" cried Conky. "What new game is on?"

"It's a blow up somewhere," said Curler. "Let us go and see what it is."

They dropped down into the stable below, and keeping close company, came upon the scene of ruin brought by the explosion.

A greater part of the front of the palace had fallen down, and the hall was filled with the ruins of the central part of the roof. Over this a man was clambering, seeking in vain to enter by one of the doors into the wings, but they were all blocked up.

After Conky and his friends the men came up in small batches, all eager to know what was the matter.

But little explanation was necessary. The great sad item among the news was that the "chief was buried."

In the first flush of the panic none thought it possible for Jack to escape death, but it occurred suddenly to all these gentlemen that it was just possible he might be alive.

This thought arose from the fact of their having once assisted to remove the ruins of a house which fell in one of the streets of London, where they worked like niggers in seeking for property, and found an old man in a shut-up bedstead, who, beyond the fright he received, was very little hurt.

"Clear away the ruins!" they cried, and all the men took up the cry.

Jackets and hats were tossed aside, and great blocks of stone rapidly cleared away, Conky, Curler, and Pigeon, looking on with smiles of self-satisfaction.

Having originated the idea they had done their share of the work—men of slower mental capacity might do the rest.

And, really, the idea was a great one.

Trimmer acknowledged it, and reproached himself bitterly for not having thought of it at first. But who, seeing the huge masses which descended, would think that aught beneath it would escape being crushed to pieces?

He did not, could not, believe that Jack had

escaped, but he encouraged the men with words of hope.

"Quick!" he said. "Work on. It was here he fell—close under the steps. Be careful, and let none of the stones slip, or he may be crushed to death. Was that his voice I heard? One moment, men."

"Chief, are you there?"

No answer, and with a wave of his hand he bade the men go on.

"He is hurt," he said, "and unable to speak. Get out of the way, you lazy brutes!"

The lazy brutes were Conky, Curler, and Pigeon, who had already elected themselves as the saviours of their buried chief. Their indignation knew no bounds.

"That's just the way," said Conky. "People with ideas never get no credit. It is them as robs their brains who make their fortunes."

"Steady, men!" suddenly cried Trimmer. "What is here?"

An arm, brown with exposure from the sun, peeped out from under a great stone resting at an angle upon the steps.

Trimmer stooped down, and saw Broad Arrow Jack lying in the triangular hollow its position made.

"Steady men," he said. "Don't shout yet. Help me to take him out. Gently there; look at these awful bruises."

He put a hand upon his heart, held it there for a moment, then said—

"Cold and still!"

CHAPTER LXXXVI.
ON THE BRINK.

THE men were stunned as the vastness of the calamity which had befallen them became apparent. "Cold and still!" He—the brave—the beautiful—the noble. He whom they had almost worshipped—dead. What else could they think of as the words fell upon their ears?

Cold and still!

They uttered not a word, and made no sign, but silently they stood as if some spell had transfixed them; only their eyes moving showed they were living men.

The silence was broken by a wild shriek from the river bank, and then came bounding towards them a little dark form, covered with dust, and bearing every sign of fatigue. It was the Tiger, and as he approached he looked like one who had run a great race and was spending all his remaining power in a final effort to gain the goal.

He came into their midst panting, with eyes staring.

"Massa Jack," he said, "where is he?"

Trimmer pointed to the prostrate form of the leader, and the boy, with a wail that found an echo in every heart around, threw himself down upon the ground.

"Oh! Massa Jack," he cried, "I dream ob dis many—many mile away. In de night, when I lay down to sleep, I see you pale and bery sick, and den you die, so I come, run—run all de way—all de way, oh! so long, to find dat dream am true. Oh! Massa Jack, my heart am broken."

He crept towards the form of his master, and taking the lifeless hand, kissed it passionately, the hot tears falling from his eyes like rain. Strong men felt a rising in their throats, and many brown hands, hard with toil, were raised towards eyes dim with the salt water of sorrow.

"Massa Jack—Massa Jack," cried the boy, "oh! come back to de life again. You am too good to die. Why leab de poor Tiger? You was de fren to him when all de rest was brutes. You speak de kind word, and you make de Tiger feel dat he was a libing creatur, and not a ting to be shot at for fun like de wild cat. You make de Tiger's heart big wif joy. Oh! Massa Jack—Massa Jack, you was bery kind to me. Come back—come back!"

His passionate grief convulsed his frame, and creeping up, he laid his head upon the bare breast of his master, and lay there sobbing.

"Better let the lad be for awhile," said Trimmer; "he'll be better presently."

But as the moments passed the grief of the wild untutored boy increased, and mingled with his sobs there came short sharp cries of pain, with exclamations of anger, as if he reproached death for being so cruel.

At length Trimmer and Nat Green exchanged glances, and the former advancing, stooped down and touched the boy on the shoulder.

"Get up, my lad," he said; "we want to carry him away."

"Where to?" asked the Tiger.

"To a grave fit for such a noble creature," replied Trimmer.

"No—no," said the Tiger, "Massa Jack must not be put in de ground."

"But he can't be left here as food for the crows, my lad. Get up."

"What you take him away for?"

"Because he is dead."

"No—no, he never can be dat. Massa Jack not dead—NO."

The last word was uttered so loudly that it made the ears of the men ring again. The Tiger put his ear to the heart of our hero, and listened. His eyes shone with the fire of hope, which presently flashed into flames of joy.

"No—no," he cried, bounding up, "not dead—not dead. I hear de tick-a-tick ob Massa Jack's heart. Listen. Do you hear him?"

"By the blessed sun," cried Trimmer, as he knelt down and listened, "the lad is right! Broad Arrow Jack still lives!"

One great shout rent the air; then Trimmer called for silence.

"Quick, lads!" he said; "each man to where I shall send him. Green, get some water. Mathers, you and the three by you break down some boughs, and make a litter. Benson and Noakes, go forward across the stream, and sling a hammock between the two great oaks under which the chief loved to sit. Tiger, raise his head gently, and let it rest upon your knees, while I see what a few drops of wine will do for him."

The Tiger, with all the care of a trained nurse, raised Jack's head, and, still sobbing, placed it on his knees. Trimmer drew a flask from his pocket, and poured a few drops down his throat.

As a rule Jack drank very little wine. He seldom tasted it, except at the periodical feasts he gave to the men; so the few drops given him acted more efficaciously than they would have done in the case of a man accustomed to strong drink. The warmth of life returned to his cheeks, and he opened his eyes.

"Oh! Massa Jack," said the Tiger, "glad to see dat you larf at death! Oh! so pleased dat you come to us again!"

"Have I been hurt?" asked Jack; and then his eyes fell upon the ruined front of the palace, and he remembered what had passed. "Something struck me on the head—yes, and then all was darkness. But tell me how I have been spared?"

"By the mercy of God," replied Trimmer, taking off his hat. "It was a miracle."

"It must have been."

"You fell close to one of the steps," said Trimmer, "and a great stone, sliding down, covered and shielded you from the falling ruins. It was a miracle, and nothing less."

"Give me your hand," said Jack. "I will try to rise."

He made the effort, but it failed.

"I am more seriously hurt than I supposed," he said; "but a little rest will set me up again."

"Let us hope so, chief."

"Meanwhile examine me, to see if any bones are broken."

"I am but a rough surgeon, chief; but I will do my best."

The examination revealed no fracture, and, with the exception of a wound in the side of the head, there was nothing to show that Jack had been injured in any way. The shock was a general one, and for a time his nervous system was prostrated.

The arrival of the litter followed the examination, and Jack was laid upon it by men who showed all the tenderness of women. When asked if he felt any pain, he said—

"No; I shall be myself again in an hour or two. I have no serious injury."

They carried him to the hammock and placed him in it; and the Tiger, scrambling up one of the trees like a cat, settled among the lower branches to watch over him. All his own fatigue was forgotten in the anxiety he felt for his beloved master.

"I am weary now," said Jack to Trimmer, "or I would ask you a few questions about my foes. But watch the place well, and come to me in an hour."

Trimmer saluted, and he and the others went quietly away.

Jack, unconscious of the presence of the Tiger, settled down to sleep; but, although weary, sleep refused to come, and so he fell day-dreaming.

The place and the hour were favourable to reminiscences of the past. On every side stood majestic trees with rich foliage sweeping almost to the ground, and through the openings the sun from above sent down his shafts of golden light. Birds and insects winged their busy flights, and the sweet songs of one and the busy hum of the other were the only sounds that broke the quietude of that beautiful morning.

And of what was Jack thinking?

Of that which so many of us waste time upon—of what *might have been* if his life had not been shackled with a chain of sorrow—dwelling, as we all do, upon the misery of the past, with all that has come out of it. A waste of time—a fruitless exercise of the ever-busy brain.

For understand this, my reader, the past can never be changed, or bent, or broken, or wiped away, but your future may be moulded into a pleasant form if you are wise. The past is cast in a form that can never be otherwise than what it is, but the future is all raw material waiting to be shaped. What it will be neither you nor I, nor any living man can tell; we can only toil honestly, and give our little aid to make it better than what has gone before.

And while Jack lay dreaming there came out of the shadow of a tree the form of a misshapen man, in whose face malevolence, vice, and brutality had set their seals. Dagger in hand he crept up, the light of murder in his eyes, and Jack, dreaming on, neither heard nor heeded his approach.

CHAPTER LXXXVII.
THE FLIGHT IN THE DARKNESS.

"I CAN see—I can see, for what care I for the darkness? What has light to do with people without eyes, and and am I not king of the headless people?"

So raved Jeb Jaundice in the dark, and the Ogre, more terrified than ever he had been in his life, was befooled by a madman, and believed him.

It was a fearful position for a man to be in—helpless in a darkness that shut out everything, in the presence of an armed man supposed to have his powers of vision as good as in daylight.

The strong, burly brute cowered and trembled. Each moment might bring him death.

"Ha—ha!" shrieked Jeb Jaundice. "I have you at last. Hear this," and the swish of the axe as he whirled it round his head fell upon the Ogre's ears, "and that," tapping the stone walls with it,—"is it not musical? Bend your knee, knave. How dare you enter my kingdom with a head on? It is an insult to my people. You must be docked as they are, and become one of them. Bend your neck!"

"It is bent," replied the Ogre, and immediately shifted over to the other side of the passage. A light was breaking in upon him, and he wondered if Jeb Jaundice could really see. The madman was befooled in his turn, and struck in the direction of the voice. The axe rang upon the stone floor, and the Ogre chuckled to himself.

"The fool has lied," he muttered; "he cannot see. What ho, there!"

As he spoke he backed a few paces, and Jaundice, again deceived, struck out, and hit the wall. The Ogre, in his glee, laughed aloud, but he narrowly escaped paying the penalty of his imprudence with his life. Jeb Jaundice, springing forward, struck at him, and the axe whistled, as it fell within a few inches of his face.

"A curse upon him!" muttered the Ogre, and commenced slowly backing up the passage, feeling his way by the wall.

"I have not slain thee yet," cried Jeb; "but the axe and the hand is ready. Bend thy neck."

The Ogre, without answering, continued his retreat, but without any knowledge of whither he was going. The predicament he was in, viewed from any point, was a most unpleasant one.

The voice of Jeb Jaundice calling upon him to bend his neck, and become a subject of his headless kingdom, died away in the distance, and the Ogre hurried on, scarce caring whither the passage led him to, so long as he escaped from his wild companion. With great rapidity he covered about a hundred yards of a winding way, and then suddenly stumbled over a heap of stones and fell.

A fall in the dark is always unpleasant, and the eye gives the mind no chance of estimating how far a man is to fall. The Ogre in consequence fell heavily upon a pile of broken stones, and hurt himself terribly.

He cut his face, hands, and knees, and was at first so stunned and staggered by the fall that he could only lie still, and give vent to his feelings in a string of oaths and furious growls.

In his agony he forgot the consequence of speaking. The busy echoes carried the sound of his voice to Jeb Jaundice, and the madman came on in angry pursuit.

"The knave!—the knave!" he muttered. "To mock and defy me by going about with his head on; but I'll cut short his impudent folly. What ho, there, I am coming! Get your neck ready for the blow."

The Ogre heard his coming, and got upon his feet, with fires of rage dancing before him; but these fires, alas! gave no light, and he could only hear—not see—Jeb Jaundice coming.

Rapidly he felt about him. The passage was narrow where he stood, and blocked up with fallen stones.

He was in a trap, and there was no escape unless he fought with and overcame his foe.

But how could he fight him?

He asked the question, and a rolling stone answered him. Stooping down the Ogre armed himself with two, of, perhaps, ten pounds apiece, and awaited the advance of the madman.

He was coming on boldly, talking and threatening as he came.

"What ho, slave!" he cried. "You dare to mock me—me—Jeb the First, King of the Headless! Poor fool, you little know what you do! You trust to the darkness, but you trust in vain. Darkness and light are the same to me."

Notwithstanding this boast his majesty was feeling his way with one hand as he came, and poking the axe about with the hope of finding his rebellious subject.

The Ogre heard him coming, and, carefully poising the stone, waited until he calculated Jeb Jaundice was within half a dozen yards of him, then he hurled it.

A short, gasping cry, and the fall of a heavy body followed. The axe rattled on the ground, the echoes took up its ring, and when they died away silence came.

"I've done for him—knocked the senses out of him, at least," muttered the Ogre, groping about. "All I want now is to have hold of him—for a moment, no more."

He groped to the right, to the left, backwards and forwards, and found nothing. Again he went over the ground with the same result.

"What is the meaning of this?" he muttered, as a fresh terror came upon him. "Am I the victim of a dream? Am I going mad?"

His brain whirled for a moment, and the strong man fell back against the wall. Then his iron will came to the rescue and rallied him.

"He was here, and I hit him," he said. "Perhaps he is foxing. Jeb Jaundice."

"Jeb Jaundice—Jaundice—dice," said the echoes, in reply, but that was all he heard.

"I'll find him—he is here!" growled the Ogre. "I'll not be a victim to childish fears. I defy all the powers that can be brought against me!"

He stepped forward with a resolute air, but the next moment paused, for a sudden roar, like the voices of a thousand wild beasts, was heard above, the palace trembled, and the loose stones came rolling down.

The Ogre staggered and fell.

"God have mercy on me!" was the involuntary exclamation that escaped his lips. "Forgive and pity a wretched man!"

A curious light—or what seemed a curious light to him—streamed through an opening down upon his face. He veiled his eyes, and lay there shuddering, for he believed it to be the light of another world.

The hardness of his heart was shattered for a time, and, under the influence of the complicated fears which beset him, he descended to the level of a child scared by a horrible spectacle. He prayed, he grovelled—yea he wept, and vowed, if his life was spared, to live as became a man.

There was no answer to his prayers, and no new terrors heaped upon him. Little by little he gathered strength and courage, and slowly raised his eyes. The light was still there; but he laughed as he looked upon it, for it was but the light of day pouring through an opening made by the shifting stones.

And was he grateful?

No—the sight hardened him again, and, rising with a laugh upon his lips, he crept up, and peeped out upon a tangled mass of brushwood at the back of the palace.

"What an ass I have been!" he said—"frightened by a mere chance. If what men preach is true there would have been no loophole left for me. No—it is all a sham. Creation is a whirlpool of chance—it has no governing power."

And, secure for the time in his unbelief, he crept out, and stood, bold and hardened, in the sunlight.

"Free from the palace," he muttered; "but whither shall I go?"

He paused to look upon the scene. It was a wild spot, seldom if ever trodden by the foot of man for many a long year. To the left he could see the roof of the shanty which served for stables; to the right a piled-up mass of rock, and a murmuring waterfall. Around were the great hills, purple in the morning light.

"I'll skulk about all day," he said, "and at night I will climb those hills, and be gone. But food and drink I must have—I am almost famished."

Lying down, he crept like a snake round to the front of the palace and looked out.

The men were bearing Broad Arrow Jack across the stream to the wood. Jack lay quiet, as if dead.

"That noise was an explosion," muttered the Ogre. "There has been some accident. Broad Arrow Jack looks as if he had gone over the border. I'll follow and see how it fares with him. If he is in need of a few finishing touches, perhaps it may fall to my lot to give them to him. Oh! my worthy Ogre, the game is not played out yet!"

CHAPTER LXXXVIII.
THE ATTEMPT FRUSTRATED.

IT was not difficult to keep in the wake of the men without discovery, for, being all absorbed in their grief and anxiety, they had no thought for aught else but their chief.

The Ogre, therefore, with very little precaution, followed to the spot where the hammock was slung, and, lying down in a clump of bushes, saw Jack deposited within it, and watched with much satisfaction the retreat of the men.

Like Jack, he did not see the Tiger—for the huge trunk of a tree shielded the active youngster from his observation—and when he crept out, fancying Jack was left helpless and alone, he had no idea that the eyes of any one were upon him.

Taking out his knife, he opened it, and cursed it for the click of its spring—so fearful was he of the least noise betraying him. It was a great habit of his to curse anything that was against him; but, fortunately, the curses of men are of little avail. If the Ogre's had taken effect, half creation would ere then have been blighted.

It is a foolish habit—this cursing. It lowers and debases a man, without bringing him profit in any shape or form. Cursing shows weakness, too: a true man is—and ought to be—above it.

Hunger, thirst, and all else were forgotten in the great opportunity now offered him for revenge. Jack lay helpless, with his eyes closed. The colour had again left his cheeks, and the paleness of the dead was there.

"What can save him now?" said the Ogre, as he crept up. "One swift, sure blow now, and the race which has been my bane will be wiped out."

He took a careful look around, and saw nothing. But he did not look up. Had he done so he would have seen a pair of glittering eyes upon him.

Without making more sound than a snake would have done he crept under the hammock, and rising slowly, elevated his arm to strike. He could see the outline of Jack's form through the canvas, and calculated the spot for the blow to a nicety.

"What can save him now?" he asked himself again, and the knife flashed upward.

But immediately the teeth of some wild beast apparently were fastened upon his wrist, and the claws or paws, or what not of the same creature were all over his head and face. Great bundles of matted hair were torn up by the root, deep red lines furrowed in his cheeks, and blinded and dismayed he staggered back and fell to the ground, dropping the knife from his wounded hand.

"What is going on there?" asked Jack.

"Dis willan ob an Ogre," said the Tiger, who had come to the rescue, as he danced about flourishing the knife he had picked up. "Oh! I gib him sumfin for a keepsake, and I hab his hair. Golly! I gib it to him!"

"So it's you!" cried the Ogre, wiping the blood from his face with his hand. "You confounded imp, I'll settle you now."

Wild with fury the Ogre took out his pistol, and fired his last shot. He missed the Tiger, for he might as well have aimed at a dragon fly.

"But I'll not be foiled!" cried the Ogre, springing up, and clutching the hammock rope. "I'll have your life if I die for it the next moment."

Jack tried to rouse himself, but his strength had not returned. As the hammock fell he lay as helpless as a child upon the ground.

"Demon!" he cried, "do your worst."

"Ask mercy of me," grinned the Ogre.

"Never! What you have to do do at once," said Jack.

The Ogre, with a smile of grim satisfaction, stepped forward, but again the Tiger was upon him, in a style that would have done credit to a young namesake of his. His lithe sinewy hands clutched at the Ogre by the throat, and tore at the flesh furiously.

The Ogre took the boy by the waist between his tremendous hands, and squeezed him until every rib cracked, but the boy was iron. His hardy life and constant travelling to and fro had given him a form as tough as leather.

"At him, Tiger!" cried Jack—"at him, brave boy! Well done!"

"All right, Massa Jack," gasped the Tiger, "me hold on while I hab breaf. Oh! shake away, you debilish Ogre, I keep on."

"A rot take him!" growled the Ogre, half out of his senses with pain and rage. "Let go, or I'll murder you."

"Murder me, Ogre," said the Tiger, "and me still hold on."

"Keep to him a moment, Tiger," said Jack, "help is coming."

It was true. Men with hasty steps were crashing through the bushes, and the Ogre heard them. His thoughts now turned from revenge to flight, and he strove to shake the Tiger off. But, like a limpet to a rock, the boy held on, and could not be removed.

The sound of men approaching drew nearer, their voices could be heard, and the Ogre, panting with passion, turned and fled, with the Tiger still holding on to his throat with the grasp of a vice.

CHAPTER LXXXIX.

IN WHICH WOBBLES DOES A DARK DEED.

OF all the trials and troubles of his varied life Wobbles had never known anything like the trouble brought upon him by Big Ben. It was very unkind of Billy Brisket to insist that Wobbles himself had fired it upon the memorable occasion when that boy of Skewball's had put a match to the touch-hole, and still more unkind when he insisted upon Big Ben being fired every night at sunset by the hand of the man who, during the day, so unwillingly bestrode it.

"It is no use your arguing the matter," said Billy. "You've got the eye and the build of an artilleryman, and it is only your modesty that keeps you from blazing away every hour of the day. That gun is to be fired every night at sunset, and you are to fire it."

"It aint a reg'lar gun," pleaded Wobbles. "I wouldn't mind a fust-rate piece of hartillery, for that wouldn't jump about like a blessed goat when it goes off."

"That is all playfulness," said Billy. "Just a little skittishness that will wear off with time."

"If time does its dooty with that ere gun," said Wobbles, gloomily, "time will bust it. But I hope I shan't live to see it."

"You won't live long when you have seen it," said Billy, with a consoling nod. "All your troubles will be over then."

The most painful part of the business was that the men who once believed in and feared him had found him out, and treated him with open contempt or indifference.

Some even had the audacity to laugh at him—even Giles did that.

"Don't you laugh at me," said Wobbles, putting on an expression such as Richard the Third is supposed to have worn when soliloquising over his villainous deed.

"Why shouldn't I larf?" asked Giles. "Ha, ha! he, he!"

"Shut up, will you?" said Wobbles.

"Shut up, thyself!" said Giles, in defiance.

Wobbles reflected a moment, and decided upon kicking Giles.

In his heart of hearts he believed it could be done with safety.

Advancing upon that individual he commanded Giles to turn round. Giles declined to do so. Wobbles, therefore, sailed in a circular direction with great rapidity, and Giles, being a very slow man, he received a kick before he knew what Wobbles was up to.

"Now, sir," said Wobbles, "will you laugh at me again?"

Giles made no reply, but took off his hat and placed it carefully upon the ground, then he took off his coat, folded it up, and deliberately rolled up his shirt sleeves.

These preparations, occupying something over ten minutes, were watched with much curiosity and satisfaction by his friends, and, when completed, they instinctively formed a ring, enclosing Wobbles and Giles therein.

"Now," said Giles, putting up his arms like a double railway signal, "come on."

"Oh, pooh!" returned Wobbles, turning white, "you don't mean fighting?"

"Oh, yes, I do, dang it!" replied Giles; "so come on."

"But you can't fight—ahem! your superior officer."

"I don't know about sperior office," said Giles, "but I aint going to be kicked for nuffin. Now then, be ye ready.

"I—ahem!" said Wobbles, "fall back upon—ahem! my dignity, and decline to fight."

"Then," said Giles, "I'm danged if I don't make yer."

"Oh! but where is Captain Brisket?" said Wobbles. "He ought, as the legal and truly justified authority, be here to stop this unmanly wiolence."

"Captain Brisket is a-lying down there, a-smokin' and larfin'."

"I see no help from that quarter," said Wobbles, cold with fear. "Oh, what a pass my property has brought me to! But look here, Mister Giles, can't we settle it by harbitration?"

"I don't know what that is, and I don't care," said Giles; "come on."

Wobbles then flatly refused to come on, and Giles, with great care and deliberation, went at him. Wobbles backed with much agility, and it is doubtful if Giles would ever have caught him if some friend, who formed part of the ring, had not basely given Wobbles a push, and placed him in his enemy's arms.

Having got him, Giles, who was a strong man, proceeded to put his head into a position favourable for "punching," and having got it tight under his left arm, regardless of the expostulations, pleadings, and wriggles of Wobbles, he gave him some half-dozen violent digs—they scarcely came under the head of blows—any one of which would have staggered a prizefighter.

Fortunately most of them were delivered on the crown of the head, which was the least vulnerable part of the Wobbles frame, or Giles would most likely have pounded all his features into one. As things were, Wobbles escaped with a black eye, and a nose like a very fine Orleans plum.

When Giles let go Wobbles fell to the ground, and lay there apparently between life and death.

"I am done for," he said, "but the awenging harm of justice shall come at ye. Take this message to my mother. No, I don't mean that. Let Hengland know how I fell, but I'll tell the chief of this, and see if he don't make you dance for it."

All night long Wobbles nursed his nose and eye, in company with his revenge, and out of the dark thoughts that ran in succession through his brain he singled out one which was to bring confusion upon Giles, and the instrument he selected to aid him was Big Ben.

"I'll get him to look down the muzzle," he said, "and when nobody is looking I'll blow his 'ed orf. Meanwhile I will dissemble."

So Wobbles dissembled, and feigned a friendship for Giles. In hollow mockery he smiled upon that man, called him friend Giles, offered him tobacco, and took drink with him the next time they camped at eve.

Perhaps he took in Giles, and perhaps he did not. Apparently Giles buried the hatchet, as well he might, having come off victorious, and returned the proffered friendship with as much warmth as could be expected from one of his stolid nature.

"The work is complete," thought Wobbles. "This night I will complete my work. Let me retire and arrange my plans. Ha, ha!—rewenge!"

He retired to a tree, and by its trunk conned over his plans.

Wobbles had a habit of thinking aloud, especially when excited, and this habit he now freely gave vent to.

"He's a hinnocent sort o' chap, this Giles," he said, "and I've seen him more than once looking down the muzzle. His skewriosity shall be his destruction. But I must proceed with caution. How shall I lead him on to-night?"

It was a difficult and dangerous task, but genius overcomes everything, and Wobbles hit upon a plan. Not a very brilliant affair, but one which he hoped would in every way answer the purpose.

"I'll tell him that it aint to be fired no more, and so I've made a peep-show of it. All yokels are fond of peep shows, and he's sure to go at it. Meanwhile I will load the gun, and dissemble yet the more."

The bloodthirsty, diabolical nature of this plot can only be spoken of with loathing and strong condemnation, and how Wobbles could get into a frame of mind to conceive it is difficult to understand. But it must be remembered he had suffered much, and had been thrown a great deal into the society of hardened ruffians. Moreover, his eye and nose still pained, and the wound made in his dignity rankled deeply still.

"I'll do it," he said, as he sauntered towards the unsuspecting Giles, who was engaged in some interesting game with a friend, with four smooth stones and five round ones.

How he lured Giles from the game, and ascertained he was fond of peep-shows, and how he inspired him with a belief that Big Ben had been turned into one, it boots us not to tell, but he did, and Giles fell into the trap.

It was but an hour to sunset, and Wobbles stole away to spend that hour alone. He had told Giles that the show would be ready by sunset, all illuminated and fair to look upon, and Giles had promised to be there.

"You are the only one who is to have a private peep," said Wobbles, carelessly. "But I want to get your opinion of it. I think it will amuse the chief, and win him from his sadness when we return. What thinkest thou, Giles?"

"I thinks that if a peep-show won't wake up he, nothin' will," said Giles.

"Right well spoken," returned Wobbles. "Remember, at the hour of sunset."

"I'll be there," said Giles.

Big Ben had been stowed away in a sheltered nook a little removed from the camp, a dark dell, where a man might be excused for not seeing any one near the muzzle in the dusk at eve. It was placed there to hide it from the eyes of any chance party of travellers who might be passing, and Wobbles chuckled as he thought how everything fell in with his arrangements.

"I'll blow his head orf," he said, "and stow away his body in the bushes. He will be missed, but they will not seek him here. I can say he went on at early dawn. All will be well, and this eye and nose awenged. Ha—ha!"

He passed a restless hour away from the camp, and as the sun touched the horizon he stole softly round, and crept into the dell where Big Ben reposed.

A dreadful gloom was on the place—a gloom that would have appalled many stout hearts, but Wobbles was strung up by a desire for revenge, and suffering had made him remorseless.

He peeped in through the bushes, and there was the form of Giles, with his head well jammed up against the muzzle of the gun, seeking no doubt to find the exhibition which had only existed in the fertile brain of Wobbles.

It was no time to pause. Wobbles ran forward, struck a match, and placed it to the fusee, which wisdom prompted him to place in the touch-hole. Then he tried to retreat, but all his strength failed him, and he sank down upon his knees.

One—two—three—bang!

Big Ben leaped, and came down upon his nozzle. Wobbles turned, and, with staring eyes, looked where Giles had been, and there lay the figure—headless.

Then came remorse.

He leaped up, and, with eyes out of his head, staggered away, but not far, for a man stepped out from the shade of a tree, laid a hand upon his arm, and, in a deep sepulchral tone, asked—

"What have you done?"

CHAPTER XC.

WOBBLES BECOMES A SLAVE.

FEW men or women ever committed a crime believing they might, could, would, or should be found out, for a criminal is generally a very cunning person, who thinks that, in his or her case, sufficient care will be exercised to cheat the law and defy all ordinary chances of discovery.

But, as is also generally the case, the criminal is discovered, and if particular care has been taken to conceal the crime justice comes up and takes them red-handed, just as it did Wobbles, who had no sooner let off Big Ben than, as we have recorded, a strong hand was laid upon him, and he was asked what he had been up to.

His first impulse was, like the clown in the pantomime, to say "nothing," and being a bit of a fool he said it.

"Nothing!" repeated his captor; "come that's a good un. Is that nothing?"

He pointed towards the headless trunk, but Wobbles dared not look. He only shuddered, and asked who it was who had come down on him.

"I'm Marks," said the other, " one of your men as was, but isn't now."

"Oh! Marks, is it?" returned Wobbles, "the chap as have got a squint."

"None of your cheek," said the man, shaking him. "I've got a bit of a turn in my eye and nothing more."

"I'm so confused," replied Wobbles, humbly, "that I don't know what I'm saying. I'm not sorry you were here to see my *haccident*, as you can tell people how it was done."

Marks had considerably obliquity of vision, and as he turned his face full upon Wobbles, his two eyes seemed to be keenly examining his nose. He was a tall, stout fellow, and barring the little defect alluded to, would have done for the Horse Guards.

"If I do tell 'em," he said, "you'll get into trouble. Giles told me you had axed him to come and look into a peep-show you'd fitted up."

"Giles," said Wobbles, warmly, "have perwerted the truth."

"If you say that I'll shake the life out of you. Giles was a pertikler friend," and Marks raised his coat cuffs to his eyes, and brushed away a briny tear.

"Any how," said Wobbles, "he must have made a mistake."

Broad-Arrow Jack.

THE SHADOW CAME TOWARDS BROAD ARROW JACK, WHO THRUST AT IT WITH HIS SWOP, BUT IT PASSED THROUGH THE IMPALPABLE FORM.

NO. 14.

"He have, but that won't clear you," said Marks. "Come afore the cap'en."

Wobbles, damp with fear, sank upon his knees and clasped his hands.

"Spare me," he gasped, "and I'll make you rich for life. Indeed I will."

"You make me rich!" sneered Marks; "how?"

"I've got a little property, a few diamonds as you can have," said Wobbles.

"Where?"

"In a place close by. If you let me go I'll fetch 'em. I swear it."

"Well," said Marks, "I'm a great lover of justice, but I'm sure if Giles was here he would be only too glad for me to make a little money out of him. How many stones have you?"

"About a dozen, reg'lar beauties," said Wobbles, eagerly.

"I'll take 'em," said Marks, "but let us bury poor Giles. It's getting uncommon dark, and we must be sharp."

"I daren't touch him," replied Wobbles, shuddering.

"Then you go and get the stones, and I'll bury him while you are gone."

Wobbles was only too glad to get away, although he had no intention of attempting to get clear off. Retiring towards the camp, he selected a lonely spot, and cutting open his belt took out a few of the stones acquired after the decease of Jereboam Bounce.

"Thee and I must part," he said, turning them fondly over, "but I've got a little fortune still."

Having allowed about ten minutes for the interment of his victim, he returned to Marks, who had got over his work very quickly, and was waiting for him. It was now so dark they could scarcely see each other, and Wobbles was all in a tremble.

"Here are the jewels," he said.

"Stop a minute, I'll put them into my handkercher," replied Marks. "I say," he added, as the brilliants flashed in the feeble light, "these are first-raters. Where did you get them from?"

"I received them," replied Wobbles, faintly, "from Broad Arrow Jack as a reward for my bravery."

"Oh! did you? Then he is easily pleased."

"He recognises true valour," returned Wobbles, "of the persevering sort; not the slap-dash business where a man goes head first at a thing, and repents of it ever afterwards."

"Well, you've got off cheap," said Marks, as he knotted his handkerchief. "But remember this, if anybody else finds you out I've nothing to do with it."

"Who else is to find me out?" asked Wobbles, aghast.

"I can't tell. There is an old saying that 'murder will out,' and if it's coming neither you nor I can stop it," said Marks, as he coolly walked away.

Wobbles hurried after him, too terrified to be left longer alone, and together they returned to the camp, where the men lay round a fire, lighted to ward off the wild beasts from the spot. Most of them were asleep, and Wobbles, creeping into the ranks, also sought repose.

But how could he hope to sleep?

Had he not the stain of murder on his soul?

By base art and devilish cunning he had lured an innocent being to his destruction. Poor Giles! with a soul thirsting for peep-shows, he had put his head into the mouth of a cannon, and found—a grave. The thought was horrible, and Wobbles with great difficulty stifled the groans of his troubled spirit.

In addition to the stain of guilt he had been robbed that night—yes, robbed by Marks, who had taken, say, a hundred and fifty pounds' worth of precious diamonds out of his little store as the price of silence. The groan that rose with this thought would not be silent, but burst forth dismally on the night air.

"Can't you keep quiet?" asked the man next to him.

"I'll try," replied Wobbles, softly, "but I was thinking—of my mother—that blessed old woman," he added to himself, "who lived a long life, and worked hard to leave me a stock of misery."

"The next time you disturb me," said the man who had been roused, "I'll put you out of the ring smart."

"I'll do my best endeavours to get to sleep," said Wobbles. "Good night."

"Go to Bath," was the amiable reply.

Wobbles did his best, but sleep would not come. His comrades fell off one by one, until he alone remained with open eyes, gazing upon the stars. A faint breeze rustled among the trees, and the leaves whispered "murder!" The owl upon the wing hooted the same word, the wings of the bat rustled it, and the stars of the heavens became eyes full of reproach looking straight at him.

He tried to shut out all these things by stopping his ears and shutting his eyes, but the singing in his head became the murmur of thousands of far off voices, singing in chorus "Murder—murder!" and in the darkness of his brain he saw the deluded Giles walking about with his head under his arm, in search of the man who had slain him.

So on, up to perhaps the midnight hour, until the light in the west had quite gone, and then for the hundredth time or so he opened his eyes, and looked —oh, horror! upon Giles.

Aye, there he was with his shattered head restored —just as a ghost ought to have it—and everything in order about him, even to his clothes. There he was on the opposite side of the dying fire, squatted down, with his eyes on Wobbles.

A curious creeping sensation came over the murderer. He felt as if his skin was shifting about all over him, and gradually he was drawn, apparently against his will, into a sitting position, too. There they sat—the murderer and his victim face to face.

The ghost was not inclined to sit there long, but, raising its hand with the horrible slowness of the spectre world, beckoned to Wobbles to come away.

He could not—dared not—disobey. Wobbles got up, with legs so limp that he swung round like an expiring humming-top, and scarce heeding what he did, walked through the hot embers of the fire in the track of the ghost, backing away—oh! so silently.

He fell over one of the sleepers, who, strange to say, did not awake, got up again, and, bent almost double, tottered after the spectre of the departed Giles.

Hamlet's father might have taken a lesson from this solemn midnight visitant, who, short as his stay had been in the spirit world, was already up to the business of making night hideous, and to horribly shake the disposition of men. With Wobbles this ghost was a perfect success.

Slowly and mournfully the shade of Giles backed to the wood, and, pausing on its verge, spoke for the first time.

Even the vernacular of the departed Giles was preserved by his spirit.

"Dang 'ee," it said, "come along; ye be a slow un!"

"Come," moaned Wobbles; "where to?"

He asked the question, discarding the answer. But the ghost was mystical, and left him in that worst of all states—doubt.

"Ye come along," it said, "and when ye get there ye'll know where ye was tuk to."

Again it beckoned, and again Wobbles obeyed, but his progress was stilty and uncertain. A drunken man with two wooden legs would have got along more gracefully.

Down into the depths of the wood they went.

Wobbles, with his eyes fixed on the shade of Giles, looking more horrible now that it was but dimly defined, and cannoning against trees as he went upon his awful way. His brain was in a whirl, fires flashed before his eyes, his tongue clave to his mouth —still he kept on.

At last the shade of Giles halted, and in a warning voice, which plainly told it would stand no nonsense, bade Wobbles—

"Stop!"

Wobbles stopped, and put a hand to his clammy brow.

He was enduring torture worse than death.

"I shan't be long gone," said the spectre. "I'm only going to fetch t'other ghaists."

"Oh," returned Wobbles, feebly; "so there are more of 'em!"

"Lots," replied the ghost, and as it melted away tripped up most unexpectedly over the roots of a tree.

Wobbles fancied he heard it swear, but was inclined to think he was in error.

Left alone he tried to think over his position; but, like most men in great and awful peril, or in imminent danger of severe punishment, he could not fully realise what was going on. One thing he was certain of—he was in a hopeless fix, and was a doomed man.

Even the most cowardly, when all hope of being saved is past, will pluck up a spirit. Death does not have everything all his own way, and sometimes the weakest of men and women will show him a bold front.

Wobbles tried to do so now.

"I don't care," he said; "I can only die—and there's an end of me."

His eyes were now growing accustomed to the darkness, and by degrees he made out objects around him. There were trees, a few pieces of rock, and —oh, horror!—Big Ben.

He was on the very spot where he had done that ghastly deed.

The little pluck he had summoned forsook him, and he fell upon his face.

"Mercy!" he cried; "mercy!"

But in response there came an awful chorus of shrieks and groans, and above all was heard a voice—

"Wobbles, base murderer, rise, and look upon the spirits of the dead!"

CHAPTER XCI.

IN A RING FENCE.

WITH the Tiger clinging like a leech to his throat, the Ogre fled through the wood, choosing the denser parts, with the hope of finding a hiding-place where he could for a few moments lie secure from his pursuers, and rid himself of the burden he bore.

The pursuers came on apace, but the cunning of the Ogre soon put them at fault. Skilfully doubling, he let them go on ahead, and, pausing at last in a deep dell, he prepared to avenge himself upon the Tiger.

But in a moment the boy let go, and sprang off to a few yards' distance, where he stood in mocking defiance of him, making signs of derision and contempt.

"You, Massa Ogre," he said, "bery bad man; but de Tiger see you hang one day."

The Ogre, with one hand upon his throat—lacerated by the Tiger's nails—shook a fist at the imp-like boy in impotent rage.

"I'll settle you one day!" he said.

"No, Massa Ogre," replied the Tiger—"'taint possorbul! Jest as likely to bring down de swaller bird wif a pea-nut as to catch and kill me."

"But, by the light of day," said the Ogre, "I'll o it! It was an accursed day when I found you under a tree, and took you home. I raised a viper then."

"No, Massa Ogre—you neber found me. You kill my fader; den I crawl affer you, and you let me come home, so dat you might hab sumfin dat was bery lilly and weak to kick and swar at."

"It's a lie, you young imp!"

"Anyhow, Massa Ogre, you kick and swar at me. I was like a ball in dat house ob yourn, and it was when I run away and hide from you dat I learn how to run and climb. You bery cruel, Massa Ogre; but I tank you for it. I neber be de Tiger I am wifout you."

"You would have died without me, you whelp," said the Ogre.

"But you neber sabe my life for lub," returned the Tiger; "and you neber feed me. I allus bery hungry, and, but for Missus Jaundice, I starbe right off. She gib de poor lilly debil ob a Tiger food, and so he libed on—no tanks to you, you downright black ole willain! But look here, massa, I hab sumfin to say to you."

"Then say it, and get away—confound you!" returned the Ogre.

"It am jes dis, and no more," replied the Tiger— "dat, go whar you may, I hab an eye on you, Massa Ogre, until de day when de noble Broad Arrow Jack gib you what you deserbe! So look out—de Tiger neber leab you!"

And, as a parting gift, the Tiger hurled a lump of moss and clay at the Ogre, and bounded off into the wood with a shriek of laughter, which made the listener shudder in spite of himself.

"I remember finding that boy," he muttered, "and as I looked into his childish face something seemed to say to me, 'Strangle him;' but I did not—I wanted something to torture. The boy was right—why should I lie to myself?—I wanted something to kick and cuff when the humour took me; and a pretty monster I have built up for myself! But I'll away—far away—give up all thoughts of the wealth in that palace—at least for a while, and hide—hide where even that little devil, the Tiger, shall not find me!"

Bent upon escaping, he went away from Black Rock, and travelled all day. At night he was suddenly challenged by two men, who called upon him to stand. He turned and fled, pursued for awhile, but again escaping.

Another track he tried, and ere long was challenged again. Once more he made his escape, and went another way; but, turn where he would, the result was the same. Weary and worn, he lay down on the second night, convinced he was surrounded, and without a present chance of escape.

"I must back to the palace," he thought, "there are hiding places there, and food—and drink. If Jeb Jaundice is only dead —— then I will pluck up a heart, and stand a siege alone."

With no other refreshment than a few roots and a drink of water he crept back to Black Rock, to the spot from whence he had emerged, and cautiously crept in. Then, upon the broken stones, he lay down his head, utterly worn out, and slept.

When he awoke, the sun was shining through the opening above, and he could hear the birds singing, rejoicing over the advent of another day. It brought little joy to him—weary still, sick at heart, half-famished, he looked at the patch of blue above, and wished that he had never known creation.

"But all is still," he said, "and I'll back to the store-room, if I can find my way. Oh! for an hour's light down here."

He had often cursed the light, as he had cursed everything except himself, and now that he most needed it there was none at hand. Slowly he crept up the passage with his hand upon the wall, trying to map out in his mind the road he had taken when he had fled from Jeb Jaundice.

He might as well have tried to map out a place

he had never seen. All he could do was to trust to chance, and, with hope and doubt alternately ruling him, he slowly moved on.

Through passage after passage until he feared he must have wandered quite away from the great building above; but he kept on. He might as well die there like a rat in a hole, as give himself up to his enemies. In either case it was but death, and dying down there he would at least disappoint Broad Arrow Jack of the pleasure of killing him, or seeing him die.

So he argued with himself, and passed on. Suddenly his foot struck something metallic, which rolled away from his touch.

He knew the sound. It was the lantern he had brought with him down there, or another like it. What if he could find it? A knife—a flint, and a piece of rag would give him a light, and there might be oil in it for half an hour.

Groping about he found it, and hugging it to his heart, crept back again to the opening which led outside. Then he sought for a flint, but failed to find one. Again despair ruled him.

Another thought. Fire could be got from rotten wood, and regardless of the risk he stole out and looked about him for what he wanted. There was wood about, some of it rotten enough for anything, and with a huge piece he once more returned below .

Then with his knife he formed a hollow in it, and with a stout stick worked in it, as he had read of African women doing, putting forth all his strength until the veins in his forehead stood out like knotted cords.

A spark at last, which found a companion in the light which flashed from his eyes. Fresh strength came to him, and soon the rotten wood was a smouldering mass.

Drawing out the wick of the lamp, he placed it on the touchwood, and blew up a flame. The lamp was lighted, but the little oil in it would not burn more than a few minutes. He had no time to lose.

Holding it above his head, and with his knife in his hand, ready for use, he hurried down the dark passage, turned a corner, and stood face to face with Jeb Jaundice, with the axe raised to strike.

"Stand!" cried Jeb; " who are you?"

"The Ogre," was the reply.

"Where have you been?" said Jeb. "Why did you leave me, and what treachery have you been plotting and carrying out?"

He was wild and haggard in his looks, but no longer mad. The Ogre saw the fit was over, and was, incredible as it may seem, glad to have his old companion with him again.

"Surely, Jeb," he said, "you have forgotten what has been going on?"

"I don't know how I came here," replied Jeb, wearily; "but I seem as if I have been ill for a long time."

"You have had an attack of the D. T.," replied the Ogre; "and what could you expect after drinking enough to float a ship?"

"I am thirsty now," said Jeb.

"No doubt. But do you know where you are?"

"We were in the palace when I was taken," said Jeb.

"Yes, and are here still—in a maze of cellars. But let us be quick—I am only burning the wick of a lamp. How long have you been in your sober senses?"

"Weeks, it seems to me," replied Jeb. "I have been lying here in the darkness, not knowing what to make of it, with a dreamy feeling upon me—a sort of don't-care-whether-I-live-or-die sensation. It was your coming that roused me."

"Aye!" said the Ogre; "but come on. I will tell you of the pranks you played by-and-bye. You have led me a pretty dance. Stay a moment—I must turn up more of the wick. That's it. Steady—here we are. I know this place. Hurrah!"

CHAPTER XCII.

A MIDNIGHT SPECTRE.

THE Ogre was so excited that it seemed as if he, in his turn, had gone mad. Jeb Jaundice, weak and wretched, followed him with very doubtful looks.

"Up this way, Jeb. Quick—the lamp is going out—here's the place! Now give a cheer, if after it your throat is closed for ever. Hurrah!"

"I wish you would not shout so," said Jeb Jaundice. "Hear those echoes!"

"The echoes be—buried!" cried the Ogre. "Hold the lantern."

He was under the opening he had made in his old cell—the spot where Jeb Jaundice, when mad, had kept him at bay. Jaundice took the lantern from his hand, and he drew himself up. Then he gave Jaundice a little help, and in a few moments they were safe in the passage, where daylight came from one of the outer rooms.

"Saved!" said the Ogre. "And now, Jeb, let us have something to eat."

"No—drink first," replied Jeb Jaundice.

"Drink in a mild form for you," said the Ogre. "No spirits."

"Anything, so that it is drink!" muttered Jeb. "I am running down again, like an old clock. All my life is leaving me."

The room where the drink was stored was only a few paces away; but just beyond it was a great pile of stones from the ruins of the wall of the hall beyond.

"We are shut into this wing," said the Ogre; "but I think we have stores to stand the siege as well here as anywhere."

"What is the meaning of this ruin?" asked Jeb Jaundice.

"A little bit of mining work," replied the Ogre. "They have blown in the front and roof of the hall."

"I knew nothing of it," said Jaundice, with a bewildered look.

"No," said the Ogre; "you have been ill for several days. But don't trouble your mind about that—you are all right now."

"All right—am I?" said Jeb, with a shiver. "Then no man was ever wrong. I'm a mere shell of a man—the life has left me."

"A little drink—mild drink—now will put you right," returned the Ogre. "Come in and have some of Broad Arrow Jack's white claret. I'll warrant it is rare stuff."

Together they entered the store-room, and the Ogre went over to the bin where this particular wine was stored. Some of the bottles had been shaken a little out of their places by the explosion, but none had fallen.

"Now we will see what this boy drinks," said the Ogre, taking down a bottle. "Perhaps it has some particular power which gives him his enormous strength."

"Heaven grant it gives a little to me!" said Jaundice, as his head sank upon his breast. "I am as near dead as a living man can be."

He looked like it. No corpse was ever more livid, and his sunken eyes were covered with a film. The Ogre saw he was going, and thrust a goblet into his palsied hand.

"Hold it up," he said, "while I set the nectar free. Have you a corkscrew?"

"No," said Jaundice, feebly.

"No more have I. But here goes," said the Ogre quickly, as with a most skilful tap of his knife he broke off the neck of the bottle close to the cork.

"Drink," he said, and taking up the bottle poured out—

DIAMONDS!

A good constitution speedily pulled Jack through his illness. At the end of the second day he had left his hammock, and resumed his usual active life, feeling a little weak, but not showing it.

The men were all rejoiced, and Jack Trimmer, in a neat speech, expressed their general congratulations, and regret at the ill-success which had attended the pursuit of the Ogre.

"And the luck that do attend that darned skunk," he said, "makes my blood bile. He's got clear off and away now."

"I fear so, but not for long," replied Jack.

"And then he's murdered that poor little chap, the Tiger."

"Let us hope not. The boy is active, and may have escaped him."

The Tiger came home a few hours later, apparently none the worse for his adventure. As usual, when he had anything to report he presented himself before his chief.

Jack was sitting in his tent when the boy came in, indulging in a habit he had cultivated of late—dreaming. The Tiger stood with his eyes down, waiting to be addressed.

"Come here, boy," said Jack, in a voice as tender and as musical as a woman's—"nearer. Give me your hand. Do you know what you have done for me?"

"No, massa."

"You have saved my life at the risk of your own."

"No, massa, me only jump on de Ogre, and scratchee him face a lilly bit."

"More than that, Tiger, you saved my life. Now tell me what I can do for you."

"Nuffin, massa; kind word all I want."

"You shall have nothing else while I live. Nay more—you shall hear them every day if you will. From this hour you shall be my constant attendant."

"Who do de scouting den, massa?" asked the Tiger.

"Oh! some of the men."

The Tiger laughed, and clasped his hands together.

"Berry bad scouts they make, massa," he said. "No, I be de scout until de war am ober; den I go away to some place wif Massa Jack, whar he marry some beautiful lady, and I be de servant to bring de coffee and fan away de flies."

The nearest thing to a smile Jack now indulged in crossed his face, and with another shake of the hand, he replied—

"You shall be what you like, when what you call the war is over. What news have you? Any of the Ogre?"

"Yes, massa."

"Has he got clear away?"

"No, massa, he go dis way and got stop, den dat way and stop; den he go straight up palace way, whar I lose him quick."

"That was unlike you, Tiger."

"Yes, massa, but a lilly berry sick. No food—no drink, and de head go round, so dat me fall. Den me hab long sleep, and wake up too stupid to follow de track ob de Ogre."

"You have done your best, and nobody could do more," said Jack. "The Ogre is yet within the circle I have formed. To-morrow I will draw it closer. Lie down here and rest."

"What! in dis tent massa?"

"Yes."

"But dis place too good for de Tiger," said the boy. "Let me hab sleep just outside, on de ground."

"No, here," said Jack, "when at home. You must be with me. I am going for a stroll; rest here until I return."

Jack was very restless. He was never merry, but there were times when the sadness of his life became intensified and almost too great a burden for him to bear. When it was so he could not remain upon one spot—naught but rapid motion relieved him.

It was his custom on these occasions to walk out, choosing a rough and, if possible, a perilous road. He would ascend hills, climb crags, scale precipices, and cross dangerous streams—do anything in fact which would bring all his mental and bodily energies into play.

On this occasion he crossed the stream, and stood for a moment in front of Black Rock. The great semi-ruin looked magnificent in the moonlight, and a feeling of awe came over him as he thought of what a great past it must have known.

"Kings," he said, "must have revelled in your halls, but see how time turns things about. Ye have become a skulking hole for two rats. But be patient, thou noble pile; I'll rid thee of their loathsome presence ere two days have passed."

He had decided upon no particular path, but in a half mechanical way went straight on up the great slope beyond, scaling rocks and breaking through thorny barriers, regardless of the roughness of one and the poignant points of the other. Onward and upward he went, until he stood half-way up the hill.

Turning he looked down upon the great valley below, with its innumerable patches of bright light and deep shadow. Black Rock looked like a pretty fairy toy, and the stream a narrow band of silver. Around and above all was the solemn stillness of midnight.

"A mighty work this world," he said; "sublime when calm, awful in its grandeur, when storms spend their fury on it. A wondrous earth, holding so many secrets which man with all his learning cannot fathom—above all the great secret of life. What is life?"

He asked the question as most of us ask it, knowing the answer would not come to him. But he thought of it as we all do, standing with his eyes fixed upon the beauteous valley below, until he became conscious of something behind him.

He heard no sound, but he knew it was there. What it was he could not tell, but he was certain it was not of this world.

Who has not felt the sensation? Standing in a dimly lighted room, perhaps alone, there has come to all a feeling that although alone in the body we are not so in the spirit. But it has fallen to the lot of few to have experienced more than the sensation, the majority have seen no fleshless form, no midnight visitant from the great boundless spirit world.

But others, with a peculiar gift, have seen more than the material, let scoffers say what they may. As Jack turned with hesitation he looked upon that which he knew was not mortal.

Dim and shadowy like mist it changed from one shape to another, retaining through all some resemblance to the human form; but through it Jack could see the light of the moon upon the rocks.

"Whoever you are," he said, "if you have power I bid you speak."

As the words came forth from his lips the shadowy figure became more defined, and reminded Jack of the pictures he had seen of vampires and ghouls. There was no feature in it like any creature he knew; yet, as he gazed, his mind was drawn to the Ogre.

"Is he dead, and can this be his spirit?" thought Jack. "Shade of the grave," he cried, "speak, if thou hast the power!"

A grim smile passed over the awful feature of the shade, and it opened its lantern jaws. No sound came forth; but, raising its arm, it pointed with a long lean finger to the valley below.

Jack followed the direction of the hand, and saw far away upon the ledge of a rock two figures—coming, as it were, out of a mist. The moon shone full upon them, and ere many moments had elapsed they stood out clearly, and he saw—the Ogre and himself!

Side by side they lay in the attitude of lifeless-ness which death alone can give. The completely motionless forms had the stamp upon them which the King of Terrors puts upon his own.

"Mysterious shadow," said Jack, "is that a prophecy?"

Again the grim smile passed over the awful face, and the form, with a motion of its hand, gave an affirmative reply.

Again it pointed for him to look down.

Now a change had come. The two bodies were fleshless, and around the whitening bones stood vultures, satiated with their horrible feast. With dim eyes and drooping wings they rested, and waited for a return of their strength to carry them to other prey.

"And is that to be my fate?" asked Jack.

Once more the grim smile and the assenting motion of the hand.

"Shadow, I defy thee!" cried Jack. "There is but One who has power to read the future, and who can guide it as He wills. By what devilish art thou hast shown me this scene to-day I know not; but, be it what it may, it is but a puny power. Go! You have wasted your wandering time in vain. Back to the dark haunts where the light of heaven never shines, and brood over my defiance!"

The figure raised both its hands threateningly, but Jack stood firm.

"If such as thou hadst power over man," he said, "then hell would reign; but thou hast none, except a man give it thee. The Ogre may fulfil your prophecy: his bones may whiten—nay, *shall* whiten —on a barren rock; but I will on, in spite of thee! Should ill luck befall me, it will not be your work. Avaunt, poor spirit—back to thy skulking place, or the sun will soon be here; and that thou darest not look upon!"

The shadow came towards him, floating like a cloud, and the two long arms were stretched out as if to embrace him. He thrust at it with his sword, but it passed through the impalpable form. Then the arms closed upon him, and a deadly chill ran through his veins.

The horrible face bent down close to him, and the mouth moved. He could hear no words, but the motions of the lips were interpreted by him—

"Dost thou fear me now?"

"No," he cried, "I fear nothing—save my God!"

The arms tightened on his—he could feel them now, and the face bending yet lower down, breathed on his an icy blast, that froze the blood in his veins.

"Dost fear me now?"

"No," he said; "I can but die."

And again the shadow breathed, and darkness came upon him.

CHAPTER XCIII.
ANOTHER SORT OF GHOST.

"AWAKE!" cried Billy Brisket, as the rising sun roused him from his sleep. "Now, men, be brisk, and we shall reach Black Rock before sunset."

The men of the camp were already awake—most of them looked, indeed, as if they had been asleep all night.

As usual they fell in, and Billy bade them number themselves.

"Two short," Billy said, when this was done. "Who is it? Let me see. Ah! Where is Wobbles and Giles?"

"Giles went away last night, sir," replied one the men. "But I saw Wobbles by the camp-fire."

"Well, we cannot stop for either of them," said the ex-pedlar. "Bring up Big Ben."

The men whose duty it was to drag it first went after it, and in a few minutes returned with it—and Wobbles also, in a state which words can only faintly describe.

He looked like a prisoner just let out of the Bastile, or like a lunatic, or an idiot—in short, like anything but a man in his sober senses.

"Has anybody seen my old mother?" he asked, staring wildly about him; "she's got a little property as I saved up for her, and I'm sure she'll lavish it."

"Bother your mother!" replied Billy. "What is the matter with you?"

"Fourteen ghosts," muttered Wobbles, "dancing all round me at the same time. I've lost a peck of diamonds. It was the ghost of Giles as come first, and led me into the thick of 'em. Have anybody seen that spiteful old party, my mother? I wish somebody would knock her on the head!"

"Does anybody know what all this means?" asked Billy. "I don't understand it."

Marks stepped forward and saluted.

"I think I can explain, sir," he said, and a short whispered conference ensued.

At the end of it there was a smile upon Billy Brisket's face.

"Like all cowards," he said, "Wobbles can be very spiteful. But I thought he would have stopped short of murder. However, let him suffer for his crime. Put him on the gun, and if he won't keep still, strap him there."

Wobbles was put upon the gun, and as he would not keep still they did strap him. He made no particular objection, and with the exception of a few references to his departed parent, which were neither complimentary nor true, he said nothing, and shortly after fell asleep.

He slept until they stopped for breakfast, when he awoke in a little more collected condition, and as he asked like a sane man to be set free, they took his bonds off, and handed him some breakfast.

Brisket sat next to him, and again asked what had caused the slight derangement of intellect which he had shown a few hours before.

Wobbles hesitated before replying, but at length said it was "spasms of the 'ed," which he sometimes suffered from.

"You seem to have more than that the matter with you," rejoined Billy. "You look as if you had murdered somebody."

The eyes of Wobbles came out, and the knees of Wobbles smote each other as he staggered back two or three paces.

"If so be," he said, "as I could get people to believe me I'd pint out how the haccident came about."

"What accident?" asked Billy.

"The cannon, we will say, was here," said Wobbles, entering upon his defence, "stuck away in among a lot of bushes, and he was a-walking home, and haccidentally stuck his 'ed into it, and jammed it fast."

"He—who?" inquired Billy Brisket.

"Having got his 'ed there," pursued Wobbles, too much engrossed with the working out of his defence to heed questions, "he couldn't holler, or I should have known he was there, for it aint likely that a man of my tender feelings would have gone to blow him into a hearly grave—is it?"

"All this is Dutch to me," said Billy.

"Of course being done no man could put his head on agin," continued Wobbles. "If it could be done I'd be the first man to get up and do it. I'd even give him my head."

"Well, it isn't much use to you."

"Which it isn't, sir, but the poor fellow would be quite welcome to it, if it was a Shakesperian 'ed. However, he's gone, and there's an end of him."

"Now, look here," said Billy, with sudden sternness, "you leave off that wandering explanation, and come to the truth. What have you been doing?"

"Nothing," replied Wobbles; "Big Ben did it."

"What did Big Ben do?"

"Blowed poor unfortunate hinoffensive Giles' 'ed orf."

"And you fired Big Ben?"

"Oh! no, I let him orf in a kind of mechanical way."

"You infernal bloodthirsty scoundrel!" cried Billy, seizing him by the throat, and shaking him to and fro. "For some base purpose of your own you have killed this man. I'll take you back to the chief, and have you tried for murder. Here, bind this fellow to the gun, and guard him well."

Wobbles said nothing. Petrified by the perilous nature of his position, he allowed himself to be rebound without a word. He was as limp as a doll, and lay quite passive as Big Ben was drawn away.

He could neither think nor act, and if they had hanged him then he would have done as much as the bravest—died, and made no sign.

CHAPTER XCIV.

BROAD ARROW JACK'S WHITE WINE.

AS the Ogre tilted the bottle, and the glittering diamonds ran freely out, the blood of both the lookers-on coursed like liquid fire through their veins.

It is impossible to give even a faint idea of the feelings of those who suddenly come upon a treasure. Only those who in poverty have suddenly acquired wealth can understand or grasp the feeling.

Hunger and thirst were forgotten. The diamonds ran out, dropped upon the floor, scattered right and left; but still the Ogre poured on, until the bottle was empty.

"So this," he said, drawing a deep breath, "is the drink of this mighty chief! Jaundice, let us drink a bumper."

Jeb, who held the goblet filled, raised it to his lips, kissed the jewels, and held them at arm's length. The Ogre gathered a handful from the floor, and kissed them, too.

"The wealth of a nation," he said, "is ours. Brace up yourself, Jeb. Kings shall bow before us!"

"I," said Jeb, with a wild haggard look, "can never live to enjoy it. Oh! why am I, when the grave yawns for me, tortured with the sight of this, which would make me one of the princes of the world?"

"Pooh, man!" said the Ogre, "you are only hipped. Here, I will give you some of your favourite spirit. Drink of it."

It was brandy he gave him, and Jeb Jaundice took a deep draught. His eyes lighted up, and again he held the goblet of diamonds aloft.

"Let us drink," he said, "to the god of man—riches!"

"The despised mammon," said the Ogre, "or rather the mammon men affect to despise. The preachers of the world all say, 'Give not your hearts to gold,' and yet they seek high places and good fat livings—they love ease and comfort, which poverty cannot give. In the world they revile gold—in private they bow the knee to it. Let us drink to the ruler of the carnal world—wealth!"

Both were intoxicated by the sight before them, and they drank—not the jewels, but rich wine and fiery spirit, which raised their blood to fever heat.

Then the Ogre took down the bottles from Jack's white-wine bin, and cast them down. Each and all contained jewels, which were scattered over the floor in wild profusion. Scarce have the eyes of man looked upon such a mass of wealth gathered in one place before.

It more than intoxicated the two men into whose hands it had fallen—it drove them mad. In a frenzy, grown out of the lust of the riches, they danced among the glittering stones, trod them down, scattered them right and left, and on every side, and finally threw themselves down, and grovelled among the vast riches.

"Life—new life!" cried the Ogre.

"Let us drink to it," shouted Jaundice.

"Better eat to it now," said the more prudent Ogre.

But Jaundice would not hearken to the voice of the wisest.

"Eat!—who can eat?" he said. "Children and youngsters love solid food, but drink is the food of man. Drink—drink—let us drink! Here, what's in this?" he knocked off the neck of a bottle, and thrust his lips to the shattered glass. "Port, as I live; good red wine!"

"Not after spirits, man," said the Ogre, as he knocked the bottle from his hand. "Do you want to kill yourself?"

"Good wine shall not be wasted!" cried Jaundice, and lying down he lapped it from the floor like a dog.

It was indeed a trying time for these men. Before them lay more jewels than fifty nobles could boast of—representing wealth sufficient to buy up a country.

Gold and jewels were the only gods these men had ever recognised, and here was their god in glittering glory before them. They bowed down the body, soul, and spirit, and worshipped as few men worship in the world.

But in the midst of their abasement a noise outside attracted them. It sounded like a footfall, and immediately a terror came upon him. The ferocity of a dozen tigers about to be robbed of their young took possession of both.

It was awful to look upon their faces as they turned towards the door, ready to grapple with any man who disputed with them the possession of that treasure.

After all there is no passion like avarice. Men sell and part with anything for gold—with a pang perchance at times, but with no pain like that which would spring from parting with the gold itself.

But, whatever the sound was, it was not made by man—the door remained closed, and silence came again.

"It was a rat perhaps," said the Ogre. "Now, Jaundice, let us get a sack, and fill it with these glittering baubles. You will find one in the storeroom next door."

"No, you get it," returned Jaundice. "I am very tired."

Each man mistrusted the other, and with good reason, for, as the Ogre went out in search of the sack, Jeb Jaundice stooped down, and gathering some of the largest and brightest stones, thrust them into his pockets.

The Ogre came back with a sack, and cast it upon the floor; then, turning to Jeb, he calmly said—

"Before we begin—empty your pockets."

"My pockets," returned Jeb; "what of them?"

The Ogre laughed hoarsely.

"Am I an ass?" he said. "Do you think I do not know you? What man, with your thievish propensities, could be left alone two minutes with a sack of diamonds? No man. I know you. Empty your pockets."

"I did but jest," said Jeb, as he turned out the capital he had appropriated for private purposes, "and surely you would not think meanly of me for a joke."

"Not at all—when I understand it," rejoined the Ogre. "Now fill up, and when the sack is full I will carry it."

"Nay," returned Jeb Jaundice, "I will carry it. I am stronger than you are."

"Fill up," said the Ogre, impatiently, and let us quarrel—and, if need be, fight about it—afterwards. But why should we fight? Is there not here enough for us both?"

"Perhaps," replied Jeb Jaundice, "but division must make a difference."

"So," said the Ogre, drily, and opening the mouth of the sack, held it while Jeb Jaundice gathered the diamonds with his hands and dropped them in.

He gathered every one, and with one eye upon the holder of the sack scraped out each corner of the room.

At last all were put together, and a tremendous store of precious stones accumulated.

"Tie up the mouth," said the Ogre.

Jeb Jaundice found a piece of string, and bound it tight.

"Now hoist it on my back," said the Ogre.

"No, mine," returned Jeb Jaundice.

"What folly!" said the Ogre; "I have ten times your strength."

"So you think," returned Jeb, "but for all that I'll carry it."

"Here, a curse upon you!" rejoined the Ogre, "take it, but go not too fast—remember I am behind you."

Jeb Jaundice tossed the sack upon his shoulder, and crossed the room with a jaunty step. At the door he paused.

"I wan't a little more drink," he said. "I can't get on without it."

"May it burn him," muttered the Ogre, as he knocked the neck off another bottle. "The sooner he is ashes the better."

Jeb drank pretty freely, holding the sack tightly, and refreshed went down the narrow passage leading to the cell. It was their only way out, and turning into the place where the Ogre had been imprisoned, he threw the sack down the opening in the floor.

"We want a light," he said.

"Then go and get it," replied the Ogre.

"No, you go," said Jaundice.

"I will not trust you," returned the Ogre; "we will both go."

So they went back together, and obtained a lamp from the store-room. Prior to leaving, the Ogre carefully trimmed it, put in oil, and provided himself with a box of matches. He remembered the last visit he paid to the cells, and wisely made arrangements for an emergency such as he had before experienced.

It would have given an observer much amusement to watch these two men. Each was as suspicious of the other as he could well be, and every movement was watched. Both were armed, Jeb having procured weapons from the store-room previously spoken of, where a large assortment of rifles, pistols, and swords were kept. Jeb armed himself with a brace of pistols and a sword.

The Ogre carried the light, and together they jumped down into the passage where the sack lay. Jeb shouldered it again, and they moved on.

"You must be the guide," said Jeb, "I do not know the way."

A thought flashed across the Ogre's mind.

"Why not," he said to himself, "lead him to and fro, until the strength drink gives him is evaporated? He will then be at my mercy."

At present, Jeb Jaundice, like himself, was very much on the alert. He watched every movement of his "friend," as the Ogre watched every movement of his. Any attempt to stab or shoot down might have resulted in failure and defeat, and with such a prize as the treasure at stake it would be unwise to risk failure.

"It is a long way," said the Ogre.

"It cannot be far," replied Jeb. "You go forward—I will follow."

"Would it not be better if I went behind?" suggested the Ogre. "It would give you a better light."

"If you will have it so," muttered Jeb, angrily; "anyhow, let us get out of here."

The path of the cellars, now grown familiar to them, was speedily trodden, the Ogre leading the way with the lantern, and Jeb Jaundice close behind with his precious burden.

Each had thoughts which he dared not put in words.

"Once clear away," were the Ogre's thoughts, "and I'll get rid of him."

"Only give me a chance," thought Jeb Jaundice, "when we are free, and I'll get away from him."

They reached the opening which the explosion had made, and the Ogre signalled to his companion to stop.

"We must run no risk," he said. "If discovered now, all is lost."

"All," muttered Jeb, hugging the sack, "and such an all!"

The Ogre crept up the hills of shattered masonry, holding the lantern so as to hide the light from the outside. It was well he had used this precaution. Men were speaking outside, and one voice he distinguished—the voice he hated more than any other. Broad Arrow Jack was speaking.

"You will guard this place," he said. "Let no creature leave. I will return by-and-bye."

"Perhaps," muttered the Ogre, as he drew a pistol from his belt; "at last I think I have you, Jaundice!"

"Well."

"Go back a few paces and wait for me. I am going to put out the light."

"I won't be left in the dark," said Jaundice. "I hate it."

"But you must."

"I won't. This is mere subterfuge. You want to murder me."

"Don't be a fool," growled the Ogre; "didn't you hear that voice outside?"

"I heard no voice," said Jaundice, "and if I had, it would make no difference to me. I am not to be deceived. You are in league with Broad Arrow Jack against me."

"What a madman's idea!" said the Ogre, with a short laugh.

"Mad or not, I act upon it," replied Jaundice, obstinately; "if I go back, you go back too, and bring the light."

"I tell you," hissed the Ogre, "Broad Arrow Jack is outside!"

"I do not care."

"He is coming down."

"Let him come. But I will not be left in the dark. If you put out the light I'll shout for help. I may as well be hanged by him as killed by you."

"Go on," said the Ogre, his face swollen with passion. "Was ever man so cursed with the companionship of a fool?"

"I'll not be your companion longer if you object," said Jaundice, putting down the sack. "Come, now, how shall it be?"

"Let us be friends," said the Ogre. "This way. We'll hide in one of the cells for awhile."

They had no time to lose, and the Ogre hurried Jeb Jaundice back past the opening in the ceiling by which he had so oft descended up the other route, towards the spot where he had first escaped. On this route there were many cells, long empty, and into one of these they hied.

"Put down the light so that I can see you," said Jeb Jaundice. "No tricks. Here, close by me, and you sit further away. No tricks. I will not trust you."

The Ogre put down the lantern, and, squatting on the ground, calculated the chances of a struggle, but he could not see his way to bringing it to a successful issue. As Broad Arrow Jack and his men probably were about, the greatest caution was imperative.

"If I thought he would not be found by that boy," muttered the Ogre, as he glared at Jeb Jaundice, who sat hugging the treasure like a monkey with a sack of nuts, "I'd shut the place up, and keep him here. Two days without drink would kill him, and if he was ever so hungry he could not eat diamonds."

Here was another happy thought, and he would have carried it out, but for an intervention in the form of Broad Arrow Jack. He was alone, and it would not be safe to leave Jeb Jaundice.

They sat quietly for half an hour, Jaundice never letting go of the bag, or taking his eyes off his companion. There was a light in those orbs of his which the Ogre, with his experience, ought to have understood. He was going mad again.

"That light won't burn long," he said, suddenly.

"I know that," replied the Ogre.

"Go and get another," said Jaundice. "Get a dozen—fill the place with them. Let us have as near a thing to daylight as we can get."

"Are you mad?" asked the Ogre.

CHAPTER XCV.

TRIED AND CONVICTED BY A GHOST.

"MAD! ha—ha!" roared Jeb Jaundice; "come, I like that—mad. I, King Jaundice, ruler of the world, mad! A good question that —coming from a subject who himself has been idiotic from his birth."

"He *is* mad by heavens!" muttered the Ogre, shifting back.

"Mad!" yelled Jaundice. "Ha—ha!—ho—ho! *I*, King Jaundice, mad? A brave thought coming from an idiot. Oh! it is good, indeed."

"I must quiet him at all risk," growled the Ogre, opening his knife quietly, and holding it behind his back. "Your majesty."

"Yes," replied Jaundice.

"May I have audience with you? I bring a message from the far corner of your kingdom."

"Give it forth," said Jeb Jaundice, graciously.

The Ogre made motions with his mouth, but cunningly uttered no sound.

"I cannot hear you," said Jaundice.

"My king," returned the Ogre, "I am hoarse with travel. I cannot make myself heard. Allow me to approach nearer."

The absurdity of the assertion, in the face of the fact that he was speaking and being heard, did not strike his majesty, who gravely beckoned for his subject to advance.

The Ogre, bent upon carrying out his amiable intention, drew near with both his hands behind his back, bowing at every step. In another moment he would have settled accounts with Jeb Jaundice, but an interruption was at hand. A trap in the ceiling was raised, a lantern thrust through, and a voice exclaimed—

"Stand villains; I have you now!"

It was the voice of our hero, Broad Arrow Jack.

* * * * * *

The journey home came to a conclusion, and Billy Brisket, bringing his prisoner and Big Ben with him, entered the camp as the sun was going down.

Already a great shadow lay in the valley, and the dew was rising from the marshy parts of the ground in all sorts of fantastic shapes such as lovers of the weird and supernatural are apt to turn to fairies, hob goblins, and what not, and the glow-worm was lighting up to be ready to attract his mate when darkness came.

Wobbles, closely guarded, was in a very dejected condition. Every step brought him nearer to the gallows, which was now before his eyes; and as they passed a spot where old Joss and Fireworks were feeding, he felt it would be bliss indeed if he could get astride either, and go for a wild ride over the plains.

Thus it is with man. What is misery to him one day may be joy in another. But a week ago and he would have shuddered at the thought of riding upon either.

It did not strike him as being odd that these horses should be there. He had sent them away with Conky, Curler, and Pigeon, to what he believed to be certain death. They were to perish in the wilderness—horses and men—was the sentence he in his arrogance and hatred had passed upon them. He had now no thought for anything but his own peril and misery.

They came to the main body of the men camped on a piece of ground to the left of the palace, and here Billy Brisket asked for his chief.

He went away that afternoon, they told him, but no man could say whither. As there were times when Jack chose to come and go quietly without observation, Billy Brisket was not surprised. Wobbles was rather relieved; he had another night perhaps to live, he thought, but again he fell into the pit of error.

Billy Brisket announced an alteration in his programme. He would try Wobbles, and place the records of the trial before his chief; he would, if the prisoner was found guilty, execute him, and ask his chief afterwards if the sentence were just or not.

This he calmly told Wobbles, who had a strong sense of justice where he himself was concerned and he demurred.

"You can't do that," he said. "Suppose the chief says the sentence is wrong, how are you going to put it right?"

"That we will talk about by-and-bye," said Billy, gravely; "one thing at a time. My present purpose is to try and hang you, if possible."

"Here's a nice state of things," groaned Wobbles, as Billy Brisket proceeded to arrange the court of inquiry. "A man is to be hanged first, and declared innocent arterwards. Oh! what an awful thing it is to have a cursed obstinate old mother, scraping and hoarding money to bring her only child to the scaffold! But I can't die—I won't die," and he sank all in a heap among the half-dozen men guarding him.

A circle was formed, and Billy sat upon a mound for a throne—twelve men were sworn in to act as jury, and the prisoner was commanded to stand up before his judge.

Standing up was out of the question with Wobbles. He doubled up like a well-worn two-foot rule, and lay nose and toes together.

"Put his head up," said Brisket, "and let me see his face."

As Wobbles was turned up his eyes lighted upon Conky, Curler, and Pigeon, standing just behind the seat of the judge, in various stages of unbrotherly gloating over his misery. Then, and not until then, he remembered what he had done to them, and having been a great deal in the shadowy world lately, he put them down as ghosts.

As his eyes became fixed and a stiffness came into his hair, one of the spectators laughed, then another, and finally all up to the judge were roaring.

In the ears of Wobbles it was the laughter of demons.

"Silence!" cried Billy Brisket; "silence in the court!"

The men settled down, and all was still. The sun was gone, and over the hills the moon was rising. It was an impressive scene. Few could have looked upon it without a deep emotion of some sort.

"This trial," said Brisket, in solemn tones, "will be conducted on French principles. I will interrogate the prisoner. Wobbles, stand forth, and answer to your name."

"I'm here," replied Wobbles, faintly, "and all I've got to say is—"

"You are charged with the murder of one Giles. Are you guilty or not guilty of that crime?"

"Hinnocent," was all Wobbles could answer, and then he got into the two-foot rule attitude again.

"Prop him up," said the judge, and there was some chuckling in court, which was promptly suppressed, as it ought to have been.

"Remember, prisoner, your answers will be taken down and used against you. When did you see the missing man last?"

"Which missing man?" asked Wobbles, glaring

Conky, Curler, and Pigeon—"there's so many of 'm."

"Giles."

"I never see him in all my life," said Wobbles, and he doubled himself up again.

He was not a heavy man, but those who raised him up were black in the face, as if the task were a very severe one. They got him up again, and the trial went on.

"Call the accusing shade of Giles," said Billy Brisket.

"Call who?" shrieked Wobbles.

"The spirit of the murdered man," returned Billy; "we have subpœnaed him, and he ought to be here."

"No, no," shrieked Wobbles; "don't. I'll plead guilty."

"Too late," said Billy; "you must be tried on your first plea. Where is that blessed ghost?"

The blessed ghost, wiping its mouth as if it had been liquoring up, stood forward full in the light of the moon. It was Giles indeed, dim and shadowy in the sight of Wobbles, but inclined to be solid in the sight of others.

"Are you the shade of Giles?" asked Billy Brisket.

"No, zur," replied Giles's shade, with a puzzled look.

"What the devil are you then?" asked Billy, who was not so polite as he ought to have been to a visitant from the other world.

"I be his ghaist," was the reply.

"But is not a shade and a ghost the same thing, you noodle?"

"I bean't aware on it, zur."

"You know it now," said Billy—"look at the prisoner."

Wobbles could not stand those eyes, and but for support would have curled quite up. The ghost looked him up and down.

"You see him?"

"I do, zur."

"Do you remember seeing him when you were last on earth?"

"Last on where, zur?" asked the ghost, who had been indulging in something which had the same effect upon shades as stimulants have upon mortals.

"Where did you see him last?"

"I've had a hye on him all the day. You told me to foller on, and let him not see me."

"If I was near you," returned Billy, "I'd knock your head off your shoulders. You are not the ghost of a man—you are the ghost of an ass."

"I be as good a ghaist as ye can get," replied Giles, who, if he had been in the flesh, might have been set down as defiantly drunk.

The judge descended from his bench, took the ghost by the shoulder, turned it round, and kicked it. His leg did not go through it as Wobbles expected, and the dawn of the truth broke in upon him.

"I've been sold," he cried, and a roar of laughter followed. Billy Brisket walked away, and the men gathering near Wobbles performed a wild dance round him, while he sat on the ground and reflected on the many disadvantages of being a born fool.

CHAPTER XCVI.

A BOLD STROKE FOR LIBERTY.

THE first thought of the Ogre on seeing Broad Arrow Jack was to seize the bag of diamonds and make for the door, but Jeb Jaundice, clinging to the sack, foiled him in the attempt, by throwing his weight upon the treasure and holding it tight to his breast.

"Mine, all mine," he shrieked.

"Yield, villain!" cried Jack.

"Never, proud boy," answered the Ogre, and dashed at the door.

Jack came down recklessly, and lit upon his hands and feet. He was up in a moment and fired, but the aim, nervously rapid, was faulty, and he missed. With a shriek of derisive laughter the Ogre fled along the vaulted passages.

"If you are a man," cried Jack, "turn and face me."

But another shout of laughter was all the answer he got, and he turned to Jeb Jaundice to wreak his vengeance on him, but one glance told him that he had only a gibbering idiot to deal with, and taking up his lantern which he had dropped in his hasty fall, he went in pursuit of the Ogre.

"Yield!" he cried, as he hurried along, "come and meet me hand to hand."

He got no answer now, only in the echo of his own voice. Passage after passage he explored, and found them all empty.

"Is it ever to be thus?" he murmured; "is this villain ever to defy me?"

By-and-bye he came to some of the many dungeons beneath the palace, the doors of which he knew how to open. One after the other he threw back, and found nothing to reward him for his pains. At last he came to one which he knew had been used as a powder magazine, and held a considerable store of powder still.

The door of this place stood open.

"If he is there," he muttered, "I'll meet him if we both go to destruction."

"Stand back," replied the Ogre's voice as he entered, "or I'll blow both of us into eternity."

"Stand back!" returned Jack, scoffingly, "when you bid me! No, villain, if you have the courage to do it, there is a powder cask close by."

"I have the courage," said the Ogre, "but I have no light."

"Take this," said Jack, tossing him the lantern. "Now let me see if you are all brute, or whether you have a little of the courage of a man."

The Ogre caught the lantern, opened the door, and took out the piece of candle inside. Then he smoothed the powder in the cask—there was no lid—and thrust the candle into it. Had one spark fallen, both of them would have been blown to fragments.

"The true test of courage," said the Ogre, "is to face a slow but sure-coming death. Dare you do so?"

"Have you the courage, Ogre?"

"Yes, I have."

"Then why ask me if I have? Stand firm, man, I will not flinch."

It was a short piece of candle, and only about an inch of it remained above the powder. In a quarter of an hour at the latest all would be over, unless the candle could be safely removed.

But there was a greater risk in doing so than in putting it there, as the wick had gathered into a crown, which might fall off with the least shaking. Jack saw it must remain there.

How calm he was, so different to the Ogre, who had performed the first feat in a spirit of bravado! Now that death was apparently inevitable his courage failed him.

Brutes and monsters of his type dare not face death.

But his cunning stood by him.

He saw that Jack was absorbed in thought, the door behind him was open, and by a sudden rush there was just the chance of saving himself. In a moment he had dashed by, and was outside.

Jack awoke from his reverie and followed, but the door was closed, the iron bar outside fixed, and he was left alone in the magazine with the candle slowly but surely burning down.

* * * * * *

Outside there was a sentry pacing up and down—a tall strong fellow, full of life and strength. He was smiling as he thought of the trial of Wobbles and the misconduct of the ghost. By-and-bye three other men came up to relieve guard.

"Is all well, sentry?"

"All well."

"You have seen nothing?"

"No."

"Nor heard?"

"N——"

The word was never finished, for the earth beneath was suddenly rent up, and a great flame of fire spurted up to the sky. The four were flung high in the air, and came down blackened shapeless masses.

And with their fall the palace came trembling down. The splendid walls were rent on every side, great stones were tossed far and wide, and the mountains echoed as they thunderingly fell. Black Rock was a heap of ruins.

A scene of wild commotion and horror ensued. From all parts men came running in, and from the stables, blown down by the explosion, the horses dashed frantically away into the wood. The structure was light, or half of them at least would have been destroyed.

"What is it? Who did it?" asked fifty voices, as the Broad Arrow men, with blank faces, stared at the heap of ruins. And none could answer.

There was Billy Brisket, raging like a madman—ordering, inquiring, imploring, and questioning men who were questioning and imploring in their turn—"What was it? Who did it?" None could tell.

But by-and-bye there staggered upon the scene a man, with blackened bloody face, who tossed his arms wildly, crying—

"The chief—the chief!"

Billy Brisket sprang forward, and seized him by the arm.

"What of the chief, man?"

"Below in the vaults, where the explosion took place."

"Then heaven help us!" cried Brisket; "we have lost him."

"The Ogre," gasped the man — "he — has escaped"

"When—how?"

"As the earth was rent," replied the man, "I saw him leap up like a devil from a fiery pit, and ere I could lay a hand on him he was gone."

"He is a demon," muttered Billy. Then aloud he cried—"Men, we have no time to lose. The chief is below. We must have him out dead or alive. But what is here?"

It was one of the blackened forms of the men who had been killed by the explosion. At first Brisket thought it was the chief, but a moment's examination showed it had never been so powerful in build.

"Fall in!" he cried. "I must see who is missing."

It was soon done. Four men and the chief absent. Of the four men one lay there and the rest were speedily found.

Next began the work of excavation. Great fires were lighted to guide them at their work, and the men stripped to their waists worked liked giants. In half a dozen places openings to the vaults were soon laid bare.

Into one of these Billy Brisket plunged, bearing a torch in his hand. Ten feet down he found his way barred by fallen rubbish. He went back and sent down half a dozen men to clear a way.

Trimmer dived into another of the openings made. He came back with the news of a blockade there too. Other men were put to work and another opening tried. Rubbish again—earth and stones mixed together in confusion.

"The whole place is shattered from end to end," said Billy, in despair.

"It don't matter," said Trimmer, coolly; "he aint dead."

"You are a hopeful fellow," returned Brisket.

"I know a man that's born for a great work when I see him," replied Trimmer, "and Broad Arrow Jack is one of 'em. Listen."

They were in another of the openings, crawling on their hands and knees. Both paused, and lay perfectly still.

"I hear nothing," said Billy.

"I must have been mistaken," said Trimmer; "I thought I heard—— Ah! I did. It is the chief!"

"What ho, there!" came the voice of their leader, muffled through the pile of rubbish.

What a cry Billy Brisket gave! It was heard outside, and a score of men came tumbling down.

"The chief is here!" he said, and they began to pull away the rubbish, and toss it behind them, with a vigour passing that of common men.

CHAPTER XCVII.

THE RESCUE—THE CHASE.

IT was soon known all round that the chief was safe, and all the men gathered round the spot where his voice had been heard. But none were idle.

Some got spades and picks, and others what they could. Some dug with their swords, and others pulled up the earth with their hands, and the morning sun came down upon them still toiling as if their work had just begun.

They made a great hollow in the earth to avoid the danger of a landslip, and every half-hour or so Billy Brisket called upon them to pause from their labours, while he spoke to see if Broad Arrow Jack was still alive. Each time he got an answer, but as the hours crept on the well-known voice grew fainter and fainter.

The pile of rubbish was immense, and sometimes they came to great stones so firmly imbedded that it seemed impossible to move them; but the men had double strength that day, and every obstacle yielded to their resistless attack.

At last a small hole was made, and the hand of Jack was thrust through. Brisket seized it, and held it until they increased the opening so that it was wide enough for him to creep out of it.

"A thousand thanks, my brave men!" were his first words.

"And you," said Brisket, "are you hurt?"

"No; but I was growing weary. Impatience tried me more sorely than all else. The Ogre—what of him? Has he been seen?"

"He has escaped."

"Which way went he?"

"Up this hill."

"Then I will follow!" cried Jack.

"Nay," said Brisket, "you are worn and weary. Rest awhile, and let some of us go upon his track."

"Rest!" said Jack. "No—never, until I have the villain. Each hour I hate him more. I want no rest."

"But was he alone? Where is Jaundice?"

"I left him below, a gibbering idiot. His sins have turned his head. Whether he is dead or alive now I cannot tell."

"Dead, I should say."

"Then let him lie. He has a noble tomb in the ruins of this palace. Farewell, Brisket, I am going."

"But not alone, chief. I will go with you."

"Then come, if you will; but at once."

"Will you have no food?"

"I need none. The men can wait my return, or orders to follow. Where is Trimmer?"

"Here, chief."

"When the Tiger returns, send him on our track. He shall bring such message as I have to send."

And then with a wave of the hand he left them, leaping up the rocks as if he had never known fatigue. Brisket, not quite so active, followed, and found it very hard work, but he persevered and kept within a few yards of him.

The men watched them until a clump of trees hid

Broad-Arrow Jack.

A LIGHT FLASHED THROUGH THE TRAP IN THE CEILING AND A VOICE EXCLAIMED "STAND VILLAINS—I HAVE YOU NOW!"

NO. 15.

them from view, and then went in search of the horses, which had been scattered in every direction

Jack, in his pursuit, had an indefinite idea that he might come upon the Ogre. A long series of disappointments had made him impetuous, and at times irritable. He ought to have laid down a plan, and worked it out as he did at first, with coolness and precision.

But here he was now, worn with confinement, weak from want of food, exciting himself to the utmost, and who can wonder that even his hardy frame gave in before he got to the summit of the hill, and he was obliged to sit down to rest.

"Brisket," he said, "I fear I can go very little further. Have you anything with you to eat?"

"No, but I have a flask," said Brisket, as he came up.

"I'll not trust to drink," returned Jack, impatiently. "It is only a spur to a jaded horse, and yet give me the flask—I must on, as I feel the villain is not far away."

"You have known that instinct before."

"And it has never failed. He is here. Why, look—even now I see him. Stand, Ogre."

It was, indeed, the Ogre crawling like a serpent up the hill. As he heard his name called, he turned round and drew a pair of pistols from his belt, two weapons he had secured outside the palace during the confusion of the explosion.

He fired both, but his aim was hasty and the bullets flattened harmlessly against the rocks. Then springing forward with wondrous activity he climbed over the brow of the hill and disappeared.

For a moment Jack had his old strength again, and he was close upon his track, but it was only a flash and died away again.

"Brisket," he said, "I am worn out," and staggering forward he fell upon his face.

Brisket lifted him in his arms, and as he raised him saw his eyes were filled with tears.

They were tears of bitter disappointment. The heart of Broad Arrow Jack was almost broken.

CHAPTER XCVIII.

SKEWBALL'S PROMISE.

MAGGIE JAUNDICE was pursuing her old vocation of singer at the diamond-fields, and although her voice had lost much of its power through suffering there was quite enough of its sweetness to charm the rugged diggers still

She drew still, and drew universally; but it is doubtful if she would have remained there long but for her finding friends in Richard Skewball and his wife, who gave up their best room to her, and waited upon her as if she had been Queen of England.

"For she's a good un and a true bred un," said Richard, "and she's seen some ups and downs, I reckon; so, Sal, if you don't mind, we'll give her the company room, and make her as comfortable as we can."

The "company room" was almost a state apartment as rooms went down there, for it contained three real Windsor chairs, a table, and a couch, carefully concealed by a screen, which Richard Skewball made with his own hand, and pasted all over with lovely pictures cut out of the illustrated papers which occasionally fell into his hands.

"It makes the place look so private," said Richard.

The attentions of Mr. Richard Skewball did not stop here. Every night he went to the music-hall and escorted Maggie home, and Sal was not a bit jealous. Not that she trusted Richard any more than women generally trust their husbands, but she knew the stuff Maggie was made of, and trusted her

"A woman with lines of sorrow like them in her face," she said, "doesn't want any nonsense from any man."

And she was right. Women are seldom if ever mistaken in these matters.

Maggie was quiet. When not at the music-hall she sat quietly at home sewing, occasionally having the society of Sal, who had a tongue quite equal to one of the old watchmen's rattles worked by steam power. She listened, but said little. What Maggie could have talked about lay in her breast deep down, and it was better there.

One night Mr. Skewball went to fetch her home, and as it was raining he gallantly took with him some wraps and an umbrella, which was the pride and envy of the diggings, having only two broken bones and two or three holes in it, which only the proudest would have noticed. This was Sal's property, and only brought out on state occasions. Seeing Maggie home was a state affair.

"The rain's come uncommon soon," said Richard, as they walked through the mire. "I hope it's only a storm."

"I think it is nothing more. I thought I heard thunder an hour ago."

"There was just a bit down west. Now, ma-am, here's a tremenjous puddle, and you must let me lift you over."

"Very well," she said, and he lifted her over as tenderly as a child.

"You are a good man," said Maggie, looking into his face; "and your wife is a fortunate woman."

"I've tried to make her think so," said Skewball, smiling, "but she don't think so. Now, if you was married, I should say your husband was a lucky party."

"I am married," said Maggie, sadly.

"Lucky party dead?" hinted Skewball.

"Don't ask me any more," said Maggie.

"I won't," replied Skewball. "You do what you like in my house and out of it, and I won't bother you in any way."

"Thank you!" said Maggie, wearily. Her spirits were heavy that night.

On reaching home Maggie declined to have any supper, and retired. Richard Skewball sought the society of his wife in their own apartment. As it was a wet night, they had no customers to speak of, and he had a long spell of almost uninterrupted domestic felicity.

In the midst of a conversation on their usual theme—their lodger—they were interrupted by the subject of it, who came in with a face graver and quieter than usual, and closed the door behind her.

"Richard Skewball," she said, "you and your wife have been good friends to me."

"Don't mention it," said Richard.

"It's hard if two honest women cannot be friends," said Sal.

"Thank you!" replied Maggie. "Now, Richard Skewball, you made me a promise to-night."

"Which I did."

"Don't interrupt her, Richard," said Sal.

"It was that, do what I might in or out of your house, you would not question or trouble me."

"That's the substance of my promise, if it aint the words," he said.

"Does your wife say the same?"

"Of course I do," said Sal, quietly. "Do you think I'm going against Richard?"

"Then I call upon you to fulfil it now," said Maggie, speaking hurriedly. "Let me keep my room to myself—do what I like in it—lock it when I am out, and bar it against you when I am at home."

"All right!" said Skewball.

"It's your own—do what you like with it," said Sal.

"If you hear voices—nay, groans, or what not—you will not heed?" pursued Maggie. "Trust me through all."

"Certainly," said Sal.

"As good as done," assented Richard.

"How shall I ever repay such friendship as this?" asked Maggie.

"Now look here," said Richard, rising to give emphasis to his words, "what I says I means, and what I means I does. You are free and welcome to that room. It's yourn—do what you like with it—pull it down if you like. We know it will be all right, if nobody interferes. Aint that right, Sal?"

"A true woman never forgets herself," replied Sal.

"Again I thank you," said Maggie, as she wiped away the tears which would come in spite of herself, and with a shake of the hand with Richard, and a kiss exchanged with Sal, she left the room.

"There's allers been a mystery about her," said Skewball. "I wonder what is up?"

"Never you mind," replied Sal; "it was not Bluebeard's wife who was curious, but the man himself, and like some men he punished the woman for his own sins."

CHAPTER XCIX.
MAGGIE'S SECRET.

WHEN Maggie reached her own apartment she closed and bolted the door, and taking up the candle burning on the table, went behind the screen and sat down on the couch, on which lay a man heavily breathing.

It was Jeb Jaundice, but so worn and torn, so marked by suffering, that few of his old associates would have recognised him. He was in the dead sleep which follows a long waking, arising from illness or great bodily exercise in active life.

Maggie held the light aloft and looked down upon him long and earnestly. The sad expression of the face might have deepened a little, but there was no other change.

"And this," she said, "is the man I worshipped—this the piece of living clay I gave up my soul to. But he was a handsome man then, and I—was a woman."

He groaned in his sleep and turned towards her. She moistened his lips with a little water and sat down again.

For hours she sat there. The house closed, Richard Skewball and his wife retired, the noisiest of noisy diggers had gone to his rest, the rain had ceased, and the stillness of space was around. Maggie never moved or closed her eyes, but sat watching her husband, and thinking dreamily and disjointedly of the present and the past.

The sleeper awoke at last with a start, and sat up on the couch.

"Where is it?" he asked; "is it safe?"

"What are you speaking of?" asked Maggie.

He turned his sunken eyes upon her and put a hand to his forehead.

"What is this, or where am I?" he asked. "Is it Maggie?"

"Yes," she replied. "You came here hours ago."

"I remember," he muttered; "they told me I should find you here."

"And you have found me," was all she said.

He lay back upon the pillow for awhile in silence. He could not look at her fairly while she had her eyes upon him, although he made two or three attempts. She saw this and looked the other way. Then he spoke.

"Maggie," he said, attempting to speak lightly, "like a bad penny."

"You have come back," she said, "like what you are."

"And what is that?"

"Would you have me tell you?"

"If you wish to do so," he said.

"No," she replied. "Why should I? You are sick and suffering, and I will tend you. When you are well again you can leave me, and go back to your old courses."

"That," he said, "I will never do."

"That," she answered, "you must do. I pray you do not renew the subject."

"Shall I tell you how I came here?" he asked.

"If you desire to do so."

"Give me something to drink first—not water."

"I have a little wine here."

"Have you nothing stronger?"

"No," she said, and mixed him some wine and water, about half and half, in a cup. She did not put it to his lips as she had done when he slept, but handed it to him, and he drank it.

"Maggie," he said, "I can only tell you half my wanderings, for I have, I think, been light-headed more than once. Indeed, I must have been so; but as much as I can remember you shall know."

He told her everything except the discovery of the diamonds; that, for his own reasons, he kept to himself.

We will take up his narrative at the point where he was left in the cellar.

"I must have been wandering about in a delirious state when the explosion took place, and how that explosion came about I cannot tell, but the shock restored me, and although I was in the dark my head was clear, and I began to grope my way along to find a path out of the ruins."

"You found it, and are here," she said. "Why tell me more?"

"I must tell you all I suffered," Jaundice said, "for then your heart may soften towards me. Oh, Maggie, if——"

"Tell me the other story, or none at all," she said.

A bitter look passed over his face, and it was nearly a minute ere he proceeded with his narrative.

"I crept here and crept there," he said, "finding all the outlets blocked by stones and rubbish. I tried every side, and found it all the same. At last I began to burrow like a mole, tearing my way upwards. See here, my fingers are covered with half-healed wounds."

"Go on," said Maggie.

"It may have been the work of days, or only hours. I don't know. All I remember is that despair gave me strength, and torture guided me to a spot where the ruins lay thinnest, and at last I crept out in the night, and turned my face hither. It has been a weary journey, an awful wandering, with hunger and thirst and suffering. But I am here at last, beside the woman I love."

"You must not let your presence be known," Maggie replied, "for there are tongues which speak very angrily of you and the Ogre."

"And what would they do if they caught me?"

"Lynch you," said Maggie.

Jeb Jaundice shuddered, and cast an apprehensive look at Maggie.

"You will not betray me," he said.

She gave him a contemptuous look, but made no reply:

"It would be so hard to die now," he said:

"Was dying ever easy to you?" she asked.

"No," he rejoined, "but it would be harder now as I am rich—rich beyond calculation. Oh! Maggie, if we can only get away from here, and over the sea we might ride and dress with the bravest of the land. Kings would admire and queens envy you."

"Are you sure this is not another stage of your delirium?" she asked.

"I swear it is true."

"Prove it," she said, "not that it would make any difference to me, but prove it."

"No, no," he said, cunningly; "I will not trust any one. I have the wealth in safe hiding, and I'll watch over it. I must go to it when I am better. Perhaps I ought to go to-night."

"Have you to go far?"

"Ha! would you try to fathom my secret?"

"I only asked because the morn will soon be here,"

she replied. "Unless you can go and return before daylight you run the risk I spoke of—being lynched."

"And what may happen in a day?" he muttered.

"A thousand things," she said. "How got you this wealth? Is it yours? Is it honestly come by?"

"Fair spoil all of it," he replied.

"What you consider to be fair spoil the world calls plunder," she said; "but sleep if you can."

He slept after awhile, but she did not. The daylight appeared—she put out the candle, and quietly arranged the room. The bustle of life about the house and outside was resumed, and through the window she could see Skewball digging in his little garden. He was there for hours, but he never once looked towards her window. Her desires were fully respected.

All that day she never left him, and at night she went to the music-hall, where she sang sweeter, so they said, than she had done for weeks. When she returned home Jeb Jaundice was away.

But not gone for good. At midnight he came back and tapped at the window. She opened it, and he crawled in, footsore and weary. He had performed a task beyond his strength; that she could see, and staggering to the couch he fell upon it, feebly muttering—

"All safe—all safe!"

"This is how he came last night," thought Maggie. "Is there really any treasure, or is he mad still? If so, ought I not to be kinder to him?"

And bending over the prostrate man she looked at his pallid face, until the hot tears rained down upon it.

CHAPTER C.

TWO MONTHS LATER.

TWO months have elapsed since the events narrated in the last few chapters, and the scene of our story shifts to an island upon the sea. Not a beautiful island such as we love to read of in books written by travellers, who have seen much and imagined more; but a rough sterile island, for the most part with ugly black rocks like huge coal clinkers scattered all over the coast, and barren sandy plains, with here and there an oasis, covering the inland.

Here the foot of man had often trod before, and here he who trod had too often found a grave. Shipwrecked seamen had been cast upon the shore only to find a more dreadful death than drowning at sea. Thither adventurous travellers had come and pitched their tents, hoping to find the red gold or glittering stone, and found nought but disappointment and death. A rugged, forbidden, awful island, cast up from the deep to show how hard and cold the earth can be when it chooses.

At high noon then, two months later, we find ourselves there, watching a ship lying at anchor and a boat approaching the land. That boat contains the first mate of the ship, four sailors, and an old acquaintance of ours—the Ogre.

The boat grates upon the hard beach, and the Ogre stands up to look about him.

"Will this be lonely enough?" asked the mate—a huge broad-shouldered fellow—with a grin all over his sunburnt face.

"It will do," replied the Ogre. "Toss out the provisions, and go."

There is very little ceremony about the men. The Ogre had paid to be brought there, and paid for the half-dozen casks of biscuits, salt meat, and a few other stores, which are cast ashore. He takes a look at the ground, and sees it is low water.

"Better roll them higher up," he says.

"No," says the mate; "we've done what we contracted for, and there's an end of it. If you object to their floating roll them up yourself."

The Ogre favours him with one of his pet curses, and the boat pushes off. There is no love between these men, I say, and those leaving the land scarce look at him. The ship is reached, the anchor hoisted, and away goes the gallant canvas-crowned vessel, leaving the Ogre to make the best of his new home. The prospect is not pleasant.

He takes a brief glance of the land, and then begins to roll up his stores. An hour is spent in this way, and then sitting down on a barrel to rest, he proceeds to look more leisurely about him. The prospect is very unpleasant.

"Anything more dismal than this," he muttered, "I never looked upon. I don't think I shall be followed here."

It was just one month before when the Ogre made his last attempt on the life of Broad Arrow Jack—an attempt which was as near success as a miss can be.

He had been pursued hotly by Jack and his men—so hotly that although he had been fortunate enough to obtain a horse, he had in his mad desire to escape ridden the poor brute to death, and while it lay upon the plain, and he was striving in vain to rouse it to life again, he saw Broad Arrow Jack and Billy Brisket approaching.

Crouching down beside the dead horse he lay there unperceived, until they were within shooting distance, then covered Jack, as he thought, and fired. But the bullet did no more than graze the smoking cap of Brisket, and the Ogre had to flee on foot.

His capture seemed as certain as anything could be, but Brisket's horse, which happened to be leading at the moment, stumbled and fell. Jack's horse went over it, and both were disabled. Night, too, was at hand, and covered the earth with her black mantle; a few minutes later and the Ogre was enabled to escape.

He hurried to the coast, and there embarked in a vessel homeward bound, asking to be put ashore on a lonely island for geographical exploration. He particularly desired for the island to be lonely, so that his labours might not be interrupted, and he was obliged by being put ashore on the most desolate island of the south.

"Lonely enough in all conscience," he muttered. "Broad Arrow Jack can never come here."

But while the thought was with him he saw over the plain a figure advancing. He knew the outline well. Tall, handsome, half-naked and determined, he recognised Broad Arrow Jack. The shadow, for it was nothing more, came up to within a few yards of him, and melted away.

"I am getting as fanciful as Jaundice was," he said, "but he and all his fancies are buried deep enough, and I ought not to be troubled. Why cannot they rest with him? Here I am where I want to be, alone—for a time at least. If a strange ship comes in a month or two, I'll leave by her. If none comes, then I must make the best of things here."

He slept that night by his stores, and on the morrow stowed them in the hollow of a rock to save them from injury by exposure. He had a good store of tobacco and spirits with him, and, as the sun was going down, he squatted on the ground to think and smoke.

"A life after my own heart," he said. "I shall soon love it."

The next day he went upon an exploring expedition, but not far. He was in a lazy humour, and lay down upon some rocks in the sun, and went to sleep. Another man would have been baked to death there, or had his liver upset for ever; he was in no way inconvenienced, and awoke in an hour or two quite refreshed.

But there was a shock in store for him.

A little way out to sea, just where the ship which had brought him anchored, was another ship at anchor too, and the instinctive feeling of self-preservation which men who live hunted lives all more or less possess prompted him to roll back over the rock, and watch the movements of the stranger with great care and caution.

Possessing capital eyesight he was not long in discovering a familiar form coming over the side—a form familiar to our readers, and once seen not likely to be mistaken. It was that of Broad Arrow Jack, and close behind him was Billy Brisket, who looked as if he and the sea had not been on very good terms with each other.

"I have seen one vision," growled the Ogre, "this may be another."

He half hoped it would prove to be so, but there was too much reality about it all. Broad Arrow Jack had arrived with Brisket, and a score of men, and the Tiger.

As the last skipped upon the shore and began to leap about in his usual way, the Ogre saw who had tracked him to the coast, and reported whither he had gone. This the Tiger had indeed done as far as informing his chief of the Ogre's going to sea. Pure good luck had given Jack the rest.

His vessel had fallen in with that which had taken the Ogre, and the last-named being in want of medicine had signalled for some. While receiving it the landing of the Ogre had been given as an interesting piece of intelligence.

A mere outline of description was sufficient to tell Jack it was the Ogre, and he set sail for the island. The ship was his own, although he had never been on board before, and it was his intention to keep her there until his task was done.

"Surely the Ogre is caged now," he said.

"Most surely," replied Billy Brisket.

Stores were sent from the ship, and Jack as usual established a camp. Rough tents were made, each man appointed to a duty, and in an hour there was a settled look upon the little canvas settlement as good as six months on the spot could have given.

The Ogre looked on with amazement. He was aghast at the failure of his flight, and saw how he in his cunning had overreached himself.

Wilfully and deliberately he had not only formed a trap, but had shut himself in it; but in all this he could not and would not see that this was inevitable.

Knaves plot nothing so successfully as their own ruin.

The camp pitched, the boat pulled off for the ship and was hoisted in. All the canvas was furled, and the usual steps taken when a ship is in harbour or going to be anchored for some time off the coast.

All this the Ogre watched from his place of concealment, and dared neither move nor stir until the sun went down.

In the darkness he fled, but could not keep in any one path. The limits of the island, which he had been told did not exceed a circle of ten miles, distracted him, and like a rat in a cage, he went up and down and here and there.

Hunger and thirst came upon him, and the latter he quenched from a spring, but hunger would not be appeased without solids, and all that he had lay near the camp of his pursuer. One of the tents was almost on the very spot.

"Perhaps on the morrow they will move and go on board," was his hope, and with it in his heart he crawled into a crevice and lay down to sleep.

He was tired and fell off into a sound repose, from which he did not awake until the next day was some hours old. Confounding his folly for sleeping so long, he was creeping out, when a voice hard bye caused him to draw it in again.

It was the voice of Wobbles, who was thinking aloud as he strutted along the beach.

"Of course," he was saying, "they must bring me, but it's all that Brisket chap's doing. He says he likes old customs, and wants a fool about him to get fun out of. Then he must have Conky, Curler, and Pigeon to. A quartette of fools he calls us, but perhaps we are not such fools as we look. I for one am not, and I shouldn't have been half such a fool as I am if I had had another mother. But there, you can't divorce your parents, and having got 'em, we must put up with 'em."

He sat down with his back close to the Ogre's hiding-place, so close that the Ogre could reach him with his hand. The Ogre debated with himself, and decided upon making use of the opportunity. Stretching out his arm, he seized poor Wobbles by the collar, and pulled him over on his back.

"Murder! What hannimal's that?" asked Wobbles.

"Silence if you wish to live," growled the Ogre. "Don't you know your old friend?"

Wobbles, in his position, got a view of the Ogre upside, but he knew him, and his heart grew cold.

"Oh, oh!" he said, and closed his eyes, "but don't be hard on me, Mr. Ogre."

"Be quiet and listen," hissed the Ogre. "I want food."

"Oh yes, sir, you was allers pretty reg'lar with that."

"Get some and bring it here, and no tricks, mind you, or I'll settle your business. Now go and get it, I give you ten minutes."

"But where am I to get it from?"

"Anywhere you like, only get it. Now be smart. Only be aware how you attempt to betray me."

"Oh! there isn't much fear of that," groaned Wobbles. "No need to do it—I'm sure to be found out. I always am."

CHAPTER CI.

A TRUST.

WOBBLES was successful in obtaining food and taking it to the Ogre unobserved; but the consciousness of his being a traitor to his chief troubled him sorely, and it was a marvel he escaped notice.

Jack kept to his tent the first day, busily writing— a thing he had never been known to do before.

Brisket looked in two or three times, but he found him absorbed in his work, and only stayed a few moments.

"What can he be doing?" thought Brisket. "If he is letter-writing it is the longest letter I ever saw."

All day he went without food, but in the evening he partook of a simple meal of fish and bread, without wine. Then he resumed his labours, and wrote throughout the night. On the following morning Brisket found him still hard at work.

"What is he doing?" asked Billy Brisket of the air, as he walked out again. "He has often said he hasn't a friend in the world, and as for writing a book of travel, such as gents allus go in for when they've been about a bit, I don't think he could do it. He's too proud to boast and brag of what he's done."

Billy was, in short, on pins and needles. His curiosity, when aroused, was as bad as that of a woman.

Fortunately for his peace of mind Jack intended to gratify it in part.

He sent for Brisket in the afternoon, and laid before him a roll of manuscript carefully tied and sealed.

"You have often asked me who and what I am," he said; "it is all written here. This is a history of me and mine, briefly given, but sufficient for you to understand who they were, and what I am."

"Thank you very much," replied Brisket. "I feel honoured by this confidence. I'll go and read it carefully through at once."

"Nay," said Jack, half smiling, "it is not written for that purpose. If I intended you to know my history now I could have given it to you in a quarter of the time it has taken to write. No, you must keep that by you, and only read it in case of my death."

"Which won't come about before mine, I hope," said Billy, fervently.

"God alone knows," returned Jack, and there was something in his tone which told he had forebodings at heart."

"So I am to keep this?" said Bill.

"Yes."

"And read to others—if—if ever you should—die."

"Why, Brisket, you seem to be quite affected at the notion of my dying."

"My lad," said the ex-pedlar, turning aside to hide a tear, "when that comes about I won't care to live. You've twined yourself about my heart, you have, and it's a shame to talk of dying. You ought to be kinder to a poor old man."

"Well, Brisket," said Jack, taking his hand, "I'll promise to live as long as I can, if only for your sake. But I tell you honestly I have no desire to die. I am not such a fool as to be really anxious to throw away the precious gift of life simply because all things do not work as I wish them."

"I am glad to hear it," said Billy, brightening up. "And now about this Ogre chap. When shall we make a move?"

"I shall send the Tiger out to-night. He will do more good than a dozen men. In three days at the outside he will scour every nook and cranny of the island. Is he about?"

"I saw him half an hour ago."

"Find him, and send him here."

The Tiger was soon found, and received his commission. He was delighted with it, for he was a born explorer, and was only too glad to find another land to conquer.

"If de Ogre on de island, massa," he said, "I'll find him."

"I am sure you will," replied Jack; and the Tiger, delighted with the confidence he inspired, went off with the speed of a greyhound.

For two days Jack did not move, and the Ogre skulked in the same hiding-place. Its very proximity to the camp was its security. Nobody ever thought of looking for him there—indeed, nobody but the Tiger was looking. All the rest were permitted to lead an idle life.

Except Wobbles, for all his energies were exercised in providing food for the Ogre, who was gifted with a tremendous appetite. As rations were served out by Brisket, who kept his eye upon the others, Wobbles had his work cut out to get what was required. All the scraps he could lay his hands on he took, and added half his own; but this was not enough.

"You must get more," said the Ogre. "I am not going to be starved by you."

"But I can't," pleaded Wobbles. "I risks my life in getting this."

"You risk it in getting so little!" returned the Ogre. "Now, mind you get me a full meal."

"I'll do it somehow," said Wobbles, desperately, "if I hangs for it!"

As if to oblige him, Billy Brisket served out a three days' biscuit on the morrow, and Conky, Curler, and Pigeon—who messed together—made a pillow of their shares, and put it into the tent where they slept with half a dozen others.

The next morning their pillow was gone, and, with the prospect of their being starved during the next week before them, they went and reported the circumstance to Brisket.

He listened attentively, and had the camp searched. Each man had his own rations, and no more.

"You must have eaten it all up in your sleep," said Brisket.

Conky, who looked as if he had not eaten anything for a month, solemnly vowed he had not touched the food. Curler said he was never vulgar enough to eat in bed, and Pigeon asserted that men who ate a sack of biscuits in the night did not feel as if they could eat the hind leg of a horse in the morning.

"Which it is my feelings now," he added, pathetically.

"Well," said Billy, "It's a mysterious affair, and I'll give you another lot. If it is a matter of theft I hope I shall find the thief. He will never steal again."

So he gave them more biscuit, and they made arrangement to watch over it by turns, but when it fell to Pigeon to watch he fell asleep, and while he slept the bag disappeared. He, however, woke before his comrades, and vowed he had not closed his eyes.

"Who took it then?" asked Conky, in despair. "Only one meal out of it, and now it's gone. Who took it? You went to sleep."

"I didn't," said Pigeon; "but I was sitting here, just by the feet of you two, and I kep my eye on the bag. All of a sudden I was in a sort of mist, and then it was gone."

"It's a pretty go," said Conky, savagely; "we shall surely be starved. Who'll report the job?"

None of the three was particularly anxious to do this, and at last they drew lots, and it fell to Pigeon to perform the ungrateful task.

He went to Brisket, who heard the story, and told him to go to Jericho.

"The fact is," he said, "you fellows are regular cormorants, and if you swallow up a week's food in a day you must go without for the rest of the time."

"But we aint touched it, sir," pleaded Pigeon.

"Bosh! Get out of my sight, and don't trouble me with that tale again."

The dismay of the other two gentleman was very great when they heard the report of Pigeon. Conky shed tears, and Curler cursed his hard fate.

"What's to be done?" said Pigeon.

"Somebody's prigged our grub," replied Conky, "and we must prig other people's."

But this plan was not successful.

Conky was discovered at the first attempt, and was most deliciously cobbed by half a dozen energetic men. Curler and Pigeon were also honoured with a small dose of the same stuff on suspicion, and hungry and sore they went to bed.

Hunger kept them awake, and reflection came to all. Knaves and villains, all their thoughts caught a suspicion of each other.

Conky was certain Curler or Pigeon was the thief, and so all round, and their long-established friendship tottered to its base.

They held out with scraps, such as the most kindly-disposed gave them, until the third day, when more biscuits were served in the evening.

Each took his share, but nothing was said about the old partnership, and each went away with his biscuit, like a dog with a bone, to hide it.

Conky ate what he wanted, and burying the rest in the shingle, marked the spot with a big white stone. Curler, with great delicacy and care, stowed his away in an old pair of boots, and Pigeon most foolishly intrusted his to Wobbles.

The thief—whoever he was—again went to work. The white stone was taken away, Curler lost his boots, and Wobbles, with tears in his eyes, vowed he had lost Pigeon's rations as well as his own.

"We shall all be dead men if this goes on," groaned Conky. "Who is it?"

"Aye!" said Wobbles, with a leaden stare, "who is it?"

Conky turned quickly upon him and read his face.

"By the old woman of Banbury Cross," he said, "you've done it!"

Wobbles did not deny it, and the enraged trio got him down and called upon him to reveal where he had hidden his ill-gotten bread.

"'Taint hidden," said Wobbles.

"Where is it, then?" demanded Conky.

"Eaten," replied Wobbles, shortly.

"Now come," said Curler, "tell the lot of it."

"All—I swear it," returned Wobbles. "I aint got a bit about me."

Conky, Curler, and Pigeon exchanged glances of astonishment. Then they looked at the spare form of Wobbles, and the question arose—

"Where has he put it?"

He was asked the question, and he answered it lightly.

"A change of hair," he said, "gives me a hawful happetite."

Wobbles was getting reckless. The web of fate around him was of such a nature that he did not care whether he lived or died.

Conky, Curler, and Pigeon took the law into their own hands, and fell upon him tooth and nail.

Wobbles, roused into a sort of mild desperation, fought feebly for a while; but he went down at last, and in five minutes they made a wreck of him.

The same good fortune which had attended the Ogre did not attend his stores. They were discovered, and appropriated by Brisket, who shrewdly guessed who they belonged to, and carried the news of the perfect certainty of the Ogre being there to his chief.

"It confirms the story, it is true," said Jack; "but I knew he was here, and here it is that he or I will conquer."

CHAPTER CII.

THE SACK OF DIAMONDS.

"JEB JAUNDICE, you will be mad if you go out to-night. It is raining hard, and the floods are out."

"I must go, Maggie; I cannot rest. I had a dreadful dream last night—I thought I was robbed of my treasure."

"Go then, if you will," she said, and threw back the wooden shutters that served for a window.

A great gust of wind rushed into the room, and extinguished the candle. The rain was falling in torrents, broad bands of lightning were flashing across the sky, and the thunder rolled heavily.

"Jeb Jaundice, you must not go to-night."

He turned upon her with a smile.

"You have ceased to love me, and yet you care for my coming and going."

"As I would care for that of a stranger. I would not send a dog out to-night."

"Do you think no more of me than of a dog?"

"Had you been half as faithful as a dog, Jeb Jaundice, you and I would have been happy."

"Am I not faithful? I love you still."

"You love me now—or think you do. But what will you sacrifice for it? Will you give up this treasure if I bid you?"

"No," he said, "for that would be madness."

"But it is not yours."

"It is mine. I hold it, and that is enough."

"Go," said Maggie, smiling bitterly. "You have neither love nor honesty in you."

"I'll not be long," he said.

She did not answer him, and he crawled out into the dismal night.

Maggie stole softly to the door of the room, and, opening it, tapped twice upon the wall outside.

Immediately a boy came tumbling out of the room opposite. It was that boy of Skewball's, young Dick, the eldest son and heir of Mr. Richard Skewball.

There was a candle in the room he left, and by its light Maggie could see his eager, wild face.

"Dick," she said, "you have always been anxious to serve me."

"Yes," he said, "I would die for you."

"Can you keep a secret?"

"If it is yours."

"I will trust you. A man has just left my room. Follow him, and see where he goes, but do not let him see you. He is ill, and limps along. You will be sure to find him."

"I'm off," said Dick, and, capless as he was, sprang through Maggie's room, and jumped out.

Maggie returned to her apartment, and sat in the darkness, listening to the thunder, and watching the vivid lightning as it sprang from the murky clouds.

Five minutes after Richard Skewball was heard calling aloud for his son, who, of course, did not answer him.

"Sal," he said, "why isn't that imp in bed?"

"He went to bed an hour ago," replied his wife. "He aint here now."

"That's a good beginning," said Skewball. "But you spoil him, Sal. He'll live to be a trouble to you yet."

"Richard Skewball," said Maggie, going out, "I have sent your boy out on an errand."

"You don't say so," said Skewball, with a puzzled expression of face.

"Yes I have, to follow a man."

"Who on airth——"

"Now, don't ask questions, but remember your promise."

"Ay," he said, "I remember it. But dashed if I don't understand now what Mrs. Bluebeard felt, and I don't wonder that she gave in."

And, as he expressed it to his wife, nearly bursting with curiosity, he went to bed.

Maggie sat far into the night, and the time passed wearily with her, for she was thinking of what her life might have been, and what it was. A line of thought sad to us all, but sad indeed to her.

Young Dick Skewball was the first to turn up. She heard a low tap on the shutter, and let him in literally sodden from head to heel with rain.

"Well," she said, "did you find him?"

"Rather," said Dick, "and never lost sight of him for five seconds, until a few minutes ago."

"And where has he been?"

"To the Chalk Pass, outside the fields, to a cave there."

"I did not know there was a cave, Dick."

"Well, it's only like a large rabbit's burrow, but a man can get in on his hands and knees. It's a deepish place, and very few would care to go down, but I've been there."

"I'll warrant you have."

"Many a time, and to-night, too. After he left, I dived in."

"And did you find anything?"

"Yes, a small sack of small stones, or something like it."

"Dick," said Maggie, suddenly, "are you very tired?"

"Not over and above, but I'd go to bed without grumbling," he replied.

"But supposing you were wanted to go back to that cave, would you go?"

"For you," he said.

"Then go, but ere you leave, get me a spade."

"A spade," said the boy surprised.

"Yes, I am going to dig up your little garden. I want to bury that sack there. You won't mind?"

"Not a bit."

"And you won't betray me?"

"Not if they roast me on a gridiron, and tear the flesh off me in strips."

"Brave boy! Now get the spade and hasten away."

He brought her what she wanted, and was off again. A little later, Jeb Jaundice, wet, miserable, and groaning, came in.

"I am almost dead," he said.

"Take off your wet things," she replied, "and lie down. I will make a fire and dry them."

"Do you never sleep?" he asked.

"Sometimes," she cried, "but at least I close my eyes. Sit down man."

He was only too glad to take off his wet garments, and get between the blankets. In a few seconds he was sound asleep.

Maggie lit the fire, hung his clothes around it, and then went out by the window, taking a candle with her. The rain had ceased, and the wind fallen, so that she could see to dig, and with incredible energy she speedily dug a hole about ten feet deep, and as wide and long as a child's grave.

Dick came back with the sack shortly after she finished it, and as he threw it down, said with a grin—

"I know what's there, mum. Anybody could tell the rattle of 'em."

"Hush, Dick!" said Maggie, alarmed. "You fancy something."

"No, I don't; but I shan't say a word, although there's enough good stuff there to put *murder* into the heart of every man in this place."

"Dick," said Maggie, "you are a sharp boy, but a good one. Help me to put in this sack. There—now we will cover it, and smooth it down."

"Leave that to me. I'll make a big mud-pie over it, and dad will then think he knows how the ground came to be muddled about. Besides, I like to make mud-pies."

"I wonder if I can trust him?" thought Maggie, as she watched the boy filling in.

The next moment he looked up, and, although the light was feeble, saw her face.

"If you doubt me," he said, "I'll knock my brains out against a wall, and then you'll know I can't betray you."

"Dick," she said, "forgive me," and stooping down, she kissed him on the cheek.

His eyes flashed with pleasure, and taking her hand he raised it to his lips.

It was a curious action for a boy so born and bred, and Maggie wondered as she looked at him.

"I love my mother," he said, "for she is kind, but I wish she was like you—proud, and noble, and handsome. Now, I must go in."

"You have a mother who is happy—be thankful for that," said Maggie.

"Ah! you are not happy," replied Dick. "Are you married?"

"Yes."

"Is your husband alive?" asked young Dick Skewball.

"Yes."

"Have you any children?"

"I had one," said Maggie, "but—it died."

"Ah! then you may be sad. But where is your husband? Why is he not with ye?"

Maggie did not reply, and the boy's ready wit told him all.

"I understand now," he said. "That fellow I have followed to-night is your husband; but he is not a man—he is *a brute!*"

"Hush, Dick; if you speak ill of him I shall quarrel with you."

"Don't do that," said the boy, piteously; "you don't know how I love you. If I was a man I—"

"Now, Dick, you must go in. Good night!"

"Good night," said the boy, and Maggie kissed his rough cheek again. Then he went away with a light step to the rest he so much needed.

"Ever thus—ever thus," groaned Maggie. "If I could go back a score years I might be thrown in the way of that boy's true heart, but I am old—I am worn—the beauty I was proud of—God help me!—is gone, and—and I have Jeb Jaundice for a husband!"

But in the midst of her regrets the woman showed itself. She was proud that she could touch the heart of a boy. Dick loved her as a child should love, and the love he had shown her that night brought back more vividly to her the memory of the child who left her all too young, and sent her back to her room weeping.

But what was Maggie after all?

Only one of the untold thousands of women who love the semblance of a man. In her youth she looked, as they do, at the husk and forgot the kernel.

CHAPTER CIII.

JEB JAUNDICE AWAKES.

THE exposure of that night almost killed Jeb Jaundice. Racking pains and delirium followed, and had he been in the hands of a woman one degree less kind than Maggie he must have gone into the futurity which had ever been his mortal dread.

But she nursed him day and night, only leaving him when her professional engagements called her away, and then young Dick Skewball—now fully in her confidence—watched and tended him.

It was a strange sight to see that boy, with his wild eyes and coarse dress, showing all the tenderness of a woman towards Jeb Jaundice. And yet wild Dick hated him with his whole heart.

Yes, with his whole heart, for he saw in Jeb Jaundice the brute who had wrecked the goddess the boy worshipped.

But Maggie had said, "Be kind to him, Dick," and the boy was kind—for her sake.

There was great depth in young Dick. The boy had a soul, but the soul won't speak out as it would do unless it is educated, and Dick had known no education beyond the rough tutoring of the diamond-fields. That was very rough tutoring indeed.

Is it a marvel that simple people should have geniuses for their children? Perhaps you may think it is impossible that a great light can come forth from a cotton candle, but don't forget that Shakespeare's father was, as far as we know, a very ordinary rushlight, and yet his offspring will shine while this world goes tumbling through boundless space.

I do not say Dick was a Shakespeare or a Milton, or anything else in particular. I only say he had a great soul in a rough shell, and if he gets the opportunity, as I hope he will, he will make a noise in the world. Every boy may have greatness lying dormant within him, but he does not always get the chance of awakening it.

To return. Dick watched in Maggie's absence unknown to Jeb for some time. Jeb was delirious for some days, but that iron constitution of his brought him out of it at last, and one evening he awoke and found Dick by his side.

He did not know the boy, and asked him who he was. Dick replied—

"I'm Skewball's boy."

"And who the blank is Skewball?"

"He's the master of this house," replied Dick, "and if you tell him he aint he'll chuck you or any man out of the winder."

"Does he live here?" asked Jeb.

"Yes, he do," replied Dick.

"With—with—my—the woman who lives here?"

"You mean the dark-eyed, beautiful lady?"

"Well, yes, I do."

"Oh, yes," replied Dick, simply, "they live together!"

A pang such as Jeb Jaundice had never felt before shot through his heart. Always resting secure in the devotion of his wife he had never conceived the possibility of another man supplanting him.

But the boy's words seemed to point to that undesirable state of things.

"And is—is he fond of the dark-eyed woman?" he asked.

"I should think so," said Dick; "he takes her to the music-hall every night, and brings her home. He is like me—he would die for her!"

"Perhaps he will die—soon!" growled Jaundice, with an oath, and lay back glaring.

Strong jealousy was a new feeling to him, and in his weak condition it was a little hard to bear. In fact, he did not bear it, but presently sat up and asked the boy for his clothes.

"Where are you going?" asked Dick.

"Out," said Jeb, shortly.

"Then you can't have 'em," said Dick.

"But I will."

"But you won't," returned Dick. "The lady said you were not, and I've put them away where you can't get at them."

"Excellently well done," muttered Jaundice. "She always did carry out her plans cleverly. She takes good care not to be interrupted in her infamy. What time is she coming back, boy?"

"I expect her directly," said Dick. "Ah, there's father, and she is sure to be with him."

"Don't let him come here!" hissed Jaundice.

"He won't come," said Dick, "for he don't know anything about you."

Every word the boy said was only adding fuel to the flame. Jeb Jaundice was at boiling heat when Maggie entered. As soon as she came in Dick retired.

"So you've come back," said Jaundice.

"Yes," said Maggie; "you are better to-night."

"Ay, better and worse," he said.

"How better, and how worse?"

He leant over towards her, shaking his fist.

"And dare you ask that question?" he said.

"You know I dare anything," she replied, "but why should I not dare that?"

"Can I be better when I know that you have been out this night with your lover—your paramour?"

Maggie turned upon him quickly, and looked him full in the face.

"Jeb Jaundice," she said, "you are a pitiful fool!"

"I may be," he said, "but I'll not endure this."

"I will not endure you and your insolence any longer," she replied.

"Give me my clothes."

"They are here," she said, taking them from a small cupboard. "Put them on and go."

"I may not go far," he said, as he dragged on his garments. "I shall live to avenge my wrongs, so look to it!"

"Your wrongs!" she said, with a hard laugh—"your wrongs! Come, this passes the arrogance of man."

"It may be; but your infamy passes that of woman."

"You are mad," she said. "Go!"

"I have wealth," hissed Jaundice, "enough to buy the services of a hundred men. I will live to torture him and you—to wreck your lives—to persecute you—to drag you down to hell together!"

"Big words from a man for whom the grave is digging," she said.

"I will not die until I am avenged!" he replied, hoarsely. "I would kill you now but that it would spoil my sport. Oh, I'll have a good return for your falsity!"

She answered him no more, but let him rave on until he was tired; and then he crawled out by the window, and went staggering away towards the place where he had hidden his wealth.

As soon as he was gone Maggie took a pistol from the cupboard, and loaded it carefully, then sat down, awaiting his inevitable return.

He came back—as she knew he would—with foam upon his lips, and hands clenched. He bore a huge stake in his hands, and there was murder in his eyes.

She had placed the light so that it would fall upon his face, and keep her in the shadow. As he came up she called upon him to stand back.

"Another step," she said, "and I will shoot you! See here—I am armed."

"You hag," he hissed, "you have robbed as well as dishonoured me!"

"I could not dishonour that which has already dragged itself down to the lowest depths of dishonour, and I cannot rob him who has nothing of his own to lose," she replied.

"They were mine!" he shrieked—"mine—all mine!"

"What were yours?" she asked.

"The jewels—the sack of jewels!"

"Are you sure," she asked, "that you have not been dreaming? You have been lying delirious here for days, talking of strange things."

He put a hand to his forehead and staggered back.

"It could not be a dream," he said. "It was all true."

A peal of laughter rang from Maggie's lips, and in mocking tones, quite strange in her, she asked—

"And are you more than mortal—you, who have lived a life bad enough to kill a dozen men? Can you claim exemption from the phantasies of the brain—a brain you have poisoned with debauchery? Poor Jeb Jaundice—he is arrantly mad!"

"If I thought——" he began; but she interrupted him.

"Think what you like," she said; "but come here no more. And put a wide tract of land between you and this place, or you will find a rope spun for your neck, and many a hangman ready. Now begone; for I will have no more of you!"

And, drawing the shutter close, she barred it, and left him outside—bewildered.

CHAPTER CIV.

A BOY'S TEMPTATION.

THE secret which young Dick Skewball held for Maggie lay heavily upon him. A boy's idea of money is different to that of man. He thinks of shillings and sixpences as men think of sovereigns, and the great wealth which he knew lay hid a few inches under the mould of the garden —great enough to be fabulous to most people—was incalculable to him.

His father had always been rich in his eyes, for he had always money in his pocket, but now he sank to the utterly insignificant position of a poor man, and ere Dick's knowledge was six hours old he began to feel sorry for his home.

But great as he thought that wealth to be, it is just possible that even his ideas were below the mark, for such jewels as those whose light was hidden in the earth assumed on some occasions a value widely different from that of another.

A king may give, and indeed has given, the value of a country for jewels to wear in his crown; but if the heavens had rained diamonds upon him, would Crusoe, on his lonely isle, have given the handful of wheat, which provided him food for so many years, in exchange for them all? I fancy not. But to Dick and his friends this bag of glittering gems were of real value, and the boy knew it. Thus he soliloquised—they don't belong to Jaundice, and Maggie does not want them. What good will they do lying there, if, as I think, she means to let 'em remain.

Fevered and restless he walked about for two days, dwelling upon this thing. His mother thought he was ill, and proposed to give him physic; his father said he was sulky, and suggested a good thrashing to put him into a better humour; but Dick was neither sulky nor ill, and in his excited state would probably have taken either or both the suggestions indifferently; luckily he was spared them both.

At last he went to Maggie.

"I've come," he said, "to talk about what we buried in the garden."

"Dick," she replied, "better let it and all thought of it lie buried together."

"Well," returned Dick, "I'll only ask you a question or two, and then never name it again."

"You may ask," she said, "but I won't promise to answer."

"First," said Dick, "does that money belong to him?"

"Jaundice? No."

"Will you ever use it?"

"Oh, no! I have all and more than I need."

"But you have to work for what you have."

"I am content," replied Maggie.

After this Dick went across the diamond-fields into the woods, where he lay with his face among the ferns, thinking.

His thoughts ran—

"If I take it who is to know, who is to care? I shall be rich. Father and all will be rich. He won't have to keep his spirit shanty then, and have to sham fight a dozen times a day when some big blackguard comes in to bully him. No, we can go back to 'Old England,' and have a big house and servants and carriages and horses, with the best of them, and I'll go to a crack school and be made a gentleman of, instead of running about like a wild beast. It can't be a crime to take it, and by JINGO I'LL HAVE IT."

CHAPTER CV.

BROAD ARROW JACK'S STORY.

TWICE the Tiger made the circuit of the island, and found no signs of the Ogre. This was disheartening, and Jack was inclined to think he had been imposed upon by the captain of the ship who professed to have landed him there; but he knew the cunning of his foe, and would not abandon the search without another effort.

"Go again," he said to the Tiger; "and take your time. I can wait two or three days, if need be."

"Yes, sar," said the Tiger, and, tightening a narrow belt he wore, was off and away like a swallow.

An hour after he was gone a cloud arose in the west, and with marvellous rapidity spread over the sky. Shortly after the rain began to fall—first in scattered big drops, then in a pelting mass of water so heavy that one might have thought a second deluge had come upon the world.

It rained all that day, all the night, and far into the next day. The island became a quagmire. In hollow places pools and ponds were formed, and in broad fissures in the earth rivulets and streams sprang into a brief but noisy existence. When the rain ceased myriads of wild fowl came from over the sea to drink.

As it was impossible to travel while the island was in that state, even if the Tiger had returned, Jack gave the men leave to go and shoot the wild fowl, and they went, glad enough of the sport.

Wobbles and his triplet of old acquaintances were of the party, and what they did in the way of shooting we shall presently see.

For the present it will suffice for me to state that Conky and Curler both let their guns off by accident within two minutes of starting, and were duly anathematised by all around them for putting up the first flock of birds without giving any one a chance of a shot.

Billy Brisket alone remained behind, partly to act as a body guard to his chief, and partly to keep him company.

Jack had one of his gloomy fits upon him, and Brisket, knowing they were good for neither mind nor body, tried his best to dispel the shadow from the young hero's brow.

"I never saw any use in being down," he said; "and I've had good cause now and then. I once tramped a hundred miles, and never sold so much as a stay-lace. I hadn't a copper, and when I asked a brute of a fellow for a bit of bread he set his dogs at me."

"You are a brave good fellow," replied Jack, "and I feel ashamed for being downcast. But I am thinking of the past, and not the present."

"Oh," returned Billy, "the past—that in your case must have been very unlike the present."

"The past was day, the present is night," said Jack.

He was silent for a few minutes, and sat with his eyes fixed upon the swampy island before him. Billy Brisket, after a sniff of sympathy, filled his pipe and began to smoke.

"Brisket," said Jack, suddenly, "would you like to hear the story of my life?"

"Ay, I would, lad, if you would not think I was prying, and if it aint too painful for you to tell."

"As for the first I know you too well to suppose such a thing. For the second, I fancy its relation would relieve me."

"Then go on, my lad; and I'll not budge from here if it takes a month to tell."

For a few moments only Jack sat silent to collect his thoughts, and then began.

"My name," he said, "is Ashleigh. I am the last of the Ashleighs, who have held Warton Manor for five hundred years. The first who lived there was a giant, and a race of big men have followed him. It is on record that no son of our house could ever pass under a six-foot standard without stooping."

"I can believe that," said Brisket—"in fact, I shouldn't be astonished if some of 'em had to bend double."

"Hardly so much as that," said Jack, with a faint smile, "but at any rate we were all big men, and it would ill become me to boast of our deeds; yet if you will look o'er England's roll of fame, you will find the name of Ashleigh here and there."

"I don't want to look," said Billy, "I know it by instinct."

"My father was Sir Gerald Ashleigh," pursued Jack, "and he, perhaps, was the least warlike of our race. That may have been because he lived in such peaceful times, when wars at home are unknown, or may have sprung from his love of books, for he was a great student, and preferred warring with ignorance to quarreling with his fellow-men."

"He was right, unless it was dealing with varmints like the Ogre."

"True, Brisket, of him I will soon speak, and then you shall know the full measure of his iniquity. My father was an only son, and both his parents died whilst he was in his minority. He spent the greater part of his youth under the guardianship of a distant relative, and at the age of twenty-one came into a fair property. We never were a rich family, but there was enough to keep up our estate with credit.

"Ere he was twenty-two, Sir Gerald, my father, fell in love with the daughter of Lord Mordenton, and found that love ardently returned. Lord Mordenton offered no objection, and all looked fair. Three weeks prior to their union, an adjoining estate was bought by a certain Rajah Rala Singh, and that rajah was the man we call the Ogre."

Billy Brisket, who had been peacefully smoking like a man quietly interested in a story, gave a start, and dropped his pipe. It broke off close to the stem, but even that misfortune scarcely troubled him. He was so utterly taken by surprise.

"That fellow a rajah?" he said.

"So he said," replied Jack, "and repulsive as he was, society received him. He in fact became the rage, and when that is the case, the world will go mad over a gorilla. The rajah, or Ogre, as I call him, was courted on every side. Among other places he visited the house of Lord Mordenton. Then he calmly and confidently proposed love to my mother."

"What darned cheek!" muttered Brisket.

"He was a young man then, but had all the qualities we are acquainted with, and what made his profession of love particularly repulsive was his knowledge that my mother was already engaged."

"But surely she would never have married him?" said Billy.

"She would not," replied Jack, "but there are

too many women in England who will marry anything with a title, and this Ogre had one then, although it was afterwards proved to be spurious. He was rejected with calm contempt, and he apparently took his rejection as he did other things, with the utmost coolness.

"In addition to other things, he was a gambler, and it was soon noticed that luck or skill favoured him. It was generally supposed to be the latter and the sort of skill knaves use to further their base ends. However, nothing could be proved; my father and mother were married, and the Ogre rajah was invited with the rest. He came, and showed no sign of animosity in his heart. My father was polite to him, nothing more, for he never liked the man, and when he heard of his audacious proposal, hated him.

"Nothing, however, came of it. A whole year elapsed, and I was born. The Ogre still dwelt in the country, courted almost as much as ever, except by people whose purses were too short to lose money with him.

"A few of these prudent people dropped him quickly, but the rest held on, and this mock rajah, in spite of all his coarseness, held his own with the best.

"The events I am about to relate were told me in after years.

"I was too young at the time to be a witness, or understand then. In fact, the opening event occurred at my christening. On that occasion my father gave a dinner party, and the Ogre was one of the invited.

"After the dinner there was gaming, and the Ogre sat down with a young fellow from Oxford to play ecarté.

"Luck favoured the Ogre again, and he was continually marking the king. The play was high, and quite a pile of notes lay beside the winner. Gradually the greater part of the company gathered round the pair, my father among them.

"He had long had suspicions, and this night they were verified. The Ogre usually waited before picking up his cards, to see if his opponent marked the king. If he did not he raised his own, and somehow the king was generally there.

"At last the exposure came. His opponent looked over his cards, and made no sign. The Ogre raised his, and cried—

"'I mark the king!'

"'Oh, no,' said the other, 'I have it here.'

"My father fixed his eyes on the Ogre, and saw the blood flee from his face under his dark skin. He felt he had the scoundrel at last, and showed him no mercy.

"'Two kings of clubs in the same pack,' he said—'how can that be?'

"The Ogre had shown his, and could not say he had made an error. His opponent threw the one he held upon the table. There they lay, an accusing pair, from which there was no escape.

"'Gentlemen,' said my father, to the company, 'I think this mystery ought to be solved at once.'

"'Certainly,' they said.

"'Somebody has cards concealed about him,' said my father.

"The Ogre's opponent stood up, and turned his frank young face upon the company.

"'You may search me,' he said, 'I am not a cheat.'

"'There lies the evidence in your favour,' said my father, pointing to the money he had lost. 'Now, rajah, do you object to being searched?'

"'It is an insult a man of my birth cannot brook,' said the Ogre, making an effort to stand upon his dignity, but it was a failure. The detected knave and thief was cowed.

"'Of your birth,' said my father, 'we know little. We have only your word for it. So little faith have I in that that I have sent a trusty agent to inquire into your antecedents.'

"'That was kind of you,' sneered the Ogre.

"'I am hourly expecting his return,' said my father. 'Hark, you! I hear the bell. He has returned. Can you face his report?'

"The Ogre rose, and glared on those around him like a wild beast.

"'This is a plot to ruin me,' he said, hoarsely, 'but I will be avenged. This money is mine—won in fair play, and——'

"'You must leave it then,' said my father, 'what say you, gentlemen?'

"'If he objects to be searched!' they said.

"That was an ordeal the Ogre dare not undergo! One last effort he made to make a safe retreat.

CHAPTER CVI.
JACK'S STORY CONCLUDED.

"'AND this,' said the Ogre, 'is your civilisation. You get a foreigner here—you cheat at play—you rob him—you get your false witnesses to asperse him, and then you band yourselves together to hide your guilt.'

"My father rang the bell, and when the servant came, asked if a message had come for him. The servant went back to inquire, and returned with the envelope.

"'Will you face the contents?' he asked the Ogre.

"'Face that or anything you like,' was the impudent reply.

"My father broke the seal, spread out the paper and read aloud—

"'The so-called Rajah is a convicted thief, and is wanted now in Paris for forgery. The officers are on the way. He is sure to be sent to the galleys for life.'

"'You hear?' said my father.

"'Yes,' he said.

"'Then go—I have no desire to play the policeman. But get out of my grounds—there is nothing but flight to shield you from arrest.'

"He went without another word, but as he passed the door he gave my father a look that made many of the lookers-on shudder.

"'Ashleigh!' said Lord Mordenton, 'that fellow will murder you unless you drive him out of the country.'

"'I do not fear him,' replied my father, but he had good reason to know these words of warning were not to be despised."

"That Ogre seems to have flown at high game once upon a time," said Billy Brisket; "but who would have thought such a coarse brute would have been received?"

"He was not so coarse then," replied Jack, "although I believe he was coarse enough for anything. But what are ill manners in an Englishman are only eccentricity and naiveness in a foreigner, particularly if he has a dark skin, and calls himself rajah or pasha."

"How did he get off that night?"

"Clear," replied Jack, "for no steps were taken to detain him. He disappeared as if he had been a shadow. Not one of his servants knew what had happened until the following morning, when they awoke and found themselves minus their master and wages. They thought, however, of making something out of the furniture; but here again the rascal outwitted them—he had sold the whole in a lump to a Jew, who came and cleared it out ere the sun had twice risen.

"Some years elapsed without any signs of his whereabouts coming to the county, and he was almost forgotten. Cecil, my brother, was born, and, as in my case, there were in due time rejoicings at his christening. My mother was rather unwell at the time, and retired early—my father remaining up to attend to the requirements of his guests.

"I believe they were much the same people, with a few additions perhaps. I was one, being

Broad-Arrow Jack.

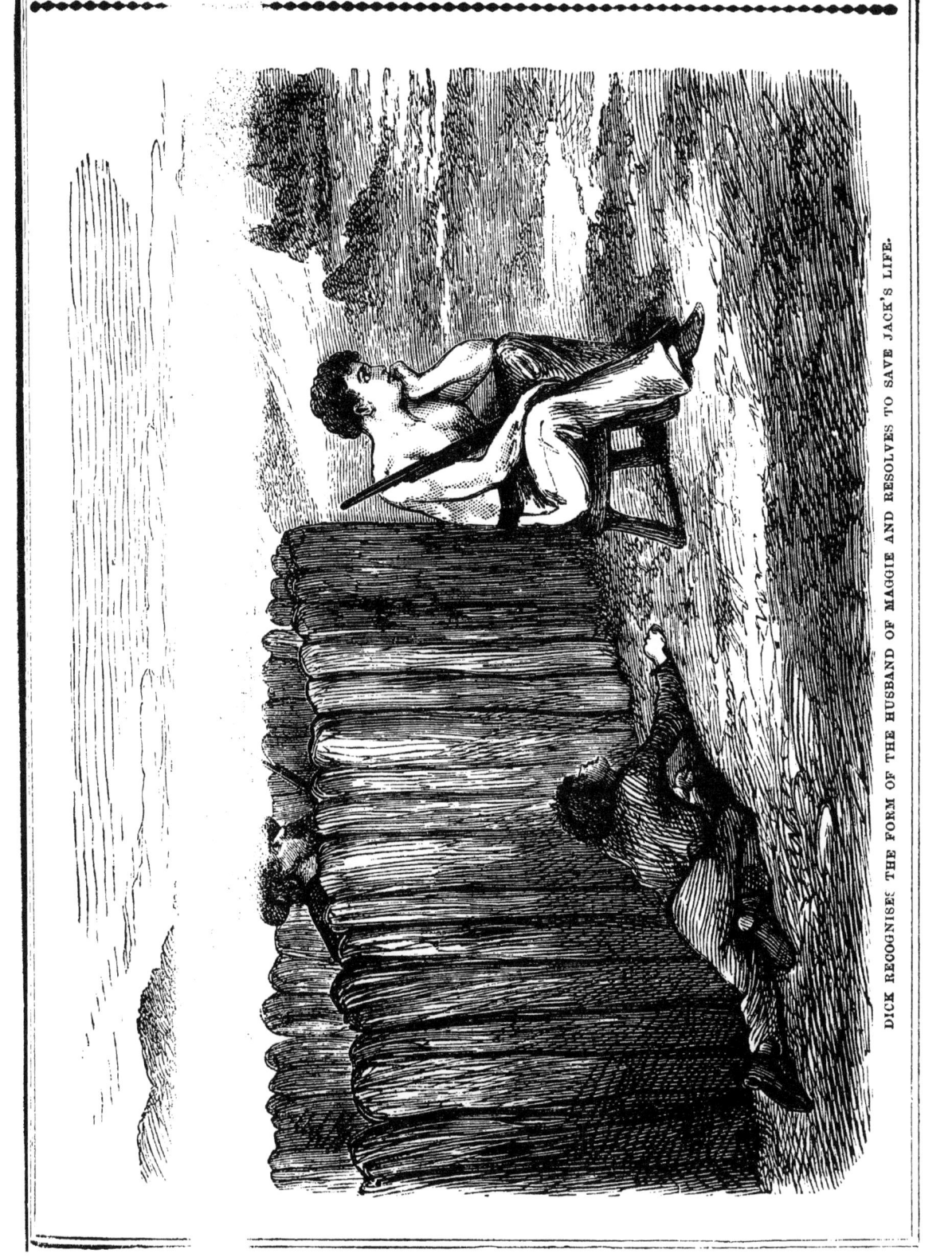

DICK RECOGNISES THE FORM OF THE HUSBAND OF MAGGIE AND RESOLVES TO SAVE JACK'S LIFE.

NO. 16.

rather a sturdy lad, and just old enough not to be an absolute nuisance to my elders. I had already learnt that it was unmanly to cry for everything I wanted, and was, I really believe, rather a good-mannered youngster——"

"And a good-looking one too," put in Billy Brisket.

"Perhaps so," said Jack; "but my looks have nothing to do with this story. I am prouder of my strength than anything else. However, to get on. Let me recall the scene of that night. Young as I was, it was imprinted on my mind with a brand of iron, and while I live it will never be effaced.

"Our drawing-room was a magnificent apartment, richly furnished, and embellished with good taste. At either end was a large fireplace, and on either side a door. One led into a corridor overlooking the hall, the other to the sleeping apartments of the house.

"I was standing with my face to the first-mentioned door, talking some childish nonsense to Lord Mordenton, when Drew, our butler, entered with more haste than a well-bred gentleman's servant usually shows. His face was deadly white, and he made straight for my father.

"'What is it, Drew?' he asked.

"'I've been into the village, sir,' began the man, 'and I've come back through the park.'

"'It appears to me you have forgotten yourself in the village,' said my father. 'I wonder at you, Drew!'

"'No, sir,' said the man, interpreting what my father meant; 'I've not been drinking—I've only been scared.'

"'By what?' asked my father.

"'By a ghost of that black devil who used to live hereabouts.'

"'I must beg of you to moderate your language here,' said my father, angrily. 'To whom do you refer?'

"'To the rajah, as they called him, sir,' replied Drew.

"'Well, what of him?'

"'I've just seen him in the park.'

"At this announcement, made in a clear voice, so that it was heard all over the room, everybody looked up, and many people drew near—I foremost.

"'You must have been mistaken,' said my father.

"'No, I was not, sir, asking your pardon,' replied Drew. 'There's a full moon and a clear sky, and, what's more, he spoke to me, and gave me something for you.'

"'Something for me! What is it?'

"'I'll give it to you outside,' said Drew, drawing back.

"'No—here, at once! There is nothing to conceal.'

"Drew still hesitated, but a peremptory command brought forth the thing sent. He drew it from his pocket, and gave it to my father—a long keen knife, stained with blood!"

Again Brisket started with amazement, and his eyes were wide open and fixed as Jack ripped up the seam of his trousers and produced from a pocket a long narrow leather case.

"That knife," he said, "is here. It was my father's until he died, and then it became mine. I hold it until the hour of vengeance."

"How came it stained when the Ogre sent it?" asked Brisket.

"You shall hear," replied Jack. "The moment my father beheld it his face became white with a new-born terror. I marked the change, and, with my arms extended towards him, uttered a bitter cry.

"He did not hear it—his thoughts were elsewhere. Turning to his guests he said, 'Remain here a moment, my friends. I have a horrible fear upon me.' Then he went out of the room, and I followed unheeded.

"He left by the door leading to the sleeping apartments, and sprang up the stairs leading to the next floor, where his own rooms here. I followed him as quickly as I could—very quickly for a child—but I was not there in time to see his entrance upon the dread scene. When I entered he was standing still, transfixed with horror.

"It was an awful scene," said Jack, his breast heaving with emotion, "for there lay my fair young mother with the life-blood oozing from her breast. The villain had stabbed her to the heart, and in her hand she still clutched a tuft of his hair.

"I was terrified, and crept up to his side, scarce knowing what to make of the scene. As I touched him he looked down, but spoke no word. I do not think he knew me.

"How long we stood together in silence I know not, but somebody came upstairs and peeped in. Then I heard a shriek, a trampling of feet, and the room was full of men and women, and the air echoing with a babel of voices.

"But all they said finally settled down into one word, and I heard it shouted in the house, and in the gardens, and across the park, as men ran forth in search of him who had done the awful deed.

"That cry was 'murder!'

"If you have never heard it uttered by men when they have just witnessed that dread crime you can have no idea of how it chills the blood and pierces the brain.

"I heard furious, terrified, horror-stricken men cry it that night, and the sound rings in my ears at this moment."

"That," said Brisket, in a low tone, "I can verily believe."

"But although they cried loud enough to be heard far and wide, although they roused the people, and filled the country with pursuers, the murderer was not taken.

"The woods were searched, and every engine put in motion, but in spite of this no trace of the Ogre, not even a footstep, could be found.

"Then the police took up another scent.

"'Whose knife is that?' they asked.

"My father examined it more closely than he had hitherto done, and recognised a blade from his armoury.

"'Ay,' said the head of the police, cunningly, 'a weapon from your armoury. What sort of servant is this Drew?'

"'Very fair,' was all my father could say, as Drew had not given entire satisfaction for some time.

"'Has he ever quarrelled with his mistress?' was the next question. 'Has she ever desired him to be discharged?'

"It could not be denied. Only the day before my mother, in the presence of Drew, had lodged a complaint against him, and urged my father to discharge him. It was only after some pleading he was allowed to remain.

"'Just so,' said the police. 'We are on the right track now. It was a clever idea, but it did not take us in.'

"Then my father understood them. Drew was suspected.

"With all his energy he insisted upon the innocence of the man, and the truth of his story. He spoke of the lock of hair in my mother's hand, a darker colour than that of Drew, but when it was sought for it could not be found. Drew was sent for, and on being questioned admitted he had seen it upon the table where it had been put by those who composed the limbs of my murdered mother, and had thrown it away, thinking it was of no value.

"'Just so,' said the inspector, with another smile, 'it was the wisest thing you could do. I charge you, John Drew, with the wilful murder of Lady Ashleigh!'

"I was present then as I was at many scenes just then, for I came and went almost unheeded; and again I have a picture burnt into my brain. It is that of Drew falling back with a face awful to look upon as this charge was made.

"'Me!' he cried—'me!—wilful murder. It's a joke of yours.'

"'You will not find it so,' returned the inspector, and put the iron cuffs upon his unresisting hands.

"'Sorry to do this, Sir Gerald,' he added, addressing my father, 'but duty is duty.'

"'Drew was an idle servant, but never a vicious one!' cried Sir Gerald. 'I will swear he is innocent!'

"'Very kind of you, sir,' replied the inspector, 'and I hope it will clear him, but I don't think it will.'

"'I a murderer!' cried Drew, as the tears ran down his cheeks. 'I, who never hurt man, woman, or child.'

"'Call the servants together, Sir Gerald,' said the inspector, 'and ask them if he has ever threatened his mistress?'

"They were called, and again poor Drew had things against him. The page-boy on the previous day heard him express a wish that his mistress was dead.

"'I can get over master,' he said, 'but she is too much for me.'

"'Pretty clear, you see,' said the inspector.

"'I'll never believe it,' said my father.

"'Thank you, Sir Gerald,' cried Drew. 'They can't hang me if you don't come against me.'

"'Sir Gerald must do his duty,' said the inspector, firmly. 'A man's kind heart must yield to the call of the law.'

"They took Drew away, and the next morning he was examined before a magistrate. Everything was dead against him, and in the eyes of most people he was a cunning guilty man.

"Of all around only my father stood out. 'Drew is not guilty,' he said; 'I will never believe it.' But he had to give evidence, to swear to the knife, and in the end Drew was committed for trial.

"Meanwhile my mother was buried, and all around went into mourning. Their grief was real, for she was beloved, and the name of Drew was execrated. 'He is guilty,' everybody said, and when my father declared his innocence they shook their heads, to imply it was very kind but foolish of him to take sides with the murderer of his wife.

"On his own account my father employed people to track the Ogre. He spent thousands, and for the first time raised a mortgage on his estate. All his efforts failed, and the day of trial for Drew approached.

"I went with my father to see him in his gloomy cell, and remember when I entered how a conviction of the man's innocence came upon me. I held out my hand and called him 'poor Drew.'

"'God bless you, young master!' he said. 'I don't care much if they hang me now. I am quite broken.'

"So he was, and at his trial his physical depression was put down as a sign of his guilt. Again, the evidence, skilfully arranged by the police, and learnedly tapped by counsel, ran clear. The jury never left the box—only whispered half a dozen words to each other—and the foreman stood up. I was there, for I had begged and cried to come, and my father humoured me. I call to mind that foreman—a white-haired yeoman, sturdy and honest, with a face full of conviction.

"'How say you, gentlemen of the jury? Is the prisoner at the bar guilty or not guilty?'

"'Guilty!'

"A deep sigh passed through the court. All but my father and I had believed in Drew's guilt, and everybody was relieved to find he would meet with his reward.

"Then he was asked if he had anything to say why the sentence of death should not be passed.

"But he only stared and muttered 'No—no—nothing to say,' and the judge put on the black cap.

"Drew listened to the sentence until it came to the awful part, 'To be hanged by the neck until you are dead, and may the Lord have mercy on your soul!' then he fell in a heap, and they carried him out senseless.

"'If that man is hanged,' said my father, rising, 'it will be murder!'

"'Hush, hush, Sir Gerald!' said the judge, and the ushers cleared the court.

"You know the usual grace given to a man lying under sentence of death. It is not too much for any man, and too little for poor Drew. My father laboured and spent money like water to help him—appealed to the Crown—called upon the press to exert its powerful sympathy—but he was looked upon as a mistaken man, blinded by a belief in his old servant, and one morning they gave Drew up to the common hangman, and he died upon the scaffold."

"Great God!" exclaimed Brisket. "And was he indeed innocent?"

"Yes," said Jack, sadly, "and what proof was needed was afterwards given. He was not naturally a brave man; but I have heard that he walked up to the fatal beam with a firm step, and before the gaping noisy crowd cried, with a loud voice, 'I am innocent!' and called upon God to witness it, and then he died."

"A sad end!" said Brisket. "But you spoke of proof just now?"

"I did, and the proof came from the Ogre himself. He wrote a mocking letter to my father when all was over, complimenting him on the clever way in which he had brought the wrong man to justice. He also coolly sent a similar epistle to the superintendent of the police and the higher officers of the Crown. The postmark was Spanish, and agents were despatched to arrest him; but all in vain.

"Of the sums spent in search of him it would ill become me to speak. Had our fortune been ten times as great all ought to have been freely spent in bringing this scoundrel to justice; but it was not all devoted to that purpose. Some of it was lost, as money often is, by the failure of a great bank, and one morning my father awoke a ruined man!

"Then we came over the sea, and all that befel us since then you already know."

"You met the Ogre at Peaceful Village?" said Brisket.

"Yes."

"And did not know him?"

"Not at first. He was changed. My father was ill, and you must remember I had never set eyes upon him. But my father knew him ere we left, and then was powerless. What could he do in his weak state? And how the scoundrel and his companions served me my shoulders bear witness to, and will do so until I have mingled my bones with the dust."

"I have often marvelled why your hatred should have been so especially great towards the Ogre," said Brisket, "but I cease to do so now. He is a greater monster than ever I dreamt him to be. You wish your story to be kept secret?"

"Yes."

"It shall be so. And now to change the subject. I wonder how they are getting on with the excavations at Black Rock. Do you think they have come upon your white claret yet?"

"I hope so. How are the funds, Brisket?"

"We have some in hand, but we shall soon be running short."

"You go, then, and see how they are getting on," said Jack. "You can go and return in a fortnight."

"And if you capture this scoundrel I shall miss the pleasure of seeing him in his confusion."

"Nay, Brisket, he will keep here. He shall live until you return."

An hour later Brisket was sailing back to the diamond-fields, on an errand which our readers know will be fruitless.

The white claret he sought was in peril of falling into bad hands, and likely to be lost to him and Broad Arrow Jack for ever.

CHAPTER CVII.

A SHOOTING PARTY.

WHEN Wobbles and his three friends found themselves armed for wild-bird shooting a feeling of pride sprang into their manly breasts, but this speedily gave way to dark doubt as they reflected upon their inexperience in the use of fire-arms and shooting in general.

Wobbles had fired a gun many times, but he had never been known to hit anything he aimed at, and the experience of Conky, Curler, and Pigeon was also limited. It was not until they came into the service of Broad Arrow Jack that they had handled fire-arms at all, and since then their efforts had been confined to firing two or three times with their eyes shut.

But they all affected to be professed sportsmen, and made strenuous efforts to conceal their ignorance from all around, and even from each other. Wobbles, with his gun at full cock, and the muzzle pointing straight at Conky's head, was quite jaunty in his walk and talk.

"Birds," he said, "is poor sport. "I'm more inclined for letting fly at helephants, tigers, and rhinosterers."

"Did you ever shoot a helephant?" asked Conky, incredulously.

"Of course I did."

"Where?"

The question was exceedingly impertinent, and Wobbles put on an air of indignation. The word of a gentleman should never be doubted, but in this case an answer was necessary.

"Oh, up there among the hills," he said, waving his hand round two-thirds of the horizon. "Me and Broad Arrow Jack used to bowl 'em over like skittles."

"When?" asked Conky.

This question was too much, and Wobbles turned round to resent it. The movement brought the barrel of his gun against Curler's head, and down went the hammer with the usual result.

"Who's that firing there?" roared Nat Green, from the front. "There's nothing to fire at here; and, see, you've put up about two hundred fowl."

"It was an accident, I think," suggested one of the men, "and that Curler chap is hurt, I believe."

Curler appeared to be suffering from the report, and indeed he was. One side of his head was singed, and one ear for the time was deafened. He fancied he had received a mortal injury, and lay upon the ground wriggling like an eel.

"Who did this?" asked Nat, angrily.

"Wobbles," replied Conky and Pigeon together, and Conky added, "He aimed at his hye. I saw him do it."

"How could I haim with the muzzle of the gun behind me?" asked Wobbles, wrathfully. "He comes and shoves his head agin it and then it went off."

"Get up," said Nat, who had been examining the victim, "you are not hurt. The next time you go to the barber's you will only have one side for him to cut, and see that you get it done half price. As for you," turning to Wobbles, "don't you load your gun again until you are told. If you do I'll make you swallow the barrel."

"Which it isn't my intention," murmured Wobbles.

Curler was got upon his feet, but his mind was very vacant for the next few minutes; suddenly, however, he came round, and asked—

"Who did it?"

On being told it was Wobbles he made preparations for retaliation by cocking his gun, and without doubt he would have favoured that brave man with its contents if Conky and Pigeon had not wrested it from him. In the act of doing this that gun went off also.

"Well, I'm blowed," cried Nat Green. "What fool is blazing away now?"

"Him was a going to shoot he." Giles explained. He had been a spectator of the scene, and bore witness like a man.

"Is anybody hurt?" asked Nat.

"Not yet," replied Wobbles, gloomily. A prophetic spirit was upon him, and he saw that something more than wild fowl would have to be carried home. How often it comes over man when the dark shadow of —— But let us not anticipate.

Conky and Pigeon were now of the quartette the only possessors of rifles in a dangerous state, and, as was quite natural, felt a little superior to their friends. They had not been such dunderheads as to fire fruitlessly, but had, in a more sportsmanlike manner, preserved their charges for the proper use.

"I suppose," said Conky, carelessly, "that when the birds get up you let fly into the thick of them?"

"What ignorance!" exclaimed Pigeon. "No—nothing of the sort. Pick out your bird, and bring him down."

Little did he at that moment think what bird he would bring down! But again let us not anticipate.

"But suppose," argued Conky, "two men pick out the same bird. Why, then ——"

"He may get blowed into bits; and a good thing too," said Wobbles.

"If I hear any more of that chattering," said Nat Green, "I'll let fly into the thick of you four, and see how you like that."

This gentle hint brought silence, and with great caution the whole party crept up to a large pool. There was a fringe of bushes on one side of it, offering good covering to advance by, and Nat had hopes of finding something to shoot at. He was not disappointed.

Everybody trod lightly, and every heart, except those beating in the bosoms of Wobbles and Curler, beat with anticipation. The two noble sportsmen named had little interest in the game; birds had lost all savour in their nostrils. They were, in fact, very much like a couple of unarmed warriors going into battle—able to look on, but deprived of the power of taking part in the fray.

Whirr, whirr! and up rose a cloud of birds.

"Look out!" roared Nat Green.

Bang—bang! went a dozen guns, and Conky and Pigeon pulled away like two maniacs, Conky with his eyes shut, and his weapon aiming at the small of Nat Green's back, Pigeon with the muzzle of his pointing at Curler's toes. Both, however, were at half-cock, and neither would go off.

About thirty birds dropped, and the men plunged into the shallow water to gather them. As they were brought out a happy idea occurred to Nat Green.

"Here," he said, to Wobbles and Curler, "you are fit for nothing else, carry the game—string the birds round their necks, boys."

"That's a nice thing," muttered Wobbles, but he knew better than to openly rebel, and in a few seconds he and Curler were garnished down to their waists like the outside of a poulterer's shop.

"I can't make out what's the matter with this gun of mine," said Pigeon, "it wouldn't go off."

"I think mine is a blessed dummy," growled Conky, "the sort of thing they gets out of a cheap-Jack. I remember once Tom Diddler buying one that was a reg'lar do. You remember Diddler, Pigeon?"

"Rather," said Pigeon; "was took for burglary at Mother Keary's."

"That's him," returned Conky, "he was allus a bold and sporting sort of chap, and he took it into his head to have a little sparrer-shooting on

Sundays. 'We'll go down the Lea-road,' he says to me, 'and when the people are gone to church we'll shoot the sparrers and bullfinches in the front gardens of the willas.' He was flush o' money just then, and that werry night we comes across a cheap-Jack as was selling aperiantly the werry things we wanted—a gun with a mahogany handle——'

"Stock you mean," put in Wobbles.

"A mahogany handle!" insisted Conky, "and a barrel that was a picter. He put it up for seven pun ten, and finally said he'd take seven bob and a tanner for it, which is a playful way them chaps has. 'That's the gun for me,' says Diddler, and goes up to the chap. ' Is it a good un?' he axes. 'The best make,' replies the cheap-Jack; 'was 'riginally made for the Duke of Sarney, but was a little too long in the barrel—a sort of misfit.' 'But it aint got a ramrod,' said Diddler. 'Don't want one,' said the cheap-Jack. 'All you've got to do is to put the powder and shot into the barrel, and there's a mechanical arrangement to ram it home.' Diddler takes it in his hand, and looks doubtful. 'It's uncommon heavy,' he says. 'All good, solid, double compressed gun-metal,' says the cheap-Jack. 'I'll bet you never bust it.' Diddler took it, and on the way home we bought some powder and shot, and going into the tap-room of the Merry Fiddlers, we tries to load it. Diddler put in some powder and then some shot, and the barrel was quite full. 'It must be rammed,' he said, and we tried to jam it down with the poker, which wasn't a bad fit; but it wouldn't go down, and just then in comes the Stepney Ripper—fighting chap, you know."

"Sold his party?" said Pigeon.

"Allus," returned Conky. " Well, he sees what we was doing, and taking the gun pours out the powder and shot, and shoves his finger into the hole. ' It don't go no further,' he says, and you should have seen Diddler's face; but it was true—that blessed gun was a dummy, and the barrel was only solid cast-iron. Diddler didn't say much, but he went about for weeks with that barrel down the leg of his trousers, bent on giving it to the cheap-Jack; but he never found him, so it was at last hung up in the bar of the Merry Fiddlers, as a kind of troffy and a warning to others, and I dare say it is there now."

By the time this painful narrative was concluded all the slaughtered birds were gathered together, and the party was ready to go on again. Pigeon, much troubled by the inactivity of his gun, brought up the rear.

"I believe I'm sold," he said to himself, as he fingered the lock, "and yet the powder went down, and this hook thing came up. Bless me, if I can understand it."

Better for him, and better for that unfortunate man in front of him with a huge frill of dead game about his neck, if he had known more about firearms. But he was ignorant, and another suffered for that ignorance.

"Let me see," said Pigeon, as the lock gave a second click, "that's just how it did afore, but it seems to have got higher up. Now, I ought to ketch hold of this, and pull it—like this."

Bang!

Pigeon staggered back, and Wobbles, the unfortunate man with the frill of birds, staggered forward. A cloud of feathers rose into the air, and the already slain bled from twenty additional wounds. Conky, who had likewise been examining his gun, dropped it in affright, and then that went off too, and lodged some score additional shot in the prostrate Wobbles and his burden.

The confusion was very great, but Nat Green might have contented himself with hard language without bestowing such vicious kicks upon the whole four sportsmen. To say the least it was wrong of him to kick Curler—who had done nothing—and Wobbles—who was perhaps on the high road to an untimely end.

"Get up, and get home," he said to Wobbles. " You never can come out and enjoy yourself like another man."

Wobbles turned upon him two eyes, in which white predominated, and in a faint voice said—

" I'm shot all over."

" I'm shot if you are hurt much," said Nat; " only peppered here and there. G, back, the lot of you."

"I can't get up," insisted Wobbles. " I'm covered with gore."

No doubt of that, but very little of it was his own. The frill of birds had mainly received the charge, and saved him. But small shot are painful things to have inside you, and Wobbles had enough to justify him in considering himself wounded.

Nat Green knew there was no danger, but reason was thrown away upon Wobbles.

" I shall not survive the night," he said.

"Carry him back," said Nat Green to Curler.

" How?" asked Curler.

"On your back, to be sure. Put him up, birds and all."

So Wobbles was put upon his back, and Curler went staggering home with his burden, the other two dejected sportsmen following behind as chief mourners.

"We were rash," said Conky. " We ought to have had a lot o' private practice afore showing off in public."

"But did you ever see sich guns," asked Pigeon, "going off in that way—doing, as you may say, just what they like with you? Them triggers are reg'lar take-ins."

They got Wobbles back, and Broad Arrow Jack, who saw them approaching, came out to know what was the matter. Wobbles, whose sufferings were not overpowering, thought proper to become sentimental in the Christy minstrel fashion.

"Put me under the willow," he said, "and let hangels waft me to my home. Tread lightly where I sleepeth. There's music in the hair, for the breezy morn is—what are you up to? Oh!"

Curler, unable to bear his burden further, had suddenly dropped him. Jack looked at the wounded hero for a moment and then turned back and re-entered his tent. He saw there was no real danger.

CHAPTER CVIII.

LOST.

BILLY BRISKET duly reached the diamond-fields, and hired a horse, on which he rode alone over to Black Rock, where a score of men, under Tom Larkin, had been employed in excavation.

Tom Larkin was a man who could be trusted, and, although his name has not often appeared in these pages he was one of the few in whom Jack wholly relied. Tom would, indeed, have died rather than betray his chief. Thus it happened he was employed in an affair of so much importance.

He and his men had laboured hard, resting little night or day, but the work was very heavy, and their progress rather slow.

When Billy arrived the store-room still lay under the ruins.

" Got a tough job," he said.

"Very," replied Tom; "but I think we shall get at the store to-night. Every bottle, I will bet, is broken."

" In that case you and I had better be alone when the place is searched."

" Why?" asked Tom.

"Because, if the men tasted the chief's white claret it might drive them mad."

" Is it so strong?"

" The most intoxicating thing on earth," replied Billy. "Only the very strongest heads can keep cool under it."

Tom looked a little puzzled, but curiosity was not his great fault, and he had no desire to know more. Late in the day he informed Billy Brisket that an entrance into the apartment in question could be easily effected.

"I am ready," said Brisket, rousing himself from a sleep he much needed, for he had ridden thither almost night and day.

The palace was a wreck, as we know, but the wing where the store-room lay was not completely shattered. The upper débris being cleared away, Tom, by the removal of some loose rubbish, made an opening into what remained of the passage in the palace.

Brisket and he entered, and found—empty bottles. The contents were, of course, gone. When Brisket crept back into the evening air his face was so deathly that some of the men, thinking he was fainting, ran forward to support him.

"My horse!" he cried—"quick! I must away at once!"

Tom Larkin, who had followed him out, gazed at his pallid features in dismay.

"You are ill, sir," he said. "The close air has affected you."

"How long am I to wait?" cried Brisket, with an impetuosity that was new to him. "My horse, I say. Are you all asleep?"

"But you are only just come," Captain Brisket, urged Tom; "you are worn and tired."

"If I were dying," cried he, "I must ride forth to-night! My horse, or a stronger one if you have it. He must get over a hundred miles ere the sun sets to-morrow."

"He's gone mad," thought Tom; "the sight of them empty bottles seemed to upset him."

They brought him a horse, and without another word he dashed in the spurs and made it leap into the stream. The most reckless of riders would not have done more, and the men stared at him aghast.

"I wonder what it is they've lost?" muttered Tom; "by the stars I have it. The money that kept us all going is gone. Lads—the chief has been robbed. Let us ride after Captain Brisket and help him to find the thief."

In a few minutes they were all in the saddle and following upon the track of Brisket; but he was already far away, riding over a rough road at a pace few sane men would care to emulate.

He rode without getting out of the saddle all that night and far into the next day, although he often stopped his horse to rest and drink, until he reached the diamond-fields, and made straight for Skewball's shanty.

That good gentleman was enjoying an afternoon pipe by the door, and hailed Brisket with his accustomed cheeriness.

"Take this horse," said Brisket, "and give him the best of food and a week's rest. He has earned it."

"Why, man, what ails you?" asked Skewball, "you've got a face as white as a summer cloud, and a brow as black as thunder."

"Broad Arrow Jack has been robbed," replied Brisket.

"Robbed of what?"

"Of a fortune that kings might be proud of."

"Then you have come to where it is to be found again," said a woman's voice, and Maggie, advancing from the shadow of the house, stood before them.

"What do you know of it?" asked Brisket and Skewball together.

"Everything," she said. "My husband, Jeb Jaundice, took it, and brought it here. I took it from him, and have it in safe keeping."

"See now," said Brisket, as his face flushed with delight, "what a woman this is! I always thought you one of the prettiest, but now I know you to be one of the noblest of your sex."

"Spare your compliments," she said, "and follow me."

"Shall I come?" asked Skewball.

"If you wish," said Brisket, and they all went into the little back garden together.

"Here," she said, "I buried it. Take that spade and turn up the earth."

Brisket thrust the spade into the earth and turned out a good barrow load. It was Maggie now who was deadly pale.

"It is not here," said Brisket.

"Dig deeper," she said.

And he dug until the garden was level with his eyes, but nothing was found.

"Deeper," cried Maggie, hoarsely.

"Nay," said Brisket, "I have come to black clay, and I will swear that has not been turned for centuries.

"Then it is gone," cried Maggie, and fell forward upon her face.

"She has been in an excited state lately," said Skewball, as he raised her, "and must have dreamt she had it."

But Brisket said nothing. He knew Maggie was not given to dreaming.

CHAPTER CIX.
ANOTHER ATTEMPT.

IT was strange that Jack, after having written and given to Brisket the story of his life, should have taken the trouble to recite it, but in this it is probable there lay a desire for others to know it too, which would not have been the case if Brisket had only received it verbally, and died, as he most likely would, without revealing it.

As for any people misunderstanding Jack in his lifetime he cared very little for it, but he was the last of a noble house, with unstained honour several centuries old. And he could not bear the thought that he or any of his house should die with a reputation otherwise than that his family had hitherto borne.

"So," he may have said to himself, "I will write this story, and give it to Brisket, to read after my death, and if he should die, others will find and read it too, and finding will believe."

It is just possible that the telling of the story may have been an impulse. But when it was told he did not regret it. After Brisket was gone he was pleased to think that, whatever might happen, he had left in the hands of his friend that which would put the story of his wrongs truthfully before the world.

He was a boy still in years—a man in suffering and sorrow—and he had, as we know, all the vigour of intellect and body to carry out a great set purpose.

What he has done we know. At the outset of his extraordinary career, when pursuing his enemies, he had accomplished with wonderous speed a number of feats that brought confusion and death to the major portion of the band of villains who had made plunder a pleasure, and murder a pastime, and now there only remained the Ogre and Jeb Jaundice. Only those two.

Well, they had given him a vast amount of trouble, and fickle fortune—that sometimes goes with the strong and deserts the weak, and will sometimes smile upon the basest, passing by the honourable and good—had stood by, and favoured the two scoundrels named.

"But surely the net is closing in," thought Jack. "Surely I have at least one of them in the toils. What can save the Ogre if he is here?"

He went to the entrance of the tent and looked out. The waters had almost subsided. The great pools, the rivulets, and cascades, created by the heavy fall of rain, had either evaporated or run down to the sea to add their mite to the great deep.

A few wild fowl, which had grown hardened to

the sound of the sportsmen's guns, yet lingered on the island, but when perched upon the trees watched with restless eyes every movement around them, and flew high when moving from place to place.

In vain had Larkin and the other men endeavoured to add to their store.

After the first day's sport not a bird could be obtained—so the men lay idle, and smoked or strolled upon the beach for nine or ten days, while the waters went down.

It is undoubtedly true that Satan finds employment for idle hands, for these men were as good fellows as ever breathed, but they felt the influence of the absence of work. Some took to gambling, and gambling, as it generally does, led to quarrelling.

Once there was bloodshed, although no fatal wound was given. Jack, who, with his own hands, separated the struggling men, saw it was necessary to be up and doing—so he looked gladly out upon the drying land, and said—

"To-morrow we will search the island."

All this time the Tiger had been away, but his master was not uneasy about him, for the boy was as hardy and active as a monkey, and his movements had doubtless been impeded by the rains and floods; but as Jack looked with joy upon the change he heard a cry upon the shore, and, turning his eyes seaward, beheld the white sails of a ship approaching.

He knew it.

It was his own vessel, so soon returned, he thought.

"Brisket brings either very good or," here he paused—"or bad tidings."

But Brisket was not there. The good ship came into the shallows, dropped her anchor, and as the canvas was being furled, swung round to the tide, and lay at rest.

Then a boat was lowered, and some half dozen men with an officer came to the shore.

It was not Jack's habit to show any emotion, but this time he had some difficulty in curbing an impetuous feeling which prompted him to rush down and ask what had brought them back.

But he sat still, and when the mate of the vessel appeared, received him quietly and courteously.

"Have you returned," he said, "without Captain Brisket?"

"We have, sir," replied the mate. "But I have a note from him."

"Where did you leave him?"

"At the diamond-fields, and I fancy, sir, he looked pale and flurried."

The mate, a young, sharp-looking fellow, involuntarily exhibited a curiosity which Jack was not at all likely to gratify.

He merely said Captain Brisket had ridden hard of late, then he opened the letter and read it.

Thus it ran:

"You must return at once. The white claret has been stolen, and passed from hand to hand until all clue is lost. I have a suspicion, but nothing more, but pray do not pause a moment. Come—you can finish your present work anon.—BRISKET."

Not a muscle of his face moved—no shadow deepened on his brow, although he read that the mightiest fortune ever held by one man had been wrested from his keeping. The mate, who had never taken his eyes from him, said to himself—

"There is nothing in this white claret after all; I was mistaken."

He was, as I have said, a sharp-looking fellow, and having been more than once employed in Broad Arrow Jack's business, his curiosity had been aroused. When aroused, he had allowed it to master his honesty and discretion, and he opened the envelope, which was merely gummed, and reclosed it again carefully.

But if the envelope told nothing his face spoke plainly, and Jack, accustomed to read men, saw the man was not trustworthy. Rising, he walked up to him and looked steadily into his eyes.

After one faint effort to return the gaze the eyes of the mate fell.

"You have read this letter," said Jack, abruptly.

The man could not and dare not deny it, but stood silent, covered with confusion.

"If I punished you as I ought," said Jack, "I should wring your wretched neck. But begone, and remember this—do not let your petty desires master you when my affairs are concerned again Send a boat ashore for me."

"I have one ready, sir," said the mate, humbly.

"Send another," exclaimed Jack; "I will not go with you."

"This," said the mate turning pale, "will be my ruin. Have mercy upon me!"

"I suppose it is scarce worth while treading upon such a worm," said Jack, contemptuously. "Go—prepare the boat—I will follow you in a few minutes."

As soon as he was gone, Jack called out Trimmer's name, and in a few seconds that cool and collected individual presented himself before his chief.

"Trimmer," he said, "I am going away from here for a time."

"All of us, sir?" asked Trimmer.

"No, I alone, and I leave you to prosecute the search for the Ogre. If you capture him, harm him not, but keep him safe until I return."

"It will be hard work," said Trimmer, "to keep hands off him."

"Nevertheless," said Jack, "you must do it. I cannot tell you how long I shall be away—a few days or weeks perhaps. You have all here in charge."

Trimmer bowed, and looked pleased with his responsibility. It was an honour he had not expected.

Jack went on board, hoping to find all ready, but just as they were going to weigh anchor it was discovered that there was no water on board. He asked how long it would take to fill the tanks, and was told it would not be finished before sunset, and, therefore, it would not be prudent to set sail until the morning.

He was very angry, and chafed at the delay, inasmuch that he would not sleep on board, but returned to his tent, where he remained writing until night-fall. Then, leaving word with Trimmer to call him at dawn, he lay down to rest.

This step proved of serious moment to him, for in the middle of the night, just as he was in his soundest sleep, a dark form crept under the canvas of the tent, and crawled towards him. It was the Ogre, bent upon another attempt to take the life of his pursuer.

Inch by inch the villain had crept past the sentries, his swarthy skin helping to hide him from their sight, and the tent was reached without his being observed. All seemed to promise well now—he was safe within the tent. Jack was soundly sleeping, and he held in his hand a knife as keen as a Spanish stiletto.

"At last!" he muttered, as he drew near—"at last!"

And Jack slept on—not dreaming of an enemy—not even when the swarthy villain stood up exulting, and raised his arm to strike.

CHAPTER CX.

WOBBLES DOES A GOOD THING.

CONKY, Curler, and Pigeon sat at supper. The hour was late, and they were partaking of it by the light of the moon; but they were not having it together. Conky sat inside the tent, Curler outside, and Pigeon was walking up and down at a short distance.

The events recently described, in which it was shown how these gentlemen lost their rations, made them suspicious of their fellow-men. The confession made by Wobbles relieved their minds to a certain extent, but did not set them at rest. Each and all vowed in their hearts that thenceforth they would trust no man.

But the trouble their rations gave them was boundless. Hard biscuit is a convenient thing for a march, if you have not much of it to carry; but when it comes to having enough for four or five days, with a pound or two of salt junk, and a couple of pints of peas for soup, the bearer of the whole is likely to find his burden somewhat troublesome.

It was Conky's idea—that of putting his food up his back—and Curler and Pigeon followed his example. All went well until Conky's little bag of peas burst, and they ran down into his boots. Curler also had a little mishap with his of a somewhat similar description; but at night they all suffered most.

It came to this—they must either sleep upon their little store or run the risk of losing it. Wobbles, reckless and defiant, was ever prowling about like a wolf in search of prey, and all he wanted was half a chance to get at and pillage their respective larders.

They were always warning him off, but he would come, and only that very evening alluded to in the opening of this chapter he had crept up behind Conky and fairly "boned" a biscuit just as he was preparing to attack it.

Wobbles, in addition to his suddenly-acquired daring, was armed with a club of immense proportions, and the gallant trio quailed at the sight of it.

"I think he's gone mad," said Conky, and the others thought so too.

And so he was mad—with terror—for the Ogre had complained the past two days of short rations, and poured into the ears of Wobbles a long list of tortures if he did not bring more. Wobbles knew the Ogre, and went about picking and stealing in a sort of frenzy.

The Ogre had said among other things—"I'll tear you to pieces, I'll gouge you, I'll skin you alive, I'll lop off your fingers and toes one by one, if you don't bring more."

"I've given you half mine," replied the terrified Wobbles, "and I'm whopped by somebody for prigging at least once a day."

"All that is not my business," said the Ogre; "I must have more."

"I'll get it," said Wobbles, and now, while his friends are partaking of their midnight meal, he is coming upon them stealthily, like a footpad, with his club behind him.

Conky saw the dark deed, so did Curler, and Pigeon had a big bump on his head to prove it. Wobbles went up behind him and gave him a whack on the head that laid him on his back, pounced upon the biscuit in his fist, and then turned him over and robbed the larder up his back.

All this Conky and Curler saw, and for a moment were unable to lend assistance in any shape or form, but when the crime in all its ghastliness made itself clear to their intelligent brains, they with one accord darted forth and cried aloud—

"Stop thief!"

It was such a cry as had never been heard there before, and many a man deep in dreams started from his sleep.

"Stop thief!"

It roused Trimmer and all those within his tent; it startled Larkin, and they came rushing out to see Wobbles flying across the camp, followed by Conky and Curler. Pigeon could not pursue, as he was occupied in ascertaining, apparently, the exact dimensions of the bump upon his head.

"Stop thief!"

Broad Arrow Jack heard it, and awoke to find the hot breath of his foe upon his cheek, and to see the cruel knife glittering in the moonlight. He sprang up, and the Ogre, dismayed by his awakening alone, escaped out of the tent for his life.

He was just in time to meet Wobbles, who came down upon him at a right angle, and was sent over upon his back with a force that knocked all the breath out of his body, and left him lying quite still, until Conky and Curler came and precipitated their manly forms over him.

Conky was pitched upon his head with such a nicety that for quite a second he stood upright working his legs, undecided which way to go. Finally he decided on settling upon his back, and did so.

Three such carcases upon the ground could not remain there without working further confusion. Trimmer, Larkin, and a dozen others got piled up in a heap, and the pursuit of Broad Arrow Jack was checked. By the time the hetacomb was dissolved the Ogre had disappeared, and all further pursuit was useless.

CHAPTER CXI.
SEEKING A CLUE.

WHEN the loss of the diamonds was known a curious sort of apathy settled upon Maggie. For three whole days she kept her room, not seeing, or apparently caring to see, anybody.

And during this time Dick Skewball was absent.

Billy Brisket remained at the stores, and he and Skewball senior, had many a long and serious conversation together.

Up to this time the latter had known nothing of the secret of Broad Arrow Jack's fortune, but now Brisket told him all, except the noble generosity of his own conduct, which, as we know, was the secret of the fortune referred to.

"Now you have told me all," said Skewball, "I must ask you to let me do one thing."

"What's that?" asked Brisket.

"To bring Sal in with us."

"I never," said Skewball, lightly scratching his chin, "do anything without her. She is a woman, but you may trust her—upon my word you may."

"I'd rather trust a woman than a man any day," said Brisket; "and as for Sal, I'd just as soon she knew all as you, old fellow."

So Sal was called in, and to her the story of the fabulous wealth discovered at Black Rock was revealed.

Well indeed might she open her eyes and hold her breath, for it seemed something beyond the marvellous to hear of all those glittering stones gathered together, and lying untouched for hundreds of years, to be at last discovered by one man, while thousands around her toiled, and dug, and sifted the earth day after day, and year after year, to realise but a tenth of this great fortune.

But when she came to learn that all had been lost, and that all had mysteriously evaporated, as if it never had been, a smile, half incredulous, spread across her face, and, laying her hand upon Brisket's shoulder, she said—

"Ah! Billy, you were always a good hand at a story; but you will never beat this."

"Upon my word it's true!" replied Brisket. "Isn't it, Skewball?"

"You say so," replied Skewball.

"But don't you believe me?" asked Brisket.

"I believe you—believe what you say!" said Skewball.

"Here, confound it!" exclaimed Billy. "Call in Maggie Jaundice, and ask her."

"Perhaps it will be just as well," returned Skewball. "Sal, fetch Maggie;" and she came willingly enough, but she had the appearance of one stunned by some sudden misfortune.

Skewball questioned her, but she declined to say more than that she had had the treasure in her possession, had buried it, and lost it.

"But who could have taken it?" asked Brisket. Maggie said nothing, but Skewball replied—

"Goodness knows, that back garden is my holding, and I never allow so much as a strange tom cat in it if I can help it. I have put a fence round it, and if any man so much as put his leg across that he runs the risk of getting a charge of shot—don't he, Sal?"

"You've peppered one man," replied Sal, "and I've never seen another near the place."

"I should think not," said Skewball, grimly. "By-the-way, Maggie, are you going to sing at the hall to-night?"

"No," she replied.

"Why not?" he asked.

"Because," said she, "I'm tired of it all. Tired of doing that which is right and just—weary of the great struggle to put down evil with good—weary of endeavouring to leaven the wrong with right—weary even of my life. I've fought the fight long, but I'll do no more."

"But what will you do?" asked Skewball, while Brisket turned suddenly round and eyed her very keenly.

"I don't know," she said, leaning back in her chair. "A longing has come upon me to enter into the great rest. I feel as if I should like to walk out from here, turn my footsteps towards a great wilderness, and there, in the midst of its vast solitude lay down the remnant of my most wretched life."

She rose from her chair and left the room. They heard her go up the passage, ascend the two steps leading to her own apartment, and until they heard the lock click as she turned it, none uttered a word. Then Brisket spoke.

"Skewball!" he said, "have you a thought in your head?"

"I don't know," replied Skewball. "I am all in a maze. I feel as if I wanted somebody to help me."

"That's nothing new," put in Sal.

"If you haven't a thought," said Brisket, "I have one."

"Then out with it," returned Skewball.

"It's this—but stay, before I give it, answer me a question."

"A dozen if you like."

"Can this Maggie Jaundice act?"

"I should think she could," said Skewball. "She doesn't always sing, you know. Sometimes at the hall she tips us a bit of the poets, and does that—what's her name in 'Hamlet?'"

"Ophelia!" suggested Brisket.

"That's the part," said Skewball, "and she carries everybody quite away. I've seen some of our roughest men blubbering like children."

"Thank you," said Brisket; "I've got a clue now. She wants to go away—doesn't she?"

"So she says," returned Skewball.

"May I keep her here?" asked Brisket.

"You may," replied Skewball, pursuing his favourite amusement of scratching his chin as he added, drily. "if you can."

"I'll try it," said Brisket. "Can you give me a hammer and a few nails?"

"What's the game now?" asked Skewball.

"I am going," said Brisket, "to nail her window up first; then I'll search her room."

"Hear that, Sal?" said Skewball, chuckling with delight. "I say, Brisket!"

"Well?"

"Make your will, old fellow, before you go there. What's your adwice, Sal?"

"I've none to give," said Sal.

Brisket and Skewball left the room together, and in a few minutes Sal heard the noise of hammering. Looking up the passage, she saw her husband holding the handle of the door of Maggie's room, while the occupant was apparently endeavouring to open it.

"Richard," said she, "have nothing to do with it."

"I must," he replied. "I am bought over. I am to have a couple of thousands if we find the treasure here."

"As you will," she said. "But two men against a woman is not fair any day."

Richard Skewball gave a short grunt, which was as far as he ever expressed dissent from an opinion expressed by his wife, and stood his ground.

In a few seconds Brisket came round, and, as he entered, said—

"I've got her hard and fast that way, Richard, and now I will come and have a parlez vous with her."

Richard made way for him, and Brisket knocked at the door.

It was thrown open by Maggie, who stood calmly confronting him with a pistol she had originally intended for Jeb Jaundice, in her hand.

"What do you want?" she asked.

"To search your room," he replied.

"You may do it," she said, "but not now."

"When?" he asked.

"When I am dead and gone," she replied. "And if you or any other man dare set your foot here before, then let him prepare his soul for another world."

And she went back, closed the door, and bolted it.

"What do you think of that?" said Richard.

"I think," replied Brisket, "she's just the woman to keep her word. But I won't be done. I'll sit here until she comes out; where she goes there I will go, until I know what's become of the treasure she's robbed us of."

"All right!" said Skewball, easily. "It's a strange start; but it's a little bit of fun, and will take the edge off the dulness of this life. But, I say, Sal, I wonder what the tarnation's become of our boy Dick?"

CHAPTER CXII.
DICK GIVES SOME TROUBLE.

WHEN a man pits himself against a woman he sets himself no common task. Maggie possessed one of those natures which may occasionallly be led, but never be driven, and when she heard the resolution fall from Brisket's lips, what little intention she had of telling them all, was scattered to the winds.

She had not revealed to them the fact that she had a partner in her secret.

Had she done so, much of the mistrust with which she was treated would never have come into existence. But she had chosen to hold the secret until she was fully assured the boy had betrayed her.

Herein lay her difficulty.

For, as we know, Dick was gone—had left his home many days. No one knew of his whereabouts.

It was not the first time this young gentleman had been absent without leave, for he was just the sort of youth who gives endless trouble to their parents, until they send their grey hairs down with sorrow to the grave.

And it was on that account, no doubt, that his mother was particularly fond of him.

Give a mother ten sons, nine of whom are all that should be—steady, sober, loving, and anxious for the peace and happiness of their home, and they shall be as nought beside the tenth, who wastes his substance in riotous living, and shows a careless and almost brutal indifference to the happiness of those who should be near and dear to him, and wilfully and deliberately destroys the harmony of that home which others have so studiously endeavoured to keep unbroken.

That it is so I know. Why it should be so I cannot tell.

Up to this time Dick's perambulations had never extended over two or three days at the outside, but now he had almost doubled his self-given furlough, and Richard Skewball, having parted with Brisket, went to prepare an instrument of punishment worthy to meet the extra offence.

He got it out of his back garden—a long slender specimen of the ground ash, which he selected with great care, cut and trimmed at handy length. He took it into the bar, and sitting down beside Sal, began to wind a nice waxed piece of twine round one end of it.

"Who's that for?" asked Sal, shortly.

"You ask that question," replied Skewball, "and you know it doesn't need an answer."

"If that's for Dick," said Sal, "you may as well put it in the fire, for I don't mean you to use it about Dick."

"Now don't you stand, Sal, between the boy and what is due. He knows I don't like him roving about with all the tag-rag-and-bob-tail of this place. He might as well be allowed the free run of any of the streets of London. And here comes the confounded young imp."

"Give me that stick," said Sal. "You've thrashed that boy a hundred times and it never did him any good; let me see what a little persuasion will do."

Richard Skewball gave up the stick, as he did everything else to his wife, and leant back with a quiet, sarcastic smile upon his rosy countenance. He believed there was more virtue in the ground-ash than in all the persuasive words ever spoken.

Dick entered by the open entrance to the bar with more audacity than most boys would have shown upon the occasion, but with a little less than he was wont to exhibit.

His eyes were wilder than usual, and his hair was matted—he had the general appearance of one who has either been hunted over a large tract of country, or who by stress of circumstances has been obliged to pass several sleepless nights.

He did not look at his father, but rather showed a desire to avoid him altogether.

Stopping short near to his mother, he said—

"I've come back."

"Oh! Dick," she answered, "why do you give us all this trouble? What have you been doing, and where have you been?"

"Ah! that's it," muttered Skewball, "and if you don't tell the truth I'll——"

He stopped short, for having given up his instrument of punishment, he was rather uncertain about what he would do.

"I've only been doing—as usual," replied Dick. "I feel sometimes that I must go and wander about the woods. I want to be a trapper or a hunter."

"In short," interrupted his father, "you want to be a man before you are a boy."

By this time Brisket had seen the boy, and hailed him from his post beside Maggie's door.

"Hollo, Dick!" he cried, "I've got a job for you if your father can spare you."

"Spare him," said Skewball. "I wish he was gone altogether."

"I can go, then," said Dick. "I can live without you now."

"No quarrelling," said Brisket. "I want you, my lad, to go down to the port."

"I've just come from there," answered the boy, "and a nice thing it is, with all ships coming in, and none going out. As soon as they came into port all the sailors skedaddled off to the diamond-fields, and they say that there won't be a chance for any one to go to England for perhaps a month to come."

"And who wants to go?" asked his father.

"That don't matter," replied Dick, and turned to Brisket again. "There's a ship," he said, "sailed in just as I came away, and I think it's the one you have often had things from England by."

"Why, that's rare news," said Brisket. "Do you know Broad Arrow Jack, my lad?"

"Who doesn't know him?" replied Dick.

"He is on board," said Brisket. "Run down and bring him here."

Away sped Dick like a greyhound.

And during his absence, which extended over the better part of an hour, Brisket kept silent at his post, and Skewball only now and then exchanged a word with his wife.

It was a quiet part of the day. All the men of the place were occupied in the race for wealth, and no outsider entered before the boy returned.

Close behind him was a tall, stalwart form, grown familiar to all that country round, striding easily along, as if no great care or anxiety lay beneath the breast so deeply bronzed by the sun.

As he entered, Skewball and his wife rose to their feet, and passing them with a graceful salute, he went to Brisket.

"Any news?" he asked. "Good or bad?"

"I have the thief here," replied Brisket."

"Who is it?"

"Maggie Jaundice."

"I can never believe that," said Jack, "until I have the proof before me."

"Go and see her for yourself," said Brisket.

Jack knocked at the door—there was no answer.

"She's only sulky," said Brisket, "try again."

Again he knocked with the same result.

"Skewball," said Brisket, quickly, "will you go round to the back and see if all is right there? She can't have forced the place, for I have not heard a sound."

Skewball went out in double-quick time, and in a minute or so came back, choking with suppressed laughter.

"Darn me," he said, "if you didn't make a mistake! You've nailed up our pantry window, and the bird has flown!"

CHAPTER CXIII.

JACK AND DICK SKEWBALL.

"AND it's a pretty mess I'm making of it," said Brisket; "who would have thought I could be such an ass?"

"The wisest of us," returned Jack, "make a mistake sometimes."

"But I never was wise. I was born a fool and have lived true to it."

Billy was very bitter against himself, and for a time was inconsolable. Richard Skewball insisted upon his having something to drink, and a couple of glasses of brandy and water did him a lot of good.

"I've known Maggie, off and on, for years," he said, "and I did not think that the wealth of the world would have tempted her to be dishonest."

"You never know 'em," said Richard, philosophically, "they are so changeable."

"Thank you, Dick," said Sal, from her corner of the little rough parlour, where the husband and wife sat with Brisket. Jack was in Maggie's room, and young Dick outside lounging up and down uneasily.

"I was only speaking ginerally," replied Skewball, "and you needn't get huffed, for you know my opinion of you. If there is perfection on airth, I've got it."

"Too late," said Sal, smiling good-humouredly, "you should have said that before."

"Well, talking of women as a body," said Skewball, "I say you can't trust 'em, and that's why I wally you. You remember the signor's wife, don't you, Sal?"

Sal nodded, and Billy Brisket, who wanted distraction from his thoughts, asked who the signor's wife was.

"A very pretty party," replied Skewball. "The signor—a furrin chap—Italian, I think, came over to the diggings and brought his wife with him. He was a jealous sort of chap, afraid to leave her behind, and not too trustful of her here; so he made her dress up in man's clothes, as if *that* would conceal a woman of good figure. Bless her innocence, there w... n't a chap in the whole fields as didn't see thro... it, but the times were busy and men didn't bot... about her."

"Do you re... think she was pretty?" asked Sal.

"Fairish," r...ed Dick, with a glance at his wife, "but no... to make people go off their heads, like s... folk. She was uncommon mild-looking, as if ...r was too stiff to melt in her mouth, but for ... hat she was a bad un."

"Right dow... ..." said Sal.

"Another f...r... came this way, and got intimate with the signo... They used to go up and down to work together. ...d waited for each other, but presently I no...d the second furriner wasn't so reg'lar at his w..., and one day I seen him sneaking off to the s...r's hut, and I guessed what was going on, and ... says to misself, 'Lud ha' mercy on you if you are caught.'

"Apparently ... signor didn't notice anything, but one morni... I went over to his place, and opening the door as we do about here, I walks in and sees him a sitting by the table, and she a-kneeling at his feet. She was apparently imploring for merc..., but he stopped her as I went in. Neither of 'em saw me."

"It's no use, he says, "it's too late. I've cut his throat and ...d cut yours if it wasn't for the pleasure of kee...g you alive to torture you."

Thinking i... ...e to make myself beknown, I gives a cough, ...d they both starts. I pretends I hadn't seen any...ng, and arter a casual observation or two, I takes m... leave.

For days tha... woman went about subdued like; she followed h... like a dog, and he snarled and swore at her ... a wild cat, but she seemed to enjoy it. Ble... ..., though, if within a week he warn't found w... his throat cut, and the signora, his wife, went ... fits of grief, as if she hadn't done it, but we all k...w she had, although we couldn't prove it. As ... matter of decency we told her to cut, and she w... off in the night, and we haven't heard of her si... But I dare say she's working mischief wher... she is—womanlike."

"Dick," cri... ...l.

"Yes, my love..."

"What do yo... mean by 'womanlike?'"

"Oh, nothi... spoke ginerally. If all women were like you ... iness would be dirt cheap."

"Oh, you've ... mooth tongue when you like," said Sal, and t... they all laughed.

The voice of ...ck interrupted the conversation. He was calling ... Brisket, who got up from his seat and went ... im.

"Brisket," h... ...d, "do you really think Maggie Jaundice has ... ...ved us?"

"Sure of it."

"I am not. ... ...lieve she is innocent."

"You believe... because you don't like to be hard on a woman."

"Of course, t... has some influence, but I formed my opinion up... ...mmon sense."

"Common s... ... in this business won't do," said Brisket, shaki... ... head.

"Just think ... ...sket, she need not have named that she knew a... ...hing about it. I fancy her secret was discovered, ...d she has been robbed."

"But who to... it?"

"Aye, that i... the question," said Jack. "We must proceed w... great caution, and then we may have a chance ... ...ning to the bottom of it. Is that Skewball's boy ...ide?"

"Yes,"

"Send him ... here," said Jack, "I've taken a fancy to him."

"Shall I co... ...ack with him?"

"No, I want ... speak with him alone," said Jack.

Brisket wen... ... his errand, and presently Dick, with a sullen ... dog look upon his face, came in.

"Well, my ... said Jack.

"Well, sir." a...swered the boy.

"You are Skewball's son they tell me."

Dick nodded and rubbed his hair with his hand.

"What is your name?"

"Dick."

"Come closer to me. I want to look at you, Dick. Closer."

Inch by inch Dick drew up, until Jack could take him by the shoulders. This he did, and bent him back, so as to get a view of his features.

"Raise your head a little," he said.

Dick did so, but he kept his eyes down, and dared not look at the commanding countenance so near him.

"You have honest features," said Jack, "and you are a lad of spirit. I want such a lad as you to be always with me."

"But I can't come," said Dick, sullenly.

"But you must come," replied Jack; "nay, you shall come."

"Shall is a hard word," said Dick, in a low tone.

"It is one I often use," replied Jack, "and I always enforce it when I utter it. You will please attend upon me, Dick Skewball, until I tell you I no longer require you."

A frown passed over the boy's face, and words of rebellion rose to his lips. But they were never uttered. The powerful will of Jack was too much for him. He was awed.

"What am I to do?" he asked.

"To be within call all the day and night," replied Jack. "No more."

"I wasn't born to be a slave," muttered Dick.

"Of course not," replied Jack, "neither will I make you one for long. I want your services to find something, and I am sure you will help me."

"You are much surer than I am," growled Dick, turning away.

Jack seized him by the collar, and swung him smartly round.

"Say that again," he said.

Dick's lips moved, but no sound followed, and his eyes were almost closed, as if he would fain hide them from Broad Arrow Jack.

"Remember this," said Jack, with quiet determination. "I allow neither man nor boy to trifle with me. Those who attempt it will but too surely pay dearly for their temerity. Go outside and wait."

Dick went into the passage, and squatted down close to the wall. There presently his father found him.

"This is a new fit, Dick," he said, "lolling about in the house during the daytime."

"I am waiting on Broad Arrow Jack. He wants me."

"Waiting on him. How?"

"I am his servant. He took me on this morning."

"Well, that's news. You a servant, Dick. I never should have thought it, but I aint sorry—it will keep you out of mischief, and it is an honour to serve such a noble fellow."

"I am glad you think so," said Dick, drily, and his father left him.

A little later on Sal heard of the appointment of her son, and knew not what to make of it. Like her husband, however, she was glad of it, as she hoped it would cure Dick of his idle habits. She and her husband had a long talk over it, and gave it up as a puzzler.

"I never thought any man would have made a servant of Dick," cried Skewball; "but boys are like women. You can never understand them."

All that day Dick sat sullenly in the passage, without receiving a summons from his master. Jack did not even come to the door to see if he was there, but as the night fell he called out his name.

"Here, sir," said Dick, springing up with alacrity.

"I see," said Jack, looking at him as he came in, "you have made one step in life. You have learnt to obey."

"Yes—sir," replied Dick, relapsing a little into his old sullenness.

Broad-Arrow Jack.

STEALTHILY THE OGRE CREPT NEARER AND NEARER THE FORM OF BROAD ARROW JACK.

NO. 17.

It was a great struggle with Dick. Of course he had a physical master, but that was not all. He had defied strong men a hundred times; his father was a strong man, and he had defied him. The real secret of his subjugation lay in the awe-inspiring presence of Jack.

"I shall not want you any more to-night," said Jack.

"Yes, sir."

"You may sleep in your usual room."

"Thank you, sir."

"And be here by six in the morning at the latest," said Jack. "You may go."

Dick retired, and Jack, tossing off the better part of the clothes from Maggie's bed as superfluous, lay down to sleep. Repose came almost as soon as courted, and he slept until Dick knocked at the door in the morning.

"Who's there?" said he.

"Dick, sir."

"What is the time?"

"A quarter to six by the sun, sir."

"He has studied nature a bit," thought Jack; then gave his orders aloud. "Get me some bread and fruit for breakfast; eat what you want yourself, and be ready to go with me."

"What will you drink, sir?" asked Dick.

"Water."

"We have some good whiskey here, sir," suggested the boy, "and most people have a drain here in the morning."

"I do not drink it," replied Jack. "I can get bone and muscle enough on water."

Dick brought his breakfast, and looked at Jack for the first time. His eyes beamed with admiration. The simple life of the big noble fellow charmed him.

"I'll have water, too," he said, "although I've often had rum and milk, and I like it."

"Eat your breakfast here," said Jack. "Share mine with me."

The boy sat down, more at his ease than he had hitherto been; but there was a reserved look upon him, the shadow of something hidden in his soul, as he glanced up now and then furtively into the face of his master.

"Can you ride, Dick?" asked Jack, after a long pause.

The boy laughed as if the question amused him, and he answered—

"I could ride before I could walk, sir."

"Then you shall ride with me this day," said Jack. "Where can we get horses?"

"My father," replied Dick, with a sly look, "has two colts—unbroken."

"They will do," replied Jack, calmly. "Have them ready in an hour."

"I can't do anything with 'em alone," said Dick, "for the devil's in 'em both. They are in a loose box."

"I will come with you," said Jack. "Have you finished breakfast?"

"Yes, sir."

"Nobody seems to be about but ourselves," remarked Jack, as they went down the passage to the rear of the house.

"We sit up late here," returned Dick, "and we are not early risers. My father and Mr. Brisket were up later than usual last night, and went to bed with as much as they could carry."

"It does not matter," inquired Jack. "I do not want either."

Skewball's stables, like the rest of his premises, were roughly but strongly built. He had room for a dozen horses, and occasionally as many were put there. In a loose box were the two colts which Dick had spoken of—small but very powerful mustangs.

"Twins, sir," said Dick, "or as good, and that's why they are so friendly. The mother of the one with the black spot on his forehead was killed by lightning, and the mother of the other suckled them both."

"A strange story," said Jack.

"But quite true, sir," said Dick, looking fully at him.

With his mind only on horses Dick could be as open and honest as the day.

"And they have never been ridden?"

"No, never, nor had a halter on. I think, sir, if you lean over here, and catch hold of the mane of that one, I can get the bridle over his head."

"I do not think we will be quite so ceremonious," said Jack, opening the door of the loose box. "Hand me a bridle here. I will get it on."

Dick was amazed, and the two mustangs stared at him as if they were overwhelmed with astonishment at his audacity. Up to that time they had had everything their own way, and were perfectly aware of the fact. Horses are not such asses as some men take them to be—they know who is afraid of them and who is not.

Jack took the bridle, and seized the nearest mustang by the mane. His grasp was of iron, and the mustang, after one attempt to rear, gave in. The bit was slipped into his mouth, and Jack led him outside, and fastened him to an iron ring in the wall.

In all his life Dick's eyes had never been so far out of his head before. He mentioned the two unbroken colts without thinking it at all likely that Jack would press them into his service, and the prospect of having to mount one himself was rather disagreeable—in fact, Master Dick began to wish himself out of the business.

The second mustang, having had a few moments for reflection, was disposed to show a wicked and rebellious spirit, and began capering and kicking about the box, but Jack, watching his opportunity, darted in, and seized it as he had done the other. In a second the other bridle was on, and both mustangs captive.

"Now, Dick," said Jack, "no saddles at first. Get them used to the bridle before completely equipping them. The first out secures the quickest. Mount, and be off."

"Where to?" asked Dick.

"Over the plain. Give them a long run to take the go out of them. Stick on, and keep him as straight as you can. If he rears or kicks you must do your best to keep your seat."

Dick drew a deep breath, and tightened the belt round his waist. There was no going back without showing the white feather, and that Dick was much too proud to do.

Having temporarily fastened his own mustang, Jack released the other, and held it by the head while Dick scrambled upon its back. The moment the boy was seated he let go, and off it went with the speed of the wind.

In three seconds he was mounted too, and followed in the wake of the other. There was no need to guide his steed, as it naturally went in pursuit of its constant companion.

"Give him his head, Dick," he cried, "until I tell you to pull up—then stick to him!"

"All right!" shrieked Dick. "Hurrah! hurrah! Here's a bit of fun."

CHAPTER CXIV.

A MORNING'S RIDE—TAMING TWO DEVILS.

IT was indeed excellent fun while the mustangs were allowed to go straight away, but the moment Jack called upon Dick to rein up, and himself set the example, the struggle began.

The mustangs, revelling in their new-found freedom, wanted to have an hour's hard running, at least, but Jack, knowing how necessary it was to have an understanding with them as soon as possible, only waited until he was well clear of the diggers' huts before he called for a halt.

BROAD ARROW JACK.

Dick reined his animal up, and immediately it stood upright. The boy clung to the mane with one hand, and struck it between the ears with the other. Neither he nor Jack had whip or spur.

"Steady, my lad," cried Jack. "Try kindness first. Gently—gently!"

His own steed was plunging and rearing about in a very angry manner, hoping to shake off his newly-acquired burden; but the brute might just as well have tried to shake off his head or tail. Jack sat still, calm and immovable, as if he had been a part of the mustang.

"Off again, Dick!" cried Jack. "We must run a little more of his pluck out of him before you can manage him."

Away they went again, over a couple of miles or so of level road. Jack's horse made no more of him than Dick's did of the boy. Then they came to a brook about twenty feet wide.

"Shall I go at it, sir?" cried Dick.

"No," replied Jack.

He knew the boy would have another struggle with the mustang, and was testing his courage. Dick made an effort to rein up, but his steed, with a dexterous movement of his head, got the bit between its teeth, and dashed at the brook.

The bound it gave was tremendous, clearing the water by several feet on either side, and Dick was thrown completely over its head, and went to mother earth with a force that threatened to dislocate every bone of his body.

But he held on to the reins bravely, and although the mustang backed quickly, dragging him over the ground, he would not let go until Jack had also leaped the brook, and came to the rescue.

Seizing the bridle, he held both horses, while Dick got up and carefully felt himself all over.

"Any bones broken, Dick?"

"None, sir, but what a bang I came down!"

"I thought you were too good a horseman to be thrown."

"Well, I didn't expect it, but he went up about four feet higher than I expected, and its rather scared me."

"Well, will you get up again?"

"I don't think so," said Dick, doubtfully.

"Mount at once," said Jack, and Dick, hesitating no longer, got across the mustang. As a matter of choice, he would rather have kept off, but a command from Broad Arrow Jack he did not care to disobey.

"Now, you follow me," said Jack, "and go exactly where I go."

"All right, sir," said Dick, his wild eyes shining with excitement. "If I break my neck ten times over I'll stick to you."

Jack, who had succeeded in getting some control over his mustang, turned its head towards a small steep hill to the left, and on reaching it he began the ascent.

As sure-footed as a cat, the mustang scrambled up the steep slope, and stood on the summit, with a fair amount of wind left for further exercise. Jack reined up, and the brute was quiet enough until the other stood by its side.

Then they began their pranks again.

First on their hind legs, then on their fore legs, then all feet in the air, they reared and capered about with the quickness and activity of goats, and finding all their little tricks in vain, for Dick and Jack kept their seats, they both, with one accord, bolted back down the hill.

The ascent was dangerous, but the descent was terrific. The two riders leant back until their backs almost touched the haunches of their steeds. It was impossible for any horse to keep his feet long, and Jack perceiving a stiff tumble was at hand, called out to Dick to throw himself off. Before the boy could do this his mustang suddenly pitched forward, and rolled over and over.

Dick was thrown half a dozen yards ahead, right in the track of the other animal, and lay still.

"Killed," thought Jack, and with a shout he urged his mustang to clear the boy.

It gave a bound, came down, slipped, and rolled down towards the plain.

Jack fell heavily, but his hardy frame, inured to every kind of vicissitude, did not suffer beyond the shaking, and a few scratches and bruises. He was on his feet in a moment, and by Dick's side.

Raising his head, he found the boy's neck was not broken, then felt his heart, and found it beating.

"Alive and not seriously injured," he said. "A plucky youngster, but—I have to tame him further yet."

Dick had not even a bone broken, and soon came round, opening his eyes like one aroused from a dream.

"Have you any pain?" asked Jack.

"Nothing," replied Dick, "but a singing in my head."

"That won't injure you," said Jack. "Now, keep quiet here while I have a look at our nags. I think they are pretty well broken in by this time."

Both were cowed by their fall, and lay panting, with their eyes wildly rolling. Jack took the bridle of the nearest, and, with cheering cries, urged it to get up. It scrambled to its feet, and stood still, trembling, while he raised the other. With one in each hand, he led them down to the level ground, where they stood as quiet as lambs.

Dick followed, pausing occasionally to feel his head, as if he was not quite certain of its being on his shoulders. He was very pale, but the determined look about his mouth was there still.

"We can ride home quietly enough now," said Jack.

"Quiet or not I am going to ride," replied Dick.

"You are a brave lad," said Jack, patting him kindly upon the shoulder, "and I should be proud of you if you were my brother."

"Don't say that, sir," said Dick, drawing back, and turning livid.

"But I mean it," returned Jack. "You have a great spirit in you, and it would take a strong temptation to induce you to do a mean or base action."

Something rose in Dick's throat, and tears came into his eyes. His mouth opened, as if he were going to speak, but he suddenly looked the other way, and said nothing. Jack patted him again upon the shoulder, and leaped on the back of his steed.

"Home," he said, and rode off.

"That boy has a proud determined spirit," he thought, "difficult to bend or break; but I will tame him yet, and then—the king shall have his own again."

Dick, relieved of all trouble with the animal he bestrode, had his mind on other things, as he rode behind his master.

For the most part he kept his eyes down, but now and then he would look up with the glance of one who is struggling with good and evil. One might have thought that he was meditating some injury to Broad Arrow Jack, but was loath to carry it out, and when they reached home again the struggle was not yet over.

"Dick," said Jack, "take these horses in, and be within call."

"I will," replied Dick, and Jack, in a thoughtful humour, went into the garden, and sat down with his back to the wooden fence.

CHAPTER CXV.

TWO KNAVES.

FOR a few brief moments we must leave our hero and his surroundings, and spreading the wings of fancy, fly over the sea to the shores of Britain. Alighting in a private room of one of the principal hotels in Dover, we find ourselves in the presence of two well-dressed men.

At the first glance they might both be taken for gentlemen, for their apparel is of the best, and their surroundings are such as we find about men of means; but a second look tells us that one, at least, is of humble if not insignificant origin.

Neither of them can boast an honest countenance, for knave is written on their features. They belong to the class of men who sit up late over cards, "plunge" at race meetings, and go the rounds of a generally dissipated life.

Their names are respectively the Honourable Morden Crewe, and Mr. Woody Welsher—the first a broken-down gentleman, the second a turf agent, which, being interpreted, means a rascal who lives upon the weakness of fools.

Mr. Welsher has only the assurance of his class when in the presence of a gentleman who is ruined and helpless, and affects an ease which only makes his vulgarity more apparent.

"Look here, Crewe," he said, "something must be done in your business. I do not think I can go another settling day. The bills you gave me last time were not met."

"But surely you won't press me?" asked the Honourable Morden, looking up with a startled face—a face, by the way, wearing its thirty odd years very badly; but if men will turn night into day, old Father Time generally proves unkind.

"Why not?" asked Woody Welsher. "Business is business."

"Business be——"

"Now, Crewe, keep your temper. You and I are old pals, and have stood by each other pretty well as the world goes, but a man must draw a line somewhere, and I am going to draw it now."

The Honourable Morden evidently chafed under this address, but he controlled himself, and put on a calm face as he replied—

"I do not think you can lose a penny by me. You have had pretty well every penny I inherited."

"How can that be? How have you lived?"

"As others of my class do—on credit. I have debts enough to swamp a three-decker, and, upon my soul, I don't know where to turn for a penny."

"You must get some money for me, Crewe," said Woody Welsher, decidedly. "You must hurry on this business of the Ashleigh estate."

"How can I hurry it on?"

"Are you not the heir, Crewe?"

"Yes, when it is proved that my uncle and cousins are dead."

"Aye, that's it, Crewe."

"Don't Crewe me so much. It irritates me to hear my name a dozen times a minute."

"It doesn't irritate you when it comes from the mouths of your brother swells," replied Woody Welsher, a little huffed; "at least, if it does, you would not like to tell 'em so."

"I beg your pardon," said the Honourable Morden. "I am out of sorts. Things harass me. Only this morning, just before we left London, I went to my lawyer, and asked him to advance me twenty pounds upon my prospects. He, in a mildly polite way, informed me he would see me further first."

"But all these Ashleighs *must* be dead, Crewe."

"That cannot be settled by surmise. At all events the estate, which has been so carefully nursed, cannot be mine just yet."

"What is it worth, Crewe?"

"A considerable sum, almost what it was originally, for investments formerly considered ruinous have turned out the reverse."

"How long shall I have to wait?"

The Honourable Morden Crewe did not immediately reply. The question apparently required reflection before it was answered. Woody Welsher looked at him keenly, saw by his face that it could be answered at once, and took up his stand accordingly.

"Now, Crewe," he said, "you needn't answer. It will be ten years before you are allowed to touch it."

"Just so, it will. I may as well tell the truth."

"And do you expect me to wait ten years?"

"No."

"What will you do, Crewe?"

"D—— it, don't 'Crewe' me so much; but I suppose it is a habit you've got. I am thinking over what I shall do."

"Shall I help you?"

"Can you help me?"

"A little, with the aid of other friends, Crewe."

"What friends?"

"Suppose I know some people who can swear to having seen all the Ashleighs murdered by the North American Indians?"

"Are there such people?"

"Yes, Crewe, I have them handy."

And then Woody Welsher winked, and the Honourable Morden perfectly understood him.

"When can these people be produced?" he asked.

"We must not be in too much of a hurry, Crewe, especially as you've been trying to raise money: Say in a month."

"And what am I to do till then?" asked the Honourable Morden.

"Live here," said Woody Welsher.

"Without money?"

"I can let you have a little for odd things, Crewe, and don't ask for your bill. They won't trouble you, being an honourable, although they would drop on me, being a snob, and yet I could pay my bill a hundred times over and not feel it."

"But suppose this sche— this arrangement with your friends fails?"

"Why, then, Crewe, you won't get your money."

"And what shall I do then?"

"Bolt!" coolly answered Woody Welsher.

"Where to?" asked the Honourable Morden.

"That's your look-out," replied Woody Welsher. "At any rate, keep clear of me, for I shall be looking after my own. I am going to help you now, not to do you any particular good, but to save myself. It's the way of the world, you know. Here, let me give you a fiver. It will keep you in cigars."

The Honourable Morden Crewe took the note in silence, and appeared to swallow something at the same time. Woody Welsher rose from his seat.

"Come, Crewe," he said, "let us leave business for the present. It is time we showed ourselves to the gals upon the parade."

"I don't feel inclined to walk out this evening."

"But I do, Crewe, and as I like to be seen about with swells, I mean you to come with me."

The Honourable Morden got out of his chair, and taking up his hat, knocked it savagely upon his head.

"Come on," he said, "only don't bawl out my name all over the place. I've duns here, there, and everywhere."

And forth went the pair, to show themselves, as Welsher said, "to the gals" on Dover Parade.

CHAPTER CXVI.

JEB JAUNDICE PLAYS HIS LAST CARD.

BARELY had Jack taken his seat when the head and face of a man rose above the fence, and two evil-looking eyes glared down upon him.

It was Jeb Jaundice.

For many days he had wandered in lone spots, harasssed and worn with bitter thoughts, dark doubts, and miserable apprehensions. He could not realise that his possession of the treasure was all a dream, nor could he exactly bring himself to believe it was true.

A man in a healthy frame of mind might well have paused and wondered as he dwelt upon the events which had transpired within the past few weeks, and what else could be expected from one with a mind diseased?

He shunned mankind, but as he could not live without food he came stealing into the settlement at night, and picked up such scraps as people cast from their doors, but he could get no drink.

'Twas better in one way for him that he did not, and worse in another. It retarded his destruction, but roused in him to the fullest extent the worst passions of his nature.

All his sufferings he charged to his wife. When alone, lying in hiding, he dwelt upon his fancied wrongs, and out of his dark thoughts there gradually grew a resolve to murder her.

Yes, come what might, he would do it.

But he had no weapons, unless he could do the deed by stick or stone, and neither of these he would trust to.

Rendered bold by his anger he crept one night into a settler's hut, and robbed him of his rifle as he slept.

It was loaded with one charge only, and to carry out his fell purpose he strode down at early morning to Skewball's house.

His hope was that she might come to the window to catch the morning air. He knew it was her custom to stand there for awhile, and he felt sure of his prey. If he could only kill her they might tear him piecemeal for aught he cared, and in his heart he felt the infuriated settlers would do it if they got him in their power.

Under the fence he lay, waiting in vain for the shutters to open, until he heard a voice which he hated as much and more than that of Maggie.

'Twas that of Broad Arrow Jack speaking to Dick, and through a crevice he saw the majestic youth enter the garden, and take his seat as described.

The enemy present shut out the fancied enemy absent—to kill Jack would gratify him as much as the killing of his wife. All his sufferings, he considered, had their foundations from the youth before him.

A sure aim, an unfailing charge, and a swift bullet would amply repay him for all he had endured.

Jack, unconscious of his presence, was absorbed in thought; but slowly and steadily, with his nerves strung by hate, Jeb Jaundice took aim.

He was so anxious to make the shot sure that he wasted the moments which might have seen the end of our hero, and in those moments there came stealing up on the garden side of the fence the form of Dick, who had seen Jeb Jaundice, and, guessing his purpose, was coming to the rescue.

Dick recognised the form of the husband of Maggie—it was the hate he had for him which stimulated the boy to go to the aid of his master; otherwise it is just possible he might have left him to his fate.

Having taken a perfect aim, Jeb Jaundice pulled the trigger; but as the hammer fell a small brown hand seized the barrel and raised it, so that the bullet sped harmlessly away.

The would-be murderer was too amazed to turn and fly, and Dick, springing over the fence, seized him by the throat, and, boy as he was, bore the strong man to the ground.

Jack, aroused from his meditations by the report of the rifle, stepped to the fence, and, seeing who was there, vaulted over and made Jeb Jaundice a prisoner.

"Dick," he said, "get me a strong rope, and ask Captain Brisket to come here."

Dick obeyed quickly, and Brisket, followed by Skewball, in a few seconds appeared upon the scene.

"What now, chief?" said Brisket. "Surely not Jeb Jaundice!"

"Take care of him," said Jack. "I leave him in your charge until I have secured the other villain."

The rope was brought, and Skewball—who was not fully in the secrets of Jack—wondering what it all meant, lent a hand to bind the prisoner. Jaundice, with the despairing look of a lost soul in his eyes, lay still, unable to speak or move.

At last all was over with him.

He felt—nay, he knew—that he had played his last card, and from that hour there could be no earthly hope for him. He might not be killed immediately—indeed, he was pretty sure of that, for Jack had given him in charge of another to keep in safe custody for a while—but the deep conviction that he was in toils from which he would never again be free settled upon his heart, and brought the darkness of hopeless despair upon him.

"Skewball," said Brisket, "have you any place where I can safely keep this fellow?"

"He must be kept out of sight," returned Skewball. "He isn't very popular about here, and I could not answer for what they would do to him. I have no room; but when the chief——"

"And I am going away at once," said Jack.

"At once!" exclaimed Brisket.

"Yes—over to the island," returned Jack. "I feel that the end of my work is at hand. You remain here with this satellite of the Ogre's in your charge; Dick and I are going over the sea."

"So you will take my boy with you?" said Skewball.

"Yes; he is determined upon going with me—are you not, Dick?"

"I will go," said the boy, in a low voice. He too was in a net from which there was no escape.

They carried Jeb Jaundice in, and, bound hand and foot, laid him on the bed. Skewball and Dick went outside the room, and Jack and Brisket went over to the window.

"You are going back too soon, chief," said Brisket.

"Too soon! Why?" asked Jack.

"Have you forgotten what you came over to seek?"

"No."

"Is it of no value in your eyes?"

"Of every value. I am not such a fool as to despise money—I do not make it my god, but I know its value."

"And yet you will leave this place when that vast fortune is in the hands of an unscrupulous woman!"

"She is not unscrupulous, Brisket; and as to the fortune, believe me—I know where it is!"

Brisket looked like a man who has been told of something which he finds it impossible to believe, however much he may wish to credit it. Jack merely repeated that "he knew where it was."

"Or rather let me say," he added, "I know who has it. There is no hurry—it is perfectly safe."

"You take things coolly," returned Brisket; "but I'm dashed if I can. We are running short."

"We have enough to go on with, and our credit is good. If you want money for the moment borrow of Skewball."

"But where *is* the white claret?"

"When I return from the island you shall know; and, for the present, farewell. Keep an eye on yon knave—guard him as you would the treasure itself."

"I'll watch him by day, and chain him to me when I sleep," replied Brisket; "but I don't think you need fear him—he's shot his bolt, and all the pluck is gone out of him."

CHAPTER CXVII.
MAGGIE'S LAST PROOF OF WOMAN'S LOVE.

IT was impossible to keep the confinement of Jeb Jaundice a secret. No matter how silent people may be there is always in large communities a little bird to whisper abroad the things that ought not to be told, and ere night it was known through the diamond-fields that Skewball had him in his house.

Jaundice was not popular. He had long been known as one of the Peaceful Village gang, and, although for awhile he and the Ogre had got upon virtuous stilts, time and the tide of events had taken them off again, and no two men could have been more fervently hated.

Judge Lynch held high court at the fields, and fain would he have tried the prisoner. He sent a deputation to Skewball to give him up, but Skewball said—

"He's in other hands, that will deal with him as well as Lynch, and I don't give him up."

"You must," said one man.

"Arter I have emptied this lot, then," said Skewball, producing two six-chambered revolvers; and the emissaries from the court of Judge Lynch, after a brief consultation, decided to let matters take their course.

"Skewball," they said, "isn't a man to be trifled with, and what's the good of fighting about a skunk?"

So they left the skunk to the care of Skewball and his friend, Brisket, and went back to their labours like sensible men.

Now, there was in hiding among friends a certain woman named Maggie, and she, hearing of the capture of her husband, determined to set him free—not that she loved him, or yearned for him in any way, but he was her husband, and it was her duty to stand by him to the last.

"I am his wife," she said, "and will go to his aid."

But how to do this?

She dared not show at Skewball's while Brisket was there, and as Jaundice was undoubtedly closely guarded, it was next to impossible to get near him. She, however, resolved to try.

The first night Jaundice spent in his confinement there Maggie was at the shutter of her room, peeping through a crack which gave her a view of her husband lying bound on the couch, and Brisket sitting by his side, smoking.

She tried the shutters gently, and found they had only been pulled to, and not made fast. Here was an opportunity which her woman's wit made use of.

Taking out her knife—one such as settlers carry, strong and good—she wrapped it in a piece of paper, and wrote upon it, with a pencil, "From a friend." The characters were ill-formed, as they were written in the dark, but they were legible enough for any man to read.

Hour after hour she watched by that shutter. The evening mists fell like rain. The moon went down, and the chill blasts of night swept by her. Silence came upon the fields, and she alone was abroad.

Brisket watched like a sentinel whose life depended upon his being true to his work. Not many men can sit still, smoking all night, without feeling inclined to close at least one eye in the morning. Billy felt inclined that way, and, allowing one eye to set the example, speedily lost the sight of two.

But Maggie dare not venture in. To arouse the sleeper would have been to spoil all. She only drew back the shutter, and, taking careful aim, tossed the knife upon the couch close to the hand of Jeb Jaundice.

He felt it, but knew not from whence it came, and she gave him no time to see. Carefully closing the shutters again, she watched him while he read the words on the paper, and having, after several efforts, succeeded in cutting the first bond, rapidly freed himself.

Inch by inch he sat up, and glided like a shadow from the bed. Brisket slept on, and stealthily Jeb crept towards the window. With her own hands she pulled back the shutter, so gently that no creak betrayed the movement, and Jeb Jaundice, content to find it open, stole out, with his face towards the sleeper, and dropped quietly down upon the soft mould outside.

The night was far spent and the day at hand the stars in the east were paling, and the cry of the corn crake was growing faint. Maggie, stepping lightly before her husband, slipped through the gate, into the open plain.

He saw her not, but unconsciously followed in her steps. In his hand was the knife that had set him free, ready to be used for another purpose if need be.

Maggie could dimly see his form—the form she had once worshipped with all the strength of woman's devotion. He was dead to her in that sense, but he was her husband still, and she wanted one last word with him.

"I will only tell him I have set him free," she said, "and then leave him for ever—at least my faithfulness may help to turn his heart."

It was a woman's thought, such as few men would understand—Jeb Jaundice least of all. On she went beyond the settlement to a wood, and there she waited for him, knowing he must come that way if he wished to hide.

He came, and entered the friendly shade as the sun peeped up. The early light swept over the earth as he stood face to face with his wife.

She came out with a face radiant with her last good deed. He saw her, and the shade that devils wear covered his features.

"You here," he said, "always spying about me, and seeking to betray me."

"No," she replied, "I have only come to speak to you for the last time."

"Yes," he said, grimly, "for the last time."

He had his hand in his pocket as he spoke, and drew near her with slow, but apparently casual steps.

"Perhaps you do not know," she said, "what you owe to me this night."

"I know," he said, "what I owe you for the past time, and by the Lord I will repay you."

"You were ever unjust," she said; "hear me for a moment, and be kinder in thoughts for the future."

"I will listen," he said, "but speak low, or my life is in danger. May I come nearer?"

"Yes," she answered, "for the last time."

"Ay," he said, with the same grim smile, "for the last time." She let him come, not dreaming of his devilish purpose.

Then the cruel knife flashed in the morning light, and he struck her down.

It entered the bosom where beat an honest heart, if all the world cannot boast of another, and she fell at his feet without a groan or word, with her reproachful eyes upon him.

"Now," he said, "I am avenged. You can never betray or wrong me more."

"Betray you!" she said, as she covered the wound with her hands, but the blood would spurt through her fingers, to show the dastard what he had done— "betray you, who has saved you this night! Look upon that knife, there is a name upon the handle. You gave it me long ago."

He looked, and all that should have been in his heart years before came upon him. There was the name of his wife rudely graven upon it by himself, as she had said, years before.

"Maggie," he said, "did you bring me this?"

"Who else," she asked, "would have done so much? Have you another friend?"

"No!" he cried, "not one. And yet I never thought of you."

"You have never thought of me," she said, "or we should not be here as we are now."

"Oh, Maggie!" he cried, "at last my eyes are open, and I see—I know now what a blind brute I have been to you, how I have trodden on all that was good and beautiful in you—the best and most beautiful of women!"

"You see too late," she said.

"In all the past I see a reflection of my own infamy," he went on, "and now I know what I ought to have known years before—the treasure which was given me."

"Too late," she said, and her voice grew fainte

as she pressed her hand upon the wound he had given.

"Oh, Maggie—Maggie!" he cried, kneeling down, "let me bind up that cruel wound. Let me check the flow of the life's blood. Here, see, I have a scarf ready."

"Too late," she said, again.

"Here," he said, clasping his hands above him, "I renounce the past, and pray God to forgive me all my sins. I acknowlege that I have never been a husband to you, only a base-minded brute, who had no idea of your great worth. I cast aside all my own unmanly pride, that would not bend when I knew I was wrong in years gone by, and here kneeling I ask you to forgive me, and to live to be a blessing to my shattered body and soul!"

"Too late," she said.

Her voice had sunk almost to a whisper, and her eyes, though fixed upon his face, seemed to look through him into regions far beyond.

"Oh, Maggie," he continued, speaking hurriedly, and with quickening breath, "live for me—live to make a man of a monster, who without you must go to perdition. I am lost without you. Live for me!"

"Too late," she said, again, "I can only die for you. Jeb Jaundice, what woman could do more?"

"Am I forgiven?" he asked.

"You are forgiven—all," she said, and on her face there rested a smile that would have graced an angel.

The wretched man who had culminated his list of crimes with this most hellish deed, knelt by her with his hands clasped, and rocking to and fro in awful agony.

The hopelessness of one who has lost all here and beyond the grave was upon him, but his suffering found but feeble vent in words.

"Maggie!—Maggie!" was all he could cry now. "Live for me!"

"Too late," she answered, and then there was a silence.

It was broken by Maggie, who, with a last effort, raised her head a few inches from the ground.

"Jeb," she said, and so low was the tone that he scarce could hear her voice.

"Yes, Maggie—my darling—my love!"

"Kiss me."

He bent over her eagerly, and touched her lips with his.

There was a flash of hope in his heart, but it died away as the life warmth left her lips. While his lingered upon hers they became cold as clay.

At first he could not, and would not believe that all was over, but the truth forced itself upon him, and in a mad frenzy of agony he rolled on the ground, calling himself all that was vile and loathsome. Again and again he knelt by her side, and implored her to speak only one word, but the gentle, beautiful face was fixed in death, and his cries were scattered by the wind through the wood unheeded.

Paroxysms of grief do not last for ever, and Jeb Jaundice soon grew calmer. Rising, he gathered some sticks and leaves, and covered the gracefully-moulded form.

"Until I can come and bury you better," he said. "Oh, Maggie!"

Once more he kissed her face, then covered it with a branch of the magnolia tree, and so left her.

Not to pursue his retreat, but to return to the home he had left that morning. He went straight to Skewball's hut, and presented himself before Brisket, who was raging over his loss.

"I've come back," he said.

"So I see," said Brisket, "and I never thought you would be such a confounded fool."

"I want you," said Jaundice, with a wild stare, "to come into the wood with me."

"No doubt you do," said Brisket, "but I want you to remain here."

"My wife," pursued Jaundice, "lies dead, and we must bury her."

"Your wife dead?"

"Yes, I have killed her—we must bury her. She is food too fair for wolves and crows."

He seemed more like a madman than a sane being, and Brisket knew not what to make of him. Skewball and his wife came in, and Brisket told them what had transpired.

"I must keep him here," said Brisket. "You go and see if his story is true. Where is your wife lying, man?"

"Do I look like a liar now?" asked Jaundice.

"He speaks the truth," said Sal Skewball; "that noble woman is dead, and he has killed her."

"Lord ha' mercy on him if it gets abroad!" said Skewball, with compressed lips.

"It must not get abroad," said Brisket—"he is to be kept until the chief returns. Skewball, Sal, I rely upon you both—keep this awful business a secret."

"I'll not say a word," said Skewball.

"And I," said Sal, "will go out alone, and bury her. No rough hand must lay such a gentle creature in her last resting place. Where is she, man?"

"In yonder wood—over by the hill," replied Jeb Jaundice, "by a tree that has fallen, you will find her. Bury her deep, so that she may never be disturbed."

"If," said Sal, "you had shown half the care for her in life you show in death, you might now be living happily together."

Jeb Jaundice made no reply, but buried his face in his hands, and Brisket led him back to the room where he had been imprisoned before. The mesh of his own weaving was around him, and there was no escape.

"Dick!" said Sal, when husband and wife were left together, "I am going away from you to-night, to bury Maggie."

"To-night, why not go to-day?" he asked.

"Do you want the whole settlement to ask why I am going out with a pick and spade?" she inquired. "No, it must be done in secret."

"May I not come with you?"

"If you will promise not to look upon her."

"I promise."

"Then as soon as it is dark we will set out together."

CHAPTER CXVIII.
THE BURIAL OF MAGGIE—A DISCOVERY.

THAT night Skewball's bar was more than usually thronged, which arose from two reasons—the absence of Maggie from the music-hall, and a lucky find on the part of two men, who, on the strength of it, were standing treat to a large number of friends and acquaintances.

The music-hall filled as usual, but when the time for Maggie to sing arrived, and Maggie did not appear, the uproar was terrible. The proprietor came forward with a scared face to make a speech, and having hooted themselves tired, the crowd condescended to hear him.

His explanation was this—

"He had anxiously awaited the arrival of his prima donna, and finding she did not come, he sent down to Skewball, who said she had left his house, and he knew nothing about her. Where she had gone to he was unable to say, but she might possibly turn up by-and-bye."

This would not do for men who had paid their money, and came to hear a particular singer, and having refreshed their throats with liquor, they began their hooting again, and several cheerful spirits threw glasses of grog at the proprietor, and one of particularly lively disposition shied two water bottles at him, and knocked down a waiter who was giving change for a sovereign.

A comic singer, a good second favourite, was put on, and as soon as he opened his mouth one of the udience, possessing miraculous aiming powers, closed it with a wig worn by the chairman, which he snatched off, and threw straight at the gaping orifice. This was a signal for the casting of other missiles, and everything that came to hand was cast upon the stage.

"The Senora Maggie," they shrieked, which was the name poor Maggie went by, and the proprietor, feeling the wreck of his establishment imminent, tucked his cash-box under his arm and bolted out the back way.

He was not disappointed in his calculation. His place was wrecked, the chairs and tables broken up, and the lamps smashed. Having obtained darkness as an assistant to pugilistic operations, the assemblage went in for an indiscriminate fight among themselves, and spent a most agreeable half hour or so, uninterrupted by the limited police authorities of the place.

The music-hall done with, they broke up, and went to their favourite drinking places, Skewball's receiving the largest part of their patronage, and having begun riotous, they took in large stocks of liquor, with the object of finishing the evening in a way worthy of the beginning.

"Sal," said Skewball, "I never saw them so wild. We shall have rough work to-night. It is as much as we shall do to clear the place by the morning."

"It must be done," said Sal, firmly. "Be a man, and stop their drink."

This was about eleven o'clock, and Sal was anxious to get away. There was something horrible to her in the idea of poor Maggie lying out in the wood at the mercy of beasts and birds of prey, and all her womanly sympathies were fully aroused. It was on her lips a score times to let the rough men in the bar know what had been done, and give Jaundice over to them, but her husband saw what was working within her, and was constantly whispering—

"It won't do to run against Broad Arrow Jack. You leave that Jaundice chap to him, and he will be punished as he deserves to be."

Jack had a power over her as he had over most people he came in contact with, and Sal bottled her wrath, and put on a smiling face as she supplied her guests with the things they ordered. At last twelve o'clock came, the usual hour for clearing the house, and she called upon her husband to serve no more.

"If I don't," he said, "they will have a fight for it."

"With you," she said, "but not with me. Go into the parlour, and I'll settle with them."

"No, I won't," replied Skewball, resolutely. "If it comes to a fight I am not going to leave you by yourself."

"I tell you," said Sal, impatiently, "they won't fight with me. But if you say a word they will shoot you down. Go back, and if you see them touch me come out."

"Let the man who offers to do it say his prayers," growled Skewball. "I suppose you know best, but don't run any risk."

"Leave 'em to me, Richard."

He went into the little bar parlour, and Sal first cleared the tills, putting the money in her pocket, then she took up a hammer, and rapped upon the counter.

"Time's up, my men," she said, "you must clear out."

"Not yet," said a great burly fellow; "we are going to make an extra night of it. Give me a pint of whiskey."

"You will have no more to-night," replied Sal.

"But I mean to," said the ruffian. "If you won't help us we will help ourselves."

"The man who puts his hand upon a tap dies!" said Sal, drawing out a pair of revolvers. "Now then, men, you know our rule, and you can't expect us to alter it against our will."

All the men stared, some of them laughed, and a few of the most drunken yelled derisively, but the brave, buxom woman, cocked the weapons she held, and showed that she was determined, if need be, to use them.

"Clear out," she said.

"Well," said one, "I suppose we can't fight with a woman."

"You can if you like," returned Sal, "but you will find I am a match for any man among you."

"Skewball is as good a man as any of us," said a voice in the background, "and she's more than a match for him."

This raised a general laugh, which put the majority in a good humour, and the cantankerous few, feeling they would get little by resistance, gave in.

The men, in a body, lounged out, and in a few seconds the bar was clear. Sal went round the bar, and closed and bolted the doors.

"Now, Dick," she said, triumphantly, "what do you think of that?"

Mr. Skewball came out of the seclusion of his parlour, scraping his chin, and shining about the face like a freshly-oiled Egyptian. From that hour he loved his wife more than ever.

"You," he said, "are a woman for a man to look up to."

"Now, Richard," she said, "sharp's the word. We have no time to lose. Put out the lights. Get lantern, matches, and shovel ready, and we'll be off."

Brisket at that moment opened the door of Maggie's room, and peeped in.

"What news?" he asked. "Have you kept the thing close?"

"Close as wax," replied Skewball. "How's your prisoner?"

"Come in and look at him," said Brisket.

They went in together, Skewball and his wife, and saw Jaundice lying stretched out on the pallet, with his arms and legs spread-eagled, and carefully bound.

"I ease a limb at a time now and then," said Brisket; "for, although I think hanging too good for him, it is no business of mine to torture him."

"Is he awake?" asked Skewball. "His eyes are open, but he does not seem to see us."

"He sees nothing now," replied Brisket, "but the blackness of his own soul, and that is as plain to him as the sun is to better men at noonday. The weight of the Atlantic on his heart would be a trifle to what he bears. Stay a moment and you will hear him groan."

In less than the time named a hollow sound burst from the lips of the despairing man. Skewball had never heard the like before, and turned deadly pale. Sal closed her ears with her fingers, and walked out.

"Hear that?" said Brisket.

"Awful!" whispered Dick.

"A sound like that," said Brisket, "comes from a man's soul. I never had the least idea of the agony of the damned until I heard him groan."

"Better almost put him out of his misery," suggested Skewball.

"I would, even against orders, if I thought his misery would end here," said Brisket, "but one don't know that it is so—in fact, I don't think it is; so I will let things be as they are. You are going out?"

"Yes, to bury Maggie."

"Before you go I want a word with you and your wife."

"Sal," said Skewball, "come here."

"No," she said, "not there, to hear that sound again. If Brisket wants to speak to me let him come down here."

They went down to her, and Brisket, assured of the safety of his prisoner, closed the door. The three stood by the bar, on which a small candle was burning. Their three figures cast a shadow over half the place.

"I want a promise from you two," said Brisket; "your word is enough. It is as good as an oath if it comes from honest people any day."

"If you want a promise you shall have it," said Dick, and Sal gave an affirmative nod.

"It is this," said Brisket, "whatever happens you will not betray where Jaundice is, or say anything about his last atrocious deed. You know why I ask it. He will be punished in due time."

"Agreed," said Dick. "I won't breathe a word if I die for it."

"Or I," said Sal, and they all shook hands upon it.

Brisket went back to his charge, and Skewball and his wife stole out by the back way. There were groups of noisy men in the distance, but nobody near that they could see, and they started for the wood—Skewball leading the way, with the heavy implements, and Sal following with the lantern, as yet unlighted.

Several times they had to step out of their way to avoid noisy roysterers homeward bound, but they got clear of the fields at last, and struck out for the wood.

The darkness was not very deep, and they reached it in safety. Stepping within its shade Skewball kept watch while Sal lighted the lantern.

Carefully judging their way they found Maggie within an hour, and Sal, kneeling down, removed the leaves and branches with which the murderer covered her. Sal clasped her white face between her two hands, and burst into tears.

"See here," Dick, she cried, "more beautiful in death than in life, and did we not know better could we not swear she was asleep?"

"There never was a purtier creature in this world," murmured Skewball, "meaning nothing against you, Sal."

"She was a lily, and I am a coarse wildflower to her," replied Sal. "Oh, pretty darling, what an end for the likes of you to come to! But haste, Dick, dig her grave, and give me your knife. I am going to cut something in this tree—only a cross, the emblem of suffering. I think I can do that."

The lantern was put down, and Skewball began to dig the grave, while Sal commenced her work, cutting deep into the bark of a silver-birch tree.

Both worked in silence, and both worked rather slowly, owing to the tears that fell like rain from their eyes.

How many great people have been buried with much pomp and ceremony, and not a tenth of the sorrow which accompanied Maggie's burial! Half a dozen honest tears are worth all the wretched undertakers' trappings that were ever paraded in the kingdom, and what sexton labouring for hire ever dug so energetically as Skewball did that night?

Without a pause he kept on until a grave was dug deep enough for a king. The ground was of stiff clay, and came out in great blocks, as he cut them neatly with his spade. There was no need for shoring up, which a lighter soil would have made imperative.

Sal had finished before him, and crouched by the grave, holding the lantern while he laboured. When all was finished she gave Skewball a helping hand, and he sprang out.

"How shall we lower her?" he said.

"Tie our scarves together," said Sal, "and my skirt shall do the rest."

She took it off and tore it into strips, and tied them together. Thus put together it was strong enough to lower that frail form.

They placed their rough ropes into a fitting position, and having hung the lantern on the branch of a tree, Skewball took off his hat, and asked his wife to offer up a prayer. Kneeling down, Sal spoke out a few words from her heart, and all the burial service that Maggie was ever to have was over.

"Now," said Skewball, "we will lower her."

"Hush!" said Sal, "what's that? Somebody is coming. Put out the light. Quick!"

It was too late. Before Skewball could reach the lantern a man burst through the bushes and stood before them. Sal recognised the rough fellow she had refused to serve with drink.

"Darned if I didn't think something was up," he said, "by the way you got rid of us; so I watched and followed you, but I lost you a bit in this confounded wood. What have you here? A dead body! Skewball and his wife up to murder! D—— me if I should have thought it. Let me see who it is."

Neither Skewball nor his wife could move. They were half-petrified by the intrusion, which was fraught with a thousand terrors for them. The new comer took down the lantern, and cast the light upon the face of the dead.

"Darn me," he said, "if it aint our Maggie. There'll be squalls about this, I guess."

CHAPTER CXIX.

A SHIPLOAD OF VALUABLE MATERIALS IS CONSIGNED TO ENGLAND.

BROAD ARROW JACK and Dick set sail, and without encountering rough weather reached the island, where Trimmer met them upon the shore. Upon recognising Dick he looked a little surprised, but said nothing just then, and merely saluted his chief.

"Have you anything to report?" asked Jack.

"Nothing of any importance," replied Trimmer.

"You have not found the Ogre?"

"No, chief, nor any signs of him."

"Has the Tiger returned?"

"Yes, chief, half a dozen times, but as you were not here he refused to say anything, although I think he has news."

"Keep a good look-out," said Jack, "and the moment he comes again tell me."

"Chief," said Trimmer, and then paused.

"What is it, Trimmer?" said Jack; "you seem to have something to say."

"Well, chief, it's hardly worth troubling you with, but something must be done with 'em."

"Them—who?"

"Wobbles, Conky, Curler, and Pigeon. They seem to have all gone off their heads."

"What are they doing?"

"Wobbles is as gaunt as a wolf, and walks about dodging the others with a club big enough for a giant. They are all mortally afraid of him, and are shying stones at him from morning till night, which wouldn't matter much if they didn't hit other people."

"What is the fool's object in pursuing them?" asked Jack, angrily.

"Their wittles," replied Trimmer. "I never saw such a chap. All he has don't seem to do him much good, and the more he has the hungrier he gets. He was always a good feeder, but he's downright ravenous now."

"Send them all to me," said Jack. "My tent is ready, I suppose?"

"Yes, chief, and has been kept so in expectation of your return."

"You can come, Dick," said Jack, and the boy followed him like a hound that has been whipped a bit, and brought to obey.

"What's the meaning of that?" thought Trimmer, as he stared after them. "Young Dick seems to be quite broken in. A feat of the chief's. Something to do, I suppose. Now to get that lot together. Here's one of 'em. Hallo, Wobbles!"

Wobbles, truly gaunt and wretched-looking, came wandering by, with the club mentioned under his arm. Despite his naturally peaceful, not to say cowardly nature, he now presented the appearance of a wolf in search of prey.

He turned two hollow eyes upon Trimmer, and in obedience to a sign pulled up.

"Come nearer," said Trimmer. "At the same old

game, I see. Where are the other fellows—your lot, I mean?"

"They are building a stockade to eat their wittles in," replied Wobbles, "but I'll have it."

"What the deuce do you do with it?" asked Trimmer.

"It's the hair—the hair," replied Wobbles.

"Who's hair?" asked Trimmer.

"The hair we breathe," replied Wobbles. "It's an everlasting stimulant, and beats gin and bitters into fits."

"It certainly makes one peck," said Trimmer, "but your pecking doesn't seem to do you any good."

"My pecking," returned Wobbles, wailing, "is a 'ollow mockery."

"You seem to be hollow enough," said Trimmer. "But go up to the chief; he wants you."

"So he's come back? Ah! more misery for me."

"What the deuce now?" asked Trimmer. "Why should the return of the chief bring you misery? He's kind enough to us all."

"And thus it is," said Wobbles, eyeing Trimmer ferociously, "that I am sad."

"You are a rum un," returned Trimmer. "Why should you be sad?"

"Hast thou a conscience?" asked Wobbles, in a hollow whisper. "Have ye hever felt the stings of remorse? Ha—ha! Hast thou never wronged the hinnocent, and felt a wurrum at the bud? Away—away!"

"Right off your 'ed you are," said Trimmer, "and I'll trouble you to come out of it."

"Would that I could!" groaned Wobbles, "but I cannot. There is a blight upon me. The sins of my youth enwellop me. The miserable past clings to me like a garment. I rob my best friends to feed a wiper."

"Calls his appetite a wiper!" said Trimmer. "Well, go on to the chief, and I'll send the others. He wants to see the lot of you."

Wobbles, with a shudder that must have sprung from a conscience terribly racked, turned and walked towards the tent of his chief. Having reached it he paused a moment outside to compose his features, and then went in.

Jack was seated at the table, looking over some papers, and close behind him was young Dick Skewball, who grinned at Wobbles as he came in as if he recognised an old friend. Wobbles returned his look with a glare of the loftiest scorn.

"Chief," he said, "I am here."

"And being here," replied Jack, looking up, "I have a few words to say to you. During my absence you have given some trouble, I hear."

"Too true—too true, oh! chief," murmured Wobbles.

"As you are of very little use here," continued Jack, "and generally manage to get in the way when there is serious business on hand, I intend to send you to England. I am going to ship some favourite horses there, and I intend you and your three friends to look after them while they are at sea. Once in England there are people who will receive you."

"Confided in yet," murmured Wobbles, smiting his forehead. "Oh! I am too base to live."

Conky, Curler, and Pigeon now put in an appearance, all in a state of alarm. They could not imagine what the chief could want them for, unless it was to hang them out of the way. When they beheld the agitated countenance of Wobbles their fears were as good as confirmed. Never did three pairs of knees smite together so simultaneously as theirs did, and Conky in addition gave vent to a groan. Curler and Pigeon were past all forms of utterance.

But what a relief it was to their manly breasts to learn their destination! Tears of relief and gratitude were shed, and Pigeon getting his tongue loosened, was heard to murmur—"The chief is the noblest cove a-goin." To which Conky and Curler, feeling it was necessary to be a little pious on the occasion, responded—"Amen, so be it! The Lord knows he is."

"You may go," said Jack, when this exhibition of good feeling was over. "Mr. Trimmer will arrange your embarkation."

Wobbles advanced to the front, and bowed low.

"Chief," he said, "may I have a word with you alone?"

Jack waved his hand to the rest, and they went out, Dick last, eyeing Wobbles as if he suspected him of some mischief.

"Now, say what you have to say, and go," said Jack.

"Chief," returned Wobbles, "I dare say you have noticed I have been the victim of some hemotion."

Jack bowed slightly.

"Oh! chief, canst thou not guess that I have wronged thee? Oh! thou noblest of men!" cried Wobbles—"a noble man, as I may say, almost afore you are a boy."

"I am not good at guessing," said Jack, coldly. "Been robbing the stores, I suppose," he said.

"It is too tre-ew," whispered Wobbles, "and I will confess all. But not in words, chief. Let me put it in writing and promise not to hopen the henvelope until I am far away upon the sea."

"Write," said Jack; "there are the materials."

"And you promise not to hopen it, chief?"

"Yes."

Wobbles, having smitten his forehead thrice, and groaned several times to show the agony within, took up a pen and a sheet of paper, and wrote a few words. Then he gave a great sigh of relief, as if a great burden had been removed from his breast. Folding the epistle carefully he put it into an envelope, and laid it before his chief.

"When I am gone, chief," he said, mournfully, "read and forgive."

Jack bowed without looking up from the papers he was examining, and Wobbles, with his conscience apparently in his knees, staggered out of the tent.

Trimmer was already busily engaged in arranging for their departure, and the captain of the vessel, having had his instructions, sent a boat ashore for the quartette, all of whom had a constitutional aversion to the sea.

They stood on the shore in a row, while Trimmer, who had been into the chief's tent again, handed to the officer in charge of the boat a packet for England, and exchanged a few words with him.

"You are going back to the fields?" he said.

"Yes," replied the officer; "but only for the horses. We have the list."

"May I ax if there is such names as old Joss and Fireworks among 'em?"

"Yes. Mr. Brisket added them at the last moment, I believe."

"Good; and when I come to England I hope to have a look at 'em again. Those two horses are worth a mint of money."

"Old—are they not?"

"Inclined that way," said Trimmer, calmly. "But what matters age when you have bone and blood?"

"Oh! nothing of course," replied the officer, who was not acquainted with the animals in question. "I suppose they are to be taken great care of?"

"Don't let them have a hair rumpled," replied Trimmer.

While the foregoing conversation was going on Wobbles and the trio of friends were eyeing the sea as if they regarded it as a common enemy.

"Roughish this morning," said Conky.

"I calls the sea a reg'lar hass," said Pigeon, "heavin' up and down. Why can't it keep still? Then a chap wouldn't be done over the moment he gets afloat."

"It's a hevil thing," said Wobbles, "and the less you has to do with it the better man you'll be."

"Now then!" cried Trimmer, "off you go, and mind how you behave yourselves. The captain keeps capital ropes'-ends on board. You don't look very merry over going."

"I don't see how a man as have to look forrard to about a week's hagony on his back can be merry," replied Wobbles; "but still on the whole I am glad we are going."

From his tent Jack was watching them. He had begun to suspect there might be more in that letter Wobbles wrote than he at first suspected. His word was his bond of course, and although it was given to one who was both knave and fool he kept it. Until the ship was hull down on the horizon he did not break the envelope.

Then he opened it, and read—

"NOBLEST OF CHIEFS,—The wittles manely whent to the Hoger. Yule find him squatted in a 'ole about 'arf a mile up the north shore.—Your 'umble servant WOBBLES."

CHAPTER CXX.
THE DIAMOND FIELDS IN A FURY.

THE name of the man who had come so suddenly upon Skewball and his wife was Mike—Savage Mike the people called him, in acknowledgment of his often displayed ferocity. A tall, powerful, violent-tempered man, he had been the terror of scores. Many a man walked about the diamond-fields with scars due to Savage Mike, and two men lay in their graves, having fallen in a quarrel with him.

Such a fellow could have but little sympathy for any one, and as far as he was personally concerned Maggie might be as well in her grave as out of it, but he felt very sore over being refused his drink by Sal, and the opportunity offered for revenge was too good to be refused.

"I guess," he said again, "there'll be a rumpus over this job. You had better have stabbed half the field than have touched her."

"But we didn't do it," said Skewball, recovering his speech.

"Who did then?"

"What business is that of yours?" interposed Sal. "When the time comes to talk about it we shall be ready to speak. Don't you set yourself up as judge and jury."

"No, I don't," said Savage Mike, "but I means to be a witness, and take a share in the execution. You didn't do it, indeed. Who did then? That's wot I wants to know. She's made a stiffish bit o' money lately, and that's what's led you into it."

"I swear it was not done by us," said Skewball.

"All right," said Savage Mike; "swear away. It will amuse people if it don't do more."

"Sal," whispered Skewball, hurriedly; "what shall I do?"

"Shoot him down," replied Sal, "he's not a man —he's a wolf."

Skewball drew a pistol, but Savage Mike had already interpreted their whispering, and backed into the bushes before he could take aim. Skewball fired, and missed.

"Ha, ha!" laughed Savage Mike, "that's a good un, but I'm off to make this place too hot for you. Not drink at your bar, eh? I'll be in there to-night with a few pals, and we'll drain the place dry before the sun's up."

"And he'll do it, unless we stop him," said Skewball.

"Quick, here! help me to lower her," said Sal. "The poor thing, if she knows what is going on, will forgive this burial. That's it—steady. Now, off with you, and I'll stop to fill in."

"What am I to do?"

"Barricade every door and window, except the back one. Keep that till I come."

"But suppose, Sal, they catch you?"

"You trust to me. I'm not afraid of the lot of 'em."

"I know you are not," said Skewball, "but that doesn't make it better if they should come on you. What is a woman to a hundred men? Let me go and tell the whole thing."

"And break our word, Richard?"

"Forgive me, it was only a moment's thought. At least, let me ask Brisket to relieve us from it."

"That you may do. Get off at once, and I'll be back too before that savage brute has got the fields up."

Skewball only stayed to give his wife the sort of kiss he generally gave at parting, and then made the best of his way back. The fields were fairly quiet when he reached home, but lights were moving to and fro.

"Savage Mike is at work," he muttered. "The Lord help us!"

Entering by the door through which he left, he went to the room occupied by Brisket and his prisoner. He knocked, but got no answer.

"Asleep," he said, and opening the door peeped into the room.

It was empty.

"Gone!" he exclaimed. "Brisket—Brisket, come here!"

No answer. He ran all over the place. Not a soul but himself was in it.

"Here's a precious fix," he muttered. "If we are accused who's to prove our innocence? We are tongue-tied, and everything is against us. But I must barricade the house, front door first."

This was in the bar, and having examined the bolts, he piled half a dozen full casks of beer and spirits against it, and drove wedges under the lower barrels to keep them in their place. Nothing less than an absolute smashing of the whole concern could break it down.

Just as he finished this portion of his work Sal came in, very much out of breath, as if she had been running.

"Richard," she said, "what does Brisket say?"

"He's not here, Sal."

"Not here?"

"No, gone—melted away—flown in the most mysterious manner."

"Then we have nothing to do but to stand to our word," said Sal.

"I suppose so," said Skewball. "Are they moving in the fields?"

"Yes, and lights are coming this way," replied Sal. "Come and make the other places fast."

"All right, old gal," said Skewball; "but they'll get in, you know, and then——"

He wriggled his neck about, and looked at his wife with a saddened expression of face. She spoke out boldly.

"We can but die, Richard," she said. "Be a man, and don't be afraid of me."

"Darned if I don't think you'll bring us through it," he said, as he nailed up the back door and closed the shutters.

"I'll try," said Sal. "You want another nail here, Richard. Now, just go on the roof and take stock of the enemy, while I pile up the furniture and so on."

There was a trap leading to the roof, and by its aid Skewball got outside. Some distance away he could see a number of lights advancing, and the murmur of those who bore them came to his ears like the roar of a distant sea.

"They'll have us out, or burn us out," said Skewball. "Poor Sal!"

He sat there waiting until they were within a hundred yards of the house, before going down to his wife again. She had done her best to make a good barricade to the back premises.

"Sal," he said, "they are coming. What shall I do?"

"Take your gun, and go upon the roof again," she

BROAD-ARROW JACK.

BY THE AUTHOR OF

HANDSOME HARRY and CHEERFUL CHING-CHING.

WHILST BRISKET WAS INTENTLY WATCHING HIS PURSUERS JEE JAUNDICE CREPT SEA-THIEF UPON HIM.

No. 18.

"call upon them to keep off, and if they don't let fly into the thick of them."

"Good!" said Skewball, and, obedient to her at all times, he fetched his gun and loaded it.

"There's two barrels here," he said, "and I seldom miss."

"Pick out the worst characters you know," suggested Sal, "for there will be many a good man in the crowd. They are here, Richard."

There was a hammering at the door, and a roar of voices calling upon him to open. There came a voice which they recognised as Savage Mike's.

"Burst open the place. Don't parley with murderers! Down with the door!"

"We owe him a lot," said Skewball, and I'll go and settle with him."

He crept up to the roof, and lay down to take stock of the mob below. He could see them well enough by the lights they carried, but he was shrouded in darkness.

Presently he picked out Savage Mike and covered him.

"I can't shoot even a brute like that without giving him warning," he said, lowering his gun. "Hallo, below there!"

They heard him, and every voice was hushed. But they could not see him, and many were in doubt as to where he was.

"I say, you, Savage Mike," he cried, "clear out!"

"Where the tarnation are you?" roared Mike.

"Up here on the roof," replied Skewball. "Clear out, will you?"

"What for?"

"Because you aint wanted here."

"No, I should think not, nor any of us," said Savage Mike. "And you didn't want me up in the wood neither. Down with that door!"

"I tell you to clear out," said Skewball. "I've covered you!"

"You were always all boast and brag," said Mike.

"But now I'm in earnest," said Skewball, and fired.

Savage Mike tossed up his arms and fell forward upon his face. They raised him, but every pulse was still.

"Dead," said somebody.

At another time the death of Savage Mike might have been hailed with joy, but now it was a different thing. He was one of many bent upon avenging what they considered to be a foul crime on the part of Skewball. He was a partner in the administration of justice, and his fall was received with a yell of execration.

"I gave him fair warning!" cried Skewball. "You can't say I did not."

"Who murdered Maggie?" shouted a score voices.

"Not me," replied Skewball.

"You liar, you did!" shouted one of the foremost.

"All right then," said Dick, "say that I did, if you like, but I know I didn't. Who accuses me?"

"Savage Mike, and you've murdered him!" they cried.

"But that's all blarney," said Skewball. "He came here blustering with a lot of you, without telling me what you wanted, and of course I stood out to defend my place. I aint a-going to keep in bed while you rob me."

"You murdered Maggie!" they cried.

"Prove it!"

"Mike said you did it."

"Mike would say anything when he was alive. He was quite capable of committing the crime, and putting it upon another."

That was true enough, and a few voices were heard to say so.

Skewball saw he had a chance of pacifying them, and made the most of it.

"It's all very well for you to come here," he said, "but who among you knows if the poor creature is dead or alive?"

"She was alive last night," said one. "I saw her."

"And have you seen her dead to-night?" asked Skewball.

"No—I ain't."

"Then stand back, for your evidence ain't worth a noggin of whiskey. You hear what I've got to say to you all—go and prove she is dead, and then come and accuse me in a straightforward way, and I'll soon show you I didn't do it. As for that chap I've shot, well—he wasn't much good to you and me, and I've got the law on my side. He came as a burglar, and I can shoot men of that stamp any day. You all came the same, but I don't want to hurt you. Go home and go to bed."

This, however, they were not disposed to do just yet. Skewball had nonplussed them a little, but they were not quite satisfied. Finally the ringleaders held a consultation, and one stood forward to speak in the name of the rest.

"Skewball," he said.

"Well," said that gentleman from the housetop.

"Mike told us you were in the woods to-night—burying her. Is it true?"

"If I said no would you believe me?" asked Skewball.

"No."

"Then why put a fool's question? If you think I'm guilty, try to prove it."

"So we will then. A party of us are going up to the wood to see if we can find the grave. If we can't, well and good; Mike is a liar and you are free. If we can, you will have to stand trial. We shall have a guard here. Don't come out, or you will be shot down."

"All right," said Skewball.

The search would give him the respite of a few hours, if nothing more, and a hundred things might happen in that time. He felt like a man reprieved, and was very thankful for Sal's sake.

"Before we go," said the previous speaker, "we want you to give us some drink. It's chilly tonight, and we have a long job before us."

"Give you some drink! No; if you want it, you must pay for it."

"Well! we will do that. Let us have a couple of gallons."

"Stop a minute," said Skewball, taking some string from his pocket and forming a running noose at one end of it—"put the money in a bit of rag, and I'll haul it up."

"Won't you trust us?"

"Devil a bit," said Skewball.

He dropped the end of the string, and the men, after another debate, put the money in a handkerchief, and made it fast. Skewball hauled it up, and went down to Sal to count it. He told her what had taken place, and she breathed a little more freely.

"But it is only a short reprieve for you," she said; "they will find the grave."

"Sure to. But now let's put the whiskey in a keg, and lower it with a bit of rope."

This was done, and a couple of tin cups tossed down for them to drink out of. It was soon disposed of, and the searching party, with their lanterns retrimmed, went off to the woods.

"Two hours to daylight," said Dick; "and say that they find her an hour afterwards, then an hour's run back. Four hours, Sal, before we shall have them hooting and yelling again."

"It is not long, Richard."

"No; but we can do much in the time."

"Is there no way out of here?"

"I'll take a look round," said Skewball, which he did from the roof, and presently reported that there was a complete cordon round the house.

"What arms have we?" asked Sal.

"Two brace of pistols and this rifle," replied Skewball.

"A brace for each of us and the gun over for

you," said Sal. "Load all, and give me my share. We have five men at our mercy."

The weapons were prepared, and by Sal's advice they took up a position in the bar, commanding the approach from both back and front. For a while they sat silent. Sal put her hand upon her husband's shoulder, and presently spoke.

"Richard," she said, "you have been a very good husband to me."

"No more than middlin'," he answered, modestly; "but I've meant well."

"You have been all that a man can be," she said. "Now, tell me, Richard, if there is anything I have ever done which you remember with scorn and anger."

"Nothing, Sal."

"Have I not been hard upon you?"

"Never."

"Not with my tongue?"

"No more than I wanted for my good," said Skewball.

"Aye! so you say, Richard; but do you think so?"

"I'll take an oath of it if you like, Sal," he said.

"No, I believe you," was her reply. "Kiss me, old fellow."

This Richard did most heartily, and then there was another silence, which was not broken until dawn peeped through a crack in the wooden walls of the room.

"They are hard at work now, Sal," said Richard. "I'll go aloft and see if I can spy anybody coming."

On taking a last look from the roof he saw the cordon still around the house, the men for the most part silently leaning on their guns. A few were exchanging whispers, and as he thrust his head through the trap-door in the roof several saw him and uttered a shout.

"All right, my lads," said Skewball, coolly, "shout away. Man to man I'll fight the lot. Now then, where's one who'll come forrard for a mutual exchange of pot shots?"

Nobody caring to venture upon that class of entertainment his challenge remained unanswered. Indeed, not a few were afraid that he might open the ball, and kept a wary eye upon him.

Skewball was not long at his post ere he saw in the far distance several black specks rapidly advancing. They were men running, he knew, and he could easily guess they were messengers of evil to him.

Hastening down to Sal he imparted to her the tidings. She turned pale, but only said—

"Stand to your post, Richard, and die like a man. Kiss me again—it may be for the last time."

He kissed her as before, with a tenderness born of the time, and grasping his rifle, waited the onslaught he knew was at hand. The moments sped swiftly, and soon the roar of voices was heard.

"Have him out—we have found her grave!" and then came a crash, as a body of men dashed themselves against the door.

CHAPTER CXXI.

FOUR KNAVES AND TWO OTHERS.

THE name of the vessel which worked to and from the diamond-fields was the Hope, and it safely carried its precious freight of rascality back to the port, and then, without permitting Wobbles or any of his friends to go ashore, transferred them to the Argosy, another craft, occasionally used in the service of our hero, and homeward bound.

It was commanded by Captain Bobbin, a good old-fashioned seaman, who drank like a fish, swore like a trooper, and kept his crew at work like one used to command. The man who disobeyed him when at sea usually found that the commander had an unusual amount of bone and muscle. A skittle had as much chance with a well-thrown ball as an ordinary man with him.

In the first place it was intended for the Hope to go to England, as it was doubtful if the Argosy would be in port. In case she was the transfer effected was to be made. She was also to carry back certain stores, and the horses referred to in a previous chapter, among them old Joss and Fireworks.

Captain Bobbin having been furnished with all needful information respecting his human cargo, took the first opportunity to have an interview with the precious four, and having had them all ranged in front of him, he took a seat upon a camp-stool, lighted a cheroot about seven inches long, and began—

"Look at me, you four," he said.

They looked at him, breathing heavily—like people who had been running.

"You see me?" he said.

"Ain't we got eyes in our 'eads?" asked Conky, disposed to be rude.

"Stand out a minute," said Captain Bobbin, "and I'll talk to the rest."

Conky stood out, obeying almost against his will, but there was something in the wave of that gigantic arm which told him he had better not refuse. Wobbles, Curler, and Pigeon, rather ashen about the gills, were then further addressed.

"Can *you* see me?" asked Captain Bobbin.

"Yes, sir," they all said.

"I'm glad o' that. My name's Bobbin. You hear that?"

Oh! yes, they heard it, and all said so.

"Did you ever hear of me afore?" he continued.

As it was plain he expected them to say they had, all hastened to declare his name was quite familiar. Wobbles, who had hazy ideas of the difference between the Merchant Service and the British Navy, hurriedly adding—"at Trafalgy, Copperhagen, Nile, and the Spanish Armadiar."

"Oh! indeed," said Captain Bobbin; "so you've known about me at these places."

"I've heard your name mixed up with 'em," replied Wobbles.

"What a liar you are!" said old Bobbin; "stand out!"

Wobbles stood out, and both he and Conky having an instinctive idea of a hot time coming they formed a very dejected pair.

"Now you two," said Captain Bobbin, returning to Curler and Pigeon, "where have you heard of me?"

This was a cross-examination they were ill-prepared to meet. Both looked uncommonly wretched; but Curler, like a brave son of old England, tried to make the best of a bad job.

"I say, Pigeon," he said, "where was it we heard of this noble gentleman?"

"I ain't got no head for the names of places," said the wretched Pigeon.

"Liars all!" said Captain Bobbin, "and if I do hate anything in the world it is a liar. Stand out all of you while I finish my smoke."

They stood out, a wretched row of criminals, tried and found guilty, and waiting mournfully for the sentences. Old Bobbin smoked at his cigar vigorously, got through it in due time, and rose to his feet.

"Do you know what I does with liars?" he said, addressing the four guilty ones.

It was a question they were really not called on to answer, and they all kept silent.

"I larrups 'em," said Captain Bobbin, "with a rope's end. Now just get about four yards apart, and march up and down in front of me half a dozen times."

This arrangement divided them conveniently, so that he could get a fair cut at each as he went by, without wasting time. He was a man of exceeding ingenuity, was Captain Bobbin.

"The man as flinches or tries to cut it," he said, "will get a double dose."

Their souls quailed, but they thought it better to take their dose as well as they could; but it was very trying. Old Bobbin was very strong, and the knot at the end of the rope as hard as a grape shot. At each blow the recipient leaped a foot in the air, and uttered a dismal howl.

"Now you knows me," said Captain Bobbin, "and you can guess what you will get if you gives me any of your nonsense. Sit down there, and don't move until I tell you. We are going to wash the deck presently, but you need not get out of the scuppers—a little water won't hurt any of you."

They sat there for a good two hours or more, while the horses were being slung on board. On the arrival of old Joss and Fireworks, both looking as fresh as possible, and up to any amount of work, the four friends shuddered in concert, and exchanged glances of dismay.

"'Aunted by them for life," murmured Wobbles; "the sperit of my mother is in one on 'em I believe."

"Don't speak disrespectful of your parient," said Conky.

"And don't you then?" said Wobbles.

"I can't," replied Conky; "I never knowed her."

Most of the horses were put below; but old Joss and Fireworks were accommodated with a deck stable—a fact which excited the curiosity of their late riders; but it was speedily explained by Captain Bobbin.

"You lot," he said; "you knows these 'orses and they knows you. They are getting a bit old and stiff, are them 'orses, and I've orders, with weather permitting, that you are to ride 'em up and down the deck for an hour daily, so as to keep their bones from getting fixed."

"But suppose, sir, they jump overboard!" said Wobbles, aghast.

"Then you must swim for it, for I'm d—— if I stand by for you," replied Captain Bobbin. "Now get up and groom the horses all round; you will find the curry-combs and things to do it in that box."

Left to themselves, the newly-appointed grooms opened the box and took out a number of stable requisites, of the use of which they knew as much as they did of an electric apparatus.

"What's this?" asked Wobbles, holding up a curry-comb.

"That," said Conky, with an authoritative air, "is to get the hairs of the tails straight."

"Then," replied Wobbles, "you had better use it, since you know all about it."

"Combing a tail out," said Conky, "is rather dangerous work."

"Horses kick," added Pigeon; "my uncle was kicked by a cob bang up agin a new-built wall, and shot into a garden with nine rows of bricks. It was his ruin."

"How's that?" asked Curler.

"He was only in a small way of business," replied Pigeon—"went about with a basket and trotters. He was so flabbergasted that he didn't know what he was up to for ever so long. When he came to, all his stock in trade was gone."

"Stole?" said Curler.

"And wus," replied Pigeon—"all swallered. The haccident happened just as they let the kids out of the national school."

"Are you going to get to work?" roared out Captain Bobbin.

"Come along," said Wobbles, hurriedly, "he's a-feeling for his rope."

The others needed no further stimulant, and in a body they skedaddled below, where the horses underwent a grooming the like of which they had never known before; but it is worthy of record that none of the grooms got what they richly deserved—a kicking.

CHAPTER CXXII.
A FRIEND TO A FOE.

THE letter left by Wobbles was full of important information, and would have been invaluable if the news it gave had resulted in the capture of the Ogre; but Broad Arrow Jack was again doomed to disappointment. They searched the cave pointed out, where they found signs of the Ogre's recent residence, but he himself was not there.

How Jack chafed under this continuous disappointment may be easily guessed, but he gave no sign of it to those with him. To Dick he appeared the same as usual, and to Trimmer he only said—"The rascal has dodged us; but he cannot leave the island, and we will have him yet."

Dick Skewball remained in close attendance upon him all that evening; but Jack said very little to him. He was occupied in cleaning his arms, which he seldom troubled his men to look after.

The keen eyes of the young attendant were seldom removed from the face of his chief, and through all there was the appearance of an inward struggle going on the same as was apparent in him during the ride back after the taming of the mustang. He had something on his mind—something which some of my readers may guess at—and if he was undecided what course to pursue it was only what might be expected from either man or boy.

Suddenly Jack looked up and caught his eyes.

"Dick, what are you thinking of?" he asked.

"I? nothing, sir, in particular—only—" and Dick paused.

"On the tip of his tongue," thought Jack, "it will come out anon."

"Dick," he said, after a pause, "have you a brother?"

"Yes, sir; two younger than myself."

"Where are they?"

"Staying from home at present, sir," at a school.

"So then, a school at the fields?" asked Jack, in surprise.

"Yes," said Dick, "the charge is a dollar a day, and the schoolmaster is as fat as a porpoise."

"Well he may be," said Jack, "but the diggers can afford it."

"Yes," said Dick, "most of them."

"And some people who do not dig could afford it," said Jack. "Now, I dare say there are some boys who could afford to educate themselves."

Dick made no reply. His eyes fell, and a flush overspread his face.

"I have heard of quite children," said Jack, musingly, "who have had a lucky find. In one case it was diamonds, previously dug by another and stowed away."

Dick's face became suddenly fixed, and a film came over his eyes. He bit his lips hard, and breathed short and quick.

"Did you ever see that lad?" asked Jack.

"No," replied Dick, in a low tone.

"Or hear of him?"

"No."

"Not yet," muttered Jack—"not yet!" Turning over a few papers he gave Dick a respite ere he spoke again.

"Dick, you have very honest parents."

"Yes," said Dick, and his voice could scarcely be heard.

"Honest parents! Aye! it is something to boast of," said Jack. "And how proud they are of their children if they are honest!"

Nothing was said after this for a long time. Dick bit his nails hard, and every now and then drew in a short sharp breath, as if he had received a sudden pain. The voice of the Tiger suddenly broke the silence.

"Massa—massa, quick! ship coming."

Jack was on his feet in a moment, and met the Tiger at the entrance to the tent. The boy stood at the attention in a moment.

"A ship, Tiger!" he said. "Where? I see none."

"Other side of the island, massa. Small ship— one sail—one man."

"Small ship—a boat, you mean. But who is the one man?"

"Not know, massa; too far away—too little to see im."

"Is the ship coming for the island, Tiger?"

"Straight! de man hab de nose of de ship dis ay."

As this stranger might work mischief, consciously or unconsciously, Jack called out Trimmer and the men, and leaving a few in charge of the tents, bade the Tiger lead the way to where he had seen the small vessel.

Dick was not invited to accompany the party, but he fell in behind the chief, and followed a little sullenly, as if he would rather have stayed away, but was under the guidance of a will stronger than his own. Most likely that was the case.

Jack took no notice of him, and when he dropped his handkerchief, and Dick sprang forward and picked it up, he neither looked nor spoke as he took it, but simply gave a slight nod in acknowledgment of the service.

The course the Tiger took was not in a direct line across the island. It lay a little southward over one one end of it. Two hours' smart walking brought them within a short distance of the sea again. The land on the way had risen. Now, of course, they had to descend a slope.

The Tiger ran on before, eagerly looking out at sea. As he bounded upon the sands a cry burst from his lips, and he fell into a kneeling position upon the ground.

Jack drew near and saw the boy was kneeling beside a figure stretched out upon the ground. A still nearer view of the figure showed him that it was a member of some savage tribe. His body was almost entirely naked, brown as a berry, and ornamented here and there with patches of paint.

"How came the fellow here?" he asked; "is he sleeping?"

"Dead, massa," said the Tiger, pointing to a cruel stab under the ribs, from which the blood was slowly oozing.

"This," said Jack, "is the Ogre's work." Then an alarm sprang up within him. "Where is this man's boat?"

"I see something out at sea, yonder," said Trimmer; "it is a mere speck."

"Aye, aye," said Jack, "but small as it is, I can see who is inside her. The Ogre is there, and I am left caged here until the Hope returns. Hope! I have no hope, now. Bury this poor fellow, and follow me back to the camp."

CHAPTER CXXIII.

A CALM AND A STORM.

THE Argosy lay becalmed in mid-ocean, and Captain Bobbin was in a very fretful mood. For five days his vessel had gently rocked upon the idle deep, under a copper-coloured sky by day and a deep purple star-covered arch at night.

If Captain Bobbin disliked anything it was to see his men idle; but five days' calm had left them nothing to do. In a row they lay upon the forecastle, on the shady side of the ship, like logs of timber in a timber-yard, and the bitter eye of their captain was on them.

"I've got my canvas set," he muttered, "and I've no excuse for furling it until the glass runs down. Every blessed thing on board is as clean as a new pin, and—well, let 'em rest for once; but I'll have somebody out. Where are those four skunks?"

The four gentlemen or skunks—as people may think—alluded to were below, where they spent as much of their time as they could, to be out of the way of that fiery old rascal who commanded the ship and found such delight in harassing them until their bodies had very little more substance in them than one finds in a small bundle of fiddle strings.

It was a happy thought in Captain Bobbin's eyes to have those fellows out, and accordingly he went to the companion and roared out—

"Come up, you Phary's lean kine—come up, you swine of the wilderness!"

As they had been called everything that was proposterous and insulting from the time they started, Wobbles and his friends generally accepted anything like the foregoing as being especially addressed to them, and accordingly they came up, meekly and obediently.

"Look here," said Captain Bobbin, "you fellows do something. What do you mean by skulking below? Here, I've got it; bring out them two horses, and give 'em exercise."

"Not here, sir, surely?" said Conky.

"Here," said old Bobbin, "on this deck. It's strong enough, ain't it?"

"Oh! yes, it's a beautiful deck—couldn't be a better," replied Wobbles. "Oh! my sainted mother, if you've got a eye on me now——"

"What are you muttering about?"

"I was thinking of my mother. I am a norphan," said Wobbles, pathetically.

"What else would you be?" asked old Bobbin, contemptuously. "Out with them horses, and two of you mount. You two first."

He pointed out Wobbles and Conky, and the misery of the hour restored the warm friendship of bygone years. They clasped each other's hands, and looked appealingly at Captain Bobbin. The figure-head of the ship would have given them as much sympathy.

Curler and Pigeon being directed to bring out old Joss and Fireworks, brought them forth, and the noble steeds, with the spirit of nine days bottled up in their carcases, were no sooner on deck than they neighed musically, and kicked up behind with joy.

"They are gone right wild," said the dismayed Wobbles. "Oh! Conky, friend and companion, here's a fix."

"Don't go a-hugging of me," said Conky. "It's all your fault, you hass."

"Up there!" roared Captain Bobbin. "We'll start from here, and run to the cuddy and back again. We'll have a race, and the man who wins shall be let off, and him who loses shall have a larruping."

It was another good idea, but Captain Bobbin had been drinking heavily and smoking consumedly all that day, and he was literally bloated with an expanded imagination.

There is nothing too wild or reckless for jack tars to engage themselves in, and the crew fell in most heartily with the notion of having races. A number volunteered to be the first to mount, but Captain Bobbin had appointed two men, and would have no others.

"Up you g—t," he said, "and let me see your best, or, by Jingo! I'll do mine with this bit o' rope."

"It's sartain death," groaned Wobbles, as he struggled into a seat upon the bare back of old Joss, and Conky, having with a little assistance got upon Fireworks, his lips were seen to move like those of a man upon the scaffold.

"It's one—two—three, and away!" said Captain Bobbin. "Now then. One—are you ready?—two —three—HOFF!"

The last word was uttered with a roar like that of a wild beast, but neither old Joss nor Fireworks moved a peg. They had been taking stock of the ship, and seeing its range was limited, perceived the necessity for good behaviour.

"It wouldn't take much to roll overboard," snorted old Joss.

"Just my opinion," snorted Fireworks in return. "Don't move."

"Not a peg," was the rejoinder of old Joss.

It is a well-known fact that horses, when left to themselves, will not go over a bridge that is unsafe, or over ground that is hollow, so that we need not be surprised at the sagacity of old Joss and Fireworks, who declined to accept the deck of the Argosy for a race-course; and it is also well known that men, in spite of the natural fear and great sagacity of horses, have stimulated them on with whip and spur, to the destruction of both. Captain Bobbin on this occasion undertook to stimulate both these animals before him with his favourite weapon—the rope's-end.

He chose Fireworks to operate upon first, and dealt that animal a blow in the rear that regularly galvanised him. He sprang up in the air, and came down all in a heap. Conky was pitched on his head on the hard deck, and lay quite still.

"That chap's out of it," said Captain Bobbin, coolly. "Now, you on the other horse, you must walk over the course."

The captain's idea of walking was a little different to other people's, for instead of leading old Joss gently over the ground, he gave him what he called "a touch up," the same as he had given Fireworks.

The result was simply terrible. Old Joss turned half-round and ran blindly forward, until he reached the ship's side, when he was stopped suddenly, of course, and Wobbles was shot up in the air, and then descended head first into the sea.

"Look out for him," cried Captain Bobbin. "Chuck him a rope."

"Sharks handy, sir," said one of the men.

And as the man spoke, the snouts of two of these agreeable monsters were seen bearing down upon the spot where Wobbles disappeared.

CHAPTER CXXIV.
SKEWBALL IN TROUBLE.

PEOPLE often change their minds over unimportant subjects. When Sal made it a stipulation with her husband not to look upon Maggie, she did it out of reverence for the dead; but when in the presence of the body, the sight so pitiful—so beautiful—drew from her the involuntary request for him to look upon her, and he did so with much reverence. As with individuals, so with masses; and the mob, bent upon having the lives of the Skewballs, raging like wild beasts for blood, got the door down, rushed in, captured them, but for the time spared their lives.

Skewball and his wife were armed, but when the rush came they could do but little. The mob came upon them like great waters let loose from behind a barrier, and Skewball was pinioned before he could pull a trigger.

At first there was a savage cry for their lives, but somebody—who it was never revealed—from behind cried out—

"Give them a fair trial—remember we have British blood in our veins."

There were some present who had not that blood, but they were few in number, and the rest, fortunately for Skewball, heard that voice, and heeded it.

"He shall have a trial," they said, and led him and his wife forth captives.

But although they spared him, they had no mercy on his place. That was given over to those who chose to wreck it. The temptation was great, and men who in their cooler moments would have blushed at the thought of wanton destruction, lent a hand to ruin Skewball's house.

Some of the more sober and earnest led the prisoners away—the rest remained to do the work of destruction.

And right well they did it.

The taps of the spirit casks were turned on, and the fiery fluids handed round. Men drank them like water, and went, as might be expected—mad. They danced, they sang, they raved, hooted, and howled, and their cries brought up others, who joined the desperate throng, and drank until they, too, were as excited and reckless as the rest.

Reader, have you ever seen a man downright stark-staring mad with drink? If you are townborn you must have seen such a creature now and then. If so picture some two hundred in the same condition, exciting each other into exhibitions of frenzy, each one worse than the last. Many were no worse than senseless fools—others were uncontrollable demons.

For awhile there was nothing more than riot and confusion, but at last a blow was struck. There was no cause for it being given, and he who dealt it forgot it the moment after; but the trains of evil passions were fired, and a desperate general fight ensued.

Knives were drawn, pistol shots exchanged, and blood began to flow. The sight of it was all that was needed to turn the majority of them to devils. The drink was in, and all that was good and noble and generous and manly was out.

How furiously they fought, and how savagely they struck at each other! One would have thought they had been enemies for years, and had at last met to settle old scores, which could not be forgiven. In the midst of all there was a cry of "fire!"

There is something intensely awful in that cry, and men never hear it without heeding. These mad furious men paused in their deadly work, and rushed out, leaving some dozen dead and wounded behind them.

The drinking booth was on fire. Some reckless hand had ignited the spirit casks, and the flames were spreading furiously.

There was a cry to save those within, and many who had been fighting savagely a minute before were the first to rush to save the fallen. More than one man was rescued by the hand that gave him the wound which laid him low.

All were not saved—three were in the midst of the flames when the rescuers entered, and two of the volunteers had a narrow escape, only leaving when the terrible fire had begun its work upon them. One man came out in flames from head to foot. They got him down, and crushed out the fire with their garments, but he felt such agony as no man could rest with, and as soon as he was free to rise he dashed out into the plain, and was heard of no more until his body, two days later, was found in a pond, into which he had plunged to assuage his anguish.

In an hour it was all over, and Skewball's house was ashes.

He heard of its fate from those who guarded him without a word or sign, but Sal shed a few tears.

"We made it very pretty for such a place," she said, "and now it's all gone. Thank God all the children were away!"

"I hope they will never come near the place or hear of us again," said Skewball.

"Why not?"

"Because, Sal, I think they are going to hang us both."

"Let them do it," said Sal, proudly, "and one day they will be sorry for it."

"That fatal promise!" moaned Skewball.

"If we told them the truth they would not believe us now," said Sal.

They were confined in one of the diggers' huts, and a guard kept outside. Every few minutes one or the other looked in to see they were all safe. One of them had been a friend of Skewball's, and to him he spoke.

"What are you going to do with us, Gerrard?" he asked.

"Try you first," replied Gerrard.

He was a tall man, with a face of Saxon mould, generally good-humoured, but now it wore a very stern expression.

"Try us for what?" asked Skewball.

"Murder."

"Do you believe we did it?"

"My belief will neither save nor hang you," replied Gerrard.

"But do you believe it?"

"What can I say to you?" asked Gerrard. "They have appointed me president of the court."

"Then we at least shall get justice," said Skewball. "When are we to be tried?"

"To-night, by torchlight, after they have buried one or two who came to grief at your place."

Skewball did not ask who had come to grief there. He had very little sympathy with men who had wrecked his home, and Gerrard did not trouble himself to give their names.

In places like the diamond-fields the death of a man by violence or otherwise excites very little comment.

Skewball and his wife had a long day, the hours dragged so slowly.

Food was brought them twice, but neither had any appetite, and partook of it but sparingly. Both longed for night.

"Better get it over," said Skewball; "it can only go one way. Poor Sal!"

"Don't you trouble about me," replied Sal; "if they hang you I don't want to live. We've lived all these years as man and wife, and it would be hard to part us now."

"You are a wife, indeed!" said Skewball.

When darkness came, Gerrard entered and announced all ready. A guard of a dozen men were in attendance, and the prisoners were marched to the foot of a tree, under whose branches the "court" had assembled.

There were a sort of public prosecutor, twelve men to serve as jury, and witnesses. The president, Gerrard, had the power to act as interrogator to the prisoners.

The witnesses had nothing but hearsay to give. The only man who had witnessed Skewball in the act of burying Maggie was dead, and they could only repeat the words he had uttered.

Confirmatory evidence could have been obtained in time, but the court of Judge Lynch was impatient; those who formed it did not care to lose a day—or days, perhaps—in searching the wood, and the evidence would have been sufficient, even if Skewball had denied being there.

Gerrard, the president, put the following questions to the prisoners.

"Skewball, you have heard the evidence of the witnesses?"

"I have."

"And you, Mrs. Skewball?"

"Yes."

"Skewball, is it true you were in the wood at the time stated?"

"I don't want to tell a lie about it," replied Skewball; "it is."

"And the Senora Maggie was lying dead there?"

"She was."

"Did you not kill her?"

"On my oath before my Creator," replied Skewball, fervently, "I did not."

"Did she die a natural death?"

"No."

"Who killed her?"

Skewball looked at his wife, and she answered for him.

"We cannot say."

"You know who is the murderer?"

"Yes," replied Skewball.

"And why will you not give up the name?"

"We are bound by a promise."

"To the murderer?"

"No."

"To whom then?"

"That I am not at liberty to name."

Gerrard paused, and looked round with a smile. He had his own opinion of the defence, which Skewball's answers virtually were, and thought it a very poor one. It was plain, and all the rest of the court and those assembled as spectators entirely agreed with him. A murmur of disbelief passed round the throng.

The scene was impressive, and more picturesque than any more civilised court could have been. The rough dresses, the rugged forms, the spreading branches of the mighty trees, the lighted torches, and above all, the dark sky studded with stars, formed a picture which would have delighted Gustave Doré. There were "effects" in it sufficient for a month's work, at least, for his rapid pencil.

Skewball and his wife alone would have made the fortune of any painter able to successfully depict them. Skewball, good looking, manly and bold—and Sal, the picture of an English matron, firm and upright, dauntless in the hour of trial.

"You have heard the prisoners' replies, and you have also heard the evidence," said Gerrard, addressing the twelve men who formed the jury; "what is your verdict?"

The consultation between the jury was brief. They were all men fairly representing their class, and had come in their jack boots, red shirts, and with their bowies and revolvers, just as they went everywhere. About a dozen words were exchanged, and then one who acted as foreman stood up.

"Well," said Gerrard, "what is it to be?"

"Skewball's guilty; but the woman is to be loosed," was the reply.

"You would not hang a woman?" said Gerrard.

"Of course not," replied the foreman, "she only acted with her husband."

"Richard Skewball," said Gerrard, rising and taking off his hat, "you've heard the verdict of the jury, and you know it's a just one."

"By heaven it is not," interposed Skewball.

"Hear me out," said Gerrard; "you and I, Skewball, were pals once upon a time, and I looked upon you as a man of honour. I don't do so now because I can't. You've murdered a poor woman for her money."

"Gerrard," interposed Skewball; "did you ever know me to tell you a lie?"

"Never—until now," was the reply.

"And now I speak the truth," said Skewball.

"I wish I could think so," returned Gerrard; "but there isn't a man here who believes you do—if so, let him hold up his hand."

Not a hand was held up. The belief in Skewball's guilt was general.

"You and I have been friends," continued Gerrard, and there were tears in his eyes when he turned his face towards the prisoner again, "and little did I ever think we should stand as we do now. But here we are. I've got a duty to do and I mean to do it. You have been found guilty, and I've a sentence to pass. You know what it is."

"Well," replied Skewball, "you will hang me."

"In an ordinary way," said Gerrard, "according to our rules here, it would be done at once; but I should like to give you till sunrise to think over your life a bit, and square accounts like. I think," he added, looking round, "we may give him till sunrise."

"Aye—aye!" muttered a few voices. The rest were silent.

"Then at sunrise be it," said Gerrard, hastening to take advantage of the scattered affirmatives. "And I hope, Skewball, you bear me no malice."

"None at all," replied Skewball.

"Then God ha' mercy on you!" said Gerrard, resuming his seat. "The trial is over. Release Mrs. Skewball, and see her outside the fields."

"I'll not go without my husband," said Sal, resolutely.

"Sal," said her husband, "think of our children, they will want you. Come, kiss me, old girl; we shall meet again."

Her bonds were taken off, and she threw her arms around his neck. A long kiss and a short whisper were exchanged, and they were parted again.

"Before I go," said Sal, addressing the assemblage, "I should like to tell you what a poor opinion I have of your faith and judgment. There stands my husband—a man every inch of him—did he ever lie to you?"

Nobody answered. Skewball's truth-telling was proverbial.

"Did he ever cheat, rob, or swindle any among you?"

Again there was a silence. Skewball was a man whom everybody trusted and believed in up to the time he was charged with the murder of Maggie.

"Of the money of the poor woman who is gone I know nothing for certain," Sal went on. "I believe it was sent to England, and invested in her name, with the understanding that if it was not claimed in ten years it was to go to the Society for the Protection of Women and Children. A wise use to make of her money, for women and children generally stand in need of much helping.

"Of our own money," she went on, "I may tell you this. Some is in good hands, but a great part of it lies under the smoking ruins of our home, which mad fools have robbed and destroyed; but the little that is left shall be devoted to bringing proper justice here, with men to institute good laws, and put such deeds as the murder of my husband out of your power. I have no more to say. Richard, my husband, I dare not look upon you again, or my heart will break. Farewell, dear husband !heaven bless you!"

She went her way, with her head bent down, and Richard Skewball, carefully guarded, was led back to the hut which had been his prison, to await a felon's death when the sun peeped up again above the earth.

CHAPTER CXXV.

BRISKET AND JAUNDICE.

ON the road between the diamond-fields and Blackrock walked Billy Brisket, with Jeb Jaundice by his side. The hands of the latter were bound and incapable of any movement but the nervous clasping and unclasping of the fingers, which told of disquietude within.

"Move quicker," said Brisket; "you are not done up yet. We have not walked a dozen miles."

"Dead—dead!" moaned Jaundice. "Dead!"

"You have said that before," said Brisket, sternly, "and I beg to say that I don't want any of your gammon; you understand me well enough?"

"Dead!" muttered Jaundice; "I murdered her."

"No doubt of that," said Brisket, shaking his fist at him. "Your confession comes a little late, and very much I should like to hand you over to them who would make short work of you. But it can't be done without the chief's orders, and so I've brought you along to get you out of harm's way."

"She was beautiful," groaned Jaundice, with a wild stare. "There wasn't a woman to compare with her all the country round when I married. Oh! Maggie—Maggie—my wife!"

"It does me good," mused Brisket, "to see him suffer—good in many ways. I did not think he had the feeling in him, and I never liked to think that any man was all demon. Can you walk faster?"

"I hear her voice," said Jaundice, stooping down; "she is not far behind. If you wait a little while she will overtake us."

Billy Brisket instantaneously looked behind, although he knew Maggie could not be there. It was well he did so, for a mile or so in the rear he saw a number of men coming apparently in pursuit of him.

To allow Jaundice—whom he felt they were in search of—to fall into their clutches, would be, in his eyes, a breach of trust, and taking him by the arm he hurried him forward.

"If we travel like this," said Jaundice, "she will never overtake us."

"She is gaining ground fast," replied Brisket, and with this assurance Jaundice was content.

Brisket's desire was to reach the shelter of the line of hills among which he and Broad Arrow Jack had shared so many adventures. Once there, he knew of many hiding places where he could stow away his prisoner with comparative safety.

That he was seen he soon knew, for presently a faint shout was borne to him on the wind, and looking behind he saw his pursuers gesticulating for him to stop.

It was just possible they might be friends, but he dared not risk stopping until they came within hail. The great fear was that Jaundice might suddenly take it into his head to pull up and wait for his wife, who, in his madness, he imagined was behind him.

Of this fear he was relieved by a fresh phantasy in the brain of Jaundice, who fancied he beheld his wife ahead, and increased his pace so much that Brisket had to exercise all his energies to keep up with him.

They got among the hills while the pursuers were yet far behind, and choosing a narrow path familiar to him through having traversed it in byegone days, Brisket doubled in and out like a hunted hare, until he came to a place where he had often rested when pursuing his former calling of pedlar.

It was a cave—one of the numerous recesses formed by nature, dry enough to enable a man accustomed to hardship to pass a night in. Into this he ran Jaundice, very much as a policeman would run a burglar into a station, and bidding him lie down at the far end, went rifle in hand to the mouth of the cave.

In front was an open valley lying between two hills, which an ordinary traveller could reach by a wide but more circuitous route than Brisket had taken. That way the pursuers advanced, and in a few minutes they debouched into the open, scattering about, and looking for the lost scent like hounds in a hunt.

"I was a fool to think they would pass on," muttered Billy Brisket, "but if needs be I must yield."

But he had done a more foolish thing than that. When he pushed Jaundice into the corner of the cave he dropped his knife without heeding the ring of it as it fell. The moment he turned his back Jaundice crept up, possessed himself of it, and in a minute he was free.

"He would stop me from meeting her," he muttered. "I hear her voice outside calling me, but he must die first, or he will haunt us, and mar our happiness. Maggie, I come!"

The men outside were now near enough for Billy Brisket to perceive they were no friends of his, for a more hang-dog looking lot of ruffians he had never set eyes on. They had the stamp of men who lived by plunder and violence.

He debated within himself whether it would be better to remain in hiding, or boldly declare himself, and endeavour to secure their good offices by giving up what he had, and promising something at a future time. Fighting was out of the question—their number was so great, and every man was well armed.

"Which shall it be," he asked himself, and Jaundice gave the answer.

Suddenly pouncing upon Brisket he bore him to the earth, and pinioning him by the back of the neck, hissed in his ear—

"Now I have you!"

If Jaundice had possessed half his former strength, Brisket's fate would have been sealed, but being so much broken by dissipation and recent sufferings

Billy had no difficulty in shaking him off and springing to his feet.

Only for a moment, though. With a howl such as travellers hear at midnight from some wild beast of the forest, Jaundice sprang upon him again, and threw his arm about him. Such strength as madness sometimes gives to the weakest, was upon him, and Brisket found himself temporarily a prisoner.

The noise of the scuffle speedily attracted the strangers, and gathering together in a body they bore down upon the cave, just as Brisket and Jaundice, locked in each other's grasp, struggled into the daylight.

"Hallo!" cried one of the foremost, "who have we here? Skin me alive if it aint my old pal, Job Jaundice!"

CHAPTER CXXVI.
WOBBLES HAS IT OUT WITH CAPTAIN BOBBIN.

TO be within a dozen feet of a "pirate of the ocean"—as the shark is called—is enough to try the nerves of any man, and if the two eyes Wobbles had in his head did stand clear out of it, it was no more than might have been looked for.

He saw that shark coming, did Wobbles, and made a rapid mental calculation of the number of teeth the monster had in his head. He could not see those teeth, for everybody knows that the mouth of a shark is under him, and that he has to turn upon its back to strike. But Wobbles had, on occasions like these, an inner vision—a sort of second sight, which answered every purpose.

The number of teeth he gave that shark credit for was 1,842, but how he arrived at such a conclusion he never could tell; but that was the number, neither more nor less.

"He's a coming," thought Wobbles, having settled the teeth question, "and I wonder where he will lay hold? The leg I believe is his favourite jint—ugh!"

Now the shark was coming upon him at the rate of forty miles an hour, and there were others coming on at a fairish rate from other directions. The slowest of them was bound to be upon him in five seconds or so. But do not therefore marvel at Wobbles having time for so much reflection, but please to remember the Persian fable of the man who dipped his head for a moment into a bucket of water and lived a lifetime.

In certain states of trial and excitement time seems to be suspended.

Having settled upon his leg as the point of attack, Wobbles shut his eyes, but as he did so a shark, or something, caught him round the throat, fires dawned before him, and a chorus of hideous noises resounded in his ears.

"This," thought Wobbles, "is the hend," and became unconscious.

But it was not the end for him, as, in due time, he opened his eyes again, to look upon familiar if not friendly faces, which he had known on board the Argosy.

There was even Old Joss, with his head over Conky's shoulder, almost smiling at him. In the front was Captain Bobbin, on whose noble countenance rested the light born of a noble deed.

"All right, my men," said the honest tar. "I told you he wasn't born to be hanged—just yet. What cheer, Wobbles!"

"I feel very odd about here," replied Wobbles, wriggling his neck.

"My lad," said Captain Bobbin, impressively, "be thankful you've got such a thick un. It saved you. I chucked the rope over your head, and we hauled you in right over the ship's side without slacking."

"Good gracious!" exclaimed Wobbles; "you didn't do that."

"Didn't we," said Captain Bobbin, "and be thankful we did. It was a close run with Mr. White Belly. He took the keel off our boat. But we got you in, my lad—we got you in. Now that's all fair and square we'll continue the races. Perhaps you'd like to have a change of 'orses."

"If I get on another," said Wobbles, with sudden ferocity, "may I be hanged. Mr. Captain Bobbin, you get on yourself."

"Me!" exclaimed Captain Bobbin; "what for?"

"What for!" said Wobbles, made brave by his maddening injuries; only to amuse us. Get on yourself; get chucked overboard; let us haul you in by the neck, and see what you'll say afterwards."

"Avast," said Captain Bobbin, waving his arm; "go easy, my lad."

"Go heasy yourself," replied the goaded Wobbles; "and mind where you are going to. I'm an Englishman; I've got British blood in my weins, and be I on the shore or on the sea, it's my privilege and blessing to be free."

"Hear that," exclaimed Conky, "real poetry."

"Easy both," said Captain Bobbin, with an evil gleam in his eye; "aboard here I'm master. There's no law except captain's law aboard here."

"But you don't call yourself a captain—do you?" asked Wobbles. His bravery was appalling, and Conky, Curler, and Pigeon were all amazed.

"Again—easy," said Captain Bobbin.

"Look here," said Wobbles, getting upon his feet, "I've stood enough. I knows my rights as well as any man, and I knows that although you can do as you like here, I can have the law of you when I get ashore. Now knock me down, and do what you like, and see what'll be the hend of it. Come on, you hanimated tomater."

Perhaps it was amazement that overcame the gallant captain more than anything else, for in all his life he had never been bearded in that way before. He saw he had gone far enough; but he did not like to give in—he wanted to give Wobbles what he called "a dose," but he also desired to do it legally.

"Look here, my lad," he said, "you and I didn't get on from the first."

"No, we didn't," said Wobbles.

"And where people don't get on, things come to a head sooner or later."

"They does," said Wobbles.

"Then they've come to a head with us now, and as there's no law ag'in a fair, stand-up, manly fight, let's have one."

"I'm ready," replied Wobbles. He was pale but firm. His two legs were like pillars, which was a good sign.

Conky, Curler, and Pigeon were much-impressed then. The bravery of Wobbles touched their better sympathy—they felt he was rushing into the jaws of death, and Conky in a friendly way admonished him.

"Don't go in for it," whispered he; "one blow and you'll be fiddlestrings."

"For hold England and liberty," muttered Wobbles, pulling off his wet coat, and dashing it down upon the deck like a dishcloth.

Public opinion was against Captain Bobbin. Being one of the "good old sort," he had, of course, been tyrannical to his men. In his school swearing, blustering, beating, and bruising were all at times essential to the good management of a ship, and scarce one of his crew was free from some mark or other in illustration of his discipline. There was no strong hope in Wobbles, but it was something to see a man standing up against tyranny, and he went with much encouraging support. When he dashed his coat down, and took off his waistcoat, the men encouraged him with a cheer.

"Oh! that's it, is it?" said Captain Bobbin, his two eyes shining like small lamps in his head—"all right—rank mutiny. I'll deal with you presently. Now, mister, I'm ready."

He did not take off his coat; he seldom did,

except when he went to bed, and not always then, for when a man ships a good cargo of grog every night he is occasionally indifferent to the small need of undressing himself when he feels inclined to sleep. As he stood up to fight he looked like a Colossus.

"Poor Wobbles!" said Conky, and wiped away a friendly tear. Curler and Pigeon sighed, but they rather enjoyed the business nevertheless. People may say what they like, but most of us manage to extract a little comfort or pleasure from the downfall and misery of others. That Wobbles would go down nobody for a moment doubted.

As we have seen Wobbles in several encounters, it is unnecessary here to dwell upon his pugilistic powers. They were not great, never could be—his fighting guns, his fists, were of little service, but then what does a ship do in that case? She rams, doesn't she? Wobbles rammed with his head.

The attack was so unexpected that Captain Bobbin was on his back in a moment. Those who govern fights by the strict rules of the ring would have said that the captain was not ready, but those on board the Argosy did not care about rules or anything of the sort. Captain Bobbin, in their opinion, ought to have been prepared for the assault, and it served him right when he was upset, and got all his senses knocked out of him by his head coming in contact with a ring-bolt.

He lay quite still, showed a vast amount of the whites of his eye, and the first general opinion, a joyful one, was that he was dead; but the first mate, a good-tempered young fellow, knelt down, and examining his heart, found that he still breathed.

"He had an ugly knock, however," he said, "and had better be taken below. I think the shock has brought on apoplexy."

Wobbles, the triumphant, saw his late foe carried down—a very tough job that carrying down was—without moving a muscle. What compassion could he have for the remorseless old villain? Nor did he feel any very great sorrow when the mate came up and announced the captain—"a raving maniac."

"It's brain fever, I think," he said, "and we've got no doctor on board."

CHAPTER CXXVII.
SAL PROVES HERSELF A WIFE.

SKEWBALL sat in the hut awaiting the hour of execution. He had no hope of reprieve, for he knew the men of the diamond-fields too well to think that, having passed sentence of death upon him, they would for one moment incline to reversing it.

No, he was sentenced and must die. But he felt it very hard that he, in the very prime of manhood, should have to leave wife and family and the world behind him. Notwithstanding all that has been preached against the love of existence here, there are very few of us who do not cling to this little ball of earth and its pleasures, and even some of the pains to be found upon it.

So Skewball felt it hard to die, the more so as he was to die innocent of the crime of which he was charged. Perhaps of all crimes he was the least likely to perpetrate this, for he loved and reverenced Maggie as a being above and superior to him in every way, and had felt as much infuriated at her murder as he would if his own wife had fallen a victim to the assassin.

And yet he was to be hanged, to die ignominiously, after a rude trial at which justice barely peeped in at the door, his self-elected judges being most ignorant, self-opinionated, and hard to turn from an idea once formed.

He had parted from his wife and children, none of whom he could hope to see again, and no wonder the tears coursed down the cheeks of the strong man, who would have borne pain or death without flinching.

His guard, outside the hut before his trial, were inside now, keeping careful watch lest the prey of Judge Lynch should escape. It was formed of three strong men, heavily armed.

When Skewball wept they laughed at him, and one jeeringly asked him if he would like to leave a message for his mother.

"You fool," answered Skewball; "do you think I am afraid to die?"

"Seems like it," was the rejoinder.

"Have you a wife?" asked Skewball.

"Yes," replied the man, "a wife who *obeys* me. I am not ruled by her."

This was a covert sneer at Skewball's well-known acknowledgment of the superiority of his wife. He understood it but answered calmly—

"Better for you if you were. A woman could give you what you want—a little feeling."

"I've no time to cultivate feeling," said the man; "diamond-digging is heavy work."

Skewball made him no answer, and a silence ensued. It was broken by one of the men, who, rising, said he would go and see what sort of night it was.

As he opened the door a figure seemed to glide away from it, and calling out to those inside to look after the prisoner, he ran out to see who was prowling about. The night was very dark; all the rest of the people of the fields were apparently at rest, and he could see nothing.

"I must have been mistaken," he muttered; "at the most a cat or a dog prowling in search of food."

As he turned to go back something smote him on the head. The light of life was for the time beaten out of him, and staggering forward he fell upon his face.

A woman's form knelt beside him. It was Sal Skewball, and with a rapid hand she removed the small arms he carried by his side.

Then rising she imitated as near as she could the voice of the fallen man, and softly cried—

"Come here."

"What do you want?" asked one of the men inside.

"Come here," she said again.

"You go, Harris," said one of the men.

"All right," said Harris, and he went.

When he got out he stooped forward and tried to pierce the darkness with his eyes.

"What is it, Newman?" he asked.

"Come closer and see," said Sal.

He came, and with a stout stick she carried she struck him just between the eyes. The blow was a severe one, he reeled and fell, but did not lose his senses.

"Look out there!" he shrieked. "Treachery abroad."

Sal struck him again, and he was silenced. Then without hesitation she walked into the hut, and presented a revolver at the third man.

"Move," she said, "and I fire."

He was too petrified to answer. Nor dare he put his rifle to the present—she could have fired her's three times before he was ready.

"Drop your rifle," she said. "Quick, and put your hands behind you."

He obeyed—it was a matter of life and death with him. He had no choice.

Still having the pistol levelled at him, Sal took out a knife, opened it with her teeth, and cut the rope which held her husband.

"Are you free, Richard?"

"Yes, Sal, dear."

"Go and take the small arms of that fellow, and bind him. If he moves an inch I'll settle him.

The man submitted quietly, and Dick bound him tight enough to satisfy a Davenport brother. The next thing he did was to embrace his wife.

"Oh, Sal!"

"All right, Richard, plenty of time to do all that by-and-bye. Come along."

They went outside, Skewball holding on affectionately to the arm of his wife; outside Sal paused for a moment.

"Where to?" asked Skewball.

"To the woods," replied Sal, rather louder than was necessary.

"Hush!" whispered Skewball, "that fellow will overhear you."

"I hope he will," replied Sal, in the same tone, "and believe me, as we are going just in the opposite direction."

"Just like you, Sal—up to every move," said the admiring Skewball.

"Don't talk nonsense to me, but come down to the port."

"The port!"

"Yes, you remember Captain Brown."

"Rather—he was over head and ears in love with you."

"Then we will make use of his affection. He shall hide us on board his ship."

"Now, Sal, I am not going to have him hanging about you."

"Captain Brown is a good fellow—he was 'spoons' on me, but I shall be as safe on board his ship as if he were my brother."

"You know, Sal," said Skewball; "but what of our other two children?"

"We must send for them somehow, either from the port, or from England when we get there."

"Heaven send we do, Sal, and once my foot is set down there catch me coming near Judge Lynch again."

"We have to begin the world once more, Richard."

"So we have," he said, "but what's that to a man who has a wife like you?"

"Why, nothing of course," said Sal, taking his arm. "Come here, we must skirt the fields, or we may run against somebody.

CHAPTER CXXVIII.

WOBBLES TURNS THE TABLES.

WHEN a hard drinker gets the brain fever he invariably has it very bad indeed. Captain Bobbin, who had taken a little over his share of liquor, was mentally upside down.

He had many hallucinations, but the most general one was that he was a common seaman with forty captains over him, who had all sworn to rope's-end him, at least once a day, and that he liked this rope's-ending, and was continually imploring them not to deprive him of even one cut. An ordinary seaman, begging that his grog might not be diluted below regulation strength, could not have been more pathetic.

The mate was puzzled what to do with him, for old Bobbin in his bunk was continually asking him why he didn't "lay on," and threatening to knock his two eyes into everlasting squibs if he didn't begin. In his troubles he called upon Wobbles to act as nurse, and to Wobbles old Bobbin pleaded to be rope's-ended.

He did not plead in vain.

"If he axes for it," thought Wobbles, "why shouldn't I do it? He used to put it on me without my saying I wanted it. Besides, it's unkind not to give a sick man everything he wants."

So Wobbles sought and found the identical rope's end old Bobbin had used upon him, and the next time he begged for a taste of it, Wobbles gave him a fairish dose of it.

Strange to say, it soothed the old mariner to sleep. With the hide of a rhinoceros all that Wobbles could do was mere tickling to him.

Oft when the operation was half over, old Bobbin would call for a halt, seize the hand of Wobbles, kiss it, and shed tears of gratitude upon it.

"You are a man and a brother," he would say, "now lay on again, heavily will you? There aint many captains o' your breed, or the world would be better than 'tis."

Of these performances Wobbles said nothing but enjoyed them in secret. The mate, finding he managed his patient all right, looked after the ship, and troubled his mind no more about the captain, and Conky, Curler, and Pigeon wondered what their friend could find in the society of a sick man to give him such a beaming face.

And, more than this, Wobbles was gathering flesh.

He was, as Conky said, "podgy," although he ate no more than usual, perhaps a little less. But he was contented with his lot, and contentment is capital butter to the blackest bread.

Looking after horses was not quite such good fun as nursing old Bobbin. There were perils attached. Curler had been kicked once by old Joss, whose hoofs, as we know, were none of the lightest; and Fireworks, of whom the sailors were very fond, being treated with a glass out of the grog-tub, turned up very drunk, and fell upon Pigeon, who was grooming him underneath, as a man would whitewash a ceiling.

Nor had Conky come out of the perils of the stable scatheless, although the injury he received was unintentional. But when a horse who has been nibbling at some hay upon the ground raises his head suddenly, and gives you a whack under the chin, it comes painful. Conky got a whack of that description, and was obliged to soak his biscuit for two whole days.

"I never knew what made ostlers so grumpy afore," he said, "but it's the malice of these brutes as spiles 'em."

"Nussing old Bobbin seems better work," said Pigeon, gloomily.

"And here's the nuss," said Curler, "as fat as a porpoise."

"Hall 'ail," said Wobbles, advancing with Shakespearian air along the deck. "How goeth it, comrades?"

"All right with you it, seems," said Conky. "You are laying on flesh. I reckon you get a peck at the good things purwided for old Bobbin."

"Never touch them," replied Wobbles.

"Don't tell no lies," said Conky, with the look of a stern moralist. "We don't want none of it."

"You are welcome to your turn," said Wobbles, loftily.

"That's a joke," said Conky.

"No," rejoined Wobbles. "I'll give him up to you for two hours."

"Done," said Conky. "Anything for a relief from them blessed 'osses."

So he went down, and found old Bobbin in the thick of a gentle slumber, into which he had been soothed by an extra dose of rope. Like all stimulants the quantity had to be increased as the craving for it grew.

Now Wobbles had, with professional instinct, learnt by this time to dose old Bobbin as soon as he gave out signs of wanting it, and sometimes before. The old man, therefore, had grown accustomed to being physicked without the bother of begging and praying for it.

Wobbles, indeed, had humoured him much, and quite spoiled him.

Waking up from his slumber he turned over ready for the dose, but not getting it from Conky, who was as innocent as a babe in that style of nursing, looked up with an evil glare in his eyes, and said—

"Now, then, where is it?"

"Water, sir?" said Conky, humbly.

"Water be ——!" roared old Bobbin. "Now, then, go on. If you stop it I'll mutiny!"

"Perhaps its harrowroot," said Conky, looking about him in vain for that starchy substance.

"My blood's up; I'll mutiny!" cried old Bobbin.

"What is it?" asked Conky. "I——"

Old Bobbin could bear his wrongs no longer, but rising up he let out at Conky, and gave him a blow

Broad-Arrow Jack.

GERRARD WAS JERKED THROUGH THE WINDOW BY BROAD ARROW JACK AND A MOMENT LATER HIS COMPANION JOINED HIM.

in the chest that was heard up on deck, being the general impression that somebody below had given a preliminary bang upon a drum prior to a brilliant display of the drummer's art.

Conky, on receipt of the blow, shot across the cabin until he came to an open locker, and into this he went and became tightly fixed therein.

"I've done now!" cried old Bobbin. "Mutiny is death by ——! Drum-head me as soon as you like, only give me a bit o' rope reg'lar till you turn me orf at the yardarm. Meauwhile I'll turn in a bit."

And off he went to sleep again.

Conky could not move, and he dared not attempt to extricate himself for his life. The door of the cabin was on the other side of old Bobbin, and if he was to awake and take it into his head to get out of his hammock, Conky was, in his own opinion, done for.

"Sich a bang," he thought, "is enough to knock the mortial breathe out of a cove's body. Straight from the helbore it was, and I niver remember the like of sich since I run up agin a timber cart as was backing round the corner of Haldersgate-street. Then me and a party as was behind was sent about 'alf-way down the Minories, clearing everything afore us. What a wenomous old party it is!"

Old Bobbin only partially woke up during the next two hours, and then he merely said "Mutiny, by ——" and slept again. At the end of that time Wobbles came down, and found Conky in his fixed position.

"What's up, old man?" he asked.

"Old Bobbin did it," replied Conky; "shot his arm out like a tallickscope, and nigh as possible drove a hole through me."

"Oh! he orfen does that to me," said Wobbles, lightly; "but it only amooses me. Tired, eh?"

"Of this game," replied Conky. "I wonder when we shall be out of this blessed boat?"

"The mate says we shall be hoff the Lizard tomorrow," replied Wobbles.

"Off the what?" asked Conky, his hair lifting with horror.

"Hoff the Lizard."

"Hain't that a kind o' crocklydile?" asked Conky.

"Oh, no!" said Wobbles, with a smile coming from superior knowledge, "it's a hisland in the Middleterraneam."

"What's that?" asked Conky.

"Well, if you don't know that," said Wobbles, "I've done with you. Go up, old Joss wants feeding."

"I say, haven't you——" began Conky, and stopped short, for old Bobbin woke up, sat up in his hammock, and reported himself.

"Come aboard, sir."

"Hoff you go," said Wobbles to Conky.

"Give me a hand," cried Conky, in agony.

Wobbles gave him a hand, and Conky, diving swiftly under the hammock of old Bobbin, darted up stairs, while Wobbles, getting out his rope, gave the old man a stiff dose and a little sopped biscuit, both of which apparently did him a world of good.

CHAPTER CXXIX.
BRISKET IN TROUBLE.

THE men who had come upon Brisket and Jeb Jaundice were old friends of the latter—that is, friends after the manner of their kind—and had been of material help to Jaundice and the Ogre in the days when they were for a time believed in as avengers of wrongs supposed to be perpetrated by Broad Arrow Jack.

It was these worthies who had fired many a settler's home, and impudently forged the Broad Arrow brand upon the ruins, and, mingling with the sufferers, offered them hypocritical consolation, and gave out mocking promises of retribution.

No more congenial companions could have come to the aid of Jaundice, and the only bar to their fraternising was the state of Jeb's mind, which was still wandering.

The leader of the party was a man named Morgan—about as great a ruffian as his namesake in Australia, whose ravages kept the colony in a state of ferment for years. He saw that something was wrong with Jaundice, but charged it to some injury he had received from Brisket, whom he recognised as the faithful ally and fervent supporter of Broad Arrow Jack.

"We will take care of *you*, at any rate," he said to Brisket, "until such a time as we think proper to hang you."

"Much obliged to you, I'm sure," replied Brisket, who, seeing he was in a mess from which there seemed no chance of escape, kept cool over it.

Inwardly he could not help confounding his folly. Better have remained and risked everything at Skewball's than have come to this pass. But Billy was a great philosopher in his way. "It was to be, I suppose," he said, and sat down on the ground, waiting for his captors to move.

They searched him first, and, finding a fairish booty on him, in the form of some gold and a half-handful of jewels, were much delighted.

Morgan told him that but for his having something about him he would have killed him there and then, but, in consideration of his having turned out a fat fish, he would spare him twenty-four hours.

Jeb Jaundice was in a queer way. When Morgan spoke to him he either vacantly stared and kept silent or gave an answer quite at variance with the question. If he spoke without being spoken to, it was to say something about his wife.

"She will be here directly," he said to Morgan, "and then we are going away together to a quiet cottage in old England."

"Mad as a hatter," said Morgan. "Well, come, comrades, we'll get back to the camp. We took you for emigrants or successful diggers," he added, addressing Brisket; "but you come in just as well."

They had some difficulty in getting Jaundice to quit the spot, for he was convinced he was there to keep an appointment with Maggie; but Morgan told him she was waiting down at his camp, and Jaundice believed him.

With as much haste as possible the robbers retraced their steps, taking their prisoner with them, and at nightfall came to their camp in the woods—not very far, as it happened, from the grave of Maggie.

Here Brisket's bonds were looked to and tightened, and a guard set over him. Fires were lighted, and the cooking of supper began.

As the night advanced other parties came in, and there were women among them—for the most part wild and reckless-looking—and one an old hag of seventy years.

To her Morgan addressed himself, at the same time dragging Jeb Jaundice forward.

"Here, mother," he said, "is an old friend of mine—a little cracked. See if you can repair him."

"He wants rest," she said.

"I cannot rest until Maggie comes," replied Jaundice. "I promised to wait for her."

"She will be here to-morrow," replied Morgan, winking at the old woman.

"And she sent you this," said the old woman, producing a small bottle. "You are to take a little of it."

"And Maggie sent it?" asked Jaundice.

"Yes."

"Then I will drink it all."

"If you did," said the old woman, grimly, "you would oversleep yourself. Here, hold your hand, and let me count ten drops into it. Now, steady—drink it from your palm."

Jeb Jaundice, on the faith that he was doing what

his wife desired, obeyed, and a few minutes later he was stretched upon the ground close to one of the fires, fast asleep.

There were a few tents, for the most part occupied by the women and children. The men, hardened to the roughness of an outdoor life, slept easily around the fires.

"Don't you attempt to escape," said Morgan to Brisket.

"Why not?" asked Brisket.

"Because it will prevent your living until the morning."

"Oh, indeed! Then I will take a nap; I need it."

"You are a cool hand."

"I am not afraid to die, if that is what you mean," said Brisket.

"I don't suppose any man with a bit of pluck is," returned Morgan.

"Then where is your bit?" asked Brisket. "I can see the very mention of death is enough for you."

"If you——"

"Bah!" said Brisket, "I am not afraid of you. Go and lie down, and let me have my last night's rest in peace."

Morgan went away muttering, after having put a guard over Brisket, who rolled himself up like a hedgehog, and went to sleep instantly. As he said, he was in want of rest. Of late he had had a trying time of it.

When Jaundice awoke in the morning he found the old hag and an old man close by.

"Come with us," they said.

"To see Maggie?" he asked, eagerly.

"He must have been very fond of his wife," said the old woman.

"He!" replied the old man, with a short laugh— "he was a brute to her."

"The way of 'em—the way of 'em," muttered the old woman. "Come on, Jeb Jaundice; your wife is waiting for you."

Was it mere accident, or were they guided by some spirit hand? I cannot tell. They went straight to the spot where Jaundice had killed his wife, and sat him down with his face to her grave.

Insanity saved him from the immediate recognition of it, but later on he knew it.

The old woman bled him in the arm, and her companion filling his hat with cold water from the spring, at her bidding poured it upon the wound.

"Will he live?" asked the old man in an undertone.

She bent over the blood, and watched its flowing a few seconds, keenly. Then she raised her head, and spoke.

"For a little time," she said; "but his end is not far away."

"Did you say I was doomed?" asked Jaundice.

"You will die—anon," she said.

"So shall we all." He was speaking calmly; reason was rapidly resuming her throne.

"Ay, ay," said the old woman; "but the spade is fashioned that will dig your grave."

"Is there no hope?" he asked; "I am not fit to die."

"None that man can give," she replied.

He bowed his head, and the blood from the wound in his arm slowly dripped upon the earth, he watching it fall with the curious look of a day dreamer.

Suddenly he leaped to his feet and stared about him aghast.

"Why have you brought me here?" he shrieked.

"To meet your wife," replied the old woman, hoping to sooth him.

In reply he turned furiously upon her. His mind was clear again—reason had resumed her sway, and what could he think otherwise than that she was mocking him?

"Who says my wife is here?" he asked, hoarsely.

"I do," replied the hag.

He stared around him aghast, and his eyes fell upon the new-made grave. Hitherto it had escaped the eyes of the others, but now they saw it too.

"Who says I struck the blow?" cried Jaundice; "it is a lie, a foul lie; she struck me first, too, and taunted me with the fact; she—she—was false to me. My God, what am I saying? I—I—help-help me from this. Oh! spare me from her avenging hand."

And falling down he grovelled upon the earth an agony of fear and remorse.

"He has told his own story," said the old woman.

"He has," replied the old man; "this is the grave of Maggie, supposed to have been murdered by Skewball. I heard the story at the fields. So then, it was her husband who murdered her after all."

"What shall we do?"

"Leave things as they are. What can we prove?"

"Nothing," said the old woman; "let us leave him there and hurry back, or we shall be too late for the hanging."

They were almost too late as it was, for on their return to the camp Billy Brisket was having the rope put round his neck. Morgan was performing the act with infinite relish, and indulging in a little badinage suitable for the occasion.

"If the necktie doesn't fit, sir," he said, "all you have to do is to complain; we can alter it in a moment. We have a motto in this shop—'be obliging to your customers and they will come again—if they can.'"

"I shall come again, to you," replied Billy.

"It will puzzle you to do so."

"My good man," said Brisket, calmly; "when I am hanged you will never be free of me. In every dark place, when you are alone, in your dreams, in your waking thoughts, you will find me with you. This is murder, and you have not the nerve to stand the afterthoughts of it."

There was a deal of truth in all this. Morgan turned pale, and his hand quivered, but he strove to laugh it off.

"You will make but a poor ghost," he said.

"Wait and see," said Brisket; "now get through with the job, or you won't get it over before breakfast. How your hand shakes!"

"It's a lie."

"It is truth," said Billy; "people on the verge of death don't lie. You, who would like to live for ever, do."

"Stand by to haul up," cried Morgan, tossing the end of the rope over the lower branch of a tree; "I'll show you how to bungle it."

"Dastard and villain," cried a voice that sounded like a trumpet, and Broad Arrow Jack, to the amazement and delight of Billy Brisket, dashed into the thick of the throng.

CHAPTER CXXX.
HOW JACK CAME TO THE RESCUE.

JACK was armed with sword and pistols, as usual, and although he seldom employed them whenever their use could be avoided, he had no hesitation in shooting Morgan down, who rolled over on the earth with a bullet in his side.

Shrieking for mercy, the cowardly bully grovelled before our hero, whose presence alone was sufficient to disperse the rest.

They scattered in every direction; even the children came out of the tents and ran away, and in a few seconds Brisket and Jack were, saving the presence of the prostrate Morgan, alone.

"Welcome, my noble chief!" cried Brisket— "thrice welcome! What extraordinary good luck brought you here?"

"Before answering that," said Jack, "let me release you."

Jack cut the bonds about his arms, loosened the

ope round his neck and tossed it off, and Brisket, thus set free, shook himself like a water-dog, and then ran up and down, to restore the circulation of his limbs.

While he was doing this Broad Arrow Jack gave a little attention to Morgan. The wound that worthy had received was, however, fatal, and although there was little to show the terrible injury he had received, Jack's experience of death told him the man was bleeding inwardly.

"You are dying," he said.

Morgan opened his lips as if he would speak, but the terror of the moment held his tongue fast. He who could be so jocular at the approaching death of another was ill prepared to meet the grim monster, who has a terror more or less great for every one.

Presently Brisket ceased his perambulation and came to the side of Jack, and together they stood watching the dying man. It was not in Brisket to triumph over a fallen foe, and the expression of sorrow upon his face was as genuine as ever worn by man.

"My lad," he said, "I hope there's no malice. The game looked all your way once upon a time, but there was a big trump card at the back of my hand which I did not see, and you've lost."

Morgan's face had a double expression in it—terror and malevolence fought for the mastery Again he made an attempt to answer, but only a few unintelligible sounds broke forth from his lips.

"Can nothing be done here?" said Brisket.

"Nothing," replied Jack; "look at his hands; see you not that he is in the grasp of death?"

Brisket sighed.

Now that he had escaped he would rather that this man had lived; not that Brisket was chicken-hearted in such matters.

The man was a ruffian of the worst type, and if spared would probably have lived only to work mischief.

But the pedlar was getting weary of the scenes of death, and longed for a quiet life, which he in his wanderings had so often pictured in his mind—a quiet cottage in some fair nook in old England, where the law is strong enough to check the growth of ruffianism, if not to entirely destroy it.

In ten minutes Morgan was dead. His eyes spoke hatred and unforgiveness to the last. Even after death Brisket fancied he saw an evil spirit hovering around him—so having composed the limbs of the dead man, he and Jack turned away.

They walked a little way in silence, and Jack was the first to speak.

"Tell me, Brisket," he said, "how you came into the hands of these men."

"Don't you know?" asked Brisket.

"Indeed I do not."

"Then how came you to my aid?"

"Mere chance," replied Jack; "but more of that anon—tell me of yourself."

Brisket told him.

When Jack heard that Jaundice had been in the camp an exclamation of anger burst from his lips.

"Why not have told me this before?" he said. "Again that scoundrel has slipped through my fingers."

"To tell the truth," replied Brisket, "he had gone entirely out of my mind; but when a man has a rope round his neck and fair prospects of swinging, he has but little inclination to think of either friend or foe—number one occupies most of his thoughts; then your sudden coming, and other things, all helped to drive him out of my mind."

"Ah, me," said Jack, quietly, "'tis but another link of the long chain of disappointment. The Ogre has escaped me again."

"Surely not."

"Too true," said Jack; "he got away from the island in the canoe of some wretched native, who I think must have been blown out of his latitude by a high wind, and so lost his way. Any how he came, and the Ogre having murdered him, made use of his little craft and so escaped."

"I had a weary time of it waiting for the Hope, but she came at last, and brought me hither; and landing, I learnt the extraordinary news of the murder committed by Skewball."

"Who has he murdered?" asked Brisket.

"Why, Maggie to be sure," replied Jack, "and it was to visit her grave I came hither."

"Ah!" said Brisket, "that's a part of my story I left out. So Skewball is charged with that murder—is he? I can soon clear him."

"You are rather late," said Jack, "for his home has been destroyed—naught but some blackened ruins remain. He has been tried and sentenced to death, but in the night that was to have been his last on earth, his wife, who was acquitted by the settlers because she was his wife, came to the rescue and got him away. They are now in hiding somewhere, and parties in pursuit of them are out in every direction."

"We must hurry back," said Brisket, "and give out the truth of this story."

"It will avail but little," returned Jack, "if they are captured in the mean time, for all those out on the search have instructions to shoot both down when or wherever they meet them."

"We must do our best," said Brisket, "and we can do no more. Let us return and send messengers out to call the pursuers in."

"So be it," said Jack. "And I will visit the grave of Maggie to-morrow."

And he and Brisket went their way, leaving the lone grave in the wood behind them. Had they gone to it then they would have found Jeb Jaundice stretched out by the side of it, suffering the remorse which taught him on earth what a hell might be his lot hereafter.

CHAPTER CXXXI.

WOBBLES MAKES A MISTAKE.

"STILL fond of nussing?" said Conky to Wobbles on the eighth morning of Captain Bobbin's illness.

"I loves it better than anythink," replied Wobbles. "It breaks my 'art to be away from that dear old gentleman for a moment."

"Can't understand it," said Conky to Curler and Pigeon when Wobbles was gone. "I'd just as soon think of nussing a mad helephant. I wish you chaps would go and have a turn at him."

"No, thankee," they said; "the hosses are bad enough—the wenomous brutes!"

"I've got a hidea," said Pigeon, after a pause.

"Then chuck it out," said Conky.

"It's this," continued Pigeon, "them hosses aint used to the *way we grooms 'em.*"

"Something's wrong," said Curler, sadly. "Them as I does up have got their 'air standing up like pig's bristles. I've tried all ways with the curry comb—hup and down and across, and they don't look no better."

"You know that piebald hoss in the corner?" said Conky.

"Yes."

"You know he was as quiet as a lamb at fust?"

"Lambs was raging wiolence to him," said Curler.

"Well, would you believe it? He's come out as the most infamous tempered warmint you never see. I never go near him without his curling up a hind leg ready to let fly, and t'other morning, when I was putting his oats into the place he pecks out of, he lays hold of me by the back o' the weskut and shakes me into fits."

"There will be a gap in our frindly circle," said Curler, with the light of prophecy in his left eye, "afore we gets to England."

"Yes, them hosses beat everything except that nussing of Wobbles."

It certainly was something to make them all wonder, for Wobbles had kept his secret carefully, and continued to dose his patient whenever he was in a waking condition. The old captain received the thrashing with joy, and, keeping up the sequence of ideas, was continually professing himself to be very thankful he was not deprived of that one source of joy before he was "hung out at the yardarm."

"It's a 'appy life," thought Wobbles, as he took his seat by the side of the old man's hammock; "lots to heat and drink, and a party to lay into as I hates like pison. Lor! I wouldn't have missed it for the coeynoor diamond—I wouldn't."

The mention of this celebrated jewel, which some people call the "Koh-i-nor," brought back to the mind of Wobbles the remnant of the wealth he had acquired at Hookey Settlement after the untimely decease of Jereboam Bounce. This was still considerable, notwithstanding his having been fleeced by the rapacious Giles. It was stitched up in his belt, and as his patient was sleeping calmly he determined upon having a look at the little sparkling stones.

First finding a needle and thread for re-stitching, he took his belt and ripped open sufficient of it to give him a good look at his treasures.

Yes, there they were—little glittering stones, so small in compass, and yet enough to make Wobbles a fairly wealthy man, his position in life considered.

After a quarter of an hour's gloating he stitched them up again, and turned his attention to Captain Bobbin, who had given out signs that one of his periodical wakings was at hand.

Wobbles got his rope, and having examined the knot at the end carefully, prepared to lay on.

"This," he said, "is a condishun of perfect happiness—on my word it's syripic bliss."

Now, in attending upon the patient, Wobbles overlooked one thing—and that was, that a fever at a given time either takes a turn for the worse and kills the patient, or a turn for the better and slowly leaves him.

The hour for the turn with Captain Bobbin had come.

Possessed of an iron constitution he had fought the fever down, and was awaking to consciousness. When he opened his eyes his mental faculties were as good as ever, but Wobbles believed him to be labouring under the old delusion, and got ready to begin.

There is one little part of this performance I have not hitherto alluded to, and that was the style of address Wobbles adopted when giving his patient his physic. It was of a nature calculated to relieve the speaker if he were in an angry frame of mind, but also to raise the ire of the party addressed. Accordingly he began—

"Now you fiddle-headed old idiot, I'm just a coming at you."

Captain Bobbin in an insane condition would not have demurred at the form of address, but Captain Bobbin in his right mind was so staggered by the impudence of that worm, Wobbles, that he could only stare at him speechlessly.

"Yes," continued Wobbles, winding the rope round his hand, so as to be sure of being able to lay on with effect, "I'm a going to give your old pig's hide a little hextra walloping. I means to have the skin off this morning—I do. So just heave over a bit, and I'll begin."

Still Captain Bobbin said nothing. He could not have spoken if all the kings and queens and admirals of the world had commanded him to do so. He could not speculate how he came to be lying there with Wobbles making preparations to rope's-end him.

But it was all true; there he was in his hammock, and Wobbles was before him cool as a cucumber, coming slowly at him.

Captain Bobbin had lost a lot of his strength—he could feel that, although he could not steady his thoughts to find out how he came to do so; but he had enough left to tackle a dozen Wobbles still, and Wobbles was advancing to meet his fate.

Was there no sweet little cherub aloft to look after poor Wobbles? It seemed not, for he came up to the hammock, put a hand upon the captain to turn him over, and the captain put a hand upon *him*."

Such a hand!

It was almost as big as a frying-pan, and had such bones and sinews even after his sickness! Wobbles felt it tighten round his throat, and knew that his windpipe was closed for the time.

Captain Bobbin shook him.

Not hastily, like a man who is blindly savage, but slowly and carefully, like an epicure in throttling, who has come upon a feast indeed.

The air turned red, fire flashed before the eyes of Wobbles, but the old seaman worked him to and fro until he was at death's door, and then cast him savagely down upon the deck.

"There," he said. "I've only spared you for the pleasure of doing that every morning until we get into port. What the tarnation made you try to rope's-end me?"

"Yer—yer axed for it," groaned Wobbles.

"You liar! I never opened my mouth," replied old Bobbin.

"Not to-day," said Wobbles, faintly, "but when you were ill. It was the only physic you would take."

"Do you mean to say I've been ill?" roared Captain Bobbin.

"Yes, for many days," replied Wobbles.

"How came it about?" asked old Bobbin.

"We was fighting, and I wrestled, and then you," said Wobbles, "and you went a buster on to your head."

Old Bobbin remembered all now, and lay back a moment to think it over.

"So I axed to be rope's-ended, did I?" he said, sitting up suddenly.

"You begged for it with tears in your eyes," replied Wobbles.

"And how often did you lay on?"

"On a haverage about six times a day," replied Wobbles, who felt sure he was explaining matters clearly, and putting everything in an agreeable light.

But the heart of Captain Bobbin was too much like a small cocoa-nut to be readily impressed with an apology, although it had a special opening for the receipt of personal wrong. He was only gaining time for a leap from his hammock, which was not easily accomplished in his then state.

But at last he accomplished it, if rolling out all in a heap can be considered a mild form of leaping, and as soon as he was spread-eagled on the floor of his cabin, Wobbles saw his danger and bolted.

Three steps at a time he leaped upwards to the deck, and presented himself before Conky, Curler, and Pigeon, who were engaged in the agreeable occupation of cleaning out a huge saucepan, in which stew had been made, with their fingers.

Conky saw him first, and marking his pallid face, saw that the patient had turned upon his nurse.

"I knowed it—I knowed it!" he said, jumping up.

"Clear out," shrieked Wobbles, "old Bobbin's coming."

Away went the four to the forecastle, where, the hold being open, they all plunged manfully into it, just as Captain Bobbin crept up and showed his head above the deck.

He was almost done up, but he managed to beckon the first mate, who came wondering to his side.

"Batten the lot down," said old Bobbin, hoarsely; "don't give one of 'em a bit or sup until I tell you. I shall be better to-morrow, and then I'll take it out of 'em."

"All right, sir," said the mate, and, giving the signal, the four prisoners were secured.

Then, with the aid of the mate, old Bobbin returned to his hammock, where he lay for hours, making strong reference to the livers and general anatomy of the four men cabined, cribbed, and confined within the hold.

CHAPTER CXXXII.

GERRARD IS RATHER ASTONISHED.

WHEN it became known among the people at the diamond-fields that Broad Arrow Jack had come again among them, no small excitement prevailed. On previous occasions he had always chosen the quiet hours for coming to and fro, and strange as it may seem, not more than a score of the diggers had ever seen him.

There was, as there always will be in every community on subjects generally, a diversity of opinion concerning him. Once popular opinion had been entirely in his favour, but recent events (he was known to be friendly to the Skewballs) had considerably changed the tune of the popular mind, and those for and against him were pretty evenly balanced when he and Brisket appeared boldly at the fields.

Jack had his supporters handy if he had wanted them, but he did not see any reason to fear the people, and by his desire they all remained camped outside, about two miles away, between the diggings and the port—Dick Skewball and the Tiger alone having leave to roam where they wished.

These two boys, drawn together by affinity of disposition, both being inclined to a wandering life, came down to the fields in the morning. Jack went in search of Maggie's grave, and Dick, who knew nothing of the disaster which had befallen his parents, made straight for his home.

On their way thither they passed several people, who, as Dick thought, looked at him and his companion curiously. He did not offer to exchange a word with one of them, but kept on until he stood before the ruins made by a reckless mob.

His astonishment and grief held him speechless for the time, and the Tiger stood by quietly, guessing at least half the truth.

"Who has done this?" cried Dick, glaring around him.

"Was dis your home, ole Dick?" asked the Tiger. "Ole Dick" was a form of address he had fallen into when speaking to his new friend.

"Yes, it was," replied Dick, with a fierce fire in his eyes, "and I want to know who has done this. Here's a fellow coming, perhaps I can get it out of him."

The man approaching the wrecked home of the Skewball's was Gerrard, he who had acted as president of the court of Judge Lynch. He knew Dick, of course, and would have avoided him, but the boy put himself in his path, and would not be denied.

"I say," he said, "you were a friend of my father's once. Tell me who burnt his house down."

"Be a little more civil in your asking," replied Gerrard, "and perhaps I may tell you."

"Then you know," said Dick, "and you shall tell me. As for civility, look here, I'm a boy, and you are a man, but I'll shoot you down if you don't tell me," and Dick whipped out a revolver, and presented it at Gerrard.

The man turned a little pale, but he affected to laugh, and treat the action of Dick as a joke.

"That is a very pretty toy for a boy to play with," he said. "Put it up."

"No I won't," said Dick; "and don't you attempt to get out your toys, or I'll fire. I have a man for a master, and he has made almost a man of me; speak—or I'll let fly at you!"

"Golly!" cried the Tiger, rolling his eyes, "dis am delightful," and to express his appreciation of the joke, he turned two somersaults in one second and then became attentive again.

"It's absurd your playing these tricks," said Gerrard, "but I don't mind telling you, because, as you say, I was a friend of your father's."

"Who burnt this house?" asked Dick.

"The people ginerally."

"What for?"

"Because he murdered the Senora Maggie."

"*My* father commit a murder? Its a lie."

"A jolly smash double big lie," put in the Tiger.

He knew nothing whatever about the case, but he felt bound, out of friendship for Dick, to give him some support.

"Anyhow your father was tried, and sentenced to be hanged for it."

"But you did not hang him?"

"No, he escaped."

"Woe to you if a hair of his head had been harmed," said Dick, and there was so much of the man in his air that Gerrard could scarcely believe he was talking to a boy.

"You talk loudly," he said, "but I tell you if he is caught hereabouts he will be shot like a rat."

"Look out if you harm him. Broad Arrow Jack will avenge my father."

"Broad Arrow Jack," sneered Gerrard, "who is he?"

"As if you did not know," said Dick.

"All de worle know him," said the Tiger; "if any man say dat it am not so dat man am a big lie."

"Broad Arrow Jack is nothing here," said Gerrard.

"We shall see," replied Dick. "I will ask him, and he will demand justice for my father."

Dick put up his pistol, and Gerrard swaggered off. At one time he had been a friend of Skewball's, but having in a way injured him, he had now become his enemy. There is no enemy like the man who has done you a wrong, or one who has been your friend; in either case the hate is remorseless.

"So," said Gerrard, "this Broad Arrow Jack is back again, and he will avenge Richard Skewball —will he? We will see."

As there was no time to lose, he hastened about among his fellows, and spread a story about that Broad Arrow Jack had come to bully them out of their verdict against Richard Skewball, because he was privy to the murder of Maggie, and had abetted the same for his own private ends.

When a man allows his tongue to be governed by hate it invariably runs wild, and Gerrard's tongue was no exception to the rule.

"That is how the fellow has got his money," he said, "by murdering and plundering people, and this Maggie must have been a rich booty. They are a bad lot altogether, and the sooner they are exterminated the better. That boy Dick, of Skewball's, is in the fields, and I don't think we shall be the worse if we turn him out."

The result of this and other inflammatory addresses was that ere the day was half over Jack had lost the better part of his former adherents, and when Dick and the Tiger came down they were chased and stoned out of the place.

Fortunately neither of the boys was hurt, for it would have required a good marksman to have hit either with a rifle. They were very masters in the art of dodging, and in general activity had no equal thereabouts.

But they did not go far, and hung about on the outskirts of the community until Dick espied Broad Arrow Jack and Brisket approaching. They made for them, and Dick, after a respectful salute, worthy of the humility of the Tiger, told the story of the day's adventures.

"And I heard some of them say, sir," said Dick, "that if you showed down there they would shoot you down."

"Indeed," said Jack, "then I will go down there and give them an opportunity to keep their word."

And with his usual calm majestic step he strode

towards the diamond-fields, with Brisket at his side and the two boys easily trotting in the rear.

"Golly for Massa Jack," said the Tiger, in a low tone.

"He's a good un," returned Dick, "and I've a good mind to—but no, I won't. It is too much to do."

"What am too much?" asked the Tiger.

"I'll tell you—one day," said Dick.

"One day. Why not now? I tell you ebery-ting," said the Tiger.

"To-night then," said Dick, speaking so low that the Tiger could scarcely hear him, "I will tell you everything. But you must promise not to say anything."

"Neber split on you," said the Tiger, fervently, and Dick gave him a slap on the back in acknowledgment of his promise.

Broad Arrow Jack was very angry at the threats of the diggers, whom he had certainly not harmed or inconvenienced in any way. But on reflection he felt it would be difficult for him to call them to account in a body, and halting, he asked Dick if he could name one who had specifically threatened him.

Dick, with great promptitude, named Gerrard.

"And where does he live?" asked Jack.

"On the west side of the fields," replied Dick "You can't miss his place, sir. It stands alone on a bit of a hill, with a clump of bushes about a dozen yards away."

"Good," said Jack. "I am going on. You need not hurry. Meet me at this man's house in an hour."

Brisket, as well as the boys, knew it would be useless proposing to go on with him, and he hastened on alone. Skirting the diamond-fields he made for Gerrard's house, and from the description given by Dick had no difficulty in finding it.

Gerrard was at home, having done his day's work, and was sitting at the rude window of his tent, enjoying an evening pipe with one of the other diggers. When Gerrard and his companion saw who was approaching—for Jack's figure was familiar to them by repute at least—both appeared to be rather uneasy, but neither budged from their seat. Had there been but one of them the window would soon have been clear, but the fear of ridicule kept them to the spot.

Jack came up, and, without any preliminary address, asked—

"Which of you men is named Gerrard?"

"First tell us why you ask the question," said Gerrard.

"Which of you is named Gerrard?" asked Jack, again, and there was an ominous look in his eyes which wiser men than they were would have interpreted as an indication that he would not be trifled with.

"It is a cool question," said Gerrard, who was anything but cool himself.

"Will you answer it?"

"No."

In a moment Gerrard found himself seized by the collar, jerked out through the window, and thrown in a heap upon the ground. Another moment and his companion joined him, and the pair lay in a state of amazement which would be difficult to describe.

"Now which is Gerrard?" asked Jack, for the third time.

The other man, having had enough dealing with Jack, betrayed his friend.

"That's Gerrard," he said, "and I wish he was at the deuce before he brought you down upon me. He is always getting into some mess or other."

"Enough," said Jack; "you are safe. Now, Gerrard, I understand you have aspersed my character, and charged me with complicity in a base murder."

"I could only speak of things as I found them," muttered Gerrard.

"I will trouble you to retract what you have said."

"I don't mind doing that," returned Gerrard, "for I can't prove it."

"And you will do the same in public."

"Where?" asked Gerrard, sullenly.

"Which is your favourite gambling saloon?" asked Jack.

"I generally go to Martin's."

"Then I will be there to-night, and I will trouble you to come, and, what is more, I shall be there alone; but beware of any attempt at trickery!" and without another word he returned by the way he came, without once looking behind him.

"Alone!" muttered Gerrard, looking after him. "Will he keep his word?"

"He has never been known to break it," replied his companion.

"Then I will prepare a reception for him," said Gerrard, "that shall rid the world of this bold bully boy, Broad Arrow Jack."

CHAPTER CXXXIII.
TIMES OF TRIBULATION.

"THIS," said Wobbles, "is a kind o' fix that it's difficult to see the hend of." He was in the hold and in the dark. His three friends were in the hold and dark also. Captivity and darkness were upon them all.

"It's all through you," said Conky, whose voice sounded as if he was speaking into a jug—it was that hollow and forlorn.

"Through me!" returned Wobbles. "That's like you, and it's mean."

"You keep a quiet tongue in your head," growled Conky.

"I won't!" said Wobbles, who of late seemed to be gifted with a courage a little above mortal man. "Come here, and I'll punch your head."

"I'm a-coming!" said Conky.

"Go it!" said Curler, who wanted a little excitement to relieve the monotony of confinement.

"Lay into each other!" said Pigeon, who was also delighted with the prospect of a fight in which he had no share.

But both these gentlemen soon changed their tone, for in the dark Wobbles laid hands on Curler, and Conky on Pigeon, and a lot of damage was done to the two unoffending ones.

When the mistake was discovered, Curler and Pigeon were intensely disgusted at finding Wobbles and Conky already satisfied with fighting, and they declined, although earnestly requested, to have any more of it.

After this little error there was a period of silence, broken only by Wobbles making an attempt to whistle the fragment of a tune; but it sounded so horribly melancholy in their dismal prison that a general request was made for him to give over, and he did so.

"I wonder," said Conky, after a time, "how long we have been here?"

"About three days," said Pigeon.

"Oh, no!" said Curler; "not more than two."

"Nearer four," insisted Wobbles.

Now the fact was that these four gentlemen had not been imprisoned more than four hours; but in darkness and misery old Father Time is but a poor traveller, and he had lagged especially with these unfortunates. Many men would have judged by their returning appetite; but these captives had no such guide, for their appetites never left them. The moment one meal was over they were ready for another, if they could get it.

Had their fate been entirely in the hands of Captain Bobbin they would, in all probability, have travelled far on the road to starvation.

But the first mate was a kindly man, and at the expiration of the fifth hour he opened the hold, lowered a can of water, and tossed half a dozen biscuits down to them; then he battened down the hatches once more, and left them to fight for their provisions in the dark.

Wobbles, who had long experience in foraging, secured four of the biscuits and the can of water, and got away into a corner, hoping to enjoy them in solitude and peace

Conky got the other two biscuits, and Curler and Pigeon, in a frenzy of hunger, went groping about in vain, their movements accelerated by the sound of munching proceeding from their more fortunate friends.

"Somebody's got more than his share," said Curler at last. "Here, shell out—will you? Come on, Pigeon."

They bore down upon Wobbles, and got him under them before he knew an enemy was at hand. Then ensued one of those struggles which would have been famous in history if Wobbles had borne the name of Cæsar instead of that which he inherited from his father.

The can of water was upset over him, but, ignoring the discomfort it gave him, he rammed the biscuits inside of his waistcoat, folded his arms over them, and prepared to die rather than yield them up.

"He's got 'em 'ere in his weskut," gasped Curler, who was lying full length upon the prostrate Wobbles. "I can smell 'em."

"So can I," groaned Pigeon, and the two pulled Wobbles about, and dashed him up and down, and tugged at his hair, and smote him on the other parts of his body, and cursed and insulted him, but still he held on and would not yield.

"Go it!" said the delighted Conky from his corner. "I'll back somebody for sixpence."

Suddenly Wobbles threw off his assailants, and, springing to his feet, dashed forward, reckless of the way he was going. As the hold was limited, he soon ran against the side, and, scattering what little sense was in him, tumbled down in a heap upon the floor. Curler and Pigeon went over him, and this brought them into contact with Conky.

In a moment Conky was a robbed and ruined man, and the two plunderers, each with a portion of a biscuit, retreated to enjoy their ill-gotten gains; but they had got no further than the first bite when the hatches were lifted, and the voice of Captain Bobbin called upon them to come up.

All thoughts of appetite fled, and Wobbles returned suddenly to sensibility, as if he had received a galvanic shock. One by one the four walked up, and stood in a row before the old captain, who was seated in a chair, but otherwise showed no signs of weakness.

By his side stood the first mate, and the crew formed a semicircle in front.

Old Bobbin, true to his race, opened the proceedings with a string of oaths—each a regular curling-iron to the prisoners—and then asked them what they meant by "larruping" a sick man.

"But I didn't do it," said Conky; "I never touched you."

"Don't lie," said the old man, sternly, "for you are on the point of being 'turned off.' I'm a reg'lar mash of bruises and lines made by the rope. I've had a lookin' glass to see, and I ought to know."

Then came explanation, and presently the whole of the business settled upon Wobbles, who made an effort to deny his guilt, but signally failed.

"But you axed me to do it," was his last feeble excuse.

"Stand out, you there," said Captain Bobbin, addressing Conky, Curler, and Pigeon, "and as you've done nothing I'll simply give you a dozen each, and stop your prog and grog. That won't matter much, as in four hours we shall be off the Lizard, and I don't suppose we shall be much more than a day in the Channel. As for you," turning to Wobbles, " yours is a case of attempting to murder the captain, and by all the law of the land I'm entitled to shoot you down, and, by Jingo! I will, as soon as I can get my pistols put into order."

"It can't be the law," said Wobbles.

"It is, and I'll make a target of you," replied old Bobbin. "I'll have you stuck up against the mizen mast, and I'll take pot shots at you until I bring you down. Lay hold there, and have him ready when I want him. Now, is there any man on board who says I shan't do this?"

None answered him, not even the first mate. There was no combination against the old tyrant, and individually they were afraid of him.

"I'll see who is master here," he growled, as he glared around him. "Am I the captain of this ship, or am I not?"

Nobody answered him.

"Look here," he said, "I am captain, and you all know it. And I'm going to drink the health of the captain in a drop of something. And here it is," he added, dragging out a brandy bottle from his breast pocket. "Health to the captain!"

"Don't drink that now, sir," whispered the first mate; "you have not been well."

"Who says I'm not to drink?" he asked.

"Nobody, sir; but you have not been well, and I was only saying it would be better if you did not drink it."

"Oh! thank you," said old Bobbin, sarcastically; "but you see it's just this way. A captain of a ship knows what he's about—doesn't he?"

"Yes, sir."

"And he doesn't take his orders from anybody—does he?"

"No, sir."

"Then I'm the captain of this here ship, and I'm not going to follow the teachings of any skunk aboard. I'm going to drink, I am"—here he took a copious sip from the bottle—"and it's the health of the captain I'm drinking"—here he took another sip, a long one—"and I says this, I says health to the captain"—here he took a third sip, finished the bottle, and dashed it down upon the deck, breaking it into a thousand pieces.

"Now who commands the Argosy if it ain't old Bobbin?"

Who could dispute his authority? Those who have been to sea know the perils of standing out boldly against a captain. He may be guilty of the grossest crimes, of the most palpable outrages upon maritime law, but at sea he has it all his own way. It is only when land is reached that those under him are able legally to call him to account for his misdoings.

"I see," said old Bobbin, "that you know who is the master here, and I'm just going down to have a nap. Mr. Mapper," that was the first mate, "will take command, and report to me if anything happens. And you, Mr. Mapper, will be good enough to wake me in an hour, and have that fellow ready for me to take a pot shot at him. He's tried to take my life, and I'm entitled to do it."

Rising, he went below, with a fairly firm step considering what he had drunk, and Mapper, the first mate, appointed two men to take charge of Wobbles. The others were ordered below to await the punishment assigned to them by this wise captain—old Bobbin.

"This is murder!" said Wobbles to the first mate.

"If it is," replied Mapper, "we will bring him to book for it as soon as we get ashore. At present it is rank mutiny to say a word against him."

"Is that the law?" asked Wobbles, faintly.

"As far as we know," replied the mate; "at least, I have been taught no other. At sea the captain is a king, and if he does wrong he must be hauled up when he gets ashore."

"And do you think he will really shoot me?" asked Wobbles.

"All depends upon his being able to hit you," replied Mapper. "As he is half drunk now, he may be wholly drunk by-and-bye, and then you will have a chance to get off. But he is sure to hit you somewhere."

"Oh, lor!" gasped Wobbles, and became as limp as a doll that has been a month in a nursery.

It must be remembered that at the time of our story the power of a captain at sea was of the most despotic nature. However he might err it was mutiny to stand out against him, and mutiny was a capital crime. Can we then wonder that the men of the Argosy hesitated to lift up their voices on behalf of Wobbles?

He was put under arrest, and remained so, carefully guarded while the ship sped towards the Lizard; and Captain Bobbin having uncorked another bottle of brandy, added fuel to the fire within him.

At such a time it was doubly dangerous for him to fill his stomach with the liquid fire, as some advocates of temperance not inaptly call it; but a man like him was not likely to reflect upon the consequences. He was fond of brandy—he had a love for it—and as he had drunk it all his days he saw no reason why he should not drink it still.

And so he drank and drank, and smoked big cigars until the hour had passed, and the mate came down to report a fog rising.

"A fog!" said the captain; "let it rise then."

He had a rising fog within him, and was not likely to be dismayed by one outside.

"Who cares for a fog?" he asked. "You've got your bearings, haven't you?"

"Yes, sir."

"Then that's enough for you. Go up and keep her head right, and I'll come and take a shot or two at that mutinous varmint."

CHAPTER CXXXIV.

ASHORE—MOST UNPLEASANTLY.

MAPPER returned to the deck with a heart not so light as most men of his years carry in their bosom. He saw danger ahead, not only in the fog, but in the foggy condition of his captain, which could be seen at a glance; but he was a sailor all over, and having learnt to obey, was prepared at all risks to follow the commands of his superior.

"I fancy we are nearer the Lizard than we thought," he said to himself, "and if we should in this fog— But why should I think of it? Watch, have you the prisoner safe?"

"Yes, sir."

"Helmsman, keep her head nor'-west by west."

"Yes, sir."

The fog he had spoken of was fast coming upon them. Already the sun was shut out, and lights fifty yards away could not be distinctly seen. Each moment it grew more dense, and anon the bowsprit grew shadowy and indistinct.

Mapper went below again to the captain. The bottle was more than half-finished, and he had mounted another cigar.

"Fog thicker, sir."

"All right. Keep her head nor'-east."

"North-east, sir!" exclaimed Mapper, aghast.

"Yes, sir; do you hear? I'm going to run her in close to shore, then round the point like a sailor."

"But, sir——"

"Who's captain here?" roared old Bobbin. "Put her head nor'-east!"

"I won't, sir," said Mapper, firmly but respectfully, "as it is certain destruction."

"You won't! Why, that's mutiny!"

"I'll stand my trial on it," said Mapper.

"So you shall!" roared old Bobbin. "And meanwhile I'll come on deck, and give the order myself."

"Heaven help the Argosy!" said Mapper, as he followed the old bully on deck.

"Keep her nor'-east there!" roared old Bobbin. "Can you hear?"

"Aye—aye, sir!" replied the helmsman, and over went the Argosy in obedience to her shifted helm.

Each moment the fog grew more dense.

The bowsprit and upper sails were invisible to a clear brain. Old Bobbin, foggy in and out, could absolutely see nothing.

But at the same time he forgot nothing.

"Where is that mutinous chap?" he asked.

"Here, sir," replied the men guarding the almost unconscious Wobbles.

"Lash him to the mizen-mast," said old Bobbin. "I'm ready to have my first pot shot at him."

"Lash him to the foremast," whispered the first mate. "You can easily make a mistake in the fog."

"Aye—aye, sir!" said the men, softly, and Wobbles was taken forward, and bound there.

"All right there," said old Bobbin, producing a pair of pistols, "I'm ready for him."

"The mizen-mast, sir," said the mate, pointing out to sea, "is just over there. You can see the prisoner bound there."

"Aye!" muttered old Bobbin, "I see him, and I'll riddle him like a sieve."

And forthwith he began to blaze away, loading again and again, and firing with much satisfaction.

"Did that hit him?" he asked the first mate.

"Yes, sir, you haven't missed him yet."

"Then he must be full of holes."

"He is perforated all over," replied the mate.

"Still I think he can bear a few more."

"Very well, sir; but shall I shift our course?"

"No, certainly not. Keep her nor'-east by east, will you?"

"Aye, aye, sir," replied the man at the wheel.

Darker and darker grew the fog. All objects a few yards away became indistinct, but Captain Bobbin, happily associating this condition of things with what he had taken to drink, kept on blazing away for a good hour or more.

"He must be dead now," he said.

"Dead as a door-mat, sir," replied the mate.

"Then I think I'll take a shot at somebody else. Where are those other three fellows?"

"All in irons, sir."

"Bring 'em up."

"Aye, aye, sir! and lash 'em to the same mast?"

"No, I'll have 'em just here, so that I may see them fairly; but I say, before you go after them, bring up my brandy bottle. And mind this, keep her head nor'-east by east."

"Won't you take a rest before you punish the rest, sir?" asked Mapper.

"No, I won't, was the reply; "why should I? I am as strong as a lion. What rest can I want? Hallo, there!"

"Aye, aye, sir!" replied the helmsman.

"Keep her head nor'-east."

"Ay, aye, sir!"

"That's the way to run her in," muttered old Bobbin.

"But, sir," said Mapper, "hadn't we better cast off a bit until the fog rises, or until we can see the shore lights?"

"The shore lights be d——," growled old Bobbin; "they are put up for landsmen. I can feel my way in the dark. I know where I am and what I'm doing—don't I?"

"It is to be hoped so, sir—ahem!" replied Mapper.

"I haven't lived all these years without knowing which way to go," pursued old Bobbin; "I've been round the world a dozen times and more, and I know my way out and home as well as a rabbit knows his way about the warren."

"Oh! yes, sir; but suppose we should be to the west of the Lizard."

"The Lizard be bothered! We are a good two hours from it yet."

"I don't think so, sir. I am afraid we are—"

But what the mate would have spoken was never

attered, for the Argosy suddenly pulled up with a crash, heeled over, and a lot of her top hamper came tumbling down upon the deck.

"She has struck!" burst from every lip, and the men who were below came tumbling up, bent upon making an effort to save their lives.

Another crash and the Argosy lay almost upon her beam ends, a huge wave swept her deck, and all loose things were carried away, among them old Bobbin in his chair.

Clear of the ship he floated for awhile, quite contented with the new state of things; then turning his head he shouted out—

"Keep her head nor'-east by east, and she'll run in like a duck;" and having given this last command he slipped from his seat into the sea, and was seen no more.

CHAPTER CXXXV
AT THE JOLLY TARS.

AT the mouth of the Irish Channel there is a small fishing village, which we will call Sandstone. It would, perhaps, if a muster-roll were called, and all answered, show about three hundred inhabitants. But small as it was, it could boast of a lifeboat, the gift of a generous lady, who lived within a few miles of the place. It was served entirely by volunteers—that is, fishermen, who went out when there was need for their services, and took their chance of getting a reward for the toil and trouble they met with on the deep.

The coast is somewhat dangerous, for there are shifting sands and hidden rocks, fraught with peril to ships drifting or blown out of their course, and in stormy weather the volunteer crew were always ready for active service, and generally met in th evening at the Jolly Tars tavern.

On one particular evening they mustered there, with their coxswain as usual occupying the seat in the chimney corner, which was the acknowledged chair from whence all oracular sounds proceeded.

The name of this coxswain was Jones, but then it was never mentioned and never heard, for as Blow Hard had he been known from the time he was able to pull an oar or steer a shrimp boat. And it is more than likely that if any one had addressed him as Jones he would have failed to recognise it as the name he inherited from his parents.

The night in question was quiet, but out at sea there was evidence of a thick fog, which led Blow Hard to remark, as he took his seat in his chair, " he fancied there would be a job for them to-night."

To this one of his crew, a man with a cast in his eye and the shoulders of an ox, replied " that he didn't see no reason for it."

"Aint a fog reason enough?" asked Blow Hard.

"No," replied the other.

"Now that's so much like you, Jim—allus on the opposite tack. What's worse than a fog at sea, where you have no more notion of where you are going than a toddling baby? I've known more jobs come out of fogs than thunder and lightning and high wind."

"You have seen some rum things," remarked another of the men from an opposite corner.

"Who says I aint?" said Blow Hard, whose answers were often of a defiant description. "I've been in all kinds of wrecks, collisions, and fires."

"A fire must be awful," remarked Jim.

"Yes," said Blow Hard, "especially that of the Tower of Bristol, homeward bound from North America with a cargo of oil. I was in the White Eagle then, and we were bound for Montreal, when we comed across her a-flaring and spluttering away under a full moon. Immediately the captain ordered the long boat out, and we pulled towards her, I standing in the bows with a boathook, looking out for any poor creature who might be floating about. The wreck seemed to be deserted, but as I drew nigh I saw a woman tossing up her arms, as people do just before they go down. I cries out, 'Give way, my lads!' and we were just in time for me to hook on and haul her in, and in a mighty bad way she seemed to be; so after pulling once round and finding nothing else, we took her name from the stern and went back to the White Eagle. As we lifted the woman on board—and we did it tenderly enough, poor creeter—she heaved a deep sigh, such as I often fancy I hear again when lying awake at night, and then fell back dead."

As Blow Hard allowed a full minute to elapse without continuing his narrative, Jim ventured to put a question. "Died—did she?" he said.

"Yes," replied Blow Hard.

"And who was she?"

"Don't know," replied Blow Hard.

"And the rest of the crew—where were they?"

"Never heard of again," said Blow Hard.

"How then did you know all about the Tower of Bristol?"

To this Blow Hard, after a glance of contempt at the other, replied—"Know'd her as a trader between Montreal and Liverpool, and could tell what was burning by the flames."

"Hear, hear," said the crew in chorus, in acknowledgment of Blow Hard's maritime experience; and Jim's confusion was covered by the entrance of the landlord.

"The fog's come up from the sea like a white wall."

"A job for us to-night," said Blow Hard.

And hardly had he closed his prophetic mouth when the boom of a gun seaward came upon the ears of the crew.

Blow Hard was not elated. Why should he be? Had he not been prophet before, whose unfailing predictions had brought confusion to unbelievers? Why should he rejoice? Merely rising with a calm face, he said, "My lads, the boat's wanted; let's run her out."

The boat-house, owing to the wisdom and foresight of its giver, was opposite the public-house, and despite the thick fog, it was in little over two minutes run down to the sea. As its bow kissed the waves another gun was heard.

"She's on the Blue Rocks," said Blow Hard. "I could steer you to it blindfold!"

Meanwhile the host of the Jolly Tars made preparation for the reception of those who might—with the good offices of the lifeboat—be saved. It was not the first time he had done so, for many an unexpected guest had come to him from the sea—the old and the young, the weak and the strong, and among them many a ghastly form, out of which the life had been beaten by the cold cruel sea; and in the room where the crew of the lifeboat were wont to make merry had lain many a form still in death. And he, the host of the Jolly Tars, had looked upon bronzed faces still as wax models, which, but for disaster, would then have been full of light with the joy of returning home; and he had looked, too, upon the faces of fair women coming to meet those who had long looked for and sighed for them, and only found them wrapped in the chill arms of death.

The constant association with these sad scenes might make you and me, dear reader, reflect a little, and give to our thoughts and words a sadly sentimental tone. Not so the host of the Jolly Tars, who, after arranging the chairs and tables for the convenient reception of the living and the dead, opened the door and cried out to his wife—

"Martha, put the boiler on, and have some hot water ready. There won't be many corpses to-night, the sea aint rough enough." He, like Blow Hard, was guided by experience, for presently the lifeboat came back with a huge cargo of living men from the good ship Argosy.

There was Conkey, there was Curler, there was Pigeon, there was Wobbles, the first mate, and all the crew; and out of all that were on board the good ship only one had gone down, and that was Captain Bobbin.

On the death of this old salt we need not further speak. On the sea he had lived, and his grave was under it. What more could a seaman desire?

But although rescued the crew had suffered much. Every man was drenched to the skin, and all were only too glad to crowd around the bright fire.

As the host thrust the poker into the burning mass to raise a blaze, he turned to Blow Hard with a business-like air and said, "Gone to pieces?"

"Not a bit on it," returned Blow Hard. "Barring her top hamper she's as sound as she was the day she set sail. There's a cargo of horses on board, and if the weather holds calm we will try to swim them ashore in the morning. I caught a peep of two of them in a deck cabin, and I am afeard it will be all over with them."

"Don't you fear about them," said Wobbles, turning suddenly upon him; "them two horses will never die. If you perforated them with cannon shot, or took 'em up in a balloon and throwed 'em hout, they would run a race in five minutes with anything you have got here."

"Your horses, sir?" said Blow Hard, respectfully.

"They are their property," replied Wobbles, pointing to Conkey, Curler, and Pigeon, "and my own."

The three gentlemen in question uttered a low groan of assent, and drew nearer the fire to warm their shivering limbs.

CHAPTER CXXXVI.

HIGH AND LOW GAME.

WHEN a man is what is termed "cock of the walk," he doesn't care for another bird to come crowing about his country, and Gerrard, who was no small cock of the diamond-fields, was considerably upset by the arrival of Broad Arrow Jack.

If he had arrived without any demonstration or assertion of power, it would have been bad enough; but Gerrard, in addition to having a rival in the field, had met that rival, who proved himself the superior.

There was gall and wormwood in the heart of the miner as he went towards his favourite gambling saloon, where he generally spent his evenings, and whither Jack had promised to come.

"It shan't be my fault," he muttered, "if he's not shot down the moment he shows his face. Who's this boy that he should come riding rough-shod over men like me?"

"I'll try to get others to do it," he said, after a pause, "and, failing help, by heaven I'll do it myself."

The saloon he sought was one of many about the fields. A long low shanty, with a roulette table at the further end, over which the proprietor presided; and fixed at different points at the sides all down the room were places for the convenience of the card-players. The bar was at the entrance, to be handy for those who only desired to drink and not to gamble.

Gerrard went in with the air of a frequenter, and found himself with a few select chums having little drinks at the bar prior to the more serious business of the evening. They were, for the most part, of the rowdy order, and were armed with the usual bowie and brace of pistols.

"Good evening," said Gerrard.

A series of nods responded to his greeting, and his next words were—

"What's your drink?"

Each man named his drink, and Gerrard gave the order for a generous quantity. This made a favourable impression, and paved the way for other business.

Gradually he worked his way, and, with the aid of further drinks, enlisted the sympathies of his audience. Before any one of them was fairly drunk they had all sworn to have the life of Broad Arrow Jack whenever and wherever they might meet him.

Gerrard had told some of them that they might expect him there that night, which, to say the least, was a diplomatic proceeding.

By-and-bye the general public began to arrive, and an active serving man put up a partition with a door in it across the centre of the building, so as to shut in the roulette-players from the general public. Those who went in for that game crowded around the table, and the proprietor taking his seat the play began.

Gerrard took a seat opposite the proprietor, with the double object of getting a good seat to gamble, and to leave Broad Arrow Jack the chance of meeting his friends, some of whom still lingered fondly at the bar, and were just in the frame of mind to shoot anything or anybody on the smallest provocation.

Luck was in his favour; whatever he played turned up trumps for him, and at his elbow there slowly grew a pile of notes and diamonds—the two forms of currency there—which made the mouths of less fortunate players water considerably.

His play was generally high, and when the luck of the others was out, they sought to follow Gerrard, but he changed his tactics instantly, and fortune followed him whithersoever he went.

His winnings were double and treble the earnings of ten years in the diamond fields—enough for him to leave the place and go back to Old England a rich man. He saw himself going back to friends he had left behind, laden with wealth. It had been his dream from the first, and now it seemed about to be realised.

"When the luck turns," he thought, "I will leave off."

But the luck did not turn until the general players were pretty nearly cleared out and the bank broken. The proprietor rose and announced that fact, and Gerrard got upon his feet with the light of triumph in his eye.

"I'm done now with the fields," he said.

"But not with me," said a voice close by, and before him stood Broad Arrow Jack.

That tall commanding form could not fail to receive respect, and as he drew near the crowd of players made way for him. Not one of Gerrard's friends came forward to fulfil their vaunted promises, although several were in the crowd close by.

"I need not announce who I am," said Jack, "for I see you know me, but it is necessary for me to tell you why I have come here. It is to clear any aspersions cast upon the character of a friend. Will you hear me?"

"No," said Gerrard; but there was a chorus of "Yes," and he went on.

"I know I run a risk of exciting your ire, but I cannot help that. The name of my friend is Skewball."

"A murderer!" said Gerrard, and there was some hissing, but the majority remained silent, wondering what was coming.

"He was accused of the murder of as noble a woman as ever breathed," proceeded Jack, "but he was also too noble to commit such a crime."

"That's what *you* say," said Gerrard.

"It is what I mean," replied Jack. "You in your heart feel him to be innocent. You were friends once."

"I have had enough of this," said Gerrard, sullenly, "and am going home."

"Stay," said Jack, "I have yet another word to say with you. It seems that from your lips a threat which bears upon myself has fallen."

"There has not," replied Gerrard, with an oath.

"I have heard it from those I can trust."

"Then those you trust have lied to you."

"Massa," said a voice just behind Broad Arrow Jack, "don't let de big tief say dat, for I hear him,"

BROAD-ARROW JACK.

BY THE AUTHOR OF

HANDSOME HARRY and CHEERFUL CHING-CHING.

"HEAVEN GRANT THAT WE DISCOVER THE PERPETRATORS OF THIS FOUL DEED!"

No. 20.

and the Tiger, followed by Dick Skewball, wriggled to the front, looking fully prepared to stand to their accusation.

"And who are these whelps?" asked Gerrard.

"My witnesses," replied Jack, "and I do not believe either of them would lie to me."

"I never uttered a threat against you in all my life," said Gerrard, with a sullen air.

"Don't lie, old man," said one of the bystanders. "I heard you myself."

"You," returned Gerrard, turning upon him fiercely, glad of any device to divert his attention from Broad Arrow Jack, "and who may you be when you are at home?"

"My name is Bob Slasher, out and at home," was the reply, "and damned if I'm afraid of a man who is a born cur."

Gerrard, with a ferocious cry, turned upon him, and the two men closed, but they were parted instantly by Jack, who held one in each hand as if they had been children.

"This is my quarrel," said Jack, "and I will not let it be foisted upon another man. Now hark you, sir"—here he gave Gerrard a shaking—"listen to me. Either you publicly retract the words you uttered, or take the consequences!"

"I will not retract them," said Gerrard, and with a quick movement he drew out a revolver and fired.

Jack saw the intention, and leaped aside. But the small bullet did deadly work nevertheless. Bob Slasher received it in his chest, and fell forward upon his face without a groan.

He was a great favourite with that rough community, for he was a light, warm-hearted, merry fellow, and a howl of execration burst from the lips of those around. Gerrard would have fallen a victim to public vengeance if Broad Arrow Jack had not interfered.

"Leave him to me," he said. "Now, Gerrard, you have your choice—a trial by Lynch law or a duel with me."

"Why should I be tried?" asked Gerrard.

"The dead," replied Jack, "gives you the answer. There's the man"—pointing to Slasher—"he died by your hand."

"It was an accident," muttered Gerrard.

"It was not," returned Jack; "he only changes places with me. How say you, men, am I just in my demand—a trial or a duel?"

"You are just," they chorussed; "he shall hang or fight."

"Suppose I fight," said Gerrard, "and this big bully-boy should fall, what then?"

"The demands of justice," said Jack, "will be satisfied, and you'll be free." Again he referred to the crowd, and one and all said that the duel, end how it might, should terminate the affair.

"Then," said Gerrard, "I will fight."

In that selection lay his only hope. Slasher had fallen before too many witnesses for him to escape by trial; and although he doubted if he could come off victorious with his young opponent, luck might be in his favour.

"I will fight," he said again.

"Choose your weapons," said Jack.

Gerrard debated for a moment, and then said, "Revolvers, and if you don't mind, we will have a novel way of settling it. Start, thirty paces between us, and run in, firing how you like!"

CHAPTER CXXXVII.
THE DUEL BY MOONLIGHT.

"IT only remains now," said Jack, "for us to adjourn outside and get this business over."

"What! so soon?" said Gerrard, "will to-morrow not do? We must have daylight."

"Nay," said Jack, "to-morrow never comes; and if there's daylight lacking we have the moon. It is enough for me if it is for you."

"But neither I nor you have a second," pleaded Gerrard.

"There is enough here," pleaded Jack, "to see fair play. Let a man be appointed to measure the ground and give the word. If either fall, I dare say there will be many kind enough to dig a grave."

"Grave!" thought Gerrard, and his blood grew cold. Hard at all times as it is to die, it was doubly hard to a man like him, and trebly hard that death. Was he to die on the eve when wealth had fallen to his lot? Was he, with riches o'er which he had gloated with the hungry eyes of the miser, to leave the world and all its pleasures behind him? Was he, with the dream of youth and the hope of his manhood realised, to fall by the hand of this proud young hero?

It seemed so! All around him there was not one pitying face, but he saw in all the look as he knew in his heart he must have cast upon Skewball the night he was sentenced to death.

No hope, no chance, no loophole, save in conquering his majestic opponent. There was cowardice in his face, and the look was read with eager eyes. Somebody laughed; and Gerrard, nerving himself, began to stuff the notes and gold he had acquired at the gaming table into his pockets. When this was done he said "I am ready."

In a place where violence in its varied forms is to be seen daily, men get experienced in conducting affairs of this description. A committee was formed to carry out the preliminaries, which were of the fairest description.

In the first place some score or so of revolvers were cast in a heap upon the table, and little Dick Skewball was blindfolded to select two. It was unnecessary to load these, as the owners invariably kept them in that condition.

Next, two men were appointed to carry the weapons to the scene of combat; and, finally, the company formed themselves into an escort to conduct the two opponents to a spot suitable for their meeting.

It was an agreeable piece of excitement for the rowdy gentlemen there collected, and forthwith they began to bet on the result.

"I'll lay on the big stranger," said one.

"What's odds?" asked a gentleman, who was picking his teeth with a bowie knife.

"Two to one!"

"Not enough; take three."

"Done," said the other; "sixty dollars to twenty."

A great number of other bets were booked with a shake of the hand, and Dick offered to bet the Tiger anything he liked that Broad Arrow Jack would make Gerrard skip once and never skip again.

"What de take me for?" asked the Tiger, indignantly. "Me bet 'gainst Massa Jack! Do ye take me for big born fool?"

"No," said Dick; "come along, or we shall be out of it."

The party passed out of the roulette-room into the card department, where the play was going on, not having been interrupted by the disturbance which had taken place. Gambling in that place was not likely to be interrupted by a single pistol shot or the brawling of a few tongues.

But when the players saw their brethren coming out in a body, a few inquiries were made, and some who had not a very exciting game on, came out, too, to see the fight.

At another time Jack would have disliked this crowd and all the show; but now he had a double purpose in view—to save Skewball's name and perhaps his life, and to raise up a few friends to aid him in the capture of Jaundice and the Ogre.

Jack was, to put the case in plain terms, getting rather hard up.

The loss of the great bulk of his wealth had left him almost without funds, and it would be impossible for him without support to keep up his large staff of servitors at present engaged. He had a hope of recovering that wealth, but hope is hardly substantial enough to feed some hundred men, and be needed for a day, a month, or it might be a year perhaps, a few good men who would be willing to serve him without recompense.

There were many in that crowd in a position to do so if they were so inclined, and Jack was resolved to secure their aid, which could only be done with such men by exciting their admiration by an exhibition of skill and bravery.

The spot chosen for the duel was a hollow piece of ground with a ridge round it, naturally formed, which gave it some resemblance to a Roman camp, and such of my readers as have seen these ancient earth-works will easily understand how favourable such a spot would be to those who desired to be spectators.

They could sit or stand round like people at an amphitheatre, with little or no risk.

The moon was high in the heavens, and shone down straight upon the hollow space, shortening the shadows of the men appointed to mark out the ground and the two foes, who had met there to fight a duel to the death.

In spite of their natural callousness, the rough men gathered in a circle on the ridge were impressed by the scene at their feet.

Four men only stood in the hollow—Broad Arrow Jack, Gerrard, and two others, who, with steady steps, measured out the ground, placed the men, and gave each his weapon.

Jack and his foe were placed with their back towards each other, and were only to turn when the word was given.

Which was to do this was settled by the two men, who fell back upon the favourite mode of procedure—tossing. One spun a coin in the air, and so still was the night that the sound of its fall upon the soft ground was distinctly heard.

"Heads," said the other, and "heads" it was.

The man who had lost joined the circle above, and he who had won, withdrawing a little aside, addressed the foes as follows—

"Now you two attend to me. I am just a-going to say—'Are you ready?' and then you can do as you please—only don't come any tricks, and fire any where, but at each other."

Another moment's stillness then his voice was heard again—

"Are you ready?"

Gerrard swung round instantly, and had fired two shots before Jack, in his leisurely way, had turned to face him, but as he neither staggered nor fell it was supposed that these shots had missed him, until the keen eyes of the Tiger noticed a dark streak streaming down his side.

"Massa Jack hit," he said, and Dick Skewball fell upon his face, and lay there until the duel was over.

It was expected that Jack would immediately return the firing of his opponent, but to the amazement of all he only advanced a pace, without even raising his arm.

A whisper ran round the circle, and some one was heard to say—

"He's mad or drunk! Gerrard's a smart shot, and will bring him down like a pigeon next fire.

Gerrard heard those words, and inspired thereby he too stepped forward a pace, and fired another shot.

Jack was seen to start and stagger as if he would fall, but he recovered himself, and came steadily on.

One, two steps, and Gerrard, drawing a deep breath, suddenly ran forward, firing as he came. As the last shot from his revolver echoed on the night air Jack was seen to reel, and there was a cry—

"He's done for, the mad fool!"

But with a mighty effort he regained his feet, raised his weapon, and fired.

Gerrard leaped quite a foot in the air, then pitched forward on his face, and lay still as a great stone half imbedded in the ground, close to which he fell.

The same moment Jack put his hand against his side and swung round, so that the light of the moon fell upon his features and showed his eyes were closed, and with a gasping sob stretched his full length upon the cold clay.

The circle broke up, and the men came tearing down, but foremost was the Tiger, who, with half a dozen wild leaps, reached his master's side, and knelt down, sobbing.

"Oh, Massa Jack, if you am dead the poor Tiger will die!"

"I guess," said the man who had given the signal, "that neither of them will ever show in a fight of this sort again."

CHAPTER CXXXVIII.
DOING THE GRAND.

THOSE who know anything of Brighton are fully aware of its being considered a fashionable watering-place. There are some who delight in calling it the "metropolis of the sea-side," and no doubt it is worthy of its name, for go where you will it seems to be always full of people, and to have each gay fashion in its season.

Brighton has not one season like most watering-places, but a string of seasons, and although its most aristocratic time is chill November it is never so gay and gorgeous as in summer, when the sons and daughters of Israel resort thither, thronging the King's-road, and choking the pier in their gay and manifold attire.

In the summer there is much to be seen of an interesting nature, for at no other time and in no other place can you hope to find such coats, waistcoats, and neckties, such silks and satins, and last, but not least, such horsemen.

There are some men who fancy they can sit at a desk from childhood to the prime of life, then suddenly bloom as perfect horsemen. Not a few of them, I verily believe, would, if permitted, ride in the Derby, or accept an engagement in the Grand National Steeplechase.

It might not be such a bad thing after all if they could obtain such an engagement, for then it is possible that once in a way the best horse might win, for there would be an end to "roping and jollying," and all other form of "barney," so extensively practised upon the race-courses of England.

To return, however, to Brighton. The inhabitants of that favoured place have grown accustomed to the equestrian who thinks he can ride in five minutes, and seldom bestows more than a passing glance on those who bump, and shake, and quiver upon the animals they are permitted to hire.

But on a certain day, when the Israelitish season was at its height, the oldest salt upon the shore and the most blasphemous of the bathing women had their thoughts and eyes drawn from their respective vocations to look upon the two strangest horsemen that ever trotted down or tumbled off a horse in the King's-road.

Both horses and men are well known to our readers, and it is only necessary to describe the garb of the men, which is new.

Both had white hats, bright brown cut-away coats, and trousers of a bright yellow ochre colour.

And these said trousers had in the course of a short ride worked well up their legs, revealing that both these gentlemen wore short Wellington boots.

It was Conky and Wobbles, and coming up close behind them at a sort of shambling trot, were Pigeon and Curler, who every now and then uttered a few short words of encouragement to their companions.

How they came there a few words will explain.

Wobbles and the others, we know, were rescued from the wreck, and on the following morning old

Joss and Fireworks, the steeds alluded to, were rescued also.

The rest, I regret to say, were drowned.

The question then became, whose horses were they? and Wobbles, having boldly laid claim to them, stuck to the point, and insisted upon their being the property of himself and his companions.

Why he did so was best known to himself.

It might have been greed, or a sort of love growing out of associations that prompted him, and the mate of the Argosy, who looked upon these noble horses as a pair of worthless old screws, allowed him to take them away.

"And what are you going to do with them?" asked Conky in confidence of Wobbles.

"Keep 'em," was the reply.

"Keep 'em!" repeated Conky; "it's as much as you can do to feed yourself."

"Oh!" said Wobbles, lightly, "I've got a little property here in old England, which was left me some time ago."

"And who left it?" asked the sceptical Conky.

Wobbles hesitated for a moment, thinking at first he would give his mother credit for it; but having for years systematically abused his parent for the little she left him, he decided upon falling back upon a more distant relative, and said it was his grandmother.

"And I'll tell you what I'll do," he added, if you fellows behave straight, "I'll make swells of the lot of you. I am going up to London for a few days, and when I come back you shall have a jolly time of it."

Conky, Curler, and Pigeon stayed at the Jolly Tars while Wobbles was away, where they ate, drank, and were merry, on credit, the landlord having old Joss and Fireworks as security for future payment.

In due time Wobbles returned, paid all the bills, and gave a grand drinking entertainment in the taproom for one whole day and night, and then he, his friends, and the horses started on the road for London.

How long they were getting thither, two up and two down, would seem incredible to our readers, but what with losing their way and stopping here and there to make merry, and being twice locked up on suspicion of having stolen old Joss and Fireworks, it was more than a month before they sighted the great metropolis.

There they only waited to lay in a large stock of the loudest clothing that could be had for money, then started for Brighton, the sea-side being, in Wobbles' opinion, the most fitting place to air his gentility in.

Wobbles was supposed to have inherited half a million of money, but the sum his store of diamonds realised was little over four thousand pounds; and in his eyes the amount seemed sufficient to last him through an extravagant lifetime.

He had no difficulty in selling his little stock, for many of the men were returning from the fields just then, and a good business was being done in the gems newly dug from the earth.

At Brighton, then, we find the party riding down the King's-road, followed by an excited and admiring crowd, such as one sees at the heels of a well-known man who is walking for a wager.

Old Joss and Fireworks were apparently on their best behaviour, but on reaching the pier the music of the band fell upon the ears of old Joss. The sweet strains, softened by the distance, carried him back to his early days, and brought back a vivid vision of the circus before his eyes. Every nerve and pulse throbbed, and with a wild sideward leap he got over the rails which bounded the pathway, and made a frantic effort to get through the turnstile.

Wobbles went upon the pier without paying, and alighted, as usual, on his head.

Fireworks, not to be outdone, essayed to follow his companion; but the iron railing was too much for him, and getting his legs somehow tied up in the top of it, he pitched upon his head and laid out Conky full length upon the gravel walk.

"Did you iver see the like o' that?" said Curler to Pigeon. "I told 'em not to come out, but they would. Some people niver will learn to ride."

By this skilful address Curler implied that he and Pigeon could ride, and among the crowd there were a few believers. One man, who was helping to raise Conky, said—

"Friends o' yourn, gentlemen?"

"Oh! yes, we knows 'em," replied Curler. "Hurt, old man—eh?"

"Your wusship," said Conky, looking round him with a bewildered stare, "I'll swear I was niver in this court afore, and as for pickin' the gent's pocket of his dirty wipe, do you think I was likely for to do it when I have a clean un of my own, as come 'ome from the wash this——"

"Bring him this way," said Curler, hurriedly. "His mind is a-wandering, and he's a-thinking of the days when he used to sit on the bench with his father, the magistrate."

"A month!" said Conky, scornfully; "I'll do it on my 'ed."

"Can't you stop his jaw?" whispered Curler to Pigeon. "Purtend you are a-going to wipe his nose, and stick the handkercher into his mouth; then ketch hold of his 'ed, and I'll take the feet."

"Wot about the 'oss?" asked Pigeon.

"Blow the 'oss!" replied Curler. "He's at it agin."

"I niver did like the mill," pursued Conky, "acause it give you such a happetite, and prison 'lowance is cut down to a point when a man hangs on starvin'. Now, for a short bit, give me hoakum."

"Where's your handkercher?" asked Curler, in an agony.

"I put it in my trousers' pocket," replied Pigeon, "and the stitches have given way, so that it's gone down my leg, but I'll have it out in a minute."

"Oh! blow you, and your handkercher, and your leg!" growled Curler. "Come on; let's carry him to the nearest pub, and give him something to drink."

"I don't like the lock-up at Clerkenwell," pursued Conky, still troubled in his mind; "there's too much wentilation. Marlborough-street's better, but Winestreet is a'most as good as a private residence Now——"

The rest he had to say was lost as he was borne away by his companions, Curler calling out as he went—

"Somebody bring the 'oss, and I'll give him a bender."

Bringing the horse was not so easy, for Fireworks lay curled up, and seemed to be either dead or asleep. A cabman hard by, experienced in the shamming of horses, gave him a playful kick in the ribs, brutal enough, in spite of its fun, to have killed some horses, and old Fireworks got up, gave himself into the hands of a bystander, and was led away.

While all this was going on old Joss and Wobbles had fallen into pretty good hands—old Joss, extracted from the turnstile, in the hands of a policeman, and Wobbles in the care of two fashionably-dressed men, at whose feet he had been thrown when he first went upon the pier.

These two men are known to our readers, being no others than the Honourable Morden Crewe and Mr. Woody Welsher, who, not being possessed of very sympathetic hearts, would have let Wobbles lie where he had been deposited but for his extraordinary get up, which caught the attention of Mr. Welsher, who exclaimed—

"My eye! here's a fly cove come abroad. A ginger-beer maker come into his property, I should think."

"The fellow seems hurt," said the Honourable

Morden Crewe, coldly. "I suppose we ought to pick him up."

"What a rig!" exclaimed Mr. Woody Welsher.

"I wish you would leave your slang at home when you come out with me," said the Honourable Morden, savagely. "Put the fellow there on the seat, and come along."

But Wobbles would not let them go. He was not much hurt, and seeing they were well-dressed men he was anxious to express his gratitude.

"My friends—my preservers!" he exclaimed, clasping each by an arm, "how can I ever repay thee?"

"Oh, botheration!" exclaimed the Honourable Morden, trying to shake him off, "there will be a scene; quite a crowd outside the barriers; and whose horse is that looking over?"

"Mine," said Wobbles. "I tried to take the turnstile for a lark, but my hanimal was unhequal to it."

"You fool!" exclaimed the Honourable Morden, "you might have killed your horse."

"Then," said Wobbles, with the air of a millionaire, "I could have bought another, or a dozen if I wanted 'em."

The Honourable Morden pricked up his ears. Here was a man of money and a fool to boot. The Honourable Morden was in want of money, and being a knave, looked to fools for his supplies. The look of old Joss alone debarred him from an immediate rush of friendship.

"Your horse seems old," he remarked.

"I rode him," said Wobbles, pathetically, "when I was a boy. I only come hout to hexercise him."

"Most likely took the ginger-beer cart round," whispered Woody Welsher. "Hang on, he's got blunt. You will get some feathers to fly with."

"I am only too glad to be of service to you," said the Honourable Morden Crewe. "Shall we exchange cards?"

Wobbles was not unprepared for such an emergency, as the old hankering after "society" was not quite dead within him, and brought out a neat thing about the size of an ordinary playing card, on which his name was printed in alternate letters of black and red.

"Will you dine with me to-night?" said the Honourable Morden, as he gave his card. "I am staying at the Bedford. Six is my hour."

"With pleasure," said Wobbles. "And now, gentlemen. I will bid you adoo, as I see my hoss is gettin' himpatient."

CHAPTER CXXXIX.

GETTING UP IN THE WORLD.

A MEAN, close nature, like that which lay enshrined in the body of Wobbles, could not fail to prompt him to partially keep secret the meeting between the Honourable Morden and his friend Woody Welsher.

He threw out a few vague hints about having to meet some great people, whom he said he knew in former days, but who they were or what they were he declined to state.

Nor did he say anything about the dinner, lest his companions should follow him to the Bedford, and there by inquiries obtain the information he had declined to give.

The curiosity of Conky, Curler, and Pigeon, was fully aroused, but as their present subsistence rested entirely upon Wobbles they were careful enough not to be persistent or personal in their inquiries.

A little before the appointed hour Wobbles, having made a few striking additions to his attire, stole forth, and by a slightly circuitous route made his way to the Bedford.

There it seems he was expected, for the head waiter took him in charge and ushered him up into a well-appointed room, where the Honourable Morden and Woody Welsher were ready to receive him, both in evening dress, and offering a striking contrast to the appearance presented by Wobbles.

Greetings were exchanged, and Wobbles talked loudly, so to appear at his ease; but the very waiter engaged in putting the dinner on the table awed him, and he felt about as much at home as a chimney sweep would in a state apartment at Buckingham Palace.

The dinner was served—a very good one; Wobbles, always an excellent feeder, having his plate kept well supplied, did not care to indulge in much conversation; but when the dinner was over, the waiters gone, and cigars and wine put upon the table, Wobbles' tongue was loosened, and he began to talk of his travels in the distant country where diamonds, according to his account, could be gathered in with a rake or a shovel!

"I am only here on a visit," he said, "and have brought a few over to keep me a-going. Just shoved a handful into my pocket, and came away to see how the old country was looking."

"And when do you go back?" asked Woody Welsher.

"Not certain," returned Wobbles. "You see, if if I gets into society here—the society has I used to mix in before I hemigrated—I think I must stop a year or two. But," he added lightly, "all depends, you know!"

"Do you smoke?" asked the Honourable Morden.

"I have smoked," replied Wobbles, "but the bacca of this country aint up to much, and I am rather afraid of it."

"Try these cigars. They are uncommonly good."

Wobbles took one, sniffed it, pinched it, lighted it, and finally began to smoke with the air of a man who is handling an infernal machine which he fears may explode at any moment.

He smoked a little, drank a great deal, and talked vastly—of himself, of course; and at length began to boast of his adventures with his pal, Broad Arrow Jack.

"A fine young fellow," he said patronisingly; "werry good at hexercises. Can shoot a bit; and after a few lessons from me could handle the cutlass fairish. We was the terror of the place—we was, both on us!"

"Oh, the terror, were you?" said Woody Welsher. "What made you so?"

"We had a wengeance to hexicute!" replied Wobbles, mysteriously.

And so he talked on; and as the evening proceeded he gave in fragments a pretty good picture of Broad Arrow Jack.

Woody Welsher, who first had listened like a man who was amused by the vain boasting of another, gradually grew interested, and with a grave attentive face marked each word that fell from the lips of Wobbles, and made mental notes of many things he said.

"Can you play écarté?" asked the Honourable Morden, when Wobbles had arrived at a condition in which he ought not to have played at all.

"Rather!" replied Wobbles, who had seen it indulged in by the Ogre and his lot at Peaceful Village.

"Shall we play?"

To which Wobbles replied, "I am on."

They played, and Wobbles speedily lost thirty pounds. Then Woody Welsher intimated by a wink to the Honourable Morden Crewe that for the present he had better not pluck his pigeon further.

The cards therefore were put aside, and after another drink or two Wobbles rose to go.

A few inarticulate words escaped his lips, and having fervently shaken hands with his new friends, he asked for another cigar. They gave him a big one, and with this in his mouth he went staggering down the stairs, leering at the impassible waiters as he went by, to let them know that any liberties they might feel inclined to take with him would be promptly resented. He got outside, and being in a sentimental mood thought he would take a stroll upon the beach; but when he got there it seemed to him that all the lights upon the pier were dancing a Scotch reel, and after staggering forward a few paces he fell upon the hard shingle, dropped his cigar, and underwent the agonies which novices in the art of smoking invariably endure.

His companions, after he left, each lighted another cigar, and drew up to the window. Their heads being seasoned to drink, were but little affected by the potations of the evening, and they could discuss business as coolly and calmly as an ordinary merchant in his counting-house.

"Poor game this," said the Honourable Morden; "why did you check me? I could have had another fifty out of him at least!"

"Bah!" exclaimed Woody Welsher. "Confound his fifty! Whatever he has I will get out of him in a lump; but we must be careful."

"Careful—and why? You may toy with the bird until you lose him!"

"But suppose the bird is only a decoy for another."

"I don't understand you."

"Perhaps the word decoy is scarcely suitable; let me call him a jackal, for he has given mouth to-night, and shown me where our prey is to be found."

"Again I am in the dark."

"Listen to me, Crewe. What property are you waiting for?"

"The Ashleigh estate."

"And who stands between you and that?"

"Young Ashleigh."

"Then," said Woody Welsher, with a triumphant air, "I know where he is. Young Ashleigh and Broad Arrow Jack are one!"

"Nonsense!"

"Why? I have compared the descriptions this fellow gave to-night with what I know of your cousin, and I also have thought over such scanty information as we have received of his fate; and I say they are one and the same."

"Impossible!" said the Honourable Morden, "for my cousin was far too proud a spirit to associate with a snob like this fellow."

"Ah! indeed, Crewe," and here Woody Welsher settled his collar, as much as to say, "I have nothing in common with our guest to-night." "But the fellow is a liar," he went on, "and I dare say he was a servant of your cousin, has robbed him probably, and came over here to spend what he got. Anyhow, we have found your cousin and a man who knows him."

"All the worse for me," said the Honourable Morden. "Him alive, I have no chance of getting the family chips."

"He may be alive, Crewe, but we will soon prove him to be dead."

"How?"

"By affidavit. This fellow is not alone, and I think when he has been cleaned out we can get both him and his friends to be of service to us."

"But even then, supposing Ashleigh returns?"

"First of all," said Woody Welsher, with a sardonic grin, "get hold of his property, and that will give you the means of preventing his ever returning. Talk of Spanish bravoes, if you like, but they were poor creatures to many men. I know I could put my hands on a hundred who, if they could do it safely, would stab their own fathers for a five-pound note."

"These," said the Honourable Morden, sarcastically, "are, I presume, not entirely unconnected with the turf?"

"They hang about it, Crewe," replied the other, "and a precious lot of rascals they are. It makes me ill to think of them, but if they can be of service why not give them employment?"

"I cannot appear in this," said the Honourable Morden, "for my family name——"

"Your family grandmother!" interposed the other. "I am not going to be made a catspaw of, we go hand in hand, and we sink or swim together."

CHAPTER CXL.
ON THE BORDERS.

THERE was a hush upon the diamond-fields, for it was whispered about that one whom all there had at length learned to respect was dying. With three wounds, received in his late encounter, Broad Arrow Jack lay in one of the huts upon a couch of straw, watched by Brisket, the Tiger, and Dick Skewball. From the hour of the duel he had been unconscious, and though borne home with the utmost care, and tended by men with all the delicacy of women, his life for days had been ebbing fast.

Brisket was not at the duel, but he met the cortège returning—with what feelings you may guess; and day and night, with only short snatches of fitful sleep, which nature insisted upon, he watched over the young hero whom he so fondly loved.

And the Tiger did his part, for he was ever journeying to and fro for cooling herbs from the forest, and bringing fresh fruit, gathered on distant plains.

Dick Skewball alone of the three was most helpless. There was a scared and terrified look about him which was more than the grief of one who fears to lose a friend. A hundred times a day he would ask Brisket, "Will he live?"

To which Brisket would reply, "God only knows;" and then the poor boy would wring his hands and cry, "Oh, I do so want to speak with him!"

Brisket knew not what to make of the boy, and his thoughts were too much absorbed with Broad Arrow Jack to trouble about the eccentricities of Dick Skewball.

Gerrard was dead! The convulsive leap he gave in the air came of the last wild throb of his heart as the cold lead entered it; and ere he had grown cold some vulture-like companions had stripped him of the wealth he had acquired that night, and left him as poor and almost as naked as when he came into the world.

Whether he merited his fate or not my readers must judge. He was not all bad, but there was not much good in him, for he had shown much alacrity in bringing Richard Skewball to trial, had sat as president there, and finally passed sentence upon one whom, a few days before, he had called his friend, Not content with this, he had been the first to organise parties of pursuit when Skewball made his escape; and it was his voice that first said, "Shoot him down wherever you may meet him!" He might perhaps have escaped punishment for the sudden desertion of an old friend but for his boastfulness and his audacity in thrusting himself in the pathway of Broad Arrow Jack, and threatening his death at a time when, of all periods in his life, he least wished to die.

In all likelihood Broad Arrow Jack would have spared the man but for the fact that he was gratuitously and without cause endeavouring to raise the public mind against him. It was necessary for Gerrard to be put down—and it was done.

Of duelling as it used to be I can speak with scorn and contempt; but the "calling out" in a civilised peaceful country is a very different thing to the rough and ready meetings in a land where laws and order are but little known. In a country like our own Gerrard would have no power—in the place we write of he had a great deal.

But he died in fair fight, and there is an end to him. We have now to concern ourselves with Broad Arrow Jack, his adherents, and his living foes.

Dick Skewball, as I have said, was troubled, and

although of little use to his wounded master, was ever hovering by his bedside with that one question—"Will he die?"—upon his lips. One day the answer was definitely given.

"He is going," said Brisket. "I do not think he can live many hours. The noblest spirit ever encased in clay is about to leave us."

The grief of the old pedlar was intense, and Dick Skewball, as he heard the words, stopped his ears with his fingers, and ran out of the hut. The Tiger was away, and companionless this wretched boy walked up and down outside—a prey to remorse and despair.

A bitter cry from Brisket drew him back again, and opening the door he peeped in. Broad Arrow Jack lay white and still, and the pedlar was kneeling by his side passionately weeping.

"Dead!—dead!" cried the old man, and Dick Skewball, with a wild look in his eyes, turned and fled away!

CHAPTER CXLI.
DICK SKEWBALL REFLECTS.

THE course Dick Skewball chose led him across the diamond fields, and as he ran on many men looked up from their labour to watch the frantic flight of the boy, with some amount of curiosity. But some were very much startled by the appearance he presented. He had always been eccentric, and they had grown accustomed to seeing him travel to and fro in various fashions, walking, running, or leaping, according to the whim of the moment.

Only two spoke to him. One said, "Hullo, Dick! whither away?" and the other advised him "to put his eyes back an inch or two, or he would lose them!" He gave no word in reply—indeed, he did not hear them—but fled, occupied with the thoughts that surged about in his brain.

And what were those thoughts?

First, that Broad Arrow Jack was dead, and that he—Dick Skewball—had lost an opportunity for relieving his breast of the burden of a great crime.

Yes! the great mass of wealth which Maggie, in a measure, had entrusted to his keeping, he had stolen and hidden away; not at first with any settled idea of appropriating it for his own use, but with the notion of placing his father and mother above the necessity of toil.

But it is astonishing how different our thoughts are before and after the possession of wealth. Poor humanity is always willing to give when it is poor; but the niggard hand too often comes with riches. It is a rule, with a few rare exceptions.

Dick was never selfish until this fortune for a time became his, and then the bare possession of it started the germs of selfishness within him, and in a few hours it had overgrown his better nature, as the ivy covers the trees of the forest. He began to live for self, and as a matter of course began to suffer.

After possession of the wealth came a knowledge of Broad Arrow Jack, and then there grew up in the boy a love for his chief that fought boldly with his baser spirit, and although it could not master it, held it at least at bay, and gave it no rest. Day and night the fight went on for days and weeks, and the result was still doubtful when the duel took place.

Dick, looking on his wounded chief, bitterly repented of his deed. The keener sympathies of his nature were touched, and he would have given all that he ever could or would have—nay, his very life—to have gone back a few short weeks, to undo the crime he had been guilty of.

And when Brisket cried "He is dead," the cry had a double meaning. It said, "Dick Skewball, you have lost your chief, and you are everlastingly accursed as A THIEF. The time has gone by for you to retrieve the past. Go forth, accursed;" and so he fled.

But as he ran, thought the second came to him, roused the selfishness which had lain dormant for awhile, and gave him such consolation as the possession of worldly wealth can give.

The second thought was this: "You have now that which will make you a great man in time to come. He to whom it belonged is dead, and you have as good a right to what he leaves behind as any other living being. It is yours, and none have a right to dispute your possession of it."

CHAPTER CXLII.
THE TIGER'S GRIEF.

AGAIN selfishness was in the ascendant with Dick Skewball, and all his grief was being scattered to the winds when he saw the Tiger approaching at a rapid pace, bearing in his arms a bundle of herbs for his chief.

"He is ten thousand times better than I am," thought Dick, bitterly. "Although he has a black skin, and can neither read nor write, I do not believe he would have robbed his noble master."

He would have passed the Tiger, but he was seen, and the active young imp came bounding up with the grace of his namesake.

"Ah! old Dick, dat you? Whar am you going?"

"I am going away," replied Dick, "for good."

"What de matter?" asked the Tiger, looking eagerly at him. "You hab tears in your eyes—you am pale. What am de matter? What bout Massa Jack?"

"Dead," replied Dick, "about an hour ago!"

The Tiger cast his burden of herbs down upon the earth, and sank upon his knees, with his hands clasped before him. For awhile he spoke no word nor shed a tear, but rocked himself to and fro, with his dry eyes fixed ahead, like one in a maze of thought. At length the relief came in the form of tears, heralded by a wild shriek.

"Oh! Massa Jack—Massa Jack, what am you dead for, wif so many bery bad men left alive?"

Who even among the wisest of us have not asked ourselves a similar question?—why does this good man die and this bad one live on? But who are we that we should doubt the wisdom of the Ruler of all things? Whoever lives and whoever dies let us not question the fitness of his dying, for it is presumption in us to do so.

But the poor Tiger, ignorant of all things save his own rude instincts, and with all his heart set upon Broad Arrow Jack, who had been the first in the world to show him what kindness was, went on with his fruitless wailing.

"Oh! Massa Jack—Massa Jack, why am you dead?"

Dick stood by, more and more racked by remorse, as he looked upon his dark-skinned friend in an agony of grief.

"He is better than I am," he kept saying to himself; "he has a noble heart. He would not have robbed Broad Arrow Jack."

Anon the Tiger rose, and turning to Dick, asked him where he was going.

"To the woods," replied Dick. "I am going to live there for a time."

"And I'll go too," said the Tiger.

"But will you not go and see the dead chief?" asked Dick.

"No," replied the Tiger, "he is not there now; he has gone away."

"But there is his body, Tiger."

"Oh, nuffin in dat!" replied the Tiger. "Dat am not de massa any more dan dat ole coat am you."

He plainly had no interest in looking upon the dead, and Dick, with a puzzled look, dwelt upon his words as they trudged on in silence together.

"He is wiser than I am," was the thought that came out of Dick's meditation.

"Tiger," he said aloud, "where is the chief gone to?"

"Dunno," replied the Tiger; "but he am not here. We see him again one day."

"How do you know that?"

"Dunno, but I feel dat it will be so," replied the Tiger.

"Face him again!" thought Dick. "How can I ever face him, and I a thief?"

But this feeling—right as it was undoubtedly—was at the same time transient. Dick was young, and easily led from sad thoughts, and in a few minutes he was running and shouting after a herd of startled deer, and the Tiger, with dry eyes, ran by his side, shouting too.

Once in the forest the ruder instincts of their natures ruled them, and although Broad Arrow Jack was not forgotten, and never could be by at least one of them, they could not repress the excitement which arose as the various forms of life came under their notice.

The startled hare, the nimble rabbit, the flying deer, all in their turn became the object of an eager but fruitless chase.

"But we will catch them by-and-bye, Tiger," said Dick, as he stopped, panting; "for I know how to make a snare, and to dig a deer-pit."

"All right, ole Dick!" replied the Tiger, laughing; "but me know how to catch dem wifout dat."

"But you can't catch them," said Dick, "for you tried just now and could not do it."

"All right, ole Dick," said the Tiger, with a knowing shake of his head, "you see by-'em-bye."

The day was far spent, and neither of the boys seemed to trouble their heads where they were to pass the night. It was not the first time by many that they had been out on a wild excursion alone, trusting to chance where they might lay their heads, and being in company they were not likely to have much thought about the matter. It was nearly dark when Dick Skewball referred to it.

"Tiger," he said, "we must have something to eat, and then sleep."

"Eat first," said the Tiger, sagaciously; "look out for de heddegehog chap."

The Tiger found two of these animals without loss of time, and Dick having some matches about him, they collected a lot of leaves and dry sticks, and made a fire. Wrapping the hedgehogs into some damp clay, they cast them in, and in half an hour their dinner was ready.

The clay having been drawn out of the fire and given time to cool, it was broken into pieces, the prickles and skins of the animals came off, and the well-cooked and really eatable flesh was ready for the youngsters.

Having eaten every scrap of it, they drank some water from the neighbouring spring, and making up their fire again, so that it would burn and smoulder through the night, lay down just as they were, and sleep soon followed.

When Dick awoke in the morning he found himself alone, and but for the impression of the Tiger's form, still visible on the turf, might have thought that he had dreamt of passing the dark hours with his companion. While wondering what had become of him the dark-skinned young imp appeared, bearing a fawn upon his shoulders.

"Me kill him," he said, as he cast it at Dick's feet.

"How did you snare him?" asked Dick.

"Not snare him, ole Dick," replied the Tiger, laughing.

"How did you kill him then?"

"Dat my business—me kill when wanted. Plenty ob fawn—neber want food."

Dick examined the graceful form carefully, but could find no sign of a snare, or wound, or bruise; the body was yet warm, and the fawn could not have been killed half an hour.

"I don't see how it's done," he said.

"No, ole Dick, and you not do it if you did know," returned the Tiger. "But dere am plenty ob him. Skin first, den cook, eat what we want, and hide de rest."

Both had knives, and the Tiger proving an adept in the art of skinning, that operation was speedily performed. Three or four of the ribs were roughly roasted, and they made a hearty meal.

But while eating Dick was pondering, and when he had finished he gave utterance to his thoughts.

"Tiger," he said, "now that the chief is dead we have nobody to serve."

"Noborry worf serbing," returned the Tiger. "I neber go bout to find anoder massa."

"No more will I," said Dick, "and I mean to live in these woods until I grow to be a man."

"And affer dat," grinned the Tiger, "lib here too—lib and die. No good to go bout wif men—dey make slabes ob eberybody."

"I shall live here until I am a man," said Dick. "Then I shall go to some great place and be a prince."

The Tiger grinned, and shook his head incredulously. Dick, a little netled, went on.

"You may grin," he said, "but I tell you I mean to be a prince. I have got a lot of money, more than any prince ever had, but I dare not show it now, because I am only a boy, and men would rob me of it. But when I get to be a man I shall be able to take care of it."

"Whar you get dat money?" asked the Tiger.

Dick paused a moment, and then replied—

"I found it."

"Found him whar?"

"I'll tell you one day," said Dick. "But I have got it hidden away, and I don't mean to tell anybody about it."

There was a thoughtful look in the Tiger's eyes as he turned to his companion and said—

"Money bring no good to me or you. What we want it for? It brings fighting, bloodshed, gives blows; men kill each oder for it. Berrer trow dat away and lib here free."

"No," said Dick, shaking his head, "it is too good a thing for that. I've lived long enough to know that you can do anything if you only have money enough, and I mean to be a big swell in a better land than this; to have horses and carriages and servants, and to have people touch their hats to me, as father says the big nobs have in the old country; and if you will stand by me and live here with me until we are both men, you shall be a big swell too."

The notion tickled the Tiger tremendously, and he roared again with merriment.

"Me a big swell," he exclaimed, "golly smash—how funny!"

"Yes," said Dick, "it shall all come about; and you shall ride in a carriage with red velvet linings, and have horses with silver harness, and fat-legged footmen to hang on behind and open the door when you want to get out."

"Scrubshous!" said the Tiger.

"And instead of having to hunt about for your food, and cooking it in this way," pursued Dick, "you shall have people to get it for you, and to cook it, and to serve it up on gold plates. And we'll have a big bell to ring when it is time to go to dinner, and people to do everything for us but eat the food and swallow it!"

"Am dat true?" asked the Tiger, with glistening eyes.

"I wouldn't lie to you," replied Dick, "for you have been a pal to me ever since I knew you. I've got it, and I know pretty well *what it's worth*, and I swear that when we are grown up there won't be two bigger swells going than you and me!"

"But whar am all dis to come about?" asked the Tiger.

"Not here," said Dick, "but in the country where my father was born. There the houses are a hundred times as big as they are here, and all made of bricks and stones, and fitted up inside with velvet and satins if you have the money to pay for it; and you and I, Tiger, will marry two beautiful women, and live as happy as the day."

"You are sure of all dis, ole Dick?" asked the doubting Tiger.

"Do you think I don't know what I am talking about?" said Dick, impatiently. "I tell you it is so, and that's enough. My father told me what money is worth, and I've got more money than all the men in the diamond-fields put together."

"How long shall we be growing up?" asked the Tiger.

"Oh! I think we may be men in about four years," said Dick, "and the time will soon pass, for it is rare fun roaming about here without anybody to bother us."

"Real fun, ole Dick," said the Tiger; "but I tink dat perhaps you make a mistake."

"I wish I may die if it isn't true!" said Dick, fervently.

The Tiger believed him then, for that in his eyes was an oath which could only emanate from one who spoke the truth; and the boys in their mutual joy hugged each other and danced about like sprites.

They were young, and may be pardoned, I hope, if for the moment, in the contemplation of the future, they forgot the past, and the great chief who had played so conspicuous a part in both their lives.

CHAPTER CXLIII.

LIGHTLY COME AND LIGHTLY GO.

WOBBLES was again in society. With the aid of his two new friends, the Honourable Morden Crewe and Woody Welsher, he was once more in the whirlpool of fashionable life—on the outer ring of it it is true, but still in it.

The part of fashionable society in which he found himself was that which is given to the turf.

Wobbles was on the turf.

He went to Ascot and Goodwood with Woody Welsher, and there he met the Honourable Morden Crewe, who spoke to them both, and to Wobbles in particular, quite affably, but he seemed to be shy of travelling to and fro with either. What of that? When a swell speaks to a man like Wobbles in public he gives him a position—doesn't he? Wobbles felt he had attained position.

His get-up on these public occasions was a thing to sit and dwell upon for years during our lonely hours. It was a thing to bring the hypochondriac and the bilious and other sufferers to gaze upon, for if they had not laughed for years they would have had a fit as soon as they beheld him. Wherever he went he was an object of interest.

The boys perhaps were rude, but boys have no idea of dress—so Wobbles said—and they have, we all know, an inborn aversion to originality of attire. Wobbles having bought a hat with a brim that had no rival in the known world, the boys pursued him with low chaff, and occasionally pelted him with harmless missiles of the cabbage-stump order.

The Honourable Morden Crewe, when first he saw that hat, retired to curse it, for he knew every one would be asking him—"Who is that fellow in the hat you spoke to just now?" and sure enough he was pestered with questions right and left, to all of which he gave one answer—

"A rough, but not a bad sort of fellow, who has made his fortune in the diamond-fields."

Then certain fashionable gentlemen, rich in name and family, but poor in pocket, took an interest in Wobbles, and asked his advice about horses, and made bets with him, which he invariably lost, and if he did occasionally win it was remarkable how bad the memories of those fashionable gentlemen became. They one and all forgot to pay him.

But Wobbles did not care. He was in society, and walked arm-in-arm with "real nobs," who never laughed at him, but said kind things, and ate and drank at his expense, and borrowed a fiver now and then, like the good-hearted fellows they were.

And in all this glory Conky, Curler, and Pigeon had no share.

Like three Peris they hovered round the gate and looked at Wobbles strutting about in the turfy Paradise with envy in their hearts.

They lived upon Wobbles still. He allowed them a pound a week each to keep away from him, and not by any chance to look as if they knew him when they met in the streets or elsewhere. If the conditions were broken their pay was to cease.

A pound a week is not much to live upon, but with discreet moving from their lodgings the night before their bill was due, and leaving it of course unpaid, they managed to support their heads above water, and to keep up as respectable an appearance as well-worn shoddy clothes and a villainous cast of countenance would enable them to do.

They also went on the turf in a small way. They laid the odds against the horses when anybody would take them, and if the horses won they all put on blue spectacles and melted away from the race-course.

They welshed or robbed those who betted with them, but their gains were not large, as they only got people who had small sums to invest to deal with them.

Meat, drink, shelter, and a roving life are four good things in their way, and Conky, Curler, and Pigeon were as happy as the general run of men.

Old Joss and Fireworks meanwhile were out to grass on Woolwich-common, where they were free to roam through the kind permission of a captain of the Engineers, who was a friend of the Honourable Morden Crewe, and there they gave immense delight to the general public by their occasional bouts with each other.

The waltzing and other circus tricks of old Joss gave unqualified pleasure to hundreds of simple, hard and horny sons of toil as they walked on the common with their little ones on Sunday eve.

Before putting these noble steeds out to grass Wobbles conceived the idea of driving the pair tandem, and they were put into harness at a great expense, but the result was sad indeed. They got the trap and horses into the street, with Wobbles on the box, but there was an end of the journey.

Old Joss, who played leader, kicked Fireworks in the jaws, and Fireworks in return bit old Joss in that part of his anatomy which would have been turned to steaks if fate had made a bullock of him instead of a horse, and then they both backed, and got the whole concern into a heap up against a greengrocer's shop, and Wobbles beat a judicious retreat up a long sloping board covered with vegetables.

The greengrocer in person received Wobbles on his arrival at the summit, and, first giving him a black eye, so that he might know him again, demanded a "fiver" for the damage done. Mrs. Greengrocer also aimed a blow at him with a bunch of early turnips, but the damage she did was not material.

Is it to be wondered at, then, that when Wobbles offered to "tool" Woody Welsher to Hampstead and back with old Joss and Fireworks, he said he would see him "somethinged first?"

It must now be clear to everybody why those two gallant steeds were put out to grass, and we will get on with our tale.

It was the cup-day at Goodwood, a glorious day, as it generally is, with a sun hot and strong enough to bake a man, and everybody was panting with heat. The dust along the road was tremendous, and as the coaches arrived they seemed to bring nothing but millers with them, and the wash-and-brush-up place was crowded to excess.

Among the early arrivals were Woody Welsher and Wobbles, who came in a fly hired at the Dolphin Hotel in Chichester, and the pair entered the

Inclosure like the real gents they were, and sought the refreshment-room, to have a brandy and soda each while they looked over their betting books.

Wobbles had not much to look at. He had, by the advice of Woody Welsher, "peppered" one horse—that is, laid against that and nothing else. The name of that horse was Trouble, and it was first favourite.

"I see that Trouble has arrived," said Wobbles, looking over a paper he had brought with him.

"You said that fifty times coming along," replied Woody Welsher, angrily. "Of course he has arrived. Who said he wouldn't?"

"What's the good of his arriving if he isn't going to run?" asked Wobbles.

"I said I was told he was not going to run," said Welsher. "The horse isn't mine, and if the owners have changed their minds I can't help it—can I?"

"No, but I'm as good as bust up if he wins."

"I don't see how he can win unless all the other horses go dead lame," returned his companion. "Go on peppering. You'll come out of it all right."

Several gentlemen lounged in at this moment, and they all began to talk about this horse, Trouble.

Nobody seemed to fancy him, but just to "square their books" they wanted to put a few pounds on. Wobbles went on peppering, and betted with them all.

"Don't forget," whispered Woody Welsher; "here we settle immediately after the races."

"All right," replied Wobbles.

"Have you brought enough, do you think?"

"I have brought every penny I have in the world," said Wobbles.

Woody Welsher slyly smiled, and, lighting a cigar, said—

"Come, old fellow, and let us see the preliminary races."

"Is Trouble in them?" asked Wobbles, with a groan.

"Trouble of some sort is in every race," was the reply.

"I say," said Wobbles, nervously, "are you sure my Trouble will lose?"

"I am sure as any man can be who doesn't know the horse."

"Don't you know him?" exclaimed Wobbles, aghast.

"Never seen him. But what's the odds? I got my tip straight from the stable."

"I hope it is all right," said Wobbles, and he groaned again, for he had deep and sore misgivings.

Conky, Curler, and Pigeon were on the course. They came in no hired carriage, but footed it all the way, each bearing a three-legged stool, for a purpose which will presently be seen. At certain corners of the road they halted and played a little game with three cards, in which an occasional member of the general public played, and when he did so he always lost.

It is a cheerful thing this three-card trick—the end of the game is so certain. If you are one of the public you put your money down. If you lose, the owner of the cards keeps it, and if you win he can't pay you, but makes all sorts of excuses, and if pushed into a corner will pay you back in "duffing" money, which is a polite name for counterfeit coin.

The precious trio got on very well until a big broad-shouldered man betted with them and lost two sovereigns—fairly enough as the game goes; but having made up his mind to win, and having a strong objection to the calculations of his mind being upset, he knocked Conky, who worked the cards, into a ditch, and in a trice turned his pockets inside out.

This nefarious deed exposed the worldly wealth of the three friends—about four pounds won in this way, and about a quarter of a peck of Hanoverian medals, which are brass coins made to look something like sovereigns. Selecting the good coins from the bad the burly man pocketed them, and went on his way rejoicing.

"You must be a pretty couple," said Conky to his friends, "not to come and help a fellow."

"Wot! arter we saw the way he floored you," replied Curler. "One on us knocked about at a time is enough."

Conky was very savage, but he was helpless. The money was gone, and with only the brass in their pockets and the other brass on their faces they swaggered upon the race-course.

CHAPTER CXLIV.

THE RACE—TROUBLE AHEAD.

SELECTING a place at the end of a row of betting men, who were vociferating the odds with voices already hoarse, Conky, Curler, and Pigeon put down their three-legged stools, and stood thereon. Then each took a printed bill from his pocket and pinned it on his waistcoat, so that it looked like an apron.

On Conky's placard was seen, "Jones and Co., of Manchester."

On Curler's, "Smith, from Liverpool."

And on Pigeon's, "Turf agency, established 1412."

The three knaves lent their voices to the dreadful din, shouting "I'll lay on the field!" "Two to one bar one!" and "Who'll bet?" "Who's got any money?" and so on; and as they shouted or sung, gents came to listen and to put their money into a business which was "all profit and no returns!"

"What's agin Trouble?" asked a squint-eyed man, with a licensed victualler's build of body.

"Two to one," replied Conky.

"Not enough."

"Three to one."

"Done with you for half-a-quid."

Conky took the ten shillings, and handed the stranger a small piece of pasteboard, on which was written in ink, "J. & Co."

"There's no number on this," said the man.

"You bring it to me when the race is over and I'll settle with you," replied Conky. "I've got a private mark as I knows on."

The man took his word and went his way. The confidence the public have in these betting rascals is one of the phenomena of the age.

Others came, and Conky, Curler, and Pigeon got enough money to live on for a month if they could only get clear away with it. The bell rang for the course to clear for the big race, and they held a whispered conference.

"Cut and run now—eh?" said Conky.

"No. Wait till the people breaks into the course arter the race," replied Curler, "then make for that bit o' wood yonder, and lay up till dark."

"That's the game," said Pigeon.

So they waited, and continued to call the odds up to the last moment, and caught many a flat.

There were but five horses in the race. The Goodwood cup has seldom called out a very large field. The names of the horses that ran that day were Black Jenny, Spitfire, Runaway, Leo, and Trouble.

As they passed the grand stand in a preliminary canter every eye was on them. Each had its admirers, but Trouble found favour with most. There was a rush to get "on" him, and he rose to even money, and in some places with odds in his favour.

Wobbles' book was full; he had laid until he could lay no more. White and nervous, with Woody Welsher complacently grinning at his elbow, he saw the horses go by, stretching their limbs so freely, and holding their heads so proudly.

"That Trouble seems to fly," he said.

"All the better. He will lose his wind, and then you will be as right as a trivet," replied Woody Welsher. "Steady now—they are at the post."

"They're off!" cried a thousand voices, and Wobbles involuntarily sank a foot or so. Limp and ghastly to look upon he awaited the issue.

The race, briefly described, was as follows:

Trouble jumped off with the lead, was never headed by any of the others, and won in a canter by five lengths.

Wobbles saw him come flying up, heard the shouts, "Trouble!—Trouble!" and clutched the arm of Woody Welsher with the grip of desperation.

"I'm a ruined man!" he said, "I can't—I won't pay all my money away; I shall be a beggar!"

"Hush!" whispered Woody Welsher, "don't talk in that way. You must pay or they will murder you. Did you read what they did to a welsher the other day?"

"No," said Wobbles, faintly.

"He was seen and recognised by a man he had swindled at Epsom; it was at Hampton races where what I am going to tell you took place. The man knew him, and calling out "Welsher!" collared him. Then up came an angry ferocious mob, thirsting to beat and bruise, and they cut him about the head and face with their walking-sticks until you could not tell one feature from another, and the blood ran in streams down his neck. Then they stripped him and kicked him about the course like a football, and they would have killed him if the bell had not rung for another race, and the police came down to clear the ground. Then he was allowed to go, and he crawled away like a maimed rat that's been worried by dogs."

"But is that true?" asked Wobbles, with staring eyes.

"Every word of it."

"But it aint considered fair for a lot of people to pitch into one man. Besides, he couldn't have robbed them all."

"Oh!" said Woody Welsher, coolly, "it was a bit of fun for them."

"A nice lot there must be on the turf," groaned Wobbles.

"As nice a lot as you would meet with anywhere," said his companion; "but the race is over, and here they come for their money. Pay up like a man, and I'll see that you don't want."

Wobbles paid up, as much like a man as he could; but it was hard to part; his sorrow had no sweetness in it, and in a few minutes he was as poor as he had been in the old days.

"Don't look like that," said Woody Welsher. "You should lose with spirit, as you win. Go and have a brandy and soda; I will come to you presently. If we miss each other, meet me at the Dolphin to-night."

Woody Welsher, after parting with Wobbles, sought for the Honourable Morden Crewe, who was smoking and drinking with some of his own set.

"Well," said the Honourable Morden, "is it done?"

"Done completely!" replied Woody Welsher; "and in a fortnight the affidavits of the death of your cousin will be ready."

"Can they be trusted?"

"Up to a certain point; but when we have done with them we can ship them over the sea. Leave it to me, Crewe, and I will put you right."

And he slapped the honourable familiarly on the back, to show people around on what terms he stood with that gentleman.

The Honourable Morden took it very well; but there was a glitter in his eye that ought to have told Woody Welsher he was going a little too far; but if he saw the expression he did not heed it. Lighting a cigar, he said, "Ta-ta, Crewe," and went in search of Wobbles.

CHAPTER CXLV.

SEE HOW HE LIES.

CALM and still, like a statue that had fallen from its pedestal, lay Broad Arrow Jack. The tall muscular form was as quiet as a stone figure on the monument of a knight of old.

The face was rigid, the eyes, half-hidden by the drooping lids, glassy and without expression, and above the broad white forehead the rich curls, emblematical of strength, hung listless.

And was this the end of all?

This was the question that Brisket asked himself as he knelt beside that silent form.

His eyes were full of the tears of sorrow which comes from the heart, and the finger-tips of his hands were white as he pressed them together.

Here was sorrow indeed, but hours passed on and no sound escaped his lips. He could only kneel and gaze and wipe away the tear-drops that rolled one by one from his eyes as the waters of grief welled up and overflowed.

There was no word, no sound that could have expressed what the simple honest pedlar felt.

He might have knelt and died there for aught I know but for the entrance of a man, who, in the unceremonious ways of that part, came in without knocking.

Coming from the light he did not fully grasp the scene at first, but the question came from his lips—

"What news, master? How fares the chief to-day?"

Brisket heard the words, but failed to associate them with aught he had heard before.

There was no meaning in the sounds, no recognition of even the human voice. He was lost to all but the great grief that lay like a mountain on his breast.

The man drew nearer, and saw that Brisket was kneeling, and then he looked from him to the still massive form, and beheld what he conceived to be the presence of death.

He had lounged into the house with his hat upon his head. Now doffing it hastily, he drew up to Brisket's side, and laid a hand upon his shoulder.

"Master," he said, "he was a noble fellow, and has met his end like a man."

Brisket raised his head, and, with a vacant stare, asked—

"What news of the chief? Will he soon return?"

"Come—come," said the man, giving Brisket another gentle shake, "if you lose your senses it will not bring him back to life again. Be content; he might have died less worthily."

Brisket passed his hand over his eyes, and sighed wearily. That sigh acted upon the clouds on the brain as the breath of wind on the morning mist, and cleared them away. Speedily he came back to all the misery arising from a knowledge of what he had lost.

As he rose from his knees the visitor said—

"That's right, master. 'Twas something to have known such a man, as you have known him, and a proud thing it must be for you to be able to stand here and say 'He was my friend.'"

"Ah!" returned Brisket, "he was. Heaven knows it. He was more than a friend to me; no son and father ever had a greater bond between them than that which held us together. I loved him."

The listener, with a glance at the prostrate form of Jack, nodded his head slowly, as he replied—

"I can well believe it."

"What was I before I knew him?" said Brisket. "Who among the men of this wild land so lonely as I? Without a friend, without a companion, plodding wearily over the great waste, and gathering a bare existence as I went, burdened with the great secret, which if I had revealed to any other but the noble lad who lies there, these bones ere now would have whitened in the wilderness, or murder must have

Broad-Arrow Jack.

THE OGRE APPLIED THE MATCH AND THE FLAMES UPROSE AROUND THE DOOMED MAN.

NO. 21.

followed. The wealth of a kingdom was mine, but I dared not touch it. There were power and all that follows in the train of riches at my command, yet in my weakness all would have lain idle but for him."

"You speak strangely," said the man.

"I can speak as I like now," returned Brisket, "for that which I tell you of has, as I fear, been lost to him and me. It matters little, for now that he is gone what have I to do but to put my pack upon my back and wander as I have done before, hither and thither, until it shall please God to call me from this world to a reunion with him I love?"

And so he talked on, and the man listened for awhile, and then went out to spread the news abroad.

He went hither and thither, and this is what he said, "Broad Arrow Jack is dead"—no more, but it was enough. Men cast down the pick and spade, and left their search for wealth to get confirmation at the hut where he lay.

Brisket received them, and they came in one by one, removing their hats, and standing for a few seconds in that silent chamber, and passing out with stealthy tread, as if they feared to awaken him.

"He's a better man dead than we are living," said many, and went home to tell their wives and little ones as much as they knew of the story of our hero.

The drinking booths, the gambling saloons, and he music-halls were all deserted that night.

Only a few of the most reckless and indifferent went out to spend their hours in dissipation, and even they spoke in a lower tone, gambled less, and forbore to quarrel. So strange an eve had never been known in the diamond fields before, and it led one of the men to remark "it is like a Sunday in the old country."

It was indeed a quiet night, and before midnight, usually the most riotous hour, the favourite haunts were closed and dark, and save for one light there was no sign of life about the fields.

All nature lay hushed. The broad dark arch above, spangled with stars, which seemed dim that night, as if they too had tears to shed, and appeared fixed and immovable. No sound was heard—not even the hoot of the night-owl fell upon the ear—no brawling, no shouting or singing, not even a footstep broke the stillness, and the diamond-fields were in mourning.

You will think it strange perhaps that the death of one man in this lawless, reckless land, could have so affected the multitude; but Broad Arrow Jack was no common being, his history no common one, and the last scene of it was calculated to enlist the sympathies of the community gathered there.

While Jack lay ill, with his mind in the land of unconsciousness, those who had witnessed the duel told the story of it a hundred times—how he had given his foe every chance of taking his life and getting off free, and how, when sinking from his wounds, he had at last brought down Gerrard with unerring aim. To men accustomed to take every advantage of a foe this story had a peculiar charm, and he never was so great a hero as the day when it was given forth that he was dead.

"We will give him a rare funeral," said some; "there shall be no work in the fields that day."

They chose his grave where he had fought and fell, and they dug it deep, so that no chance prowling beast might disturb him, and a young oak sapling was to be planted o'er the grave as an emblem of the strength of him who lay beneath.

Brisket helped but little in the preparations. His mind was lost in sorrow when the day at last dawned for the ceremony, and a multitude of those who had undertaken to bear Broad Arrow Jack away, and to follow, gathered round the door. The pedlar in a passion of grief, cried, "It shall not be! I will not have him taken away." Kind hands gently thrust him aside, and on a bier, constructed with great care by skilful hands, and fringed all round by wild flowers of the forest, they laid the hero, and bore him to the open air."

Outside there were women assembled, and one of them, whose wrinkled face told of three score years or more, shading her eyes with her hands, said: "No need to hurry with his burial—there are no signs of change in him."

It was but a passing remark, but it struck many around, and curious eyes were bent upon Broad Arrow Jack, who was pale and still as a marble figure, but otherwise unlike those from whom the spirit has fled.

Brisket heard it, and with an eager look he stooped over the prostrate form. At the same moment, like a brief light flashed from a moving mirror, something came and went from the handsome face.

With a new hope, so keen, that had a disappointment immediately followed it would have killed him, the pedlar opened the broad blade of his bowie knife, and held it for a moment over the slightly parted lips; then reversing it he looked upon the blade.

A slight shadow was there, and in an instant it was gone; but brief as its coming and going, it told all, confirmed the old man's hope, and brought from his lips a shout of joy that echoed far and wide.

"Great God!" he cried, "I thank Thee—he lives."

The cry was taken up and carried from mouth to mouth until it reached those who were standing by the grave, ready to perform the last offices for the dead.

Instinctively guessing the cause, they cast down their picks and spades, and rushed down to the hut, where they found the crowd opening out to a response for a cry for air.

With wonderment they saw the form of Broad Arrow Jack rise slowly, like one coming back from death, and sitting up, look around him dazed, as if he had been long in the dark, for the light of day was blinding him.

The trance, for such it was, that had held Broad Arrow Jack in stillness for so many days, was over, and the community of the fields, casting aside their grief, made it a day of merriment instead of mourning. The grave was filled in by men who sang as they worked, and at night a great bonfire lit up the sky with its radiance, to the amazement of settlers far away, who stood by their doors watching the red sky, asking themselves if the prairie which surrounded their homes was on fire.

Some mounted their horses and rode down to the fields, where, learning the story, they stayed to make merry with the rest, until the light of another day eclipsed the burning fire.

CHAPTER CXLVI.

ANOTHER YEAR.

THE winter, mild enough at the diamond-fields, but winter still in comparison to their summer, came and passed away, and Jack and Brisket were still there.

Although he did not die, Jack came out of his trance in so weak a state that full three months were spent ere he had gathered up his strength, and when he was himself again no man in the fields was poorer.

No news of his lost treasure, no news of the Ogre or Jaundice, and heavy claims against him from his agents at the fields and abroad.

He satisfied such credit as he could, and paid to the uttermost farthing, then worked like the rest in the field for his daily bread.

Good fortune did not smile upon him; the darkest part of his life seemed to have come, but he made no complaint, and living on the poorest fare let the rest of the little he gained go to those to whom he was indebted.

"My revenge can wait," he would say to Brisket, "but these men are more impatient. The darkest hour is that just before the dawn, and the sun will rise again ere long."

"But money would do much," was Brisket's answer, "and surely there is some to be obtained from home."

"How mean you?"

"Why, see here," said Brisket, "your family estates were left to nurse, and——"

"No, no, Brisket—to reclaim them I must go back to England, and that I cannot do if I keep my oath. My estates, like my revenge, must wait."

One day Brisket suggested that the Ogre might be in England.

Jack merely said that he was not such a fool to run his neck into a halter.

"They would hang him for certain," he said, "for there is not any officer of standing in the police force who does not know his history, or could mistake his physique. No, no, Brisket, he is still in this or some land hard by, and we shall be sure to find him."

It has been stated in a previous chapter that among the men in the diamond-fields there were many both ready and willing to serve him, but as they had no more than what they gained by their labours, and Jack nothing, the will for a time had to be taken for the deed.

'Twas late in spring, and the sun was beginning to give a taste of the heat to come in the summer, insomuch that at midday only a few of the hardiest ventured to continue their labours.

Among these was Broad Arrow Jack, who gave himself no more rest than he absolutely needed. Heat and cold were both alike to his hardy frame; he could defy them both.

Brisket was indoors preparing the daily meal. There was not, perhaps, more than a dozen at their daily toil, and most of them took frequent rest to wipe the labour drops from their brow. Jack himself was not free from these signs of toil, and during a slight pause he, while brushing back his locks with his handkerchief, beheld a stranger approaching.

First he fancied the form was familiar, as it was something of Trimmer's build, and there was the same cool, easy, lounging gait which had distinguished that individual; but Trimmer, with many others of his men, was far away on a trapping expedition, which was expected to cover a good two years.

They left the day after Broad Arrow Jack's supposed death, and had not been heard of since—so it could not well be he.

As he drew nearer Jack saw that he had his ears, which Trimmer had not, and on a closer inspection he found the stranger to be a good ten years younger. His form was well built and strong, for the signs of youth were on him still, and at the outside he barely reached the years of manhood.

The stranger paused in front of Jack, and with a cool easy nod, such as we generally bestow upon a familiar acquaintance, said—

"I reckon it's hot, young fellow."

"Indeed," said Jack.

"I reckon too," continued the stranger, "that if you don't put something on that head of yours you will get your brains baked. Put a handkerchief or something over it—do, man."

"My head," said Jack, "has not been covered for years, and, as far as I know, may not be covered again until it is under the earth."

"I say, mister," said the other, opening his eyes, "you must have had an extra nip or two this morning, and yet you don't look like a fellow given to gin-sling and cocktails."

"I rarely," replied Jack, "drink anything stronger than water."

An amused look passed over the stranger's face, and putting his finger to the side of his nose, he said—

"Now, don't you talk gammon, for if there's anything on airth I hates it's a teatotle chap, who's always swearing he never takes anything. I know it's all bosh, for they take a little, in some form or other, to a man."

"I am not given to lying," said Jack, coldly, and turned away.

As he did so the brand of the broad arrow was exposed to the view of the stranger, who opened his eyes and gave vent to a low whistle.

"Darn me," said he, "if this aint the creetur I heard talk of up at Black Rock Mountain."

He spoke aloud, and Jack, hearing his words, turned again.

"Who has spoken of me?" he asked.

"Well," said the stranger, hesitating, "they were a scratch lot that I got mixed up with. I shouldn't be over proud of them as relations, but when a fellow goes a-pottering about a country, digging here and digging there, just as the fancy takes him, he can't ask everybody he meets for a character."

"You have been in strange company," said Jack.

"Unkimmon," said the stranger.

"Thieves?" said Jack.

"Tarnation ones."

"Murderers perhaps?" asked Jack.

"When the fancy took 'em," replied the stranger, calmly, "they did a little throat-cutting."

Jack's heart was beating a little quicker than it was wont to do, for he felt that this stranger had brought him welcome news. Still preserving a quiet face, he asked—

"Shall I describe one of them to you? A dark swarthy villain——"

"Hooked nose, bleary eyes, and legs a little bandy," interposed the stranger. "Yes, that's the one that spoke of you—quite friendly of course. He would very much like to have you up at Black Rock Mountain for a week."

"I shall be there ere long," said Jack, striving to keep down his exulting feelings. "Who else was with him?"

"Oh! there was a pretty pile of 'em," replied the stranger, "but they were all understrappers, except one—a tall, good-looking fellow, but mighty shaky, as if he'd been drinking his own share of liquor as well as that of a numerous circle of friends."

"Jaundice!" exclaimed Jack. "How could they have come together?"

"I heard all about that," said the stranger. "They were old pals, it seems, and got separated somehow. The dark chap—Mr. Ogre, I think they called him—was put on an island, and escaped in a canoe, and being set up with fine weather steered back to this country, where I believe he was already pretty well known. Not wishing to show too much in public he went skulking about in the woods, and was, I should guess, in a general way pretty hard up. One day he was found by his old pal, who was wandering about, picking up a living in his old style. He had a few friends, and with these Jaundice and the Ogre entered into business again."

"And what may be their business now?"

"Bird-catching," replied the stranger.

"Bird-catching!" echoed Jack.

"Yes, sea-bird catching. Black Rock Mountain, as you may know, aint many miles from the shore."

"I know—I know," said Jack. "Go on."

"This is how they work," said the stranger. "They have got a pole fixed on a promontory, with a signal of distress flying at the top. Ships pass, and see it. Some go on, but now and then one stops, and sends a boat ashore. Then they have got a dummy ship and a wrecked seaman, generally played by Jaundice, who tells a lying yarn about a dozen of his comrades lying in a dying state inland. Then the better part of the crew are sent to bring them down. Then out of hiding-place comes the Ogre and some score of his precious lot. They seize the boat, pulls out to the ship, and boards her, for who is to stop them? The crew gone, no man armed, no quarter's given, and the ship's their own. You understand?"

"Yes," said Jack, sadly, "I understand."

"The crew ashore falls into ambush," continued

the stranger, "and when they have got all they want out of the craft, they sink her."

"Knowing all this," said Jack, "how is it they have allowed you to come away?"

"They did not allow me," was the reply; "I ran off. Now, mister, you be mighty curious, but you haven't asked anything about me; but still I don't mind telling without asking. My name's Grip, and I haven't a cent in the world, and I am hungry enough to eat a flint."

"Such as I have," said Jack, "you are welcome to—come home with me."

CHAPTER CXLVII.

ON THE ROAD TO BLACK ROCK MOUNTAIN.

BRISKET was putting the plain fare he and Jack were accustomed to upon the table as Jack and Grip, the stranger, entered.

"Ah!" said the latter, as he entered. "You are the 'tother party I've heard speak on. They would be glad to have you up on Black Rock Mountain too."

Brisket looked at Jack for an explanation.

"At Black Rock Mountain," said Jack, "we shall find those we seek. This good friend has brought news with him."

The eyes of Brisket lighted up. "Good news, indeed," he said; "doubly welcome here. I wish I had a better dinner for you; but we have, as you see, nothing but bread and a piece of goat's flesh."

"There's plenty of it," returned young Grip, "and that's all I care about just now." He ate well, and he talked all the time. Judged by his conversation he had many qualities in common with our old friend Trimmer. A careless wanderer without home or friends, apparently indifferent to the past—content for the present, so long as he got a little sunshine from the clouds of life, and giving no thought to the future. A waif, a stray, a drifting straw—the busy world is full of them.

The great longing and thirst of his life was to get change.

"I might stop a week in a place," he said; "but I think on the eighth day I should run away. Of course I have stopped longer in places. Them varmints at Black Rock Mountain kept me close on a month, and I once drifted a fortnight in an open boat with two other men, and when picked up we had eaten our shoes and the leather off our braces; but them were exceptions, and don't count with my ordinary life."

"How far is it from here to the mountain?" asked Jack.

"You can't do better than follow the river," he said. "There's an old boat as I've picked up on my way down, and you are welcome to it; but you will have to pull against the stream. I floated down—just the way I like to travel."

"I am obliged to you," said Jack, "and take your offer. Are you ready to start, Brisket?"

"Of course I am," was the reply.

"Will you come with us?" asked Jack, addressing Grip.

"What's your game?" asked Grip.

"Going to drag these villains from their haunt," said Jack.

"You two alone?"

"Yes."

"The odds are too heavy," replied Grip; "but I'll jine you. I'll pick you up some time to-morrow. I know the road well, and want to have a look about this place."

They took down full directions where they would be likely to find the boat, and with a shake of the hand with their new friend, Brisket and Broad Arrow Jack within an hour left the diamond-fields.

It was not until the morrow they found the boat. Grip had spoken of a roughly-constructed thing of the canoe type, and originally intended to be paddled, but fitted up by some former possessor with rowlocks and oars.

The moment Jack beheld it he saw that it was a familiar object to him, and after a little reflection was convinced that it was the canoe by which the Ogre had escaped from the island.

"It saved him once," said Jack, pointing to the canoe; "but let us hope it will carry to him the ruin and destruction he so richly deserves."

They had brought their rifles with them, and having first loaded them in case of emergency they laid them in the bottom of the boat, and pushing off, sallied forth on their upward voyage.

Jack took the oars first, and pulled steadily for a good hour. There was not much current, and he made excellent headway against it. The land on either side was for many miles naught but a barren plain; but anon the scene changed, and clusters of bushes and groves of trees shut out the inland view.

As they progressed, each taking turn at the oars, the stream narrowed, occasionally running between high sloping banks, and piles of high broken rocks, and at last a waterfall checked their course.

Pulling into the bank they drew the canoe up high and dry, and Jack, with sheer strength, carried it to the calmer waters above. Here they rested, for the night was at hand, and Jack having shot a hare, Brisket prepared supper.

He lighted a camp fire to leeward of a rock, and with their backs against it the two friends sat chatting of the past and their future prospects. Amidst their conversation footsteps fell upon their ears, and, looking up, Grip stood before them.

"I guessed it was you," he said; "nobody but them that is strange to the country, or wanted to be killed right away, would get up an illumination at this spot."

"Is there any danger here?" asked Brisket.

"I don't suppose," replied Grip, coolly, "you could find more in any spot if you travelled all your life for it. I should think the thieves in these woods are as plentiful as blackberries, and the great wonder to me is they haven't taken a few pot-shots at you. As I came down I ran the gauntlet from a good bit of file-firing."

"At all events," said Jack, "we at present have not been disturbed. Won't you have a bit of something to eat?"

"Yes," replied Grip.

But fate was against him having anything there that night, for as he sat down beside Broad Arrow Jack the sound of a rifle was heard, and a bullet struck the rock between them with a dull thud, and bespattered them with fragments of lead.

"I told you so," said Grip, coolly. "What will you do—stay here?"

"I think not," replied Jack.

They arose and scattered the fire with their feet, being favoured with a couple of harmless shots from their unseen enemy as they did so; and then, shouldering their rifles, they marched to the canoe, and once more put out upon the stream.

"If I could spare the time," said Jack, "I'd stay here and teach my impertinent friends a lesson; but I have more to do than knocking a miserable brigand on the head. How dark it is! and the moon will not be up for an hour or more."

"Yes," said Grip, "the river here winds about like a corkscrew, and at every bend there's a little patch of ruffianism. I saw their huts as I came down. Hear that! they've signalled to each other, and will be on the alert all the way to your destination."

"But who and what are these men?" asked Jack. "I never heard of this band."

"I fancy they are part of the Ogre lot," replied Grip. "He is making a rich booty, and he knows that sooner or later he must be called to account, and these men are set to guard one of the roads to his stronghold. They are all a bad lot, and while out on their master's business cannot help doing a little for themselves."

"We are too near the bank," whispered Jack, after a pause. "Pull your left, Brisket."

Either his voice or the sound of the oar was heard, for one of the worthies on the shore took a chance shot at them. It struck the water close to the stern of the boat, and splashed a few drops into Grip's face as he stooped down and endeavoured to pierce the darkness with his eyes.

"That's the champion shot of the lot," he said. "Ah! now I know where I am. Further out, or we shall be ashore."

On the many perils of that night it is needless here to dwell. They ran the gauntlet of them all, and escaped to find themselves in the morning with a broad stretch of open land on their left, and low bushes, scarce affording concealment for man, on their right.

They were all tired and worn, and needed rest, but as it was scarcely safe for more than one to rest at a time, and none of them would be the first, tired as they were, lots were drawn with three pieces of stick, and Grip drew the fortunate one for reposing. He stretched himself upon the ground and seemed to sleep instantly, the others sauntering up and down to keep themselves awake.

A little way ahead there was a mound of fine red sand, cast up by the current; and as they increased the length of their perambulations their steps led them up to it.

On the other side was a sight which gave them a thrill of horror.

Bound to the trunk of a tree was the form of a man whose bearded and bronzed face told a tale of wandering. He was dead, and had been dead, they judged, three or four days. His clothes were soddened, and the water was dripping from his hair—not many minutes could have elapsed since the current carried him ashore, and left him beyond its reach.

"I wonder," said Brisket, "what new story of villainy this body could tell us if it could speak?"

"It tells me enough," replied Jack, "for this is the Ogre's work—who can doubt it? It nerves me on; I have now no need of rest. Let us rejoin Grip, and on again."

A determined expression was common on Jack's face, but when Grip was aroused he remarked the change in him. The lines about his mouth were deeper, his brows more bent, his eyes more fixed, and lines hitherto almost strange to the smooth broad forehead had gathered there.

"Go on at once!" said Grip, in surprise, when he had received the command. "You have had no rest."

"I need none," replied Jack; and in his voice there was a change too. It was deeper than heretofore, and Grip, as he heard it, thought of a deep-toned bell he had been wont to hear in another land booming out a knell for the dead.

"I am glad this Broad Arrow Jack is no enemy of mine," he thought. Aloud he said, "Your friend looks tired and worn."

"He can rest while you and I go on," replied Jack.

They launched their boat. Jack took the oars, and pulled out sturdily up the stream.

"I will never relinquish these," he said, "until I stand in sight of the Ogre's hiding-place."

And he kept his word.

CHAPTER CXLVIII.
DICK AND THE TIGER.

ANOTHER year had wrought its changes—amongst others especially in the two lads, Dick Skewball and the Tiger. Throughout all the time which elapsed since last we left them and the time now being dwelt upon these two boys had seldom seen a human face except their own. Occasionally, while hiding in the wood, they had seen some wanderer passing by, and now and then at night, when the all-prevailing desire to mix with their fellows was upon them, they stole down to the outskirts of the diamond-fields, and listened to the hum of the pleasure-seekers in the booths.

It was music in their ears, especially pleasing to Dick, who had known less of a lonely life than his companion. Many a time there was a strong prompting within him to go down to see and speak to those who lived in the fields; but by a strong effort he would put it aside, always muttering the same sentence to himself—

"You will soon be a man, and then you can go down and be greater than them all."

In the Tiger's heart there was only the natural longing for change in his desire to see and speak to others; but he was so bound up in Dick, so much a slave and yet a friend, that his slightest expressed wish amounted to a command, which he was ready and willing to obey. Their life in the wood was simple, barely above that of the rudest savage of a land where civilisation is unknown.

In a deep dale, surrounded by a fence of tangled brier, through which they had to creep upon their hands and knees, was a rude hut—their house. Without implements they could do little, but there was still no little ingenuity displayed in the way they had drawn down the branches of a tree, and laced them together, so as to form a perfect shelter from the night wind.

A thatch of broad leaves kept out the rain, and a couch of moss was their resting-place. This was all their hut could boast of.

Outside, in the midst of a circle of stones, a smouldering fire of touchwood was constantly kept burning. Of such wood there was plenty around, and a goodly store was kept up near the hut. Dick had a few common matches left, but they were too precious to be used, except in case of an accidental extinction of their fire, by means of which they cooked their food.

It had been extinguished once by a heavy rain, but this led to an improvement in their oven, if I may so term it. A rude roof of sticks, tightly bound together, and thatched with leaves, was kept ready for covering it in case of emergency, and from thenceforth there was little fear of its dying out except through neglect.

Their food was roots, wild fruit, and the flesh of such animals as the Tiger occasionally brought home.

How he caught these was a secret of his own which he had never given up to Dick; indeed, it would have been useless for him to do so, for it was simply through his cat-like activity that he was able to secure his prey.

His plan was this.

Selecting the branch of a tree that swooped down to within a few feet of the ground, he would stretch himself out like a panther, and lie still as that beast while waiting for its prey, until a foe or some other creature halted to carouse beneath. Then swift as a thunderbolt he would fall upon his prey, and seize it round the throat, holding on with an iron grasp until its life was gone.

The sinews of the Tiger were of iron, and this feat would have been impossible to Dick Skewball, in whose case, although he was of heavier build, failure would have followed any attempt to perform it.

Still the Tiger kept his secret for a reason of his own. To him he often said, "you hab a secret, ole Dick, you keep him berry close. You tell me and I'll tell you."

To which Dick would answer, "Not yet—wait until we are men."

And so we find them living their savage life in the woods, unconscious, through their keeping aloof from all and visiting the fields only at night, that their hero-master, Broad Arrow Jack, was still alive.

A few days before Jack started in fresh pursuit of his enemy, Dick was in his hiding place, blowing up the fire ready for cooking their mid-day meal. The Tiger, tired with many hours' wandering in search of game—a pursuit that always took him away from the settlement—lay stretched upon the sward, watching his companion with lazy interest.

The boys had both grown—Dick wonderfully so. He was nearly a head taller than when he begun this novel life, but he had gained height at the expense of strength, and looked very thin and rather pale.

They had been silent for awhile, until Dick, who had been blowing energetically for awhile without much success, turned to the Tiger and said—

"The wood is all damp; we shall get no fire for some time."

The Tiger did not immediately answer—he was thinking of something else. Beneath that lazy air there was a restlessness such as we see in those who have something to reveal yet hesitate to speak.

"Dick," he said, suddenly, after a lengthened pause, occupied by Dick in renewed attempts at the fire, "are you 'fraid ob ghosters?"

"Lor'! no," replied Dick, looking up, laughing. "I don't believe in them. Do you?"

CHAPTER CXLIX.
GHOSTERS.

THE Tiger, opening wide his eyes, exclaimed—"Not blieve in ghosters, Ole Dick; why dis wood am full ob dem." Dick stared at him in dismay. He fancied his companion had suddenly gone mad. He had never mentioned such a subject to Dick before.

"What nonsense you are talking," he said—"the wood full of ghosts."

"Dat quite true," insisted the Tiger. "I hab seen 'em by de score bout de wood in de night. When people die den ghosters go bout affer dark. But I neber see one till to-day in de day time."

"And whose ghost was that?" asked Dick, a little overcome by his friend's earnestness.

"Massa Broad Arrow Jack's," replied the Tiger. "I see him coming dis way."

Dick turned pale as death itself, and sank into a sitting position.

"Broad Arrow Jack!" he said.

"Yes," replied the Tiger, nodding.

"Coming this way?"

"I reckon he was goin' to make straight for hyar," replied the Tiger.

"Let me hide somewhere," cried Dick, staring about him wildly.

"What for?" asked the Tiger. "What am dere to be 'fraid ob?"

"I dare not see him," muttered Dick, shuddering —"anybody but him."

The Tiger could not make it out. This terror of his friend was a new thing to him. It lasted all that day, and during the night Dick started up many times from his dreams, shrieking for help. The Tiger began to think his friend was not so very brave after all.

The next day Dick absented himself a few hours, leaving the Tiger to look after the fire and prepare the food. It was close upon nightfall when he returned, and he was pale still, but calm.

"I've been thinking, Tiger," he said, "that I shall not stay here until I am a man."

"Am you going back to de fields den?" asked the Tiger.

"No. I wish to go further—to England, where my father's home was."

"What sort ob place am dat?" asked the Tiger.

"A big city, with tall houses made of stone, and broad streets full of people dressed magnificently. A place where you can get the best of food and drink by paying for it."

"Ah! dat it, but how you pay, ole Dick, wif no money?"

"I have a little," replied Dick—"a diamond or two, which I can sell, and pay for our passage over the sea. When we get there I'll find lots of money, and we will ride about and be big swells."

"I t'ink I rader run 'bout de place," said the Tiger.

"You can do as you like," said Dick, "but I shall ride in a coach lined with red velvet. I shall go soon, but before we start I want to make a bag. The skin of a fawn would do; I have a knife, and we can lace it up with the sinews."

"But what you put in de bag?"

"Another bag, that belonged to—to—a lady I knew. She is dead, and I don't want to part with it."

"Am dere any wood in Englan'?" asked the Tiger after a little reflection.

"Oh! yes," said Dick.

"And big plain?"

"Yes—oh! you can run about as long as you like."

"But if I not like de place—how den?"

"Go out of it."

"Whar to?"

"Anywhere—all over the world, if you like. England is the middle of the world, and the biggest place in it."

The Tiger was satisfied. He would go anywhere with Dick, especially to a place that was the "middle of the world." That evening he brought in a fawn, and the boys between them skinned it and hung up the skin to dry, prior to making it into the bag Dick required.

On the morrow Dick took it away with him, and was absent until very late. When he returned, he had the bag under his arm, laced up and tightly bound.

"Am dat what de lady gabe you?" asked the Tiger.

"Yes," replied Dick.

"What am in it?"

"Clothes."

"Oh! no, ole Dick," said the Tiger, laughing, as he rubbed it with his hand, "it sound more like lilly stones."

"Don't say that wherever we go," said Dick, trembling; "if anybody asks you what is in it, say clothes."

"What for am I to tell a lie?" asked the Tiger.

"Only to oblige me. Now to-morrow I am going down to the fields, to change a few little diamonds I have for money, and to ask about a ship, and then we will be off. You take care of the bag while I am gone."

"All right, ole Dick."

On the morrow Dick started. It was the very day Broad Arrow Jack left on his fresh search for the Ogre, and Dick was therefore not likely to meet him. He gave the Tiger so many injunctions about the bag that he must have been an idiot not to perceive it held something more than old clothes.

His curiosity was aroused, and after Dick's departure he sat for a long time looking at his charge, poking it with his finger, and turning it over and over. It was firmly laced together, but with a little perseverance he got his finger in between two of the stitches, and felt another skin inside stitched also.

He stuck to his work and got his finger eventually between the second line of stitching, and then his face assumed a comical expression.

"It am small stones," he said, "but what ole Dick do wif dem?"

In a moment a chain of circumstances flashed through his brain, and the truth burst upon him.

"Dis," he said, "am Massa Broad Arrow Jack's lost diamonds, and dat why him ghoster came dis way. Oh! Dick, I neber tink dat you was a tief," and overwhelmed by the discovery he sat down and wept bitterly.

Let us now follow Dick down to the diamond-fields, where avoiding the more crowded portions, he made his way to the hut occupied by one of the many dealers who bought the stones found by the diggers.

It was no uncommon thing for children and youths to be sent to the dealers by their parents to offer diamonds at a certain price. Dick's entrance therefore excited no surprise in the breast of the Jew whose establishment he patronised. Putting four stones upon the counter, Dick said, "I want two hundred dollars for these."

The Jew looked at the stones, and saw they were worth a thousand dollars at least, but he had the craft of his nation, and pushed them back, saying, "They are not worth twenty."

Dick, equally cunning, put them into his pocket again, and was marching to the door when the Jew called him back.

"What is the least price, good Bank of England notes down," he said.

"Two hundred dollars," replied Dick, "not a cent less," and eventually he got it.

Hurrying down to the port with the notes in his pocket, he asked for a ship that was about to sail, and one was pointed out to him. It had been waiting three months for a crew, and was even now going to be worked home by men who had made money in the fields, and were glad in any way to get back to their native land again.

Dick heard that his services would be acceptable, and volunteered, on behalf of the Tiger and himself, to be there on to-morrow. This was a good stroke of business. Dick had saved his dollars, and with a light heart he hastened back to the wood.

He reached his hiding-place, crawled through the thorny bushes, and was confronted by the Tiger.

"Back again, ole Dick?" he said, but his voice sounded strange.

"Yes," replied Dick. "I have settled all; we sail to-morrow. But where's *the bag—my bag?*"

"Gone away," replied the Tiger.

"Away!" said Dick, trembling all over.

"Yes," said the Tiger, "I put him dere. It am Massa Jack's bag, and not yours."

"It's a lie!" cried Dick, hoarsely.

"It am de trufe," returned the Tiger. "Oh! no, Dick, you shall not steal dat."

"It's mine, and I'll have it. If you don't give it up," yelled Dick, "I'll kill you! Now then, where is it?"

"Me not tell you," said the Tiger, firmly. "Kill me if you like, but *how find you it den?* Me hid him safe enough."

Although Dick was but a boy, his passionate fury was terrible to look upon.

He was livid to his hair, and there was murder in his eyes as he glared at his friend. Drawing out his knife he opened the blade, and raised his arm to strike, but the Tiger stood firm and quailed not.

"No—no, ole Dick," he said; "me will not let you be de tief. When I see de ghoster of Massa Jack I ask him if you may hab it. If he say yes I tell you where it am; if he say no me neber tell you what I hab done wif it."

Dick's arm fell by his side, and bursting into tears he threw himself in an agony of mortification upon the ground.

CHAPTER CL.

FOUR PERJURERS.

THERE are men who, if they escape temptation and the society of evil-doers, will themselves do very little harm. Wobbles was one of these, and if he had lived and died in a small village community as a tradesman he would probably have done no more than the average amount of cheating, and lived and died respected; but unfortunately for him his lot was cast among a blacker portion of the world. It was his luck to be constantly associated with villains and exposed to temptations, and he was continually coming a series of moral and criminal croppers.

Having lost all his money upon the race-course he was for the time deserted by Woody Welsher, and he and his three companions fell upon hard times.

They lived for weeks in a rough and humble sort of way, getting a little credit when they could, and pawning their clothes when they could not, till at last they had no more in the world than what they stood in, and the direst poverty loomed in the future.

Then it was that Woody Welsher suddenly turned up, and offered to be their friend.

It would be useless to describe in detail the arts he used, but he got the affidavits out of them at last, and the Honourable Morden Crewe became possessed of what was not his own.

The affidavits were very perfect, being drawn up by a clever lawyer. They set forth a full description of Jack abroad, gave a full account of the life he led there, described an imaginary death, and a confession as to who he was. All this Wobbles, Conky, Curler, and Pigeon signed their names and swore to.

And for this precious piece of rascality they were all furnished with a free passage to America, and bank notes for one hundred pounds.

Woody Welsher had instructions to see them safe out of the country, but he considered he had done his duty when he saw them on a Gravesend boat at London-bridge.

The four rascals ought to have gone to their vessel, which left the docks that morning, and was lying at Gravesend to pick up passengers, but instead of doing so they all went to Rosherville Gardens, spent a very happy day, and at night returned to London.

For a brief time we must now follow the fortunes of the Honourable Morden Crewe, who, by the most dishonourable means, had obtained possession of the property of his cousin.

"I'll have a big fling with the money," was the inward comment he made when the court announced its decision. "He may one day return—nay, the real Simon Pure will return—but I'll spend his estate before he comes, and then deny his identity."

There were two residences attached to the Ashleigh estate, and one named Rookholme Castle he resolved to make his country seat. It was a splendid place in the heart of an excellent hunting county, where he could find plenty of society congenial to his gentlemanly tastes.

For some years he had been rather out of good company. His character had been none of the best, and indeed some of the turf and gambling transactions he got mixed up with were rather shady, but now that he had come into large estates the upper part of the world could conveniently forget the past, and hail him as a gentleman and a brother.

"To mix with them again as one of themselves," he thought, with glistening eyes, "to have no more of the cut direct, or worse still the doubtful nod, and cool 'how d'ye do?' of the world. I am indeed a man again. No more of the cut-throat, seedy, needy, skulking scoundreldom I have been mixed up with for years."

But here he reckoned without his host. Woody Welsher was not to be shaken off. He declined to accept a pension and retire from the society of his old friend.

"No," he said. "I've always fancied I should like the society of nobs, and now I'm sure of it. I am coming to live at the castle with you."

"The deuce you are!" said the Honourable Morden Crewe; "and what sort of figure do you think you'll cut with the people you'll meet there?"

"Look here, Crewe," said Woody Welsher, with a warning look, "my society used to be good enough for you, and it must be good enough now.

You leave it to me. When I get among the nobs I'll soon pick up their ways."

"There never was a silk purse made out of a sow's ear yet," muttered the Honourable Morden Crewe.

Woody Welsher overheard him, and turned upon him a white, savage face.

"Birth," he said, "is a mere matter of chance. A man who makes the best of a low birth is better than he who degrades a high one. I am as good as you any day."

"All I can say is," returned the Honourable Morden Crewe, "that people will wonder who the deuce I've got with me."

"You must pitch some yarn—tell them that I saved your life, and that you keep me out of gratitude. I shan't bother the people much if they don't talk to me; I'll keep quiet enough. All I want is to *live* in the same house with nobs as a nob."

Eventually he carried his point, but only by threatening to expose the scheme by which the Honourable Morden Crewe had acquired the property.

"I'll get rid of him somehow," muttered the owner of Rookholme Castle. "There are plenty of snug corners and deep pools on the estate where a dead man can lie for a year and nobody find him."

It was a great day for the people around the castle when these two knaves went down to take possession—great at least as far as the expenditure of money went. There were cakes and ale in plenty for all comers, and a dinner for the tenantry, who, in the innocence of their hearts, tired of the land being so long without a real master, hailed the coming of the new squire with joy.

They gave him a hearty reception, the bells rang and the loafers shouted, and the farmers on horseback met him at the entrance of the village, and accompanied him to the castle grounds.

Then a long line of servants bowed a welcome. A number of gentlemen from the surrounding estates met the Hon. Morden Crewe as their friend.

They looked a little askance on being introduced to Woody Welsher. Morden Crewe muttered something about being saved from drowning by the gallantry of his friend, and overcame their doubts.

It was only natural that a man whose life had been saved, would show a little gratitude, although his saver was the most arrant cad.

The working classes were regaled in the village, after having shouted themselves hoarse welcoming their new landlord, so that the grounds were tolerably clear when the tenantry and gentry sat down together beneath a large and handsome tent to enjoy the feast.

It was a splendid repast, and a good two hours were spent in relieving the table of its toothsome burdens.

Then began the usual speeches; one of the tenant farmers getting upon his feet proposed the health of the Honourable Morden Crewe.

It was a hazy production, with the inevitable coughs and break-downs, but it answered every purpose, and was received with tremendous cheering.

Then the Honourable Morden arose to reply.

As he did so he looked out of the entrance of the tent and saw a carriage with one horse coming across the grounds at full gallop. There was a driver on the box, and four men inside—men who seemed familiar to the Honourable Morden, and he turned as pale as death.

"A gang of turf rascals," he thought, "presuming upon our old acquaintance to come here to-day!"

But it was more than that. Turf acquaintances such as he had fancied would have been bad enough in all conscience, but the four individuals proved to be Wobbles, Conky, Curler, and Pigeon.

The vehicle dashed up to the tent, and the precious quartette hastily descended, Wobbles foremost.

He entered the tent, and made straight for the Honourable Morden, who stood like a man turned into stone.

"We come in such a hurry," he said, "that we have left all our traps at a public on the road. Was afraid we should be too late for the wittles."

"Indeed!" was all the Hon. Morden could say.

The tenantry were all silent; the gentry raised their eyebrows and exchanged glances pregnant with meaning.

"Yes," pursued Wobbles, "and we've got old Joss and Fireworks there too. The party as I gave them to to sell, when we was jolly hard up altogether, had 'em on his hands all this time. We think of doing a bit of 'unting."

While this was going on Woody Welsher, thoughtfully scraping his chin with his finger, kept his eyes fixed upon the roof of the tent. The arrival of the four friends gave him much food for reflection. He could see that he was not the only individual thirsting for the society of nobs, and that he was not likely to reign alone over the Honourable Morden Crewe.

CHAPTER CLI.

THE PHRYNE.

AFTER the last speech made by Wobbles there was a dead silence. Nobody seemed inclined to speak; in fact it is doubtful if any one knew what to say. The circumstances were peculiar, and it would have required a man of no ordinary talent to have spoken to the point without making matters worse than they were.

"The table," said Wobbles, "seems to be chock-full. Don't any of you get up; me and my pals can pick a bit on the grass."

The gentry had arisen while he was speaking, and seemed to be making towards the entrance. As they passed the Honourable Morden he made a gesture of despair, and hoarsely whispered—

"Gentlemen, all this can be explained. I beg of you not to leave."

To which the grey elderly man of noble presence replied—

"We shall be glad to receive your written explanation to-morrow."

Then they went out in a body, and the next minute were heard calling for their carriages. The tenantry shuffled uneasily about, and at last one arose, then another, and finally all went out unchallenged by their landlord.

The Honourable Morden Crewe was left alone with his five accomplices.

"And what brought you here?" he asked savagely, addressing the late arrivals. "What has prompted you to this impertinence?"

"Well," said Wobbles, looking towards his companions for support, "me and my pals have been talking it over——"

"We has," said Conky, Curler, and Pigeon, in a low deep tone.

"And have come to this conclusion," continued Wobbles—"that, having done all the work, we means to have a proper share of the fruits of our labour."

"Of the sweat of our brow," added Conky.

"Which it are," said Curler and Pigeon.

"Come to the point," said the Honourable Morden Crewe. "What do you mean to do?"

"We means," replied Wobbles, "to live here, and mix with the hupper suckles."

"A curse upon you!" said the Honourable Morden Crewe, addressing Woody Welsher, "and upon the day I was fool enough to fall into this trap! Eat your fill—make merry," he continued, turning to the others. "Drink yourselves blind—all here is yours."

And, kicking aside his seat, with a bitter oath he strode out of the tent.

The moment he was gone Wobbles and his friends

fell upon the remnant of the feast like starving wolves.

* * * * * *

"Land ahead, sir!"

So cried the man on the look-out of the good ship Phryne—Captain Murray—outward bound from Liverpool to the Brazils with a mixed cargo. The Phryne had been driven out of her course by severe weather, and, notwithstanding a week's incessant sail, was getting short of water.

"All right," replied the captain. "We'll run in and fill the tanks and barrels."

The good ship speedily brought land nearer, so that those on board could see a very promising little bay, with a sandy shore, and hills beyond. 'Twas the very place to land in, with every prospect of getting what was wanted.

"All hands to shorten sail," shouted the captain, and the men came tumbling up, glad of an opportunity to put their feet ashore if only for a few hours.

"Signal ashore, sir."

"Where away?"

"On the point of land south, sir."

Captain Murray took his glass and scanned the part of the shore alluded to. There he saw a tall pole with a white rag like a piece of linen flying on the top of it.

"A signal of distress," he said, to his mate, "some castaways, I reckon. We can do two things at once. Help ourselves and help others."

He was a thorough good fellow—this Captain Murray—and beloved by all on board. He was obeyed without any bullying, rope's-ending, or any of the usual stimulants too often resorted to by captains at sea. A few simple words from his lips, and the Phryne ran into the bay, and anchored in seven fathoms, with the order and precision of a man-of-war.

The signal was plain enough then—a pole, an old topmast of a ship raised, with a rag on its head, and close by it the form of a man lying.

"Cutter and longboat ready," cried the captain, and the two boats swung over the side, and dropped into the water together.

"All hands but Mr. Grey and two men for the shore," was the next order. "Mr. Grey, choose your men."

Mr. Grey, the first mate, called out two, and they came willingly, although their hearts were bursting to have a few hours' run ashore. "Out with the barrels, my lads."

"We shall have to go twice," said the captain, kindly, "and then I and ten others will relieve you."

"Just like you, sir," said one of the men, touching his forehead. "Thanky, sir."

The second mate was put in command of the long boat to go ashore, and the captain himself in the cutter took half a dozen men, and went to the rescue of the castaway.

As the cutter drew near land the figure of a tall spectral-looking man rose up apparently in great pain, and slowly waved his arms above his head.

"Coming, my lad," shouted the captain, "you are all safe now."

The men of the cutter cheered, and the crew in the long boat answered with another. The cutter grated on the beach, and the spectral figure, in tattered sailor's shirt and trousers, staggered towards those who had come to save him.

He fell into the captain's arms gasping for breath. He seemed incapable of giving vent to his thanks in speech, and the men, full of sympathy, gathered around him.

"Take a drop of this," said the captain, giving him a flask. "How now? Do you feel better?"

The man took a long draught out of the flask, and in hollow tones replied, "Much better."

They gave him some biscuit, and he devoured it eagerly. Renewed strength seemed to come back to him, and the colour gathered in his cheeks.

"Now, my lad," said the captain, "I think we can leave you for a little time. We are going inland for water. When we return, we will take you aboard."

"All going?" asked the fellow, in a hollow voice.

"Yes, unless you are afraid."

"Oh, no!" he said, a little eagerly; "I am not afraid. You can pick me up on your return."

"Will you have another drop of this?"

"Thanky, sir."

He took a second drop, emptying the flask, and the captain put it back into his pocket. The rescued man turned round to hide his emotion, and winked at the horizon.

"You can make yourself comfortable in the cutter if you like," said the kind-hearted captain. "You will find the cushions softer than the ground."

"Thanky, sir."

"You can give me your history by-and-bye, when you are stronger."

Again the man turned to hide his emotion, and again he winked at the distant sky, his face undergoing all sorts of curious contortions, which might, under other circumstances, have been taken for suppressed laughter.

"I have come ashore in search of water," said the captain. "I suppose I shall find some hereabouts."

"Yes, sir," replied the man. "You see that big rock over yonder which stands up like a pillar. You'll find a spring there spurting up like a fountain."

The captain thanked him, and with his crew hurried off to rejoin them of the long boat, who had got the barrels ashore, and were lying about waiting orders.

The man who had been the object of the captain's kind intentions, instead of lying down in the cutter as desired, followed slowly, and was half-way towards the long boat, when the sailors, in obedience to the captain's command, began to roll the barrels up the country.

In a few minutes they were well away, with Captain Murray trotting in their rear, and the long boat and cutter were left unprotected.

Then the man thrust his finger into his mouth, and gave vent to a shrill whistle.

What followed Grey, the first mate who had been left on board the Phryne, saw with horror and amazement.

It was this.

Some thirty ruffians suddenly sprang from behind masses of rock scattered upon the promontory. Foremost among them was a mis-shapen man of muscular power, whose dark skin shone in the sunlight like polished mahogany.

Dividing into two parties of unequal proportions, the smaller took possession of the cutter, and the larger made for the long boat.

Grey, with a sickness at his heart, turned to the two men with whom he held sole charge of the ship, and said—

"My lads, we are the victims of a pirate's ruse, but let us die like Englishmen. We have no arms on board; with Captain Murray there has never been need to keep any, but there are iron bars about. Let us each take one, and ere we give up our lives let us thin the ranks of those villains."

"Ah! ah!" said the men.

"In five minutes," said the mate, taking off his cap, "it will be all over with us. God have mercy upon us."

The men bowed their heads for a moment, then, with fixed looks, armed themselves with iron bars, and stood ready to meet the remorseless foe.

The boats, laden with yelling demons, not men, came up speedily, the Ogre, for it was he, standing in the bow of the long boat with a boat hook in his hand.

In a few moments the wretches were tumbling over the sides. The mate dealt the Ogre, as he scrambled up, a blow that would have split any other skull but his, and sent him back into the long boat.

"Spare that man," shouted the Ogre hoarsely, as he lay clasping his head with agony, "keep him for me; I'll have a rare revenge for this."

The struggle on board was soon over. Some half-dozen of the pirates lay on the deck with battered heads, and their villainous faces, distorted with pain, up towards the sky. Then the mate was secured, and the two seamen who had made such a gallant defence received a dozen death wounds, and while yet warm and bleeding were tossed into the sea.

The fight was over, and Jeb Jaundice, who had commanded the cutter, went to look after his leader. With blood-stained hands he helped him over the side, and the Ogre, still smarting terribly from the blow he had received, faced the undaunted mate.

"Better for you," he said, "if that blow had never been struck. Ere the sun sets you shall curse the day that you were born."

"I will never curse that," replied the mate. "Now, devil or beast, whichever you may be, do your worst; you can but take my life."

"Yes," said the Ogre. "I'll take it inch by inch; I'll find a death for you which will give me full revenge."

"And you," said the mate, with contempt, "can talk of revenge! You, who carry upon your face the shadow of untold hellish deeds. You—a murderer, a robber, a cunning, treacherous villain, grown fat and gross with crime, for whom there is no hope in this world, and who dare not think of the world to come!"

"Gag him," said the Ogre, "and bring me something to drink."

"Aye, drink—drink," said Jaundice, who had grown more gaunt and conscience-stricken than when we met him last. He was but the skeleton of a man, and had no rival in wan looks in the gang, save the wretched fellow who had played the part of decoy.

Some of the men went down to find the spirit-room, and while they were gone Jaundice drew near to the Ogre and whispered in his ear—

"Did you see her? Maggie is on board."

"More of your cursed fancies," growled the Ogre. "Here is some brandy, man; fill yourself up with it so that there is no room for these fools' visions."

They each took a deep draught of the liquor, and Jaundice brightened up. The Ogre, on the contrary, became sullen and ferocious, and eyed the mate malevolently. "What shall I do with him?" he muttered? "I have it—I'll burn him!"

This awful resolve, so in accordance with the general nature of the Ogre, was a little too terrible for his companion. Shuddering violently, he gave the Ogre an appealing look, and said—

"Not that. Kill him, if you like, but be not so merciless. Let me shoot him."

"I'll burn him," growled the Ogre.

"And I," said Jaundice, made bold by drink, "will have no hand in it—I am bad enough. I know I am a lost creature, but I'll stop here."

"Do as you please," returned the Ogre, with a shrug of indifference; "I'll have this rare treat to myself. Drink, my men," he shouted to his followers—"help yourselves freely. One can be as merry here as the king in his castle. None can touch us."

And they drank—drank as fiercely as the hunted wolf laps water—drank as men drink who are tortured by conscience, and who have no hope of rest save in a sodden brain—drank as the lost soul would drink of the waters of Lethe—until half lay like helpless logs upon the deck, and the rest, maddened by the fiery liquid, ready for any crime.

The Ogre looked towards the shore, where he saw the captain and his crew running to and fro in helpless horror, and in derision he waved a salute with his handkerchief.

A shout of fury came in answer back, the seamen in helpless anger casting stones towards the vessel.

These poor weapons fell short, of course. The Ogre danced and yelled in derision until he was tired; then lay down panting and calling for drink.

And so the day passed, and night came on. The sun went down fiery-red, as if in anger at the spectacle beneath him, and the moon arose, the bright stars came out, to look sadly and sorrowfully down upon the devilish orgie on board the good ship Phryne.

CHAPTER CLII.
AT THE STAKE.

HAVING conceived his cruel project, the Ogre was the sort of man to carry it out. Before it was light a boat was lowered, and he and a picked dozen of his crew bundled the prisoner into the boat and pulled away.

Knowing the coast well, his plan was to pull round the promontory, and land a little lower down where a wood ran almost down to the sea. Then he was assured he could carry out his fiendish plan in safety.

And it was carried out as well as he could have hoped for. The party landed, and carried poor Grey, bound and gagged, to the verge of the wood. Here they fastened him to the trunk of a tree, blasted by lightning during a late storm, and the men gathered sticks and bushes, and piled them around him.

This done, the Ogre gave orders for the gag to be removed, so that Grey might speak if he desired to.

The mate was a man of forty years of age—a good sailor, and an honest fearless man. Fixing his eyes upon the Ogre, he regarded him with calm contempt.

"Beg for mercy," said his persecutor.

"Never!" was the reply. "Why should I?"

"To have your life spared," returned the Ogre.

"I know how little you intend to spare me," said Grey. "Do your worst and get it over. You are a brute—worse than a brute. But your turn will come. There is retribution in store for such devil's work as this."

"You mistook your vocation," sneered the Ogre. "You should have been a parson, not a sailor."

To this the mate made no reply, and the Ogre went on—

"Those who wrong and injure me never get off scot free. I never forgive. I swore as you struck me down that I would have ample revenge, and see I keep my oath."

"And you call a blow struck in self-defence an injury?" said Grey. "You, who came upon a piratical expedition, and would have met no more than your just fate if I had split your skull and sent you down to hell. You are spared, but only for a worse end."

"Indeed!"

"Yes. Dying men have sometimes the gift of prophecy, and I can tell you that in the future there lies for you a fate so awful that all you inflict upon me now shall seem light to it. Aye! and you will count such a death as is to be mine as a thing to be envied——"

"Peace, fool!"

"I must speak—look to it. In the dark distance of your life I see wandering accursed an outcast of God and man—bearing a burden to which a mountain would be a feather—enduring a pain to which all earthly suffering would be as naught—accursed—accursed for ever—doomed to bear through all the ages of eternity."

"I'll hear no more!" cried the Ogre. "Light the fire."

"I see," cried Grey, in triumph, "my shaft has struck home. You *know* that all I say is true! For all eternity ——"

"Light the fire!" cried the Ogre, and with his own hands he lighted the first match and placed it in the brushwood.

Up rose the flames, curling round the doomed man, who, with moving lips, turned his eyes heavenwards, as if praying.

It was an awful spectacle—this helpless man at the stake, and the triumphant devils around him. As the fire increased in power the savage wretches began to dance in ferocious excitement, and the Ogre, more like a madman than aught else, leaped and shouted to the flames.

"At him!" he cried. "Burn him—roast him! Ha! ha!—a good fire, and a most excellent roasting! Cry for help now—for mercy. What! no sound?"

A violent shudder ran through Grey's frame, and his hands worked convulsively; but he compressed his mouth, and made a strong effort to keep from shrieking out with pain.

"Ha! ha!" laughed the Ogre, tauntingly. "I can see you suffer—that you feel all I would have you feel! Beg for mercy, you fool!"

The fire and smoke gathered around the unfortunate man, hiding him from view. The Ogre and his vile companions ran round and round, stirring up the flames, and shouting with glee.

Higher rose the fire, but still no sound.

"He shall not die," cried the Ogre, "without one shriek for mercy! Scatter the fire, and let me look upon him."

They kicked the blazing mass away, and the wind wafted off the smoke, revealing a ghastly sight. Of poor Grey only the charred trunk of a man remained. A bald and ghastly head hung down on a blackened breast; but the lips were still moving, and a few words, spoken in a hollow whisper, reached the Ogre's ears—

"For all eternity this fate be yours!"

Then the lips, like the rest of the body, were still, and all was over.

"He died pluckily," said the Ogre, turning away. "Come, let us go back to the ship."

But the men did not move. The excitement was over, and the horrible spectacle their work presented had brought about a revulsion of feeling.

"What is the matter with you?" said the Ogre. "Back to the ship, I say!"

But they remained motionless, each man with his eyes upon the ground, as if afraid—as indeed they might well be—to look up to the light of heaven.

"What's come to you?" asked the Ogre. "Haven't you served an apprenticeship to this business?"

"Not to this," said one of the men, with a shudder. "We have all been bad enough, God knows, but it was an evil day when we met you."

"If you've turned soft," snarled the Ogre, "you can leave me. Go back to the diamond-fields, and there you will meet with a warm reception."

"Anything is better than this," said the man. "I, for one, am going to take my chance elsewhere."

"And I"—"and I," said the others.

The Ogre glared at them, and growled like a wild beast.

"Go," he said; "I can do without you. The world is full of better stuff than you are made of."

"And hell holds no worse than you," was the reply. "Come, mates, let us go, and pray for forgiveness for the work of to-day. It was the infernal drink as did it—it made me mad."

In a body they moved away, and never once looked back upon the leader they had renounced. He remained watching them until they were lost behind a distant hill, and then strolled slowly to the boat, thinking.

"So," he said, "they have left me. Well, let them go; I have enough to carry out my purpose, and a stout ship to carry me and what I have. I'll away from this spot and seek some island, where Nature's beauty has never yet been touched by man. There are many such in the broad Pacific, and I will away. And yet—no. How could I live there the dull monotonous life which must be mine in such a place? I *must* have excitement, which can only be had among men, and where they are I dare not go while my curse—Broad Arrow Jack—is alive!"

Suddenly, as he walked, a new-born terror came upon him. He paused and quailed before some invisible horror, which had no distinctive reality to him. It had no recognisable connection between himself and anything past or present, and the like of it he had never known before.

Sinking down until he crouched upon the ground, he looked around as one who dreads to meet an all-powerful foe. Every limb of his body quivered, and two dark cunning eyes stood out from their depths like balls of fire. For a few moments the terrible terror held him, and then went as it came—without warning.

What was it?

He could not tell, although he had a dim idea that the awakening from a life of crime was at hand. This he had ever mocked at, as strong men governed by vile passions often do. He knew not what to think of it, and rising to his feet he walked moodily to the spot where he had left the boat.

"They say that rats shun a falling house," he said to himself. "Am I falling? Is the end near?"

He was answered by a distant shout, mingled with the clash of voices, and high above all a voice he knew so well.

"'Tis he," cried the Ogre—"my curse—my ban. What fiend has guided Broad Arrow Jack hither?"

He ran forward in a stooping position until he came to the shore, and crouching down behind a large stone he looked towards the Phryne.

"All is lost," he hissed between his set teeth. "I am ruined—and alone."

CHAPTER CLIII.

JACK TO THE RESCUE.

WHEN Captain Murray discovered how he had been duped and imposed upon he was overcome with horror. The fact of having lost his ship, and left his mate and two of the men to certain death, drove him almost to distraction.

A man of tender heart—though brave—he had always more sympathy for others than for himself. He could suffer, he could endure, but he could never hear of the sufferings of others without a pang.

The helplessness of his position added to his anguish. Could he have rushed at his treacherous foe, even with the prospect of death before him, he would have been content; but to know that his enemies had, by cunning, triumphed, leaving him without an opening for retribution, was doubly and trebly trying to him.

In his first despair he formed the idea of making a raft by lashing the water barrels together, and he and his men tore their shirts to strips to make a rope for this purpose. Whilst thus engaged three strangers stood before them.

They were Jack, Brisket, and Grip.

The foremost—Jack—addressed Captain Murray in the tone of one accustomed to command. "Where is your leader?" he said.

"My leader," replied the captain, "who is he?"

"The piratical demon—called the Ogre."

"Nay," said Captain Murray, "I am a victim of this villain. In me you see the captain of that fair ship lying there. I came ashore for water, and they have seized my boats and taken possession of my craft."

"And what are you doing now," asked Jack.

"Getting materials for the building of a raft, my man. We think of lashing the water barrels together."

Broad-Arrow Jack.

BROAD ARROW JACK'S TEMPER GOT THE BETTER OF HIM AND HE SHOOK THE BOY UNTIL HIS TEETH RATTLED IN HIS HEAD.

No. 22.

"A wild idea."

"A wild idea is better than none."

"So it is," returned Jack, but nevertheless it may be a false one. The sun is now sinking, and shortly it will be dark. Why not swim to the ship and recapture her. How many of your men will risk it?"

Alas! for the bravery of those gallant men. Out of the whole body only one fancied he could reach the ship, and he was not certain he could do it without aid.

"There is nothing left then," said Jack, "but to fetch the canoe."

He spoke to Brisket, who nodded assent. The raft was the wild idea of a desperate man, and could not have been constructed even if they had persevered. Jack explained to Captain Murray that he had a canoe lying in the middle of a river about ten miles away, and asked him to lend his aid to bring it thither.

"It will hold half a dozen," said Jack, "and while five are engaged with the enemy, the sixth can bring back the boat for more."

"You are a bold fellow," said Captain Murray, looking at him keenly. "I fancy there is a strange story attached to you."

"Too strange to tell now," replied Jack. "Come, let us go."

They all went, but shortly after starting the sun went down, and unhappily they missed their way. It was a strange country, and the landmarks in many places bore a strong resemblance to each other, and so it came about they took one wrong turning and lost their path.

It was close upon morning ere they came to the boat, and the sun was well up when they reached the bay again. Not one of them had eaten or drunk throughout the night, but without pausing a moment, Jack, Brisket, Grip, Captain Murray, and two of the sailors put off, and pulled quietly to the Phryne.

They boarded without opposition, for all on board were either drunk or asleep. Close to the mainmast lay Jeb Jaundice with a brandy bottle beside him, and strewn about the deck were half a score pirates just as they fell after their debauch.

"Secure that scoundrel," said Jack, pointing to Jaundice, "and toss the rest overboard."

He was so used to command that for the moment he forgot he was aboard a ship belonging to another, but immediately remembering, he turned with an apology.

"Pray forgive me," he said, "I forgot where I was."

"I am only too glad to follow," replied Captain Murray. "For the present, pray take the command."

"All I want," said our hero, "is that villain and his partner in crime. Arouse and bind him, Brisket. I will settle with him anon. Now to find the Ogre. My hour of triumph has come at last."

Alone and fearless he ran down below, where he found some half-dozen of the pirates waking from a soddened sleep. They stared at him standing at the door of the cabin with his cutlass drawn, doubtless wondering whether they were awake or dreaming.

There was no need to tell those men who stood before them. They were old associates with the Ogre, and the majestic figure of Broad Arrow Jack was as familiar to them as the dome of St. Paul's is to a Cockney. Like frightened sheep they huddled into a corner, and stared at him in terror.

"Where is your leader," thundered Jack—"the Ogre?"

"He was aboard last night," said one, "but—"

"Well, speak out."

"He threatened to go ashore this morning and burn the mate, and he may be gone."

It was not often Jack showed temper in his language, but now he could not keep back the angry expression which arose to his lips.

"Down with your arms!" he shouted to the pirates.

With trembling hands they cast them down, and he gathered them up and tossed them away.

"Remain here until I return," he said.

Outside he met Grip and Brisket, to whom he gave the prisoners in charge, and then made a search over the ship from end to end.

Pirates awake and asleep he found, but of course no Ogre. It was a bitter disappointment, but he was calm under it. He had one of the villains in his power who he determined should not escape him.

"I must be content," he said—"must be patient. The turn of the Ogre will come."

On returning to the deck from an unsuccessful search of the hold, he found all the pirates prisoners, blinking like owls in the sunlight. Convinced that no appeal of theirs would be of any avail, they stood dogged and sullen, awaiting their fate.

With one exception—Jeb Jaundice.

CHAPTER CLIV.

RETRIBUTION.

IN addition to the terror the presence of Broad Arrow Jack inspired, Jeb Jaundice had all the vague apprehensions and nervous tremours of the broken-down drunkard in the morning. The reaction of his night's debauch was in itself a fearful thing—combined with his fear of the young avenger it was worse than death itself.

He lay upon the deck, shivering like a cur in the presence of a body of medical students bent on vivisection, and not for a moment did he take his eyes off Jack, before whom the other prisoners were arraigned.

Of their guilt there could be no doubt, and what sentence but that of death could he pass upon them? To keep them as prisoners was impossible, to let them loose upon society would be a crime.

So he passed the sentence—to be hanged at the yard-arm.

When they heard it, these wretches, so ready to shed the blood and take the lives of others, began to howl and shriek for mercy. And thus it ever is with those who love cruelty and live by rapine and murder, when their own safety is concerned.

The crew of the Phryne may be forgiven if they were ready and anxious to execute the pirates, for they knew the fate of the two sailors and the mate. No wonder their blood boiled—no wonder they ran forward and swung the fatal noose at the yard-arm. —a short shrift and a long rope was as merciful a death as the scoundrels could expect from them.

The first who suffered a just death had to be carried to the spot. His face was the picture of horror and unutterable despair—his lips moved as if beseeching for mercy, but no sound came forth, and silently they swung him over the sea.

In a minute all was o'er—then the next was called upon to advance. He, unlike his late companion, would shriek and bellow, and make piteous appeals or that which he had never given—for the sake of a wife whom he had coolly deserted years before, and children on whom he scarce ever bestowed a thought, he begged that his life might be spared.

He cried to men hardened for the time with anger, and in a few brief moments his tongue was still, and he had joined the other in the land of the great unknown.

And so one by one—some crying for help, others dumb with fright, but none going to their end like men—they were cast into the sea.

Jeb Jaundice alone was left.

In the pride of his strength, years before, he would have accepted defeat, and died boldly enough. Of all these he alone would probably have uttered a jest or a defiant word with the rope around his neck and died as he had lived, without an expression of remorse or repentance.

But now how different!

Broken and bowed down with dissipation, and long days and nights of agony—haunted by the memory of a thousand crimes, above all that of the murder of his wife—the woman who had loved him as man is seldom loved.

From the hour when he struck the fatal blow which took away her life and opened out to him the brilliancy of the treasure of her love, her fair image had seldom been absent from his thoughts.

Judge, ye who have lost some trifling chance of happiness through your own folly, and have felt the mortification which came with after knowledge, what were the feelings of this man.

Before him on one side there was the bright vision of what might have been receding ever further and further from his view, while on the other side drawing nearer and nearer was the dark picture of the black doom before him.

In past perils he had often felt that he was in a position from which there was no escape, yet the feeling had never been before what it was now—one of positive conviction.

He knew he must die.

"I have to ask you," said Jack, addressing Captain Murray and his men, "to leave me and this man awhile together. We have an account to settle which I fain would close without spectators."

"Your wish is law," replied Captain Murray. "Let us go below, my men."

There was a slight look of disappointed curiosity upon the face of many, but they all obeyed without a murmur.

Grip and Brisket were the last to go—the latter on his way pausing to whisper a few words to his leader.

"Give him no chance this time," he said.

"Fear not," replied Jack; "either he or I will fall. Even now I cannot kill him without giving him a chance for his life. As man to man we will meet, and should he prove the conqueror put him ashore and let him go free."

"That would be a hard trial for me," said Brisket.

"Nevertheless," returned Jack, "you must promise it. I would spare his life but for my oath. Look at him—is there any mercy in giving life to him? Could he ever escape the torture which lies within? No, Brisket, living or dead what has he to hope for?"

"You shall be obeyed," replied Brisket, "come what may," and holding out his hand he gave Jack a hearty grip, and went down below.

CHAPTER CLV.

ANOTHER.

AS soon as the deck was clear Jack cut the rope which bound the arms of Jaundice, and set him free.

"Rise," he said; "be a man again, if only for a few moments more."

"Mercy!" moaned Jaundice.

"You shall have it with its kindred spirit, justice," replied Jack. "Rise, I say, and meet me as a man should meet his foe."

"I have never wronged you," said Jaundice, hoarsely; "it was the Ogre. I would have spared you that night, and begged for you to be set free, but the Ogre was the terror of us all."

"That he was the leading spirit I admit," replied Jack. "He was the cunning workman who devised the work, but you and the others were ready tools enough. Is the wrong you did me your only crime?"

"No, no!" returned Jaundice, "but the Ogre was at the bottom of them all."

"Your wife," said Jack, sternly. "What of her? Did the Ogre urge you to take her life? Was he present when you struck the blow? And what was your life before you knew him? No, man, your lie is unavailing. Stand up!"

"I am too ill to fight," replied Jaundice.

"Pistols," said Jack, "were at one time your favourite weapon. You were renowned as a skilled marksman, and with these you cannot deny our equality—at least, what advantage there may be is yours."

As he spoke he drew out his revolvers and off red one to Jaundice, who raised his hand as if to take it, but let it fall by his side again.

"I will not fight," he muttered.

"If you will not get up," said Jack, "I must treat you like a sulky hound, and lash you until you obey."

He turned aside in search of a piece of rope, and at the same moment Jaundice, with a wild idea of flying he knew not whither, sprang to his feet and ran to the side of the vessel. His first idea was to spring into the water, but there before his eyes was the fin of a shark slowly sailing about. The monster, gorged by the last feast, was yet unsatisfied, and was looking for further prey.

At the sight Jaundice drew back in horror, and without a thought of the folly of attempting to escape by the rigging, leaped upon the ratlins, and ran with the activity of a cat to the cross-trees.

"Come back," said Jack, from the deck; "there is no escape."

But Jaundice, to whom every moment was as a year, only answered with a further appeal for mercy.

"Come down," said Jack, "or I will fetch you."

There was a curious dazed look upon Jaundice's face as he ran higher, and without pausing he went up to the royal cross-trees and crouched there.

Jack immediately began the ascent.

As he went up he kept his eyes fixed upon Jaundice, who returned his gaze with a stare. He was so much like a corpse that Jack was inclined to think that he had died upon reaching his present elevation. But he went on calmly and deliberately until he was within reach of the other; then Jaundice, with a wild shriek, so awful in its power that Jack remained still with his hand outstretched, relaxed his hold and fell back.

Down he went, fell upon the lower cross-trees upon his back, then, bounding over, struck the side of the vessel, and so on to the sea.

He did not sink—the frantic tossing of his arms kept him afloat, and now with wild hoarse shouts he uttered the name of his wife—"Maggie! Maggie!"

It echoed along the shore even to the blue mountains in the distance, and came back like the voice of mocking spirits, and as he shouted the dark fin of the shark came again to the surface and glided swiftly towards him.

He saw it, and the light came back to his eyes—not the light of life, but the fire of the great terror which comes to the like of him when grim death is near.

In a few seconds the shark was upon him, its white belly flashed under the water, and its deadly teeth were fixed upon his body. He was dragged under, and all that ever came to the surface again of Jeb Jaundice was a streak of blood, which spread out, mingled in the waters, and was lost; but if the ancient fable is true, Jaundice in those two brief seconds lived a thousand years of pain, and who could wish him more?

CHAPTER CLVI.

A BAD NIGHT.

MATTERS at Rookholme Castle were not quite so satisfactory as they might have been. The Honourable Morden Crewe, to begin with, was left entirely to the society of the five gentlemen who had come uninvited to his lordly halls.

The upper circles of the county, forming their own opinion of affairs, deliberately cut the Honourable Morden. Not one of them called after the dinner, and when by chance the owner of the castle met them, they were all afflicted with short-sightedness, for which the best spectacles ever manufactured would be of no avail.

"I must live it down," he muttered, "when I've rid myself of these leeches. Ah! rid myself, but how?"

No easy matter, for it is one thing to desire to kill a person, and another to find an opportunity to do it with safety. Woody Welsher belonged to a canny school of men, and knowing pretty well what was working in the mind of his associate, gave him no opportunity for violence. By day he kept to the grounds about the castle, and at night he locked and barricaded his door, as if he were going to withstand a siege.

As for Wobbles and "the precious three," they kept close to each other almost night and day—at night particularly so—until they went to bed. But their principal source of terror lay in the castle, which, according to the servants, with whom Wobbles freely conversed, was more or less haunted in every nook and corner.

The dreadful tales he picked up Wobbles freely imparted to his friends with sundry embellishments naturally arising out of his gifted mind.

Scarce a day passed without his making an addition to the ghost catalogue, and the lives of these four gentlemen after dark became one broken round of miserable terror.

At first they all slept in separate rooms. Wobbles had an apartment big enough to hold a public fancy ball in, with more dark corners in it than ever he dared to count.

The fireplace alone was big enough for a bedroom, with a huge overhanging chimney-board shaped like an extinguisher, and the way the wind would howl and whistle and shriek at night beneath it would have daunted a more courageous man than Wobbles.

He usually slept in the middle of the bed under the clothes, and curled up like a periwinkle, but his sleep was always broken and troubled until he arranged for all his friends to rest in the same apartment.

They were glad enough to come, for each and all had a terror of being alone, and with their own hands they moved their beds into the room occupied by Wobbles.

But, be it understood, none of these valiant gentry admitted their fears; on the contrary, they all assumed a boldness, and openly expressed wonderment at the servants, who, after dark, went about in pairs.

"Ghost!" said Wobbles; "nonsense! I should like to see one very much—it would amuse me. Yes, I likes the stories of 'em," he added; "they give a hair of barrystocratic flavour to a place."

"If I was too see a ghost," said Conky, "I'd herff with my boot and chuck it at his 'ed."

"I'd hit him under the jaw," said Curler.

"And I'd larf at him," remarked Pigeon.

All very brave and bold when together, but if left alone by any chance, afflicted with mortal fears.

Occasionally such a thing would happen, and one night Conky, on leaving his room to go down to dinner, saw, or fancied he saw, a white figure gliding towards him. He made for the grand staircase and went down head first with a noise like far-off thunder, meeting Pigeon half way and taking him back again.

The pair descended with a thud upon the pavement of the hall, and Pigeon saw a multitude of stars, rockets, and catherine wheels. He also personally exploded, and called Conky a beast, an ass, and sundry other names.

This was on the evening previous to their all taking up their abode in the apartment of Wobbles. Here they hoped all terrors would be at an end. By day and night together what was there to fear?

The room they arranged themselves, and very pretty they made it. All the beds were put pretty close together, with just room enough to walk between. "For," said Conky, "being here we may as well be near enough to talk a bit when we get into bed. I likes being talked to sleep."

So they all did, and not one of them was even the least bit afraid. Of course not—so all the beds were put opposite the big fireplace, and the first night they went to bed as happy as birds in a tree.

Happy until they had been about five minutes in bed, conversing upon the advantages of living in an aristocratic mansion, "where," as Wobbles said, "the grub was good and reg'lar, attendance fust rate, and no fees to waiters." At the end of the time alluded to, a curious scratching was heard apparently just in front of the beds.

"What's that?" asked Conky in a hollow whisper.

He got no reply, simply for the reason that his valiant comrades had all retired under the clothes, where they lay shaking until their couches creaked again.

"I say," said Conky, "no larks. I hate gammon of this sort. It aint manly and fair. Drop that scratching."

But the scratching went on, and was soon accompanied with an odd kind of whistling, such as Conky, in his vivid imagination, fancied the wind would make as it ran through the jaws of a skeleton.

"I wish I was out of this house," he gasped. "Are you all dead there?"

It may be wondered why these gentlemen remained in such an uncanny place; but excellent board and lodging, gratis, are things not to be found everywhere. They wanted an allowance to live away; but the Honourable Morden, enraged at the disgrace they had brought upon him, said he would see them further than this earth first.

To return to the four friends in bed. Conky having followed suit in retiring under the clothes, endeavoured to go to sleep; so did the others, but not a wink could they obtain.

Anon Wobbles put his head out and listened.

"What now?"

Something moving about the room with a rustling sound.

Frou-frou—swish—swish—what could it be?

"I say," said Wobbles, "are any of you awake?"

No answer. He listened intently, and could not even hear them breathing.

"They're all murdered," he groaned, and down he went again.

In the same way the others put their heads out in their turn, and hearing the noise in the room Curler and Pigeon also made appeals to their friends and got no answer. Each man, then convinced that all the rest were dead, lay tremblingly awaiting his fate.

It would have been very edifying to a spectator if it had been possible to look upon those four arrant knaves trembling in their beds, but imagination must supply the picture to my readers.

At last a happy thought came to Wobbles.

"If I step quietly out of bed, and make a bolt for it, the ghost perhaps won't know me. I'll go to Welsher's room, and sit up all night."

As he carried out his plans, and slipped from his bed, Conky put out his head and saw his dim figure. Then a happy thought came to him.

"It's Wobbles larking. I'll chuck a boot at him."

With much stealthiness he felt about, and secured one of his boots—a heavy article, not entirely without nails. Taking careful aim he hurled it at Wobbles, and smote him in that part of the anatomy known in pugilistic circles as "the bread basket."

"Oh, Lord! my hend is near," shrieked Wobbles, as he went down all in a heap.

"And sarve him right," growled Conky, as he felt about for his other boot, "a getting of us all here and a-coming all sorts of larks to frighten us. I'll have another shy at him."

But Pigeon received this boot. Hearing the shrieks, which he assumed, for some reason of his own, were the triumphant cries of a vampire drunk with the blood of his companions, he rose up with the idea of beating a precipitate retreat, and, getting that boot under his left ear, went to bed again smart, and lay incoherently babbling of the days of his youth.

As for Curler, he got so far down the bed that his feet stuck out at the bottom—a fact that he discovered as soon as they became chilly—and in his frantic struggles to get them back again he burst through the sacking of his old-fashioned bedstead, and went headlong to the floor.

Wobbles heard him go, and, dreading a further attack from the spirits about, made a plunge for the door, and would have reached it had he not gone in a wrong direction and shot himself into the ancient fireplace.

The moment he arrived there something or somebody began to peck and claw at his head, and another something or somebody to dig a hole in his back. His yells would have aroused anybody a mile off, and in a few seconds some half-dozen male servants came tumbling into the room with lights.

The sight they looked upon, so far from alarming them, drew further peals of laughter. Conky sitting up like a man in a dream; Pigeon wildly gesticulating; Curler peering out from under his bed, and Wobbles in the fireplace fighting frantically with a pair of owls, who had somehow got down the chimney.

Order was soon restored. The owls on seeing the light went blundering up the ample chimney, and took themselves off to their nightly hunting grounds, and Wobbles hearing familiar voices rose up and in broken tones thanked his preservers, and Conky, Curler, and Pigeon all came to their senses again.

Explanations followed. Nobody had been at all afraid, only Wobbles for one was not going to be disturbed by two owls, nor was he going to wait for lights, but fought 'em in the dark as he used to "tackle the roaring lions on the boundless perairies."

The servants listened respectfully enough, and believed as much of the lion-hunting business as was necessary. They were civil, of course, for whatever these men were, they were their master's guests, and who or what they were was not at all a dependent's affair. Curler's bed was replaced, a fire was lighted to keep the owls out, and the four friends all prepared for sleep again.

"What a jolly night it's been," said Wobbles. "I don't know when I've had such a lark, but who hit me with a boot?"

"I did," replied Conky. "I thought you was a howl."

Wobbles did not say any more aloud, but with that blow rankling in his heart he lay down, and after a little tossing and turning fell asleep. The rest followed suit, and there was no further disturbance that night.

At breakfast on the following morning the Honourable Morden Crewe, who was never known to be in the best of tempers, asked Wobbles what he meant by disturbing the whole of the house as he had done.

Wobbles explained, and the Honourable Morden laughed grimly.

"And so," he said, "you think they were owls, do you?"

"Of course they were," replied Wobbles.

"Indeed," said the other, "then you will see them again *in another shape*."

"Wot do you mean?" asked Wobbles, turning pale enough to play the part of a ghost himself.

"Oh! nothing particular," replied the Honourable Morden, carelessly. "Only I know this castle better than you do, and I can tell you this much. That those who begin to see owls and such things here in the night *don't live long*."

"Oh!" said Wobbles, dismally, and a huge round of brawn upon his plate seemed to grow suddenly distasteful to him.

"There was an uncle of mine," pursued the Honourable Morden, calmly knocking the top off an egg, "who came here only for one night, and saw but one owl, and yet he never left the estate alive. The next day he was found under the great oak yonder with his throat cut. Won't you have some bacon? That brawn is not very good, I fear."

"I've no happetite this morning," replied Wobbles, looking at his three particular friends, who also appeared to have fallen off in their gastronomical powers.

Woody Welsher ate as usual, but the conversation made a deep impression upon him. He occasionally cast a keen glance at the Honourable Morden, as if he had found in him a new and puzzling cause for reflection.

He said nothing, however, until after breakfast, when he was left alone with his patron; then as they strolled on the terrace for a morning cigar he said—

"By the way, Crewe, that story of your uncle was all true of course?"

"Every word," was the reply. "He came here on business which did not concern him, and he lost his life. This place is infested with poachers, and although he had nothing to do with the game he was continually having fellows brought up for trespassing. At last he brought up one too many, and he was murdered."

"Was it brought home to the fellow?"

"Near enough to hang him, although he died protesting his innocence. But innocent or guilty it did good, for the game was plentiful enough next season."

CHAPTER CLVII.

THE TIGER SEES THE GHOST AGAIN.

"I DON'T want to defend poachers," retorted Woody Welsher, as the Honourable Morden Crewe ceased speaking, "for no honest man can call them anything else but thieves; still, I think you swells pull the cord too tight."

"I should like to pull it tighter—round some necks," muttered the Honourable Morden, as he strolled away.

"No doubt you would," said Woody Welsher, softly, as he shook his fist at him; "but you will not find I am ass enough to put my head into the noose."

Like all vulgar cunning natures, he had perfect confidence in his powers; and yet there was a better head than his, with all his cunning, at that moment compassing his death.

* * * * * *

Within Dick Skewball there lay a very subtle disposition, which, with proper training, would develop into a very valuable possession in after life. It was not the cunning of a crafty soul, but the greater gift which enables people to read others as if they were open books, and to plan and deal with them accordingly.

He read the Tiger, and saw in his nature something which at present he did not possess—unswerving honesty—and there were times when he felt bowed down with shame to think how mean he was in comparison with the dark-skinned untutored boy.

Dick also felt he had committed a crime which could never be blotted out—a crime that, as events had come about, brought him no valuable return—and, doubly harassed by the weight of the sin and the loss of the proceeds of it, the boy became moody and irritable.

They continued to live together in the woods, but the old companionship was at an end. Without absolute mistrust they held aloof from each other, and took to wandering alone here and there, sometimes days apart, suddenly going and suddenly returning, as the whim took them.

Dick spent his leisure time in looking for the lost diamonds. He tried to persuade himself that, once again in his possession, he would not use them for his own purposes, but apply them in some sort of way—he knew not how—for the benefit of others. "It is a pity they should be lost," was his argument, "and the talk of the Tiger was all nonsense."

He might say so, but at night—especially when alone—the thought of the shade of Broad Arrow Jack wandering about terrified him, and oft he crouched upon his rough bed, shuddering and shivering in mortal fear.

The rustle of the trees was Jack's warning whisper—the moaning of the wind the groaning of his wandering spirit; and when Dick heard them the childish prayers he had learnt at his mother's knee would burst from his lips with a fervour unknown in the earlier times of his life.

"I don't think I shall live here much longer," he said to the Tiger one day; "it's so lonely and so miserable. You were away all yesterday and the day before."

"Me left you plenty of food," said the Tiger.

"Food is not everything," returned Dick. "I want somebody to talk to—something to do more than we have here. Where were you yesterday?"

"Looking at Massa Jack's ghost."

"Nonsense, Tiger—you don't see ghosts in the daytime."

"Me see him yesterday," replied the Tiger, "not far from dis place, wif a tent, and men, and all sorts of tings dat he used to hab in de lifetime."

Dick looked at him incredulously. He had just the slightest possible suspicion that the Tiger was going mad.

"I should like to see this ghost of yours," he said, "just once."

"Come wif me to-morrer and me show him to you."

Dick was not really very anxious to look upon the spirit of his chief, and had the visit been proposed for the night he would most certainly have refused; but a ghost in the daytime he need not be afraid of, and freely consented.

"How far is it away?" he asked.

"'Bout fifteen mile," replied the Tiger—"just a good run afore we hab breffast."

"Thank you," said Dick, "but I think I will take breakfast before I start. You can do as you like."

Half the night Dick lay thinking. The truth was vaguely shadowed out before him, and he felt easier than he had done for a long time; but if—it was only an "if" to him—Broad Arrow Jack was alive, how should he act?

Mark his position.

He could not got go to Jack and say, "The Tiger has your property, and will give it up to you," for Jack would naturally ask how the Tiger came in possession of it, and then the whole truth would come out.

Nor dare he go and confess his sin to Jack, for he had not sufficient knowledge of his chief to feel assurance of forgiveness. He had seen and understood more of the sterner side of Jack's nature than the tender portion of it. He did not know how ready he was to forgive a sin confessed.

Again, suppose it was a real ghost—a veritable spirit—he was going to see. What then? Suppose he was brought face to face with a being of another world! Would not the very contact kill him? In the night Dick half repented of the promise he had made.

But when the dawn came the light of the sun reassured him, and he was ready to set forth with the Tiger. Dick ate a little breakfast, but tho Tiger partook of none. He preferred eating when he had time to rest after it.

Striking out eastward, away from the diamond-fields, the Tiger led the way to the mountain fastnesses wherein so many scenes of our little play have been enacted. Most of the ground they traversed for the first hour was familiar to Dick, but after that time he was in a strange land.

The Tiger, however, appeared to know every inch of the ground, and pointed out to his companion paths and gulleys among the mountains, telling him where they led to, and many strange things he had heard and seen there.

They principally concerned Broad Arrow Jack, and are for the most part familiar to those who have read this story, and need no repetition here.

A little before noon they came to a barrier in their path, which lay in a canyon between the mountains.

Great masses of rock had either fallen or been hurled down from the mountain side, completely blocking up the way. Pausing in his talk about the past, the Tiger softly whispered—

"Behind dere we see de ghost of Massa Jack. Follow me, and make no noise."

An ordinary traveller might have hesitated to scale the barrier, but the boys were as sure-footed as goats, and swiftly and surely they leaped from rock to rock, until they reached the summit, some fifty feet in height, and peeped over.

"See dere—see," whispered the Tiger, "dere am de ghost."

Dick looked and saw, in the continuation of the gulley beneath, Broad Arrow Jack seated upon a stone, in the attitude of one who is deeply thinking.

A little beyond him were four tents, apparently quite new; lying outside in easy attitudes were about a dozen sailors; and hard by was a fire burning, over which Brisket and a man strange to Dick were engaged in cooking.

It was only the natural simplicity of his mind that prevented the Tiger realising the truth. Having heard and once believed that Jack was dead he assumed that the figure before him was that of his ghost.

Not so Dick. He understood all, and quickly reviewing the position in his mind, determined what to do.

"Stay here, Tiger," he whispered; "I'll go down and speak to him."

"What! speak to de ghost?" exclaimed the Tiger.

"Yes," said Dick. "Why not?"

"If you speak to a ghost," rejoined the Tiger, "unless him speak fust, he is sure to kill you."

"I'll risk it," said Dick.

With a boldness that made the courageous Tiger shudder, Dick began the descent on the other side of the barrier, leaping down with his usual activity, until he stood before Broad Arrow Jack.

CHAPTER CLVIII.

THE TIGER IS SCARED.

THE party with our hero was composed of Brisket, Grip, and a number of sailors from the Phryne. The latter Captain Murray had lent at vast inconvenience to himself, but the men were so eager to avenge their comrades, and Jack so intent upon the capture of the last of his living foes, that, considering the services which had been rendered him, he could do no less than spare the men.

On landing they sought out traces of the Ogre and tracked him to the spot where the ghastly tragedy had been enacted, and there the sight they looked upon redoubled their anger and thirst for vengeance.

At first they could only guess that it was the mate, for all that remained was a blackened mass of charred flesh and bones; but on raking the ashes over they found his watch, partially destroyed, but his name still legible on the inner-plate.

They buried the remains with reverence at the foot of a tree, and cut his name upon the bark.

Then with set lips they pursued their search for the author of this diabolical deed.

The traces of him were few—a foot-mark here and there and a fragment of clothing clinging to a thorn-bush—but, such as they were, they proved sufficient for the keen eager eyes of the pursuers, until they came to the barrier, and there all trace of him was lost.

Further pursuit of him was vain until they had ascertained his whereabouts. As the search might prove a long one in any case, two men were despatched to the fields for certain necessaries, which Jack believed he could obtain on credit until his return.

Now indeed did he miss the great wealth which had ever been his. With it at his command he could have employed a hundred agents to aid him in his pursuit, but now he was groping in the dark and knew not whither to go. He had not even a single purse to aid him, and such provisions that they had were obtained in the chase.

He was brooding over this when Dick Skewball suddenly presented himself before him, with a curious look of mixed fear and sullen defiance on his young face.

Hitherto Jack, knowing full well that Dick had robbed him, had nevertheless restrained himself; but now an almost resistless impulse came upon him to seize hold of the boy and shake the truth out of him.

He extended his hand, but drawing it back he looked straight at Dick, and put a question to him.

"Where have you been?" he said.

"Living in the woods," replied Dick.

"Alone?"

"No," said the boy, "I have had the Tiger with me."

"And why are you here now?"

"I thought you were dead," replied Dick, "but now I find you are alive I am come to serve you again."

Jack's temper now for a moment got the master of him. Dick's answer sounded like a gross piece of impertinence, and taking the boy by the arm, he gave him a shake which made his teeth rattle again.

"You serve me," he said, "you thief! Where are the jewels you robbed me of?"

"I—I don't know," stuttered Dick; "the Tiger has hidden them."

"And pray," said Jack, "what has the Tiger to do with the robbery?"

"He found I had them," replied Dick, "and took them from me. He has hidden them from me, and will not tell me where they are."

"And where is he?"

"Before I tell you," replied Dick, "I want you to say that you forgive me. It was a great temptation, and I am only a boy. I have suffered for it since."

"Especially since you lost them again," replied Jack. "I have watched you through all, and saw how the evil conquered. But I do not war with boys. You are forgiven. Where is the Tiger?"

"Up there," replied Dick, pointing to the spot where he had left his companion. "He dare not come down, for he thought you were a ghost."

Jack waited to hear no more, but, with a step as sure as that of the Tiger himself, clambered up the barrier of stones, but on reaching the summit all he saw was a small black figure retreating in the distance.

"What new trick is this?" he thought. Then he shouted out—

"Stop, Tiger—stop, I say!"

But the fleet-footed youngster fled on, and in a few seconds disappeared.

Jack, unable to understand this new turn of events, thinking he had been the victim of some fresh trick, went back to Dick, who quailed before his stern gaze.

"Now, Dick Skewball, I will have the truth. What is this plot between the Tiger and yourself?"

"I swear I told you the truth. The Tiger has the treasure. He said that he hid it from me because it was yours."

"Why, then, does he fly from me?"

"I suppose," replied Dick, hanging his head, "that, like me, now he has the bright stones he feels that he must keep them."

Jack made no answer to this, but turned away with bitterness at heart. The trial of what might be called the second loss was as much as he could bear.

CHAPTER CLIX.

A NEW LANDLORD.

ATTACHED to the village near Rockholme Castle was an inn that bore the sign of the Bold Brigand. During the absence of a resident owner at the castle the business flagged, and the original landlord took his goods and chattels to another part of the world, being, as he said, unable to "live on air and give credit to people who couldn't pay."

So the inn, failing another man to take it, was shut up. The little boys broke all the windows with stones, as boys unhappily will do when there is a house long to let, and the natives fell back upon their own home-brewed beer, or went without, and nobody seemed the worse for it. It is astonishing how well people can get on without a public-house if they will only try.

But shortly after the arrival of the Honourable Morden Crewe it was whispered about that another landlord was coming.

Painters, glaziers, and other artisans went to work, and not only made the front of the Bold Brigand as good as new, but a good deal better, and within a month the enterprising individual who had embarked his capital in the said inn came down with his wife and a small family to take possession of it.

It was no other than Richard Skewball who came to Rockholme, by the merest chance as men view things, for he was a stranger to the Honourable Morden Crewe, and knew nothing of the estate being in reality the property of Broad Arrow Jack.

But then he was a landlord all over, ready and willing to oblige, with a knowledge of his business, and a nice little bit of capital at his back, which enabled him to be quite independent of customers.

If they came he would be the landlord to perfection, but if they stopped away he and Sal and the children could do very well without them.

The money he had, it will be remembered, was saved in the diamond-fields, and sent over to England prior to the mishap which befell him there, and it was enough for him to live upon. But Richard Skewball never could, and never would if he could help it, be idle, and his tastes turning in the direction of a snug public-house in the country, he advertised for one, got an answer from the agent of the Ashleigh estate, and there he was.

"And a very roomy old-fashioned place it is," he said to Sal, when describing it to her after a preliminary visit alone. "Stabling for a regiment of cavalry, styes for a score pigs, good garden and paddock, and a yard big enough to rear five hundred fowls."

"If it suits you it will suit me," said affectionate Sal. "The country is just the thing for the children. Ah! if Dick were only here."

That was their great trouble—the absence of Dick. After his return to England Richard Skewball sent copies of a printed notice, to be put up about the diamond-fields, offering a handsome reward for any one who could give him news of his son, but owing to Dick's secluded life nobody was able to give the information required.

After waiting some time patiently a letter came from Broad Arrow Jack, informing them of Dick's disappearance during his chief's illness, and then as a long time elapsed without further news of him they began to mourn him as dead.

"He was always wild and reckless," said Sal, "and I fear some accident has happened to him.

It is hard for so bright a boy to come to a violent end in the wilderness."

"It seems so to me," returned Dick, "but 'taint for us to dispute the working of things. There was something wrong about Dick for a long time before he left us. He seemed to be much troubled in his mind."

"I hope he has not got mixed up with any bad lot," said Sal. "I would rather he died a hundred times."

They were still uncertain of the whereabouts of Dick when they came down to the Bold Brigand, where for a few days they were fully occupied in arranging their new home.

In the midst of their work their landlord, the Honourable Morden Crewe, accompanied by Woody Welsher, called.

"I like to know all my tenants," said the former, "and to know if they have any complaints to make. Has everything been done that you would desire?"

"Well, not exactly, sir," replied Richard. "The front's been painted and patched up, and looks quite pretty, but——"

"Not a place that isn't just under your nose has been touched," put in Sal.

"Indeed," said the Honourable Morden. "I will just mention it to my agent. He sees to all these things, and of course has to—to look after money matters; for the present rents of my estate are low, and I barely receive two per cent. on the value. I see you have brought a bagatelle-board with you."

"Yes," said Richard. "I'm fond of the game, and Sal can play like a Trojan."

"Don't talk nonsense, Dick," said Sal, sharply, "but stick to business. Ask the squire when the back part of the house is to be done up."

There was no need to put the question, for he heard it from Sal's lips, and most politely and courteously he replied—

"I will lay the matter before my agent."

After a little more chat he shook hands with them both, and retired, followed by Woody Welsher, who did nothing but suck the top of his stick throughout the interview, and vote the whole thing a perfect nuisance.

"Civil and perlite—aint they?" said Dick, when they were gone.

"Too much so," replied Sal. "You will get nothing more out of him."

"Well, Sal, I don't want it. The place will do well enough for me, and if there's a few pounds wanted to put it right here and there I've got it handy."

"That fellow," said Sal, referring to the Honourable Morden, "has rascal written all over him. He'll be a regular grinder here. 'Spend all and take all,' is his motto. He's a wolf, that's what he is, and that fellow with him is a fox. I shall call 'em the Wolf and the Fox."

"I don't know much about people's looks, but I'll bet you are right, Sal," rejoined Richard. "Left to myself he would have taken me in, for I do like perliteness."

"Any one with a soft word can do as they like with you," said Sal. "Now, here's some customers coming, and I do wonder what they are."

The new customers were no other than Wobbles and his charming associates, who hearing their aristocratic friend intended to visit the public-house, determined not to be long behind him.

"We must make ourselves known," said Wobbles, "or we shall niver be treated with proper respect."

They all came swaggering in, to let the landlord of the Bold Brigand know he had real gentlemen to deal with. Richard and Sal both recognised their guests, having seen them occasionally, and heard much of their doings from Brisket; but neither Wobbles nor any of his friends knew either their host or hostess, not having patronised their establishment in the diamond-fields.

"How on airth did these fellows come here?" was Richard's natural question.

"It's very odd," replied Sal. "But don't let them see that face. Go and serve them as if you had never met before."

"What can I do for you, gentlemen?" said Dick, advancing. The last word would stick in his throat, in spite of his efforts to send it out freely.

"We are going to try your drinks, my good man," said Wobbles, patronisingly. "We are friends of the Honourable Morden Crewe, and are staying at the castle. Ahem! Can you show us into a private room fit for gentlemen?"

"The bagatelle room is the only one that is ready, replied Dick. "Walk in there, please."

"And bring us some hot brandy and water, my friend," said Wobbles, adding in a whisper to Conky, "nothing like being civil to them people; they likes soft words from harrystocrats."

"He seems to be more flabbergasted than anything else," said Curler, as they entered the bagatelle room.

"It's our hair," returned Wobbles. "He saw we belong to the hupper classes, and he's overcome with our condescension."

Sal brought in the brandy and water, and as she put it on the table she eyed each man in his turn very keenly.

"Half-a-crown, please," she said, and Wobbles put the money down.

"Would you like to play?" she asked, before leaving. "If so, you will find the balls and cues in this cupboard. The table is new, so mind the cloth. If you cut it you will have to pay for it."

"What a eye that woman 'as got," said Conky—"a reg'lar gimlet."

"It pierced me like a harrow," said Curler.

"I feel as if I had been stabbed," said Pigeon.

Wobbles took a different view of that eye, and gave it credit for softer expression.

"When she looked at me," he said. "I felt a kinder feeling. She's a fine woman, and I think she's got a brute of a husband."

"Wot put that into yer 'ed," added Conky, scornfully.

"Because she looked at me as if she wanted protection," was the reply.

Wobbles was, to speak mildly, a very plain man—a pikestaff was more ornamental than he; but the uglier the man the quicker he is to jump at the conclusion that every woman he meets is in love with him.

Wobbles bore that character.

"You fellows go on with bagatelle," he said, "and I'll go into the bar and have a talk with that uncommon fine woman."

"Mind the husband," said Conky; "he's a big 'un."

"And got a fist like a shoulder of mutton," added Curler.

"Don't you trouble yourselves," said Wobbles, with a wink; "it's not the first affair of the sort I've been mixed up with. In the hold days I was always up to something and was never bowled hout yet. Putting his hat carefully on one side of his head he swaggered into the bar, leaving his companions in a state of admiration.

"I never thought it was in him," said Conky.

"You can't tell," said Curler. "Sometimes a chap like he have got a lot of devil in him."

"Anyhow," said Pigeon, "I hope he won't bring us into it. I wouldn't have a big chap like that about me for twenty pounds."

Sal and Richard Skewball saw Wobbles enter the bar from their little private room behind. Sal read the would-be gallant as plainly as she would the heading of a newspaper. Drawing her husband close, she whispered in his ear—

"Now, Dick, you leave this fellow to me, and don't take notice of anything that you may see. I'll soon let you know why he and that lot are here."

"All right, old gal," said Dick; "but do you think it is any business of ours?"

"I have a strong impression upon me," said Sal, "which makes me think they are somehow mixed up with us—I can't tell you in what way just yet, but I'll let you know all about it in a day or two."

CHAPTER CLX.

THE JACKASS IN LOVE.

WOBBLES saw Skewball and his wife in the bar, and marked with a self-satisfied smile that the latter came out to attend upon him.

"Good morning, sir," said Sal, with a little curtsey, uncommonly taking in its way.

Wobbles pulled his collar up a bit, and not having yet got his conversational powers in full swing, merely replied—

"Charming day, mum."

After this cordial greeting there was a slight pause—Sal Skewball waiting demurely for an order, and Wobbles endeavouring to work up an insinuating gleam into his left eye.

It has been asserted that Wobbles was a plain man, but now he was more so, looking, as he did, intensely ridiculous. Sal, scarcely able to keep her countenance, took out her handkerchief and coughed gently.

"Did you say you wanted a cigar, sir?"

It was about the last thing in the world Wobbles really desired, for after his Brighton experience he had shunned the narcotic weed; but thinking it would look manly and bold to indulge for once, he rashly replied—

"Yes, if you please—one of your best."

Again it may be said that Sal thoroughly knew who she was dealing with, and brought down a box containing some long cigars as thick as your thumb, and almost as black as liquorice.

"These," she said, "are called the gentlemen's regalias. The prince smokes them."

"They look rather dark," said Wobbles.

"That's the nature of the tobacco," returned Sal. "Shall I send you a light into the bagatelle-room?"

"No," said Wobbles, with a leery look, "I am going to smoke it here, and screwing up his courage he came out with a little piece of gallantry which did him much credit. "Chatting here with you is better than bagatelle."

Again Sal had much difficulty in concealing a smile: Turning to her husband, she said—

"Dick, I think you had better go and feed the pigs."

These words made the blood within Wobbles run quicker; he saw that his gallantry was received with favour.

As soon as Dick was gone he asked for a light. Sal brought him one, and as he took the burning paper he secured the tip of her forefinger and gave it a gentle squeeze.

"Oh! go away, you wicked man," said Sal.

But Wobbles did not go away. He only stretched himself up, and lighted his cigar with a swaggering smirk upon his face which only a conceited cad could possibly produce.

"That's the way with you travellers," continued Sal. "Always up to your nonsense!"

"How did you know I was a traveller?" asked Wobbles.

"You have the look of it," was her answer. "I should say you had been all over the world."

"So I have, pretty nigh," said Wobbles; "and I have just come back from a run over to the diamond-fields."

"From the diamond-fields?" said Sal, with an innocent look. "That's the place where they find the bright stones that ladies wear—isn't it?"

"I've been there," said Wobbles, "and picked them up in handfuls."

We will pass over sundry romances Wobbles poured into the ears of his hostess, and let the history of certain little gallantries go bye. Sal did so, with the greatest patience. She let him run on, while he drank two glasses of brandy and water, and then suddenly put a question to him.

"I have a relation of mine there," she said; "at least, I was told he went there. I wonder what's become of him. His name was Brisket. Do you know him?"

"Brisket," said Wobbles, turning white. "I think there was a party of that name about—a pedlar chap."

"Yes, that's him, and no good, I'll warrant," said Sal, shaking her head; "all the respectable part of his family have done with him long ago."

"He was a downright bad un," said Wobbles, much relieved.

"You met him then?"

"Oh, yes, I've seen him lots of times. The best of us get mixed up with a rum lot over there."

"No doubt."

"He was with thieves," said Wobbles, "as was ruled by a party of the name of Broad Arrow Jack."

"What sort of a man was he?" asked Sal, carelessly.

"Well, a biggish sort o' fellow," replied Wobbles, "but a little touched in the 'ed."

Here the affidavits he and his friends had lately taken came into his head, and he added hastily—

"But he's dead now—dead as a tenpenny nail."

Sal had much difficulty in controlling herself now, but she succeeded, and said with as much indifference as she could assume—

"Dead, is he? How did he die?"

"Of fever. Me and my mates—friends, I mean—attended him through it, and buried him. He was more than Broad Arrow Jack, you know."

The brandy and water led up to the admission, and Sal led him further. She saw there was a mystery behind.

"Who was he?" she asked.

"Young Ashleigh, heir to these estates," said Wobbles.

Things were getting clear now, and Sal a little feverish. Taking Wobbles's glass, she filled it without an order, and passed it over to him. The cigar had long been out, although it was not a third smoked, and she did not ask him to have another light.

"Dead!" she said again; "and was he a very fine fellow?"

"Uncommon, as far as muscle went," replied Wobbles, "but wrong in the 'ed. Oh! what a dear creature you are! I never saw such a hye in my life."

"Don't, sir, please—my husband will be here directly, and he is very jealous," said Sal. "He will go on at me after you have left—he will."

"Oh! never mind his going on," said Wobbles, trying to get possession of her hand, without succeeding. "I'll purtect you. I—I adore you!"

"So you think now," returned Sal; "but you will go away and forget me to-morrow."

"Niver—niver!" said Wobbles, fervently. "If I love once I love hever."

"But about this Broad Arrow Jack," said Sal. "I am so fond of stories, and you tell them so prettily. Tell me all about him."

It was the old fable of the fox and the crow with the piece of cheese all over again. Wobbles, being praised for his sweet voice, opened his mouth and dropped the piece of cheese Sal wanted.

"He died," he said, "and we come all this way to take haffurdavys on it, so as to put my friend Crewe into the property. He couldn't get it without us, you know, and that is why we lives with him."

All clear now. Sal read the villainy from end to end, and, although unable to keep her hands off Wobbles without exercising much self-restraint, she managed to talk with him until he got into a state of maudlin drunkenness and began to cry because she was cold and cruel to him.

"Rejected love is a thing as rooins a man," he said. "You've broken my 'art—you have!"

"Come to-morrow," said Sal, sweetly, "and I'll mend it."

"How?"

"Oh! in the usual way."

"With kisses sweet and other cauoollings?" asked Wobbles.

"Wait until to-morrow."

"Can't you give me one now?"

"Oh, no!"

"Just one, hangel as thou hart!"

"You are in too great a hurry," said Sal "Come to-morrow."

CHAPTER CLXI.

THE KING GETS HIS OWN AGAIN

WOBBLES shook his head and feebly smiled at Sal's advice. Brandy and water, with part of a strong cigar, combined with the affection by which he was so suddenly inspired, made a bigger fool of him than he ordinarily was. He would have said something, no doubt; but speech was denied him, and suddenly, without any warning, he disappeared from the gaze of Skewball's wife.

Looking over the counter she saw him seated upon the ground, opening his mouth, and working his head like a wax figure, apparently unconscious that he had taken a seat upon the floor. Retiring to the back she called for her husband, and when Skewball came he bade him rouse the friends of the afflicted Wobbles, and make them aware of his condition.

On being made acquainted with it they left an interesting game of bagatelle, and, raising Wobbles, led him forth. As he left the door in a very limp condition, he muttered "Morrow!" and that day Sal saw him no more.

"Well," said Skewball, when they were gone, "what news?"

"Bad," she said. "Broad Arrow Jack is the real owner of this property, and they have got up a sham death, and put that scoundrel who was here this morning into it."

"It was no sham," said Skewball, sorrowfully. "I have just been reading the paper, and here is a letter from the correspondent in the diamond-fields. Hear what he says."

Dick turned the paper back, and read as follows—

"'The mysterious individual called Broad Arrow Jack, whose exploits caused so much excitement here, died this morning from wounds received in a duel. He is to be buried with much ceremony by the diggers, on whom his undoubted bravery has made a great impression.'

"So you see," said Dick, as he sorrowfully put down the paper, "that our brave young friend is gone and we can do no good by interfering in anything."

"I am not so sure of that," replied Sal. "Newspaper correspondents can be humbugged as well as other people. I mean to keep my eye on these rascals here."

* * * * * *

The terror which inspired the Tiger caused him to keep on straight away for a good five miles before he pulled up; and even, although it was daylight when he stopped, he looked round with the idea of seeing the spirit coming bounding in his rear.

The Tiger would not have been afraid of the spectre but for it having, as he supposed, seized Dick either to murder him or to bear him away to the great unknown world of which the Tiger, in common with many people, both wise and foolish, had an overpowering dread.

But the first stage of his fear over, and finding he was not pursued, the Tiger began to reflect, and reflection soon brought with it a conviction of his having been rather mean in deserting his friend in the time of trouble.

"Perhaps if I stopped," he thought, "Massa Jack not hurt him, for he was allers berry kind to me, and to Dick, too. Perhaps he not hurt him bery much after all."

This thought had a little comfort with it, and also brought a little additional reproach. Perhaps, indeed, Dick was not at all hurt, and if so, the Tiger felt he had behaved most miserably.

"I go a lilly way back and see," he thought.

Not quite divested of his fears, he crept cautiously back, with his eyes restlessly roaming here and there until he came to the spot where he had last looked upon Dick. Here he halted, and went through the process of screwing his courage up before he began the ascent.

He was a long time about it, for a hundred vague fears oppressed him, and as the time of eve was approaching he felt the influence of the terror. Already the sun was behind a distant mountain, and in a few minutes darkness would be there.

The boy had a stout heart and knew nothing of common fear, and little by little, as he slowly made the ascent, he regained his strength and courage.

Arriving on the summit of the barrier he peeped over, and, to his astonishment, beheld Broad Arrow Jack seated in a similar position to that in which he was before, and Dick standing behind him.

"Golly!" exclaimed the Tiger, "what am all dis? Am Dick's ghost dere, or—or," fire flashed from his eyes at the thought, "am *Massa Jack alive*? I go and see if I die for it."

Leaping over the top of the barrier he ran down impetuously, and threw himself at Jack's feet.

"Massa Jack—brave Massa Jack," he cried, "if you am dead don't hurt de poor Tiger, but if alive—"

"Of course I am alive," said Jack, "you foolish boy. What do you take me for—a ghost?"

"Ah! dat it," cried the delighted Tiger, springing to his feet and capering about. "I take you for de ghost ob yourself. Dick dere told me dat you was dead."

"I thought so," said Dick, sullenly.

The arrival of the Tiger was not very agreeable to him, for he foresaw in it certain contingencies which might prove to be anything but agreeable.

"Be quiet, Dick," said Jack. "So, Tiger, you thought I was dead."

"Yes, Massa Jack, replied the Tiger.

"But why did you not come and see for yourself?"

"Because I believe ole Dick. He say you was dead."

"And how is it you have never been near the fields since?"

This the Tiger explained in short chapters, with capers of delight between, which were of a particularly lively nature when he came to speak of the various occasions when he saw Jack in the flesh, believing him to be a spirit.

"And so," said Jack, "you have been living in the wood?"

"Yes, Massa Jack, and me and ole Dick was bery happy until——"

He paused, and looked slightly embarrassed; but the truth was on his lips, and it would come out.

"Until I find out dat Dick hab sumfin dat not belong to him—sumfin dat was yours."

"Oh! forgive me," cried Dick; "it was such a great treasure, and I am only a boy."

"You are forgiven," said Jack, "but you can never be a servant of mine again. Where are my jewels?"

"I don't know, sir," replied Dick—"the Tiger has them."

"Yes, Massa Jack, all safe and sound in a bery snug place. Me go and bring dem to-morrer."

"Stay! is it far from here?"

"It was close to whar we lib," said the Tiger, with twinkling eyes.

"We will march at once," said Jack. "Tiger, call Mr. Brisket; he is in that tent yonder. As for you," he added, turning to Dick, "I have news of your father, who is in England. You shall be sent to him at once."

"I would rather die with you," said Dick, "than live with him."

"Mere idle talk," said Jack.

"Oh! no, indeed, replied Dick; "you don't know what a struggle it was when I took that money— how I felt—how I have thought over it—sometimes through the night. It was so much that I don't think a man could have resisted the temptation, and I only a boy. Let me remain with you while you are here."

Jack looked at him, and saw now that the burden of his sin was removed he was again truthful and honest. It had, indeed, been a great temptation, such as many an older one than Dick might have succumbed to, and if the boy really desired to serve him why should he thrust him aside?

"Dick," he said, "I have trusted you once, and will trust you again. It is enough. I shall never name the subject again."

Dick, in a wild passion of gratitude, threw himself at the feet of his new master, but Jack bade him rise.

"And keep the secret of this from the men around," he said.

"I will," replied Dick; "if I do not—kill me!"

The arrival of Brisket with the Tiger checked his further utterance, and darkness rapidly setting in Jack and Brisket retreated to the tent of the former, when a torch was lighted, and the two sat down to talk.

Brisket was soon enlightened as to all that had passed, and agreed with his chief that it would be better to march at once to the spot where the Tiger had secreted the treasure, and also as to the advisability of its existence being kept secret for the present.

"I can obtain what money I want through the channels I used before," said Jack, "and I will send out scouts all over the country to find the Ogre, and when he is found——"

"We will go and capture him."

"No," replied Jack, "I will go alone. I feel when next we meet the end of one of us will come."

The word was passed, the tents struck, and leaving two men to follow them on two pack-horses, Jack, Brisket, the boys, and the rest of the men, returned in the direction of the spot where the Tiger and Dick had lived for a year or more.

The Tiger was their guide below, and the stars their guide above. With the aid of the two the party reached the wood before the dawn, and with torches of pine entered its dark recesses.

Back to the very spot they went, to Dick's amazement, and into the very hut where they had lived went the Tiger, and from under the bed of leaves where the boys had slept he brought out the long-lost treasure.

"It was just dis, Dick," he said. "I tought you would go a poking bout out ob de place, but, like mose people, neber look under your nose, and dat was whar I hub you."

CHAPTER CLXII.

CLEARING AWAY.

ROOKHOLME was a very handsome, stately mansion, but was peculiarly likely on that account to get dull without society. This Mr. Woody Welsher found out ere his noble head had been two months under its roof.

He had in reality no society after the first week or so.

With Conky, Curler, Pigeon, and Wobbles, he would have nothing to do. They were altogether knaves of another colour—rogues of an inferior caste—and Woody Welsher, like the rest of the world, drew the line somewhere, and he drew it at them.

The Honourable Morden Crewe had grown moody and taciturn, smoking and drinking much alone, and keeping a very painful silence when in company. With Woody Welsher he was growing positively morose.

"I say, Crewe," he said, one morning at breakfast, "can't you cheer up a bit?"

"Why should I cheer up?" asked the other.

"Because it would be better for you and me— better every way," said Woody Welsher. "Let's be jolly as we used to be."

"How am I to be jolly?"

"Why, drink and smoke, and so on."

"I do nothing else from morning till night."

"Eat more, then."

"I eat fairly well."

"Hunt, shoot—do anything."

"Oh! don't bother me," said the Honourable Morden, looking at him viciously. "Go and be hanged!"

"You are uncommon polite this morning," said Woody Welsher. "Got out of bed the wrong way I should think."

"I," said the Honourable Morden, "have not been to bed at all."

Woody Welsher stared at him, as well he might.

"Not been to bed at all!" he repeated.

"No—I have not closed my eyes?"

"What has kept you awake?"

"Thinking."

"And what have you been thinking about?"

"Do you think that *you* could understand my thoughts?" said the Honourable Morden, scornfully.

"I'd try to," said the other, coolly.

"How should you? What know you of my feelings as I sit here *alone?*"

"Oh! come, you are not alone. I'm with you."

"You!" exclaimed the Honourable Morden. "It is not such as you that I want to be sitting there. No; and you need not flush up and look like that, for I'm cursed if I care what I say! I've lost all that in my life is worth living for. I'm burdened, and tied to people that I loathe; and I would to heaven that I had never listened to your voice, but kept as I was—a beggared gentleman."

"Dunned right and left."

"Yes, but not tied to my duns."

"No—they hunted you."

"I know it; but I could fly. Now I am chained."

"Go it!" said Woody Welsher. "Go and blow the whole gaff! *I* don't care—it won't hurt me, and you will get lagged. Did you ever see the inside of a prison?"

"No, but I have no doubt you have."

"Right for once," said Woody Welsher, with a chuckle; "and that is why I'm so mighty particular not to get there again. But look here—as you won't have any company here I will."

"You!"

"Yes, I mean to have a few of my old pals here. There's Cocky Davis would like a change of air and rest. He's been to a mighty lot of meetings this year, and is quite wore out."

"I'll not have those fellows here," said the Honourable Morden.

"You must," said Woody Welsher. "I shall write to them to-night. If you think you are going to stop me you are mistaken. Don't put your back up too high, or I'll pull this house about your ears!"

"Go your own way," said the Honourable Morden, with a sudden calmness, far more awful to look upon than his anger; but Woody Welsher was blind. "I suppose I am helpless."

"Now you speak sensibly," said the other. "Ah! I like a sensible man. Not going? You have eaten no breakfast."

"I have had enough," was the reply.

The Honourable Morden Crewe left the room.

Broad-Arrow Jack.

"YOU ARE IN MY POWER, VILLAIN, SO YIELD TO BROAD ARROW JACK." (See page 94.)

NO. 23.

and passed through the hall. There the butler was standing by the door and opened it for him.

"Benson, keep the letter-bag late to-night," he said—"up to the last minute, as I have something to send."

"Perhaps, sir, it will be better to keep the bag until you speak to me again," said the butler. "If too late here the boy can run across the fields and catch the mail-cart on the common."

"Ah! just so, Benson; perhaps it will be better. Where are the four gentlemen?"

"All out, sir, for the day," replied the butler; "gone on an excursion to the Shipney Rock to see the caverns. Mr. Wobbles is driving."

"What horse has he?"

"The only one fit for the work was Green Dragon."

"That brute! He will kick the trap to pieces."

"He went off kicking, sir," said the butler, with an imperturbable face.

"Well, I hope no harm will come to them," said the Honourable Morden; but as soon as he was outside he said, "May the whole crew be shot over the precipice! If so, there will be only one remaining—but one—and when he is gone I can live down the darkness about me."

"Only one," he said again, as he crossed the common—"only one, and he will come round directly by the Beeches for his usual morning walk, enjoying his cigar as if he were lord of the manor."

The Beeches was a clump of trees on the southern side of the park surrounding the castle—a quiet spot, with no path or high road near. Outside lay a great waste of land, occasionally used by wandering gipsies, but otherwise seldom visited by man, woman, or child.

The Honourable Morden Crewe went to this spot—not direct, but by a circuitous route, taking a wonderful deal of care to avoid meeting with any one. A labourer and a little girl were the only creatures he met, and these he avoided by hiding behind clumps of bushes.

Why all this caution? Why that secrecy during a morning stroll?

Here is the answer—among the bushes was a grave he had dug in the night, and there was murder in his heart!

Yes, it had come to that. He was resolved, at all risks, to murder Woody Welsher and rid himself of that incubus, as he believed, for ever.

He had no thought of how sacred life is—how valuable is the meanest of God's creatures. He had no care for that—all he wanted was to be free of the burden he had made for himself, and he could see only one way to do it.

The grave was dug, and his plans were laid so carefully that he thought detection was impossible. There was to be no noise about it. A blow with a heavy instrument—a body thrust into a grave—earth over it—moss, tufts of grass, and even shrubs over it—all so cunningly planned, and only wanting a clever execution to insure success.

Crouching under a bush, close to the border of the Beeches, he awaited his victim, and presently he came, jauntily smoking a cigar, and revelling over his fancied triumph that morning. The castle was as good as his own he thought—he could have his friends there and do what he pleased.

"After all," he thought, "it will be a jolly life."

And while the thought was with him he received a fearful blow on the side of the head, and staggering, fell to the ground, where, with dimmed eyes, he made out the figure of the Honourable Morden Crewe standing over him, knife in hand.

"Crewe, would you murder me?" he gasped.

"Yes—I'll do it, by ——!" was the reply, and then the man whom he had ruled so long knelt down upon his chest and grasped his throat with a hand of iron.

CHAPTER CLIII.
THE OGRE'S PATH.

BOWED down by the weight of his own iniquities, the Ogre wandered along a sandy plain.

There was little of the old arrogance in his walk, none of the old brutal defiance in his eyes; all the dare-devil spirit which had made him a ruler among his kind had fled, and only by his copper-coloured skin and huge misshapen limbs could he have been recognised by his old associates.

For fourteen days he had been alone.

During that time he had seen the face of no man, and the lagging hours, laden with awful memories of the past, had each and all been long days to him. As he wandered over the plain he felt like a man who had not seen his fellow-men for many—many years.

Loneliness at last had grown unbearable, and he was seeking society again in a place he knew of by name, but where the people were all strange to him, and, as he fondly hoped, he strange to them.

The misery of this brutish man was unbearable, and all the more terrible because it was new to him. No harder nature was ever enclosed in clay. That which we call conscience had been so girded about with the armour of brutal indifference that it had defied the stings of remorse until he spent those fourteen days alone.

But at last he felt them—not as a man who desires to lead a better life, but like one who is galled to find that, having striven to be a scourge to others, he is the greater scourge to himself; that for every wound he had inflicted he had laid up tenfold suffering for himself.

Now was the day and now the hour for him to turn and repent, to throw himself down and—prostrate—confess how vile he was, and seek forgiveness of the merciful God whose laws he had outraged, and whose warnings he had so persistently ignored.

But he would not hearken to or obey the call.

The last chance of saving himself from everlasting perdition he cast aside.

"Among men," he muttered, "I shall soon be myself again. Conscience! Pshaw! It is the monitor of babes and old women, and the guide of cowards."

He was bending his footsteps towards another of those settlements dotted about the country around the diamond-fields, known as Garker's Folly.

At first he intended to go to Taegur-town, which was upon the coast, but he feared that would prove to be too public for a man of his mark, and so he turned his steps to the Folly aforesaid.

Mr. Garker, the founder of the Folly, who built a part of it a little oddly, as we shall soon see, was still alive, and was—or he ought to have been—the leading spirit of the place that bore his name. He it was who farmed all the arable land around, and grazed all the cattle. He it was who fed all comers for a stipulated sum when they had money, and gave a bit and a sup to those who had none, with the understanding they were not to "come sliding that way again or he'd trip 'em up." He it was who gave work to those who would work, and confounded those who would not. All the laws by which the Folly was governed were of his making, and he expounded and carried out the same.

"I'm big enough and strong enough to do so," he would say. "I'm six feet three in my stockings; I can carry an ox upon my shoulders, and I never had a day's illness in my life."

His code of laws was very simple, and when once heard was never forgotten. It was this—

"If you come here and do as I bid you, no great harm will happen; but if you come here with a notion that you can do as you like you will soon be either out of the Folly or out of trouble altogether."

On the whole the Folly was a fearful place—remarkably so when the frequenters of it are con sidered. Mule-drivers, loafers, gamblers, half-castes, and others of a like nature, with a sprinkling of men bent upon doing honest work, generally made up its community; but what with those who moved on themselves and those who were moved on by Garker, the Folly might be looked on as being a moving population.

It was towards this place the Ogre was bending his steps. He was half-famished, in addition to his other well-earned miseries, and although the plain was only a few miles from the place he sought, it seemed to him that it would never be reached.

With faltering steps he pursued his way, pausing now and then to give vent to a deep curse, or to shade his eyes with his hand as he looked ahead for the settlement.

But those eyes of his were dim, and even when the Folly was in sight he could not see it until he was almost at the door of Garker's house.

It is not necessary to analyse the sufferings of the Ogre; indeed, it would be difficult to do so, but his bitterest foe could not have desired to see him more afflicted than he was during that journey across the sandy plain.

When he found himself close to rest at last he broke down, and losing the little remaining strength he had, fell in a heap against the long wooden building which had Garker for its owner.

Night was closing in when the Ogre fell, and darkness was upon the land when he had regained sufficient strength to knock at the door. There was a noisy party of gentlemen inside playing euchre, and the knock was unheard.

Summoning all the energy he could command, the Ogre got slowly upon his feet, raised the latch, and walked in.

There was no intermediate hall, and he went straight into the kitchen of the establishment.

A girl was cooking something over the fire in a frying-pan, and hearing the noise she turned her eyes upon the repulsive figure of the Ogre, made ten times more repulsive than usual by his recent sojourn in the wilderness.

First giving vent to a scream she ran from the room, and the Ogre, with wolfish eyes, bore down upon the frying-pan, from which he took the food, burning hot as it was, and crammed it into his mouth.

It was a delectable dish of eggs and bits of bacon and potatoes, relishable to any hungry man, but a rich and splendid feast to the starving Ogre.

He was in the midst of it when Garker came in with the servant-girl trembling behind him. Being a man of action rather than words he first knocked the Ogre down and then asked him what he was doing there.

The Ogre, on whom the food had acted like a reviving charm, clambered up from the ashes on the hearth into which he had been sent, and put a hand upon his knife. Mr. Garker drew a revolver and covered him.

"Put up that darning needle," he said. "At three I fire. One, two——"

"I was starving—dying!" grunted the Ogre, as he left hold of his knife.

"So you might have been, and you look like it," said Garker. "But still it is more polite to ax a man's leave before you eat his supper."

"So it is," returned the Ogre; "but I was mad. I have had no food to speak of for days. I can pay for what I've had."

"That's a good afterthought," said Garker. "A couple of dollars will put it square."

The Ogre paid him and found he had but another dollar left.

When leaving the Phryne he had not anticipated the events which followed, and was on that account unprepared to meet any heavy expenses.

"It's almost all I've got," he said. "I've heard of you before. Can you give me work?"

"Will you work?" asked Garker.

"Yes, to-morrow; but I must rest to-night."

"I put the question," said Garker, "because I've had lots of chaps here who seem to think that lying on their backs and smoking is hard labour. I've got a lot of digging on hand, and if you do your share I'll pay you well."

"I'll do it," said the Ogre.

"It's a lonely bit o' work," said Garker.

"The lonelier the better—in the daytime. Can I sleep here at night?"

"Yes; there's an empty loft overhead. The wages is seven dollars a week, and food and drink found —food unlimited—drink limited to half a pint of whiskey a day. You can buy more if you like. What's your name?"

The Ogre was not prepared for the question, but he answered promptly—

"Grey."

"What are you?"

"Seaman."

"What ship?"

"Late—of—of—the Phryne. She's gone down, and I was wrecked in the bay yonder."

"All right," said Garker, satisfied. "Go to bed when you like, and get to your work in the morning."

"Can I have some drink now?" asked the Ogre.

"Yes, if you pay for it."

"Here's my last dollar then," said the Ogre, with a growl; "can't you trust a man with anything?"

"Not a man of your stamp," replied Garker, coolly; "I should be an ass if I did. I should say that of all men on airth you are least to be trusted."

"Candid, at any rate," growled the Ogre.

"I generally am," was the calm reply.

The Ogre swallowed the bitterness he felt as best he could. It was neither the time nor the season, nor was he in a condition to quarrel with any one, but he smarted terribly under the blow and contemptuous treatment he received.

Having had his drink, he ascended the steps leading to the loft, and gladly threw himself down upon the loose straw he found there, but he lay long before he closed his eyes, and when sleep came at last it seemed to him he had slept but a moment when he heard the voice of Garker calling him up.

"Now, lazy bones, you won't kill yourself with work. Get up and come along."

He arose and descended to the kitchen, where Garker was waiting for him, and together they went out, Garker carrying a small basket in his hand, which he presently gave to the Ogre, saying it was his food and drink for the day.

The portion of arable land which the Ogre was required to dig lay near a piece of wooded ground, part of which had been recently cleared. The digging was of the roughest character, and would have tried an English gardener very considerably with its hard clay and gnarled roots running in every direction.

It was just the sort of land the ordinary emigrant encounters when he leaves the comforts of old England to prepare a virgin soil for those who will come after him.

Garker measured out a piece of ground—a very fair day's work for the Ogre—and told him he could go back to the house when it was done, or at least not to show himself before sundown. The Ogre said he would do it, and was left to his labour.

The recuperative power of this man was most marvellous. Food and a night's rest seemed to have wholly restored him to his former vigour.

Having made a morning meal from his basket he began to dig as a man who desires distraction from his thoughts would dig, turning up the heavy soil with the strong spade as if it had been sand, like the plain lying in the horizon.

Apparently insensible to fatigue, he kept on for an hour before pausing, halting only now and then for a few seconds to clean the implement with a piece of stick. Then he rested, and filling a clay pipe which, with some coarse tobacco, was in the basket, he sat down for a smoke.

As the blue cloud rose up in the still morning air he began to think, first of all of the present and then of the past. Returning strength had brought with it his hardness of heart; conscience was asleep again, and charging, as he had always done, all his late misfortunes to Broad Arrow Jack, he cursed him loud and deep.

"All was well with me," he muttered, "until I met the Ashleighs. I had comforts, luxuries, and fools unnumbered to gull and live upon, and what am I now? Where could I be if *he* was dead?"

The rustle, it was no more, of a few leaves in the bush behind him drew his attention in that direction, but he could see nothing. Whatever had been moving there was still again.

"Some bird or hare," he thought, "and yet the sound seemed to be of ominous import to me. Bah! I have been a child of late. Let me be a man again."

He knocked out the ashes of his pipe, and went to his work again. He was resolved to do it to please his employer, with whom it suited his purpose to live for awhile. As he thrust the spade into the earth a light figure crept from the bushes and darted into the wood.

It was the Tiger, and as he bounded along he chanted or sung—

"Good news for Massa Jack—good news! Me am de chile to take it to him. Good news for Massa Jack!"

CHAPTER CLXIV.
UP A TREE!

"HOW many scouts have returned this morning, Brisket?"

"Eleven, chief."

"And no news of him?"

"None. They have gone straight out and home, some alone, others meeting people by the way, and they bring nothing concerning him."

"Do you think, Brisket, he can have got out of the country again?"

Brisket shook his head.

"Impossible," he said; "we have stopped every road that way. Here comes the twelfth—Grip."

Grip came in, and it was easy to see by his face that he had no news worth hearing. But he told his story.

He had taken the river with the canoe, as he called a rough boat Jack had bought of a settler for his use, and, in company with another man, had gone up many miles without making any discovery worth recording. Only one adventure worth mentioning had befallen him.

On the second day he saw something moving among the reeds on the banks, which looked like the bent back of a man skulking, and at once he went ashore, to find himself close to a brown bear, who came at him, bent upon mischief.

Taken by surprise he fired and missed. The bear came on steadily, and he made for a tree, fortunately clambering up to a place of temporary security before Bruin could put the hug on. He was never more up a tree in all his life, for the brute, cunningly sheltering itself from the fire of the other man in the canoe, slowly commenced the ascent, and Grip, having left his flask of powder in the boat, had nothing but an empty musket for a weapon.

"And I never guessed," he said, "how hard the skull of any critter could be until I let into that brute's head. I hammered and hammered at him as he came up, but I might just as well have tapped the paving stones of New York with a toothpick and tried to crack 'em, as to split the bone of that skull. If Rowland, who was with me, hadn't come up, and given him a couple of shots behind, I should have been fixed up that tree. But we've brought him home, and bear rashers aint bad. When I've had one I shall be ready to start again to the Himalayas if you like."

"Come in an hour," said Jack.

Grip saluted and retired to enjoy his rasher, and Brisket took up a position at the mouth by the tent to watch for the coming of others. There was a silence of some minutes before he spoke again.

"Scout number thirteen," he said, at last.

"Who is it, Brisket?"

"The Tiger."

"Ah! if he fails me I verily believe I shall despair."

"Don't do that. Men like the Ogre cannot escape for ever."

The Tiger had good news, as we know, and both Jack and Brisket saw it in his face before he spoke.

"Where is he?" asked Jack.

"Ober dere," replied the Tiger, "across de plain, near big house wif a fox on de top."

"He means a weather-cock," explained Brisket. "I know the place. It is called Garker's Folly. I can guide you there."

"I want no guide, thanks, old friend," said Jack, rising. "Give me the distance and the direction, and it will be better for me to go alone."

"Better have somebody with you."

"No, he is but one, and I one. And what would I care if he were ten? At last I am convinced we shall stand face to face."

"It is a good two days' journey from here," said Brisket.

"Then I will do it in one. Give me a handful of food and I will begone."

In vain Brisket urged him to have a companion. He would not hearken. Strapping a small wallet, containing a supply of food, he set forth, leaving strict injunctions that nobody should follow him.

"Not even you," he said to the Tiger. "All here must await for my return."

"And when will that be?" thought Brisket, as he watched his retreating figure. "What heaviness is this that lies upon my heart? Can it be that we have parted now for ever?"

And as the thought came the figure of Jack was suddenly lost to him, for his eyes were filled with tears.

CHAPTER CLXV.
AT LAST.

IT was the third morning of the Ogre at Garker's Folly, and he was digging as he had done before, like a man who has something in him to be worked off.

The sun had been up about two hours, and shone undimmed by a cloud.

To ordinary men that morning would have brought joy and gladness—to the Ogre it gave naught but dark despair.

The feeling was upon him, growing deeper each moment—that great terror which he had experienced after the awful death he had inflicted upon the mate of the Phryne was again advancing, and he knew he could not ward it off.

Ordinary fear of death was as nothing to this growing dread.

He had, as it were, against his will, taken the name of the mate when asked who he was, and through his fears he began to see something ominous in having done so.

The apprehension of coming vengeance drove him almost mad.

And so he dug and dug, tossing the soil aside like water, until the perspiration rolled down his face in big drops, and fell to the ground like rain. Fatigue was upon him, but he dared not halt, for he felt if he did so the dark mysterious terror would come with all its force.

At last he could toil no more, and sank down panting upon his knees. Involuntarily, as it seemed, he looked up then and saw before him—Broad Arrow Jack.

Fear of the most deadly nature bound him to the very earth, and he lay crouching, with his eyes fixed on the noble form of his foe, unable to move.

How easily Jack could have killed him then!

But no! To one and all of his dastard tormentors he had given a chance of life, had met them all as man to man, and conquered them in fair fight.

Should he do less for the Ogre?

No. And yet not for the Ogre's sake, but for his own. He would not for worlds have had the after reproach of having slain him—brute as he was—while he lay helpless and in his power.

"Ogre!" he said, "we meet at last. I have you now, and what or who can save you?"

The Ogre spoke not. The horrible terror was upon him in its full force, and lying there he died many deaths in a few seconds.

"To the others, your accomplices," pursued Jack, "I have given the choice of weapons, but that I must refuse you. See here—I have two stilettoes, which I have carried with me for many a year. This one you know—you have grasped it before. Villain! it was with this you took the life of my noble mother!"

He held up the blade, and the glittering reflection it drew from the sun lighted up the face of the young hero. The Ogre saw that light, marked and knew the weapon, and in one brief moment mentally beheld again the murder he had committed.

"This is mine," said Jack, "and I will use it now. What!—cowed?—the valiant Ogre with less courage than a rat! Come—will you disappoint me? Am I to find that while I supposed I was chasing a wolf I was on the trail of a skunk?"

But the Ogre only lay and stared, quivering in every limb.

"There have been times," said Jack, seizing him by the collar of his shirt and dragging him to his feet as if he had been a child, "when I have felt half inclined to forego my own vengeance, but that was long ago. Gleams of earnest repentance might have turned me aside; but what remorse have you ever shown?"

It was the Ogre's voice that spoke, but he seemed to have no share in the answer—

"None!"

"Truth from your lips," said Jack, grimly, "is something new, but I am glad you have found your tongue at last. Up, man!—here is your weapon, but first let me take those you have. We must have fair play to-day."

He took away the Ogre's knife and pistols without resistance, and cast them far away into the brushwood, then thrust the second poniard into his grasp.

The Ogre held the weapon, but never moved.

"Dastard!" cried Jack, and struck him openhanded upon the face.

The blow aroused him from his trance of terror, and with a growl he sprang back a pace and took up an attitude of defence.

"That is better," said Jack, with gleaming eyes; "defend yourself, Ogre, for I will have no mercy now."

"What in the name of my grandmother's tom-cat is all this about?" broke in the voice of Garker, as the giant—who had advanced unperceived—strode forward. "Fair play—whatever it is."

"Don't put yourself between us," said Jack, in tones that rang clarion-like on the morning air, "or this moment shall be your last!"

CHAPTER CLXVI.

THE CHOICE OF A PLACE.

GARKER pulled up without scarcely knowing why, and looked keenly at the singular form before him; but one glance up and down the noble form threw light upon the young stranger. He had heard of him from men who once had sojourned at the Folly and knew him.

"Ah!" he said, "you are the young fellow called Broad Arrow Jack—but what are you doing here?"

"As you know me," replied Jack, "perhaps you know him. That is the Ogre."

"Darn me if I didn't think I ought to know him," said Garker, smiting his huge thigh with his hand.

"Well, now there is a treat in store for me. So you two have come together. Fight it out lads and I'll see fair."

"I cannot fight here," said the Ogre, hoarsely. "I have no chance with him. I have been ill, and he is strong and well."

"Rest an hour," said Jack, "and choose your place so that it be easy of access."

The Ogre did not answer for a moment—he was thinking. Suddenly a flash passed over his face and turning to Garker he said—

"In the centre of the Folly you have a room where no ray of light can come."

"It's as dark as the devil's house," replied Garker, "and that is why my house is called the Folly. I built that ere room without thinking of the windows, and rather than anybody should get the laugh of me I keep it still, and give out that I keep my money bags there. Ha, ha, ha! More than one beggar has tried the door."

"Enough of the history of your room," said the Ogre, impatiently. "If that boy is not afraid of the dark *I'll fight him there!*"

He had put on some of his former bravado, but it was not like the courage of old. He was afraid of his young adversary and Jack knew it; and he was fool enough to fancy that Jack would fear to meet him and fight him, as it were, blindfold, and Jack knew that also.

"Let it be there," he said, "and at once."

"I must have a little drink first," said the Ogre, "for I have been hard at work this morning."

"And I," said Jack, "have walked all the night and need none. Give him none; I deny him the gift of a sodden brain. He shall die with a clear head, so that he may know and fully feel the terror of the time."

"It's a bitter disappointment to have you fighting it out in that way," said Garker, "for I should like to see you have your little kick-up. There's also some brave lads at my house who would enjoy it—but it's not for me to dictate. The room is yours, only I must have two dollars an hour for this sort of work, and if you give me three I'll undertake to bury the party as—as—won't survive It may seem mean of me to make a charge, but the Folly cost me a pile of money and labour, and I live by it."

"Here is all and more than you ask," said Jack, emptying one of his pockets of a number of crisp bank notes. "Let us get back now. I trust to you to see fair play."

"I'll settle everything," said the delighted Garker. "Ah! you are a prince, indeed, and I should like to see you have, at the price, a fighting job on ever day at my house for a month."

Jack, a little impatiently, waved his hand for him to lead the way, and drew up to the Ogre's side.

"Ogre," he said, "we will walk together, but do not waste your time in idle tricks, as they are sure to fail."

It was not the intention of the Ogre to try any. His one last hope now was the darkness of the room, by the aid of which he hoped to slay his adversary. He had the **gift of** nocturnal creatures, and if he could not see in absolute darkness, his eyes were capable of penetrating a deep gloom.

"What men call darkness is seldom so to me," he thought; "let me be wary and the victory is mine."

Nothing more was said on the way back to the Folly. Garker walked at a smart pace, and the two bitter foes came on together behind him, each with his weapon in his hand. They entered the house by the back door, and Garker asked them to wait in the kitchen, which was empty, while he fetched the key of the dark room.

"That's the door," he said, pointing to one near the fireplace, "a strong un, I'll promise you, for I built the house well, and made no mistake in it 'cept that room. It was a stupid thing to do, but I never thought of the windows until the place was finished.

"Sit down and make yourselves comfortable. Sure you won't have anything to drink?"

"Nothing for me or him," said Jack. "I will have no Dutch courage at this hour. As we are by nature, brave or cowardly, we will meet."

The Ogre licked his coarse lips, and glared about him, but made no demur to what Jack said, and yet how gladly would he have drowned his fears and sinking heart with some of the fiery liquid which cowards in their terrors fly to.

He would no more have disputed a word Jack spoke at that time than a slave would the word of his master.

Garker did not absent himself very long, and on bringing the key he was found to be accompanied by some half-dozen friends, who appeared to have been making merry over night, and to be suffering in the morning, as merry-makers are wont to do. They were all big muscular men, accustomed to hardship and peril, but they were quiet enough when they came into the presence of Broad Arrow Jack, contenting themselves by commenting in whispers on his appearance in very complimentary terms.

He, on his part, did not appear to be aware of their presence, but remained quiet with his eyes fixed upon the Ogre, until Garker unlocked and threw open the door, disclosing a bare gloomy apartment, with rough walls, and ceiling coarsely plastered.

"That's the place, gentlemen," he said, "and it's yours for the time. If," he added, with a grin, "you are more than an hour, I ought to charge overtime."

"Go," said Jack to the Ogre, "and cross to the far end. The moment I enter," he added, addressing Garker, close the door, and keep it so until you hear my voice."

"You make sure of victory, my young friend," said Garker.

"I *am* sure," replied Jack.

The Ogre, after a moment's hesitation, entered and crossed to the far end, as he was bidden. Jack waited one moment, and the door closed, leaving the two deadly foes together in the darkness.

CHAPTER CLXVII.

THE DUEL IN THE DARK.

AS soon as they were left alone the two enemies prepared for the fight, which both knew would be of the most desperate character. But each went to work in his own way, the Ogre stealthily removing his shoes and shifting his position, while Jack merely bound an arm, and stooped slightly, so as to be able to catch the slightest sound.

The darkness was intense. Every crevice appeared to have been filled up, and as a piece of workmanship the apartment was highly creditable. The Ogre, who had eyes that could penetrate the ordinary gloom of night to a considerable distance, found himself in a very unexpected position.

He could see nothing.

A darkness that might be felt was around, and he was deprived of the advantage he hoped to have had over his mortal foe.

Jack relied principally upon his hearing, which was very keen, and now and then, as the Ogre moved stealthily about, he heard a slight sound, but the darkness deceived him, and had a peculiar effect upon his hearing. He could not tell for certain whence the sound proceeded.

Time, as usual in such cases, lagged dreadfully, and a half minute to the unnerved Ogre seemed an hour. The stillness was unbroken; the men outside were all as quiet as mice, so that they might lose no indications of the struggle.

Jack had ever been generous, even to his foes. At any risk or sacrifice he scorned to take advantage of them. Perhaps he gave them more latitude than men of their stamp deserved, but it is always better to err on the side of generosity in both public and private warfare.

He broke the silence at last. The monotonous waiting did not please his fiery nature, and he wanted the struggle to begin and end.

"I am here, Ogre," he said. "Advance—I will not move."

The Ogre did not reply, but making a calculation of the spot where Jack stood, crept towards him.

His calculation, like most of a like nature made in the dark, was erroneous, and he crept past him a yard to the left. The wall was a little beyond, and mistaking it at the first touch, he struck his stiletto deep into the wood.

Jack sprang upon him, and seized him by the neck behind. A horrible yell burst from the Ogre's lips.

"You are a coward!" he shrieked. "I am unarmed."

"Where is your weapon?" asked Jack.

"In this accursed timber," replied the Ogre.

Jack cast the Ogre from him, and sent him staggering to the other end of the room. Then he felt for the stiletto, found and released it, and cast it towards his enemy.

"Pick up your weapon," he said, "and meet me like a man."

It had fallen clattering near the Ogre's feet, and a little groping about restored it to him. Laughing in his sleeve, as much as he could laugh at the time, he began to creep forward towards Jack.

And Jack was advancing too in a direct line towards him.

Suddenly and unexpectedly they met, and both dealt out a deadly thrust. Jack felt the cold steel graze his side, and the Ogre, with his arm ripped open, staggered back with a shriek of pain.

The duel began in earnest now. Jack pressed upon his foe, and endeavoured to seize the Ogre in his grasp. He just touched his skin, but the agile villain slipped from him and fled.

All silence was at an end now. The Ogre reached the wall, and guiding himself by it with his hand, hastened round and round the room, while Jack using a similar guide followed close upon his heels.

A stern chase, they say, is a long chase, and so Jack found it. Quite a dozen times he went round and round the room, and seemed to be no nearer to his enemy.

Despair lent the Ogre additional strength and swiftness, and he could have kept on his retreat for an hour but for a ruse on the part of Broad Arrow Jack.

Swinging round suddenly, and advancing in the opposite direction as silently as a shadow, Jack came up with the Ogre, and the pair met with a violent shock. Each again struck, but a ready instinct enabled each to seize the arm of the other in his left hand and so to ward off the blow.

No mercy now—no more generous yielding, but a duel to the death. With every nerve strained to break down the guard of the other, the pair went struggling over the room.

Both endowed with immense muscular power—one animated by the thirst to avenge, the other stimulated by despair—the fight was as desperate as ever took place between two mortal beings.

The force and intensity of it were felt outside, although no word was spoken by the combatants and those shut out from the scene grew bloodthirsty and hoarsely called upon Garker to open the door.

"It's the biggest fight going," they cried. "Why can't we see it?"

"No," replied Garker. "I've promised not to. Besides, I don't want to get the temper of that youngster up. He might turn on me."

"Are you afraid of him?" asked one, derisively.

"Yes," replied Garker, candidly, "and so are you, I guess. Silence now. One of 'em is down."

It was Jack who had fallen, his foot having slipped, and the Ogre uttered a yell of triumph. But the cry was premature, for Jack turned him over and gained the uppermost position, both still holding the right arm of the other.

"Ogre," said Jack. "I have you now. If you have a prayer to offer, say it quick."

"Mercy!" gasped the Ogre, as he felt his left arm being slowly bent down.

His right held firm by Jack was stretched out upon the floor. He was helpless and felt all was over.

"Mercy, mercy!" he cried, "let me live."

"What mercy did you show to my innocent mother—to my noble father—or my poor brother Cecil?"

A thousand fires danced in the eyes of the Ogre. His blood bubbled and boiled in his veins one moment, giving way next to a chill of fear. At last the awful terror which had visited him twice before came upon him.

Still he held on, and Jack could only bring down his stiletto inch by inch. All the worse for the Ogre. A victim of the Inquisition, lying beneath the awful pendulum knife, which came down a hair's breadth every time it swung, slowly but surely hacking its victim to pieces, suffered not so much as he.

The stiletto he could not see, but he knew it was descending. And yet it was not the pain of the wound he dreaded, but the awful thought that his end was near.

Why has the scoffer this dread of death?

Why should the man who has lived all his days in hellish infamy, knowing he must sooner or later yield up his breath, have such an overwhelming horror of the great change from this existence to another?

Reader, the answer is in yourselves.

There lay a monster, hardened in sin, steeled to remorse, pitiless towards others, full of a dark and fearful dread, now that he felt his time had come. Death with eternal oblivion might have been welcome to him, but death with the knowledge of a terrible future opening out to him was inconceivably horrible.

He could not express his agony in words, but he moaned for mercy. Jack, with his blood on fire with his wrongs, gave him none.

Slowly he bore down the Ogre's arm until the point of the stiletto touched his breast. A shriek of horror escaped the Ogre's lips, and Jack struck home.

Once—twice—and his foe lay still.

Rising, there came upon him the reaction which often follows great efforts, and staggering forward he sank upon his knees.

"Open the door," he cried.

Garker willingly obeyed, and the men outside came in with eager looks upon their faces. A flood of light filled the room.

"Stand clear," cried Garker; "let's have a look at them. Ah! I knew who would be victor. You are wounded and bleeding freely, young sir."

Of this Jack took no notice, but merely asked—

"Is he dead?"

Garker, again asking his friends to stand aside, knelt down and examined the Ogre.

"He will never trouble you or any one else again," he said.

On hearing this Jack got upon his feet, and went without another word.

After he was gone there was a silence among the men, who stood near the outstretched form of the Ogre. It was broken by Garker.

"He was a bad un," he said. "But did you ever see such muscles? An ox might be proud of 'em."

"But t'other was strongest," said one of the men "or he couldn't have got him under."

"That young chap is a living wonder," returned Garker, "strong as a lion and as handsome as paint. But what shall we do with this chap? He must be buried of course, as I contracted for it, but I want my revenge of Modler. He aint a-going to clear me out at euchre if I knows it."

"Put him in the woodhouse, and bury him to-morrow," suggested Modler—"a man with gambler printed by nature all over him."

"It's good enough for him," said Garker.

So they put the Ogre in the woodhouse and went back to their cards, and played euchre all day, until Garker had obtained his revenge of Modler by clearing him out, and leaving him without a "darned cent;" and so pleased was Garker with his success that he stood drinks all round, and gave a start towards a merry evening.

There are few examples more readily followed than that of standing drink. Once it is begun it becomes infectious, and too often ends in fuddled heads, disordered livers, and a general quarrel.

Thus it was at the Folly on this occasion. The example of Garker was followed until it came to his turn again; and, led away by a feeling of generosity, he opened the ball afresh, and at it they went again, and very merry they all were until Modler, who had been dwelling upon his losses, suddenly dealt Garker a blow between the eyes.

It was a rash act, but Garker took it kindly. He did not absolutely kill Modler, but he pommelled him until he was as soft as a bag of feathers, and then kicked him out of doors with the usual hint not to come there again.

Modler went his way, and in the course of a night of wandering over a lonely country had an opportunity for reflecting over the folly of euchre and the miseries of being homeless and penniless. Whether he benefited by such reflection, or whether he indulged in it at all, does not matter much, as here he falls out of our story as quickly as he came into it.

But at the Folly they made a night of it, and as morning approached it was suggested by somebody that they should bury the Ogre. It would have been a good suggestion if they had not all been so very drunk, but drunk or sober they resolved upon doing it.

In a body they went to the woodhouse, and tumbled through the door in a heap. Garker, who was foremost, became sober in an instant, not from anything he saw, but from what he could not see.

The body of the Ogre was gone.

CHAPTER CLXVIII.

HAUNTED.

"SAL," said Richard Skewball, "what do you think of our squire?"

"Bad," replied Sal—"bad as bad can be."

"But don't he seem changed to you since we first saw him?"

"He seems to me," said Sal, "to be like a man *who is haunted.*"

"That's it," cried Skewball, smiting his thigh. "You have got a head to be sure. There never was such a woman. I couldn't make the look out at all, but now it's as plain as a pike-staff."

"I should fancy he is the most miserable of men," said Sal.

"I used to think that he missed his friend," said Skewball, after a moment's thought, "that flashy betting chap, who took himself off so sudden; but they never were real friends—didn't seem to agree a bit—did they?"

"There never was the least friendship between them," said Sal.

"You are a woman," exclaimed Skewball, admiringly—"see and know everything at a glance. But about the squire. Matthew, the keeper, told me he thinks he is going off his head. The Beech Copse is to be enclosed to keep off intruders, and yet nobody goes there once in a twelvemonth. People hereabouts says it's haunted."

"So the squire is going to enclose it?"

"Yes."

"He's got a reason for *that*, I'll warrant," said Sal.

"Of course he has—to keep people out of it."

"More than that, Richard."

"If you say he has of course he has, but I don't see it."

"Did you ever see anything, Richard?" asked Sal, with a smile.

"Never," replied Skewball, good-humouredly, "except you, and I've always got an eye for you."

"And so has this gentleman just coming into the bar," said Sal.

Skewball took a peep through the blinds of the little parlour, and saw Wobbles, gorgeously arrayed in a suit of clothes which Sal recognised as having been once worn by Woody Welsher. He also carried an ivory-topped cane, which had likewise been the property of that gentleman.

"I think I'll go to him," said Skewball.

"Do. Say I'm out if he asks for me."

Sal, with a laughing nod, slipped out of the side door leading to the kitchen, and Skewball went into the bar and gave Wobbles a good morning.

"How-de-do," returned Wobbles, with his most lofty air. "I hope Mrs. Skewball is quite well."

"Middlin'!" replied Skewball. "Her body's all right, but she's a little troubled in her mind about something."

"Nateral," thought Wobbles. "Tied to a person she cannot and will niver love. Give me—ah! a little bre-andy cold," he said aloud, "and a cigar."

Skewball helped him, and as Wobbles was lighting his weed he said—

"So Mrs. Skewball's out?"

"Yes," said her husband, "and much obliged she will be to you for your anxious inquiries when I tell her of 'em."

"Of that," thought Wobbles, "there can be no doubt. Oh! woman—lovely woman—that twineth like—like—scarlet runners round the 'art."

"Any news of Mr. Welsher since he left?" asked Skewball, after a silence.

"No," replied Wobbles. "I put the same question to my friend, Crewe, this morning, and he threw a ham at me—in a playful way, of course—but still it hit me. He's allus up to some lark or other with me."

"I was told that he had a good joke with you t'other day."

"What's that?"

"Kicked you downstairs."

"Hangels and minsters of grease defend us!" exclaimed Wobbles. "What his people has the hinsurance to speak about! That story come about this way. Says Crewe to me, 'I've got very strong legs and can kick a man downstairs.' Says I to Crewe, 'I'm a man, and I'll bet you don't kick me.' 'Done,' says Crewe to me. 'For a fiver,' says I to Crewe. 'That's the sum,' says Crewe to me. So we went upstairs, and he gave me one which only landed me 'arf way, and so I won my bet. What liars there are about to be sure."

"How are all your friends?" asked Skewball—not that he cared to know, but to change the conversation.

"Not wery well," replied Wobbles, "for to tell the truth we have a hanxious time of it at the castle, specially at nights. It is such a place for noises and rum sights."

"There's been some queer things done there," said Skewball, shaking his head sadly, "not to my knowlege, for I'm a stranger there; but Matthew, the keeper, was telling me all about it."

"Oh! he was—and what did he say?" asked Wobbles, turning a little pale, but that might have arisen from the cigar, as he was not a very practised smoker.

"Have you ever seen the woman without a head?" asked Skewball.

"Is there sich a thing?" said Wobbles.

"Yes," replied Skewball, solemnly; "she comes out about midnight and marches about with her head on a sort of silver tray. They say it's the sperrit of one of the wives of one of the owners of the castle. He was a wicked old man and cut off her head as she lay asleep."

"And she walks about, you say?" asked Wobbles, with affected indifference.

"She doth," answered Skewball, "and sometimes puts the head on to the foot of people's beds, and walks about without it. They say she used to do that to her husband every night."

"I think I'll have a little more brandy," said Wobbles, hurriedly. "It's like these country people —so superstitious."

"Matthew aint, for he don't mind the ghosts a bit," said Skewball; "he have seen too much of 'em."

"It's an awful place," returned Wobbles, "and I'm only staying there for a time to oblige Crewe, but I'll get away as soon as I can."

"And yet I hear you've got your horses down."

"Yes, me and my mates clubbed—that is, we sent the money for 'em. Good hosses—plenty of sperrit, if they don't look up to much. We think of going out with the 'ounds next week, me and Squire Conky."

"Hope you will enjoy yourself," returned Skewball. "This is a good bit of country, with stiff fencing, but horses like yours will make nothing of it."

"I shan't spile my hosses at the fences," said Wobbles, "but keep 'em on the roads. Conky's delicate, too, and it won't do for him to over-ride hisself."

"I should think not," returned Skewball.

Their conversation was interrupted by a shouting at the door, and Skewball on going round saw the Honourable Morden Crewe on horseback.

He looked pale and haggard, and his dress was very much neglected—a thing unusual in him, as he was invariably very neat.

"Give me some brandy, Skewball," he said, "a stiffish glass."

"Any water in it, sir?"

"None. I want it neat. I am not very well this morning."

Skewball went in, and half filled a tumbler with brandy from a bottle he had in a cupboard. The public taps would not do for the squire, he knew.

The Honourable Morden Crewe tossed it off at a draught, and gave him a shilling. He was about to ride off when he caught a glimpse of Wobbles cautiously peeping round the corner.

"Who's that?" he asked, with a frown.

"Only me," replied Wobbles, coming jauntily forward. "I thought I would come out and have a breath of fresh hair."

"And gossip about what doesn't concern you," said the Honourable Morden. "I know you—an old woman every inch of you. Get away to the castle and keep there."

Worms will turn when trodden on, and the meanest of men have a great objection to being spoken to like a dog. Wobbles was mean, but he was also to a certain extent independent, and he resented the order.

"I shall go home," he said, "just when I like— so you shut up!"

It was a daring speech for him; but Wobbles had been drinking brandy and smoking, and moreover, just at that moment Mrs. Skewball, with her bonnet on, came out of the stable-yard, and advanced towards the door. Before her Wobbles felt he must assert his authority.

Mrs. Skewball glanced keenly at the Honourable Morden as she passed, dropping him a curtsey. He did not heed her, being blind with passion at the reply he received.

"You miserable cur," he said, "get home!"

"You—be jiggered!" replied Wobbles, folding his arms and leaning against the door-post. "Say another word to me, and I'll ruin you!"

The Honourable Morden sprang off his horse, and before Wobbles could guess what was coming he felt a hand upon his throat, and his head knocked against the wall.

The effect of this blow was that he saw Skewball, his wife, and the house in the air, and the sign-board, multiplied by eleven, waltzing about anyhow. But all was not yet over. He was shaken until he was in a state of confusion impossible to describe, then kicked into the road, where he spun about like a humming-top until he came to a heap of mud newly scraped from the road, and in the middle of that he came to an anchor.

"What are the wild waves a-saying?" he asked, wildly. "Kiss me, darling, for your mother! Who dat knocking at de door? Man the lifeboat! Who did it? What is it? Where am I?"

He asked these questions with the air of one whose wits are scattered, tossing his arms recklessly about. The Honourable Morden, who had followed him up, replied with another kick.

"You ruin me!" he cried, "you low-bred pot-house sot! Get up and go to the castle—do you hear?"

Wobbles came round more quickly than might have been expected, and, with his usual acumen, realised the situation. Rising from his soft but uncomfortable seat, he tried to assume a waggish look.

"So like you!" he said—"so 'asty! Hitting a chap for a joke, and chucking him down for nothing. Go home! In course I will, for I am ever happy in them lordly bow-wowers. Oh!"

It was the whip this time that made him skip as it was laid across his shoulders.

"Get home," was the order, firmly repeated, "or I'll ride over you!"

Wobbles went home at a round trot, exhibiting to all who passed by a very muddy condition of attire behind. Allowing for what dropped on the road, he must have started with ten pounds about him, as he arrived at the castle with five. The Honourable Morden rode a short distance behind, cursing him every step he took.

Wobbles could have borne all that and more if Sal Skewball had not been a witness of it, but her presence added a sting which was more bitter than his humiliation.

He made straight for his bedroom, where he found Conky, Curler, and Pigeon doing what they were pleased to call washing themselves—that is, they were each and all damping the nobby part of their countenances, and rubbing them gently with a towel.

"Good gracious!" exclaimed Curler. "What's the matter?"

"Don't ask me till I've got my breath," replied Wobbles, sitting down on Conkey's bed. "Me and Crewe have had sich a kick-up. I don't know whether he's dead or alive!"

"Here, come out of that," said Conky, catching sight of a lovely piece of mud printing, worked by Wobbles on his counterpane. "Did you ever see the like o' that?" he asked of Curler and Pigeon. "Couldn't he sit on his own bed?"

"Oh! bother your bed," growled Pigeon. "Let's hear about the fight."

"Well, then, it happened this way," began Wobbles, shifting his seat to Curler's couch, but Curler was at him instantly.

"Get off," he said, "and sit on a chair."

Wobbles left behind him a tolerably good imitation of the map of the world upon Curler's couch, and, as requested, took a chair. From that he told his story.

"Me and Crewe," he said, "met in the village, and went to the public and had a glass together, and while we were drinking it I haccidentally trod on his toe. 'You do that again,' he says. 'So I will,' says I, and did it. Then we closed and got all over the bar into the road, and rolled about like anything. You never saw anybody in the state he's in."

"It's a rum story," said Conky.

"Hush!" exclaimed Curler. "Somebody's coming."

The somebody turned out to be the Honourable Morden Crewe himself, who, throwing open the door, advanced a pace and thus addressed the startled four.

"I've a word to say to you fellows. You are not to go beyond the castle or the park."

"Which it was niver our intention for so to do except accidental," murmured Conky.

"If I find you out," continued the Honourable Morden, "I shall whip you home. Do you hear?"

"Oh! yes, sir," they murmured in chorus.

"And mind you do not disobey."

With this the Honourable Morden went out and closed the door with a bang that made them all jump in their boots. But as soon as he was gone their British blood—if they had any of the real stuff in their veins—got up, and they asserted their liberty.

"Shall the tyrant crush us?" asked Wobbles.

To which the others answered "niver."

"Are we to be shut up in a wile place perwaded by ghostesses?" asked Conky.

To which there came the same response—

"Niver."

"We will strike off our chains and shake off the dust from our feet," said Wobbles, and as a preliminary to get rid of the soil of the district, he began to scrape off the mud he had acquired that day.

The castle, indeed, was haunted, if ever castle was. Haunted by spirits good and bad, some of the latter ever hovering about with its master, the Honourable Morden Crewe.

He had one grim spectre with him that bore a strong resemblance to Woody Welsher, bloody and threatening—the Woody Welsher lying in his grave in the Beech Copse.

By day and night it was ever with the murderer, and never so much with him as when he was alone. If he sat with his eyes down it was before him. If he raised his face it was behind him.

He never saw it as we see things of the earth, but he knew it was there—none the less terrible for being invisible—none the less horrible for being in his mind's eye alone.

There were times when he thought of leaving the castle and in the excitement of a fast life try to forget the deed he had done; but then came the thought, "Dare I leave it in the wood?"

Men wander about, dogs scratch the earth, moles burrow it. There were a hundred things which might help to bring the ghastly corpse to light.

It never struck him that no mortal man had seen him do the deed. It was enough that he knew himself guilty, and believed, if once the crime came to light, there was but one step between Rockholme Castle and the gallows.

Every morning he stole down to the spot to see if the grave had been disturbed. Every night he wandered there to see if the eyes of the curious had found out his secret. And the feeling for the necessity of watchfulness grew upon him.

He never trusted the light, but he had some confidence in the dark, until the thought came, "What if some fox should burrow there?"

"I'll have no foxes," he said, and gave orders for all upon the estate to be destroyed. He even went forth himself with his men and helped in the work, which, in the eyes of country gentry, is a sin that hath no forgiveness.

The feeling of terror grew upon him. He was never an hour away without fancying somebody prying about that grave. So he took to felling trees, for amusement he said, and he lopped off great branches from stately monarchs of the forest, and piled them above the awful hiding place. His servants asked him if the wood should be brought home and he cursed them. Then, when those who were engaged, at last, in fencing round the wood asked if they might cut up the fallen timber, he cursed them too and bade them fetch it from elsewhere.

Haunted, indeed—the castle and its owner. The murdered Welsher was already avenged.

The loneliness of his life at last grew insupportable, and as he would not have anything to do with the four friends, he invited Skewball to the castle, and Skewball came and told him stories of distant lands, which pleased him; but while he drank Skewball scarce touched the wine cup.

"I've no head for it," he said; "I can make merry on a little, but a lot poisons me."

Wobbles often met Skewball, and once asked him how his wife was. To this Skewball replied that "she was as merry as a cricket, allus a-larfing at the way Wobbles went into the mud that morning." After that Wobbles became gloomy, cursed the faithlessness of women, and stuck to his friends for society.

At last they all settled upon leaving the castle if the Honourable Morden would make an allowance, and Wobbles was called upon to lay the proposition before him.

Wobbles did so, and came back with his necktie awry, his hair rumpled, and the general appearance of a struggle about him.

"And what did he say?" asked Conky.

"Nuffin," replied Wobbles.

"What did he do, then?"

"He *led* me out of the room," replied Wobbles.

"What can we do to amoose ourselves?" asked Pigeon. "I suppose we shall have to stop here."

"Have old Joss and Fireworks out in the park for exercise," replied Wobbles.

They led both these noble steeds out of the stables, but having grown fat and lazy they both struck work. They would not take exercise, but lay down and went off into sham sleeps, from which nothing could arouse them, until the would-be riders left them. Then the cunning brutes went back to the stable and ate and drank again.

There old Joss would readily go through his tricks, to the great delight of the stable-boys, who were not less amused at the efforts Fireworks made to imitate him. Both were established favourites, and their feeding was carefully looked to.

The friendship, or what passed for such, between Skewball and the Honourable Morden increased. If Skewball was not at the castle the Honourable Morden Crewe was at the inn. Sometimes he slept there, and Sal, hearing a cry in the house one night, bade Skewball get up and listen.

He crept to the door of the room occupied by his squire, and heard him talking aloud in a beseeching tone.

"Spare me, leave me, or I shall die. It was a hasty deed. I never meant to kill you, but you persecuted me."

Skewball crept back to his own room and told his wife what he had heard.

"The squire's done murder, but who is it he's killed?" he said.

"That flash fellow who lived with him," replied Sal.

"Right for a thousand pounds," said Dick, "but how are we to prove it?"

"It will all come out in time," said Sal, and then they went to sleep again. Not being haunted themselves, repose speedily came again.

CHAPTER CLXIX.

HOMEWARD BOUND.

ON the deck of a ship, homeward bound, stood Brisket and Broad Arrow Jack. Thinking that he had accomplished his oath—and whether he was right or not we shall presently see—he at last had assumed an attire little likely to attract much attention—the ordinary apparel of a settler.

Brisket wore the same, and in wearing it they had no choice, for no other was to be obtained at the diamond-fields. Both travelled first-class, in company with many successful men returning home to spend the fruits of their labour in their native land.

The name of the ship was the White Eagle, a first-class sailing vessel, originally belonging to an Australian line, and her captain was therefore accustomed to men of the class he had on board, and preferred them to the usual run of passengers, composed of querulous old maids, bilious bachelors, half-pay captains and colonels, and occasionally a few runaway bankrupts.

There was nothing particularly uncongenial in the society on board, but Jack held aloof from it, for he had yet another trouble and task ahead, which was the subject of conversation between him and Brisket, and they stood side by side watching the line of seething water the White Eagle left in her wake.

"Of this Morden Crewe," said Jack, "I know little, except that he is my cousin, and was, when I was a boy, one of those fast men about town who are a curse to society."

"And no particular blessing to themselves," said Brisket.

"Quite the contrary, but I suppose there must be something fascinating in the life they lead or they would not pursue it. Still I can hardly believe he is a party to the fraud and usurpation of my property.

"The mystery to me is how he became acquainted with that gang of rascals," returned Brisket, "and how they ever dared to put their original names —"

"Say rather the names they bore out here," said Jack.

"Yes, that is better—how they dared put them to the affidavits. The letter you received gives no information on that point."

"No, for Skewball does not seem to understand it, and appears himself to be in doubt as to the truth of the story. He writes in an uncertain manner—'If you are alive, pray come here at once.' That's rather amusing. If I were dead I could not obey his summons. Nor, pressing as the case is, would I have done so but for the completion of my vengeance on that nest of villains."

"I am almost sorry it is all over," said Brisket. "After a life of unbroken excitement, I do not see how we shall settle down to a quiet country existence."

"I do not think we shall settle down just yet."

"How is that?"

"I intend to have some quiet amusement at Rockholme."

"When you have turned your cousin out?"

"No—before. It is not my intention to declare myself at first, but to sit by and quietly watch these knaves at play. My life has been serious enough hitherto, and I do not think a little relaxation will hurt me."

"Goodness knows it won't," returned Brisket "What is your plan?"

"To assume the title and dress of a Spanish don, and put up at Skewball's."

"But they will find you out at once."

"No; for I shall be mysterious, and not show myself in the day, and at night we will haunt Rockholme. I know how to get in and out of our old family seat without troubling the servants at the ordinary doors."

"That will be rare fun."

"You like my plan?"

"Uncommonly; but won't it come expensive? This Morden Crewe may be making ducks and drakes of your property."

"No. I have written to my agent to put an end to that, and to question the veracity of the affidavit. Legal quibbles and arguments will keep him at bay for a time."

"It will be rare sport."

"On arriving at Liverpool I will communicate at once with Skewball—we can trust him; and I will travel down by easy stages—being an invalid, you see."

"Ha, ha! An invalid—that's too good!" said Brisket. "It does me good to see you in this humour, for I never hoped to see you smile."

"My heart grows lighter every day," returned Jack; "and yet I fear there will ever be a tinge of sadness upon it. The only thing we must be careful of is the two boys."

"You can trust the Tiger," said Brisket.

"And so I think I may Dick,' replied Jack. "He is thoroughly repentant, and will not grumble at a little confinement."

"You have some game in your woods, I suppose?"

"There ought to be a lot, though no doubt poachers have been at work. But the mischief may not be very great, as Rockholme is a long way from a large town."

"Turn these two boys into the wood by night," suggested Brisket, "and keep them locked up by day. They won't grumble."

"I was sorry to part with the other men," said Jack, thoughtfully.

"You paid them handsomely for their services."

"With your money."

"If you say it is mine again, I go downstairs, bring it up, and throw it into the sea."

"Mine, then, if you will have it so," said Jack, smiling. "But to return to the men. I was sorry to part with them, but I could do nothing with them at home."

"Most of 'em would die away from an adventurous life," said Brisket, "and so we'll say no more about them. What's that—another row in the fo'castle?"

"Yes, and as usual, between those two boys and the nigger cook. I think we must stop that, Brisket."

"And take away the only amusement the people have on board. Look at them clustering round the caddy. I'll go for'ard and see what it is."

Brisket hastened forward, and pushing his way through a circle of amused passengers, came upon the Tiger and Dick Skewball engaged in a violent dispute with the nigger cook—a true African, as black as the blackest night, and looking more so in his white shirt and trousers. In his hand he held a saucepan, which he was brandishing at the two boys.

"You come my way agen, d'ye hear," he said, "a-shoving your ugly fist in dis pot, and taking away de dinner ob a specterable born African genciman, dat more fit to walk on de carpet ob de sloon dan you am to go a-kicking your dam cussed feet bout in a mudhole."

"Who put his hand into your pot?" demanded Dick.

"How de debil I know?" returned the cook. "You come and go like de ghose ob de ole man dat stab him under. It am one ob you, I swar."

"But it's not exactly reasonable," said Brisket, advancing, "to accuse these boys unless you are certain of their guilt."

"Massa Griskin," said the nigger, with the aptitude of his race to mispronounce names, making a strong effort to control himself, "I neber make de cusation wifout habing grouns to put my lily foot on. It aint de fuss time, nor de second, nor de tird, dat tings come roundy bout dis way. My life's one eber ... g dam roun ob misery trew dem boys."

"Don't swear," said Brisket, calmly, "but explain yourself."

"It don't marrer a blessed bit," pursued the nigger, "what I be doing—wedder it de capen's dinner, or de passagerers' mess, or a lily bit ob picking for meself—dem boys must hab a bit ob it. Now it am a taty, den it am a lump ob meat, and by-em-bye it am whole loabs ob bread."

"I don't quite understand you," said Brisket. "What do you mean, and how does it all come about?"

"A nigger don't hab no more eyes in de back ob him head dan a white man," was the reply. "Not dat I am a nigger—for de moder dat gabe me birf, and so in a roundyabout way made me a fernally unfortenet cook, had more dan a common orinary spicion ob white blood in her body; but, as she had ony two eyes, it am unreasonable for you to spect dat I habe more."

"I don't expect any more," replied Brisket. "But what have these boys been doing?"

"Ebery blessed moral ting dat boys can do, and more," replied the nigger, clutching angrily at his wool with his left hand, and shaking the sancepan savagely. "Ony dis day, when I pretty nigh wore out, and dead faint wif gettin up de dinner, I get a lily flour, and a lily lard, and de smallest bit ob meat dat eber you did see, and I make dem into de wee-weeist dumpling dat was eber put into de plate ob moral man. Den I put him into dis sarsepan to bile."

"Well, go on."

"I swar to de sarsepan, and I swar I put him in. Den I jest turn round to peel one taty—no more—to eat wif him, for I was dat bery faint dat eat sumfin I must or die under de grate——"

"You are always stuffing yourself," said Dick.

"He swell out like a frog," said the Tiger.

"If I get one bash at you," said the cook, aiming a couple of futile blows at them, "I settle dis business and yours for eber!"

"You must keep cool," said Brisket, signalling to the bystanders not to indulge in unseemly laughter, "or we shall never understand your story."

"I just peel dat taty den," said the nigger, "and turn round to de sarsepan, and I see de lid off, and de lilly dumpling gone. Let me get a bash at dem —only one."

"All this," said Brisket, gravely, "is mere suspicion. You did not see either of them take your little dumpling."

"See dem!" exclaimed the nigger, overcome with surprise at the preposterous idea. "Whoeber see de debil at work?—but still *we feel him*. We know when he am bout de place, and so I know day hab my dumpling. Oh! let me get de smallest bash at one of dem, den I neber say any more bout it."

"It is a great pity you cannot agree with the boys," said Brisket—"one of them of your own colour too."

"*Which?*" asked the nigger, as if there could be any doubt about it.

"This lad—the Tiger," replied Brisket.

"He my colour!" said the nigger. "It well for you dat my moder am not present at dis moment, or she hab all de ugly tow off your head. But I see, you am in leagle wif de boys, and no doubt had your share ob de dumpling, and so rob a poor man, faint wif him work, ob him dinner, and so I treat you wif de scorn ob a genelman. As you hab de dumpling take de sarsepan too," and, dashing it down upon the deck, the indignant nigger walked away.

Broad-Arrow Jack.

Broad-Arrow Jack came staggering down a few paces, then he fell, and great masses of masonry rolled over him. (See page 125.)

NO. 24,

CHAPTER CLXX.

THE FAIR.

THE village of Rookholme boasted an annual fair, and that fair was the pride and glory of the inhabitants. They talked of the fair when it was coming, and dwelt upon it when it was over. They saved money to spend there, and groaned over it when it was gone, owning, however, that they had received an equivalent for it; and as soon as one little stock was disposed of they began to accumulate another, to be got rid of in a similar way.

The fair day was their one red-letter day of the year. All the rest was plodding weary working in all weathers; eating, drinking, and sleeping, as people of their station eat, drink, and sleep; round and round, day by day, grinding everlastingly at the same mill.

But when the fair was at hand these dull sons of the soil brightened up, bought new clothes or mended old ones, put more briskly into their money-boxes, and gathered smiles upon their sunburnt faces.

The fair—the fair—a time to put aside sorrow and groaning; a time to laugh as well as they could, and dance as lightly as hob-nailed boots would permit.

Wobbles heard of the approaching fair from the servants, and communicated the good news to his fellows. Three weeks' confinement to the castle had not entirely broken their spirit, and they resolved for one day to be free.

"We will go," said Wobbles, "if he kills us for it hafterwards."

"We will," said Conky.

"How?" asked Curler, and then there was a silence. Wobbles came out with the answer.

"You two can walk," he said to Pigeon and Curler; "me and Conky will ride old Joss and Fireworks."

"That aint the pint," said Curler. "How are you going to get away?"

"Sleep in the stable," said the audacious Wobbles, "and get away as soon as it is light. Once there he dursn't fetch us home."

"But we must come back again," suggested the cautious Curler, "and then—ahem!"

"Come back at night," said Wobbles, "just about the times he gets drunk; go to bed and swear we have all been laid up with sore throats."

As the Honourable Morden Crewe was now seldom sober during the day and never so after dinner, there was a fair chance of this bold scheme being carried out, and accordingly on the eve of the fair the four dauntless adventurers, each with sufficient food and drink for breakfast in his pocket, crept into the stable and prepared to pass a night in the stalls with old Joss and Fireworks.

Those invaluable animals had evidently caught the excitement of the time, for neither showed the slightest tendency to go to rest, but remained standing and occasionally snorting joyously until midnight.

"It will never do to lie down on the straw," said Conky, "for it's ten to one but they fall down upon us."

"Can't we go somewhere else?" asked Curler.

"No," said Wobbles; "those two brutes have got this small stable to themselves, and all the rest are locked up. Be easy and don't talk and they will soon go to sleep."

Fireworks was asleep by this time, although they did not know it. He was a hardy creature, and slept as often standing as he did lying. Old Joss, however, was uneasy; he sniffed the battle from afar, and would have gone through a little waltzing but for his halter.

The four friends, mindful of the injunction to be silent, leant against the walls of the stable, and nibbled little bits of their food and drank little sips of their drink until both were consumed. How gladly would they then have gone to sleep, but the only straw in the place was under the horses, and they could not make up their minds to rest their bones on stones.

"I can't stand any more of this," said Curler, suddenly. "I shall get into the manger."

He got into the manger, under the nose of Fireworks, and that sagacious beast immediately smelling the blood of an Englishman, and desiring to make oats of him, woke up and gave Curler a nibbling bite that made him come out of his resting place with the activity of a sprite. Fireworks after this went to sleep again—still standing.

"That beggar never sleeps," said Curler. "I shall try the straw."

He lay down, and Fireworks being often afflicted with visions, dreamt a dream. He thought he was out upon a lonely prairie in a wild state. He sniffed the air of freedom, he tasted the food of liberty. All was joy and peace with him until a cunning hunter crept up and levelled a rifle at him.

Fireworks, in his dream, knew then that only one thing could save him, and that was falling down. He accordingly fell, in his dream and in reality too, and rolled upon Curler, who, in stifled gasps, called upon his friends for aid.

Easy to call but hard to obey that call in the dark. They did their best, but when you are feeling about a horse's hind legs in the dark you ought to know exactly what sort of horse he is, or to take such precautions as will ensure your safety.

And even the most cautious make mistakes. Wobbles got into a posititian where he thought he would be secure, but Fireworks lifted a hind leg and caught him under the jaw. His teeth met, his eyes flashed fire, and with a mutilated tongue he swore.

Whether it was the language that startled him, or merely a desire to get get up again which prompted Fireworks, we know not, but up he got, and Curler, with a crushed-bandbox sort of feeling, crept out of the way and took a seat upon a stable pail, groaning dismally.

After this disaster they all sat on upturned buckets and slept in wretched snatches until the dawn peeped through the windows of the stable. Weary and languid they rose up and opened the door.

"Shall we wash," asked Conky, gloomily regarding the pump in the yard.

"You must be orf your 'ed," replied Wobbles, and the others said "Quite orf."

"I thought," said Conky, sadly, "it would be something to do."

"I'd like to peck a bit," said Curler.

After this ensued a reflective silence.

"If there is anything," said Wobbles, breaking silence, "that is trying to a man it is a hempty stomach. I think they keeps mangel wurzel in the loft overhead."

"I've had many a one on tramp," said Conky, brightening up; "let's pick a bit."

"If you have tramped," suggested Wobbles, with a vicious eye, "you needn't go a hollerin' it on the 'ouse tops."

After a heavy but unsatisfactory meal of mangold wurtzel they brought out Fireworks and Old Joss and put the saddles and bridles on. This feat was successfully performed except as far as Old Joss was concerned, and he had the bit outside. But bit or no bit made very little difference to that learned brute.

It was too early to go to the fair, so they went off to a distant wood and hung about there until they heard the beating of gongs and drums summoning the revellers. Having given a few touches to their attire, Wobbles got upon old Joss, Conky mounted Fireworks, and off they went to the fair, leaving Curler and Pigeon to follow as best they could.

Old Joss knew there was a fair going on. He heard the gongs and he sniffed the odour of distant sawdust. Cocking his tail he let out his feet and gave Wobbles a taste of what a horse of his stamina on long rest and unlimited corn could do.

Fireworks, of course, followed him.

Age ought to bring discretion with it, but in the case of many people it does not. With Old Joss discretion was a laggard, or he could not have gone at fences and gates in the way he did.

Don't suppose he jumped over these obstacles. Jumping he despised as a mean art. On principle he went through them, tumbling into ditches and getting out again without hurting himself or Wobbles, in a manner that ought to have obtained a medal for him.

Curler and Pigeon were speedily outdistanced, and saw with envy their two friends disappear. But of this Conky and Wobbles knew nothing. All their faculties, all their energies, were concentrated on keeping in their saddles.

They succeeded tolerably well, and were really entitled to be considered good horsemen, although Wobbles arrived at the fair with the reins dangling down in front of Old Joss, and Conky put in an appearance seated upon the tail of Fireworks.

The fun of the fair was at its height. Gallant knights and fair ladies prevaded the platforms of the dramatic entertainments. The barrel organs of the peepshows sent forth demoniacal strains. Men beat gongs, banged drums, waved whips, and shouted themselves hoarse as they called upon people, as cabmen call upon a horse, to come up.

Into the thick of the fair went Old Joss, and, having singled out a travelling circus, he went round to the stage entrance and carried Wobbles into the midst of a number of ladies and gentlemen engaged, in the artless manner of their tribe, in arranging their dress for the coming performance.

"I've nothing to do with it," gasped Wobbles, "it's this brute."

And, exhausted nature giving way, he fell out of the saddle and lay upon his back blinking.

Barely had he fallen when Fireworks, without Conky, whom he had left on a pickled mussel-stall, came in, snorting defiance and expressing in his eye a determination to go through with whatever Old Joss might attempt. The new animal created no end of additional confusion. Women screamed, men swore, and some tried to back the horses, but Old Joss was firm. He broke his way through them all, and, dashing into the ring, where the band happened to be playing a selection from Norma, he immediately struck up a waltz.

There was a crowded audience, the applause was terrific, and the enthusiasm increased when Fireworks, with the ring master clinging frantically to the pommel of the saddle, appeared. The ring master was the only one of the establishment at liberty to check this volunteer business. All the rest were engaged in pommelling and scratching Conky and Wobbles.

"Stop that infernal music!" roared the ring master, and the music stopped. Old Joss, with a mind and memory impaired by age and trouble, and yet a little stimulated by beans, immediately conceived that the battle of Waterloo was over, and lay down to die.

If he lay down, was there a law to prevent the emulative Fireworks following his example? I trow not. Fireworks therefore lay down, and with one eye open prepared to follow the next move.

The next move, however, was made on the part of the company, and it consisted in the united efforts of the ring master, two clowns, and four stablekeepers, to get the recumbent brutes upon their feet again.

Vain the effort. Old Joss had died professionally, and was not to be raised by such efforts as are common among night cabmen. Nor was Fireworks the horse to be got up while Old Joss was down, and both having hides of leather—and uncommonly tough leather too—the frantic men kicked, tugged, and were without success.

"Who do they belong to?" asked the ring master, wildly; "who brought them here?"

"The party as brought 'em here," replied one of the men, "is a-being wolloped in the dressing tent."

"Kill 'em!" hissed the ring master, grinding his teeth; "smash their heads orf."

This suggestion could not be carried out as the parties in question, much mauled, had made good their escape, and were at that moment behind a peep-show engaged in removing the stains of conflict.

"We must get 'em out somehow," said the ring master; "this brute," pointing to Old Joss, "has died in the very houter circle. You must carry them."

The grooms of the ring did not object to carry a horse they knew, but with a stranger it was a different thing, and there was considerable hesitation among them. At last threats and persuasion united made them resolve upon making an effort to remove them.

They got the usual hurdle for Black Bess and White Surrey, and they put Old Joss on it first. The public, in happy ignorance of the true state of things, cheered tremendously, and Old Joss, overcome with emotion, quivered visibly. Again he was among the happy scenes of his youth, and once more his bosom throbbed in response to public applause.

As soon as they put him outside of the ring he got up of his own accord and marched off to the stables on the left, where he took possession of a stall and lay down with sweet content.

"That horse is worth having," said one of the men.

So thought the proprietor, who came up from the money-taking box at that moment to see what was going on, and he said "Let him be." The next moment Fireworks was brought out, and, catching sight of old Joss, he marched up and shared his stall.

"They are hold uns," said the proprietor, "but money is to be made out of them. Don't make any fuss about what's happened, and unless they are axed for you needn't advertise 'em."

So said and so done. No inquiries were made, and old Joss and Fireworks entered then and there upon a new career of glory, with which our present story has nothing to do. So take off your hats and, with all good wishes, bid them adieu. Thank them for such amusement as they may have given you, for at the fair at Rookholme you hear of them for the last time. Adieu, Old Joss! Farewell, Fireworks! Joy and comfort and plenty of corn attend you throughout your latter days.

CHAPTER CLXXI.

THE SPANISH RESIDENT.

IN the humble and contented mind there is much joy to be found in stewed prunes and pickled whelks, and to Conky, Curler, Pigeon, and Wobbles, there was especial joy that day.

They stood at a stall and first cleared away all that was displayed to tempt the passer-by, then they called for more and pegged away until the one-eyed man who was proprietor of the stall saw a dearth in the distance.

Mentally he said—"If I had thought of this I would have prepared another barrer-load;" but as he had not thought of it, and neither whelks nor prunes being a product of Rookholme, he was obliged to extract comfort from having sold out his stock with unprecedented rapidity.

His joy and the joy of his consumers would have been perfect but for one trifling defect. Not one of the consumers was blessed with a single penny wherewithal to pay his lawful and just demands.

How this state of things came about need not be told. Impecuniosity was a familiar acquaintance with all four, so familiar that it is possible they did not notice its presence, or it may be each and all relied upon his brother to settle the account.

They cleared out the stock of that aged man and gathered breath. He, like a prudent dealer, immediately began to cast up the account, first asking if they would pay separately or in the lump.

"In the lump," said Wobbles, loftily, and having so far committed himself his three friends drew back and left him to fight it out.

"Eighty-seven dishes of whelks and thirty-nine of stewed prunes," said the man; "eighty-seven is seven and three—thirty-nine is three and three, which put together make ten and six."

"Yes," said Wobbles, "ten and six—my friend here—hallo—they're all gone!"

The one-eyed man, although limited in respect to the organs of vision, could see as well as most people, and he was round his stall in a moment and had Wobbles by the collar.

"This sort of thing," he said, "can't be done with me."

"What sort of thing?" asked Wobbles, putting a bold face upon it.

"A swallering whelks and prunes like camels, and then not paying," replied the man; "come, you shell out."

"My friend," said Wobbles, "I've left my purse at home."

"Where do you live?"

"At Rookholme Castle."

"Then I'll just go up with you," said the man, "and stick to you until you find your purse."

"Would you hintrood on that lordly domain?" asked Wobbles.

"Yes, I would," was the stern reply, "and we'll go at once."

There was no help for it. Wobbles felt he must go home and take that man with him—but, oh! how degrading it was to one of his lofty spirit to return in the society of a man who sold whelks.

"The other gentlemen live there too," said Wobbles, "and I think we had better go and have a look for them."

"Well," said the man, "I don't mind going once round, but if we don't find 'em then I must take you home."

They went the round of the fair, the one-eyed man clinging to Wobbles's arm firmly if not tenderly. During the perambulation Wobbles passed many servants from the castle and Richard Skewball, all of whom stared at Wobbles and his companion with natural surprise.

Wobbles was cut to the quick. Here was a bitter pill and degradation indeed.

"Don't hang on in this way," he said; "they think you must be a relation or a friend of mine."

"They must be asses to think as I'd own you," returned the man, gruffly. "Now then, your friends beant about, and we will go up to the castle. What are you there? Bottle washer?"

The eyes of Wobbles flashed fire, and he breathed hard, but after taking stock of the muscular development of the one-eyed man he offered no reply.

"If you wish to go to the castle," said Wobbles, after a pause, "I think we had better start."

He was reckless. Anything was better than stopping at the fair, where so many eyes were upon them. The man declared his willingness to go at once and on the road they started.

Not unseen, for Conky, Curler, and Pigeon had been upon their track, and followed stealthily behind the pair to see what was to be the fate of their companion. On this point they were speedily enlightened.

At the park gates they met the Honourable Morden Crewe strolling gloomily up and down smoking a cigar. Wobbles, still desperate, walked up to him at once and said—

"I want a sovereign."

"What for?" asked the other.

"To pay this man."

"Who is he?"

"Dealer in whelks," said Wobbles, shortly.

"Yes, and here I mean to stop until I'm paid," said the man.

"Go out of my place," said Morden Crewe, fiercely. "Who next am I to be pestered with?"

He levelled a blow at the nearest and Wobbles being the nearest he went under. The one-eyed vendor of whelks backed a bit and put himself in an attitude of defence.

"If that's your game," he said, "come on."

The Honourable Morden Crewe hesitated a moment. Should he contaminate his aristocratic fist by striking a vendor of whelks? And yet—why not? He had fallen low enough in all conscience, and a little extra lowering would do no great harm.

He resolved to fight that whelk man.

In a moment the pair were engaged, and the Honourable Morden Crewe speedily found himself overmatched. His opponent had been a lower-class member of the prize ring in his early days and knew how to work round his man. He did it very cleverly considering his loss of an eye, and put the gentleman speedily into a ditch, with many records of his fistic art upon him.

Wobbles watched his patron's defeat with mingled joy and terror. Joy on account of his own wrongs and fear because he had a pretty clear idea that the Honourable Morden would take it out of him for the defeat he had endured.

"You rascal," gasped the defeated one, "I'll have you locked up for this."

"Pay me for my whelks," said the man, or "I'll let into you again."

The threat was a real one, and the Honourable Morden in no way desirous of being further punished, took a sovereign from his pocket and tossed it towards the man. He tried it with his teeth, spun it in the air, caught it deftly, and departed.

Left alone with his patron, Wobbles thought it time to retreat, and he accordingly scampered off at a good rate. His patron followed him with a lowering scowl upon his face.

"I'll clear them out," he said, "one by one. The beeches will hold them all."

A man who is in earnest when he contemplates a crime does not go blustering about, and Wobbles was agreeably surprised to find the Honourable Morden very quiet when they met again later in the day. He merely said to Wobbles—"See that you don't disgrace me again, will you?"

"It isn't horften we gets out," said Wobbles, "and then a vile fate seems to pursue us."

"Go out as often as you like," was the reply. "Keep clear of me."

Wobbles lost no time in taking advantage of this offer, and having asked for five shillings and most unexpectedly got it, he went off to the Bold Brigand to explain matters to Sal Skewball.

Gifted with great powers of invention, of which he was fully conscious, he had no doubt about being able to clear away the cloud upon him, brought down by his meeting with the Honourable Morden at the inn.

"If I don't explain things," he thought, "she will have an hidea that I ain't so plucky as most people."

Sal was in the bar when he entered and did not take any notice of him. Wobbles felt the sting of a woman's indifference in his heart and moaned. Whenever Wobbles suffered he became poetical and soon burst forth into a few quotations most suitable for the occasion.

"From sport to sport they hurry me to banish my regret, but when I think of you, ma'am—we may be happy yet," he said. "Why leave me alone to pine within them lordly bowers? Oh! come and cheer my life, and give me back them golden hours. Oh! Mrs. Skewball, is it possible that the little contrary-temps which you witnessed houtside of this 'umble but 'appy 'ome can have lowered me in your hesti mation? I was obliged to content myself, for if I'd let out in my bold style I must have killed him."

"I really," said Sal, "have no time to talk to you."

"Time," said Wobbles, softly, "was not made for canoodlers."

"I don't understand you," replied Sal, with surprise.

"Time was," said Wobbles, bitterly, "when you warn't so deaf—but no matter."

"I have a Spanish gentleman here," returned Sal, and he requires all my attention."

The green-eyed monster Jealousy fastened upon the breast of Wobbles. A Spanish gentleman taking up all the time of the woman he adored! Bloodshed would come of this.

"Spanish," he said. "Is the party handsome?"

"As paint," replied Sal.

"Young?"

"Yes—the blossom of manhood."

"Perhaps," said Wobbles, faintly, "he don't care for the fair sex."

"He dotes on every one of us, old and young," replied Sal.

Wobbles knocked his hat over his eyes to hide his tears.

"A little brandy, warm," he said.

"If you stop a minute," replied Sal, "I'll send the servant girl to serve you."

This was too much. Wobbles in the main was not proud, but if stung in the right place he could kick as well as any horse or ass going. Drawing himself up to his full height, and keeping his balance with consummate skill, he said—

"Woman, you have deceived me, but bewair. There are some things as can't be endured, and some as must be avenged. Hide your guilty head, and again I say bewair."

With a lofty wave of the arm he swaggered out of the Bold Brigand and got as far as the horse trough. Then, with the hope that Sal might see him through the window and repent of her cruelty, he took up an attitude intended to convey dejection.

But it did not succeed for two reasons. First, Sal Skewball was not looking out of the window; and secondly, a low country boy mistook the cause of his emotion.

"I say, measter," he cried, "be ye drunk already?"

"Go away, boy," replied Wobbles, regarding him with the eye of the Melancholy Stranger. "What know ye of slighted love?"

"Yah!" was all that boy said, and went off to his toil at a distant farm.

"Be he who he may," groaned Wobbles, referring to the Spaniard, "I'll wait and wait for him, and he shall feel the strength of my hiron arm."

CHAPTER CLXXII.

WOBBLES SEES A GHOST AND NO MISTAKE.

"A MAKING an ordinary ass of himself may pass without much notice; but when he strikes into the extraordinary line he inwariably secures unto himself much attention," was the joint opinion of Wobbles's companions.

Wobbles—on the subject of Sal—went into the extraordinary, and literally forced his sufferings upon the attention of his friends. They came home from the fair very tired, and, having partaken of a hearty dinner, wanted to go to sleep, and with that object uppermost in their minds went to bed.

When they got there they put themselves into attitudes conducive to repose, and would have gone off if Wobbles had not come to bed too, and entered upon a course of groaning sufficient to keep any man, however tired, awake.

"What's the matter with you?" asked Conky, after being roused on the verge of repose for the twelfth time.

"Oh—oh!" groaned Wobbles, "henceforrard there is no peace."

"Wot's up?"

"Wronged, deceived," said Wobbles; "but let him beware."

"I wish you would stop that row," said Curler.

"If you was in my place," replied Wobbles, "you'd hexpire."

Eventually the curiosity of the tired trio was aroused, and little by little Wobbles, in language all his own, revealed the scene and substance of the story of his wrongs.

"A Spanish gentleman," said Conky; "I wouldn't be done by a furrinar."

"Nor I—nor I!" said Curler and Pigeon.

"What shall I do with him?"

"Waylay and wollop him," said Conky.

"I will," said Wobbles, and after a little more groaning he lost all memory of his sufferings in sleep.

Having committed himself to a course of vengeance, Wobbles was obliged to make preparations to carry it out, and Conky kindly assisted him to a weapon from the armoury in the form of a short battle-axe with a spike at the back, an instrument of the most murderous nature.

With this wrapped under his overcoat Wobbles, backed up by his friends, took to haunting the neighbourhood of the Bold Brigand, occasionally entering therein for a liquor.

He was cool to Sal and she was cool to him, uncommonly cool, and a casual observer at these meetings would have supposed they had never met before. At these interviews Wobbles suppressed his feelings, but when away he dwelt upon them moodily, and ground his teeth savagely.

One day he met Skewball out for a walk, and accosted him on the subject of the stranger.

"You have a Spanish gentleman in the house," he said.

"Yes, Spanish gentleman and sweet," replied Skewball.

"And he is young?" said Wobbles.

"Very young."

"And fair—I mean handsome?"

"As fine a man as ever I saw in my life."

"And what is his name?"

"The Don Doutyouwishyoumaygetit," replied Skewball.

"Don what?"

"Dontyouwishyoumaygetit," replied Skewball, skilfully running the words one into the other and giving them a foreign twang.

"I'll try and think of that name," said Wobbles, "but it's a difficult one to get hold of."

"So it is," said Skewball.

"He don't seem to come out much."

"He never does—by day."

"So he walks at night?"

"Sometimes," said Skewball, "but he don't like to be seen. He's a murderous sort of fellow and would settle the hash of any one who pryed into his actions."

"Would he?"

"Yes. The last place he was staying at there was a man who tried to follow him about. That man was found dead with his head cut off."

"And did the Don Donterumbertumble something kill him?" asked Wobbles.

"That was never known—it could only be guessed at," said Skewball. "Good morning."

"I think I had better let him alone," thought Wobbles, as he walked away, "and I must stick some yarn into Conky and t'others to account for it."

The story he told them was that the Spaniard was confined to his bed and not expected to be up for a month.

"But I can wait," he said, with assumed ferocity; "he shall not escape me."

That night the Honourable Morden Crewe did not come home to dinner, but where he was or what he was doing nobody in the establishment had the least idea. Nor did the four friends trouble themselves much about it, for there was a glorious spread, and, having ordered the servants to put everything upon the table at once, and leave them to themselves, they fell to.

It was a sight to see this little congregation of greatness feed. The indiscriminate way they mixed the solids and drinks would have taxed the digestion of any living thing, but they had a motto, implied if not uttered—"Eat first and suffer afterwards," and very faithfully they acted up to it.

The dining-room of Rookholme was a handsome but somewhat sombre apartment, and unless thoroughly lighted—which it seldom was—had dark shadows in more that one odd corner.

The furniture was very solid, and quite two hundred years old. The walls were wainscotted, and suspended here and there were family portraits of the old school—well-defined figures standing out against dark backgrounds.

One of them hanging at the far end of the room was that of a cavalier of the time of Charles the Second—the figure standing in an easy attitude, with the right hand upon a pedestal and the left resting upon the hip.

Wobbles had often seen and noticed this portrait. He, more so, as his seat at the dinner-table put him face to face with it. There was just light enough for him to see the outline of the form, and it had grown into a habit with him to look at this portrait while eating and create within his fertile mind all sorts of fancies concerning it.

The dishes were too good for conversation, and his friends eating silently Wobbles soon fell into his habit of looking at the cavalier, and raising his eyes in that direction received such a staggerer as he had never known before.

The figure of the cavalier was gone and in its place was—Broad Arrow Jack!

Yes, there he was, as Wobbles had known him—bare breast and arms, bare head, and the loose trousers hanging easily from his hips. No mistaking that figure at all events.

When that awful and terror-striking apparition met his gaze Wobbles had a large piece of meat on a fork raised half way to his mouth. There it stopped until Conky, who sat facing him, beheld the extraordinary phenomenon of a man holding a luscious morsel for a minute or more within two inches of his mouth without making any attempt to swallow it.

"What's the matter?" he asked. "Good 'evens! keep your eyes in your head."

Wobbles opened his mouth, and a curious clicking sound came forth, such as we hear when moving wax-work is a little out of order. Curler and Pigeon were likewise drawn towards him, and stared in surprise.

"If you are choking," said Conky, "swallow some water."

"There—there," gasped Wobbles, but unable to point in the direction he alluded to.

"Get it down or hup," suggested Conky, " or you'll be gone in a minute. A man can't live with wittles in his throat. Is it a bone?"

"There—there—its HIM!" groaned Wobbles, and slipping from his seat he disappeared under the table.

They got him up, and in a fever of excitement sought to administer restoratives. Conky put some wine to his lips, Curler emptied a decanter down his back, and Pigeon threw water over him generally.

Their united efforts were crowned with a success they richly deserved. Wobbles came too, and was able to offer an explanation.

"He's a standing in the frame yonder," he said.

"He—who?" chorussed his listeners.

"Broad Arrow Jack."

"Which frame?"

"Why that—marcy on me—he's gone."

The cavalier was in his old place, and Conky regarded Wobbles dubiously.

"You've been a little hupset," he said; "your brain's haddled."

"Yours may be," said Wobbles, savagely; "but I'll swear I saw him there."

"Anyhow, he ain't there now," said Curler, cheerfully, "and I'm going to finish my dinner."

"Ay, just so," said Pigeon, and all but Wobbles took their seats again.

"I don't think I can eat any more," he said, "and yet—here, give us hold of the wine. I suppose I'm unnerved—I want touching up."

He drank a lot, and his courage came back again. Once more he took a seat at the table, but not his old seat. He chose one by the side of Conky, and Curler took his place.

What is that that suddenly stiffens Curler's hair and gives to his face a ghastly expression, and why should he point with his fork towards that picture of the cavalier.

The rest understand all this, but none dare to look round. Gradually their faces reflect the expression of Curler's, and they sit transfixed like figures of stone.

"Uck—uck!" gasps Curler.

"Can you see anything?" asked Conky, in a whisper.

"*Him*," said Curler, and fell back in his chair.

They knew who "him" was, and as Conky afterwards expressed it, they felt as if they all had "penny hices down their backs." Curler lay groaning under the table for full five minutes before Wobbles looked round. It was no act of volition on his part, but an involuntary movement—his head was "drawed round" and then he saw—the cavalier.

"Most strordinary," he said, "he's gone again."

The others, reassured, plucked up an atom of spirit and looked round too. Then they all laughed —a listless unmeaning laugh—and bade Curler get up.

"There's nothing to be afraid of," said the valiant Conky. "Get up and have a drink."

"I'll have a drink first," whispered Curler, and they gave him one—a stiff one.

"I don't like this room," said Conky, "it's gloomy and not at all comfortable. Suppose we each take a little snack upstairs with us and have 'em in bed; we can also have a smoke and a drink there."

A charming proposition, hailed with delight by his friends. Bed was the place where you can put your head under the blanket the moment you hear or see anything to be afraid of.

Each man filled up a plate of "mixed goods" and armed himself with a decanter. Wobbles in addition carried a box of cigars, taken from the mantelpiece, and with candles and matches they made their way upstairs.

How close they kept together, and with what joy they heard the click of the lock as Wobbles secured the door. With haste they one and all got into bed.

"This is indeed comfort," said Wobbles, as he put his plate upon his knees and stood the decanter upon a chair by his side.

"It's more than airthly bliss," was the comment of Conky.

The size of their bedroom has been previously alluded to, and it may therefore be easily understood how imperfectly four candles lighted it up. The gloom of the dining-room was almost day in comparison to the gloom of this chamber.

Still it was not so bad as the dining-room, for they were in bed.

There are some appetites that grow on what they feed on. The four friends appeared to be gifted with such appetites and were just about to begin another feed when—

A faint click was heard in the darkest corner of the chamber.

Wobbles started and upset his plate. They all started and upset their plates.

"What's that?" asked one.

"Was it the lock of the door?" asked Wobbles; "perhaps I didn't fasten it properly."

"It came t'other way," said Conky. "Hush!"

A sound scarcely above that which would have been made by a fallen feather, and then a soft rustling footstep.

Hush! again—sit frozen ye four cowardly fools—stare and gasp and moan—endure an agony worse than death on the scaffold—for see—he comes—Broad Arrow Jack!

With slow and stately steps he passes by, regarding them with the scornful dignified air they were so familiar with—up and down the room, and then passing away in the darkness, leaving them frozen with horror.

For awhile they neither move nor speak, but at last Wobbles sets the example and dives beneath the bedclothes, the rest follow, and there they lie quailing through the livelong night.

CHAPTER CLXXIII.

NOT DEAD YET.

MR. GARKER and his companions on discovering the loss of the Ogre were at first puzzled to account for his disappearance. They were inclined to think that beasts of prey had something to do with it, but on remembering that the door was fastened when they came in search of him they were obliged to abandon the supposition.

Next it was suggested that Jack had borne him away, but again no was the answer, for Jack had gone straight away, leaving the Ogre, according to agreement, to be buried by Mr. Garker. This suggestion, in the eyes of Mr. Garker, was absurd, for what man, after paying another to do a certain work, would do it himself?

"The truth is," he said, "the beggar wasn't dead. He either feigned death or was only wounded very badly and came out of it."

"He certainly seemed dead," said one.

"I once knew a man," said another, "who could put himself into such a state that you would swear he was dead, and come round again the moment he liked."

"This chap must have had the power," said Garker.

Drops of blood were soon discovered and traced as far as the edge of the wood. This was tolerable good proof of the Ogre being alive, and Garker proposed to hunt him down.

"After breakfast," said one.

"After breakfast of course. There's no hurry. He can only crawl at the best. It will be rare fun."

"And what shall we do with him when we catch him?"

"We'll talk of that when we have the luck to get hold of him."

They had breakfast of a sort, and with renewed strength set out upon the trail of the Ogre. The drops of blood were easily distinguished as they lay upon the moss and fallen leaves, and they followed them for two miles or more, until they came to a very dense part of the wood, where broken rocks, shrubs, and tall trees abounded.

Here the signs of blood ceased and all trace was lost.

"He's a good plucked 'un," said Garker, "and I wouldn't mind giving him a lift in the world—darned if I would."

Little did he think those words were overheard by the Ogre, weak from loss of blood, weary with flight, crouching among the thick branches of a tree into which he, with a superhuman effort, had managed to climb.

Not dead yet—only wounded sore. His death had even been like the man in the story told above—a counterfeit.

There was a lot of the spider in the Ogre and he had feigned exceedingly well—not dead yet, still only spared for a more awful doom.

It was high noon, and Mr. Garker, with a house empty of all save himself and his servant, was taking his siesta. All his friends had gone their several ways and he had nothing else to do, or intended to do nothing else, which was much the same thing, until more customers or men willing to work came that way.

Garker loved his siesta, especially after a hard night's work in gambling, and it was always a risky thing to disturb him, as he occasionally showed a very uncertain temper.

Disturbed, however, he was on this particular occasion by the Ogre, who crawled into the room where he lay asleep and shook him by the arm.

"Get out," growled Garker. "You clear off, whoever you are."

"Give me food and drink," said the Ogre, hoarsely. "I am dying."

"Not dying but lying," said Garker, opening his eyes. "Who are you? Oh! what? My black friend back again?"

"Yes," replied the Ogre, "for a mouthful of food. Give it to me and I will be your slave."

"You won't be much use to me," said Garker—"not for a month or so. Why, man, you are half dead."

"Are you fond of money?"

"Rather."

"Do you love to gull fools, to live at their expense, to empty their pockets, and get their thanks for it?" asked the Ogre, hoarsely.

"I like all that," said Garker, "if I only saw the way to do it."

"I'll show you. We can work together—only give me food."

"You shall have it," said Garker; "only I expect to be paid back some day."

"I'll pay you back with interest," was the reply.

Food and drink were set before the Ogre, and he devoured both eagerly. His dress, which had long been in a bad way, was now made worse by portions of it having been torn up to bandage his wounds. Garker, looking at him, thought he had never beheld a more miserable spectacle.

When he had finished he asked where he might lay down to sleep and Garker told him "where he was." Nodding his thanks for the permission the Ogre curled himself up like a dog in the corner and went to sleep.

No man ever had more of the brute in him, and yet he was endowed with high gifts, which, properly applied, might have made a man of mark of him. All, however, was shadowed over by evil passions, and in the wide world there was no more callous monster than he.

While he slept Garker finished his siesta and did a little work about the house. No strangers arrived, and at eve the Ogre woke up, weak from loss of blood, but most astoundingly recovered from his injuries.

"If you will talk to me now," he said, "I'll tell you my plans."

"Go ahead," said Garker; "do you smoke?"

"Yes."

"Then put a pipe on. It is a great help to a talker or a thinker."

The Ogre lit a pipe and Garker gave him some coarse whiskey.

Then the Ogre unfolded his plans.

"You are not in love with this life, I suppose?" he said.

"No," returned Garker; "I've bore it pretty well, but its often lonely."

"Would you like to go to the old country—England."

"Unkimmon; but what could I do there?"

"Nothing. I would do the work—if you will only give me a fair start."

"What's that?"

"Turn up as a rajah or pasha, as I've done before. It's a paying game."

"But isn't it risky?" asked Garker, doubtfully.

"Not at all, if worked well. The last time I did it I went about too much; but now I've a fancy that coming the retiring dodge will pay. Go out in a carriage with blinds down, receive only a few people, and so on. Don't look surprised, man. In a month I will get a circle of the best people about me."

"But you are sure to be found out?"

"Not at all. Certainly not for a year. By that time we shall have made a little fortune."

"How?"

"Gambling, the purchasing of goods, mortgage of my estates—tea plantations or tobacco grounds. It's easily done. In addition there are plenty of things to lay your hands on—jewels, plate, and so on. I did it before and was never found out—at that."

"It seems to me to be a wild scheme," said Garker, "and yet there's a method in it."

"So you will find," said the Ogre. "Give me a little money to play with and I'll make your fortune?"

"But how am I to go?"

"As a faithful follower, who has been all over the world with me, and thrice saved my life," grinned the Ogre. "They will make as much of you as me. The last time I was a rajah—I will be a pasha now, and those who were acquainted with me before will never dream of me being one and the same. I'll get a dress that shall completely disguise me. Trust me—you will never know me."

"I'll try it," said Garker; "it will be an amusing run, at all events. I want a change, too. I'm on. They can't hang me for it."

"Good," said the Ogre, and went outside the Folly to walk up and down and reflect.

"One last fling," he thought, "one more spell of ease and luxury and then the end may come. I know it can't be far away. I feel that I am like a wolf that has escaped the hunter's spear many and many a time, but know he must eventually conquer. But what care I? One last spell of comfort, one last fling among a race of fools, and then farewell to this world. Men must die—and I will die like a man—or monster—as some deem me."

"It was a mad and foolish infatuation, for he was rushing into the jaws of the lion, and was almost certain of it, but he was in the hands of Fate, and he could not turn out of the road in which an unswerving and unbending hand was guiding him."

CHAPTER CLXXIV.

WALLAH PASHA.

THE Honourable Morden Crewe had left his castle for a time. Driven to desperation by his doubtful position and the unsought-for and repulsive association with the four leeches who hung upon him, he resolved to go away for a time.

He chose Brighton for a temporary resting-place. There he, even if society cut him, was sure of finding some means of relaxation and distraction from his thoughts. So having given commands for his guests to be well cared for he went to Brighton.

There he speedily found that the best society had cut him. His story was already abroad and the best people, independent of anything below him, turned upon him the sightless eye and bestowed upon him the look of non-recognition which is so very painful for a gentleman to bear.

He affected to laugh at it even to himself, but the arrows of scorn and indifference rankled deeply in his heart, and he sought balm for his wounds in a more questionable circle of men—those who had been cast out by debt, dishonour, and open vice, from the aristocratic fraternity.

It was among these that he first heard of one Wallah Pasha, an Ottoman dignitary who had just arrived from Turkey, either on a secret mission for the Turkish government or in pursuit of pleasure. The latter was the most likely, as the said Wallah Pasha was very fond of gambling, drinking, and other pursuits, all in direct oppositon to the teachings of the wise and good.

He sought and found this Wallah Pasha at one of the leading hotels, where he had put up, with a rough but faithful attendant, Garry Garker, of American blood, who had from his youth been his constant attendant, and had, according to the pasha, saved his life fifty times.

The Honourable Morden Crewe went to the hotel, sent up his card, and was admitted after a little delay. He found the pasha in simple but rich raiment of the East, and thought he had never looked upon a more repulsive fellow. Garry Garker, also in Eastern robes, was in attendance, getting two hookahs in order, and as the visitor was ushered in he made a grave salaam and stood up behind his noble master.

"I am glad to see you," said the pasha, in perfect English. "Pray sit down. Will you recline as I do or take refuge in your stiff fashion of a chair."

"I prefer a chair, thank you," replied Morden Crewe; "what one is accustomed to is generally the most comfortable."

"Just so, Sir Morden. Will you excuse the presence of my attendant. He cannot babble like your valets. He is a mute."

"A mute?"

"Yes. We take measures in our country to ensure the silence of those who are immediately about us."

"I would like to exercise that measure on some I know here," was the reply, "but the laws of England do not permit it."

"I am well acquainted with your English laws," said the pasha, and there he spoke the truth. He had known about them many years before, and was particularly anxious not to come under them again.

The call so far was very pleasant, and the Honourable Merden Crewe would have followed the English custom of making his first visit a short one, but the pasha was hospitable and insisted upon his smoking a hookah and drinking either coffee or wine. The visitor took wine and the pasha—contrary to pashas in general—drank it too.

The mute attendant seemed to be a little troubled with peculiar swellings in the head, for as the two men chatted his cheeks would now and then swell out and, his eyes protruding, threaten to start from his head.

These attacks of indisposition were soon observed by the pasha, who—probably to give him a chance of recovery—bade him leave the room. Outside the mute danced about and spat on the mat and talked much like Mr. Garker of the Folly.

"I shall bust, I shall," he said, "if this game goes on. He's more than real. No Turkey cove could ever come it so strong; and to see that British ass a smoking his weed and a talking about the Ottoman Empire is enough for to bring about a bust—that it is. And I'm a mute, am I? Well, it was a good dodge of his, for until I breaks with him I've very little chance of spoiling his game."

He was very nearly caught talking by an active waiter, who came gliding upstairs with some more refreshment for the pasha and his guest. Rapidly collapsing into a mute state again, he bowed gravely as the waiter passed and walked downstairs."

An hour's quiet stroll calmed his feelings, and

he then came back again and reported himself to the Ogre—or Pasha Wallah—whom he found alone.

"That chap gone?" he said.

"Yes," replied the Ogre, "and I must counsel you to be more discreet. If you can't keep from laughing go out of the room until it is over."

"I will, but I never felt so nigh busting as I did to see that chap sitting and talking and you as solemn as a judge on hanging day—"

"Yes—yes, I know," said the Ogre, impatiently. "All that may be very amusing but I have serious business behind it. We—or rather I—am invited to his castle—Rookholme, as he calls it. I fancy they keep the family jewels there."

"Then we will have 'em."

"Softly—all in good time. Our plans must be well laid so as to divert suspicion. You will have to be careful. I shall keep you in my room."

"It's a desperate lonely life," sighed Garker.

"Yes, but it pays. Two years or so of it and we shall have a fortune."

"Two years silent imprisonment."

"You talk to me?"

"Of course I do when I can."

"Hush! here is the waiter."

"Sir Charles Graddleton," cried the waiter as he ushered in another aristocrat, "come to pay his respects to the distinguished foreigner."

CHAPTER CLXXV.

SUNDRY FACES.

ALL doubts about the castle being haunted were set at rest. Wobbles and the others had seen the ghost of Broad Arrow Jack, and they firmly believed that unearthly visitants were abroad.

Any ghost would have been bad enough, but the shade of the bold youth was doubly and trebly awe-inspiring. An overwhelming fear took possession of the four friends, and their lives sunk into the state which is supposed to be unbearable.

But still they bore it, and ate and drank to keep their spirits up. By day they were tolerably well, but when night came it opened up a fresh round of misery.

They changed their bedroom and for two nights saw nothing, but on the third night, while their candles were burning, Broad Arrow Jack came again to look at them.

From wherever he came they knew not, but there he was, suddenly, at the foot of Wobbles's bed, bearing in his hand a scroll, which he first drew their attention to, then tossed down by Wobbles's side, and melted immediately away.

The scroll was left untouched till the morning, as they all believed it to be a ghostly production, but when daylight came there it was—a genuine sheet of foolscap—and on opening it Wobbles read—

"Perjurers beware, the end is at hand."

"I knew evil would come of it," answered Wobbles. "I said so when you led me into it."

"*Me* lead *you*," exclaimed the indignant Conky. "Here, come into the middle of the room and I'll soon see who's the best man."

This Wobbles declined to do, and apologised, on the score that peace ought to be preserved in the castle at any price, and then Conky suggested an outside visit. Wobbles shirked this also, a cold in his head being the excuse, and Conky accepted it with a laugh of scornful derision.

"If you don't come out," he said, "I'll pull your nose."

"If you've got the 'art to pull the nose of a friend," said Wobbles, "do it."

Conky had the heart and he pulled his nose. Wobbles accepted the pull with all meekness and went down to breakfast, where he soothed his anguished breast with tea and toast.

All this was brought about by Jack, who, as our readers know, was the supposed grandee, and was merely indulging in a little fun prior to making an earnest claim to his estate, little thinking how that trifling would bring more serious business upon him.

Shortly after the delivery of the scroll news came down to the castle that the Honourable Morden Crewe was coming home in company with a foreigner of distinction, and Wobbles received a letter asking him in civil terms what he and his party would require to absent themselves for a month. The dicussion which followed the receipt of this letter was a very warm one.

Conky, who had wild ideas of figures generally, was inclined to stand out for a half a million, but his more sober companions brought him down to twenty thousand, and there he stuck—bent upon, as Wobbles said, "spoiling the whole business."

"It's as much as he'll give us twenty pounds a-piece," he said.

That sum was, indeed, what they were eventually offered, and all but Conky took it. He resolved to remain behind to make a private and a better bargain—if he could. Meanwhile, however, he held the twenty pounds in reserve in case of failure.

A number of men came first to put the place in order for the reception of so noble a guest as Wallah Pasha, and this they did with commendable speed. After them came a French cook and a small army of servants, and the general remark was that "the squire was going it."

At last he came with his swarthy guest—who preferred a close carriage, and scarcely showed his nose to the expectant people. Behind, in the rumble, was his "mute," with his cheeks red and swollen, as if about to burst. It was all so funny to Mr. Garker, it was.

At the entrance hall the servants stood in two lines to receive their master and his guest. As the pair passed through they were greeted with bows of humility, and at the top they came full butt against Conky.

"What are you doing here?" asked the Honourable Morden, passionately.

Conky did not answer, nor did he even look at him, but, with eyes protruding, stared at the Ogre, who at first did not recognise him.

"I ask you why are you here?"

"Well," said Conky, still staring at the Ogre, "of all the jiggery dashed things. Here, I say—come—who—what—I don't know what I'm talking about, but am I awake or dreaming?"

"He seems to know you," said the Honourable Morden Crewe.

"He was my prisoner once," replied the Ogre, calmly, "and I made him a present of his life. He suffered much in prison and I intended also to offer him compensation. The charge against him was an error of my followers. Here, slave, is gold. If you have a grudge against me let this be balm to your wounds."

"Yes, sir—thanky, sir!" said Conky, as he mechanically took the money tendered him. "But of all the dashed jiggery—well, I never! Who *could* have thought it?"

He stood aside and master and guest passed on. The line of servants broke up and Conky was left alone in the hall.

"How came *he* here?" he mused, rubbing his hand through his bristling hair. "It's a most mysterious thing. Is everybody coming over—the living—the dead? Perhaps," here his hair stood up like the wires of a sweep's broom, "*he is a ghost too!*"

His meditations were interrupted by the arrival of the pasha's mute, who beckoned him to follow upstairs. Conky naturally hesitated, as it was a little uncertain what might be in store for him above, but Garker, the mute, took him by the arm and half dragged half led him from the hall.

Into the presence of the Ogre he conducted him, and, standing by his side like a goaler guarding a prisoner, he heard all that passed.

"What brought you here?" asked the Ogre, scowling at him from the shadow of a high-backed chair. "Don't you know how dangerous it is to spy upon me?"

"I wasn't spying," said Conky, tearfully. "I didn't even know you were a-coming over—less likely did I think you'd show here."

"Well, here I am," said the Ogre, "and I want to say this simply—if you talk of me or my affairs I will silence you for ever. You understand me!"

"Oh! yes, sir."

"Then tell me how you came here."

This Conky did, making a full confession of the iniquity done, but shouldering the main burden of it upon his friends.

"Alone," he said, "I should niver have thought of anythink wrong, but I'm weak and easily led."

"No doubt," said the Ogre. "And now attend. While I am here I shall attach you to my person. You will be one of my followers and will please to keep in the society of my mute."

"Yes, sir," said Conky, casting a curious look at Garker.

"I am going to dinner now," pursued the Ogre, "and you will wait here till I return."

"I won't budge an inch," replied Conky. "Consider me glued to the floor."

The Ogre nodded and rising went out, leaving the mute and Conky together.

CHAPTER CLXXVI.
ANOTHER FACER.

CONKY and Garker remained quietly looking about the room and occasionally glancing at each other for some time after the departure of the Ogre. It was the first occasion on which these gentlemen had met and they were therefore strangers to each other.

"I wonder whether he's deaf as well as dumb?" thought Conky.

Garker, whose Oriental costume but imperfectly disguised his real origin, seemed to interpret the thoughts of Conky, for he answered them at once.

"My being a mute," he said, "is all gammon."

"Good graciousness!" exclaimed Conky, staggering back; "I thought you couldn't speak."

"Then you thought wrong," said Garker, coolly. "I say, you seem to know *him.*"

Garker jerked his thumb over his shoulder towards the door. He referred to the Ogre, and Conky nodded.

"Knowed him well," he said, "years ago."

"Where?"

"Over yonder, near the diamond-fields."

"Then you," said Garker, "was mixed up with that affair of Broad Arrow Jack's."

"I was—fout for him many a time."

"Then why don't you now?"

"Wot's the good? He aint here."

"That's true," said Garker. "But look you, he's a bad un—aint he?"

"Couldn't possibly be a worser," replied Conky. "It's no use sticking to him. He'd sell his best friend for sixpence."

"So I've been thinking," said Garker, reflectively. "He's made use of me to get a lift here, and now he don't seem to care a cuss whether I stands by him or not. I spent every brown I had to get him over here."

"More fool you," said Conky, gruffly.

"True."

A silence followed. Both were occupied with very painful thoughts. Both felt the Ogre was a little too much for him.

"I say," said Garker, suddenly, "how long have you been here?"

"Months."

"Then you know the house?"

"Every hinch of it."

"Is there any plate?"

"Lots."

"And jewels?"

"A werry fair sprinkling," replied Conky. "Crewe has a good thousand pound's worth of diamond rings."

"We must have that lot," said Garker.

"What!" exclaimed the horrified Conky, who was not quite certain whether he had found a real pal or was being tried a bit—"rob a benefactor and a friend."

"A grandmother and a fiddlestick," returned Garker. "Come, no gammon, I'm a pal of yours if you are on. Beggar the Ogre, let's collar what we can and cut it. You tell me where the brads are and I'll take 'em. Then we will go off together."

"Share and share alike?"

"To the last copper."

"Done then," said Conky. "The plate is kept in the butler's pantry, and he sleeps close to it."

"Where is the pantry?"

"At the bottom of the staircase, first turning to the right."

"Good, and the jewels—the rings?"

"Crewe's room is two doors from this."

"Does he sleep sound?"

"Goes to bed drunk as a fiddler every night."

"Better and better. We'll work the job off as soon as everybody is in bed."

"Must we go about in the dark?" asked Conky, shuddering.

"Yes. Why?"

"This confounded castle is haunted from end to end."

"Gammon—there isn't such a thing as being haunted."

"I tell you," exclaimed Conky, "I've seen 'em."

"Seen ghosts?"

"Lots of 'em. The ghost of Broad Arrow Jack is here."

"Whose ghost?" exclaimed the amazed Garker. It must be remembered he knew nothing of our hero being the owner of the estate, and had good cause for surprise.

"Broad Arrow Jack's, I tell you."

"And you've seen it?"

"As plain as I see you."

"I never could quite think he was mortal," said Garker, "and now I begin to believe in what you say. He knowed the Ogre was coming over afore he knew it himself and came here to wait for him. We'll be off to-night. One bold rush and then away. Can you get anything to drink?"

"The servants will fetch it if you will ring."

They rang the bell and the servant appearing Conky asked for spirits for the "dumb gentleman," and something to eat for himself. A liberal supply was shortly forthcoming and they enjoyed themselves intensely.

Meanwhile the Ogre and the Honourable Morden Crewe sat at dinner, both eating lightly and drinking heavily. The Ogre sat facing the picture of the cavalier as Wobbles had done, and his eyes, like those of that valiant man, were drawn towards it more than once.

"That's a good painting," he said.

"Yes," replied Carew; "an ancestor of mine—killed at Naseby."

"It seems very life-like."

"It is considered to be a splendid piece of work."

"One almost expects to see it move."

They went on eating for a time and the Ogre raised his eyes to it again. The cavalier was gone and in its place was Broad Arrow Jack, regarding him with a gaze of mingled sternness and amazement.

He uttered a shout of fear and, springing to his feet, staggered back across the room.

"What ails you?" asked the Honourable Morden.

The Ogre, before whose eyes a mist was swimming, pointed in the direction of the picture. The

Honourable Morden looked and beheld nothing but the famous portrait of the cavalier.

"There is nothing," he said, "but the portrait."

"Ah!" returned the Ogre, drawing a deep breath, "it must have been my fancy. I am not well, and yet it was so real. I am unnerved—I must drink."

And filling a tumbler with rich brown sherry he drank it off at a draught.

"There, I am better now," he said. "Do not regard my foolish fancies. It is only now and then I am subject to them."

"I have them too," replied the other, "and as nothing but drink drowns them we will drink together."

CHAPTER CLXXVII.
THE MYSTERY OUT.

WOBBLES, Curler, and Pigeon, went no farther than the Bold Brigand, and then they put up to wait for Conky, who was coming thither to report the result of his interview with the Honourable Morden Crewe.

On inquiring for beds Sal Skewball told them they could have them on the first floor next to the Spanish gentleman, requesting them at the same time to talk quietly as the distinguished guest was an invalid.

"We will play bagatelle till twelve, and then go to bed," replied Wobbles.

"You can't sit up here till twelve."

"Eleven then, fairest of the fair."

"Well, eleven be it, but I should advise you not to talk nonsense to me as my husband has just bought a brace of pistols and I fancy he is going to use them. He's mad jealous, he is."

Wobbles made rapid tracks to the bagatelle-room and gave up love-making for that night, and evermore as far as Sal was concerned. He and his friends commenced to play, cheating each other and wrangling all the evening.

While they were thus engaged an interview of striking interest took place between Brisket and Broad Arrow Jack, the supposed Spanish invalid, in the room above.

Brisket had prepared to spend an evening alone, as Jack had gone on one of his secret visits to the castle, but in less than an hour his chief came back, with more excitement depicted on his face than the old pedlar had ever seen before.

Casting aside a thick cloak he wore, Jack drew a chair up to the fire and put a question to his companions.

"Do I look well to-night?" he asked.

"Uncommon well," replied Brisket.

"Are there any signs of fever about me?"

"Fever! good gracious! No. Whoever would dream of such a thing?"

"You would consider me sane?" asked Jack.

"What else could I consider you? What's up?"

"I put these questions because I doubt the evidence of my own senses. I have either seen a vision or the Ogre living to night—"

"The Ogre?"

"Yes, he is in the castle, dining with my worthy cousin. He's got up as a pasha."

"Oh! that can't be."

"It is but too true," said Jack. "Come and see."

"Well, if it is true, you didn't kill him."

"Just so. I have often fancied, or rather felt, as if I had left some work undone, but this feeling was vague and I paid very little heed to it. Come and see if I am mistaken or not."

"I'm ready."

A knock at the door was heard as they arose, and Brisket went to see who it was. He reported Richard Skewball at the door.

"Let him come in," said Jack.

Richard Skewball, pale as King Death, entered the room, leading a huge bloodhound by a chain. The dog's nose and paws were covered with earth, and it was well for Richard that Sal did not see him bring the dog into her best apartment.

"Axing your pardon, chief," said Skewball, "but I felt I must come to you before I did anything. I've awful—horrible news for you."

"For me?"

"Yes, chief. I was out with Tartar, here, for a run, just about dusk, and as he is rather a fierce chap with other dogs I took him on to the common by the Beeches. I've generally led him, but he wanted exercise, and I thought I would let him run free."

"This is the first time I've seen the dog."

"I bought him of the keeper, Marks, a few days after he came here. He's afraid of Tartar, but I fear no dog. However, we went out on the common to-night and I set him free for a run. The moment I did so he made straight for the Beeches and leaped over the new fence that's just been put up. I followed, calling as loudly as I could, thinking he was after game, but I soon came upon him tearing away the earth at the foot of a tree like a mad thing."

"I understand now," said Jack; "somebody lies there."

"Somebody murdered," replied Skewball, in a hoarse whisper, "and I've seen enough to know who it is."

"Well, who is it?"

"The chap the missus used to call the Fox. He was staying at the castle and disappeared quite sudden."

"Do you suspect any one?"

"I'm afeard I do, chief. He seemed to have a hold upon your cousin—"

"Go at once for the police," said Jack. "I do not wish to play the detective against one of my own kin. Besides, I have other work to do. What noise is that below?"

"Some of them flash gents from the castle playing bagatelle."

"Keep them here until I return."

"I will chief," said Skewball; "and I think I shall put them into the stable."

"Where you please, only do not lose sight of them. Now, Brisket, are you ready?"

"Quite."

They went out together by a back staircase, and Skewball sought the gamblers below. As he entered the room Wobbles turned deadly pale, and, having made a miss, put the cue into Curler's eye in his agitation.

"You lot," said Skewball, curtly, "follow me."

They made no objection, but, inwardly quailing, followed him in Indian file through the bar, down the passage, across the yard to the stables.

Unlocking the door of the harness-room he bade them go in, and they went, without daring to offer any objection.

"Keep there," he said, "until I send or come for you. Don't attempt to escape as I shall be watching for you. I've a brace of pistols and I'm an uncommon good shot."

He closed the door and left them in the darkness. A short but painful silence was broken by Pigeon.

"What's in the blessed wind now?" he asked.

"I don't know," replied Wobbles, "but I've got a sort of feeling on me as if the hend was nigh."

CHAPTER CLXXVIII.
FLIGHT.

BROAD ARROW JACK, followed by Brisket, made his way to the south side of the castle, which was the part devoted to the stables, kitchen gardens, and out-houses.

Outside the domestic portion of the establishment there was a piece of ground covered by gorse and briar, and in the midst of it was a small round house, built of stone, and thickly thatched, with a strong iron door and no windows.

This was reputed to have been once used for those who broke the laws, but had not, to the knowledge of the villagers, been opened within the memory of man, as it was reported to have been the scene of a desperate struggle between two malefactors who were accidentally incarcerated together, and each owing a grudge, they fought out a ghastly fight of tooth and nail, resulting in the death of both.

This round house was said to be haunted, and consequently a place to be avoided, and no man, woman, or child living in those parts had the slightest desire to enter therein.

But Jack made straight for it in the darkness and entered without a key by simply pressing one of the iron knobs upon the door, which was supposed to be the nails of an age when iron work was rude and primitive in its construction. The door yielded to his touch, and he and Brisket entered together.

Materials for travelling through dark places were at hand, in the form of a dark lantern and matches. Lighting the lantern he raised a carefully concealed trap door by touching a cunningly hidden spring, and the pair descended a flight of stone steps leading to an underground passage.

From thence, by tortuous ways—now up, now down —they arrived at the back of the picture of the cavalier in the dining-room, and through a small hole in the canvas Jack took a peep at the room.

It was deserted, but the remnants of a fire still flickered in the grate, and half a dozen wax candles guttered in the solid silver candelabra upon the table. An overturned decanter, a broken glass, and the remnants of dinner showed that for some reason the servants had not been into the apartment since the meal was partaken of.

"Not here," said Jack; "tell me the time, Brisket."

Brisket produced his watch, and by the light of the dark lantern they saw it was half-past eleven o'clock.

"So late," said Jack; "they must have retired. What room have they put the monster in? We must find out that, and then I will make sure work of him this time."

"There is great risk," said Brisket, uneasily. "Remember what country we are in now."

"I forget everything," replied Jack, "except the wrongs of me and mine."

Vain to argue with him, that Brisket knew, and so said nothing more. Jack turned back the picture upon the pivot on which it worked and lightly they both dropped into the room.

Brisket felt in his pocket for a revolver he carried and found it safe. With great care he cocked it ready for use.

"The moment I see the Ogre," he thought, "I will shoot him down, and the deed will be upon my head. What matter if they hang an old scarecrow like me so that my brave boy lives?"

Out into the corridor they went to the top of the grand staircase—no shadows ever moved more silently.

"Steady," whispered Jack; "somebody is moving in the hall."

Stealthy footsteps below broke in upon the silence of the house, and presently they heard voices.

"Be careful—this is the room where he sleeps."

"I know that voice," said Jack in Brisket's ear, "but it is not the Ogre. There is foul play going on."

The click of a lock, a shout, and then the struggling of men, one crying aloud for help!

Jack turned on his lantern, and saw them in a heap fighting on the floor by the door of a room, which he knew was where the butler slept. The latter in night attire was undermost, and one above him was opening a knife with his teeth.

"Villains!" he shouted. "Now, Brisket, to the rescue."

"Throw a light upon him," said Brisket, hurriedly. "I'll bring him down."

Jack threw a flood of light upon the struggling mass, and Brisket took careful aim and fired. Mr. Garker, of the Folly, received the shot originally intended for the Ogre and rolled over in the agonies of death. Conky, his very amiable assistant, sprang to his feet and fled.

But in his haste and confusion he ran straight at Broad Arrow Jack, who dealt him a blow between the eyes that scattered all his wits and laid him like a log upon the stone floor.

The house was now aroused. Shouting and banging of doors was heard above and the voice of Morden Crewe reached the ears of Jack.

"Attend to them," said Jack. "I must go above or I shall lose my man."

He leaped up the staircase just as the Ogre, in his dressing-gown, with a light in his hand, appeared upon the landing. The recognition was mutual and with a yell that rang through every part of the castle the Ogre dashed back to his room, closing and locking the door in a moment.

Jack rushed at it and bore the oaken structure from its hinges with an impetuosity that nothing could resist. The light the Ogre had carried lay flickering upon the floor, and, raising it, Jack took a rapid survey of the apartment.

The window was open, and without a moment's hesitation he leapt through and fell heavily upon the ground beneath.

He was hurt in one of his legs, but he cared not for that. Rising he glared around him like a hound upon the scent. Nothing living was in sight, but round by the main entrance he could hear a knocking at the door.

Thither he limped, and saw Richard Skewball with half a dozen police officers, one of whom bore a lantern.

"Hush," he said. "Search the grounds. The greater villain has escaped."

"The Honourable Morden, sir?" said one of the men.

"No, the Ogre, the murderer of my mother. Scatter yourselves, rouse the country, he must not escape this time. I am lame and cannot assist you. Stay, Skewball, and get me a horse from the stable. I will ride round and direct the search."

"You are not fit, sir."

"I am the best judge of that. A horse, I say."

Skewball delayed no longer, but ran off with the speed of his youth, and in a few minutes—hours they were to Jack—came back with a horse saddled and bridled, and a little knot of grooms following.

"Men," cried Jack, "I am your lawful master, come to claim my own. The murderer of your mistress is about those woods. Seek for him. A thousand pounds reward to the man who finds him."

There was no need to offer the reward, but it acted naturally as a stimulant, and the men, arming themselves with sticks and pitchforks, darted off in pursuit. Half the police followed, but the rest, with a sergeant in command, remained behind.

"I have a duty to perform," said the officer. "We have to arrest Mr. Crewe."

"Do your duty then," said Jack, and pressing his knees into his horse's sides he rode fearlessly away, shouting encouragement to the searchers.

CHAPTER CLXXIX.
TARTAR CALLED INTO PLAY.

THE first thing the police did on entering the house was to put the handcuffs upon Conky, who was just recovering from the blow he had received from Broad Arrow Jack. He accepted his bonds quietly, merely whining that "he had allus tried to live spectably but was constantly being led away into something or t'other."

Skewball was left in charge of him, the butler, still shaking from the fright he had received, remaining with him to assist. Close by Garker lay, in the stillness of death, with blood slowly oozing from a wound in his side—a ghastly sight.

Up the stairs the policemen went, and the Honourable Morden Crewe heard them coming. No need to tell him their misson. Instinctively he felt the hour of doom was at hand, and locking his door he barricaded it with the heaviest furniture he could move in the room.

They knocked, and the voice of the sergeant called upon him to open. To the demand he made no reply.

"Break down the door," said the sergeant.

They threw their might against it but failed to accomplish what Broad Arrow Jack had done. The Honourable Morden Crewe smiled grimly.

"I have five minutes more to live," he said.

With a terrible calmness upon him he sat down by a table and drew out his pocket-book. From an inner part of it he took out a small packet containing a powder, which he mixed with a little water in a tumbler, and sat down to await the issue of the attack.

They beat and hammered for a long time in vain, but at last one of the panels split, and a strong foot kicked it to pieces.

There was little more room than a dog would have required to enter his kennel, but the bold sergeant, without hesitation, thrust his head and shoulders through, and began to push aside the furniture which formed the barricade.

The Honourable Morden Crewe drew out a pistol, and, walking over, placed it against the head of the courageous man.

"Sergeant," he said, "I can blow your brains out."

"Can't help it, sir," was the calm reply; "I've a duty to do."

"Live, my good fellow," said the Honourable Morden, casting the weapon aside. "Why should I stain my soul with a needless crime? I'm doubly damned already."

He walked over to the table, took up the tumbler, and drank the contents, then went to his bed and lay down.

"Ask my cousin," he said, "to let me lie in the family vault. I learnt this night that he is here. Say I died as became my race."

He said no more, and when the sergeant got through into the room he found the blue eyes of the fallen man with no light in their depths. He was dead, and his spirit had gone to answer for his crimes.

"He had some of the family backbone in him at all events," said the sergeant, as he covered the face of the lifeless man; "it is a pity he did not make a better use of it."

Then he shouted to his men, "You are not wanted here. Go and help to search the wood."

Gladly they went, for the prospect of so great a reward was very tempting, and all night long they wandered hither and thither, with scores of other searchers, and found nothing. Broad Arrow Jack went to and fro like a mad rider on a mad horse, and the dawn of another day revealed a fruitless search.

Fatigue and pain at last mastered the gallant hero and he fell from his horse. They bore him in, and his last words ere he swooned away from sheer exhaustion were, "Ten thousand for the man who takes him. He must be found."

They gave him restoratives, and with renewed strength came fresh thought. "Skewball," he cried, "where is your dog? How mad of me not to think of it before. Brisket, remain with me, I shall want your arm. I am going out with the dog."

"You can't do it," said Brisket.

"I *will* do it," replied Jack. "Skewball, get the dog, I say, and speedily."

CHAPTER CLXXX.
FOUND.

STRAINING at his chain, lolling out a great red tongue, and showing his gleaming fangs, Tartar came up to the castle eager for the trail. He knew what was expected of him and he was ready to do it.

They took him beneath the window from whence the Ogre dropped and showed him a footprint there. With a deep growl he took up the scent, and straining with all his might at his chain he bounded away.

Skewball held him, and a little host of followers came behind—foremost, Broad Arrow Jack upon another horse.

Away, across the park, straight to the wood, and immediately the men began to spread out so as to form a living circle round it. The Ogre, they said, must be there, as all outside was open country, which had been scoured in every direction on horseback and on foot.

Away, into the wood to its very depth, and then at the foot of an old oak tree the hound paused and whined.

"Go on, good dog!" cried Skewball.

Round and round the tree, but no further, went the dog. Curious eyes were raised aloft, but the branches were thin, and without leaves, and he was not there.

"The dog has lost the scent," cried one.

"For the first time, then," said Marks, the keeper. "That tree is hollow I fancy—he may be there."

In a moment Jack was off his horse, regardless of his injured foot. "Raise me up," he said.

"No, no," they cried, "if he is there he may shoot you."

But Jack was imperative, and all objection went down before his authoritative air. Two sturdy men lifted him up to the first fork of the tree, and then they saw him thrust his arm into the hollow.

A moment of intense silence and then he spoke.

"Take me down," he said.

"Not there, sir?" said Skewball.

"Yes," replied Jack, quietly, "he has fallen into the hollow *head foremost* in his haste to climb the tree, and has perished most miserably."

And that was indeed how the end to the Ogre had come. He had fallen, as Jack said, into the hollow, and, wedged there, found a terrible death.

It was the task of an hour before they released him, so tightly was he fixed, and when they laid him out upon the sward, ghastly to look upon, his body was yet warm. All through the night he must have fought for life in his horrible prison-house.

His shoes were worn through by his frantic efforts to escape, the flesh of his toes was gone, and the nails of his fingers broken down almost to the very quicks. A ghastly awful punishment that which the Ogre went through within the darkness, unable to cry out even for the assistance of those he fled from.

They bore him back and placed his body in the Bold Brigand Inn, there to await an inquest, and even then he was watched for fear the life once so strong within him would return. But all was over, and a verdict of "Accidental Death" being recorded, he was buried in a corner of the churchyard, away from all honest men.

"There let him lie," said Jack, "and may he and his sins be soon forgotten."

On the same day the Honourable Morden Crewe was quietly interred in a grave near the family vault of the Ashleighs. Jack could not put him with the long line of honourable men, but out of respect for his dying wish laid him closely, and over him stands a stone with "Morden Crewe" and the date of his death upon it. His virtues and his vices alike are unrecorded there.

Garker was buried next to the Ogre, and it is said by the people that their spirits at night can be seen abroad together. Whether they speak truthfully or not matters little. Some believe in ghosts and some do not, and each and all remain firm in their convictions, so I make no positive assertion on the subject.

CHAPTER CLXXXI.

THE LAST LINE.

ROCKHOLME CASTLE has now a noble handsome owner, who married four seasons ago the most beautiful of the women of the county—the Lady Alice Mantenoy—and already there are two little babies, with a trifle more than a year between, to make music in its halls.

They keep a deal of company at the castle, for the fame of its owner has spread far and wide, and away from him he is never spoken of as Sir John Ashleigh, but Broad Arrow Jack, and so will he be until he dies. He has a shrewd idea they call him so and is not at all anxious for his name to be changed.

Brisket lives with Skewball at the Bold Brigand, where he is the most tremendous oracle that ever sat in the coffee-room of an inn. His talk, which we know is of the first water, his experience of life, and his general acuteness, combined with his apparently unlimited command of money, awes the rustic mind and keeps them admirers at his feet.

The main fortune, which was really his, Brisket says he will never touch, and it is invested in the names of the children of Broad Arrow Jack, but whenever Brisket wants money he goes to the castle and gets it. He is very often there when he does not want money, and is a right welcome guest.

"I could live there of course," he says, "but the people who come there don't suit me, and I don't fit in with them. We belong to different classes, and although they are as kind as people can be—your true gentleman is always so—all I want is a civil 'How d'ye do?' and a shake of the hand may be and there's an end."

"Just so," says Skewball.

"But with you and me, Skewball, it's different. We've got the same grain in us—rough and honest I know, as far as you go, and I hope I am the same myself. Here I'm comfortable. It does me good to see you all so happy, and Sal so blooming, and your children growing up to be a credit to you; even young Dick seems to be settling down as head groom, and is, I hear, casting sheep's eyes at that pretty girl Marmot, the carpenter's daughter."

"She cast sheep's eyes at him first," put in Sal.

"It don't matter which began it," replied Brisket; "the thing's done—they'll make a match of it, and the chief told me t'other day he should give 'em a lodge to live in."

"He was always kind to my boy," said Skewball; "he forgave him a great crime."

"Oh, Skewball, he was generous enough to make allowance for a great temptation. No man or boy on earth could be more honest than Dick now is, and let us drink to the young couple and wish 'em as much health and happiness as you and Sal have enjoyed."

The Tiger, like Dick, has advanced in years, but, unlike Dick, he has not grown much. He is the faithful attendant upon his hero master still, but a life in a civilised land has not impaired his great gift of activity in any way. The peasants are all afraid of him, and have a legend among them that he can *fly*.

More than one is ready to take an affidavit that he has seen the Tiger winging his way from place to place through the air.

Talking of affidavits reminds me of Wobbles, and "that ilk." Broad Arrow Jack did not prosecute them—he treated such small fry with contempt, but he warned them against being found hanging about his estates, and with a ten pound note each he sent them forth to begin the world again.

They began it in the old fashion, and did the great swell business for a week, then fell back upon their wits for a living. Their wits are not keen enough to fill their stomachs and to put decent clothing on their backs, and if you want to see them go to Fleet-street any day when there is a great race on. You will find the whole four outside the publishing office of a certain sporting paper waiting for the winner to be telegraphed, so that they may hasten with the news to some patron almost as needy as themselves, who makes the parlour of a public-house his club and in the most spirited manner backs horses while he has a crown in his pocket.

They talk of their adventures, these four, and suffer agonies because they can get *no* believers. This is the fruit of being known as members of the lying fraternity, and the quantity they gather is very great.

Wobbles feels his position keenly because he has such a taste for society, and has twice been into it. He occasionally talks mysteriously of a "certain party" of the name of Sal, who was very spooney on him, but here again he reaps the reward of his evil ways—he finds not a single believer. Sal herself is supposed to be a myth, and this idea is secretly encouraged by the envious Conky, Curler, and Pigeon, not one of whom have ever known the sweet and soothing influence of a woman's love, nor, as far as can be judged, are ever likely to.

And so we leave them all to dwell upon the past, to enjoy the present, and to look forward to the future, as their lives may warrant, each bearing his own burdens and reaping his own joys, according to the will of the Great Creator who gave them life.

THE END.

HANDSOME COMPLETE VOLUMES.

Eleven years ago Ching-Ching made his first bow before the youths of Great Britain, and at one bound leaped to the summit of fame—not only in our island home, but across the seas, even to the remote corners of the earth, wherever the English tongue is spoken. There is no parallel to Ching-Ching! Other stories have been popular, and are still popular, but none of them are so voluminous as the story of the incomparable "Chingy," or are in such a consistent narrative form. The records of the immortal one are like the links of a chain, and every link is sound.

One Vol. Complete. Price 2s.
HANDSOME HARRY OF THE FIGHTING BELVEDERE.

The True and Wonderful History of CHING-CHING will be found in this volume, which is the most thrilling and laughable Sea Story ever written for the Press, and everybody says so.

One Vol. Complete. Price 1s.
CHEERFUL CHING-CHING.
SEQUEL TO "HANDSOME HARRY."

The further adventures of the renowned CHING-CHING and the partner of his joys and troubles, the confiding SAMSON, are fully detailed in this volume. As the narrative developes, the real Story of Ching-Ching's life appears, and our readers only need be informed that it is *told by himself* to know that every word of it may be fully relied upon.

One Vol Complete. Price 6d.
DARING CHING-CHING;
OR, THE MYSTERIOUS CRUISE OF THE SWALLOW.

A Story of Travel in far-off lands and seas. An unbroken series of thrilling, humorous, and wonderful adventures.

One Vol. Complete. Price 1s.
WONDERFUL CHING-CHING
HIS FURTHER ADVENTURES.

One Vol Complete. Price 2s.
YOUNG CHING-CHING;
"A WORTHY SON OF A WORTHY SIRE."

Complete in Four Vols. Price 1s. each.
SWEENEY TODD;
THE DEMON BARBER OF FLEET STREET.

Complete in One Vol. Price 1s 6d
THE ADVENTURES OF
JACK SHEPPARD.
HIS REAL LIFE AND EXPLOITS.

One Vol. Complete. Price 2s.
BROAD-ARROW JACK.
By the Author of "Handsome Harry" and "Cheerful Ching-Ching."

Complete in Four Vols. Price 1s. each
SPRING-HEELED JACK;
THE TERROR OF LONDON.

The History of this Remarkable Being has been specially compiled, for this Work only, by one of the Best Authors of the day, and our readers will find that he has undoubtedly succeeded in producing a Wonderful and Sensational Story, every page of which is replete with details of absorbing and thrilling interest.

Complete in Five Vols. Price 1s. each
TURNPIKE DICK;
THE STAR OF THE ROAD.
A Splendid Romance of the Highway.

London: CHARLES FOX, 4, Shoe Lane, Fleet Street, E.C.